Masterpieces
of Fantasy
and Wonder

Masterpieces of Fantasy and Wonder

Compiled by David G. Hartwell
With the assistance of Kathryn Cramer

DOUBLEDAY BOOK & MUSIC CLUBS, INC.
GARDEN CITY, NEW YORK

Quality Printing & Binding by:
R.R. Donnelley & Sons Company
1009 Sloan Street
Crawfordsville, IN 47933 U.S.A.

ACKNOWLEDGMENTS
Grateful acknowledgment is made to the following for permission to reprint their
copyrighted material:
"Green Is the Color" by John M. Ford. Copyright © 1987 by John M. Ford. Re-
printed by permission of the author and his agent, Valerie Smith.
"Lest Levitation Come Upon Us" by Suzette Haden Elgin. Copyright © 1982 by
Suzette Haden Elgin. Reprinted by permission of the author.
"The Princess and the Frog" by Robin McKinley. Copyright © 1981 by Robin Mc-
Kinley. Reprinted by permission of the author.
"Darkness Box" by Ursula K. Le Guin. Copyright © 1963, 1975 by Ursula K. Le
Guin. Reprinted by permission of the author and the author's agent, Virginia Kidd.
"Jack and the Beanstalk" by Osbert Sitwell. Copyright Frank Magro; © 1959 by
Macmillan. First published in Fee-Fi-Fo-Fum by Osbert Sitwell.
"The Mouse Festival" by Johannes Bobrowski. Copyright © 1965 by Johannes
Bobrowski, Mäusefest, Wagenbach, Berlin. Translation © 1989 by Kathryn Cramer.
"A Proper Santa Claus" by Anne McCaffrey. Copyright © 1973 by Anne McCaffrey.
Reprinted by permission of the author and the author's agent, Virginia Kidd.
"Inside Out" by Rudy Rucker. Copyright © 1987 by Rudy Rucker. Originally pub-
lished in Synergy 1 and reprinted here by permission of the author.
"The Woman Who Thought She Could Read" by Avram Davidson. Copyright ©
1958 by Mercury Press, Inc.; renewed © 1986 by Avram Davidson. From the
Magazine of Fantasy and Science Fiction, January 1959. Reprinted by permission of the
author and his agent, Richard D. Grant.
"The Third Level" by Jack Finney. Copyright © 1950; renewed 1977 by Jack Finney.
Reprinted by permission of Don Congdon Associates, Inc.
"The Man Who Sold Rope to the Gnoles" by Margaret St. Clair. Copyright © 1951
by Fantasy House; renewed © 1979 by Margaret St. Clair. Reprinted by permission
of McIntosh and Otis, Inc.
"The Dragons" by Murilo Rubião. Copyright © 1965 by Murilo Rubião. From The
Ex-Magician and Other Stories by Murilo Rubião. Translation copyright © 1979 by
Thomas Colchie. Reprinted by permission of Harper & Row, Publishers, Inc.

ACKNOWLEDGMENTS

"On the Downhill Side" by Harlan Ellison, from the Author's collection *Deathbird Stories*. Copyright © 1972 by Harlan Ellison. Reprinted with permission of, and by arrangement with, the Author and the Author's agent, Richard Curtis Associates, Inc., New York. All rights reserved.

"The Parrot" from *The Seance and Other Stories* by Isaac Bashevis Singer. Copyright © 1968 by Isaac Bashevis Singer. Reprinted by permission of Farrar, Straus and Giroux, Inc.

"The Harrowing of the Dragon of Hoarsbreath" by Patricia A. McKillip. Copyright © 1982 by Patricia A. McKillip. Reprinted by permission of Howard Morhaim Literary Agency.

"Lila the Werewolf" from *The Fantasy Worlds of Peter Beagle* by Peter Beagle. Copyright © 1974 by Peter S. Beagle. Reprinted by permission of Viking, Penguin, a division of Penguin Books USA, Inc.

"The Drowned Giant" by J. G. Ballard. Copyright © 1964 by J. C. Ballard. Reprinted by permission of the author's agent, Robin Straus Agency, Inc.

"Narrow Valley" by R. A. Lafferty. Copyright © 1966, 1970 by R. A. Lafferty. Reprinted by permission of the author and the author's agent, Virginia Kidd.

"Beyond the Dead Reef" by James Tiptree, Jr. Copyright © 1982 by James Tiptree, Jr. Reprinted by permission of the author's Estate and the author's agent, Virginia Kidd.

"The King's Bride" by E. T. A. Hoffmann. Copyright © 1963 by New English Library Ltd. From *Four Tales* by Ernst Theodor Amadeus Hoffmann, translated by Michael Bullock, and published by New English Library Ltd. Reprinted by permission of Hodder & Stoughton Limited.

"Under the Garden" from *Collected Stories* by Graham Greene. Copyright © 1963 by Graham Greene. Reprinted by permission of Viking Penguin, a division of Penguin Books USA, Inc.

"The Things That Are Gods" by John Brunner. Copyright © 1986 by Brunner Fact and Fiction Ltd. Reprinted by permission of John Hawkins & Associates, Inc.

"The Seventeen Virgins" and "The Bagful of Dreams" by Jack Vance. Copyright © 1983 by Jack Vance. Reprinted by permission of the author and the author's agent, Ralph M. Vicinanza, Ltd.

I would like to acknowledge the contributions of the book dealers, the antiquarians and out-of-print specialists who have supplied me with such precious and scarce material over the years, without which this book would never have been done. There are too many to list, but I must mention one: my friend and ex-partner, Lloyd Currey, of Elizabethtown, N.Y., from whom I have obtained more books and learned more than from any other.

And I again offer sincere thanks for the challenging collaborative talents of Kathryn Cramer, whose contributions to this volume are interwoven throughout, as in all our joint projects, and without whose encouragement and assistance this book would not have been done.

To Alison and Geoffrey

Contents

INTRODUCTION

"Worlds of Wonder, Worlds of Difference"   xiii

ENCHANTMENTS

Green Is the Color   3
  John M. Ford
Wooden Tony   58
  Lucy Clifford
Lest Levitation Come Upon Us   71
  Suzette Haden Elgin
Prince Bull   93
  Charles Dickens
The Triumph of Vice   99
  W. S. Gilbert
Turandina   111
  Fyodor Sologub
The Princess and the Frog   122
  Robin McKinley

WONDERS

Darkness Box   139
  Ursula K. Le Guin
Jack and the Beanstalk   148
  Osbert Sitwell
Peter Pan   157
The Thrush's Nest   164
Lock-out Time   171
  J. M. Barrie
The Mouse Festival   180
  Johannes Bobrowski, translated by Kathryn Cramer
A Proper Santa Claus   183
  Anne McCaffrey
Inside Out   192
  Rudy Rucker
The Facts Concerning the Recent Carnival of Crime   213
  Mark Twain
The Woman Who Thought She Could Read   229
  Avram Davidson
The Third Level   238
  Jack Finney

CREATURES

The Griffin and the Minor Canon   245
  Frank R. Stockton
The Man Who Sold Rope to the Gnoles   259
  Margaret St. Clair
The Dragons   264
  Murilo Rubião
On the Downhill Side   269
  Harlan Ellison
The Parrot   284
  Isaac Bashevis Singer, translated by Ruth Whitman
The Gray Wolf   300
  George MacDonald

CONTENTS

The Harrowing of the Dragon of Hoarsbreath   306
  Patricia A. McKillip
The Last of the Dragons   325
  Edith Nesbit
Lila the Werewolf   332
  Peter S. Beagle
The Drowned Giant   353
  J. G. Ballard

WORLDS

The Enchanted Buffalo   367
  L. Frank Baum
Narrow Valley   375
  R. A. Lafferty
Beyond the Dead Reef   389
  James Tiptree, Jr.
The King's Bride   406
  E. T. A. Hoffmann, translated by Michael Bullock
Under the Garden   451
  Graham Greene

ADVENTURES

The Things That Are Gods   503
  John Brunner
The King of Nodland and His Dwarf   540
  Fitz-James O'Brien
The Seventeen Virgins   571
The Bagful of Dreams   596
  Jack Vance
The Hollow Land   623
  William Morris

Introduction:
Worlds of Wonder, Worlds of Difference

Masterpieces of Fantasy and Wonder offers the range and diversity of fantasy fiction, a gathering of strongly individual stories by varied talented masters. As with my previous anthology, *Masterpieces of Fantasy and Enchantment*, the present collection is divided into five sections, each of which emphasizes one of the strengths of fantastic fiction either in content or effect, and the selections are chosen from the huge repository of the best works of short fiction of the last two centuries. Here are tales filled with delights and surprises from many of the great names of the past and the present, from Mark Twain to Ursula K. Le Guin, from Fitz-James O'Brien to Jack Vance, from William Morris to Peter S. Beagle. This book is filled with writers' names you will recognize (although you may perhaps be surprised to see a few of them in a fantasy anthology) but not, I venture to say, with familiar stories that have been frequently reprinted in recent years.

Some of these stories (for instance Isaac Bashevis Singer's "The Parrot" or Mark Twain's "The Facts Concerning the Recent Carnival of Crime in Connecticut") have never been printed as "fantasy" before, although the majority are indeed written by well-known fantasy names. I have a point to make in adopting this editorial strategy. Fantasy readers often limit themselves to what has been published with an identifying label. It seems to me that this practice is rather like reading only text requiring 3-D glasses; the publisher finds and offers under the fantasy category only works that blur the registration, so that other readers who haven't got the glasses—the proper set of conventional knee-jerk responses—can't bring anything into focus.

This is important to discuss now, because the category of fantasy, as separate from the mainstream of fiction, is a recent publishing subdivision, introduced to the mass market only in the 1970s for ease in marketing. The more limited the material, the more alike the product, the easier the job of the marketer. But the true case is that fantastic fiction has been an intimate part of the body of literature from the very earliest times; from the works of Lucian of Samosata, through the Medieval Romances of the Arthurian tradition and the Alexander Romances, to the imaginary voyages in European literature that culminated in the late eighteenth century, when a multi-volumed collection of them (including such masterpieces as *Gulliver's Travels* and *Robinson Crusoe*) appeared in France. That unimaginative material is best for imaginative (i.e. successful) marketing is symbolized by the proliferation of the image of the unicorn. The unicorn can be a strong image but it has too often been diminished to a cliché by pointless repetition. At the World Fantasy Convention in Arizona recently, there was a panel discussion entitled "Where Have all the Unicorns Gone?" The first participant said, "To the hotel gift shop, of course." There was a whole shelf full of them. But the purpose of marketing is to sell, not to reproduce an accurate representation of the real individual text. We are grateful when such accuracy occurs, but we do not, cannot expect it. Marketing operates as if the imaginations of people had been boxed in to the point where they require eternal vague sameness, not innovation, not difference. I do not believe it need prevail in our time.

The fantastic tradition in prose fiction as a consciously separate enterprise (as works in which the reader was supposed to derive pleasure from the knowledge that the tale was fantasy and not truth) began sometime in the late eighteenth century, with the literary movement known as Romanticism, but only became a genre of adult reading in the twentieth century and a separate label on books in just the last two decades. Given the long historical traditions of fantasy and the fantastic, and the range of material today worldwide, it is my considered opinion that to read only fantasy offered with a category label as the real stuff is an act of literary politics tantamount to declaring red and blue the only colors in the spectrum. Authentic fantasy literature is found throughout the world, past and present, immensely varied, rich and strange. And you must search it out, and not accept the easy labels, or you will find yourself reading retreads of contemporary originals like Tolkien. This book will help, will show you the spectrum, and introduce you to other authors and wonders of other kinds than you may be used to.

This book is offered as an antidote to the limited range of bright colors offered generally as category fantasy, one trilogy after another. Herein, the door is opened to a multiplicity of worlds, light and dark, pleasant and dreadful, always different. The conventional fantasy images you will find here are alive and are treated with unusual respect by the writers, not reduced to the cute or the pretty, like stuffed animals, marketing signals. Fantasy and the fantastic thrive on the new and the strange, in all times and places. For this anthology I have sought out stories that use imagination to make new whatever familiar material they may use, or that use new images, or that take a new point of view, or that invent.

These stories as a group are intended to reawaken your imaginations to the full range of experience, the whole palette of colors of the art of the fantastic. They offer escape into wonder. The true wonder tale is an emotional and intellectual experience that, for a moment, transcends diurnal life. It is an escape from reality to a world that does not exist (and we know it), a world that we can then compare to our own. For while the initial pleasure of escape from the real world is fulfilled, the final and quintessential pleasure of the fantastic is to allow in the end a new viewpoint, a vantage point from which to see reality as you have never seen it before.

Are young girls sometimes monsters? Are dragons sometimes working-class? The use of innovation to break the link between everyday reality and the world of the story and the use of fantastic images (the dragon, the unicorn, the werewolf, the ghost, the magician—all monsters that can be metaphors for abnormal psychological states—or swords, rings, jewels that have deep psychological meaning) takes the ground out from under the reader and allows new perspectives, new comparisons. The fantasy tale intensifies meaning through its use of such images to create a pleasurable distance from the real world. Perhaps you might in the end see George MacDonald's "The Gray Wolf" as a story about a young man's fear of a hungry young woman, or Robin McKinley's and Patricia McKillip's tales as stories about the troubles young women have in dealing with young men, or Avram Davidson's and Anne McCaffrey's stories as allegories of the artist and the audience. But no matter. The stories yield up immediate rewards as fanciful fun. Let them be. Read them. Enjoy. And then use them as a guide to further and better reading in other worlds.

DAVID G. HARTWELL
Pleasantville, New York

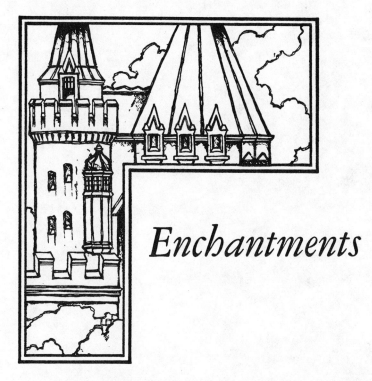

Enchantments

Stories of magical workings
in this world and others

Green Is the Color

John M. Ford

John M. Ford is the author of several popular fantasy and science fiction novels, including the World Fantasy Award winner The Dragon Waiting, *the Star Trek novels* The Final Reflection *and* How Much for Just the Planet?, *and many short stories of distinction. "Green Is the Color" takes place in the shared world of Liavek, a fantasy world invented as a literary game by Will Shetterly and Emma Bull, into which they have invited other authors to write stories for "shared-world anthologies." The characters and the story are the invention of Ford, while background elements, such as the Green Order, belong to the setting of Liavek in common. Most shared-world stories are, frankly, undistinguished when removed from their immediate game-playing context, but not so with Ford's. This is one of the finest stories of love, death, and enchantment in all of modern fantasy fiction.*

Arianai had gone two blocks down the narrow, empty lane before she realized she'd missed Wizard's Row. Or it had missed her; sometimes the street vanished on a moment's notice. It was never individual wizards' houses that came and went, always the whole Row. She wondered just who decided the issue.

It was a gray, gloomy spring afternoon, matching her mood. She half hoped for rain, though she wasn't dressed for it, in white cotton shirt and pants and a thin flannel cape. Rain would at least be something definite—she could point to it and say, "Look, it's raining, no wonder we're all unraveled."

No, she thought. She didn't need cheap excuses. She needed Wizard's Row, and that meant she needed someone to give her directions.

There wasn't anyone on the little street, and all the houses seemed to be shut tight. Some of the doors were boarded up. But a little way ahead there was a glow of light, a shopfront, two high narrow windows and a high narrow door.

There was a rattle like bones overhead. Arianai looked up. Hanging from a wooden bracket, apparently as the shop sign, was a puppet on a string. It danced in the slight breeze—didn't just swing, but actually danced, throwing out its elbows and knees. The only sound on the street was a whisper of air. There was something eerie about the marionette, dancing to no music.

Arianai went inside. It was surprisingly spacious within. The narrow storefront was only a third of the shop's actual width.

There were shelves filled with stuffed animals of cloth and fur, dozens of dolls, some with porcelain heads and arms, little ships with linen sails. More marionettes hung on the walls, and kites of paper and silk. A table displayed boards for shah and tafel and other games, dice, decks of cards; on another, two armies of toy soldiers faced each other in precise ranks, brightly painted in the liveries of Liavek and Ka Zhir four centuries ago. There were smells of sandalwood and hide glue, and a faint taste of raw wood in the air.

A long counter crossed the back of the shop. Behind it sat a pale-skinned man with long, slender limbs and very black hair. He was working at a piece of wood with a small rasp. Other tools and bits of carving were laid out on the counter within his reach. Behind him were more shelves, more toys; on the topmost shelf was a wooden train, a model of the one being built along the coast from Hrothvek to Saltigos. It had shiny brass fittings and red-spoked wheels.

"Good afternoon," the man said, without looking up. "Browsing is free. The prices are outrageous." His voice was pleasant without being friendly.

Arianai said. "Excuse me, master . . . I am looking for Wizard's Row. I seem to have gotten lost."

"You, or it?" said the dark-haired man.

"I'm not certain," Arianai said, and laughed, more from the release of tension than the joke.

"Well," the man said, "the Row is either ninety paces to the right of my door, or else it is not. Happy to have been of assistance, mistress." He held up the piece of whittled wood, blew dust from a hole. He picked up a length of braided white cord and ran it experimentally through the hole.

"That's a shiribi puzzle, isn't it?" Arianai said.

"It is."

"I'd always wondered where those came from. You see the White priests with them, but . . ."

"But you cannot imagine White priests making anything with their hands?"

"I'm sorry, I didn't mean to insult your faith."

The man laughed. "If I had a faith, that wouldn't be it." He put down the wood and cord, picked up another stick and a file, went back to work. He had long-fingered, spidery hands, quick and very smooth.

Arianai turned toward the door. An arrangement of soft toys drew her eye; in the center was a fuzzy camel as high as her knee, with a ragdoll rider perched on the hump. The rider, dressed in the robes of the desert nomads, had one arm upraised, with a yarn whip coiled down it—an ordinary pose, but there was something about the way the person was bent forward, and the camel's neck was bent back, that let Arianai hear the rider muttering and grumbling, and the camel—most obstinate beast that ever the gods devised—well, snickering. The toy was a perfect little sketch of a stubborn camel and its hapless owner, in cloth and stitches and yarn.

Perhaps, Arianai thought, there was luck in her wrong turn after all. "Who makes these toys?" she said.

"I do," said the black-haired man, "when I am not interrupted." Arianai was not certain if it was meant as a joke.

She said, "I am looking for something for a child."

"That is very usual in a toyshop." The man stopped his filing, but still did not look up. "Even if the child is oneself, many years late."

"This is a child who cannot sleep," Arianai said.

"Perhaps a music box," the toymaker said, examining the bit of puzzle in his fingers. "I have one that plays 'Eel Island Shoals' with a sound of waves as background, very restful. Or the flannel cat on the third shelf, beside the carousel . . . inside it are a cam and a spring; when wound up, it makes a sound like a beating heart. Some people find it quite soothing." The toymaker's voice had warmed. "Then again, all your child may need is something to hold. A woolen monkey, or a satin dolphin. A friendly caution—if the child has lost a pet, or greatly desires some particular animal, choose something different. Toys should not come with bad memories or unfulfilled promises attached."

"Why have I never heard of you before?" Arianai said.

The man looked up. His face was fine-boned, somewhat sharp, with hazel eyes of a remarkable clarity. "Why should you have?" The warmth was gone again.

"I am Arianai Sheyzu."

"Yes?"

"The children's physician. My house is just around the corner."

"Oh. Forgive me for telling you your trade, Mistress Healer. Please browse at your pleasure." He went back to his work.

"The child—her name is Theleme—is afraid to sleep." The toymaker said nothing, but Arianai went on, the words just spilling out. "She fights sleep for as long as she can, sometimes for days, until she falls into an exhausted sleep. And then she screams. Chamomile and valerian are no use at all, and she has become too frail for stronger drugs."

"I understand now why you were seeking Wizard's Row, Mistress Healer. I do hope that you find it."

Arianai bit her lip. "I'm sorry, master . . ."

"Quard."

"I didn't mean to burden you with my troubles."

"I never accept such burdens," Quard said. "To the right, ninety paces."

"Thank you." She turned to go.

"Take the flannel cat with you," Quard said in a quiet voice. "It's wound through the seam on its left flank."

Hesitantly, Arianai picked up the stuffed animal. As she moved it, she felt the springs inside loosen and the wooden heart pulse. Something in the mechanism purred softly.

"No charge for the loan," Quard said.

She looked at him. He was looking back, his eyes bright in his pale face like the eyes of a porcelain doll. Arianai tucked the cat under her arm, gave the man a hard stare back, and went out of the shop. Above her head, the sign-puppet kicked up its heels on a fresh wind from the sea.

Sen Wuchien was strolling through the Levar's Park when he heard the sentry call midnight. He paused for a moment, shivered, and felt an irrational impulse to touch the vessel of his luck. Instead he simply leaned slightly on his walking stick and thought on his vessel, drawing power into his bones to stop the chill. Foolish to have gone walking on such a chilly night, he thought, but the air was clean and pleasant, if damp. He would make tea when he got home, Red Orchid blend, and share it with his cat Shin; then all would be well.

His magic warmed him. With his empty hand he stroked the air, as if Shin's head were there, and tightened his abdomen, pulling power up to his eyes. Around Sen, the landscape brightened, sharpened. The images of catsight reminded him of an ink-and-water drawing; it occurred to Sen that he had neglected his brushes of late. That was not good. New rituals kept the magic responsive, the power fluid.

He stretched his vision, watched an owl gobbling a mouse, a badger waddling off toward its hole, a pair of lovers in deep consideration. He thought, amused, that he would do a pillow-book painting, the sort young people did, indeed the sort he had done as a young man in Tichen. And the text . . .

> Backs shape heaven's arches
> Dark hair braids with fingers
> As the tea grows cold.

Sen realized that he was tracing the calligraphy in the air. It was idle, no light trailed from his fingertips; he had moved, but not invoked. He was old now but not yet so careless. He wiped the power from his eyes, let the magic flush of warmth drain away, and walked on.

He heard a musical whistle, turned his head. There was a figure sitting on a boulder, a long white pipe to its lips. Sen Wuchien wondered that he had not seen this one before—he was not indeed so careless. There was power involved here. Sen looked closer.

The person wore a sashed full robe in the classical Tichenese style, all pure white with the sheen of silk, and white slippers. The face was smooth and finely featured, a young woman's or a beautiful boy's, Sen could not tell, with black hair in a long braid across one shoulder. The piper played a few notes, bowed slightly. Sen Wuchien bowed in return.

Sen said, "I had supposed to meet you in Tichen."

The piper gestured meaninglessly with the white flute, which Sen could see was made of a long bone. The bone of what? he wondered. It was too long to be a man's, or even a horse's. Sen said, "Pardon me. I spoke falsely without intent. I meant to say . . ." But he could no longer recall what he had meant to say.

The person in white stretched out a slim hand, pointing the bone flute at Sen, and spoke in Tichenese. "Come, if you are coming."

Sen smiled at the thought of having some option in the matter, and put his hand on the flute. It was very cold. Sen controlled his trembling without the use of his power, and looked into the face of the white piper.

"Oh," Sen said, "it is *you*—"

He looked at his hand. It glowed with a cool green light. He tried to let go of the bone flute, but could not. He reached for his power, but his mind was cold and would not move that far. Through the green haze that now wrapped his whole body, Sen looked again at the piper's face, understanding now why he had been offered a choice, and that in fact the offer had been real.

But as the cold caressed his heart, Sen Wuchien thought that he had already made the choice, thirty years ago.

The Levar's Park was large and not heavily patrolled; it was about an hour and a half before the two Guards came by on their rounds. They saw the glow long before they could see what it came from.

The next day was still gray, and drizzly as well. The puppet over the toyshop door seemed to clutch at himself and shiver in the wind, and there was a sad drip-drip from his nose and his toes.

Lamps were lit inside the shop; Quard sat near a lamp with a large glass lens that threw light on the doll's face he was painting. As he stroked cobalt blue on the eyebrows, he said, "Did you find Wizard's Row?"

"Yes," Arianai said, "and a strange thing happened there."

"Most who seek Wizard's Row are disappointed if one does not."

"The Magician at Seventeen and Doctor Twist both recommended you."

"As what?"

"As one who knows something about dreams."

Quard put down his work, wiped his brush with solvent. "In addition to an entire street named The Dreamers', the apothecary at Canalgate calls his boat *Dreams*. Maydee Gai at the House of Blue Leaves retails them fairly and to most tastes; Cimis Malirakhin is most to mine. Liavek has many splendid theaters, though I do not attend them. I'm a toymaker."

Suddenly a chipmunk appeared from beneath the counter, nodding and chittering, a blue nut in its paws. "Yes?" Quard said to the animal, then, "I quite agree. She has made a mistake." *Squeak, squeak?* "Yes, Doctor Twist will probably refund her money, but Trav? Never. It would offend his moral principles."

Finally Arianai realized that the chipmunk was a puppet on Quard's hand. "You do that very well," she said, "but I'm not so easily insulted."

"No insult intended," Quard said, now sounding tired. "I only wished to get a point across. Sometimes puppets are better at that than people." He pulled off the glove-puppet and put it on the counter, where it looked rather unpleasantly like a dead real chipmunk.

Arianai said, "You haven't even seen the child."

"I assume that you have confidence in your own abilities as a healer. And you have already named the most noted sorcerer in Liavek, as well as the craziest. What is there for me to look at?"

"It was the wizards who named you."

"So you said. Perhaps I've upset them somehow. They are subtle and quick to anger, you know."

"Surely you must care what happens to a child."

"Because I'm a toymaker? Bad proof, mistress."

"I think you did prove it to me. When you first spoke, about choosing toys."

"As a children's healer, you must know a certain amount about lice and worms. Do you love them?"

She stared at him. He had picked up the doll-mask, and turned the lamp lens to examine it.

"She slept last night, master. With your cat in her arms, she slept for almost the whole night."

"Then you have no further need for me. You may keep the cat."

After a moment Arianai said, "The girl is dying."

"So are we all, Healer—with all due respect to your profession."

For several minutes there was no sound in the shop. Then Quard said, "Did Trav tell you I'd be difficult?"

"Who?"

"The Magician."

"He did not tell me you would be hateful."

"Trav is like that. Bring Theleme tomorrow at five hours past noon."

It took her a moment to realize what he had said. "There's a long night between now and then."

"True. Five tomorrow."

She felt puzzled and relieved—too much of both to be really angry. "Tomorrow, Master Quard. Thank you."

The wizard Gorodain sat in his attic room, contemplating a tabletop. The wood was covered with a disk of glass, etched with a six-pointed star and inscriptions in the language that had centuries ago evolved into the S'Rian tongue. From each of the points of the star, a line led to the center of the disk; above the intersection was a small, darting green flame that burned without fuel or ash. One of the points was empty. Small objects rested on the others: a small bronze mask on a chain, a leather shoelace coiled in a complex knot, an arrowhead, a wooden doll, a silver dagger with a wickedly curved blade and an emerald in the hilt.

The previous night all the points had been filled, a little paper scroll on the sixth.

Gorodain examined the objects on the glass as a man might look over a crucial position in a game of shah—which, after a fashion, this was. The creation of the board, the collection of the pieces, had occupied most of thirty years. This was no time to rush the endgame.

He picked up the mask. It had horns, and finely crafted eyes that were chips of carnelian in onyx. He put it down again on its point, looked out the garret window at the moon rising through torn clouds. It was nearly eleven o'clock. Time to start.

Gorodain concentrated on the vessel of his luck, reached out with an imaginary hand, closed fingers of power on the bronze mask. He began to push it along the cut-glass line, toward the flame in the center.

He met resistance. He concentrated again, pushed harder. The mask wobbled but did not move. Gorodain felt his strength draining away. He ceased to push.

He raised his right hand, brushed his smallest finger against the boss of the ring he wore. A small blade, no bigger than a fingernail trimming, flicked out. He drew back his left sleeve, spoke some words, and nicked the skin of his arm. A drop of blood fell into the green flame.

The flame guttered, flattened, pooled on the glass. A darkness appeared, and Gorodain looked into it. He saw a man with pale skin, lying on a narrow bed, one arm thrown out straight, the hand clutching the bedpost.

So, Gorodain thought, the key was not yet fully in the lock, the door was closed to him tonight. It was possible still for him to send another nightmare, perhaps force the issue. But that would cost more of his already depleted magic, and the ritual of feeding the flame was exorbitantly costly. There would be time. He had waited thirty years; he could wait another day. He made a gesture and the flame went out.

It had rained all day, and by five in the afternoon showed no sign of stopping. Arianai and Theleme met no one on the street except a pair of cloaked and disgruntled City Guards, who looked after them as if bewildered that anyone would take a child out on a day like this.

They sloshed and bustled down the side street—it didn't seem to have a name posted anywhere—to the sign of the dancing puppet, which now stood nearly still, just shivering in the wet.

There was no one in the front of the shop, though lamps were lit. "Master Quard?" Arianai said. There was no answer. A small light came from a door behind the long counter.

Arianai took the damp cape from Theleme's shoulders. The girl was five, or perhaps six, but her face was ancient, hollowed under cheekbones and dull, unfocused eyes. "Wait right here, Theleme," Arianai said. "I'll be back in just a moment. Don't go anywhere, now."

Theleme nodded. Arianai went behind the counter. "Master Quard?" she said into the dimness beyond the doorway.

"No farther," Quard's voice came back softly. "How did the night go?"

"The cat did help," Arianai said. "She slept for a few hours—but then she began to scream again."

"All right. Go back to her. I'll be out."

Arianai did so. She saw that Theleme was slowly looking around the walls of the shop, at the toys. Perhaps, Arianai thought, they had made an opening; perhaps the key was in the lock.

Quard came out. He wore a long robe of blue and yellow, with a matching skullcap. Without a word, he went to the windows and lowered the blinds. The lamps were already lit. Then he bowed low to Theleme, and settled down to sit cross-legged on the floor before her, his clothes billowing around him. The effect was at once clownish and impressive.

"You would be Mistress Theleme," Quard said in a respectful tone.

Theleme nodded.

"I am Quard Toymaker, Quard of Dancing Wood, and your friend the healer Arianai has brought you to me, through the storm and the cold and the wet, because I need your help in a thing."

"Yes, master?"

"Sit down, mistress." Quard spread his arms above his lap. Theleme looked at Arianai, who nodded. Theleme sat down, cradled on Quard's knee.

"Now, mistress," he said, "do you know of the Farlands? The Countries of Always-Cold?"

"Anni has told me stories."

Quard shot a curious glance at Arianai, then said, "There is a princess in the Farlands—just about your age."

"What does she look like?"

"I have never seen her," Quard said, "but they tell me she has yellow hair like yours, and violet eyes like Mistress Anni's, and the pale skin of all Farlanders."

"Like yours?"

"There you have it. Now, mistress, the princess is to have a birthday soon. Lean close to me." He whispered in Theleme's ear, and she nodded gravely.

Quard said, "Now you understand how important this matter is?" Theleme nodded again. Any Liavekan, even the youngest, understood the seriousness of revealing a true birthday.

"Now, mistress, comes my problem. The princess must have a gift for her birthday. But there are so many things in my shop, and I know them all so well, that I cannot choose one for her. Do you think you can help me?"

Theleme put a finger to her mouth. She turned again to Arianai, who smiled and nodded.

Quard helped Theleme stand up again, and she began to wander around the shop, looking wonderingly at the toys. She put out a hand hesitantly, drew it back.

"Please touch," Quard said. "You will not break them."

Theleme searched among the toys for a third of an hour. Arianai caught herself fidgeting; Quard just sat, smiling crookedly, his hands crossed in his lap.

Arianai noticed that the backs of Quard's hands were entirely smooth, without a single hair. His face was just as bare below his eyebrows, without the shadow of a beard. Was Quard a woman? she wondered. The flowing robe made it difficult to tell. Not her business, she supposed. If this succeeded, she did not care if Quard was a troll.

Theleme had picked up a toy and was bringing it to Quard. It was the soft camel-and-rider Arianai had seen on her first visit. Quard held out his hands and received the doll. "Why, this is it, Mistress Theleme; that is just the present for the princess. I never would have guessed it." Quard stood up in a fluid motion, holding the stuffed toy in both hands. "Perfect, perfect. I must arrange at once to send this to the Farlands."

Theleme looked up at him, still as a sculpture, watching with dead eyes as the toy camel left her.

Quard turned away, then spun full circle, his robe floating out. "Wait," he said, and sat down again. "Come closer, mistress."

Theleme did so. Quard said, "My eyes are not what they once were, you know. Will you look closely at this toy, *very* close, and tell me if anything is wrong with it? A princess's gift must be perfect, you know."

Theleme took hold of the toy, began to minutely examine it. As she did, Quard reached slowly to the back of her neck, began to rub it. Theleme leaned over the soft camel. Quard stroked downward. Theleme's head tipped forward and was pillowed on the camel's hump.

Surprised and a little alarmed, Arianai said, "What did you—?"

"Let nature take its course," Quard said softly, and then pressed a finger to his lips. He leaned close to Theleme and said, "They will ask me why, you know. Not the princess—she will be delighted, I am sure—but all the lords and ladies at court, they will want to know, 'Why that toy? Why a camel?' Surely you know how lords and ladies are, when they see something that is special to you. They always want to know why."

Eyes still shut, Theleme said, "Yes, Master Quard."

"Tell me what the princess should say to them."

Theleme said, in a startlingly clear voice, "The green man is there. He has to go away."

"Is the green man bad? Is that why he has to go?"

"He wants to hurt the princess. He wants her to die."

"Do you see the green man, Theleme? Is he here?"

"Yes, Yes!" The child struggled. Arianai bent forward. Quard hugged Theleme and said, "Look away from the man, Theleme. Look away. Do you see something coming there? Do you see a camel, and a rider? I think they're coming. Do you see them?"

"Yes . . . I see them."

"And does the rider have a whip? Can you see the whip in the rider's hand?"

"Yes."

"Look, Theleme! The rider's reaching down for you. Catch the rider's hand as the camel comes by. Quick, now! Catch it!" He gripped Theleme's hand in his own.

"I have it!"

"I'll pull you up now!" He tugged gently at Theleme's hand. "Hold tight, hold tight! We have to ride fast!" He slipped his hand around Theleme's waist.

"I'm holding, master!"

"Now, we must ride for the green man. You have to be brave now, Theleme, for we must drive him out. Do you see the whip in the rider's hand?"

"Yes, I see it. I'll try to be brave."

"Very well. Here we come. And here comes the whip." Quard gestured to Arianai. She raised her hands and clapped them as hard as she could. Theleme twitched, but held tight to the stuffed camel.

"Here it comes again!" *Crack!*

"Is he running, Theleme? Can you see the green man run?"

"Yes! He's running! He's running away . . . " Theleme's voice faded, and she relaxed in Quard's arms. He rocked her gently.

"I think she will be better now," he said finally. "Here—can you take her?"

Arianai did, and Quard stood up, the stuffed toy under his arm. He put it in Arianai's arms beside Theleme, who cuddled it without waking. Then he walked to the door. "I'll go up to the corner and get you a footcab. There must be an enterprising few of them out in the slop." He opened the door, letting cool air in from the dark outside. "Well. It's stopped raining."

"Quard, I—"

"I doubt she'll remember the story about the princess as any differ-

ent from the rest of the dream. If she does, tell her that I made
another camel, just for her."

"Quard."

"Let me get the cab. You don't want to carry her home, do you?"

"I wouldn't mind. If you carried the camel."

" 'I'll carry the child if you carry the camel.' " Quard's voice was
suddenly flat. "That must be the punch line to a joke, but I don't
remember it."

"Come and have tea. I'd like to talk to you."

"What, and wake Theleme with our pillow conversation?" sounding more sad than funny.

"Do you have other appointments?"

"There's your cab," Quard said, in a tone that made Arianai hug the
child tight. He went running out the door, and was gone for minutes,
and minutes, the door wide open. Then a footcab did appear. Arianai
went to meet it, found the driver had already been paid. But Quard
was nowhere in sight. Arianai closed the shop door and rode home.
She put Theleme to bed, the camel still in the child's grasp, and then
sat in her office making notes on the case and rereading medical
books that had been dull the first time. Finally, at almost midnight,
she went to bed, and her sleep was very sweet.

Shiel ola Siska blew through the narrow bronze pipe, sending a
narrow jet of flame from the spirit burner onto the tinned wires in
her left hand, brazing them to a circular copper plate as broad as
three fingers. She tongued the blowpipe, spraying fire around the
copper, producing a pleasing rainbow finish on the hammered metal.
She slid her fingers to the other end of a wire, bent it around, then
fused it to the plate. Another wire was curved and twisted over and
under the first before being brazed in place; then the next, and the
next.

The end product was a copper brooch bearing a coil of wires,
tangled, complex, yet pleasing in form. The purpose of the item, the
ritual, was antimagic: When luck was driven through the brooch,
spells cast at the wearer would be ensnared in the coil, their energy
twisted and untuned and dissipated. Certain spells, at any rate. "The
most crucial of magics," ola Siska's instructor had taught her, "is the
illusion that wizards are infallible, but their customers can foul up any
enchantment."

And as with any magical device, it was temporary; it would lose its luck on ola Siska's birthday, or with her death. No wizard could truly create. A true adept could bind luck into a thing and make it truly magical—but only once, for the bound magic was gone from the wizard forever. The brooch was just a brief diversion of luck, as a spinning top that could stand impossibly on its point until it slowed and toppled.

Ola Siska stroked her finger across the wires. They played a faint series of notes, not quite music. She snuffed the spirit burner, took the brooch to a table covered in white linen. A high window let the light of the three-quarter moon shine upon it. She took up a pair of forceps, and with them lifted a small silver casting of a spread-eagled, naked man. She started to lower it into the nest of wires.

There was a slight rumbling beneath the floor. The copper brooch bounced into the air, rolled across the linen, and fell to the floor, where it kept rolling. Shiel muttered darkly and turned to catch it as it wheeled away—had she been thinking of spinning tops? Was that why the thing was acting so—

The brooch bumped against metal with a little tinny clink and fell over. The thing it had struck shifted; it was a boot, of lapped bronze plates.

Ola Siska looked up, slowly. Above the boot was a bronze greave, a knee-cover, then, resting on the knee, a jointed bronze gauntlet. The hand pushed down, and the knee levered up, and the figure of a man in full metal armor stood up, a bronze man shaded green with verdigris. His breastplate was heavily engraved with intricate designs, and his helmet bore winglike flanges at the temples. Its crown nearly brushed Shiel ola Siska's ceiling beams.

His faceplate was a mirror-finished sheet of metal, without features, without holes for sight or speech or air.

Her throat felt tight. So it had not been time and chill night air that had taken Sen Wuchien after all, she thought. She should have known.

She should have been *told!*

The bronze man walked toward her, holding out its hands. Ola Siska saw that its forearms were spiked down their length, like a crab's arms. She was quite certain that the jagged metal points had not been there a moment ago.

She flexed her hands. If she had not been at work, there would have been a ring on every finger, half a dozen bracelets on each of her wrists, each one the ritual of a spell. But she still wore amulets, around her neck and ankles, in her hair. And most important, she had the vessel of her luck safely on her person.

She caught her full skirts in her hands, swept them upward like a butterfly's wings, then released the cloth and touched a square pendant of interlaced steel and glass rods.

As the skirts fell, a circle of something like stained glass, though impossibly thin for glass, appeared before her. Grainy color radiated from the center of the disk, and thin black veins.

The bronze man collided with the colored disk. There were showers of sparks where his armor touched it. Ola Siska reached to the top of her head, pulled out two long golden pins. She raised her hands and breathed deep, feeling the power rise from her vessel to the pins.

A bronze gauntlet punched through the disk in a spray of colored fragments. Cracks shot through the glass, and in a moment it collapsed to the floor, and evaporated.

Ola Siska stiffened, but did not break the incantation. She threw the two pins. They flew true as arrows through the air, and pierced the bronze man's hands, nailing them to his breastplate. Ola Siska raised her right fist, slammed it into her left palm, and the pins shone with unbearable blue light, hissing as they welded themselves into place.

The bronze man struggled to pull his hands free, as Shiel ola Siska groped through her boxes of jewelry for the proper ritual device. There was a grating noise, then a rhythmic clinking, like a music box but deeper and flatter. Ola Siska seized a bracelet and turned.

The bronze man's arms had fallen off at the shoulders, and dangled from his chest by the nails through their gauntlets. From the sides of his breastplate, another pair of arms, thin and rodlike, was folding out, oiled cables gliding in grooves along their length.

Ola Siska dropped the bracelet—no use now to sever the thing's legs—and turned, and ran, out the door and into the night. She could hear the clanking of the bronze man behind her, and could not help but waste a moment in looking back: There were now spikes and hooks and blades down all its limbs, and steam hissed from its joints.

She ran up the street, trying to keep a grip on her thoughts and her skirts, unable to order her luck with the brazen thing behind her. She seemed to feel a dull red heat from it, but that was only in her mind, surely in her mind—

She paused, leaned against a doorframe, turned to face the thing. It was twenty paces behind her, taking slow long strides. There was no steam, no furnace glow, and even its steps were not overly loud; it had a sort of quiet dignity as it came for her. She held up a hand in a warding gesture, saw that her fingernails shone brilliantly green.

Into the pit with dignity, she thought, and hiked up her skirts and ran. She heard the clank of metal behind her, dared not waste the time to turn but knew it was gaining. Could it tire? *Metal fatigue*, she thought, with—irony? Ha, ha, ha.

Suddenly she thought of a place to run, a thing to run for. She had cast the spell away uncast, and now—

She stretched luck down to her right foot, felt the anklet there rattle and loosen. There was no time to stop, take the thing off, do this properly; it had to be timed just right—

Ola Siska kicked off the loop of silver. It sailed out before her, spinning, expanding from a bracelet to a belt to a loop broader than her shoulders; it struck the pavement; she leaped into it—

And landed on her hands and knees, gasping, half the city away, where Park Boulevard met the Street of the Dreamers. The shop called the Tiger's Eye was dark, its awnings folded. There was only the slight glitter of streetlamps on the items behind its windows.

Shiel tried to stand. She couldn't, not yet; the spell had drawn most of her strength. She was terribly cold. And her nails and knuckles were greenly luminous.

She pushed herself upright and went to the door of the shop, groped at her belt for a gold-and-silver key that hung there. She rubbed the pendant, pulling hard at the last of her luck.

Her hand spasmed and the key fell on its cord. Of course the shop would be sealed against magical entry. She pounded on the door, still short the breath to shout.

Behind her was a sound like a key in an unoiled lock. She looked into the dark shop, and in the glass saw the bronze man reflected, tall and shining and severe, his arms stretched out to her.

Ola Siska leaned against the door. With just a moment to recover herself, she could break the glass, reach through . . . no, that was too obvious, the inner bold would require a key. There was no sign of a stirring within, no lights, just a twinkling like stars on crystal and silver and brass. Only an inch of wood and glass between her and that whole constellation of life.

Something blurred her view: It was her face, shining green in the glass. Was that truly the way it was, then? Was she really so tired of running?

She turned, leaning back against the door, hands on knees that glowed greenly through her skirts. She looked up at the bronze man, who stood above her with his metal hands outstretched. His face was green as well . . . no, it was just her reflection.

"Come," said the bronze man, his voice rasping and twanging like a saw cutting wires, "if you are coming."

"I could have run farther still," she said, breathless but with dignity. "I could." She held out her hand, but remained sitting, so that he would have to kneel to her, like a courtier and not a conqueror. Which he obligingly did.

The sun came out the next morning, in more ways than one; Theleme woke wanting breakfast, and almost smiling. Arianai gave her some buttered toast and juice, knowing the child would be hungry but that her stomach would be in no shape for a heavy meal, and then they tossed on light cloaks and went for a walk along the canal.

As they crossed the lower bridge, they ran into a cluster of people on the street, around the Tiger's Eye, and a line of Guards keeping them away from something. Arianai recognized the officer in charge, a tall, hawk-faced woman with straight black hair, and walked up to her.

"Hello, Jem."

Jemuel, captain of the Levar's Guard, turned. "Hi, Anni." More softly she said, "Keep the little one away. It's not nice, what's over there."

"Can I help?"

"Not any longer, Anni. It's another green one."

"What? A Green priest?"

"Another glowing one—you haven't heard? The half-copper rags have been full of it."

"I've been busy, and you know I don't read the rags."

Jemuel said, "We've got two wizards dead in three nights. Not a scratch on either of them—but the bodies are glowing green as fireflies."

"Just a moment, Jem." Arianai led Theleme over to a baker's cart, bought her a sweet biscuit for distraction, then went back to Jemuel. "Glowing? Magic?"

"What it seems. Funny, though, you should even have to ask—Thomorin Wiln said that phosphorus could make a body glow so, but he tested, and there wasn't any, nor any other poison he could find.

Phosphorus, imagine that. More ways to die than you'd think, eh, Anni?"

"Who were they?"

"Um? Oh. Two nights back was that old Titch who lived up on the canal, Wuchien; found him in the park. And this morning when Snake opens up, she finds Shiel ola Siska glowing on her doorstep."

"Snake," Arianai said distantly, thinking of Snake's skill with the camel driver's whip she always carried, thinking too of a rag-stuffed toy.

"—so there it sits," Jemuel was saying, "one not far from his house, the other a long way the wrong side of the canal; a man, a woman; a Titch and a Liavekan—no pattern to it except that they both did magic, no motive, no sense. And an ola Siska dead, so the nobility are demanding that Somebody Do Something." She sighed. "Guess who."

"Captain?" It was a young Tichenese, Snake's assistant Thyan. "There's kaf."

"Enough for one more?" Jemuel said, indicating Arianai.

"Of course. Hello, Healer."

"Well . . . will Theleme be any trouble in there?"

"I'll take care of her, mistress," Thyan said. "Part of the job. Do come in."

Jemuel and Arianai sat in wicker chairs, by a tiny brass table with the porcelain kaf service; Snake, wearing an embroidered abjahin with the long whip coiled incongruously at her waist, leaned against a cabinet, stroking her cup, looking as if she wanted to pace. Arianai recalled that the shopkeeper had quietly put out word that she was to marry shortly. Death on the doorstep must have been quite an intrusion.

"You did know ola Siska?" Jemuel said.

"Of course I knew her. Everyone involved with jewelry did. But I never carried much of her work. Mostly she sold through Janning Lightsmith, sometimes the Crystal Gull."

"Too expensive for your trade?"

"Thanks, Jem."

"Well?" Jemuel said, not apologetic.

Snake gestured with her fingertips. "Not to my taste. Shiel had a particular fondness for . . . well, strange images. Skulls. Human figures twisted up. And sharp edges: she showed me a necklace once that . . ." Snake ran a hand around her throat.

Arianai said, "There's a market for that?"

Snake said, in a more relaxed voice, "There's a market for everything. I'm no prude; I'll sell you a poison ring, or a pendant with a hidden dagger. But Shiel ola Siska's work seemed to . . . celebrate death, and pain." She looked around the shop, at the multitude of trinkets and oddments that crowded the place. "Let me show you something," she said suddenly, went behind the counter and brought out a velvet-covered tray. She raised a spherical pendant on a fine gold chain. "This is one of hers. I bought it for the craftsmanship, before I quite saw what the thing was."

The pendant was an openwork ball of gold and silver pieces; the gold bars were straight, the silver ones coiled.

"It's a shiribi puzzle, isn't it?" Arianai said. "What's that in the center?" She put her finger to the pendant.

"Careful!" Snake cried, and Arianai stopped her hand, just as she saw that the object within the shirbi puzzle was a silver figure of a man, curled into a fetal position with one arm outstretched.

Then Snake's hand shook, and the metal sphere bumped against Arianai's fingertip; and the ball collapsed on its silver springs, into a tight knot of white and yellow metal from which a pale hand emerged in a gesture of pure desperation.

"Kosker and Pharn!" Jemuel said.

"It'll certainly be salable now," Snake said, "dead artists and all that. But I've wondered ever since I first looked closely at the thing, would I want to do business with anyone who'd buy it?"

"You think it had anything to do with ola Siska being at your door last night?"

"I've told you already, Jem, I don't know why she was there."

"And you didn't hear her knock."

"If she knocked, I didn't hear it." She put the pendant down. "There *was* a privacy spell on the bedroom last night."

"Thank you for saving me the question," Jemuel said. "Anni? Something wrong?"

Arianai realized she was still staring at the shiribi puzzle. "No, nothing."

From several corners of the shop, clocks began to strike nine. Jemuel said, "Pharn's teeth, it's three hours past my bedtime. If anything occurs to you—either of you—as a clue, you'll let me know, right?"

"Of course."

"Sure, Jem."

"Thanks for the kaf. I'll sleep better for it." She waved and went out of the shop, jingling the porcelain bells above the door.

Arianai said, "Snake, you sell some toys, don't you?"

"Sure. Want something for the little girl you've been—"

"No, I . . . have you ever bought from Quard?"

"Quard? Yes, some marionettes. He makes the best string-puppets I've ever seen. He'd have a reputation and a half, if his shop weren't harder to find than Wizard's Row in a dust storm."

"Hard to find . . ."

Snake put her hand on Arianai's shoulder. "Are you sure there's nothing wrong, Anni?" They locked eyes for a long moment, and then Snake said gently, "*Oh.* Yeah. Me, too . . . guess you've heard." She smiled, a little sadly. "It does make it harder to look at death, doesn't it?"

Arianai nodded and went out. In front of the shop, Thyan was demonstrating cat's cradle for Theleme, who watched in amazement as the knots appeared and vanished. Arianai said, "Time to go, Theleme. Thank you, Thyan," and handed the young woman a copper.

"I shouldn't take this," Thyan said. "It's part of serving the customers . . ."

"I didn't buy anything."

"Oh. I guess it's all right, then." Thyan grinned. From within the shop came the sound of a single clock striking nine, and Snake's voice calling, "Thyan!"

"Oops," Thyan said, "see you later," and ducked inside.

Theleme held up her fingers, tangled in brown string. "See, Anni? You pull, and snap she closes!" She tugged at the figure.

"Yes, dear, I see," Arianai said, and licked her dry lips. "Let's go home, now, and you can nap."

"Well," Quard said as Arianai entered the shop, "you are by far the most regular customer I have ever had." He had some of the miniature soldiers arrayed on the counter, with books piled up to represent hills and a blue scarf for a river.

"Tell me about shiribi puzzles," she said, trying not to look at the little metal men.

Quard shrugged. "They involve rods and strings. The object of the puzzle is to take it apart, and then to reassemble it." He went to one of the shelves behind the counter, took down one of the puzzles; it was the size of a small melon, of dark oiled wood and white cord, with a blue glass ball caged inside. "Some, like this one, have a thing inside them, which is supposed to be 'freed,' but the problem is the same."

"Where do they come from?"

Quard looked up. "Toymakers, when they're not being interrupted."

"I mean—"

"I know what you mean. I was being hateful again. I don't know who invented them, but they're old, several thousand years at least. And most of them come from the far West, beyond Ombaya." He turned the puzzle over in his fingers. "The White priests have decided they mean something important, and wear them as symbols of whatever-it-is."

"You make them for the Whites?"

"I haven't yet. But then they haven't asked me."

"Have you made them to order?" she asked carefully.

Quard blinked his clear light eyes. "I was once asked to make one as a cage for an animal—a chipmunk, say, or a large mouse. I'd seen them before; the puzzle has to be made of something the pet can't gnaw, of course, but it can easily be fed through the openings, and when it runs for exercise the cage rolls around on the floor, which also cleans it . . . however, this customer wanted a bit more. The puzzle was to be designed so that a mistake in opening it would crush the animal to death."

In her mind Arianai heard the snap of metal. "Did you build it?"

"Is it any of your business if I did?"

She said slowly, "Do you know Shiel ola Siska?"

"The jeweler-mage. I know she's dead."

"It only happened this morning."

"They print the half-copper rags so fast these days, isn't it a wonder?" He put the puzzle back on the shelf. "Time I was going back to work. Theleme is well?"

"Yes. Theleme is well."

"I don't suppose I'll be seeing you anytime soon, then. Do come back if you need a toy."

"I'm still interested in shiribi puzzles."

"Well." Quard took down the puzzle again, spun it between his palms. "There really isn't much more to be said about them. Do you

know the match take-away game, where a player can always force a
win if he knows the right moves? Well, there's a general solution to
these, a set of moves that will unravel any shiribi. Once you know it,
they're no fun any longer."

"Any of them?"

"Quite simple and obvious, once it's occurred to you." He
brought the puzzle down on the countertop and smashed it to pieces.

"Quard—"

"You *did* ask me for an answer, Healer. There it is. Good day."

Gorodain looked over his glass gameboard. The bronze mask was
gone now; the flame had been almost greedy to receive it. The key
was in the lock, and turned.

There had been a great deal of news-rag speculation on Shiel ola
Siska's apparent attempt to break into the Tiger's Eye in her last
moments. Gorodain was not displeased. It would confuse and distract
the temporal authorities in looking for an answer, which they would
not find. He had acquired the small mask from Snake's shop some
years ago, through a series of intermediaries, all of them now comfortably dead; even if Snake should recall the item's sale, there was
no way of tracing it to him. And the thing itself no longer existed.

It was just like ola Siska, Gorodain mused, to try to dispose of the
thing by selling it, casting it to the winds of luck, so to speak; it was
Shiel's habit of playing with sharp things that had brought her into
the circle to begin with.

Just as it would be the pretty young healer's boldness that would
bring them together, that would open the bottomless spring of death
and let it flow. There were, in round figures, three hundred thousand
living human beings in Liavek. Three hundred thousand deaths! The
thought alone was wine to the senses.

Gorodain reached his magic to the carved glass and touched the
knotted shoelace.

Teyer ais Elenaith lived in the entire top floor of a squarely dull old
building in the Merchant's Quarter, fronting on the Levar's Way. The
ground floor was occupied by a firm of admiralty lawyers, and the
level between was packed with the lawyers' files and records, so that
no one but the occasional tired clerk or nautically inclined mouse
ever heard the thump of a foot from above.

The loft was one large room, closets and a tiny bathchamber along one wall, heavy trusses and skylights overhead. Folding screens could fence off sleeping or dressing areas as needed. On the walls, dancing shoes and performance props, canes and bells and caps, hung from pegs. There were several full-length mirrors and a balance rail, and in a corner were a stack of music boxes and a large metronome.

A few sweet-scented candles were burning, but most of the light came from the moon through the skylights. All the folding screens had been set up on the studio floor in rectilinear boxes and corridors. Moonlight, direct and from the wall mirrors, added panels of silver light and black shadow to the maze.

Teyer ais Elenaith leaned against the wall, arms folded, one foot on the floor and one on the wainscot, examining the puzzle she had set up. She wore a loose shirt over trousers, all crimson silk of Tichen, with a broad leather belt, something she had once fancied on a sailor's hard body, riding low on her hips. Her dancing slippers were red kid, laced around her strong slender ankles. A nine-strand braid of gold wire wrapped twice around her long throat; a compromise, but one had to keep one's luck vessel within three steps—ordinary steps, not dancer's leaps—*and* make certain it didn't go flying during a particularly active movement. Probably the reason there weren't more dancer-magicians; of course, it also required a bit more working room than most rituals. She looked up at the ceiling beams; ais Elenaith was not a tall woman, barely five feet, and still the trusses were inconveniently low at times. Better, she supposed, than having columns interrupting the open floor.

She went to the corner and set the metronome ticking, its brass pendulum catching moonlight on each beat. She took a few loose-jointed steps, rolled her shoulders. One, she thought to the rhythm. Two. One, two, *three.*

She leaped into the shadow-maze, landing on the ball of a foot barely a span from one of the screens. She arched her back, stroked her hands down the screen without touching it, spun on her toe and sidestepped, froze again, leaped again.

Ais Elenaith worked the maze with her whole body, threading through it start-stop-turn-leap, moving ever faster, coming ever closer to the screens without touching them, the smell of sweat mingling with the candles, the only music the tick of the metronome, the steady chord of her breathing, the bang of her feet on the floor, all in harmony.

She came through the maze, stepped, stretched, then repeated it, faster. She came through and repeated, and now there was music in the loft, instruments called up through the luck around her neck, cittern and hammered harp and horn. Once again and there were bells and drums; once again and there was a chorus, and sparks showered from her hands and feet as she moved.

Once again, and she saw him, standing by the metronome, in front of the mirror, which did not reflect him.

He wore trousers tight enough to show every muscle—*every* one— of black silk that glistened in the moonlight, and around his broad bare chest was a leather harness with small gold bells, as the temple dancers of eastern Tichen wore. One gold earring, one bracelet, one anklet. He was barefoot, and his hair was tied back like a sailor's.

So, ais Elenaith thought, was this why so many went willingly? But she was more than a heart and a will. He would have to dance for her life. She spun, clapped her hands, stepped again into the maze, hearing the temple bells chiming behind her.

Step, turn, pause. Her music was now a bright passage for horn, counterpoint to the golden bells. One, two, leap, four. She waited for him to falter, to touch the maze. He did not. Perhaps he would not; it was not necessary. Arch, step, pivot, *kick*—

Her foot snapped out, and a panel swung on its hinges, slamming closed against another with a crack and a streak of red fire. She danced on, two, three, *kick,* and another screen closed up.

She circled the maze of screens, kicking higher than her chin, shutting the panels like a puzzle box, luck in her throat like the lump of arousal. Sweat spattered from her as she moved, the droplets crackling with waste luck. The candle flames were drawn toward the center of the room.

The spell drew close. Ais Elenaith cartwheeled heels-over-head three times and drove both feet into a painted wood panel. The screens all collapsed, one on another with a crescendo of slams. All the candles blew out.

Teyer ais Elenaith wavered on her feet. There were no more sounds of footsteps or bells or music, nothing but the metronome's tick, tick—

It stopped beating.

Ais Elenaith turned. The man held his finger on the pendulum. Then he held out his hand, palm up; he did not have to speak. She knew an invitation to the dance.

She bowed. She pulled the metal braid from around her neck; it only chafed, and she was out of magic for this night. It was a strain on the strength, so much more than dancing. She pulled the lacings of her kid slippers, kicked them off. Teyer ais Elenaith took the offered hand, and saw pale green light shimmer and bounce from the mirrors in the loft.

She began to dance. There was no hesitancy in it; she had always called hesitancy the death of the dance. And it was not hard at all, even without her luck. The stiffness that she had tried to ignore these last years was gone truly. She moved with her partner like two hands at the same task, and she danced for joy—what other way is there?

They spun to the door, and kicked it open, and moved lightly down the stairway to the moonlit street. The partner held out his hands, and she leaped into them, was lifted into the clear night sky. Something fell away from ais Elenaith, the last concealment of the veil dance she had done so long; it crumpled beneath her feet but did not hinder her step, the green light of its bones through its flesh only a backlight to her firework movements, as she danced away from Liavek with the partner she had always known would come.

The House of Responsible Life was a boxy building at Liavek's northeast corner, between the Street of Thwarted Desire and Neglectful Street. Though not far from a city gate, it was not in a heavily traveled part of Liavek. So the occupants of the House, the religion whose color was green, did see the crowd around them.

The Green order did not do anything at first. It was not their way to do anything: They were a faith of sworn suicides, concerned only with fulfilling all their earthly obligations and responsibilities before making an artistic exit from life. This was not too clearly understood by most Liavekans, and crowds had stared at the House before. The Order simply took no notice; there was work to do in the House and its gardens.

They noticed the first stone through the window.

Suddenly there were more stones, and angry shouts. Glass was breaking, and people were running, and wood splintered. A hole was battered in the garden fence, and bodies crowded through, trampling vines and crushing fruit, doing more damage by accident than design. Someone tossed in a little pig, which ran about rooting and squealing.

At the front of the House, a novice came out of the main double doors and hurried to close the window shutters; a shower of stones

drove her to cover. Voices were loud and without meaning. Someone lit a torch. The crowd, some fifty people, moved forward.
The front doors opened again, and a man in green robes came out.
He was not tall, with long hair and large brown eyes in a soft face.
He walked down the three green steps, and went straight toward the
mob, to the man holding the torch. Missiles shot past him; he ignored
them.

The Green priest put both hands on the burning roll of papers and
jerked it out of the holder's grip. He threw it down and stamped on
it.

The crowd faltered, fell back a step. They muttered in a low rumble that was not quite speech. The Green priest stood still. The crowd
started to surge forward again.

There was a gunshot, and then a voice: *"All right, that's enough!"*
To one side, pressing in on the crowd, was a line of City Guards in
gray. Most had swords out; a few carried flintlock shotguns, clumsy
but able to splatter men like thrown tomatoes. The shot and the voice
had come from a Guard captain with black hair and a fierce expression. Her double-barreled pistol was still leveled, and people were
backing away from her as from a plague carrier.

The crowd was breaking up, people colliding with one another,
drifting away from the House, falling down, getting up and running.

It was over almost as quickly as it had started, the street emptying
out as the line of Guards pressed forward. The Green priest had not
moved. The captain walked up to him.

"Hello, Verdialos," Jemuel said. "Nice morning."

"I can recall better," the priest said, "and worse." He turned to
survey the damage to the House, then walked quickly to the bush
where the novice was still huddling. "Are you hurt, my dear? No,
that's good. Go inside now, and tell Cook I said to give you two
honeycakes and some strong tea." He turned back to Jemuel. "The
gardens?"

"I've got some people back there." She took her pistol off cock and
put it away. "Dialo, I realize you're sworn to kill yourself, but
weren't you trying rather hard at it just then?"

"Oh," Verdialos said, and his eyes went very round and white. "I
didn't . . . well, it was their stoning the girl. It made me angry."

"Angry. You? If I put that in the report, no one will believe it."

"Would you then also put down that my order takes complete
responsibility for the green deaths, so that won't be believed either?"

"We're doing what we can, Dialo. Do you want guards full time?"

"I'll put it to the Serenities, but I don't think so. It might only encourage another mob. We were fortunate today."

Jemuel nodded. "I wanted to tell you that I've been put on special duty to deal with this green mess. No offense."

"None taken. If we learn anything, of course we'll let you know."

"Thanks, Dialo."

"Thank you, Jem. Good death to you."

"I'll just say good day, thanks."

Jemuel took a footcab back to the Guard offices in the Levar's Palace; the runner grudgingly took a city credit slip for the fare, but insisted on a cash tip.

Jemuel made out the reports on the night's dirty work and the incident at the House of Responsible Life. The riot—she had to call it that—was really bad news; the Regent would want to know if Liavek were being pushed to the edge by the deaths, and the truth, that in a city of three hundred thousand you could get fifty people together to throw rocks on any excuse at all, would not reassure him a bit.

Only three deaths, she thought. More people than that died every night in the Old City, of starvation or other sharp edges. But these were all wizards, and even people who knew better—like other magicians—tended to think of wizards as immortal. And it was certainly a creepy way to go. Sen Wuchien's body was four days cold in the morgue, with nobody to claim it, and still glowing. Somebody wanted to keep him on the slab, to see how long he did glow. There was a typically morgue-ish joke about saving money on lamp wicks.

Her pen was starting to wobble. So this was special duty: she was supposed to end her shift with the end of the night watch, and here it was morning with a vengeance. She shoved her chair back from her littered desk, put her feet up, and closed her eyes. Immediately there was a knock at the door.

Lieutenant Jassil put his red-haired head in. "Captain? Someone here to see you. It's Thyan, from Snake's place."

"Sure, Rusty."

The Tichenese girl came in. Jemuel gave her forehead a pat in greeting. "What news, mistress?"

Thyan held out a small shiny thing. "Snake thought you'd want to see this."

Jemuel looked at the object. *"Fhogkhefe,"* she said.

Thyan giggled and blushed slightly. "That's a good one, Captain."

Jemuel said, "You speak Bhandaf?"

"I work in Snake's shop, Captain. I can swear in sixteen languages."

"Come visit this office on a holiday night, you'll learn sixteen more," Jemuel said. "Come on, let's go talk to Snake."

Quard was reading when Arianai came in. He put the book down, said, "I'm sorry about yesterday. I was upset."

"Would you like to tell me what you were upset about?"

"No."

She nodded. "I guess the apology will have to do, then. Would you mind talking about Theleme?"

"She's not ill again?"

"No. She's fine. I wanted to ask—you seemed to slip into her dream so readily."

"You wondered if I knew something about green men?" Quard said, an edge in his voice. "Green men who kill?"

"That's not it at all," Arianai said. It was at least halfway the truth. "I was wondering . . . if we could work out where the nightmare came from, so she could be protected from having it again."

Quard nodded. "All right. What's the girl's family like?"

"She doesn't have one. She was left as an infant at the House of Responsible Life—"

"*The suicides' order?*"

"Yes, of course," Arianai said, startled. "I don't know why. Perhaps the person who left her misunderstood the name of the order, thinking it meant 'those who take responsibility for the living,' or somesuch."

"That is what the name does mean," Quard said, "in Sylarine . . . Old S'Rian."

"There's such a thing as *Old* S'Rian?"

"Everything has a past," Quard said softly. "What did the Green priests do with the child?"

"They thought about taking her in as a novice of the order. But it was decided that if she were raised entirely within the House, she could never come to an unbiased decision about her own death . . . isn't that odd, that a religion of suicides should be so particular about who actually dies?"

"Every faith excludes someone from paradise."

She laughed in the hope it was a joke. "Do you know, I cannot remember ever having heard of a member of the House actually taking his own life?"

Quard said, "They may not, until they have severed every link of responsibility to the rest of the world. The order isn't about death, really, but breaking links."

"There's a difference?"

"Yes, there is. That is another reason they would be unwilling to adopt a child, you know. Someone would have to take responsibility for her, and be bound again to life. To willingly take on such a bond would be practically apostasy."

Arianai paused. It was so hard to read anything from Quard's tone of voice. "Are you a member of the House?" she said.

"I once considered it. But we were discussing the child."

"Yes. . . . They gave her to the Levar's Orphanage. She lived there for five years. Until she began to sleep badly. Could the Green order have been the source of the 'bad green man' in her dreams?"

"It seems so obvious. But it was five years between the time the Greens had her and this . . . disturbance? You're certain of that?"

"Yes, certain."

"And she was only in the House of Responsible Life for a short time."

"A few days, I was told."

"Then . . . no. Surely that can't be it. Not with the dream so strong."

"*Does* it mean something?"

"No," he said, too quickly.

"You don't think—"

"Do you intend to adopt Theleme?"

"What? Well, I'd thought about it . . . or find her a foster family—"

"I think the best thing you can do to protect her from nightmares is to do just that. The Levar's Orphanage is, I'm sure, a fine place, but it surely can't be better than loving parents."

"I think you're right."

"Thank you. Now, please, I need to get some work done."

"All right, Quard." She held his hand; he looked at hers as if he were not certain what it was for.

When Arianai got home, Jemuel was sitting on the doorstep, in her officer's uniform.

"You're up early," Arianai said.

"I'm up late. I sleep when there's a chance these days."

Arianai said, "I've found a cure for—" and shut her mouth.

"So I hear. What does your gentleman friend do nights, Anni? Beggin' your right to privacy."

"Jem, do you know how long it's been since I've had a . . . gentleman friend?" She tried to laugh, but it came out forced and high.

"Your little patient told Thyan. Thyan's not very good about secrets."

"Third-hand gossip, Jem? Are you really so short of clues for your two dead wizards?"

"Yes. And it's three. The Hrothvek dancer, Teyer ais Elenaith, was found last night, in the middle of the Levar's Way." Jemuel reached into the pouch at her belt, put a small cool object into Arianai's hand. "Seen one of these yet?"

The item was a glass skull, not much bigger than the end of Arianai's thumb, filled with green liquid. The crown of the skull seemed to be threaded in place. "What is it?"

"Poison. Fast and neat. I'm told it doesn't even taste too bad."

Arianai sat down on the step next to Jemuel, with rather a bump. "Where are they coming from?"

"At last a question I can answer. Remember Old Wheeze the glassblower? His son, Little Wheeze, came up with the first ones. He claims it was his girlfriend's idea. Now there are five glass-blowers turning them out so fast that there's a shortage of green poison. They're dyeing white poison . . . Pharn's fangs, I didn't mean that pun."

"But what's the idea?"

"Random green death, according to Little Wheeze's girlfriend. If you never know when you're going to suddenly glow green and drop dead, well, why not carry your own?"

Arianai looked at the skull. "And are they actually using these?"

"Not yet. I'm not going to worry until they stop shocking the grownups. When that happens, the kids'll need a new shock. And then we might be in trouble."

"Are you going to do anything about it?"

Jemuel produced another of the skulls, tossed it in the air and caught it. "Legal age to buy poison in Liavek is fourteen. So far, that's been strictly observed. There's no legal minimum to *carry* poison, because who would have passed such a dumb law? And if you use the thing, you can't be charged with much, except maybe littering, or blocking a public sidewalk, which come to think of it we're guilty of now. Move along, please, mistress."

They stood up. "We *did*," Jemuel added, "put the lid on a fellow who wanted to do them in rock candy and lime."

Arianai shook her head. "Would you like to come in for tea and a biscuit?"

"I'd rather come in for tea and a clue . . . Anni, I do need help. Is there any chance that this friend of yours knows anything?"

"I don't think there is."

"Are you not thinking there is, or can you provide him with an alibi?"

"Jem, there's a line. Don't cross it."

"All right," Jemuel said, sounding nearly sorry. "I'll see you around, Anni. Say, what's your luck time?"

"Three hours. Why?"

"You might want to study magic. I think there's going to be a shortage." Jemuel went off down the street, juggling a pair of glass skulls and whistling "Positively Cheap Street."

Prestal Cade thought that her life had a rather marvelous symmetry to it: she had become a magician on her fifteenth birthday, successfully forcing her magic into a wooden doll in one long and nervous night. Then for forty more years she had practiced the mysterious and confusing art, leaving her birthplace in Ka Zhir for some time at sea, a few years in the Farlands, a few more in Tichen, before finally arriving in Liavek to stay as a quiet practitioner of the luck-craft.

She worked through dolls, composing her spells in carving and painting, dressing and detailing them; as a result, her magic was mostly involved directly with people—cosmetic spells, protection from hazards (while at sea, she had crafted a doll of cork, whose spell preserved absolutely from drowning), and the occasional bodily complaints, though always with the assistance of a healer.

And of course there had been the special doll, her part of the spell that they had all cast together, that was now coming back to them all and dressing them in green.

Well, she thought, that completed the symmetry. For after fifteen years without magic, and forty with, she had had fifteen again without. Fifteen years ago there had been a man who was jealous of her luck, her dolls, her craft. Durus had loved her, she still did believe that; she was convinced that it was because he loved her that he found the vessel of her luck and broke it, set her magic free so that all her spells failed at once.

Prestal Cade had been walking home from the greengrocer's when it happened. She felt her heart squeezed, she fell and was sick into the gutter as fruits and cabbages rolled away from her. *So this is it,* she thought, *the knock at the door and me without my magic to answer it.* But the Liavekans on the street, used to the vagaries of luck, knew better than she what was happening; someone, she never knew his name, gathered up her groceries and led her home.

There she found Durus on the floor, a knife in one hand and a small cedarwood doll without its head in the other. Had he only waited a few more months, the break in his heart would have healed, and the patch she had put on could have failed without harming him; but Durus was always impetuous.

He had not, of course, destroyed her vessel on her ill-luck day; on any given birthday since that night, Prestal Cade could have stuffed her luck into some new vessel, been a practicing magician again. But she had not. She was, she thought (when she thought about it at all) becoming old, and would inevitably start using magic to confuse that inalterable fact. She had seen all the places she had meant to see, except the Dreamsend Hills (and who ever got *there?*). She would only begin to repeat herself, another this, another that, another Durus.

Still, there was the one small thing, each night.

Prestal Cade stood in the largest room in her not-large house, as she did every night just before midnight. The only furnishings were a chair just big enough for her, and a table just large enough for a teacup and a cake plate. The rest of the room was filled with dolls, more than three hundred of them, tiny dolls made from a single piece of wood and some as high as her waist, with jointed limbs and eyes that moved; dolls clothed as kings and jesters, sailors and fops, heroes out of legend and beggars from the Two-Copper Bazaar. Some of them had been spell dolls, a luck-twisting purpose in their every feature, but most of them came after that. If not for those she had sold or given away, there would be twice as many of them in the room.

For most of those in Liavek who knew Prestal Cade, she was the Doll Lady, had never been the Doll Witch. It was, she thought (and this she thought rather often) a satisfactory name to depart with.

She looked among the dolls on their shelves, took one down. It was a little lady as tall as Prestal Cade's forearm, with a porcelain head and arms and a cloth-stuffed body, under a long, full gown of blue velvet. It had been the style of court ball dresses two centuries ago, preserved in children's stories. Prestal Cade adjusted the hem of the gown, saw that the tiny fur slippers were securely in place. She stood the doll on the floor, and waited for midnight to strike.

A wizard who could invest, but did not, had one trick left: on the minutes of each day corresponding to the moment of birth, the power flashed by. Only a little luck, the most immediate of all the instant magics, but sufficient, perhaps, to hold the line between power and the void.

The hour came by. Prestal Cade felt her luck rise. She reached out with it.

The blue velvet doll straightened up, began walking in stately fashion toward the door. When she reached it, she raised a porcelain hand, and the door swung open. The doll curtsied to the figure beyond the door; Prestal Cade bowed.

The doll did not rise. The moment was gone. Prestal Cade looked up, smiling. The room was already suffused with green light.

"Verdialos, you're crying."

"Oh. Am I?" His eyes went wide, which stopped his tears. He was sitting in the dining hall of the House of Responsible Life, over a cup of cold breakfast tea and a half-eaten slice of melon. "I'm sorry, Serenity." The title did not mean a great deal; the hierarchy of the Green Order was loose at best. It just was necessary to have something to call the people with more authority than others.

"Don't be sorry. Do you mind telling me what the matter is?"

"I was just told that Prestal Cade had died. Did you know her?"

"I don't believe so."

"She was a dollmaker."

"A wizard?"

Verdialos smiled slightly. "She had been. But her vessel was destroyed."

"*Oh.*"

"Well, no, not like that, not *quite* like that, Serenity. Her luck was just freed, not lost. She could have reinvested, but she didn't."

"Do you know why?"

"Not so well that I would be comfortable saying so." He picked up his piece of melon. "I was there the night her luck was freed, you see.

It was fifteen years ago, and I was just barely a novice of the Order, and I saw this woman fall down. . . ." He examined the melon rind.

"She had a bag of groceries."

"Groceries."

"I picked them up for her. I remember thinking, as soon as I'd sorted out what had happened, that I should convert this woman to the faith, that I should at least preach the truth to her . . ."

"But you didn't?"

"No, I didn't. There was so much going on at the time, you see."

"And now the woman is dead, and it's too late to preach to her. You shouldn't cry over what can't be mended, Dialo."

"I'm not," Verdialos said plainly. "I'm sad because I've lost something, and I can't decide whether it's a reason to live, or to die." He shook his head. "One would think after fifteen years as a priest I'd be beyond such ambiguities."

"I've been a priest rather longer than you," the Serenity said. "If it weren't for ambiguity, what need would we have for faith?"

Verdialos nodded. "Thank you, Gorodain."

"That's what I'm here for," the Serenity said, and started up the stairs to his attic room. "That's what we are all here for."

Arianai went looking for Wizard's Row, and was rather surprised to find it present.

Present, but scarcely all there: in place of the usual outlandishly styled houses, there were plain stones, shuttered windows, and silence, except for a raw wind blowing dust and trash up the street.

Number 17 was on this day a modest stone dwelling with lead-paned windows that admitted no view. A small enameled sign by the doorway arch carried the street number. The knocker on the heavy oak door was of black iron, and as Arianai reached for it, it rattled of itself and the door swung open.

Arianai entered a narrow corridor with a worn red carpet, hazy light filtering through small windows high up. The passage led to a room with one small lamp on a table: it was otherwise so dark that the objects on the walls, the walls themselves, were uncertain.

In a large leather chair next to the lamp sat The Magician. He wore a long red gown with brocade trim, black leather slippers. His face was difficult to see in the glare of the lamp, but his hands were as youthful as always. His small silver-blue cat was in his lap, the fat black one curled up at his feet.

"Arianai," he said, and that was all.

"Magician."

When he did not answer, she said, "Your hospitality is usually better than this."

"Times are usually better than this."

"What's the matter with the times? It doesn't seem to me to be a bad time at all. Unless of course you're a wizard."

"You are acquiring a bitter humor, Arianai. I wonder from where." His voice was that of a very young man, but it was shot through with ancient weariness, so terrible that she had to pause before answering him.

"You sent me to Quard."

"I referred Theleme's case to him. There is a difference."

"I'm tired of hearing about all these subtle differences! Is Quard involved with the dead Wizards?"

The Magician was silent.

"You want a fee?" She threw a handful of silver on the floor. The sleeping cat jumped up and ran away into the darkness. She took a step forward. "I think you're scared. You're afraid you're going to die, too."

"Young lady," The Magician said firmly, "I *know* that I am going to die. It taunts me every year with its presence. I ceased to be *afraid* of it before your several-great-grandparents were conceived." He stroked his cat. "That is why these . . . colleagues of mine are dead: because they had no fear."

More quietly, Arianai said, "Is Quard a murderer?"

"No."

She licked her lips. "But is he the wizard-killer?"

"There is no way to answer that question in a way you will understand."

"Then tell me enough to understand! Please, Magician . . . Quard said your name was Trav."

"I've thought about changing it." He sighed. "What you are seeing now are the last in a long series of actions. Call them moves in a game. The object of the game is power . . . a power as much greater than our magic as the sun exceeds this lamp."

"Are you playing the game?"

"At present, only observing it."

"So who are the players?"

"Originally—thirty years ago—there were seven. Their leader's name was Imbre. He was an extremely powerful wizard, with a luck time of almost two full days. There was, in fact, a time when he might have become The Magician of Liavek in my place. But he had an obsessive streak in his nature that led him into . . . experiments. And not long after the start of the one that interests you, he died."

"Did you kill him?"

"Thank you for your confidence. His closest associate in the seven killed him, fairly or not, I've no idea."

"And took over."

"There was nothing for him to take over."

"But you said the power—"

"It is not that kind of power. Not something that any of Imbre's group—or all of them together—could use or control to their own ends. All they could do was release it on the world."

"And if they did?"

The Magician said nothing.

"And if they did?"

"Do you pray to a god, Healer?"

"I . . . pray. Healers do that quite a bit."

"And what happens when you pray to whatever god it is? Does some actual being use its power to touch you back? Or does your own wish, your own prayer, give shape to some abstract power?"

"What difference does it make?"

The Magician made a gesture over the cat in his lap. It began to rise, levitating almost in front of The Magician's face. The cat seemed to enjoy it, curling and stretching in midair. "I reach into myself and do this," he said, "but I am not a god."

"How do you know?"

The cat sank back into The Magician's lap, presented its belly for scratching, and was rewarded. The Magician said, "Because I look back and regret my wasted efforts. Only mortals look back."

"Is Quard mortal?"

"If you cut him, he will bleed. But Quard is also a gateway to the power that Imbre's seven reached for."

"He has the power?"

"No one *has* the power!" The Magician's voice softened. "Because Quard has a mind and a will, he may not simply be walked over. Think of his will as being a lock on the gate. Imbre's successor has spent thirty years assembling the key to that lock."

"And the glowing dead—they're the first light coming through the keyhole?"

"Spoken like a wizard."

"But if you know all this—if you've been 'observing the game'— why in all the gods' names haven't you *done something?*"

"Because I believe that the play will fail, and by interfering I would do no good and might cause many more deaths."

"All right! Tell me what *I* can do."

"You have already done it," The Magician said tiredly. "You put the key into the lock."

Arianai stared. "I . . . what did I . . . do you mean Theleme?"

"Imbre fathered Quard to gain access to power. Imbre's successor fathered Theleme to gain access to Quard."

Arianai's throat clamped shut. The Magician just sat in his darkness, stroking his cat.

Finally she said, "Theleme . . . ? The . . . green man is her father?"

"Planted in her dreams for Quard to find."

"But you sent me to Quard!"

"I sent you *back* to Quard. His sensitivity to dreams is real. Theleme would have died without him, and the unlocking process would still have begun. Now do you start to understand just how complex this game is?"

"Tell me the rest of it! *Please.*"

"The rest of it is Quard's story. He will have to tell you."

"You could tell me more, but you won't."

The Magician sighed again. "I could tell you to leave Liavek, to have nothing more to do with Quard, but you won't. That is one mistake that I have made, and am bitterly sorry for: I forgot what it meant to be lonely, and not be proud of the fact."

"At least tell me the name of the green man."

"If I tell you, you will go to him. If I do not tell you, you will discover it anyway."

"Then you might as well tell me."

"No. I will not. So that I may pretend that my hands are clean. Good day to you, Healer Sheyzu."

The lamp went out. After a moment of darkness, Arianai found herself standing on Healer's Street, at the intersection with Wizard's Row; but the intersection, and the Row, were gone.

"I've been to see Trav," was the first thing Arianai said to Quard.
He did not look up from the piece of wood he was whittling. "On
first-name terms with him now? That's good. Did you get your money's worth?"

"He told me you were involved with . . . some sort of power."

"I thought Liavekans always called it luck."

"Don't be hateful to me, Quard."

"I'd be glad to do it in your absence."

Arianai breathed hard. "Forgive me for wearing sandals," she said.
"If I'd known the self-pity ran so deep around here, I'd have brought
my boots."

Quard put down the rasp. "That's not a bad line."

"The Magician said I was learning."

"How long is your luck time?"

"What?"

"I didn't ask your blessed birthday, just the span of luck. How long
was your mother in labor?"

"A little more than three hours."

"Not long for a Liavekan," Quard said.

"My family are healers, not magicians," she said. "We don't believe in prolonging pain."

Quard said, "Then you know that it *is* done."

"Of course. A student magician has access to power only for the
duration of his mother's labor. I've heard of it being stretched out for
forty, fifty hours." She shook her head in disgust. Then she thought
of what The Magician had said about Imbre—two days' luck—and
shivered.

"Is labor pain really as terrible as all that?" Quard said, with a sort
of distracted curiosity.

"It is."

"Then to extend it for . . . say, twelve days . . . that would be a
very bad thing, wouldn't it."

She stared. *"Twelve days?"*

"It would have been twelve weeks, if they could have done it.
Twelve months, if only they could have. Imagine that: an unending
luck time. But it does leave the question of one's ill-luck time, at the
opposite pole of the year. I think they might have been satisfied with
six months and a day . . . just to see what happened on that day
when luck and counter-luck overlapped. An irresistible force and an
immovable . . ." He gave a nasty, barking laugh.

"But your mother—twelve days? That's impossible!"

"No. Not impossible. With drugs and magic and clever surgeries, not impossible for the pain to last that long. But impossible to survive, yes." His voice rose. "My father and his little clutch of wizards stretched my mother's pain until there was no more flesh to cover it. And then, as she was dying and I was being born, just when any *human being* would have thought the obscenity could not be increased, they cast a spell. It took all seven of them, because the luck of a birthing woman is overwhelming—how else do you think the thing happens? These seven people, with enough power between them to have done anything, *anything* their souls desired, they, they—" He gestured wildly. "—they *stopped* my birth instant, my mother's death instant, and we *hung* there, me struggling to be *born,* she struggling to *die,* for an *hour* from midnight—"

He fell forward on the counter, sobbing without tears. He reached up and clawed at his hair, pulling the wig away, displaying a skull utterly smooth but for a few strands of false hair stuck in spirit gum. He tugged at an eyebrow, and it came away as well.

"Quard—" She reached around his shoulders.

"Three of them—" He shuddered, pulled away from her arm. "Three of them were *women.*"

"Quard. You have a will of your own."

He straightened up. "A small one. . . . I destroyed my vessel of luck, years ago. It was almost harder than the investment had been. I did it at the wrong time, though. The luck is only loose, not gone."

"As long as you use your will, your mind, no one can use you. The Magician told me that."

"You don't understand. I was created for a purpose."

"I don't doubt your power. But the power belongs to you. No one else can use it, if you don't let them."

"No. No. That was the experiment, but not the experiment's purpose. Do you remember when we talked about the Green faith? And I mentioned what its name meant, in the old language?"

"Yes."

"When that language was spoken, the Order was different from the one you know. Now they spend their time plotting their own deaths—and rarely succeed. But not so long ago, they contrived the deaths of others, and they did achieve them. Do you see?" He leaned toward her, and his clear light eyes shone feverishly. "Death as an art form. The death of the whole world as their masterwork." He stood up, turned away from her, braced his hands against the wall as if to keep it from collapsing upon him. He took a deep breath. "My father didn't want a powerful magician, you see. He wanted to create a god. To have Death as his own obedient son."

Arianai went around the counter, put her hands on his knotted shoulders. "But he failed," she said gently.

"*No!*" He twisted away from her, pulling the shelf from the wall. A shiribi puzzle and a stack of alphabet blocks crashed to the floor. "No, he *didn't!* The death is in my soul, just waiting to come out in the world. Don't you see? Don't you know who the rest of my father's gang were? Sen Wuchien. Shiel ola Siska. Teyer ais Elenaith. Prestal Cade. All of them dead, and still they control me. I've killed them, in my midnight dreams, and I'm still the slave of their wish." Quard stared at the shelves of toys, and began to sweep them aside. Puppets were tangled and broken, music boxes spilled their tinkling clockwork, porcelain dolls shattered.

"Stop it, Quard," Arianai said firmly. "Do you think I haven't seen an unhappy child throw a tantrum before? I said, *stop it.*"

Quard's shoulders slumped. He looked up. There were tears and dust on his face, and he smiled, a joyless doll's smile. "Tantrum? It's midnight, Mistress Healer. Allow me to show you a tantrum such as gods throw."

He stretched his hand toward a pile of ceramic bits that had been a doll's head. There was a flicker of green, and a small tornado swept the pieces into his palm. He closed his fingers around them, and squeezed; green light leaked from his fingers, and the bones showed through the skin. The hand relaxed. He flipped something to Arianai, and she caught it.

The object was a perfectly formed porcelain skull just smaller than an egg.

She threw it down. "Come home with me," she said quietly. "I'll change your dreams."

"What, in *bed?*" he said incredulously. "Wrestle and gasp and pledge the world, and then wake up counting the days till the world ends?"

She was too angry to turn away. "I'm not frightened, Quard."

"Then you're stark mad." He circled around her. "I can't stay here any longer," he said. "If I can't get away from my destiny, at least I'll be the death of someplace less than Liavek." He went into the back of the shop, paused in the doorway. "The toys are innocent," he said in a hollow voice. "Give them to children who will love them."

The door closed, the latch clicked. Arianai knocked at it, called to Quard, for half an hour. Then she went home.

Theleme was sleeping fitfully, tossing and turning. Quard's stuffed toys were beside the bed, apparently knocked aside by Theleme in her sleep. Arianai wound the spring in the flannel cat, listened to the soft beat-beat of its wooden heart, put it carefully against Theleme's chest. Theleme curled her arms and legs around the cat. Her breathing quieted.

Arianai picked up the camel and rider, carried them from the bedroom into her office. Some of the stitches on the rider's hood had broken, and it was askew; Arianai straightened it, put the toy on her desk. She poured a cup of nearly-cold tea, sat down behind the desk, and looked for a long time at the stuffed beast and its harried driver. As ever, the cloth tableau made her want to laugh out loud.

But she didn't. She put her head down on her arms and cried herself to sleep.

When Obas came to Liavek from Ombaya, he brought with him six shafts of ebony from the tree behind his house. The tree was old, and strong, and lucky; it had been planted on the grave of Obas's thrice-great-grandfather Udeweyo, a mighty wizard of earth and air, and the black tree's roots and branches kept his luck alive. Obas's mother had gone out into the yard where the tree stood to give birth to him, done the labor that gave Obas his birth luck on the ground that fed the tree, in the shade of its leaves.

Obas shaped his luck in the making of arrows, and when he left home his mother gave him the blackwood shafts, sealed in a pouch of moleskin, saying, "These are for no ordinary magic, not for wealth and not for power, not for the people of the lands you visit, for their own trees in their own earth will be strong enough for that. Someday, my son, you will need the luck of the house you were born in; these will touch you to Udeweyo's luck."

That had been fifty years ago; and in that span Obas had been hungry and poor, and he had been afraid, and he had needed luck that had not come to him; but he had not touched the ebony shafts.

Tonight the moleskin pouch was open and empty, and Obas was crafting the last of the six black arrows.

Their points were silver, and their flights were from a red fla-

mingo, taken without harming the bird. The smooth black wood was
carved with words and symbols, the carvings then rubbed with a
mixture of herbs and Obas's blood. Each arrow had a name, and the
names were Seeker, Binder, Blaster, Blinder, Flyer, and Slayer. Each
arrow had a purpose—and the purpose would come for Obas at midnight, but Obas would meet it armed with ancient luck.

Just before midnight he put the arrows in a quiver and strapped it
to his back. Around his left wrist he tied a band of oxhide. He put on
a short cloak of skin, and went out into the Levar's Park in the city's
northwest, the place where Sen had died. He did not have to go to
the park; he did not have to go to his opponent at all. He knew that
he could be found. But he wished to meet the enemy in the open,
under the sky, earth under him. Sky and earth might strengthen the
gift of Udeweyo's luck; Obas did not know. But if he was to die, let it
be in the room he was born in: the room of the world.

The park was quiet, and bright with the light of the nearly full
moon. Obas smelled damp grass and cedarwood, heard a fly buzz past
his ear; he turned, but the fly—if fly it had been—was gone. He was
alone.

No, he thought, feeling luck stir in the soles of his feet, not alone.

Obas drew out the first arrow, the one named Seeker. The vessel of
his luck, a broad silver arrowhead on a cord around his neck, was
cool against his chest. His heart was slow and his breathing was even.
He twirled the shaft in his fingers, filling it with his luck. Little light-
nings flashed from the silver head down the shaft, making the carved
chants glow, sparking from the red feathers.

With a snap of his wrist, Obas cast Seeker. It flew from his fingertips, trailing behind it a ribbon of silver light. The ribbon arched,
bent, dove. Then Seeker began to whirl, spinning a ring, a braid, a
column of light. The arrow struck the ground, its magic spent, and
fell apart in black ashes.

Within Seeker's windings stood a tall warrior with a shield and a
spear. He wore a striped skin, and his own dark skin was painted with
figures of white and red and yellow.

In Ombayan the warrior's name was Barah. He was the First
Hunter, the one who had learned to use wisdom to overcome prey
stronger than himself. Obas felt suddenly old, and weary, and small.
At the same time, he had hope: he did not fight an *inisha,* the wind or
the earth, but the Hunter, who though a god had been a man. Barah

could fail. A hunter might abandon the kill, if the prey proved too strong.

Obas raised the arrow Binder, spun it. It flashed and flew, striking the earth between Barah's feet. The shaft swelled, and sprouted branches, growing into a tree with its trunk at Barah's back. The branches reached for Barah's arms, the roots coiling to trap his legs. Barah struggled, but the tree drew luck from earth, and held him.

Obas drew the next arrow, Blinder, gave it magic, and cast it. It whistled like a diving shrike and flew toward Barah's eyes. The Hunter tried to raise his shield, but the branches pulled his arm aside. Blinder reached his face, and opened into a hood of blackness that tightened over Barah's head, covering his eyes, his ears, his nostrils, his mouth, so that Barah's face was a smooth ebony sculpture, all senseless.

Obas raised Blaster, whispering his luck into it. The silver arrowhead grew warm against his chest. The luck was there, the luck was strong. Hunter and prey had changed their skins. Obas cast the arrow, and it flew for Barah's chest.

Blaster erupted in fire that flowed down Barah's body, along his pinioned limbs, melting the skin from his bones. Dark flesh fell away, and the bones beneath showed green.

The fire spread to the binding tree, haloing it in the night. Bark began to slough from the branches, dripping thickly, like black mud.

Where the molten bark struck the Hunter's bare green bones, it clung, shining red over black over green, clothing the bones, muscling and fleshing them.

Barah stretched out his new limbs, still held in the tree's branches and roots, and tightened his new muscles. The tree groaned. Barah bent his back, and brought the tree up by its roots.

Earth fell away from the dead tree's roots, and tangled in them. Obas could see white bones: the skeleton, he knew, of Udeweyo, the breaking of his luck.

The first Hunter shook off the tree as a man throws off a cloak. Its trunk and Udeweyo's bones crunched together into black and white splinters. Barah struck his spear on his shield and took a step toward Obas.

Feeling his heart pound, his lungs strain, Obas raised Flyer. He cast the arrow, and as its flights brushed his fingers he grasped the feathers. Flyer lifted Obas, carried him into the sky.

He was afraid, he was fleeing. Could it be cowardice? The prey was too strong.

Far below, Obas saw Barah drop his shield to the ground, stand upon it. The wind rose, rippling the grass. Barah's shield rose on the wind, carrying him aloft. Barah raised his spear and flew after Obas. Together they soared above the housetops of Liavek, curving over the shining pan of the sea, riding the wind toward distant Ombaya.

Barah rose above Obas, stood on air, a dark shape against the moon. His spearpoint flashed in the moonlight. He threw the spear. Obas raised his left wrist. The band of hide around it began to grow, until it was a shield. Obas raised it as the spear flew toward him.

Barah's spear struck Obas's shield, and pierced it.

And stopped, the spearhead barely two fingers' breadth from Obas's heart.

Obas let the shield and spear fall away. They caught fire, a green shooting star toward the roofs of the city. Obas grasped his last arrow, the one named Slayer. He pulled at his magic until his heart burned, and then he cast the spell. Slayer shot burning at Barah's heart, and the First Hunter's shield was between his feet and the wind.

Barah reached out and plucked Slayer from the air. As he held the arrow, it seemed that neither he nor Obas were flying, but simply standing, two men face to face in the darkness. Obas looked into Barah's eyes. The hunter was mighty. The prey was not.

"Come," said the voice of Barah, louder than the wind, "if you are coming."

The moonlight took on a green cast; Obas looked at his open hand, empty of arrows, and saw that the green light came from him.

Barah cast Slayer back at its maker.

Obas's vessel of power melted, and the liquid silver trickled down his skin. If he cried out, it was lost on the wind. He lost his grip on the arrow Flyer, and he fell. Below him, the towers of Liavek thrust up like the bones of Udeweyo, and embraced him.

It was nearly noon when Arianai awoke. She dressed at once and went out to buy a *Cat Street Crier;* the front page had the news of Obas the Arrowsmith, found dead in the Levar's Park with the ground dented beneath him, though the earth there was not soft and there was no mark on Obas's body. Excepting of course the green glow of his bones.

Arianai crumpled the paper, shook her head. She carried the sleeping Theleme next door, leaving her in the care of that healer's nurse, and went to the toyshop.

The sign-puppet showed no more motion than a hanged man. Arianai tried the door, found it unlocked. Quard was not in the front of the shop; quietly, Arianai went around the counter and into the back.

It was a mess even by young-bachelor standards, shelves and tables and most of the floor haphazardly covered with paint jars and glue pots and tools, partially finished toys and drawings for others, odd books and dirty dishes, with dust and wood shavings filling all the gaps.

Quard was asleep. The bed was small and hard, but so finely carpentered it must have been his own work. He was sprawled on his stomach, head turned to one side. His wig was off, and the smooth complete hairlessness of his head and neck and face made him look like an unfinished doll.

She put two fingers to his temple. His pulse hammered. His eyelids twitched as he dreamed.

"Who killed Imbre?" she said into his ear. "We can stop him if only we have his name."

"No," Quard muttered. "Can't go there."

"Imbre. Who was Imbre's friend? Who killed him?"

"Die, all die."

"We have to drive out the green man. Who is he?"

"Gorodain," Quard said. "Friend, priest, kill. Gorodain."

She kissed him and went out, went north, to the Street of Thwarted Desire, and the House of Responsible Life.

She asked to see Gorodain. The clerks sent her to a small office, barely big enough to pace comfortably. Its walls were painted a pale green. Arianai thought that she was becoming quite physically sick of green.

After a few minutes an unprepossessing man came in. "Are you Gorodain?"

"My name is Verdialos," he said, in a lame little voice. "I am . . . oh, say that I deal with requests."

"I'm not here to die."

"But you are looking for someone who is?"

"I want to talk to the priest called Gorodain. Tell him it's about five dead wizards."

"I will tell him that. But he won't see you on that matter."

"Then tell him it's about Imbre."

"All right," Verdialos said equably. "Dead wizards and Imbre. Please wait here. Sit if you like."

"Your chairs aren't very comfortable."

"Most of our visitors have other things on their minds." Verdialos went out.

He was not long in returning. "Serenity Gorodain regrets that the press of duties keeps him busy for the next several days. If you would care to make an appointment, or leave your name . . ." He sounded vaguely uneasy.

"Arianai Sheyzu, eighty-five Healer's Street." Then she recalled what The Magician had said, about her discovering the green man's name. The Magician was one of the murkiest of an opaque lot, but what was in the fog was always truth.

Verdialos had started writing the address. He looked up. "Are you well, Mistress Sheyzu?"

"Yes," she said. "I've got no intention of dying anytime soon."

"A good death to you nonetheless," Verdialos said.

Shortly after the Healer Sheyzu had gone, Gorodain came into Verdialos's office. "Did she leave her name and address?" the Serenity asked.

Verdialos gave him the paper. "Forgive me for asking, Serenity . . . but my schedule is rather light this week, and if I could assist you . . ."

"I forgive you for asking, Verdialos. And I forgive you your ambition. You do know that you will succeed me as Serenity, when I finally"—he smiled—"achieve the goal?"

"I had supposed I was one of those in line."

"Good. One should not face death with false modesty." He glanced at the paper, then crumpled it. "If the woman should return, another dose of your usual kind firmness, eh, Dialo?"

Verdialos nodded as the Serenity went out.

It was in fact a busy day for Verdialos; the mob had done quite a bit of superficial damage to the House, especially the gardens, and the repairs had to be supervised and accounted. They were, Verdialos thought, very often an order of bookkeepers and tally-counters, and he wondered if perhaps the work they did for the House bound them to it, created exactly the responsibilities they were supposed to be severing in their quest for the regretless death.

And then again, he thought with a stifled chuckle, neither the tomatoes not the tomato worms would feel guilt at the gardeners' passing.

It was quite late when the last note had been written on the garden charts, the last cracked window mended against the night air. There was nothing artistic about any death that involved sneezing.

Verdialos ate a light dinner, a chop from the rioters' poor pig, and began a discussion with his wife concerning the healer and the Serenity. She ended it shortly by saying quietly, "Asking for an extra opinion never killed anyone." Verdialos laughed and kissed her warmly. Then he put on a cap and cloak of neutral gray (because prudence in troubled times had never killed anyone, either) and went out to talk to a City Guard.

He was directed to the Guard office in the Palace itself, and finally to Jemuel, who was studying reports and drinking kaf thick as syrup —"It's not supposed to taste good," she said, "it's supposed to keep me standing."

Verdialos told her about the day's event. "I am troubled by all of it," he said, "both the healer's interest in us, and the Serenity's interest in her."

Jemuel said, "It bothers me, too. I want to have a talk with your Serenity."

They shared a footcab back to the House, and climbed the stairs to Gorodain's chambers. Verdialos knocked on the door.

"Come in," said a voice that was not Gorodain's. Verdialos opened the door. His eyes widened. Captain Jemuel said, *"You."*

The Magician sat in a wicker chair, looking at a table with an etched-glass top. There was no one else in the room.

"May I ask," Verdialos said, "how you come to be so far from your usual, um . . ."

"A fool's errand," The Magician said. "I came to talk a priest out of his faith. But I arrived too late; he has already gone."

Jemuel said to Verdialos, "I have the right to commandeer the fastest horse in the neighborhood. I hope you have it."

"I have a faster horse," The Magician said, "and we all may ride. Open the window, please."

"Trav—the Serenity—"

"Is a branch of the Old Green Faith," The Magician said. "Those Who Assume Responsibility."

"Yes. I had been rather afraid of that. In our defense, he was never allowed to—well. Nothing to say now, is there." Verdialos opened the window.

Arianai had been dozing, nearly dreaming, when the knock came at her front door. It was a faint tap, hesitant. Shaking herself awake, she rushed to answer it, swung the door open. "Qua—" she said, before seeing anything in the dark, and only gurgled the rest.

Gorodain's hands were crossed in the grip called the Butterfly; they closed easily around Arianai's neck, fingertips thrusting into the hollows at the base of her skull, tightening, lifting. She lost the power of speech and movement at once. Her toes scraped the doorstep. Gorodain held her for several heartbeats, wishing that there were time for something more elaborate. So often he felt like a master chef who knew a thousand exotic recipes and was forced to prepare a single bland pudding for a toothless stomach patient.

Then, he thought, minimal art was still art, and this was the brushstroke that would complete his masterpiece, to confound a metaphor. And there simply was not time. Gorodain flexed his wrists, and there was a single sharp crack from Arianai's neck.

He lowered her, turning her on her back so that she lay across the threshhold of her front door, her head draped—quite elegantly, Gorodain thought—over the edge of the step. It might well be taken for an accident. Not that it mattered what it was taken for. Then, on impulse, he knelt beside her, stretched out a hand, tapped into his luck. The green glow would be simple enough to induce. Closure, that was what a work of art needed, a bright green line to link all the deaths.

There was a cold pressure at the back of Gorodain's neck. For a moment he thought it might be Quard—but the time was not right, it was still most of an hour until midnight. Then the touch resolved itself into pistol barrels. Gorodain looked up, saw Verdialos approaching, and with him The Magician—himself, out of his house!

The gun pressed hard against him, and a woman's voice said, "Just move, you dirtwad; just do us all a favor and make one little move."

"Don't, Jemuel," The Magician said, in that irritating pretty-boy voice of his. "The favor would only be to Gorodain."

Gorodain grinned involuntarily. The Magician was right. There was nothing they could do now, any of them. Death would come for his dead lover, and to save her be forced to admit that he was truly Death, take the power that could not be controlled. In less than an hour, Imbre's son would be loosed upon Liavek; before dawn, Liavek would be Necropolis. He wondered if the glow of all the dead would shine out upon the sea, like a green dawn.

Quard was sitting on the floor of the toyshop, arms and legs at odd angles, like a marionette cast aside.

He had intended to go away. He had started to pack a bag with everything that was meaningful to him, and then realized that such a bag would be empty. He had been sitting on the floor for most of the day now, waiting for night, for midnight, the hour of his birth and his power. There was nothing for him in Liavek but Death, but there wasn't anything more for him anywhere else.

So he would stay, and when next someone came into his shop they would find him on the floor, green.

The door swung open and Theleme came in. "Master, master! You have to come, master!" She rushed to him, and without thinking he opened his arms and hugged her.

"What is it, Theleme? What's wrong? Where's Anni?"

"Anni's sick, master, sick. The green man. You have to come. You have to ride the camel for Anni."

Quard's throat tightened. He tried twice to speak and failed. On the third try he said, "Where is she, Theleme?"

"Home," Theleme said. "Come, master. Captain Jem will take us."

"Who . . . ?" Quard stood up, walked with Theleme to the door. Just outside was a woman in Guard officer's uniform. Her face was pretty, but hard as a cliff. She had a pistol out, casually ready. "Good evening, Toymaker," she said, in a cold voice. "I've been wanting to meet you. But we've got some other business first."

Quard walked mechanically down the stairs. The Guard captain pointed at the toyshop door. "Aren't you going to lock up?"

"Why?" he said. "There's nothing in there that isn't mine."

It was not far to Arianai's house. There was a sphere of lucklight illuminating the scene, in the grainy, unreal fashion of magic.

Arianai was lying on the doorstep, half-in, half-out. The healer Marithana Govan was there, kneeling next to Arianai. Quard looked

around at the rest of them: The Magician, Verdialos the Green priest
. . . Gorodain.

"Welcome, son of Imbre," Gorodian said, and pressed his palms to
his forehead. No one paid any attention.

Jemuel took Theleme inside. Quard said quietly, "Give her something to make her sleep," and Marithana went inside as well. The
others stood out in the cold, around the body.

When the two women came out again, Jemuel said, "Well?"

"Her neck's cleanly broken," Marithana said. "She didn't suffer."

"I am an adept of my order," Gorodain said.

In a tightly controlled voice, Jemuel said, "If you speak out of turn
one more time I will surely shoot your balls off."

"Can you mend the break?" Quard said abruptly.

Marithana said, "Young man, she's—"

The Magician said, "I can mend the bones, with guidance from
Mistress Govan. Marithana, if they're splinted by magic, will they
knit?"

"Trav, she's *dead.*"

"If that changed?" The Magician said, and all of them stared at
him, except for Gorodain and Quard, who looked at one another
with unreadable expressions.

"In time," Marithana said. "Perhaps more than a year. Your birth
time . . ."

"If it takes that long, Gogo can renew the spell."

"You're serious."

Quard said, "More than you know. Do it."

The Magician said, "Marithana, concentrate on the bones as they
should be. We'll do it together."

Marithana Govan put her hands on Arianai's throat, straightening
it, massaging it. There was a faint sound of grinding, crunching.
Verdialos looked worried, Jemuel impassive, Gorodain positively
merry.

The healer and the wizard moved back. Quard stepped forward.
He said to The Magician, "If something goes wrong—if I come back
before she does, it'll mean that—"

"I'll do what I can," Trav said.

Quard knelt by the dead woman. Gorodian was speaking again;
Quard shut him out, looked up. Full moon at the top of the sky. Close
enough to the crease of midnight. Quard stared at the moon, feeling

the weight of luck tug at his heart, the tides of fortune raising his salt blood.

He stepped from his flesh and into his birthright.

Around him was still Liavek, still streets, houses, windows, rooftops, still just as lovely and hideous as any other Liavek; if anything, perhaps a little more precisely defined, cleaner of line and truer of angle, small where it should be small and grand where grandness was deserved. For it is not true that the dead know all things—indeed the dead know nothing that the living do not. But the dead have perspective.

Quard was surrounded by wraiths, human figures in translucently pale shades of green: not the dead but the living, dwelling here in their minds as they wished for death, in the degree of those hopes. Marithana Govan and Jemuel were barely even visible, delicate as soap bubbles. Verdialos was nearly solid, but without luminance; certain but not eager.

Quard looked at The Magician, who stood there with one hand already in the quiet world; Quard examined the rest of The Magician, studied his wish, and almost laughed. He did not: laughter and tears were things of the full world.

Quard looked with interest at Gorodain, who flickered, wavering to and from oblivion. Quard reached out and touched Gorodain's shade. Its eyes opened wide, and the figure knelt out of Quard's way, growing fainter as it did so. As ever with the voyeur, Quard thought, recoiling at the actual touch. He walked by.

There was no source of light in the city: it was uniformly dim, dull perhaps, though the effect was not drab but soothing. And there was no glass in the windows, nor glasses on the walls, nor puddles on the ground—nothing at all that night cast a reflection.

He moved easily on the dustlessly clean streets, passing among the shades of the still living, looking up at windows luminous with their death wishes. "I felt Death breathe on me," their living selves would be saying, in the full world; "someone is walking on my grave." Quard could see easily through the windows, or the walls for that matter, and no door was closed to him: even Wizard's Row would be present, should he desire to travel it. Nor did he have to walk; others rode, he supposed, or flew, but walking was the one way he knew.

Quard paused at a house on Cordwainers' Street: in an upstairs room, a crowd of shades stood around a man on a bed. The supine figure was deep green, and his shade was very thick.

Quard held out his hand. "Come if you are coming," he said, and there was a sound somewhere between a sigh and the pop of a cork, and the shade on the bed was suddenly a body dressed in clothes of subdued color. The man rose up and followed Quard, as the shades they left behind—some fading, some thickening—threw themselves upon the empty bed.

There were others after that, the sick, the old, the murdered and suicided, a Vavasor who had eaten a spoiled fish, and nine sailors drowned off Eel Island. Some of their bodies were young and robust, some old and elegant in appearance, but they all walked steadily, and there was among them no mark of decay, no wound, no lesion, bloat, nor worm.

They all followed Quard, winding through the streets of that other Liavek like a streak of smoke, pointing and touching and talking among themselves in a low murmur, passing through the green shades of the wishful living without notice—as indeed they could not see them. That was for Quard alone.

Finally, after he had fulfilled his duties among the lastingly dead, he returned to find Arianai, in her house, searching through the rooms cluttered with what she loved. "Theleme," she said, "Theleme, where are you?" She ran her hands over Theleme's bed, touching, seeing nothing.

Quard saw Theleme, asleep on the bed even as Arianai's hands passed through her shade. Theleme clutched the cloth camel and rider to herself, and her wish shone in the cool-colored room. Quard shook his head and took Arianai by the wrist.

She looked at Quard, and in an instant she understood. Quard did not know what the dead saw in him, and there were no mirrors to show him. He led her from the house, to the street where the column of dead waited. Arianai saw them, standing patiently and calm, but looked right through the shades of the living clustered around her, each of them waiting for some kind of miracle.

Quard knew there were no miracles.

Arianai said, "You came to bring me back."

Quard said, "This is not the story you think it is. I did not charm you free from here. There was an exchange."

"Who? *Not Theleme!*"

Quard was silent.

"It is Theleme? Or is it you? I won't accept such a trade."

"You are dead," Quard said, "and have no choice in the matter."

"If someone will die in my place, surely I have the right to know."
Quard said, "No knowledge is ever taken from this world." He
pointed at the street, where he could see the shade of Marithana
Govan kneeling. "Go, if you are going. We have a final destination,
and you may not see it."

Arianai looked at the column trailing behind Quard. She seemed
to be trying to recognize individual faces, but Quard gestured again,
and she lay down on the ground. The air shuddered, and in place of
the solid Arianai there was now a shade, even less substantial than
Marithana's.

He had not lied to her. Gods never lie, even if they then change
the world to suit their words. He had struck the bargain with himself.

Quard turned and left the square, the dead in quiet files behind
him.

"Is he dead?" Jemuel said.

Marithana held a bit of polished metal to Quard's nostrils. "To the
best of my ability to tell." She looked down. "Dear Lady around us,"
she said. "Anni's breathing."

Jemuel said, "He *could* do it, then."

Gorodain said, "Ah, but that is only the beginning."

"Shut up," Jemuel snapped at him, than looked at Quard,
crouched motionless over Arianai, who was now only sleeping peacefully. "Gods, how are we going to tell her?"

"I'll tell her what needs to be said," Quard said, unfolding and
stretching his limbs.

Marithana said, "You were—"

"I slept. I sleep very deeply."

Gorodain said, astonished, "You *return*—"

"You are a complete fool, Gorodain," Quard said, in a voice that
made Gorodain step back from him. "You wished for Death to take
the whole world down with you. But Death serves no man's wish,
nor does it wear one face. Death is particular to all it touches."

The Magician nodded. Then Quard turned to face him. "And you
sigh with relief, Magician, because your guess was right, because the
city did not die for your miscalculation? What of my mother, who
was tortured for nothing? Of my father, who died for nothing? Of
the other five?"

The Magician looked Quard in the eyes, and nodded again. "But

Anni and Theleme live," he said, without any force. "And I suppose
I shall, too."

"Kind of a shame," Jemuel said, poking at Gorodain with her
pistol, "all those other wizards dead, and not this green toad."

Quard said "I am . . . what I am. Justice is another thing entirely."

Jemuel said, "Fair enough. We'll see to justice," and pointed at
Gorodain. "I know a nice little cell just your size."

Gorodain shifted his hands. The Magician said quietly, "Don't
trust to luck." Something appeared between his fingers, and was as
quickly palmed.

Gorodain smiled grimly, shrugged, lowered his hands. "Do you
think," he said to Verdialos as if the others were not there, "that you
could provide me with one of those little green skulls the youth are
so fascinated with? Think of it as your first task as a Serenity."

"Pharn take that," Jemuel said. "You'll die on Crab Isle."

"True enough," Gorodain said, "for I am old, and once you destroy my magic—as you must—I will be older still. Better that Death
come quickly for me."

Quard began to laugh. Gorodain looked at him, and went very
pale. Quard threw his head back and laughed from the bottom of his
lungs. Gorodain put his hands to his mouth, and his eyes were wide
and black. Jemuel looked bewildered, Verdialos turned away, and
The Magician was simply gone. Quard just kept laughing as he
picked up Arianai in his wiry arms and carried her into the house.

Arianai woke damp with sweat, her neck stiff and sore as if she had
slept with it twisted. Her scalp prickled, and she struggled to recall
what her dream had been, but it had melted and run away.

She rolled over, pulling free of the sweaty sheets. Quard was on
the floor across the room, cradling Theleme in his arms. Theleme
shifted a bit, giggled in her sleep. Quard didn't move.

Quard didn't stir at all. He just sat, eyes shut, pale limbs wrapped
around the child.

Arianai felt a chill touch her eyes, her spine. Draping a sheet over
herself, she went to Quard's side, crouched, touched his shoulder.
His skin was quite cold. She bit her lip and tightened her grip.

Quard's eyes snapped open. Arianai nearly screamed.

"Hello," Quard said softly. He shivered. Theleme stirred, but

Quard rocked her to sleep again, then put her gently down, her head pillowed on the toy camel.

"You scared me," Arianai said.

Quard's face was mostly in shadow, but two little reflections stared her straight in the eyes. "Well. The world is full of possibilities this morning."

He got to his feet, and they went out of the room, with a last look at Theleme asleep and dreaming sweetly.

Arianai turned up the lamp in the office. Quard blinked in the light then said, "Is that really what you want to be doing?" and looked down at the soft, thick carpet.

She chuckled. "Then you've no other appointments."

"Not this midnight," he said, in a different voice, and looked her in the eyes again: in the better light she could see that his eyes, which had been hazel and clear as water, were now the color of green olives.

She turned out the light before she could see anything more. She felt Quard embrace her, felt him stir.

"You're like fire," he said, and pressed his cold lips to hers.

Only mortals look back, she thought, and knew that she was mortal.

He pushed her away to arm's length, said distantly, "How can you love me?"

"Day by day," she said, "until the end of the world," and pulled him close again. She felt Quard's tears, freezing down her cheeks, and prayed she would not wake up counting the days.

Wooden Tony

Lucy Clifford

Lucy Lane Clifford, a mathematician's widow, was a Victorian writer of bestsellers and children's stories (she published several collections of them, including Anyhow Stories *[1882], generally regarded as her finest work, and* The Last Touches and Other Stories *[1912], from which this story is taken). She was a notable literary hostess and friend of George Eliot, Henry James, and Rudyard Kipling, among others. Her stories are strong and unusual in their psychological sophistication, underneath a draconian moral overlay. "Wooden Tony" is a chilling fantasy set in a fairytale Switzerland. A haunting Pinocchio run backward, it is the story of how a real boy, Tony, is both granted his wish and punished horribly. There is an odd logic to it worthy of a darker Lewis Carroll.*

Tony was the idlest boy in Switzerland. Other boys of his age chopped wood, gathered edelweiss, looked after goats and cattle; carried parcels for the strangers, guided them on short expeditions; and earned pence in many ways. But Tony did none of these things, and when his mother tried to make him useful he looked so frightened that at last she left him alone and let him do as he pleased. Gradually he grew to look quite stupid, as if his wits had gone a-wandering: and he was called the "Wooden-head"—that was the name by which all the neighbours knew him.

"Poor little Wooden-head! he's no use at all to you," they said to his mother; and at this she waxed angry, for though she often called him Wooden-head herself, she did not like to hear others do so.

"Perhaps he thinks more than he cares to say," she would answer.

"But he never tells of what he thinks; and a thinker who says nothing is like a signpost that points no way, and has nought written on it to guide him who looks up," old Gaspard said one morning.

"The signpost was made before the writing, and the talking that is worth hearing only comes after much thinking. He'll tell us enough some day," the mother answered. But though she spoke up bravely she was sad at heart. "I love thee dearly, my little son," she said. "I love thy pale face and wide open eyes, looking as though they expected to see Heaven's door creak on its hinges so that thou mightest know what the heavenly city was like; but who besides will care for thee if thou art stupid? And if thou art useless who will want thee? Even thy father gets impatient." Tony turned from the faggot that was beginning to crackle and merrily lick with its long flames the black soup-pot hung over it.

"Could I be with thee and yet far off?" he asked. "I long to be far off."

"Dear mercy!" his mother exclaimed. "But why dost thou want to be far off, Tony?"

"Then would I be little and could lie in thy arms; and none would want me to do the things I cannot do and forget to do."

"But how would being far off make thee little, my son?"

"All the people are little far off," he answered. "I often watch the strangers come down the pathway from the big house. They grow bigger and bigger as they come near; they pass the door and go on by the gorge, getting smaller and smaller till they are as little as the figures in the wood that my father cuts away in the winter. When they return they grow bigger and bigger again as they come near. Yes—I want to be very little and far off."

"My son, thou art a fool," his mother said. "Is thy father ever smaller, dost thou think? It is only the distance that makes the strangers seem as thou hast said; if thou drew near them thou wouldst see that they had neither grown smaller nor larger." But Tony shook his head and would not understand.

"They are little to me," he said. "I would like to go away and be little to thee again, and then thou wouldst not be always asking me to do this thing and that, and be angry at my forgetting. There are so many things in my head that come before my eyes and make my hands useless."

"Thou are no good if thou art useless," his mother sighed. "All things have a reason for staying in the world, and the reason for the young and strong is that they are useful." But Tony answered only— "Some day I will go far off and be very little," and went to the sunshine and sat down on his little stool by the door. Presently he began to sing a song learnt in some strange fashion unknown to any near him, as a solitary bird might learn from its own little lonely heart.

"Ah, dear child," his mother said sadly as she listened. "He is no fool in spite of his talk, or if he be one, then his voice is sweeter than the wisest; there is not room for an evil thought anywhere within sound of it. While I listen to him I could even forgive Gaspard's wife for getting the fine linen to be washed for the English lady. It was a small thing to quarrel about."

But you do not know yet where Tony lived. In the summer his home was far up a high mountain in Switzerland. Beneath was a valley abounding in little meadows and winding pathways that had at one end a waterfall. The waterfall fell over a mountain side and was like a dream forgotten before waking-time, for though the spray went down and down, it never reached the bottom, but scattered itself in the sunshine and was lost. Tony used to watch the falling water, and try to feel as he imagined it felt—caught by the breeze and carried away in its arms. Sometimes he could almost fancy himself journeying with it—on and on, till he lost all likeness to himself, and, meeting the great winds, he became a part of them, and swept over the far-off sea. All about the valley and here and there on the mountains were the chälets or dark wooden houses of the peasants. Some were built on piles, so that when the storms and floods came the herdsmen and their beasts might still keep themselves dry; and some had heavy stones on their roofs, so that the winds might not blow them away. When Tony was very little, and before he had seen the builders at work, he thought that the piles were wooden legs on which the chälets had walked up in the darkness and stillness of the night, and that the two little windows in most of their fronts were eyes with which they had looked out to guide themselves. He often wished that he could see them staggering step by step upward along the zig-zag pathways. When he grew older it was almost a grief to know that human hands had built them on the mountain and in the valley, and that they would stay where they first rose till the winds and rains had done their worst. There was a little heap of rubbish on one side of the mountain; he had often wondered what it meant, but at last he knew, and then he stood looking at it and thought sadly of the children crouching over the fire, while the herdsman watched the sweeping storm gather to shatter their home and leave it in the past.

Just above his father's chälet was a big stone house, called the Alpine Hotel, where strangers came and stayed in the summer. The strangers talked among themselves in a language Tony did not understand, and were curious about the country round, professing to love it much, and day after day they walked over little bits of it. It seemed odd to Tony that they should travel from far countries to see the things he had lived among all his life—just the hills and valleys, the snow and the edelweiss, the sunshine and the infinite stillness. Was it really for these that the strangers came? He wondered sometimes what more might be in the distances beyond his home, and in what strange forms the great world stretched itself. Yet he did not trouble often about either the strangers or the world they came from, but silent and lonely let the days and nights slip by as one that swims with but just enough movement to keep himself from drowning. So Tony seemed to swim through time, and to find each day as difficult to remember from the one that went before or came after it as he would have found it to tell one mile of sea from another. Sometimes he wondered if the strangers were people easy to break, or to kill, or to get lost, for though they never ceased praising the beauty of the mountains, yet they were afraid to go alone up the steep paths or on the snow-plains that he could have wandered over in his sleep. But it was good that they had so little courage, for they gave his father money to show them the mountain ways, to carry their food, and pull them across the little precipices and crevasses that Tony scarce noticed, to cut steps on the sheer ice to which his feet clung surely, to take care of them altogether, those foolish strangers who professed to love the mountains and yet were afraid to be alone among them. All day long while his father was away Tony stayed in the chälet watching his mother scrub and clean and wash, and make the soup ready for his father at night. Or he would sit by the doorway, listening to the falling avalanche, and letting the warm sun fall on his closely-cropped head. Happy Tony! the trees made pictures and he saw them, the wind blew and he understood: surely he belonged to the winds and the trees, and had once been a part of them? Why should he trouble to work? Vaguely his heart knew that not to work as his father and mother worked had he journeyed into the world from the mists beyond it. Had he not been very little once when he set out on that first journey? Some day, when he had done his resting on the mountain, he would go into the distance, and be very little once more. And there were, besides, other thoughts than these that came into his heart, for he and nature were so near akin—thoughts of which those about him knew nothing; but he had few words with which to talk; even the easy ones of daily life his lips found difficult to use.

When the evening came, and the soup was eaten, he stood by the doorway, listening to his father's stories of what the strangers had said and done. Sometimes when they had been niggardly or very silent or the day a disappointing one, his father would be cross and grumble at the soup, or reproach Tony for being idle; but his mother always took his part.

"Nay, nay, do not be hard on him," she would say. "Now he is as one called too soon, before his sleep has satisfied him, and his dreams overtake his waking hours. Let him get his dreaming done, and he will rouse to work as men do in the morning time."

"Ah, nonsense," the father would answer; "we can any of us dream who are too stupid to wake and too idle to work. If it were not that he could sing I would have no patience with him."

The strange thing about Tony's song was that no one knew how he had come by it. He sang a little bit of it in the days when he looked for edelweiss on the mountain. To the highest ridges he went to seek for the little white flowers that grow on the edge of the snow on the Alps, and when he brought any back they were tied in bunches and offered for sale to the strangers. That was before he had grown so silent, before the time when the great cobweb seemed to have wrapped him round, before he had wandered into a dream and shut the door on the waking world. One day he came back with his basket empty.

"But where is the edelweiss?" his mother asked.

"I did not see any," he answered, and sat down beside the smoking wood. Then he began the song he had known since he could sing at all; but this time there was something that his mother had never heard before.

"Where didst thou learn that?" she asked, but Tony would not speak.

"It is hard on thee," Gaspard's wife said, "that thy son should be a fool."

"Nay, he is no fool," the mother answered.

"But he cannot tell even where he learnt his song," the woman said.

"He learnt it in the clouds, or on the mountain side, farther up than our feet can climb—what may be there—only the like of Tony can tell," and she waited scornfully for Gaspard's wife to go; but then she sighed sadly enough. "Surely he will some day awaken," she thought, "or what will be the good of him?" But from that time Tony forgot more and more the things he was told to do, and lived among his dreams, which grew so tangled that even he could not tell the sleeping from the waking ones.

It was only in the summer that the days passed thus. When the storms came and the snow descended, the hotels and all the chälets on the mountains were closed, and the peasants and the herdsmen and their families and their flocks went down to the valley for the winter. Tony and his parents lived with a neighbour at the entrance to the village, all of them huddled together in a little wooden dwelling. The floods came, and the winds swept past, and the snow-drift piled higher and higher against the windows till it was hardly possible for any light to enter the close and smoky room. Tony used to watch his father cutting bits of wood: chip by chip he seemed to take away the walls that held little animals and men and women in prison. He never realized that his father's sharp knife and precise eye shaped the toys, or understood that it was just for the sake of the money they would bring that his mother placed them away so carefully till the dealer from Geneva came to buy them, or till it was time to put them on a tray outside the chälet door so that the strangers might see and bargain for them.

One winter there was a dark knotty morsel of wood that fascinated him. Every morning as he drank his milk his eyes wandered towards it. In the evening as he crouched shiveringly by the smouldering fire beneath the black soup-pot, he kept his eyes fixed on it and wondered what strange thing it concealed. One day his father took it up, and, turning it over and over, began to cut, till there came forth the figure of a little woman who had on her face an expression of listening and waiting. Tony's father looked at her and held her up before him when he had taken off the last bits of wood that clung to her.

"Maybe thou are expecting some one to come and bear thee company," he said, speaking to it affectionately, as though it were a child; "but I do not know of any thou canst have, unless Tony here will please thee?"

Tony shrinking back fancied that the woman's eyes turned towards him.

"She is only wood, my lad," his mother said, "and to-morrow she will be sent to the dealer's far off—there is nothing to be afraid of, she cannot move, and in things that cannot move no danger lies. All things that live and move have power to frighten, but not this bit of wood that has been shaped by thy father's knife."

But Tony crept out of the chälet and trampled the soft snow under foot, and he was afraid of the little wooden woman lying still and wide-eyed in the smoky chälet. When he went back his mother looked up and said, just as if she had divined his thoughts, "Our neighbour Louis has gone to Geneva to look for mules for the summer; he has taken all thy father's carving with him, so thou needst not be afraid of the little woman any more."

This had happened more than a year ago, and Tony had forgotten the piece of wood and what had come from it. Now his father was carving again, and making ready for the dealer who arrived once a year to buy their winter's work from the peasants; and if the dealer would not buy, the little figures would be put away in a drawer ready for the strangers.

"If I were but like one of them," Tony used to think as he saw them wrapped in soft paper, "to be always little, to be handled tenderly and put to sleep in a drawer till the summer, and then to be warmed through and through by the sun. Why should they have legs that never ache and hands that never work?"

It was a cold morning when the dealer came—a dark, silent man, black haired, with overhanging eye-brows.

"Who is this?" he asked, looking at Tony.

"He is my son," the father said; "but little enough good is he save to sing."

"Is he the boy whose song the goatherds say was learnt in the clouds?"

"It may be."

"Ah, Tony's song is known all down the valley and over the mountain too," his mother said.

"A stranger came to Geneva once and tried to sing it," the dealer said, "but he could not remember it all."

"It is no good to Tony," the father said, "he is only a fool, and will not use his hands and feet." Then the mother spoke up for her son.

"Don't judge him harshly," she said. "Surely, some are made to use their hands and some their feet, and some it may be just their hearts to feel and their lips to speak. Does he not sing a song he has fetched from the clouds? Let that travel instead of his feet and work instead of his hands?"

"He is called the Wooden-head," the father went on, unheeding, "and he might well be all wooden but for his song. The rest of him is no good—"

"A song has sometimes lived longer than the strongest hands that ever worked for bread, and travelled farther than the swiftest runner," said the mother.

"—And he would be like one of those," the father added, pointing to the little carved figures he had made.

"They were hidden in a block of wood, just as thy song is hidden in thee," his mother said, looking at Tony fondly.

"He would be better without his song," his father said. "He might dream less and work more."

The dealer considered and was silent, and when he spoke again he spoke slowly.

"Let him go to the city with me—to Geneva," he said, "and I will take the song from his lips and send it over the world."

"Tony," asked his father, "wilt thou go to Geneva? Perhaps there thou wouldst get thy wish to be far off and very little."

"Ah!" said the mother, with a heart that stood still, "but I have heard it said that a wish and its fulfillment sometimes find themselves strange company. But go if thou wilt, dear lad, there is much in the world. I would not keep thee from seeing it."

The peasants came out of their chälets and stood at their doors watching Tony as he went through the village with the dealer; but Tony did not see them. He walked as one who was dazed. The icicles hung like a fringe on the waterfall, and everywhere the sun had kissed it there rested a little golden star; but he did not look up as he passed by. He kept his eyes towards the long, straight road, and wondered if in the stems of the fir-trees beside it there dwelt strange figures like those his father had set free with his knife. The dealer pulled some wire from his pocket and fashioned it carefully as he

walked on, but he said no word until the village was far behind and
they could no longer hear the trickle of the unfrozen water. Then he
looked up and said,

"Sing."

Mechanically, as though he were a puppet, of which the string had
been pulled, Tony began to sing, and the dealer twanged the wire in
his hands till it almost echoed the song. But Tony did not hear it.
Over his senses had stolen a great rest; he walked as though before
him he saw the land of his dreams and presently would enter its
gateway.

Twang, twang, went the wire.

The fir-trees swayed a very little in the breeze; more and more as
the twilight deepened, as the night came on. Tony turned his face
towards them; he felt as if he knew them, he wanted to go to them, to
walk among them as his friends, but something held him and he
could not. The trees knew him and held out their arms: they whispered a message but he did not understand it. But he was going to
understand them, to learn their language and ponder their secrets.

Twang, twang, went the wire.

The trees were wrapped in darkness at last, but Tony did not stop,
he went on, on and on without stopping, into the blackness till that
too was behind, and towards him slowly stole the morning light.
There was a range of low mountains far in the distance. They rose
higher and higher as he drew near as if to greet him.

"Sing," said the dealer.

But his song was different, it seemed no longer to come from his
heart but only from his lips, and as he sang he heard the notes repeated. The song was going out of him and on to the dealer's wire.
He did not look towards it, he did not care; he felt nothing keenly.
His legs were growing stiff and his feet were hard, yet lighter to lift
than they had been. He was not tired, or warm, or cold, or glad, or
sorry, but only in a dream.

The fir-trees were far, far behind now. Tony and the dealer had
passed other villages than the one from which they had started yesterday. They were nearer to the mountains that had looked so low at
first, and before them was a blue lake reflecting the bluer sky. Beside
the lake was a long road that led to the city of Geneva—the city
towards which they were journeying. But there were more villages
and little towns to go through first—towns with white houses on the

hill-side and others low down close to the water's edge. There were carved wooden balconies to some of them, and some were built altogether of wood. Tony wondered in what strange forest the trees of which they were made had grown. He seemed to have more and more kinship with the things that belonged to Nature's firstness—with the sky and the lake and the trees, nay, even with the dead wood that had been used on human dwelling-places. But towards human beings he felt a strangeness spring up in his heart as if between him and them had begun a separation. They seemed to be made of a different texture, of different flesh and blood from himself, and they —these people—were so tall, they overshadowed him; they took long steps and carried great loads that would have crushed him. And yet they did not look bigger than his father and mother, it was only when they were beside him that he realized the difference in height. It did not surprise him, for nothing surprised him now, or stirred his pulse, or made his heart beat quicker. He went on, on.

The dealer twanged the wire, and the music of it grew more and more to resemble Tony's song. But Tony tramped in silence looking at the lake and sky, while the sun shone, and the mountains rose higher and higher. He felt as if they were his parents or had been once in a far-off time, and now they were reaching out to him trying once more to bring him back to themselves before it was for ever too late. Too late for what? He did not know, he could not answer himself. His heart was growing still and slow, his lips were growing dumb.

"Sing," said the man again.

Then Tony opened his mouth, but the words of his song had gone, he could not remember them, he could not say them, only the notes came forth, but they had no meaning that could be written down in words, and each listener heard them differently. Gradually instead of singing he listened, for his song was all around and about, but it did not come from his lips any more. It seemed as if it came from behind him, but when he tried to turn he could not. He was clasped everywhere by the wire, and in the midst of its cold tangle he walked, strange and rigid, as if in a dream. One arm hung by his side, he could not move it; one hand was in his pocket, he could not pull it out. His clothes seemed to have changed, to have grown as stiff as he, and to be separate from him no more. Only his feet moved just enough to carry him forward, and that was all.

But now the last miles of the road were behind, and the sounds of a
city were before him with lines of houses standing up high and white,
and many little windows like gaping mouths talking in the air or
lidless eyes looking out on the people in the streets. Lower down
there were windows, reaching to the ground, filled with all manner
of things to please those who had money to go in and buy. Tony
walked by all scarcely knowing: but he understood, for he had seen
his shadow: he was in the distance towards which he had looked so
often from his mountain home.

He was far off and very little.

He knew that he was bound and a prisoner, but it did not matter,
he did not care. It was only part of a new life in the new world that he
had entered. Suddenly with a jerk he stopped by one of the great
windows; a door opened and he entered. All about him was wooden
—wooden houses and people and animals—and everywhere a sound
of ticking. Tick, tick, tick. He was lifted by the dealer's hand on to a
height. Before him was a house, a chälet, with a flight of stairs outside
leading to a balcony.

"Go up," the dealer said, and slowly stair by stair he went, his feet
growing stiffer and stiffer with every step upward. He rested on the
balcony; there were two little doors leading into the house, they
opened suddenly and disclosed a little room behind. In the room
waiting—surely waiting for him—was the strange little woman Tony
had seen his father take from the block of wood. He remembered
that he used to be afraid of her. How foolish he had been; now he
was afraid of nothing. He took his place beside her, he felt that they
would never be apart again unless great change or sorrow came:
surely it was like a marriage? He saw that the little woman was as big
as he, had she grown? or had he—but he could not think or reason.
He was jerked back, the wire twanged, the doors closed, and all was
still. He was in the darkness waiting too, but for what or how long he
did not know: all time was the same to him, he could measure it no
more.

In the distance he heard other wires twanging, and presently the
melody of his song came from many directions, as though the place
were full of it. He could hear the people in the street; they hummed
it as they passed by. Once far off he heard a band playing it. But he
did not listen long, for all things grew faint as they would have grown
dim too had he been in the light to see and know. For Tony's life had

gone into his song; only a simple little song, just as his had been a simple little life.

Life is not only in nodding heads, and work is not only for hands that move and feet that walk; it is in many other things.

After a time there were sounds of fitting and tapping over Tony's head, a loud ticking—tick, tick, tick unceasingly, and then a strange whirring, and an iron tongue struck out clang-clang up to eleven. As the last stroke fell, the little doors flew open and Tony and his companion were jerked out by the wire that bound them on to the balcony at the top of the stairs by which he had mounted, and stood together while all around and above the song was played—the song that never would come from his lips again. Before them, separating the place in which their dwelling was from the street, was a great window letting in a flood of light, and on the outer side against the glass were pressed eager faces watching; but Tony and his companion did not know this; as the last note died away they were jerked back into the little room and all was darkness till another hour had passed, and then it all happened again. Hour after hour it was always the same, day after day, week after week, month after month, in light and dark, in heat and cold.

Two weary faces once were pressed against the window, those of a woman and a man, and as the doors opened and the two little figures came forth on the clock and stood while the song was played, the woman cried.

"It is Tony, it is Tony, it is his song; there beside him is the woman you made, and he is wooden too—he is wooden."

"Thou art dreaming," said the man; "Tony is gone into the world, and we will go and seek him."

"No, no," the woman cried in despair, "his song has gone into the world, but Tony is there," and she pointed to the clock; "he is wooden—he is wooden." The man looked long and silently.

"He had always a wooden head," he answered slowly; "maybe the rest of him has gone wooden too, for he did not move enough to keep quickened. But he was useless," he added, trying to comfort his wife; "didst thou not say thyself that his song would work instead of his hands, and journey instead of his feet?"

"Ah, that was well enough for those who did not love him" said the mother, "but it does not comfort me. It is Tony that I want, my son Tony who sat by the door and sang, or by the fire watching the

wood smoulder." While she spoke the song ceased, the figures were
jerked into the darkness, and the doors closed: before the man and
woman lay the long road and the weary miles that led back to the
village and the mountain.

Lest Levitation
Come Upon Us

Suzette Haden Elgin

Suzette Haden Elgin is a linguist, writer, and folk singer known both for her science fiction and fantasy novels and her tall tales and musical performances at fantasy conventions. Some of her best fiction suggests her concern with feminism in a style free of rhetorical jargon, as with this witty and, perhaps, subversive tale in which the wife of a prominent lawyer discovers to her dismay that she seems to have become a saint, miracles and all. As her miracles become gaudier and seem likely to hurt her husband's prominence, she decides something must be done about them.

If it had been only her circumstances, her own convenience, only her own *self* to be considered, Valeria thought she might in fact have been able to manage. There would have been adjustments and accommodations, but she was a woman; and, accustomed as all women are to adjustments and accommodations, she would have coped somehow. If nothing else, she could have let a tale be leaked, one bit of trivia at a time . . . little note cards in a spidery hand with weak excuses on them, and the word going round of a chronic disease. Nothing fatal, and nothing ugly; but something that would have made coming by to see her a chore to avoid, while at the same time explaining why she was never seen in public anymore. And pretty soon she would have been forgotten, one of those enigmatic and eccentric Southern ladies with a decomposing corpse to protect in the cupboard . . . the teenager who delivered her paper, and the elderly man who could still be hired to deliver groceries if the order was kept to just a bag or two, they would have set things down on her front porch and made hasty tracks. For fear of what they might see behind Valeria Elizabeth Carterhasty's spotless white curtains.

But it was *not* like that, as she was no longer a Carterhasty, nor could she consider her own self. She was much-married, mother of three, wife to Julian B. Cantrell, up-and-coming attorney-at-law, and consideration of self was far down the list of her priorities, some-where below keeping the flea collars up to date on the requisite dog and pair of Siamese cats. Clearly, she was going to have to think of some way to deal with this inexplicable affliction an unknown deity had seen fit to visit upon her.

That Julian had been furious the first time it happened seemed to her entirely reasonable; after all, a lawyer does not maintain a prac-tice at $100,000 a year and support a family without maintaining a certain image. The elegant home, with the redwood deck. The pleas-ant wife with the knack for noncontroversial conversation. The matched set of well-groomed and well-behaved children, each with a hobby that might in time become a profession. Daryl, with his micro-scope and his white mice. Philip, with the ranks of labeled shoeboxes each containing an electronic something-or-other, and the lust for a personal computer—even without a printer—that Julian sternly re-fused to satisfy. "When you have earned and saved half the money for it, I'll match that with the other half, young man." That was Julian's way. And Charlotte. With Charlotte it was ballet. Charlotte had not really wanted to take up ballet . . . had wanted to go into baton-twirling, actually . . . but when it was explained to her that there would be a problem making that fit into Daddy's image, she had sighed, and exchanged glances with her mother, and gone duti-fully into the ballet classes as requested. Whether she ever took out the wooden baton with the gold dust and the red tassel and the cheap silver cord, won at a carnival and put away in her closet, Valeria did not know and was careful not to ask.

They had been at the Far Corner, she and Julian and a Mr. and Mrs. Tabbitt from Memphis, right between the cocktails and the trip to the salad bar, and Valeria had known Julian was satisfied by the way things were going. He'd leaned back a little in his chair, and the tension in his hands that came from trying to quit smoking had re-laxed a bit. The light was dim enough to make everyone look attrac-

tive, but not so dark you couldn't see what you were eating, and the
Muzak was doing "Rhapsody in Blue," when it happened. Mr. Tabbitt . . . Wayne? . . . she thought he had been a Wayne . . . had
leaned forward and peered at her, his eyebrows a little vee of intense
interest, and remarked that however she achieved the effect it was
surely very becoming. And when she'd asked what effect, he had said
that he was talking about the way she glowed.

"Glow? Do I?" Valeria had turned to Julian and pointed out how
nice it was of Mr. Tabbitt to pay her the compliment, and found him
staring at her too, and all the relaxation replaced by the kind of tight-
strung attention he paid to juries he wasn't sure of yet.

"It must be the light in here," he'd said slowly.

"Must be," agreed the Tabbitts, especially Mrs. Tabbitt, whose
name Valeria could no longer remember.

"It would have to be," Julian added. "I wonder how they do it?
They should make a fortune at it."

Valeria sat there, fiddling with her glass, wondering; and the
murmurs from behind their table began to work their way through to
her conscious attention. And about that time the rose petals started
falling, and that was really the last straw. Julian was a patient man
ordinarily, for the stress that he was under, but he took her out of
there as fast as if she'd thrown up on the table, and the Tabbitts not
only didn't give him their malpractice suit to handle, they were practically at a full run by the time they reached the parking lot.

Julian's main concern, after the loss of the Tabbitts, had been for
the publicity.

"How the hell are we going to keep it out of the papers?" he had
demanded, handing her brusquely into their Mercedes in a way that
made her elbow ache and coming very close to slamming the door on
her white silk skirt. She only just managed to snatch it free in the nick
of time.

"Keep what out of the papers, Julian?"

"Oh, come *on*, Valeria!"

"Sweetheart, if you don't look at the road once in a while I don't
see how you can drive—it can't be a good idea."

"Well, damn it, Valeria, just look at yourself! Go on—*look* at you!"

She had held her arms out in front of her, obediently, and sure
enough, she did glow. Not just the rosy glow of health, or the meta-
phorical glow that came from the right sort of cosmetics and a good
hairdresser. You could have read a newspaper by her.

"My goodness," she said. "How embarrassing for you . . . I'm sorry, Julian."

"Yeah." Julian swerved viciously around a dog that wasn't bothering anybody. "Your goodness. What the bloody hell is going on with you, anyway?"

Well, she didn't know, so far as that went. What it reminded her of more than anything else was one of those white plastic statues of Gentle Jesus, Meek and Mild, that came for $6.98 from a radio station that broadcasts all night long from the very depths of Texas. The statue, according to the preacher hawking it, not only glowed in the dark with the light of *Truth* and the light of Sal*va*tion and the ever*last*ing light—provided you put the batteries in, presumably—it also could be made to revolve slowly on its stand. Valeria was grateful that she was not revolving, either slowly or in any other manner. But the glow was really in very bad taste. It was not soft, it was *bright,* and it was the same shade of gold as the stuff glued to the top of her daughter's carnival baton. And it spread out from her skin to a distance of a good two inches or so.

Tacky, thought Valeria, and brushed off a rose petal that Julian had missed while he was hustling her out of the restaurant.

"My dear," she said, genuinely concerned because she could see that he was, "you don't need to worry about the papers. Really."

"I don't, eh? I suppose you think people are *used* to going out for a quiet dinner in an expensive restaurant and seeing the woman at the next table light up like a damned Christmas tree, not to mention having rose petals rain down on her from the ceiling. For God's *sake,* Valeria . . . I mean, the people who go to the Far Corner are reasonably sophisticated, but they won't have seen *that* number before."

"Julian."

"What, Valeria? What?"

"It won't be in the papers," she said.

"The hell it won't."

"It *won't,*" she insisted.

"One reason why not, Valeria—just one!"

"Because, when people see something like that, they won't admit it. Not to each other, not to themselves . . . not to the papers. By the time they've all finished eating they'll be convinced they didn't see anything at all, or they'll think it was a stunt for my birthday with the waiters throwing roses at me or something. I assure you."

"You think so?"

"Julian, if any of those people were to suddenly look up and see an angel, twenty feet tall and with a wingspread like a 747, you know what they'd say? 'Biggest damned bird I ever saw,' that's what they'd say. And then they'd order another strawberry daiquiri."

"You really think—"

"I really do, dear heart. There's absolutely nothing for you to worry about. Even the Whatsits—"

"Tabbitts. They were a damned good *case,* Valeria."

"Even the Tabbitts . . . they won't be three blocks away before they've convinced themselves they didn't see anything either."

She saw the tightness go out of his shoulders. She patted his hand, and waited.

When they pulled into the driveway he finally asked her, tentatively, if she could—maybe—explain it.

"No, Julian," she said calmly, "I'm afraid I can't. But I'm sure it won't happen again."

"Like those stories you read about it raining frogs."

"Something like that."

Valeria was quite wrong. It happened over and over again. The children didn't appreciate rose petals in their breakfast pancakes when it happened while she was cooking. Julian set out for her logically the reasons why, since he differed from almost every other American husband by not snoring, it was unfair and unreasonable for her to keep him awake by glowing at him in the dark. Her protests that she had no control over it at all, and no warning either, didn't help matters, and Julian suggested to her that she stay home as much as possible until they could work something out.

She *was* at home when the cookies thing occurred. It was Charlotte's turn to have Camp Fire Girls, and Maryann Whipple's mother was supposed to have sent the refreshments; but, Mrs. Whipple being the sort of woman she was (not Maryann's fault, and a nicer child you couldn't have asked for), there weren't nearly enough cookies to go around. There Valeria was with a plate of cookies—store-bought, too, and not a bakery, either—with only one dozen cookies on it. And seventeen Camp Fire Girls holding glasses of Kool-Aid and looking at her expectantly.

She had just opened her mouth to excuse herself, meaning to go to the kitchen and see what she had in *her* cooky jar, when she heard

Charlotte make a funny little strangled noise and cover it with a cough.

"Oh, how nice of your Mama!" the child said—she was one quick thinker, was Charlotte—and before Valeria could say anything to confuse the issue, Charlotte had whisked the plate out of her hands and was passing it around just as bland as you please. If any of the girls had seen the one dozen nondescript lemon supermarket cookies on that plate suddenly become a pyramid of dainty little cakes, each one with its own icing and its own trim of chopped nuts or candied cherries or silver sprinkles, that girl hadn't mentioned it. So far as Valeria knew, it was just herself and Charlotte who had seen it happen, and Mrs. Whipple would never remember that she'd sent a plain white plate and gotten back good china with a narrow rim of gold, and that made two things to be thankful for.

"*Really*, Mother!" Charlotte had said, when the door closed behind the last of the Camp Fire Girls. "*Really!*"

"You handled it very well, dear, I must say," said Valeria. "I was impressed."

"Thank you, Mother," said Charlotte, tight-lipped and fuming, her arms folded over her chest just exactly like Julian.

"Charlotte," Valeria chided, "that's not attractive."

"I don't care if it's attractive or *not!*" wailed Charlotte. "*Really*, Mother—what are you going to do *next? ? ?*"

"Ah," said Valeria solemnly, "if I knew that, I would be much more comfortable about this whole thing. I could plan ahead, you see, if I knew that."

"And you think *that* is attractive?"

Valeria raised her eyebrows, thinking that Charlotte had more than a touch of the Cantrell temper from her father's side, and that puberty was going to be a storm-tossed sea for the child, but she said nothing. She only looked, until the girl's eyes dropped and a high flush spread over her cheeks.

"I'm sorry, Mother," said Charlotte. "That was sassing, and it was uncalled for. I know you don't do it on purpose."

"I surely don't," Valeria answered.

"Can you stop, do you think? I mean, that's not sass, Mama, it's just that I want to know. Do you think you can?"

Valeria sighed.

"I think it will stop of itself," she said slowly. "The way everybody around a town sees UFO's or hears mysterious thumps or something for a week or two . . . and then it just stops. Provided you don't pay a lot of attention to it."

"And if it doesn't stop?"

"Well! If it doesn't stop, then I will have to get some sort of help, naturally. We must wait and see."

She stayed home more and more that summer, and Julian went so far as to let the word get out that the doctor thought she might be just a touch anemic and ought to stay in bed a good deal. But there were times when she really did have to go out, and no way to avoid it. When your next-door neighbor is in labor, and there's not a single soul around to take her to the hospital, and her husband's away in Atlanta on business and her parents clear off in California . . . might as well be on the moon as be in California . . . ! Well. Valeria had yet to see the day when she would send a woman off to the maternity ward in a taxi, always supposing they could have gotten a taxi, which was not anything you could have counted on. Before it was over she was to wish fervently that she had called an ambulance, or delivered the baby herself (which would have been no great shucks, though the mere suggestion had nearly sent the mother into hysterics); but at the time, her duty had been as clear to her as the freckles over the bridge of her nose. And she had bundled up Carol Sue and the suitcase and headed straight for Skyway Memorial without giving it one more minute's thought—as would any other woman, under similar circumstances.

That time it did get in the papers. Never mind what people might have thought they did or didn't see. The traffic helicopter that was doing the feature for the six o'clock news about the tangled mess at the intersection by the defense plant got pictures that had nothing to do with subjective impressions. There was the Mercedes, on the six o'clock news, and her, Valeria Carterhasty Cantrell, at the wheel, rising into the air every time there was a little bit of a knot in the traffic and just wafting right over it to the next empty space before settling sedately back into the row of cars and their flabbergasted drivers.

It got them to the hospital in record time, and the inconvenient glow got them past the Admitting Office without one word about insurance *or* money, which had to be a first, but if it didn't mark the baby it would be a miracle. And nobody was speaking to Valeria. Not her husband, not her children, not Carol Sue, not Carol Sue's husband (back from Atlanta) . . . Carol Sue's parents, flying in in great haste from California, had been threatening to sue until they learned that Julian was an attorney.

Julian once more had a good deal to say about last straws. Not divorce, of course; Cantrells did not divorce. Divorce, furthermore, would do nothing for his carefully made plans to move one day into the Governor's Mansion. It could be added that he was truly fond of Valeria, and aware that she could not be easily replaced.

Valeria, who appreciated both his concern for her and his concern about her, came to the rueful conclusion that it was not just going to go away of itself as she had hoped, like a spree of UFO sightings. She would, she told Julian, do something about the problem.

"The problem."

She did not like the way he was looking at her; it had overtones of *naming* the problem, perhaps *defining* the problem. Valeria did not think that would be in Julian's best interests.

"This afternoon," she said quickly. "I'll see to it."

"How? What?"

"But right now, Julian, you are late for the Jaycees Luncheon. That Municipal Center thing."

"God, I forgot all about it!"

"Well, you'd better go, dear, hadn't you?"

"I'm not sure I have the guts."

"I beg your pardon, Julian?"

"I am going to hear one hell of a lot about what they saw on the six o'clock news, Valeria. And the ten o'clock news. *This* time, it's a horse of a different color. Television cameras do not imagine they see . . . what they saw."

"Mmmmm."

"Valeria?"

"Julian," she said, tapping her lower lip with her finger, "I suggest that if they bring it up—which would be extraordinarily rude of them, I must say—you tell them that we are bringing suit against Mercedes for one million dollars. And another couple of million on behalf of Carol Sue and her baby."

Julian stared at her, and she could have sworn there was a flash of admiration in his eyes.

"I never would have thought of that, darling," he said, grabbing his briefcase.

He wouldn't have, either. Valeria had explained to Charlotte, on the single occasion when the child insisted on knowing what was the *matter* with men, anyway, that they lacked motherwit; and that this was an inherent deficiency that could not be held against them.

"I don't see why not," Charlotte fretted. "They could learn . . . they learn law stuff and medical stuff and how to blow up the whole world, don't they?"

"Not the same thing at all."

"What's motherwit?"

"Motherwit is what makes you notice the messes men get themselves into, Charlotte Rose. And what gives you sense enough not to let on you notice."

"And to clean up the messes after them."

"Precisely. And we will never mention this again."

"Can I tell Judette McElroad? We've been best friends going on three years this March."

"No."

"Not even Judette? Mama!"

"Not even Judette. It's up to Judette's mother to tell her."

"Like the Curse."

"We do not say 'the Curse,' Charlotte. It's tacky."

As was this situation.

"Can you just give me a simple description of your problem?" the priest had asked her, no doubt wondering what a nice Methodist lady like herself was doing in a place like his, crucifixes on the wall and candles flickering in niches, and him with his long black gown.

She had tried, beginning with the disastrous dinner that had lost Julian the Tabbitts case and going straight on to the end, with the trip to the hospital and the Mercedes.

He looked at her, when she paused, in precisely the way she had expected him to look, and she knew he had not watched the news. He looked at her dubiously, for which she could in no way blame him. And then the look in his eyes changed abruptly, and his fingers flickered through the sign of the cross, mutter-mutter-mutter, and she assumed she must have begun doing something convincing. Glowing. Rotating. Levitating. Whatever.

"—and the Holy Spirit. Amen," said the priest. Adding, "Oh dear. Oh dear me."

"Why, Father?" asked Valeria, as reasonably as she could after the dreary recital of her humiliations, and feeling as if she had a bit part in one of those Italian movies about devout peasants with flocks of goats. "It seems to me that *I* am the one who should be saying 'oh dear.' "

The priest, to her astonishment, lowered his head to his hands and gripped it fiercely, all ten fingers buried deep in the thick black curls of his hair, and he moaned. Moaned!

"Father?"

Valeria waited, and then tried again.

"Father!"

From the depths of his hands came a muffled "Please allow me to compose myself" and some mumbling about not having believed it even if the call *did* come from the Bishop, but now he'd seen it with his own eyes, and "Please forgive me," and then he was at last looking at her. Or perhaps through her. Beads of sweat on his upper lip and forehead, and a bit shocky-looking, but no longer in a state of collapse.

He cleared his throat twice, and folded his hands, and said, "Mrs. Cantrell, I fear I am in over my head."

"As if I needed an ophthalmologist and you were an oculist."

"An excellent analogy, dear lady."

"Nevertheless," said Valeria, "we could *discuss* this. It is, in some sense of the word, your field . . . and you are the expert, isn't that right?"

"A most inadequate expert, I'm afraid."

"That's twice now you've said you were afraid. You have nothing to be afraid of."

He shook his head vehemently—he did have beautiful curls!—and crossed himself again.

"Oh my, oh my," he said. "You're wrong there, Mrs. Cantrell."

"In what way?"

"Either you are a visitation of the Dear Lord, in which case I have good reason to be afraid—I was never in the presence of a living saint before, you see, and I don't have the remotest idea how to behave. Or you are a visitation of the Evil One, in which case I have good reason to be terrified right out of my cassock, if you'll pardon a feeble joke."

"Is that possible?"

"Is what possible?"

"That all this might be the Devil's doing," said Valeria. "It never occurred to me, but it would surely simplify things."

His jaw dropped, and then he shut his mouth in a way that made his teeth click.

"I don't see it, I'm afraid . . . there, I've said it again. But I *am* afraid. And I don't know why you would prefer the workings of the Devil to the workings of the Almighty."

"Because," Valeria pointed out, "if I am bewitched, or possessed, or whatever the label is, there's a cure for that. You just haul out your exorcism kit and fix me up, and I can go home to my family and tell them life is normal once again. I would much prefer that, Father, to the other thing."

"Tell me again," he said flatly.

"All of it?"

"All of it. This time I will be able to listen more carefully, since I know what's coming. Please don't leave out anything, not the smallest detail."

She told him again, feeling bored and hopeless, while he steepled his fingers and peered at her over them and, every now and again, made a soft noise like a half dozen bees.

"Mrs. Cantrell," he asked when she got to the end of it again, "have you always been a devout woman?"

"Never," she said promptly.

"Never!"

"Never. I'm a Methodist. I went to Sunday School when I was a child because my parents made me go, and I go to church now because my husband's law practice would suffer if I didn't—and I make my children go for the same reason. I suppose my mother made *me* go for the sake of my father's medical practice, come to think of it."

"Do you pray?"

"Of my own accord, you mean?"

"Yes."

"Father Genora—if there is a God, a matter on which I'm no authority—I would certainly have better taste and better manners than to think that He or She was interested in the kind of things I have to pray about. Can you imagine a God that would be interested in my profound hope that my daughter won't have to wear braces on her teeth? Can you imagine a God that would be concerned about that rash I get when Julian tries a different aftershave lotion. . . . Father, I don't think for one moment that God doesn't respect my ability to manage my own affairs. And I have an equivalent respect for God's ability to run the celestial mechanics, so to speak."

"You don't want to be any trouble to Him," said the priest gently.

"Or Her. As the case may be."

The priest winced visibly, but Valeria did not apologize.

"My dear child," said the priest, "there really isn't any question about it. I don't think there has been any question, from the beginning. I don't *understand* it—but then I don't understand Job, either, or Judas, or Biafra. My Bishop would have my head on a platter if he heard me say this, but I would be a coward if I didn't—my dear child, you are . . . for some utterly unfathomable divine reason . . . a saint. Not a *certified* saint; for that you have to be dead. But a saint all the same."

"Father Genora, couldn't you be mistaken? I think the Devil version is far more likely, now you've brought it up. The Devil's not nearly so choosy, as I understand it."

"If you were possessed," said the priest firmly, "you could not look me in the eye and talk of . . . the Almighty the way you have. You wear the armor of holy innocence, and I can only say that in this situation I wish *I* did."

Valeria drew a long breath, and asked: "And do you have something in your procedures manual for that? You can cast out devils in the name of God—can you cast out angels, or whatever it is I've caught?"

He shook his head, and his fingers seemed to be searching in his cassock for someplace to hide.

"You must try to understand," he told her. "The Church cannot even imagine such a thing as wishing to be . . . unsainted."

"Well, that's absurd. It's a terrible nuisance."

"I imagine it must be. The masses have always loved the saints, and their families have always hated them. Nobody wants to *live* with one . . . some of them have done the most repulsive, stomach-turning, not to mention outright demented things. But if God picks you to be a saint, my child, the Church is assuredly not going to presume to question His choice. Do you see what I mean?"

Valeria was thinking hard. Here she was, with her marriage falling apart, and her children turning against her, and Julian's entire future on the line, and all this holy man could do was make excuses.

"Father Genora, what if you were to say the exorcism service backward? Do you suppose . . . oh dear. Father, I apologize. I did *not* realize it would upset you so much—it's an entirely empirical question, you know. Put a car in forward, it goes forward; put it in reverse, it goes backward. Do an exorcism, you undevil the bedeviled; do an *anti*-exorcism, you might unsaint the besainted. But I can see that you wouldn't care to try that, so I'll have to manage on my own, won't I?"

The priest was pale and shuddering, but he managed to ask her how she intended to proceed. Valeria thought it best to be gentle with him.

"Father," she said, "you'll be far better off if you don't know."

"Mrs. *Cantrell!* How do you suppose that I am to live with my conscience, if I let you just walk out of here like this? A saint comes to me, to *me,* for spiritual counsel; and all I can do is mumble and sweat. You must give me an opportunity to discuss this, to see if there is not some solution, to . . . ."

She did not really like to cut him off in mid-stream, having learned long ago that a man frustrated in that way would tend to take it out on somebody else at the first opportunity, but she was tired. Tired, and disgusted; after all, she had not asked for this. She had *not* gone about doing good, trying to entice the birds and the squirrels and the butterflies to light upon her person, healing the sick and the maimed, praying and preaching. She had been going about her business, *minding* her own business, and not bothering anybody, and then to have this happen—it was a bit much. And this priest, this holy tinkerer who appeared not to know one end of a religious question from another, was a great disappointment to her. It just went to show how limited her experience had been.

"Father," she said carefully, "sainthood is something you get into by not sinning enough. I intend to go home and *sin* until I have become too wicked to be a saint. If you want to help me, you might save me some time by explaining to me what the *worst* sin is—that one against the Holy Ghost. I could start with that and skip some of the minor infringements."

There he went again. Oh dearing. Oh dear me-ing. It was more than she could bear, and to avoid beginning her career as a sinner by the wanton murder of a man of God, she simply left him nattering and went home. She was late in any case, and Julian did not like for her to be late.

Valeria believed in *system.* Flounder about, doing things at random, and you got nowhere. She began, therefore, with the Ten Commandments, although she was not quite willing to go through them in order.

The one about having no other gods was easy enough. Valeria went down to an import shop where she was accustomed to getting those paper lanterns you put in the garden to help people wander around outside at parties without breaking their necks. She bought a Buddha, a Kwan-Yin, an Indian deity with far more arms than any god ought to need, a very badly done Venus, and something the clerk swore was a statue of Isis—if she was mistaken it didn't really matter, it was sure to be some minor god or other. That made *five* forbidden gods, all of them graven images (or cast images, which ought to be equally wicked, given the Almighty's own knowledge of how things had changed since Moses and that calf), and she set them all up in her sewing room, locked the door, and bowed down to each and every one of the five in turn. While she was at it, getting two commandments with one stone, so to speak, she took the Lord's name in vain repeatedly, feeling that the Lord had it coming anyway.

Sunday, instead of going to church with the rest of the family, she hemmed a whole set of curtains, carting them into the sewing room where she could sit surrounded by her heathen images and getting up every now and then to bow to each one of them. And on the off chance that the sabbath day mentioned in Exodus was Saturday instead of Sunday, she spent a Saturday in there, too, taking the hems out and putting them back in again despite the fact that they'd been done perfectly in the first place. When she found that she'd spotted one of the panels with blood, sticking her finger with a pin, she turned her face up to the heavens and said aloud: "God damn it. God damn it all the way to hell and back."

When Charlotte knocked on the door to find out if she was ever coming out to fix lunch, Valeria took a deep breath and said "Fix it yourself, God damn it!"

"Mother!"

"You heard me," said Valeria. "Now, God damn it, do what I told you. I'm very, very busy."

Next came dishonoring . . . no, failing to honor was all that was required, thank goodness . . . failing to honor her father and her mother. She took care of that and worked false witness into it at the same time, telling Julian's mother on the telephone that he wasn't home when he was standing right behind her. Valeria had never lied to Mother Cantrell before, and didn't enjoy doing it now, but putting things off wasn't going to help.

"No, Mother Cantrell," she went on, "I don't know when he'll be back. He didn't say. You know how Julian is, he does as he pleases, goes where he pleases, and shows up when the spirit moves him. God damn it."

Lies, all of it. Julian wouldn't have gone around the block without giving Valeria an exact schedule, and if he'd turned any one of that block's four corners later than promised, he would have stopped to call her and let her know.

Moving right along, she tried coveting. She coveted everything she could get at. She put her back into it and coveted an awful phony waterfall in Carol Sue's yard, along with the phony boulders that made its basin, and she hoped she was making a good impression.

Stealing was a nuisance, but she did it; she stole a girdle from Macy's, ostentatiously parading it through the store inside her blouse, and throwing it into a Salvation Army pickup box on the way home when nobody so much as questioned her about it. Killing was easier; she got an assortment of spray cans and killed everything that crawled or flew within the reach of her narrow stream of noxious chemical death. She stepped viciously on spiders she would ordinarily have carried carefully out to the rosebushes. And she reminded herself that each and every time she showered, each and every time she brushed her teeth, she slaughtered tens of millions of innocent bacteria and assorted bystanders. In the long run, it must count up.

Thinking that *combined* sins were more efficient, she went to see her father and his new wife, lied to the wife about her father's age, stole a crystal vase of her mother's, stunned both father and bride with her incessant string of "God damns," and resolutely flushed down the toilet a tropical fish that any fool except her father could have seen was swimming at that bizarre angle because it was sick and in pain. As the fish gurgled out of sight, Valeria said, "Thank you, holy Isis."

By the end of her first week as a dedicated sinner, Valeria felt fouled from the gut out and wondered how the habitual sinner stood it, not to mention all the *time* it took. But it wasn't working. It seemed to her that the more she sinned, the more brightly she glowed and the worse the rose petals falling about her stank, and when Julian moved to the bed in the guest room she did not blame him one bit. In his place, she would have moved even sooner.

Somehow, Valeria had thought she would surely be excused from the last of the proscribed activities, but it clearly was not to be. Like Job, or Aristotle, or somebody, she was going to have to drink her nasty poison to its last dregs. And that meant adultery. It was not an interesting sin, but she could not think of anything wickeder, and the complicated arrangements it involved made it possible to drag in a number of associated sins in the false witness line along with it. She did it twice, with two separate willing strangers; and then to top it off she did it with a few of the husbands in the neighborhood. Afterward, she understood why so many of the women she knew were so cross and vicious, and she treated them with special tenderness. She had had no idea what they had been putting up with, or how lucky she was to have Julian competently sharing her bed—or at least visiting it.

And that didn't work, either. She'd run through the whole list, much of it dozens of times, and things were no better. Putting in tulip bulbs, and trying to keep her mind on doing that properly, Valeria fretted and wept and impatiently brushed away a herd of butterflies that insisted on settling around her, and swore terrible oaths.

"I will be *damned,*" she cried desperately in the general direction of the heavenly parapets, waving her trowel, "I will be damned if I will murder a human being just for Your satisfaction! I warn You, You will go too far, do You hear me? You hear me down here? I am *blas*pheming, damn it! Praise Isis! Praise Zeus! Praise Satan, for that matter!"

And when the pure white dove came out of the puffy cloud above her and flew down to circle over her head, Valeria lay down in the ditch she had dug for her flowers, heedless of the carefully worked-in manure, and wept in desperate earnest. And the burden of her complaint was: "My God, my God—what will it take to get You to forsake me?"

It was Maryann Whipple's mother, of all unlikely people, who finally solved her problem. Nobody would call Ruby Whipple a saint, that was for sure and for certain. A trollop, perhaps, a liar and a thief and an awesomely poor excuse for a mother *or* a daughter—but never a saint. Valeria, forsaken by everyone she loved and tormented by a god whose attentions she had never sought but could not now get rid of, went to Ruby Whipple and told her the whole story. Valeria was long past caring if Ruby believed her or not and Ruby, monumentally

fortified with straight Scotch at ten o'clock of a Tuesday morning, was
in no condition to doubt anything.

"Shoot, honey," said Ruby, leaning back on the pillows her couch
was piled with and knocking half a dozen onto the floor, "you
haven't been sinning at all."

"I have!" Valeria was furious. "I have been sinning *so* hard—"

"Yeah, yeah," scoffed Ruby. "Sure you have. Honey, I am a Bap-
tist minister's daughter, and I know whereof I speak, and I am here to
tell you that you can't sin for *shit.*"

"Nonsense!"

"Nonsense, my rosy butt," Ruby said. "You tell me *why* you're
racing around like a chicken with its head cut off, lying and stealing
and cussing and hopping in and out of bed with anything that can get
it up and plenty that can't! Not to mention bowing to Isis and Kwan-
Yin and hemming drapes on both Saturdays and Sundays!"

Ruby lay back and laughed fit to burst, spilling Scotch down her
front, and Valeria's heart ached for Maryann Whipple.

"Every one of those things," she said firmly, "every last one that
you find so funny, is supposed to be a sin. Every single one has a
special commandment all its own forbidding it. You *can't* say I
haven't sinned."

"Valeria . . . tell me *why.* You haven't been doing it because it
was fun, have you?"

"Fun?" Valeria moaned as the priest had moaned. "I have never in
my life done anything so tiresome and so boring as all these sins.
Fun!"

"Then why?"

"Because Julian and the children are entitled to a normal wife and
mother and a normal ordinary wholesome life, that's why, and I am
determined that they shall have them!"

"Uh-huh," said Ruby emphatically. "That's the problem, sweet
thing. You sin for the sake of those you love, you lay down your soul
for your friend. Valeria, that doesn't *count.* You've been wasting your
time, child."

"It's not fair!"

"No, it's not," agreed Ruby Whipple, "but then, nothing is." And
she passed out cold on the couch.

Well, even a saint has limits to her patience, and Valeria came to
the end of hers that day. She could see what Ruby meant, and was

fervently grateful that she'd listened to Ruby before she took the next step she had been contemplating. True, old Mr. Hackwood would have been released from his misery, lying there with all those tubes and monitors and lights and buzzers in a strange place he hated, with nothing but his agony for company. True, his poor wife, not really well herself, would have been released from the seemingly endless burden of watching him die by fractions of inches and hearing him plead for release around the clock; Adam Hackwood no longer knew that the woman who'd shared his life for over fifty years was in the room, but he hadn't stopped believing that there was a Jesus somewhere who would step in and set things to rights if you only asked Him often enough and nicely enough. True, the nurses on the floor where Mr. Hackwood was would have had more time to spend with other patients who were *not* dying, and would have had to spend less time comforting the ones in the rooms nearby his who had a tendency to weep at what they heard from their "terminal" colleague. True, if the Bible were to be believed, Adam Hackwood would have traded a hard bed, with a stiff rubber sheet and every invention of misery a fecund modern medical science could provide, for residence in Paradise and nothing more uncomfortable to do but learn to tolerate the brightness of the Almighty's shining face and the duty of praising Him everlastingly. All true.

Well, let it be true. All of it. She, Valeria, was *not going to do it.* Let them all suffer, let them writhe and bleed and wail; she was going to grit her teeth and let it pass her by, because nothing she had done so far had helped one bit and nothing she had in mind along the same lines impressed her as having any greater potential for releasing her from *her* misery.

She hadn't the heart to go back and torment the priest further, but she knew what she needed now, and she thought she could manage. She needed a way to work within the system, instead of against it. She needed to break a rule that the High-and-Mighty would have no choice but to pay attention to. No more Mrs. Nice Lady, no sir . . . not *this* saint! Valeria set her teeth and headed for the theology section of the University library. And it turned out that the books on fornication and adultery and murder and all their repulsive ilk weren't even *in* the theology section; if you wanted to read those, you had to go to the social science shelves, or Family Studies. No doubt Ruby Whipple could have told her that.

She learned a lot in the theology stacks. She learned that women were the gateway to Hell. She learned that despite claiming that what they had seen and experienced could not possibly be expressed in words, the mystics went right on and expressed it at extraordinary length. She learned that the Vatican had curious problems, and that it was possible to commit a crime called "fishing in Papal waters." She learned vast amounts about things that not only did not interest her but clearly had not interested those who wrote about them, and it became obvious to her that if all theology were written in Latin it would be no great loss. Her frustration grew, but she did not let that distract her from her task, and would have been ashamed to do so; she was literate, and she had been a Carterhasty, and nobody was going to tell her that she couldn't get to the bottom of this.

And there came the day when she found what she was looking for. Lying and murder and other-gods-before-me and stealing and working your tail off on the sabbath . . . those, she discovered to her amazement, were piddly little sinlets hardly worth mentioning. Those were such everyday common garden variety in the way of sinning that it was no wonder Ruby Whipple had laughed, and Valeria flushed along the delicate ridge of her cheekbones, remembering. The place to find out about sins was not in the Bible, it was in the books that mortal men had written *about* the Bible, and it was there that Valeria learned the name of the sin that would get you smacked no matter how well you might be doing otherwise.

"Hallelujah!" she said, right out loud and no reverence intended.

Who would have ever guessed that the Sin of Sins would not be something interesting like infant cannibalism, but simply *pride?* She shook her head, overwhelmed.

Pride. Pride! That was the one that wouldn't be tolerated and, from what Valeria read, it was a source of real difficulty for anybody fool enough to go out for sainthood, since the more good and pure and holy you were, the more likely you were to tumble into the pit of being proud of your own goodness. People might watch Valeria lie and cheat and fornicate (horrible prospect!) and learn nothing at all from that; the Almighty could afford to ignore that, what with everybody and his housecat doing it right and left all the day and all the night long. But pride, now! If Valeria were allowed to get away with pride—even to *seem* to get away with pride, especially now that they were trying to get her to go on television talk shows—that would set a precedent the Almighty wouldn't dare overlook.

Valeria slammed the book shut, chuckling to herself, and went

straight home to call up the television pests and say she'd be delighted to appear on their fool show. Julian roared and swore she'd
ruin him, and the children all threatened to run away, but Valeria was
not to be budged.

"You just wait and see," she told them. "I know what I'm doing."

"You do not!" snapped Charlotte. "You absolutely do not."

"This time I do," said Valeria.

"Valeria, if you go on that television show and millions of people
all over the country get a long look at your little bag of tricks—"

"Julian Cantrell," she said, thin-lipped and sounding almost snap-
pish, "I said I know what I'm doing, and I do. Now, I don't want to
hear any more about it, not one word. You just go on about your
business, and I'll go on about mine. Daryl, I'm going to need your
help."

"My help?" Daryl was bewildered.

"I need you to go shopping with me," she told him.

"Mother—"

"Valeria—"

"Mother—" That was Charlotte.

"Daryl will know where we should go," Valeria insisted, "he's the
right age." And Julian threw up his arms in despair and went off to
work.

"All right, Mother," sighed Daryl. "I don't understand, but then I
haven't understood any of this yet. Sure, I'll go with you . . . what
are we going after?"

"Bumper stickers," she said. "And those little round buttons with
the pins on the back that make a hole in your clothes when you wear
them. And maybe a T-shirt, though I'd rather not."

"Oh, I see," said Daryl.

"Well, I don't," Philip muttered, and Charlotte declared that her
mother had gone over the hill at last and should be restrained instead
of taken shopping, which obliged Valeria to explain the difference
between joking and Taking Liberties.

"You *will* see," she said comfortingly. "I promise."

She knew she had gotten it right when she appeared on the talk
show and nothing happened. They were very nice about it, considering; they explained that they were always getting people who could
bend spoons just by staring at them hard at home and in their friendly
neighborhood bars but then couldn't do it on television.

"It's the lights," they said. "And the stress. You're not used to all this confusion around you, you know." And they assured her that they firmly and truly did believe that when she wasn't on television she had showers of rose petals falling around her and doves flying over her head and that she glowed not only in the dark but even in daylight.

But they didn't. It was obvious that they didn't. They just felt sorry for her because she'd sat there in front of all those people and nothing had happened. Valeria was encouraged, and she tugged at the button on her lapel to be sure everybody noticed it, and she threw a couple of handfuls of buttons into the audience, and left a stack of her bumper stickers in the studio for anybody who wanted them.

"I'm of the opinion," she said happily, "that it's over. I really think it's all been just . . . an oversight."

And she was right. Valeria Carterhasty Cantrell is a saint no longer. The masses don't even know she exists. She is a mere codicil to a footnote in the obscure histories of religious phenomena. But her *family* adores her.

Daryl has a scholarship to Cornell, and will be going into law as his father hoped he would; he has given his microscope and his white mice to the Boys Club. Philip has just become an Eagle Scout, and he is only thirteen dollars short of the money needed to pay for his half of the computer. Charlotte is dancing in everything she can get permission to dance in and saving every penny to set up a school of baton twirling in Tulsa, Oklahoma, the minute she turns eighteen. All three children refer to Valeria's little episode as, "when Mother was so nervous," and are especially gentle and tender with her lest it happen again.

For their anniversary, Julian gave Valeria a mink jacket and a pair of diamond earrings and promised never to change shaving lotions again; for Christmas he is giving her a small vacation cottage on an island off the coast of Maine. He worships her; their marriage is the envy of every couple who knows them; he has not slept anywhere but in her arms (except on business trips) for two years. And last year he made $350,000 *after* taxes.

Valeria, for her part, no longer feels obliged to wear the lapel button, and never was forced to buy the T-shirt or go on to the sky-writing that she had saved as a backup if her first plan failed her. But she keeps the bumper sticker, and when it gets faded she has a new one made to replace it. Valeria does not intend to take any chances. She doesn't drive the Mercedes anymore; she drives her own car. (After all, putting the bumper sticker on Julian's Mercedes would have been a bit much to ask of him.) It's the bright red sports car—with the shiny wheels and the ooga-horn and the fur upholstery and the quad sound system—that costs more than an average person earns in a year or so.

It's the car you see on the freeway with Valeria at the wheel, driving along flat on the ground like everybody else, tangled up in the traffic jams like any other sinner.

It's the car with the bumper sticker that reads, in giant Gothic letters:

HELLO THERE! I AM A HOLY BLESSED SAINT! FOLLOW ME!

Prince Bull

A Fairy Tale

Charles Dickens

Charles Dickens is one of the literary giants of the English language, who upon occasion wrote fantasy stories. The best known of them is of course A Christmas Carol. *His short tales are characteristically moral, as is "Prince Bull." Usually they are conventional narratives (Dickens wrote an article deploring the use of fairy tales for polemical purposes). But in this case, Dickens cast a political allegory in fantasy form: John Bull is the stereotypical anthropomorphization of the English nation. Since "red tape" is still plaguing us today, the world over, with concern over military budgets and an annual outcry against waste, there is still bite in the satirical teeth in this allegory.*

Once upon a time, and of course it was in the Golden Age, and I hope you may know when that was, for I am sure I don't, though I have tried hard to find out, there lived in a rich and fertile country, a powerful Prince whose name was BULL. He had gone through a great deal of fighting in his time, about all sorts of things, including nothing; but, had gradually settled down to be a steady, peaceable, good-natured, corpulent, rather sleepy Prince.

This Puissant Prince was married to a lovely Princess whose name was Fair Freedom. She had brought him a large fortune, and had borne him an immense number of children, and had set them to spinning, and farming, and engineering, and soldiering, and sailor-ing, and doctoring, and lawyering, and preaching, and all kinds of trades. The coffers of Prince Bull were full of treasure, his cellars were crammed with delicious wines from all parts of the world, the richest gold and silver plate that ever was seen adorned his sideboards, his sons were strong, his daughters were handsome, and in short you might have supposed that if there ever lived upon earth a fortunate and happy Prince, the name of that Prince, take him for all in all, was assuredly Prince Bull.

But, appearances, as we all know, are not always to be trusted—far from it; and if they had led you to this conclusion respecting Prince Bull, they would have led you wrong as they often have led me.

For, this good Prince had two sharp thorns in his pillow, two hard knobs in his crown, two heavy loads on his mind, two unbridled nightmares in his sleep, two rocks ahead in his course. He could not by any means get servants to suit him, and he had a tyrannical old godmother whose name was Tape.

She was a Fairy, this Tape, and was a bright red all over. She was disgustingly prim and formal, and could never bend herself a hair's breadth this way or that way, out of her naturally crooked shape. But, she was very potent in her wicked art. She could stop the fastest thing in the world, change the strongest thing into the weakest, and the most useful into the most useless. To do this she had only to put her cold hand upon it, and repeat her own name, Tape. Then it withered away.

At the Court of Prince Bull—at least I don't mean literally at his court, because he was a very genteel Prince, and readily yielded to his godmother when she always reserved that for his hereditary Lords and Ladies—in the dominions of Prince Bull, among the great mass of the community who were called in the language of that polite country the Mobs and the Snobs, were a number of very ingenious men, who were always busy with some invention or other, for promoting the prosperity of the Prince's subjects, and augmenting the Prince's power. But, whenever they submitted their models for the Prince's approval, his godmother stepped forward, laid her hand upon them, and said "Tape." Hence it came to pass, that when any particularly good discovery was made, the discoverer usually carried it off to some other Prince, in foreign parts, who had no old godmother who said Tape. This was not on the whole an advantageous state of things for Prince Bull, to the best of my understanding.

The worst of it was, that Prince Bull had in course of years lapsed into such a state of subjection to this unlucky godmother, that he never made any serious effort to rid himself of her tyranny. I have said this was the worst of it, but there I was wrong, because there is a worse consequence still, behind. The Prince's numerous family became so downright sick and tired of Tape, that when they should have helped the Prince out of the difficulties into which that evil creature led him, they fell into a dangerous habit of moodily keeping away from him in an impassive and indifferent manner, as though they had quite forgotten that no harm could happen to the Prince their father, without its inevitably affecting themselves.

Such was the aspect of affairs at the court of Prince Bull, when this great Prince found it necessary to go to war with Prince Bear. He had been for some time very doubtful of his servants, who, besides being indolent and addicted to enriching their families at his expense, domineered over him dreadfully: threatening to discharge themselves if they were found the least fault with, pretending that they had done a wonderful amount of work when they had done nothing, making the most unmeaning speeches that ever were heard in the Prince's name, and uniformly showing themselves to be very inefficient indeed though that some of them had excellent characters from previous situations is not to be denied. Well; Prince Bull called his servants together, and said to them one and all, "Send out my army against Prince Bear. Clothe it, arm it, feed it, provide it with all necessaries and contingencies, and I will pay the piper! Do your duty by my brave troops," said the Prince, "and do it well, and I will pour my treasure out like water, to defray the cost. Who ever heard ME complain of money well laid out!" Which indeed he had reason for saying, inasmuch as he was well known to be a truly generous and munificent Prince.

When the servants heard those words, they sent out the army against Prince Bear, and they set the army tailors to work, and the army provision merchants, and the makers of guns both great and small, and the gunpowder makers, and the makers of ball, shell, and shot; and they bought up all manner of stores and ships, without troubling their heads about the price and appeared to be so busy that the good Prince rubbed his hands, and (using a favorite expression of his), said, "It's all right!" But, while they were thus employed, the Prince's godmother, who was a great favorite with those servants, looked in upon them continually all day long, and whenever she popped in her head at the door, said, "How do you do, my children?

What are you doing here?" "Official business, godmother." "Oho!"
says this wicked Fairy. "—Tape!" And then the business all went
wrong, whatever it was, and the servants' heads became so addled
and muddled that they thought they were doing wonders.

Now, this was very bad conduct on the part of the vicious old
nuisance, and she ought to have been strangled, even if she had
stopped here; but, she didn't stop here, as you shall learn. For, a
number of the Prince's subjects, being very fond of the Prince's
army, who were the bravest of men, assembled together and provided all manner of eatables and drinkables, and books to read, and
clothes to wear, and tobacco to smoke, and candles to burn, and
nailed them up in great packing-cases, and put them aboard a great
many ships, to be carried out to that brave army in the cold and
inclement country where they were fighting Prince Bear. Then, up
comes this wicked Fairy as the ships were weighing anchor, and says,
"How do you do, my children? What are you doing here?"—"We
are going with all these comforts to the army, godmother."—"Oho!"
says she. "A pleasant voyage, my darlings.—Tape!" And from that
time forth, those enchanted ships went sailing, against wind and tide
and rhyme and reason, round and round the world, and whenever
they touched at any port were ordered off immediately, and could
never deliver their cargoes anywhere.

This, again, was very bad conduct on the part of the vicious old
nuisance, and she ought to have been strangled for it if she had done
nothing worse; but, she did something worse still, as you shall learn.
For, she got astride of an official broomstick, and muttered as a spell
these two sentences "On Her Majesty's service," and "I have the
honor to be, sir, your most obedient servant," and presently alighted
in the cold and inclement country where the army of Prince Bull
were encamped to fight the army of Prince Bear. On the seashore of
that country she found, piled together, a number of houses for the
army to live in, and a quantity of provisions for the army to live upon,
and a quantity of clothes for the army to wear: while, sitting in the
mud gazing at them, were a group of officers as red to look at as the
wicked old woman herself. So, she said to one of them, "Who are
you, my darling, and how do you do?"—"I am the Quarter-master
General's Department, godmother, and I am pretty well." Then she
said to another, "Who are *you,* my darling, and how do *you* do?"—"I
am the Commissariat Department, godmother, and I am pretty well."
Then she said to another, "Who are *you,* my darling, and how do *you*

do?" "I am the Head of the Medical Department, godmother, and I am pretty well." Then, she said to some gentlemen scented with lavender, who kept themselves at a great distance from the rest, "And who are *you*, my pretty pets, and how do *you* do?" And they answered, "We-aw-are-the-aw-Staff-aw-Department, godmother, and we are very well indeed."—"I am delighted to see you all, my beauties," says this wicked old Fairy, "—Tape!" Upon that, the houses, clothes, and provisions, all mouldered away; and the soldiers who were sound, fell sick; and the soldiers who were sick, died miserably; and the noble army of Prince Bull perished.

When the dismal news of his great loss was carried to the Prince, he suspected his godmother very much indeed; but, he knew that his servants must have kept company with the malicious beldame, and must have given way to her, and therefore he resolved to turn those servants out of their places. So, he called to him a Roebuck who had the gift of speech, and he said, "Good Roebuck, tell them they must go." So, the good Roebuck delivered his message, so like a man that you might have supposed him to be nothing but a man, and they were turned out—but, not without warning, for that they had had a long time.

And now comes the most extraordinary part of the history of this Prince. When he had turned out those servants, of course he wanted others. What was his astonishment to find that in all his dominions, which contained no less than twenty-seven millions of people, there were not above five-and-twenty servants altogether! They were so lofty about it, too, that instead of discussing whether they should hire themselves as servants to Prince Bull, they turned things topsy-turvy, and considered whether as a favor they should hire Prince Bull to be their master! While they were arguing this point among themselves quite at their leisure, the wicked old red Fairy was incessantly going up and down, knocking at the doors of twelve of the oldest of the five-and-twenty, who were the oldest inhabitants in all that country, and whose united ages amounted to one thousand, saying, "Will *you* hire Prince Bull for your master?—Will *you* hire Prince Bull for your master?" To which one answered, "I will if next door will;" and another, "I won't if over the way does;" and another, "I can't if he, she, or they, might, could, would, or should." And all this time Prince Bull's affairs were going to rack and ruin.

At last, Prince Bull in the height of his perplexity assumed a thoughtful face, as if he were struck by an entirely new idea. The wicked old Fairy, seeing this, was at his elbow directly, and said, "How do you do, my Prince, and what are you thinking of?"—"I am thinking, godmother," says he, "that among all the seven-and-twenty millions of my subjects who have never been in service, there are men of intellect and business who have made me very famous both among my friends, and enemies."—"Aye, truly?" says the Fairy.— "Aye, truly," says the Prince.—"And what then?" says the Fairy.— "Why, then," says he, "since the regular old class of servants do so ill, are so hard to get, and carry it with so high a hand, perhaps I might try to make good servants of some of these." The words had no sooner passed his lips then she returned, chuckling, "You think so, do you? Indeed, my Prince?—Tape!" Thereupon he directly forgot what he was thinking of, and cried out lamentably to the old servants, "O, do come and hire your poor old master! Pray do! On any terms!"

And this, for the present, finishes the story of Prince Bull. I wish I could wind it up by saying that he lived happy ever afterwards, but I cannot in my conscience do so; for, with Tape at his elbow, and his estranged children fatally repelled by her from coming near him, I do not, to tell you the plain truth, believe in the possibility of such an end to it.

The Triumph of Vice

A Fairy Tale

W. S. Gilbert

William Schwenck Gilbert (1836–1911) became famous as one half of the collaborative team of Gilbert & Sullivan. He wrote the libretti for the most famous operettas in English, classics such as H. M. S. Pinafore *and* The Pirates of Penzance. *But he began his career as a journalist and writer of fiction, including fairy tales for adults, such as this one, in which he reverses the polarities of the standard Victorian moral tale for children. Vice triumphs over evil and there is no virtue anywhere to be rewarded. Along the way, vanity is punctured repeatedly and the witty dialogue echoes down the generations to Jack Vance's contemporary tales of Cugel the Clever, very polite and ironic. Here is a tale about Klauffenbachs and Krappentrapps, all in fun.*

The wealthiest in the matter of charms, and the poorest in the matter of money of all the well-born maidens of Tackleschlosstein, was the Lady Bertha von Klauffenbach. Her papa, the Baron, was indeed the fortunate possessor of a big castle on the top of a perpendicular rock, but his estate was deeply mortgaged, and there was not the smallest probability of its ever being free from the influence of the local money-lender. Indeed, if it comes to that, I may be permitted to say that even in the event of that wildly improbable state of things having come to pass, the amount realized by the sale of the castle and perpendicular rock would not have exceeded one hundred and eighty pounds sterling, all told. So the Baron von Klauffenbach did not even wear the outward show of being a wealthy man.

The perpendicular rock being singularly arid and unproductive even for a rock, and the Baron being remarkably penniless even for a Baron, it became necessary that he should adopt some decided course by which a sufficiency of bread, milk, and sauerkrout might be provided to satisfy the natural cravings of the Baron von Klauffenbach, and that fine growing girl Bertha, his daughter. So the poor old gentleman was only too glad to let down his drawbridge every morning, and sally forth from his stronghold, to occupy a scrivener's stool in the office of the local money-lender to whom I have already alluded. In short, the Baron von Klauffenbach was a usurer's clerk.

But it is not so much with the Baron von Klauffenbach as with his beautiful daughter Bertha that I have to do. I must describe her. She was a magnificent animal. She was six feet in height, and splendidly proportioned. She had a queenly face, set in masses of wonderful yellow hair; big blue eyes, and curly little mouth (but with thick firm lips), and a nose which, in the mercantile phraseology of the period, defied competition. Her figure was grandly, heroically outlined, firm as marble to the look, but elastically yielding to the touch. Bertha had but one fault—she was astonishingly vain of her magnificent proportions, and held in the utmost contempt anybody, man or woman, who fell short of her in that respect. She was the toast of all the young clerks of Tackleschlosstein; but the young clerks of Tackleschlosstein were to the Lady Bertha as so many midges to a giantess. They annoyed her, but they were not worth the trouble of deliberate annihilation. So they went on toasting her, and she went on scorning them.

Indeed, the Lady Bertha had but one lover whose chance of success was worth the ghost of a halfpenny—and he was the Count von Krappentrapp. The Count von Krappentrapp had these pulls over the gay young clerks of Tackleschlosstein—that he was constantly in her society, and was of noble birth. That he was constantly in her society came to pass in this wise. The Baron von Klauffenbach, casting about him for a means of increasing—or rather of laying the first stone towards the erection of—his income, published this manifesto on the walls of Tackleschlosstein:

"A nobleman and his daughter, having larger premises than they require, will be happy to receive into their circle a young gentleman engaged in the village during the day. Society musical. Terms insignificant. Apply to the Baron von K., Post Office, Tackleschlosstein."

The only reply to this intimation came from the Count von Krappentrapp; and the only objection to the Count von Krappentrapp was, that he was not engaged in the village during the day. But this objection was eventually overruled by the Count's giving the Baron in the handsomest manner in the world, his note of hand for ten pounds at six months date, which was immediately discounted by the Baron's employer. I am afraid that the Baron and the Count got dreadfully tipsy that evening. I know that they amused themselves all night by shying ink-bottles from the battlements at the heads of the people in the village below.

It will easily be foreseen that the Count von Krappentrapp soon fell hopelessly in love with Bertha; and those of my readers who are accustomed to the unravelling of German legendary lore will long ere this have made up their minds that Bertha fell equally hopelessly in love with the Count von Krappentrapp. But in this last particular they will be entirely in error. Far from encouraging the gay young Count, she regarded him with feelings of the most profound contempt. Indeed, truth compels me to admit that the Count was repulsive. His head was enormous, and his legs insignificant. He was short in stature, squat in figure, and utterly detestable in every respect, except in this, that he was always ready to put his hand to a bill for the advantage of the worthy old Baron. And whenever he obliged the Baron in this respect, he and the old gentleman used to get dreadfully tipsy, and always spent the night on the battlements throwing ink-bottles on the people in the village below. And whenever the Baron's trades-people in the village found themselves visited by a shower of ink-bottles, they knew that there was temporary corn in Egypt, and they lost no time in climbing up the perpendicular rock with their little red books with the gilt letters in their hands, ready for immediate settlement.

It was not long after the Count von Krappentrapp came to lodge with the Baron von Klauffenbach, that the Count proposed to the Baron's daughter, and in about a quarter of a minute after he had proposed to her, he was by her most unequivocally rejected. Then he slunk off to his chamber, muttering and mouthing in a manner which occasioned the utmost consternation in the mind of Gretchen, the castle maid-of-all-work, who met him on his way. So she offered him a bottle of cheap scent, and some peppermint-drops, but he danced at her in such a reckless manner when she suggested these humble refreshments, that she went to the Baron, and gave him a month's warning on the spot.

Everything went wrong with the Count that day. The window-blinds wouldn't pull up, the door wouldn't close, the chairs broke when he sat on them, and before half his annoyances had ceased, he had expended all the bad language he knew.

The Count was conscientious in one matter only, and that was in the matter of bad language. He made it a point of honour not to use the same expletive twice in the same day. So when he found that he had exhausted his stock of swearing, and that, at the moment of exhaustion, the chimney began to smoke, he simply sat down and cried feebly.

But he soon sprang to his feet, for in the midst of an unusually large puff of smoke, he saw the most extraordinary individual he had ever beheld. He was about two feet high, and his head was as long as his body and legs put together. He had an antiquated appearance about him; but excepting that he wore a long stiff tail, with a spear-point at the end of it, there was nothing absolutely unearthly about him. His hair, which resembled the crest or comb of a cock in its arrangement, terminated in a curious little queue, which turned up at the end and was fastened with a bow of blue ribbon. He wore mutton-chop whiskers and a big flat collar, and his body and misshapen legs were covered with a horny incrustation, which suggested black beetles. On his crest he wore a three-cornered hat—anticipating the invention of that article of costume by about three hundred years.

"I beg your pardon," said this phenomenon, "but can I speak to you?"

"Evidently you can," replied the Count, whose confidence had returned to him.

"I know: but what I mean is, will you listen to me for ten minutes?"

"That depends very much upon what you talk about. Who are you?" asked the Count.

"I'm a sort of gnome."

"A gnome?"

"A sort of gnome; I won't enter into particulars, because they won't interest you."

The apparition hesitated, evidently hoping the Count would assure him that any particulars of the gnome's private life would interest him deeply; but he only said—

"Not the least bit in the world."

"You are poor," said the gnome.

"Very," replied the Count.

"Ha!" said he, "some people are. Now I am rich."

"*Are* you?" asked the Count, beginning to take an interest in the matter.

"I am, and would make you rich too; only you must help me to a wife."

"What! Repay good for evil? Never!"

He didn't mean this, only he thought it was a smart thing to say.

"Not exactly," said the gnome; "I shan't give you the gold until you have found me the wife; so that I shall be repaying evil with good."

"Yes," said the Count musingly: "I didn't look at it in that light at all. I see it quite from your point of view. But why don't you find a wife for yourself?"

"Well," said the gnome diffidently, "I'm not exactly—you know—I'm—that is—I want a word!"

"Extremely ugly?" suggested the Count.

"Ye-e-es," said the gnome (rather taken aback); "something of that sort. *You* know."

"Yes, I know," said the Count; "but how am I to help you? I can't make you pretty."

"No; but I have the power of transforming myself three times during my gnome existence into a magnificent young man."

"O-h-h-h!" said the Count slyly.

"Exactly. Well, I've done that twice, but without success as far as regards getting a wife. This is my last chance."

"But how can I help you? You say you can change yourself into a magnificent young man; then why not plead your own case? I, for my part, am rather—a—"

"Repulsive?" suggested the gnome, thinking he had him there.

"Plain," said the Count.

"Well," replied the gnome, "there's an unfortunate fact connected with my human existence."

"Out with it. Don't stand on ceremony."

"Well, then, it's this. I begin as a magnificent young man, six feet high, but I diminish imperceptibly day by day, whenever I wash myself, until I shrink into the—a—the—"

"Contemptible abortion?"

"A—yes—thank you—you behold. Well, I've tried it twice, and found on each occasion a lovely girl who was willing and ready to marry me; but during the month or so that elapsed between each engagement and the day appointed for the wedding, I shrunk so perceptibly (one is obliged, you know, to wash one's face during courtship), that my bride-elect became frightened and cried off. Now, I have seen the Lady Bertha, and I am determined to marry her."

"You? Ha, ha! Excuse me, but— Ha, ha!"

"Yes, I. But you will see that it is essential that as little time as possible should elapse between my introduction to her and our marriage."

"Of course; and you want me to prepare her to receive you, and marry you there and then without delay."

"Exactly; and if you consent, I will give you several gold mines, and as many diamonds as you can carry."

"You will? My dear sir, say no more! 'Revenge! Revenge! Revenge! Timotheus cried,'" (quoting a popular comic song of the day.) "But how do you effect the necessary transformation?"

"Here is a ring which gives me the power of assuming human form once more during my existence. I have only to put it on my middle finger, and the transformation is complete."

"I see—but—couldn't you oblige me with a few thalers on account?"

"Um," said the gnome; "it's irregular: but here are two."

"Right," said the Count, biting them; "I'll do it. Come the day after to-morrow."

"At this time?" said the gnome.

"At this time."

"Good-night."

"Good-night."

And the gnome disappeared up the chimney.

The Count von Krappentrapp hurried off without loss of time to communicate to the lovely Bertha the splendid fate in store for her.

"Lady Bertha," said he, "I come to you with a magnificent proposal."

"Now, Krappentrapp," said Bertha, "don't be a donkey. Once and for all, I *will*NOT have you."

"I am not alluding to myself; I am speaking on behalf of a friend."

"O, any friend of yours, I'm sure," began Bertha politely.

"Thanks, very much."

"Would be open to the same objection as yourself. He would be repulsive."

"But he is magnificent!"

"He would be vicious."

"But he is virtuous!"

"He would be insignificant in rank and stature."

"He is a prince of unexampled proportions!"

"He would be absurdedly poor."

"He is fabulously wealthy!"

"Indeed?" said Bertha; "your story interests me." (She was intimately acquainted with German melodrama.) "Proceed."

"This prince," said Krappentrapp, "has heard of you, has seen you, and consequently has fallen in love with you."

"O, g'long," said Bertha giggling, and nudging him with her extraordinarily moulded elbow.

"Fact. He proposes to settle on you Africa, the Crystal Palace, several solar systems, the Rhine, and Rosherville. The place," added he, musingly, "to spend a happy, happy day."

"Are you in earnest, or" (baring her right arm to the shoulder) "is this some of your nonsense?"

"Upon my honour, I am in earnest. He will be here the day after to-morrow at this time to claim you, if you consent to have him. He will carry you away with him alone to his own province, and there will marry you."

"Go away alone with him? I wouldn't think of such a thing!" said Bertha, who was a model of propriety.

"H'm!" said the Count, "that is awkward certainly. Ha! a thought! You shall marry him first, and start afterwards, only as he has to leave in two days, the wedding must take place without a moment's delay."

You see, if he had suggested this in the first instance, she would have indignantly rejected the notion, on principle. As it was she jumped at it, and, as a token of peace, let down her sleeve.

"I can provide my trousseau in two days. I will marry him the day he arrives, if he turns out to be all you have represented him. But if he does not—" And she again bared her arm, significantly, to the shoulder.

That night, the Baron von Klauffenbach and the Count von Krappentrapp kept it up right merrily on the two thalers which the Count had procured from the gnome. The Baron was overjoyed at the prospect of a princely son-in-law; and the shower of ink-bottles from the battlements was heavier than ever.

The second day after this the gnome appeared to Count Krappentrapp.

"How do you do?" said the Count.

"Thank you," said the gnome; "I'm pretty well. It's an awful thing being married."

"Oh, no. Don't be dispirited."

"Ah, it's all very well for you to say that, but— Is the lady ready?" said he, changing the subject abruptly.

"Ready, I should think so. She's sitting in the banqueting hall in full bridal array, panting for your arrival."

"O! do I look nervous?"

"Well, candidly, you do," said the Count.

"I'm afraid I do. Is everything prepared?"

"The preparations," said the Count, "are on the most magnificent scale. Half buns and cut oranges are scattered over the place in luxurious profusion, and there is enough gingerbierheimer and currantweinmilch on tap to float the Rob Roy canoe. Gretchen is engaged, as I speak, in cutting ham-sandwiches recklessly in the kitchen; and the Baron has taken down the 'Apartments furnished,' which has hung for ages in the stained glass windows of the banqueting hall."

"I see," said the gnome, "to give a tone to the thing."

"Just so. Altogether it will be the completest thing you ever saw."

"Well," said the gnome, "then I think I'll dress."

For he had not yet taken his human form.

So he slipped a big carbuncle ring on to the middle finger of his right hand. Immediately the room was filled with a puff of smoke from the chimney, and when it had cleared away, the Count saw, to his astonishment, a magnificent young man in the place where the gnome had stood.

"There is no deception," said the gnome.

"Bravo! very good indeed! very neat!" said the Count, applauding.

"Clever thing, isn't it?" said the gnome.

"Capital; most ingenious. But now—what's your name?"

"It's an odd name. Prince Pooh."

"Prince Pooh? Pooh! pooh? you're joking."

"Now, take my advice, and never try to pun upon a fellow's name; you may be sure that, however ingenious the joke may be, it's certain to have been done before over and over again to his face. Your own particular joke is precisely the joke every fool makes when he first hears my name."

"I beg your pardon—it *was* weak. Now, if you'll come with me to the Baron, you and he can settle preliminaries."

So they went to the Baron, who was charmed with his son-in-law elect. Prince Pooh settled on Bertha the whole of Africa, the Crystal Palace, several solar systems, the Rhine, and Rosherville, and made the Baron a present of Siberia and Vesuvius; after that they all went down to the banqueting hall, where Bertha and the priest were awaiting their arrival.

"Allow me," said the Baron. "Bertha, my dear, Prince Pooh—who has behaved *most handsomely*" (this in a whisper). "Prince Pooh—my daughter Bertha. Pardon a father if he is for a moment unmanned."

And the Baron wept over Bertha, while Prince Pooh mingled his tears with those of Count Krappentrapp, and the priest with those of Gretchen, who had finished cutting the sandwiches. The ceremony was then gone into with much zeal on all sides, and on its conclusion the party sat down to the elegant collation already referred to. The Prince declared that the Baron was the best fellow he had ever met, and the Baron assured the Prince that words failed him when he endeavoured to express the joy he felt at an alliance with so unexceptionable a Serene Highness.

The Prince and his bride started in a carriage and twenty-seven for his country seat, which was only fifty miles from Tackleschlosstein, and that night the Baron and the Count kept it up harder than ever. They went down to the local silversmith to buy up all the presentation inkstands in his stock; and the shower of inkstands from the castle battlements on the heads of the villagers below that night is probably without precedent or imitation in the chronicles of revelry.

Bertha and Prince Pooh spent a happy honeymoon: Bertha had one, and only one cause of complaint against Prince Pooh, and that was an insignificant one—do all she could, she couldn't persuade him to wash his face more than once a week. Bertha was a clean girl for a German, and had acquired a habit of performing ablutions three or even four times a week; consequently her husband's annoying peculiarity irritated her more than it would have irritated most of the young damsels of Tackleschlosstein. So she would contrive, when he was asleep, to go over his features with a damp towel; and whenever he went out for a walk she hid his umbrella, in order that, if it chanced to rain, he might get a providential and sanitary wetting.

This sort of thing went on for about two months, and at the end of that period Bertha began to observe an extraordinary change not only in her husband's appearance, but also in her own. To her horror she found that both she and her husband were shrinking rapidly! On the day of their marriage each of them was six feet high, and now her husband was only five feet nine, while she had diminished to five feet six—owing to her more frequent use of water. Her dresses were too long and too wide for her. Tucks had to be run in everything to which tucks were applicable, and breadths and gores taken out of all garments which were susceptible of these modifications. She spent a small fortune in heels, and even then had to walk about on tiptoe in order to escape remark. Nor was Prince Pooh a whit more easy in his mind than was his wife. He wore the tallest hats with the biggest feathers, and the most preposterous heels to his boots that ever were seen. Each seemed afraid to allude to these extraordinary modifications to each other, and a gentle melancholy took the place of the hilarious jollity which had characterized their proceedings hitherto.

At length matters came to a crisis. The Prince went out hunting one day, and fell into the Rhine from the top of a high rock. He was an excellent swimmer, and he had to remain about two hours, swimming against a powerful tide, before assistance arrived. The consequence was that when he was taken out he had shrunk so considerably that his attendants hardly knew him. He was reduced, in fact, to four feet nine.

On his return to his castle he dressed himself in his tallest hat and highest heels, and, warming his chilly body at the fire, he nervously awaited the arrival of his wife from a shopping expedition in the neighbourhood.

"Charles," said she, "further disguise were worse than useless. It is impossible for me to conceal from myself the extremely unpleasant fact that we are both of us rapidly shrinking. Two months since you were a fine man, and I was one of the most magnificent women of this or any other time. Now *I* am only middle-sized, and you have suddenly become contemptibly small. What does this mean?"

"A husband is often made to look small in the eyes of his wife," said Prince Charles Pooh, attempting to turn it off with a feeble joke.

"Yes, but a wife don't mean to stand being made to look small in the eyes of her husband."

"It's only fancy, my dear. You are as fine a woman as ever."

"Nonsense, Charles. Gores, Gussets, and Tucks are Solemn

Things," said Bertha, speaking in capitals; "they are Stubborn Facts which there is No Denying, and I Insist on an Explanation."

"I'm very sorry," said Prince Pooh, "but I can't account for it;" and suddenly remembering that his horse was still in the Rhine, he ran off as hard as he could to get it out.

Bertha was evidently vexed. She began to suspect that she had married the Fiend, and the consideration annoyed her much. So she determined to write to her father, and ask him what she had better do.

Now, Prince Pooh had behaved most shabbily to his friend Count Krappentrapp. Instead of giving him the goldmines and diamonds which he had promised him he sent him nothing at all but a bill for twenty pounds at six months, a few old masters, a dozen or so of cheap hock, and a few hundred paving stones, which were wholly inadequate to the satisfaction of the Count and the Baron's new-born craving for silver inkstands. So Count von Krappentrapp determined to avenge himself on the Prince at the very earliest opportunity; and in Bertha's letter the opportunity presented itself.

He saddled the castle donkey, and started for Poohberg, the Prince's seat. In two days he arrived there, and sent up his card to Bertha. Bertha admitted him; and he then told the Prince's real character, and the horrible fate that was in store for her if she continued to be his wife.

"But what am I to do?" said she.

"If you were single again, whom would you marry?" said he with much sly emphasis.

"O," said the Princess, "you, of course."

"You would."

"Undoubtedly. Here it is in writing."

And she gave him a written promise to marry him if anything ever happened to the Prince her husband.

"But," said the Count, "can you reconcile yourself to the fact that my proportions are insignificant?"

"Compared with me, as I now am, you are gigantic," said Bertha. "I am cured of my pride in my own splendid stature."

"Good," said the Count. "You have noticed the carbuncle that your husband (husband! ha! ha! but no matter) wears on his middle finger?"

"I have."

"In that rests his charm. Remove it while he sleeps; he will vanish, and you will be a free woman."

That night as the clock struck twelve, the Princess removed the ring from the right-hand middle finger of Prince Pooh. He gave a fearful shriek; the room was filled with smoke; and on its clearing off, the body of the gnome in its original form lay dead upon the bed, charred to ashes!

The castle of Poohberg, however, remained, and all that was in it. The ashes of the monster were buried in the back garden, and a horrible leafless shrub, encrusted with a black, shiny, horny bark, that suggested black beetles grew out of the grave with astounding rapidity. It grew, and grew, and grew, but never put forth a leaf; and as often as it was cut down it grew again. So when Bertha (who never recovered her original proportions) married Count Krappentrapp, it became necessary to shut up the back garden altogether, and to put ground-glass panes into the windows which commanded it. And they took the dear old Baron to live with them, and the Count and he spent a jolly time of it. The Count laid in a stock of inkstands which would last out the old man's life, and many a merry hour they spent on the hoary battlements of Poohberg. Bertha and her husband lived to a good old age, and died full of years and of honours.

Turandina

Fyodor Sologub

Fyodor Sologub (1863–1927) was a Russian writer of short stories whose greatest popularity was in the decade or so before World War I. A volume of his stories and fables was published in English in 1915, The Sweet-Scented Name, *from which this tale is taken. Here is the story of Peter, who is an effective lawyer though poor, and a success with the ladies because of his sarcasm. A fairy-tale princess is called into his emotionally empty life, and he falls in love with her. An ideal wife changes him very little, and in the manner of supernatural beings, her presence lacks permanence. This is a fable about how little power the fantastic has to change a contemporary personality.*

Peter Antònovitch Bulanin was spending the summer in the country with the family of his cousin, a teacher of philology. Bulanin himself was a young advocate of thirty years of age, having finished his course at the University only two years before.

The past year had been a comparatively fortunate one. He had successfully defended two criminal cases on the nomination of the Court, as well as a civil case undertaken at the instigation of his own heart. All three cases had been won by his brilliant pleading. The jury had acquitted the young man who had killed his father out of pity because the old man fasted too assiduously and suffered in consequence; they had acquitted the poor seamstress who had thrown vitriol at the girl her lover wished to marry; and in the civil court the judge had awarded the plaintiff a hundred and fifty roubles, saying that his rights were indisputable, though the defendant asserted that the sum had previously been paid. For all this good work Peter Antònovitch himself had received only fifteen roubles, this money having been paid to him by the man who had received the hundred and fifty.

But, as will be understood, one cannot live a whole year on fifteen roubles, and Peter Antònovitch had to fall back on his own resources, that is, on the money his father sent him from home. As far as the law was concerned there was as yet nothing for him but fame.

But his fame was not at present great, and as his receipts from his father were but moderate Peter Antònovitch often fell into a despondent and elegiac mood. He looked on life rather pessimistically, and captivated young ladies by the eloquent pallor of his face and by the sarcastic utterances which he gave forth on every possible occasion.

One evening, after a sharp thunder-storm had cleared and refreshed the air, Peter Antònovitch went out for a walk alone. He wandered along the narrow field-paths until he found himself far from home.

A picture of entrancing beauty stretched itself out before him, canopied by the bright-blue dome of heaven besprinkled with scattered cloudlets and illumined by the soft and tender rays of the departing sun. The narrow path by which he had come led along the high bank of a stream rippling along in the winding curves of its narrow bed— the shallow water of the stream was transparent and gave a pleasant sense of cool freshness. It looked as if one need only step into it to be at once filled with the joy of simple happiness, to feel as full of life and easy grace of movement as the rosy-bodied boys bathing there.

Not far away were the shades of the quiet forest; beyond the river lay an immense semi-circular plain, dotted here and there with woods and villages, a dusty ribbon of a road curving snake-like across it. On the distant horizon gleamed golden stars, the crosses of far-away churches and belfries shining in the sunlight.

Everything looked fresh and sweet and simple, yet Peter Antònovitch was sad. And it seemed to him that his sadness was but intensified by the beauty around; as if some evil tempter were seeking to allure him to evil by some entrancing vision.

For to Peter Antònovitch all this earthly beauty, all this enchantment of the eyes, all this delicate sweetness pouring itself into his young and vigorous body, was only as a veil of golden tissue spread out by the devil to hide from the simple gaze of man the impurity, the imperfection, and the evil of Nature.

This life, adorning itself in beauty and breathing forth perfumes, was in reality, thought Peter Antònovitch, only the dull prosaic iron chain of cause and effect—the burdensome slavery from which mankind could never get free.

Tortured by such thoughts Peter Antònovitch had often felt himself as unhappy as if in him there had awakened the soul of some ancient monster who had howled piteously outside the village at night. And now he thought:

"If only a fairy-tale could come into one's life and for a time upset the ordered arrangement of pre-determined Fate! Oh, fairy-tale, fashioned by the wayward desires of men who are in captivity to life and who cannot be reconciled to their captivity—sweet fairy-tale, where art thou?"

He remembered an article he had read the day before in a magazine, written by the Minister of Education; some words in it had specially haunted his memory. The article spoke of the old fairy-tale tradition of the forest enchantress, Turandina. She had loved a shepherd and had left for him her enchanted home, and with him had lived some happy years on earth until she had been recalled by the mysterious voices of the forest. She had gone away, but the happy years had remained as a grateful memory to mankind.

Peter Antònovitch gave himself up to the fancy—oh for the fairy-tale, for a few enchanted years, a few days . . . ! And he cried aloud and said:

"Turandina, where art thou?"

II

The sun was low down in the sky. The calm of even had fallen on the spreading fields. The neighbouring forest was hushed. No sound was heard, the air was still, and the grass still sparkling with raindrops was motionless.

It was a moment when the desires of a man fulfil themselves, the one moment which perhaps comes once in his life to every man. It seemed that all around was waiting in a tension of expectation.

Looking before him into the shining misty vapour, Peter Antònovitch cried again:

"Turandina, where art thou?"

And under the spell of the silence that encompassed him, his own separate individual will became one with the great universal Will, and with great power and authority he spoke as only once in his life a man has power to speak:

"Turandina, come!"

And in a sweet and gentle voice he heard the answer:

"I am here."

Peter Antònovitch trembled and looked about. Everything seemed again quite ordinary and his soul was as usual the soul of a poor human being, separate from the universal Soul—he was again an ordinary man, just like you and me, who dwell in days and hours of time. Yet before him stood she whom he had called.

She was a beautiful maiden, wearing a narrow circlet of gold upon her head, and dressed in a short white garment. Her long plaits of hair came below her waist and seemed to have taken to themselves the golden rays of the sunlight. Her eyes, as she gazed intently at the young man, were as blue as if in them a heaven revealed itself, more clear and pure than the skies of earth. Her features were so regular and her hands and feet so well-formed, so perfect were the lines of the figure revealed by the folds of her dress that she seemed an embodiment of perfect maiden loveliness. She would have seemed like an angel from heaven had not her heavy black eyebrows met and so disclosed her witchery; if her skin had not been dark as if tanned by the rays of a burning sun.

Peter Antònovitch could not speak for wonder at her, and she spoke first:

"Thou didst call me and so I came to thee. Thou calledst to me just when I was in need of an earthly shelter in the world of men. Thou wilt take me to thy home. I have nothing of my own except this crown upon my brow, this dress, and this wallet in my hand."

She spoke quietly, so quietly that the tones of her voice could not have been heard above earthly sounds. But so clear was her speech and so tender its tone that even the most indifferent man would have been touched by the least sound of her voice.

When she spoke about going home with him and of her three possessions, Peter Antònovitch saw that she held in her hand a little bag of red leather drawn together by a golden cord—a very simple and beautiful little bag; something like those in which ladies carry their opera-glasses to the theatre.

Then he asked:

"And who art thou?"

"I am Turandina, the daughter of King Turandon. My father loved me greatly, but I did that which was not for me to do—out of simple curiosity I disclosed the future of mankind. For this my father was displeased with me and drove me from his kingdom. Some day I shall be forgiven and recalled to my father's home. But now for a time I must dwell among men, and to me have been given these three things: a golden crown, the sign of my birth; a white garment, my poor covering; and this wallet, which contains all that I shall need. It is good that I have met with thee. Thou art a man who defendeth the unhappy, and who devoteth his life to the triumph of Truth among men. Take me with thee to thy home; thou wilt never regret thy deed."

Peter Antònovitch did not know what to do or what to think. One thing was clear: this maiden, dressed so lightly, speaking so strangely, must be sheltered by him; he could not leave her alone in the forest, far from any human dwelling.

He thought she might be a runaway, hiding her real name and inventing some unlikely story. Perhaps she had escaped from an asylum, or from her own home.

There was nothing in her face or in her appearance, however, except her scanty clothing and her words, to indicate anything strange in her mind. She was perfectly quiet and calm. If she called herself Turandina it was doubtless because she had heard some one mention the name, or she might even have read the fairy-story of Turandina.

III

With such thoughts in his mind Peter Antònovitch said to the beautiful unknown:

"Very well, dear young lady, I will take you home with me. But I ought to warn you that I do not live alone, and therefore I advise you to tell me your real name. I'm afraid that my relatives will not believe that you are the daughter of King Turandon. As far as I know there is no such king at the present time."

Turandina smiled as she said:

"I have told thee the truth, whether thy people believe it or not. It is sufficient for me that thou shouldst believe. And if thou believest me, thou wilt defend me from all evil and from all unhappiness, for

thou art a man who hast chosen for thyself the calling in which thou
canst uphold the truth and defend the weak."

Peter Antònovitch shrugged his shoulders.

"If you persist in this story," answered he, "I must wash my hands
of the matter, and I cannot be answerable for any possible consequences. Of course I will take you home with me until you can find a
more suitable place, and I will do all I can to help you. But as a
lawyer I very strongly advise you not to hide your real name."

Turandina listened to him with a smile, and when he stopped
speaking she said:

"Do not be at all anxious; everything will be well. Thou wilt see
that I shall bring happiness to thee if thou canst show me kindness
and love. And do not speak to me so much about my real name. I
have spoken the truth to thee, and more I may not say, it is forbidden
me to tell thee all. Take me home with thee. Night is coming on; I
have journeyed far and am in need of rest."

Peter Antònovitch was quick to apologise.

"Ah, pardon me, please. I am sorry that this is such an out-of-the-
way place; it's quite impossible to get a carriage."

He began to walk in the direction of his home, and Turandina
went with him. She did not walk as though she were tired; her feet
seemed hardly to touch the ground, though they had to walk over
stiff clay and sharp stones, and the moist grass and rain-soaked pathway did not seem to soil her little feet.

When they reached the high bank of the river and could see the
first houses of the village, Peter Antònovitch glanced uneasily at his
companion and said somewhat awkwardly:

"Pardon me, dear young lady . . ."

Turandina looked at him, and with a little frown interrupted him,
saying reproachfully:

"Hast thou forgotten who I am and what is my name? I am
Turandina, and not 'dear young lady.' I am the daughter of King
Turandon."

"Your pardon, please, Mademoiselle Turandina—it is a very beautiful name, though it is never used now—I wanted to ask you a question."

"Why dost thou speak so to me?" asked Turandina, interrupting
him once more. "Speak not as to one of the young ladies of thy
acquaintance. Say 'thou' to me, and address me as a true knight
would speak to his fair lady."

She spoke with such insistence and authority that Peter Antò-novitch felt compelled to obey. And when he turned to Turandina and for the first time spoke to her intimately and called her by her name, he at once felt more at ease.

"Turandina, hast thou not a dress to wear? My people would expect thee to wear an ordinary dress."

Turandina smiled once more and said:

"I don't know. Isn't my one garment enough? I was told that in this wallet I should find everything that I should need in the world of men. Take it and look within; perhaps thou wilt find there what thou desirest."

With these words she held out to him her little bag. And as he pulled apart the cord and opened it, Peter Antònovitch thought to himself, "It will be good if some one has put in some kind of frock for her."

He put his hand into the wallet and feeling something soft he drew out a small parcel, so small that Turandina could have closed her hand over it. And when he unwrapped the parcel, there was just what he wanted, a dress such as most young girls were wearing at that time.

He helped Turandina to put it on, and he fastened it for her, for, of course, it buttoned at the back.

"Is that all right now?" asked Turandina.

Peter Antònovitch looked regretfully at the little bag. It looked much too small to hold a pair of shoes. But he put in his hand again and thought, "A pair of sandals would do nicely."

His fingers touched a little strap, and he drew forth a tiny pair of golden sandals. And then he dried her feet and put on the sandals and fastened the straps for her.

"Now is everything all right?" asked Turandina again.

There was such a humility in her voice and gesture as she spoke that Peter Antònovitch felt quite happy. It would be quite easy to manage her now, he thought. So he said, "Oh yes; we can get a hat later on."

IV

And so there came a fairy-story into the life of a man. Of course, it seemed sometimes as if the young lawyer's life were quite unsuited for such a thing. His relatives were utterly unable to believe the account their young guest gave of herself, and even Peter Antònovitch himself lacked faith. Many times he begged Turandina to tell him her real name, and he played various tricks on her to trap her into confessing that her story was not really true. But Turandina was never angry at his persistence. She smiled sweetly and simply, and with great patience said over and over again:

"I have told you the truth."

"But where is the land over which King Turandon reigns?" Peter Antònovitch would ask.

"It is far away," Turandina would answer, "and yet if you wish it, it is near also. But none of you can go thither. Only we who have been born in the enchanted kingdom of King Turandon can ever get to that wonderful country."

"But can you not show me how to go there?" asked Peter Antònovitch.

"No, I cannot," answered Turandina.

"And can you return yourself?" said he.

"Now, I cannot," said she, "but when my father calls me, I shall return."

There was no sadness in her voice and expression, nor any joy, as she spoke of her expulsion from the enchanted land and of her return. Her voice was always calm and gentle. She looked on all she saw with inquiring eyes, as if seeing everything for the first time, but with a quiet calmness, as if knowing that she would soon become accustomed to all new and strange things, and would easily recognise them again. When she once knew a thing she never made a mistake nor confused it with anything else. All ordinary rules of conduct that people told her or that she herself noticed, were lightly and easily followed, as if she had been accustomed to them from her childhood. She remembered names and faces of people after having once seen them.

Turandina never quarrelled with any one, and she never said anything untrue. When she was advised to use the ordinary Society evasions she shook her head and said:

"One must never say what is untrue. The earth hears everything."

At home and in the company of others Turandina behaved with such dignity and graciousness that all who could believe in a fairy-tale were obliged to believe that they were in the presence of a beautiful princess, the daughter of a great and wise king.

But the fairy-tale was somewhat difficult to reconcile with the ordinary life of the young lawyer and his people. There was a perpetual struggle between the two, and many difficulties arose in consequence.

V

When Turandina had been living with the family for a few days, an official came to the house and said to the servant:

"They say there's a young lady visitor here. She must send in her passport and have it signed."

The servant told her mistress, who spoke to her husband about the matter. He asked Peter Antònovitch about the passport, and the latter went to find Turandina and ask her. Turandina was sitting on the verandah reading a book with much enjoyment.

"Turandina," said Peter Antònovitch, going out to her. "The police have sent to ask for your passport. It must be sent to be signed."

Turandina listened very attentively to what Peter Antònovitch had to say. And then she asked:

"What is a passport?"

"Oh, a passport," said he, "don't you know, is—a passport. A paper on which is written your name and your father's name, your age, your rank. You can't possibly live anywhere without a passport."

"If it's necessary," said Turandina calmly, "then, of course, it ought to be in my little bag. Look, there's the bag, take it and see if the passport is inside."

And in the wonderful little bag there was found a passport—a small book in a brown cover, which had been obtained in the province of Astrakhan, in which was inscribed the name of the Princess Tamara Timofeevna Turandon, seventeen years of age, and unmarried. Everything was in order: the seal, the official signature, the signature of the princess herself, and so on, just as in all passport books.

Peter Antònovitch looked at Turandina and smiled:

"So that's who you are," said he, "you are a princess, and your name is Tamara."

But Turandina shook her head.

"No," said she, "I've never been called Tamara. That passport doesn't tell the truth; it's only for the police and for those people who do not know and cannot know the truth. I am Turandina, the daughter of King Turandon. Since I have lived in this world I have learnt that people here don't want to know the truth. I don't know anything about the passport. Whoever put it in my little bag must have known that I should need it. But for thee, my word should be enough."

After the passport had been signed Turandina was known as the princess, or Tamara Timofeevna, but her own people continued to call her Turandina.

VI

Her own people—for they came to be her own people. The fairy-tale came into a man's life, and as often happens in a fairy-tale, so it now occurred in life. Peter Antònovitch fell in love with Turandina and Turandina loved him also. He made up his mind to marry her, and this led to slight difficulties in the family.

The teacher-cousin and his wife said:

"In spite of her mysterious origin and her obstinate silence about her family, your Turandina is a very dear girl, beautiful, intelligent, very good and capable, and well brought up. In short, she is everything that one could wish. But you ought to remember that you have no money, and neither has she.

"It will be difficult for two people to live in Petersburg on the money your father allows you.

"Especially with a princess.

"You must remember that in spite of her sweet ways she's probably accustomed to live in good style.

"She has very small soft hands. True, she has been very modest here, and you say she was barefoot when you met her first and had very little clothing. But we don't know what kind of garments she will want to wear in a town."

Peter Antònovitch himself was rather pessimistic at first. But by and by he remembered how he had found a dress for Turandina in the little bag. A bold thought came into his mind, and he smiled and said:

"I found a house-frock for Turandina in her little bag. Perhaps if I were to rummage in it again I might find a ball-dress for her."

But the teacher's wife, a kind young woman with a genius for housekeeping, said:

"Much better if you could find some money. If only she had five hundred roubles we could manage to get her a good trousseau."

"We ought to find five hundred thousand—for a princess's dowry," said Peter Antònovitch, laughing.

"Oh, a hundred thousand would be quite enough for you," laughed his cousin in reply.

Just then Turandina came quietly up the steps leading from the garden, and Peter Antònovitch called to her and said:

"Turandina, show me your little bag, dear. Perhaps you have a hundred thousand roubles there."

Turandina held out her little bag to him and said:

"If it's necessary, you will find it in the bag."

And Peter Antònovitch again put his hand into the little bag and drew forth a large packet of notes. He began to count them, but without counting he could see they represented a large quantity of money.

VII

So this great fairy-tale came into the young man's life. And though it didn't seem well suited to the taking-in of a fairy-tale, yet room was found for it somewhere. The fairy-tale bought a place in his life— with its own charm and the treasures of the enchanted bag.

Turandina and the young lawyer were married. And Turandina had first a little son and then a daughter. The boy was like his mother, and grew up to be a gentle dreamy child. The girl was like her father, gay and intelligent.

And so the years went by. Every summer, when the days were at their longest, a strange melancholy overshadowed Turandina. She used to go out in the mornings to the edge of the forest and stand there listening to the forest voices. And after some time she would walk home again slowly and sadly.

And once, standing there at midday, she heard a loud voice calling to her:

"Turandina, come. Your father has forgiven you."

And so she went away and never returned. Her little son was then seven years old and her daughter three.

Thus the fairy-tale departed from this life and never came back. But Turandina's little son never forgot his mother.

Sometimes he would wander away by himself so as to be quite alone. And when he came home again there was such an expression upon his face that the teacher's wife said to her husband in a whisper:

"He has been with Turandina."

The Princess
and the Frog

Robin McKinley

*Robin McKinley is a Newbery Award-winning writer of children's books,
such as* Beauty *(a retelling of "Beauty and the Beast"), and the author of a
number of short stories. This one is taken from her collection of four fantasy
novellas,* The Door in the Hedge. *It takes as a point of departure the fairy
tale of the same name, but there are no kisses here. There are two princes,
strong and weak. And there is a frog and the water he lives in, an interesting
contrast to the Tiptree story (pp.389–405). Does love triumph? Indeed.*

PART ONE

She held the pale necklace in her hand and stared at it as she walked.
Her feet evidently knew where they were going, for they did not
stumble although her eyes gave them no guidance. Her eyes remained fixed on the glowing round stones in her hand.

These stones were as smooth as pearls, and their color, at first sight,
seemed as pure. But they were much larger than any pearls she had
ever seen; as large as the dark sweet cherries she plucked in the
palace gardens. And their pale creamy color did not lie quiet and
reflect the sunlight, but shimmered and shifted, and seemed to offer
her glimpses of something mysterious in their hearts, something she
waited to see, almost with dread, which was always at the last minute
hidden from her. And they seemed to have a heat of their own that
owed nothing to her hand as she held them; rather they burned

against her cold fingers. Her hand trembled, and their cloudy swirling seemed to shiver in response; the swiftness of their ebb and flow seemed to mock the pounding of her heart.

Prince Aliyander had just given her the necklace, with one of the dark-eyed smiles she had learned to fear so much; for while he had done nothing to her yet—but then, he had *done* nothing to any of them—she knew that her own brother was under his invisible spell. This spell he called "friendship" with his flashing smile and another look from his black eyes; and her own father, the King, was afraid of him. She also knew he meant to marry her, and knew her strength could not hold out against him long, once he set himself to win her. His "friendship" had already subdued the Crown Prince, only a few months ago a merry and mischievous lad, into a dog to follow at his heels and go where he was told.

This morning, as they stood together in the Great Hall, herself, and her father, and Prince Aliyander, with the young Crown Prince a half-step behind Aliyander's right shoulder, and their courtiers around them, Aliyander had reached into a pocket and brought out the necklace. It gleamed and seemed to shiver with life as he held it up, and all the courtiers murmured with awe. "For you, Lady Princess," said Aliyander, with a graceful bow and his smile; and he moved to fasten it around her neck: "a small gift, to tell you of just the smallest portion of my esteem for Your Highness."

She started back with a suddenness that surprised even her; and her heart flew up in her throat and beat there wildly as the great jewels danced before her eyes. And she felt rather than saw the flicker in Aliyander's eyes when she moved away from him.

"Forgive me," she stammered; "they are so lovely, you must let me look at them a little first." Her voice felt thick; it was hard to speak. "I shan't be able to admire them as they deserve, when they lie beneath my chin."

"Of course," said Aliyander, but she could not look at his smile. "All pretty ladies love to look at pretty things"; and the edge in his voice was such that only she felt it; and she had to look away from the Crown Prince, whose eyes were shining with the delight of his friend's generosity.

"May I—may I take your—gracious gift outside, and look at it in the sunlight?" she faltered. The high vaulted ceiling and mullioned windows seemed suddenly narrow and stifling, with the great glowing stones only inches from her face. The touch of sunlight would be healing. She reached out blindly, and tried not to wince as Aliyander laid the necklace across her hand.

"I hope you will return wearing my poor gift," he said, with the same edge to his words, "so that it may flatter itself in the light of Your Highness's beauty, and bring joy to the heart of your unworthy admirer."

"Yes—yes, I will," she said, and turned, and only her Princess's training prevented her from fleeing, picking up her skirts with her free hand and running the long length of the Hall to the arched doors, and outside to the gardens. Or perhaps it was the imponderable weight in her hand that held her down.

But outside, at least the sky did not shut down on her as the walls and groined ceiling of the Hall had; and the sun seemed to lie gently and sympathetically across her shoulders even if it could not help itself against Aliyander's jewels, and dripped and ran across them until her eyes were dazzled.

Her feet stopped at last, and she blinked and looked up. Near the edge of the garden, near the great outer wall of the palace, was a quiet pool with a few trees close around it, so that much of the water stood in shadow wherever the sun stood in the sky. There was a small white marble bench under one of the trees, pushed close enough that a sitter might lean comfortably against the broad bole behind him. Aside from the bench there was no other ornament; as the palace gardens went, it was almost wild, for the grass was allowed to grow a little shaggy before it was cut back, and wildflowers grew here occasionally, and were undisturbed. The Princess had discovered this spot —for no one else seemed to come here but the occasional gardener and his clippers—about a year ago; a little before Prince Aliyander had ridden into their lives. Since that riding, their lives had changed, and she had come here more and more often, to be quiet and alone, if only for a little time.

Now she stood at the brink of the pond, the strange necklace clutched in her unwilling fingers, and closed her eyes. She took a few long breaths, hoping that the cool peacefulness of this place would somehow help even this trouble. She did not want to wear this necklace, to place it around her throat; she felt that the strange jewels would . . . strangle her, stop her breath . . . till she breathed in the same rhythm as Aliyander, and as her poor brother.

Her trembling stopped; the hand with the necklace dropped a few inches. She felt better. But as soon as she opened her eyes, she would see those terrible cloudy stones again. She raised her chin. At least the first thing she would see was the quiet water. She began to open her eyes: and then a great *croak* bellowed from, it seemed, a place just beside her feet; and her overtaxed nerves broke out in a sharp "Oh," and she leaped away from the sound. As she leaped, her fingers opened, and the necklace dropped with the softest splash, a lingering and caressing sound, and disappeared under the water.

Her first thought was relief that the stones no longer held and threatened her; and then she remembered Aliyander, and her heart shrank within her. She remembered his look when she had refused his gift; and the sound of his voice when he hoped she would wear it upon her return to the Hall—where he was even now awaiting her. She dared not face him without it round her neck; and he would never believe in this accident. And, indeed, if she had cared for the thing, she would have pulled it to her instead of loosing it in her alarm.

She knelt at the edge of the pool and looked in; but while the water seemed clear, and the sunlight penetrated a long way, still she could not see the bottom, but only a misty greyness that drowned at last to utter black. "Oh dear," she whispered. "I *must* get it back. But how?"

"Well," said a voice diffidently, "I think I could probably fetch it for you."

She had forgotten the noise that had startled her. The voice came from very low down; she was kneeling with her hands so near the pool's edge that her fingertips were lightly brushed by the water's smallest ripples. She turned her head and looked down still farther; and sitting on the bank at her side she saw one of the largest frogs she had ever seen. She did not even think to be startled. "It was rather my fault anyway," added the frog.

"Oh—could you?" she said. She hardly thought of the phenomenon of a frog that talked; her mind was taken up with wishing to have the necklace back, and reluctance to see and touch it again. Here was one part of her problem solved; the medium of the solution did not matter to her.

The frog said no more, but dived into the water with scarcely more noise than the necklace had made in falling; in what seemed only a moment its green head emerged again, with two of the round stones in its wide mouth. It clambered back onto the bank, getting entangled in the trailing necklace as it did so. A frog is a silly creature, and this one looked absurd, with a king's ransom of smooth heavy jewels twisted round its squat figure; but she did not think of this. She reached out to help, and it wasn't till she had Aliyander's gift in her hands again that she noticed the change.

The stones were as large and round and perfect as they had been before; but the weird creamy light of them was gone. They lay dim and grey and quiet against her palm, as cool as the water of the pond, and strengthless.

Such was her relief and pleasure that she sprang to her feet, spreading the necklace to its fullest extent and turning it this way and that in the sunlight, to be certain of what she saw; and she forgot even to thank the frog, still sitting patiently on the bank where she had rescued it from the binding necklace.

"Excuse me," it said at last, and then she remembered it, and looked down and said, "Oh, thank you," with such a bright and glowing look that it might move even a frog's cold heart.

"You're quite welcome, I'm sure," said the frog mechanically. "But I wonder if I might ask you a favor."

"Certainly. Anything." Even facing Aliyander seemed less dreadful, now the necklace was quenched: she felt that perhaps he could be resisted. Her joy made her silly; it was the first time anything of Aliyander's making had missed its mark, and for a moment she had no thoughts for the struggle ahead, but only for the present victory. Perhaps even the Crown Prince could be saved. . . .

"Would you let me live with you at the palace for a little time?"

Her wild thoughts halted for a moment, and she looked down bewildered at the frog. What would a frog want with a palace? For that matter—as if she had only just noticed it—why did this frog talk?

"I find this pool rather dull," said the frog fastidiously, as if this were an explanation.

She hesitated, dropping her hands again, but this time the stones hung limply, hiding in a fold of her wide skirts. She had told the frog, "Certainly, anything"; and her father had brought her up to understand that she must always keep her word, the more so because as Princess there was no one who could force her to. "Very well," she said at last. "If you wish it." And she realized after she spoke that part of her hesitation was reluctance that anything, even a frog, should see her palace, her family, now; it would hurt her. But she had given her word, and there could be no harm in a frog.

"Thank you," said the frog gravely, and with surprising dignity for a small green thing with long thin flipper-footed legs and popping eyes.

There was a pause, and then she said, "I—er—I think I should go back now. Will you be along later or—?"

"I'll be along later," replied the frog at once, as if he recognized her embarrassment; as if he were a poor relation who yet had a sense of his own worth.

She hesitated a moment longer, wondering to how many people she would have to explain her talking frog, and added, "I dine alone with my father at eight." Prince Inthur never took his meals with his father and sister any more; he ate with Aliyander or alone, miserably, in his room, if Aliyander chose to overlook him. Then she raised the grey necklace to clasp it round her throat, and remembered that it was, after all, her talking frog's pool that had put out the ill light of Aliyander's work. She smiled once more at the frog, a little guiltily, for she believed one should be kind to one's poor relations; and she said, "You'll be my talisman."

She turned and walked quickly away, back toward the palace, and the Hall, and Aliyander.

PART TWO

But she made a serious mistake, for she walked swiftly back to the Hall, and blithely through the door, with her head up and her eyes sparkling with happiness and release; she met Aliyander's black eyes too quickly, and smiled without thinking. It was only then she realized what her thoughtlessness had done, when she saw his eyes move swiftly from her face to the jewels at her throat, and then as he saw her smile his own face twisted with a rage so intense it seemed for a moment that his sallow skin would turn black with it. And even her little brother, the Crown Prince, looked at his hero a little strangely, and said, "Is anything wrong?"

Aliyander did not answer. He turned on his heel and left, going toward the door opposite that which the Princess had entered; the door that led into the rest of the palace. Everyone seemed to be holding his or her breath while the quiet footfalls retreated, for there was no other noise; even the air had stopped moving through the windows. Then there was the sound of the heavy door opening, and closing, and Aliyander was gone.

The courtiers blinked and looked at one another. The Crown

Prince looked as if he might cry: his master had left him behind. The King turned to his daughter with the closing of that far door, and he saw first her white frightened face; and then his gaze dropped to the round stones of her necklace, and there, for several moments, it remained.

No one of the courtiers looked at her directly; but when she caught their sidelong looks, there was blankness in their eyes, not understanding. None addressed a word to her, although all had seen that she, somehow, was the cause of Aliyander's anger. But then, for months now it had been considered bad luck to discuss anything that Aliyander did.

Inthur, the Crown Prince, still loved his father and sister in spite of the cloud that Aliyander had cast over his mind; and little did he know how awkward Aliyander found that simple and indestructible love. But now Inthur saw his sister standing alone in the doorway to the garden, her face as white as her dress, and as a little gust of wind blew her skirts around her, and her fair hair across her face, she gasped and gave a shudder, and one hand touched her necklace. With Aliyander absent, even the cloud on Inthur lifted a little, although he himself did not know this, for he never thought about himself. Instead he ran the several steps to where his sister stood, and threw his arms around her; he looked up into her face and said, "Don't worry, Rana dear, he's never angry long." His boy's gaze passed over the necklace without a pause.

She nodded down at him and tried to smile, but her eyes filled with tears; and with a little brother's horror of tears, particularly sister's tears, he let go of her at once and said quickly, with the air of one who changes the subject from one proved dangerous, "What did you do?"

She blinked back her tears, recognizing the dismay on Inthur's face; he would not know that it was his hug that had brought them, and the look on his face when he tried to comfort her: just as he had used to look before Aliyander came. Now he rarely glanced at either his father or his sister except vaguely, as if half asleep, or with his thoughts far away. "I don't know," she said, with a fair attempt at calmness, "but perhaps it is not important."

He patted her hand as if he were her uncle, and said, "That's all right. You just apologize to him when you see him next, and it'll be over."

She smiled wanly as she remembered that her own brother belonged to Aliyander now and she could not trust him. Then the King came up beside them, and when her eyes met his she read knowledge in them: of what Aliyander had seen, in her face and round her neck; and a reflection of her own fear. He said nothing to her.

The rest of the day passed slowly, for while they did not see Aliyander again, the weight of his absence was almost as great as his presence would have been. The Crown Prince grew cross and fretful, and glowered at everyone; the courtiers seemed nervous, and whispered among themselves, looking often over their shoulders as if for the ghosts of their great-grandmothers. Even those who came from the city, or the far-flung towns beyond, to kneel before the King and crave a favor seemed more to crouch and plead, as if for mercy; and their faces were never happy when they went away, whatever the King had granted them.

Rana felt as grey as Aliyander's jewels.

The sun set at last, and its final rays touched the faces in the Hall with the first color most of them had had all day; and as servants came in to light the candles everyone looked paler and more uncomfortable than ever.

One of Aliyander's personal servants approached the throne soon after the candles were lit; the King sat with his children in smaller chairs at his feet. The man offered the Crown Prince a folded slip of paper; his obeisance to the King first was a gesture so cursory as to be insulting, but the King made no move to reprimand him. The Hall was as still as it had been that morning when Aliyander had left it; and the sound of Inthur's impatient opening of the note crackled loudly. He leaped to his feet and said joyfully, "I'm to dine with him!" and with a dreadful look of triumph round the Hall, and then at his father and sister—Rana closed her eyes—he ran off, the servant following with the dignity of a nobleman.

It seemed a sign. The King stood up wearily and clapped his hands once; and the courtiers made their bows and began to drift away, to quarters in the palace, or to grand houses outside in the city. Rana followed her father to the door that led to the rest of the palace, where the Crown Prince had just disappeared; and there the King turned and said, "I will see you at eight, my child?" And Rana's eyes again filled with tears at the question in his voice, behind his words. She only nodded, afraid to speak, and he turned away. "We dine alone," he said, and left her.

She spent two long and bitter hours staring at nothing, sitting alone

in her room; in spite of the gold-and-white hangings, and the bright
blue coverlet on her bed, it refused to look cheerful for her tonight.
She removed her necklace and stuffed it into an empty jar and put the
lid on quickly, as if it were a snake that might escape, although she
knew that it itself had no further power to harm her.

She joined her father with a heavy heart; in place of Aliyander's
jewels she wore a golden pendant that her mother had given her. The
two of them ate in a little room with a small round table, where her
family had always gathered when there was no formal banquet. When
she was very small, and Inthur only a baby, she had sat here with both
her parents; then her pretty, fragile mother had died, and she and
Inthur and their father had faced each other around this table alone.
Now it was just the King and herself. There had been few banquets
in the last months. As she looked at her father now, she was suddenly
frightened at how old and weak he looked. Aliyander could gain no
hold over him, for his mind and his will were too pure for
Aliyander's nets; but his presence aged him quickly, too quickly. And
the next King would be Inthur, who followed Aliyander everywhere,
a pace behind his right shoulder. And Inthur would be delighted at
his best friend's marrying his sister.

The dining-room was round like the table within it; it was the first
floor of a tower that stood at one of the many corners of the Palace. It
had windows on two sides, and a door through which the servants
brought the covered dishes and the wine, and another door that led
down a flight of stone steps to the garden.

Neither she nor her father ate much, nor spoke at all, and the room
was very quiet. So it was that when an odd muffled thump struck the
garden door, they both looked up at once. Whatever it was, after a
moment it struck again. They stared at each other, puzzled, and because since Aliyander had come all things unknown were dreaded,
their looks were also fearful. When the third thump came, Rana
stood up and went over to the door and flung it open.

There sat her frog.

"Oh!" she exclaimed. "It's you."

If a frog could turn its foolish mouth to a smile, this one did.
"Good evening," it replied.

"Who is it?" said the King, standing up; for he could see nothing,
yet he heard the strange deep voice.

"It's . . . a frog," Rana said, somewhat embarrassed. "I dropped

. . . that necklace in a pool today, and he fetched it out for me. He asked a favor in return, that he might live with me in the palace."

"If you made a promise, child, you must keep it," said the King; and for a moment he looked as he had before Aliyander came. "Invite him in." And his eyes rested on his daughter thoughtfully, remembering the change in those jewels that he had seen.

The Princess stood aside, and the frog hopped in. The King and Princess stood, feeling silly, looking down, while the frog looked up; then Rana shook herself, and shut the door, and returned to the table. "Would you—er—like some dinner? There's plenty."

She took the frog back to her own room in her pocket. Her father had said nothing to her about their odd visitor, but she knew from the look on his face when he bade her good night that he would mention it to no one. The frog said gravely that her room was a very handsome one; then it leaped up onto a sofa and settled itself among the cushions. Rana blew the lights out and undressed and climbed into bed, and lay, staring up, thinking.

"I will go with you to the Hall tomorrow, if I may," said the frog's voice from the darkness, breaking in on her dark thoughts.

"Certainly," she said, as she had said once before. "You're my talisman," she added, with a catch in her voice.

"All is not well here," said the frog gently; and the deep sympathetic voice might have been anyone, not a frog, but her old nurse, perhaps, when she was a baby and needed comforting because of a scratched knee; or the best friend she had never had, because she was a Princess, the only Princess of the greatest realm in all the lands from the western to the eastern seas; and to her horror, she burst into tears and found herself between gulps telling that voice everything. How Aliyander had ridden up one day, without warning, ridden in from the north, where his father still ruled as king over a country bordering her father's. How Aliyander was now declared the heir apparent, for his elder brother, Lian, had disappeared over a year before; and while this sad loss continued mysteriously, still it was necessary for the peace of the country to secure the succession. Aliyander's first official performance as heir apparent was this visit to his kingdom's nearest neighbor to the south, for he knew that it was his father's dearest wish that the friendship between their two lands continue close and loyal.

And for the first time they saw Aliyander smile. The Crown Prince had turned away, for he was then free and innocent; the King stiff-ened and grew pale; and Rana did not guess how she might have looked.

"I had known Lian when we were children," Rana continued; she no longer cared who was listening, or if anything was. "He was kind and patient with Inthur, who was only a baby; I—I thought him wonderful," she whispered. "I heard my parents discussing him one night, him and . . . me . . ."

Aliyander's visit had lengthened—a fortnight, a month, two months; it had been almost a year since he rode through their gates. Messengers passed between him and his father—he said; but here he stayed, and entrapped the Crown Prince; and next he would have the Princess.

"I don't know what to do," she said at last, wearily. "There is nothing I can do."

"I'm sorry," said the voice, and it was sad, and wistful, and kind. And human. Her mind wavered from the single thought of *Aliyander, Aliyander,* and she remembered to whom—or what—she spoke; and the sympathy in the creature's voice puzzled her even more than the fact that the voice could use human speech.

"You cannot be a frog," she said stupidly. "You must be—under a spell." And she found she could spare a little pity from her own family's plight to give to this spellbound creature who spoke like a human being.

"Of course," snapped the frog. "Frogs don't talk."

She was silent, sorry that her own pain had made her thoughtless, made her wound another's feelings.

"I'm sorry," said the frog for the second time, and in the same gentle tone. "You see, one never quite grows accustomed."

She answered after a moment: "Yes. I think I do understand, a little."

"Thank you," said the frog.

"Yes," she said again. "Good night."

"Good night."

But just before she fell asleep, she heard the voice once more: "I have one more favor to ask. That you do not mention, when you take me to the Hall tomorrow, that I . . . talk."

"Very well," she said drowsily.

PART THREE

There was a ripple of nervous laughter when the Princess Rana appeared in the Great Hall on the next morning, carrying a large frog. She held her right arm bent at the elbow and curled lightly against her side; and the frog rode quietly on her forearm. She was wearing a dress of pale blue, with lace at her neck, and her fair hair hung loose over her shoulders, and a silver circlet was around her brow; the big green frog showed brilliantly and absurdly against her pale loveliness. She sat on her low chair before her father's throne; the frog climbed, or slithered, or leaped, to her lap, and lay, blinking foolishly at the noblemen in their rich dresses, and the palace servants in their handsome livery; but it was perhaps too stupid to be frightened, for it made no other motion.

She had seen Aliyander standing with the Crown Prince when she entered, but she avoided his eyes; at last he came to stand before her, legs apart, staring down at her bent head with a heat from his black eyes that scorched her skin.

"You dare to mock me," he said, his voice almost a hiss, thick with a venomous hatred she could not mistake.

She looked up in terror, and he gestured at the frog. "Ah, no, I meant no—" she pleaded, and then her voice died; but the heat of Aliyander's look ebbed a little as he read the fear in her face.

"A frog, Princess?" he said; his voice still hurt her, but now it was heavy with scorn, and pitched so that many in the Hall would hear him. "I thought Princesses preferred kittens, or greyhounds."

"I—" She paused, and licked her dry lips. "I found it in the garden." She dropped her eyes again; she could think of nothing else to say. If only he would turn away from her—just for a minute, a minute to gather her wits; but he would not leave her, and her wits would only scatter again when next he addressed her.

He made now a gesture of disgust; and then straightened up, as if he would turn away from her at last, and she clenched her hands on the arms of her chair—and at that moment the frog gave its great bellow, the noise that had startled her yesterday into dropping the necklace into the pool. And Aliyander was startled; he jerked visibly —and the courtiers laughed.

It was only the barest titter, and strangled instantly; but Aliyander heard it, and he turned, his face black with rage as it had been yesterday when Rana had returned wearing a cold grey necklace; and he seized the frog by the leg and hurled it against the heavy stone wall opposite the thrones, which stood halfway down the long length of the Hall and faced across the narrow width to tall windows that looked out upon the courtyard.

Rana was frozen with horror for the moment it took Aliyander to fling the creature; and then as it struck the wall, there was a dreadful sound, and the skin of the frog seemed to—burst—and she closed her eyes.

The sudden gasp of all those around her made her eyes open against her will. And she in her turn gasped.

For the frog that Aliyander had hurled against the wall was there no longer; as it struck and fell, it became a tall young man, who stood there now, his ruddy hair falling past his broad shoulders, his blue eyes blazing as he stared at his attacker.

"Aliyander," he said, and his voice fell like a stone in the silence. Aliyander stood as if his name on those lips had turned him to stone indeed.

"Aliyander. My little brother."

No one moved but Rana; her hands stirred of their own accord. They crept across the spot on her lap where the frog had lain only a minute ago; and they seized each other.

Aliyander laughed—a terrible, ugly sound. "I defeated you once, big brother. I will defeat you again. You are weaker than I. You always will be."

The blue eyes never wavered. "Yes, I am weaker," Lian replied, "as you have proven already. I do not choose your sort of power."

Aliyander's face twisted as Rana had seen it before. She stood up suddenly, but he paid no attention to her; the heat of his gaze was now reserved for his brother, who stood calmly enough, staring back at Aliyander's distorted face.

"You made the wrong choice," Aliyander said, in a voice as black as his look; "and I will prove it to you. You will have no chance to return and inconvenience me a second time."

It was as if no one else could move; the eyes of all were riveted on the two antagonists; even the Crown Prince did not move to be closer to his hero.

The Princess turned and ran. She paused on the threshold of the door to the garden, and picked up a tall flagon that had held wine and was now sitting forgotten on a deep windowsill. Then she ran out, down the white paths; she had no eyes for the trees and the flowers, or the smooth sand of the courtyard to her right; she felt as numb as she had the day before with her handful of round and glowing jewels; but today her eyes watched where her feet led her, and her mind said *hurry, hurry, hurry.*

She ran to the pond where she had found the frog, or where the frog had found her. She knelt quickly on the bank, and rinsed the sour wine dregs from the bottom of the flagon she carried, emptying the tainted water on the grass behind her, where it would not run back into the pool. Then she dipped the jug full, and carried it, brimming, back to the Great Hall.

She had to walk slowly this time, for the flagon was full and very heavy, and she did not wish to spill even a drop of it. Her feet seemed to sink ankle-deep in the ground with every step, although in fact the white pebbles held no footprint as she passed, and only bruised her small feet in their thin-soled slippers.

She paused on the Hall's threshold again, this time for her eyes to adjust to the dimmer light. No one had moved; and no one looked at her.

She saw Aliyander raise his hand and bring it like a back-handed slap against the air before him; and though Lian stood across the room from him, she saw his head jerk as if from the force of a blow; and a thin line formed on his cheek, and after a moment blood welled and dripped from it.

Aliyander waved his hand so the sharp stone of his ring glittered; and he laughed.

Rana started forward again, step by step, as slowly as she had paced the garden, although only a few steps more were needed. Her arms had begun to shiver with the weight of her burden. Still Aliyander did not look at her; for while his might be the greater strength at last, still he could not tear his eyes away from the calm clear gaze of his brother's; his brother yet held him.

Rana walked up the narrow way till she was so close to Aliyander that she might have touched his sleeve if she had not needed both hands to hold the flagon. Then, at last, Aliyander broke away to look at her; and as he did she lifted the great jug, and with a strength she thought was not hers alone, hurled the contents full upon the man before her.

He gave a strangled cry, and brushed desperately with his hands as if he could sweep the water away; but he was drenched with it, his hair plastered to his head and his clothes to his body. He looked suddenly small, wizened and old. He still looked at her, but she met his gaze fearlessly, and he did not seem to recognize her.

His face turned as grey as his jewels. His eyes, she thought, were as opaque as the eyes of marble statues; and then he fell down full-length upon the floor, heavily, without sound, with no attempt to catch himself. He moved no more.

Inthur leaped up then with a cry, and ran to his fallen friend, and Rana saw the quick tears on his cheeks; but when he looked up he looked straight at her, and his eyes were clear. "He was my friend," he said simply; but there was no memory in him of what that friendship had been.

The King stood down stiffly from his throne, and the courtiers moved, and shook themselves as if from sleep, and stared without sorrow at the still body of Aliyander, and with curiosity and awe and a little hesitant but hopeful joy at Lian.

"I welcome you," said the King, with the pride of the master of his own hall, and of a king of a long line of kings. "I welcome you, Prince Lian, to my country, and to my people." And his gaze flickered only briefly to the thing on the floor; at his gesture, a servant stepped forward and threw a dark cloth over it.

"Thank you," said Lian gravely; and the Princess realized that he had come up silently and was standing at her side. She glanced up and saw him looking down at her; and the knowledge of what they had done together, and what neither could have done alone, passed between them; and with it an understanding that they would never discuss it. She said aloud: "I—I welcome you, Prince Lian."

"Thank you," he said again, but she heard the change of tone in his voice; and from the corner of her eye she saw her father smile. She offered Lian her hand, and he took it, and raised it slowly to his lips.

Wonders

Stories filled with
events to astonish and delight

Darkness Box

Ursula K. Le Guin

Ursula K. Le Guin is one of the finest contemporary fantasy writers, winner of many awards (the Hugo, the Nebula, the National Book Award among others) and author of many popular books, including the contemporary classic, the Earthsea trilogy, second only to Tolkien's famous "Ring" trilogy in renown. Here is a less familiar piece, a fantasy story about light and dark, life and war and magic, filled with omens of impending doom. It is sharply and cleanly written, like a fine blade honed and polished, cold steel. It's a story about death.

On soft sand by the sea's edge a little boy walked leaving no footprints. Gulls cried in the bright sunless sky, trout leaped from the saltless ocean. Far off on the horizon the sea serpent raised himself a moment in seven enormous arches and then, bellowing, sank. The child whistled but the sea serpent, busy hunting whales, did not surface again. The child walked on casting no shadow, leaving no tracks on the sand between the cliffs and the sea. Ahead of him rose a grassy headland on which stood a four-legged hut. As he climbed a path up the cliff the hut skipped about and rubbed its front legs together like a lawyer or a fly; but the hands of the clock inside, which said ten minutes of ten, never moved.

"What's that you've got there, Dicky?" asked his mother as she

added parsley and a pinch of pepper to the rabbit stew simmering in
an alembic.

"A box, Mummy."

"Where did you find it?"

Mummy's familiar leaped down from the onion-festooned rafters
and, draping itself like a foxfur round her neck, said, "By the sea."

Dicky nodded. "That's right. The sea washed it up."

"And what's inside it?"

The familiar said nothing, but purred. The witch turned round to
look into her son's round face. "What's in it?" she repeated.

"Darkness."

"Oh? Let's see."

As she bent down to look, the familiar, still purring, shut its eyes.
Holding the box against his chest, the little boy very carefully lifted
the lid a scant inch.

"So it is," said his mother. "Now put it away, don't let it get
knocked about. I wonder where the key got to. Run wash your hands
now. Table, lay!" And while the child worked the heavy pump handle in the yard and splashed his face and hands, the hut resounded
with the clatter of plates and forks materializing.

After the meal, while his mother was having her morning nap,
Dicky took down the water-bleached, sand-encrusted box from his
treasure shelf and set out with it across the dunes, away from the sea.
Close at his heels the black familiar followed him, trotting patiently
over the sand through the coarse grass, the only shadow he had.

At the summit of the pass Prince Rikard turned in the saddle to
look back over the plumes and pennants of his army, over the long
falling road, to the towered walls of his father's city. Under the sunless sky it shimmered there on the plain, fragile and shadowless as a
pearl. Seeing it so he knew it could never be taken, and his heart sang
with pride. He gave his captains the signal for quick march and set
spurs to his horse. It reared and broke into a gallop, while his
gryphon swooped and screamed overhead. She teased the white
horse, diving straight down at it clashing her beak, swerving aside
just in time; the horse, bridleless, would snap furiously at her snaky
tail or rear to strike out with silver hoofs. The gryphon would cackle
and roar, circle back over the dunes, and with a screech and swoop
play the trick all over. Afraid she might wear herself out before the

battle, Rikard finally leashed her, after which she flew along steadily, purring and chirping, by his side.

The sea lay before him; somewhere beneath the cliffs the enemy force his brother led was hidden. The road wound down growing sandier, the sea appearing to right or left always nearer. Abruptly the road fell away; the white horse leaped the ten-foot drop and galloped out over the beach. As he came out from between the dunes Rikard saw a long line of men strung out on the sand, and behind them three black-prowed ships. His own men were scrambling down the drop, swarming over the dunes, blue flags snapping in the sea wind, voices faint against the sound of the sea. Without warning or parley the two forces met, sword to sword and man to man. With a great shrilling scream the gryphon soared up, jerking the leash from Rikard's hand, then dropped like a falcon, beak and claws extended, down on a tall man in gray, the enemy leader. But the tall man's sword was drawn. As the iron beak snapped on his shoulder, trying to get the throat, the iron sword jabbed out and up, slashing the gryphon's belly. She doubled up in air and fell, knocking the man down with the sweep of her great wing, screaming, blackening the sand with blood. The tall man staggered up and slashed off her head and wings, turning half blinded with sand and blood only when Rikard was almost on him. Without a word he turned, lifting his steaming sword to parry Rikard's blow. He tried to strike at the horse's legs, but got no chance, for the beast would back and rear and run at him, Rikard's sword slashing down from above. The tall man's arms began to grow heavy, his breath came in gasps. Rikard gave no quarter. Once more the tall man raised his sword, lunged, and took the whizzing slash of his brother's sword straight across his uplifted face. He fell without a word. Brown sand fell over his body in a little shower from the white stallion's hoofs as Rikard spurred back to the thick of the fight.

The attackers fought on doggedly, always fewer of them, and those few being pushed back step by step toward the sea. When only a knot of twenty or so remained they broke, sprinting desperately for the ships, pushing them off chest-deep in the breakers, clambering aboard. Rikard shouted to his men. They came to him across the sand, picking their way among hacked corpses. The badly wounded tried to crawl to him on hands and knees. All that could walk gathered in ranks in a hollow behind the dune on which Rikard stood. Behind him, out on deep water, the three black ships lay motionless, balanced on their oars.

Rikard sat down, alone on the dune top among the rank grass. He bowed his head and put his hands over his face. Near him the white horse stood still as a horse of stone. Below him his men stood silent. Behind him on the beach the tall man, his face obliterated in blood, lay near the body of the gryphon, and the other dead lay staring at the sky where no sun shone.

A little gust of wind blew by. Rikard raised his face, which though young was very grim. He signaled his captains, swung up into the saddle, and set off round the dunes and back toward the city at a trot, not waiting to see the black ships steer in to shore where their soldiers could board them, or his own army fill up its ranks and come marching behind him. When the gryphon swooped screaming overhead he raised his arm, grinning at the great creature as she tried to perch on his gloved wrist, flapping her wings and screeching like a tomcat. "You no-good gryphon," he said, "you hen, go home to your chicken coop!" Insulted, the monster yawped and sailed off eastward toward the city. Behind him his army wound upward through the hills, leaving no track. Behind them the brown sand lay smooth as silk, stainless. The black ships, sails set, already stood out well to sea. In the prow of the first stood a tall, grim-faced man in gray.

Taking an easier road homeward, Rikard passed not far from the four-legged hut on the headland. The witch stood in the doorway, hailing him. He galloped over, and, drawing rein right at the gate of the little yard, he looked at the young witch. She was bright and dark as coals, her black hair whipped in the sea wind. She looked at him, white-armored on a white horse.

"Prince," she said, "you'll go to battle once too often."

He laughed. "What should I do—let my brother lay siege to the city?"

"Yes, let him. No man can take the city."

"I know. But my father the king exiled him, he must not set foot even on our shore. I'm my father's soldier, I fight as he commands."

The witch looked out to sea, then back at the young man. Her dark face sharpened, nose and chin peaking cronelike, eyes flashing. "Serve and be served," she said, "rule and be ruled. Your brother chose neither to serve nor rule. . . . Listen, prince, take care." Her face warmed again to beauty. "The sea brings presents this morning, the wind blows, the crystals break. Take care."

Gravely he bowed his thanks, then wheeled his horse and was gone, white as a gull over the long curve of the dunes.

The witch went back into the hut, glancing about its one room to see that everything was in place: bats, onions, cauldrons, carpets, broom, toad-stones, crystal balls (cracked through), the thin crescent moon hung up on the chimney, the Books, the familiar— She looked again, then hurried out and called, "Dicky!"

The wind from the west was cold now, bending the coarse grass down.

"Dicky! . . . Kitty, kitty kitty!"

The wind caught the voice from her lips, tore it into bits, and blew it away.

She snapped her fingers. The broom came zooming out the door, horizontal and about two feet off the ground, while the hut shivered and hopped about in excitement. "Shut up!" the witch snapped, and the door obediently slammed. Mounting the broom she took off in a long gliding swoop southward down the beach, now and then crying out, "Dicky! . . . Here, kitty, kitty, kitty!"

The young prince, rejoining his men, had dismounted to walk with them. As they reached the pass and saw the city below them on the plain, he felt a tug at his cloak.

"Prince—"

A little boy, so little he was still fat and round-cheeked, stood with a scared look, holding up a battered, sandy box. Beside him a black cat sat smiling broadly. "The sea brought this—it's for the prince of the land, I know it is—please take it!"

"What's in it?"

"Darkness, sir."

Rikard took the box and after a slight hesitation opened it a little, just a crack. "It's painted black inside," he said with a hard grin.

"No, prince, truly it's not. Open it wider!"

Cautiously Rikard lifted the lid higher, an inch or two, and peered in. Then he shut it quickly, even as the child said, "Don't let the wind blow it out, prince!"

"I shall take this to the king."

"But it's for you, sir—"

"All seagifts are the king's. But thank you for it, boy." They looked at each other for a moment, the little round boy and the hard splendid youth; then Rikard turned and strode on, while Dicky wandered back down the hills, silent and disconsolate. He heard his mother's voice from far away to the south, and tried to answer; but the wind blew his call landward, and the familiar had disappeared.

The bronze gates of the city swung open as the troop approached. Watchdogs bayed, guards stood rigid, the people of the city bowed down as Rikard on his horse clattered at full gallop up the marble streets to the palace. Entering, he glanced up at the great bronze clock on the bell tower, the highest of the nine white towers of the palace. The moveless hands said ten minutes of ten.

In the Hall of Audience his father awaited him: a fierce gray-haired man crowned with iron, his hands clenched on the heads of iron chimaeras that formed the arms of the throne. Rikard knelt and with bowed head, never looking up, reported the success of his foray. "The Exile was killed, with the greater part of his men; the rest fled in their ships."

A voice answered like an iron door moving on unused hinges: "Well done, prince."

"I bring you a seagift, Lord." Still with head bowed, Rikard held up the wooden box.

A low snarl came from the throat of one of the carven monsters of the throne.

"That is mine," said the old king so harshly that Rikard glanced up for a second, seeing the teeth of the chimaeras bared and the king's eyes glittering.

"Therefore I bring it to you, Lord."

"That is mine—I gave it to the sea, I myself! And the sea spits back my gift." A long silence, then the king spoke more softly. "Well, keep it, prince. The sea doesn't want it, nor do I. It's in your hands. Keep it—locked. Keep it locked, prince!"

Rikard, on his knees, bowed lower in thanks and consent, then rose and backed down the long hall, never looking up. As he came out into the glittering anteroom, officers and noblemen gathered round him, ready as usual to ask about the battle, laugh, drink, and chatter. He passed among them without a word or glance and went to his own quarters, alone, carrying the box carefully in both hands.

His bright, shadowless, windowless room was decorated on every wall with patterns of gold inset with topazes, opals, crystals, and, most vivid of all jewels, candle flames moveless on golden sconces. He set the box down on a glass table, threw off his cloak, unbuckled his swordbelt, and sat down sighing. The gryphon loped in from his bedroom, talons rasping on the mosaic floor, stuck her great head onto his knees, and waited for him to scratch her feathery mane. There was also a cat prowling around the room, a sleek black one;

Rikard took no notice. The palace was full of animals, cats, hounds, apes, squirrels, young hippogriffs, white mice, tigers. Every lady had her unicorn, every courtier had a dozen pets. The prince had only one, the gryphon which always fought for him, his one unquestioning friend. He scratched the gryphon's mane, often glancing down to meet the loving golden gaze of her round eyes, now and then glancing too at the box on the table. There was no key to lock it.

Music played softly in a distant room, a ceaseless interweaving of notes like the sound of a fountain.

He turned to look at the clock on the mantel, an ornate square of gold and blue enamel. It was ten minutes of ten: time to rise and buckle on his sword, call up his men, and go to battle. The Exile was returning, determined to take the city and reclaim his right to the throne, his inheritance. His black ships must be driven back to sea. The brothers must fight, and one must die, and the city be saved. Rikard rose, and at once the gryphon jumped up lashing her tail, eager for the fight. "All right, come along!" Rikard told her, but his voice was cold. He took up his sword in the pearl-encrusted sheath and buckled it on, and the gryphon whined with excitement and rubbed her beak on his hand. He did not respond. He was tired and sad, he longed for something—for what? To hear music that ceased, to speak to his brother once before they fought . . . he did not know. Heir and defender, he must obey. He set the silver helmet on his head and turned to pick up his cloak, flung over a chair. The pearly sheath slung from his belt clattered against something behind him; he turned and saw the box, lying on the floor, open. As he stood looking at it with the same cold, absent look, a little blackness like smoke gathered about it on the floor. He stooped and picked it up, and darkness ran out over his hands.

The gryphon backed away, whining.

Tall and white-armored, fair-haired, silver-capped in the glittering shadowless room, Rikard stood holding the open box, watching the thick dusk that dripped slowly from it. All around his body now, below his hands, was twilight. He stood still. Then slowly he raised the box up, clear up over his head, and turned it upside down.

Darkness flowed over his face. He looked about him, for the distant music had stopped and things were very silent. Candles burned, dots of light picking out flecks of gold and flashes of violet from walls and ceiling. But all the corners were dark, behind each chair lay darkness, and as Rikard turned his head his shadow leapt along the wall. He moved then, quickly, dropping the box, for in one of the black corners he had glimpsed the reddish glow of two great eyes. The gryphon, of course. He held out his hand and spoke to her. She did not move, but gave a queer metallic cry.

"Come on! Are you afraid of the dark?" he said, and then all at once was afraid himself. He drew his sword. Nothing moved. He took a step backward toward the door, and the monster jumped. He saw the black wings spread across the ceiling, the iron beak, the talons; her bulk was on him before he could stab upward. He wrestled, the great beak snapping at his throat and the talons tearing at his arms and chest, till he got his sword arm free and could slash down, pull away, and slash again. The second blow half severed the gryphon's neck. She dropped off, lay writhing in the shadows among splinters of glass, then lay still.

Rikard's sword dropped clattering on the floor. His hands were sticky with his own blood, and he could hardly see; the beating of the gryphon's wings had blown out or knocked over every candle but one. He groped his way to a chair and sat down. After a minute, though he still gasped for breath, he did as he had done on the dune top after battle: bowed his head and hid his face in his hands. It was completely silent. The one candle flickered in its sconce, mirrored feebly in a cluster of topazes on the wall behind it. Rikard raised his head.

The gryphon lay still. Its blood had spread out in a pool, black as the first spilt darkness from the box. Its iron beak was open, its eyes open, like two red stones.

"It's dead," said a small soft voice, as the witch's cat came picking its way delicately among the fragments of the smashed table. "Once and for all. Listen, prince!" The cat sat down curling its tail neatly round its paws. Rikard stood motionless, blank-faced, till a sudden sound made him start: a little ting nearby! Then from the tower overhead a huge dull bell stroke reverberated in the stone of the floor, in his ears, in his blood. The clocks were striking ten.

There was a pounding at his door, and shouts echoed down the palace corridors mixed with the last booming strokes of the bell, screams of scared animals, calls, commands.

"You'll be late for the battle, prince," said the cat.

Rikard groped among blood and shadow for his sword, sheathed it, flung on his cloak, and went to the door.

"There'll be an afternoon today," the cat said, "and a twilight, and night will fall. At nightfall one of you will come home to the city, you or your brother. But only one of you, prince."

Rikard stood still a moment. "Is the sun shining now, outside?"

"Yes, it is—now."

"Well, then, it's worth it," the young man said, and opened the door and strode on out into the hubbub and panic of the sunlit halls, his shadow falling black behind him.

Jack and the Beanstalk

Osbert Sitwell

Osbert Sitwell (1892–1969) published a book of fairy tales, Fee-Fi-Fo-Fum, *in 1959, collecting his contemporary versions of classic tales, such as Cinderella, Bluebeard and the present selection. A scion of the famous English literary family of Sitwell, with forty books to his credit, Sir Osbert commented upon fairy tales in his charming prefatory essay. Speaking of the appeal of the fairy story to modern authors, he said, "it should constitute for them a kind of abstract art, stylized and meticulous, and also a sort of technical exercise, while at the same time it should enable them to throw out lateral beams of light to illuminate parallels in contemporary life." Of the present selection, he explained, "Jack himself represents Man, who can make use of the gifts of nature to become rich." Sir Osbert's tale indeed fulfills his prescription.*

Whereas Jack the Giant-Killer—though it is true that not so long ago his story was summarily dismissed in the current psycho-analytic cant of the day by a writer in a weekly paper as a "simple case of Adlerian Inferiority Complex"—may by some be regarded in a different light, as a knight-errant searching for ladies to rescue, yet it appears certain that the other celebrated Jack, whose name is fabulously associated with the Beanstalk, and with whom we are first concerned, was no idealist, but the prototype of many capitalists in Europe and America during the era of unrestricted free enterprise. His career can be seen to resemble nearly that of any man who started life as an errand-boy and ended—as was always said of such people—"entirely through their own efforts," as a millionaire, a sort of magical Sir Thomas Lipton.

When he was a boy, Jack and his widowed mother lived in Hampshire, some twelve miles from Winchester. She was a typical widow, but of the French variety rather than of the English, glorying in her black, neatly and tightly clad in it, sad but voluble, with a practical outlook: while Jack for his part was equally typical of an English boy, apple-checked, as a rule reliable beyond his years, and given to slouching and sly remarks. A stranger would have guessed him to be a farmer's son, but his father had been a butcher, dead some three years before this story begins. After her husband's death at forty from rheumatic fever, the widow had been obliged to sell the business in order to pay his debts; nevertheless in later years it was often said of young Jack that in the manner of many great men (*great* was then a term reserved specifically for those who became of a sudden inordinately rich) he owed much to his mother's early training of him, because it had been her habit to din continually into his ears, even when he was a small child, such concise odds and ends of proverbial wisdom as *"Never miss an opportunity," "Don't kill the goose that lays the golden eggs," "Look after the pennies and the pounds will look after themselves,"* and, most often of all, that *"God helps those who help themselves."* And, indeed, the last and so frequently recurring adage may really have influenced him, for, as will be seen in the course of the next few pages, he helped himself to a good deal at a comparatively early age. The only assets of mother and son to start with were their mutual affection, a thatched cottage, the front of which was thickly covered during the summer with honeysuckle and small red roses, a garden, a meadow, and a cow called Buttercup, which supplied the rich golden butter and creamy milk they sold in the nearest market every morning: sold profitably, because both products looked appetising and abounded in vitamins—albeit these were then called something else.

One day, however, the cow yielded no milk, and in consequence the widow became worried to desperation. Jack tried to find work, but the Trade Union rules forbade it because he was only eleven years of age. Moreover they lived too far away from a town for him to be able to attend a school, and his mother had not been able to give him anything but practical lessons, for she had no letters herself. In consequence, when not employed by her on errands of one sort or another, he spent all of his considerable spare time climbing trees,

until he attained an extraordinary proficiency in this art of the youthful, and showed an altogether astonishing agility. This way of spending the hours used, however, to irritate his mother, who frequently
would leave her cottage, trace him to a tree-top, and call up to him,
"Why aren't you working? Climbing like that will never get you
anywhere!" (Little did she foresee the future.) . . . Soon, his
mother was obliged to sell their furniture piece by piece, and even to
get what she could for their spare clothing—though of this there was
little enough. Finally the day came when with a solemn air she called
Jack from the garden and told him to drive Buttercup to market the
next morning, and sell her for the best price he could obtain.

On the way there he met an old man with a flowing white beard,
who looked, Jack thought, rather like a hermit. He was clad in a long
black robe, and wore on his head a high conical black hat decorated
with golden suns and stars. . . . Directly the boy was near enough,
the stranger spoke to him, saying:

"Good morning, Jack, that's a nice cow you've got. I'd like to buy
her."

"Well, what do you offer, sir?" asked Jack.

"I'm a wizard, not a merchant or farmer," replied the old man, "so
I do not buy with money, but I offer you, in exchange for her, five
beans. They're not by any means ordinary vegetables, neither broad
beans nor scarlet runners; they are *magic* beans, and if when you reach
home you plant them, by morning they'll have grown to the kingdom
of the sky."

Jack, being still young, forgot his mother's careful instructions: the
thought of these beans fascinated him, and at once, without any attempt to raise the price, he accepted the offer of the sorcerer; who
then drew out from a deep pocket five small kidney-shaped objects
with a hard skin corrugated as a contour map of the world, and
counted them into the boy's hand.

Jack started off for home in high spirits, but as he approached the
cottage he began to feel a little nervous about his bargain. . . . The
widow was waiting for him at the door.

"Well, what have you brought me, son?" she called.

"I've brought you five magic beans, mother," he answered.

The poor woman, flabbergasted by her son's unexpected act of
disobedience and folly, shouted at him, "Magic, my foot! I'll give you
beans!" (which is said to be the origin of that well-known slang
phrase). She then—for by this time Jack had entered the house—

seized the beans from his hand, flung them out of the window, and sent her son straight up to bed without supper.

As Jack lay in the dark room, hungry and cold, and unable for a long time to sleep, he thought of the beans, and determined never to fall into such an error again. It was then that he for the first time comprehended fully the importance of knowing the exact value of all animals and objects, and of money itself. . . . A full moon soon shone into the room, plating the walls with its precious if intangible metal, but this began before long to fall into patches, instead of sheeting a whole surface. He wondered what the reason could be, and for a long time stared at the window, for something appeared in the past hour to be obstructing the entrance of the light, and he also vaguely wondered what could be the curious rustling that he seemed to hear, soft and rhythmic. Though he was not sleepy, he was far too tired physically to get out of bed. If, however, he had been more inquisitive, and had persevered, he would have discovered that the sound was one that no man had ever heard before, or would probably ever hear again; the sound that trees and plants and all green things make in the process of their growing; a music usually spread over so long a period, and so slowly, that the human ear cannot catch the pattern of it. He lay there, wondering whether the soft sounds were due to his imagination, until after another half an hour or so he fell asleep.

In the morning he woke up in his familiar room: but the moment his eyes opened, he realised there was a difference; it was strangely dark. He got out of bed and ran to the window. . . . A beanstalk as thick as the bole of a well-grown oak, only more flimsy in substance, and with leaves as large as those of a great-leaved magnolia, filled the space, casting a green shadow on the white walls. Craning his neck out through the various barriers, he looked upward, and saw there too the curious plant, stretching, apparently for ever, up to the very sky itself. He dressed quickly and, curiosity overcoming his hunger, slipped out before, as he thought, his mother was down, and began with ease to climb the beanstalk. He soon reached the clouds. But he had not passed beyond ear-shot when he heard his mother rush from the cottage, and shout up to him, "Jack, you come down this instant! And don't you get it into your head that, after all, it's a magic bean. It's just those hormones you read of." He was determined not to turn back for anybody, because he wanted to reach the kingdom of the sky, of which the old man had spoken. The top of the beanstalk was level with the clouds, which today were pushed up in fleecy hillocks, and a road led from it to a tall house, grey as the pastures of the angels, and its huge windows shone with reflected light, as though they were the eyes of Gods.

In the doorway, which was as large, the other way round, as the whole front of his home, stood an enormous woman. Owing to her size, her skin seemed very coarse, and the pores showed like pockmarks, but she had a kind expression, so that Jack, whose exertions had made his appetite all the keener, plucked up his courage to ask her, "Please, ma'am, could you give me some breakfast?"

"You're more likely to find yourself part of somebody else's breakfast, if you stay here," the woman replied, "for my husband is the celebrated ogre Crunchingbones, and there's nothing he likes so much of a morning as an English boy on toast."

"Well, I may as well risk being eaten myself, as die of hunger," Jack answered.

The good-natured woman smiled at this, took him into the tall house, and placed before him bread and cheese and a bowl of milk which Jack soon consumed. Scarcely had he finished when the ground began to tremble with a peculiar rhythm.

"That's *his* footstep," said the woman; "I warned you. He'll be here in a minute." . . . She seemed terrified at her husband's approach, and lifting Jack up by his collar, threw him into the oven to hide him, and shut the door: but he could peep into the room through a crack invisible on the outside. The sound of gigantic footsteps drew nearer, and in a moment Jack saw the form of a vast man enter the room. He threw down on the table two calves he had been carrying, and said to his wife, "There's my breakfast: get it ready for me at once!" For some minutes he paced up and down the kitchen— then stopped short and sniffed the air in a most frightening way, like a wild animal. Suddenly he howled out in his ferine voice:

> Fee, Fi, Fo, Fum!
> I smell the blood of an Englishman!

"You're imagining things, dear," said his wife, "you don't keep your strength up. You should take more care of yourself."

"Well, that may be so." answered the giant, mollified.

In the meantime, while Jack trembled in the oven, Mrs. Crunchingbones had set to, and prepared breakfast for her husband. He ate long and greedily, but the moment he had finished, he dragged from where it stood against the wall opposite him a large chest, unlocked it, lifted the lid, and took out of it two bags. They contained gold coins which he proceeded to count until he fell asleep. Crunchingbones's wife was somewhere at the back of the house, so Jack, creeping out of the oven, seized one of the bags of gold, dropped it into his mother's garden far below, and then swarmed down the beanstalk, home.

At first his mother was angry, for the sack was heavy, and had nearly hit her. "You careless little beggar, you!" she shouted up at him. "One of these days, you'll kill someone!" But she softened when she heard his story and saw what the bag contained.

"You acted correctly, Jack," she commented at the end. "Fair shares for all! He has no right to have more gold coins than we!" So she and Jack lived on the ogre's hoard until the last gold coin was spent. After which they existed for some time as best they could, borrowing and running into debt, for their spell of temporary prosperity had debauched them.

At last want of food drove Jack again to explore. The beanstalk still flourished, and he climbed it once more, and once more arrived safely at the ogre's house. Cautiously he entered the kitchen, and, after having made sure that the ogre was out, greeted the wife, saying, "Hello, Mrs. Crunchingbones, ma'am," in rather an offhand manner, as if he saw her every day.

"Hop it, boy!" she replied. "Wasn't it you that I hid here the very day that my husband missed one of his sacks of gold?"

"Well," he answered, "if I weren't so hungry, I could tell you a few facts about that: they might interest you—but I must eat first."

The ogre's wife again felt sorry for the boy; he seemed too young to have much harm in him, and she could see that he was hungry, so she said, "Sit down over there," indicating a corner near the oven, and brought him a bowl of milk. He had scarcely finished it when they heard—or, rather, in the first place, felt—the ogre's footsteps approaching. Once more the kind woman threw Jack into the oven, and he was able to watch as before. Once more, the ogre angrily sniffed the air. Once more he bellowed out in his angry, ugly voice:

> Fee, Fi, Fo, Fum!
> I smell the blood of an Englishman!

His wife, however, calmed him, patting him and saying, "There, there, dear: don't carry on! You're tired, and will feel better after breakfast"; and she soon produced three broiled oxen for him.

After he had finished his meal, he shouted sleepily, "Bring me my hen!"

Accordingly, his wife brought to him a large red hen fluttering and cackling in her arms, put it down and left the room. Crunchingbones commanded "Lay!": whereupon the hen cackled again, and laid an egg of gold—which puzzled Jack, for he had always understood from his mother that it was a goose that laid the golden eggs. Indeed, this discovery first began to undermine his mother's authority. However, there was no time to waste, or in which to think this out at the moment, and as soon as the ogre fell asleep and began to snore, Jack crept out of his hiding-place and grabbed the hen. The frightened cackle it put up woke the ogre, but Jack had a good start and was already on his way down the beanstalk before Crunchingbones was out of the house, so that the boy reached home safely with the gold egg in his pocket and the hen under his arm.

The next time Jack climbed his beanstalk it was not from hunger, for the golden eggs procured him and his mother all, and more than all, that they could wish for: no, now Jack wanted to get rich, and easily won treasure had fanned his greed for money. . . . The ogre's house seemed empty, and Jack slunk in without meeting the ogre's wife, and on this occasion for a change concealed himself in the copper. . . . Soon Crunchingbones returned. Directly he entered, he stopped, sniffed the air, as he had done on previous occasions, and hitting the wooden walls with a stick as big as a tree trunk to make sure that there was no hollow space behind them in which someone could hide, at the same time bawled out his theme-song:

> Fee, Fi, Fo, Fum!
> I smell the blood of an Englishman!

At the sound of his voice, his wife hurried in, saying, "If you really think you do, dear, it will be that little villain from down below again; the boy who stole our gold and our magic hen. If so, he's sure to be in the oven. That's where he was before, if you remember."

Jack was terrified that it would be the turn of the copper next, for he heard Crunchingbones rush towards the oven, open the door with a bang, and explore it with great blows from his stick. . . . However, that it had proved to be empty must have reassured the ogre, for he did not search the copper, and after his breakfast of four sheep, roasted, called to his wife: "Bring me my harp of gold!" When she had brought it and had left the room, he commanded: "Sing, Harp!"

and the harp sang in a golden voice, most touchingly, for more than half an hour, until the ogre fell asleep. Then the harp fell silent for fear its singing should wake him.

As soon as the sound of the giant's snoring replaced its melodious songs, Jack crept noiselessly out of the copper and grasped the harp: but the moment he touched it, it called out "Master! Master!" . . . The ogre first stirred in his sleep, and then, feeling that something was amiss, roused himself, and ran to the door just as Jack was disappearing out of sight down the beanstalk. Crunchingbones looked at the plant doubtfully, wondering, no doubt, whether in spite of its size it would support his weight. But from far below the harp cried again, "Master! Master!" and on hearing this, the ogre threw caution to the winds, and, first clutching the beanstalk, began to climb clumsily down it, the whole plant swaying, sagging and drooping under the unexpected burden.

By this time Jack had reached the ground in safety, and realising what was happening, called "Mother, Mother, bring me an axe!" She hurried out, but was so startled that she could not move when she saw the giant's leg protruding out of a cloud as he clumsily felt for his next foothold. Jack, however, snatched the axe from her, and wielded it to some purpose, for at the second blow he cut the stalk clean in two, and the giant like an avalanche of flesh fell to the ground with a tremendous crash, making it shake as though an earthquake were in progress, and carrying the top of the beanstalk with him: his head was broken, and after a minute there sounded a death-rattle from him, like a great hurricane. . . . Now it was to Jack that the harp sang "Master! Master!"

In London, and in the provinces too, Jack and his mother gave concerts regularly for the harp, which learned to sing Gounod's *Ave Maria,* and made much money for them. Indeed, the house was invariably sold out. With this exceptional musical instrument, and in addition with the hen, as their capital, they started the Golden Egg Bonus Company, a dairy and grocer's shop, combined with a lending library. As Jack could not read, his chief wish—for he affected to despise books, or book-learning, as he termed it—was to get every new offending volume out of the shop as soon as it arrived in it, and this gave an appearance of keenness. The business started in quite a small way: regular customers—those who had spent enough money, without realising that it was too much—were invited to draw a ticket out of a bag, and if it had printed on it a particular number, announced beforehand, the fortunate client found himself awarded an egg of gold. This novel system of bonus continually brought in new and enthusiastic clients, until the smaller competitive shops became deserted and were bought up by the new company. Soon branches of it opened in every large city and prosperous manufacturing town in England and the United States.

Jack and his mother now found themselves in the world of big business, and before long proceeded to sponsor the famous Golden Egg Television and Radio programmes, in which the Golden Harp was a favourite performer. They owned yachts and rented grousemoors in Scotland. But all this work, all this prosperity and luxury, brought their own drawbacks. He never married, and his mother was too old and set in her ways to make an ideal hostess. Moreover, Jack, unable to read, was bored in his leisure hours. His new friends thought him eccentric, for, conscious that the improvement in his circumtances had all followed on climbing a beanstalk, he persisted every day in climbing trees, though he was now of middle age, and guests could not help being surprised when they heard their host hail them from some leafy fastness at the top of oak or chestnut. His mother would try to break him of this habit, but she failed. In fact, he had developed what is now called a fixation. His move to a large mansion in London served to make his eccentricity only more evident. And one morning Lord Beanstalk, as he was now called, for he had lately been created a viscount, was found by the police at the top of an elm, known to be unsafe, in Kensington Gardens. They ordered him to come down, but he refused, and in the ensuing struggle—for ignorant as they were of his identity, they sent up firemen on ladders to capture him—he fell and was killed. His solitary and grieving mother did not long outlive him, and the nationalisation of the Golden Egg Bonus Company that followed.

Peter Pan

J. M. Barrie

Mythic figures in popular culture arise all too frequently and often decay in a generation. Some, such as Peter Pan, last. This selection of chapters from Sir James M. Barrie's novel The Little White Bird, *is the origin of Peter, who proved so charming and popular that Barrie (1860–1937), who was primarily a dramatist, brought him to the stage in the famous story of Peter and Wendy and the lost boys. Barrie's plays often use fantasy to superb effect, but his creation of Peter Pan towers over all else in the body of his work. Here is Peter Pan, the escaped flying baby, in his original habitat, Kensington Gardens, among the fairies.*

If you ask your mother whether she knew about Peter Pan when she was a little girl, she will say, "Why, of course, I did, child," and if you ask her whether he rode on a goat in those days, she will say, "What a foolish question to ask; certainly he did." Then if you ask your grandmother whether she knew about Peter Pan when she was a girl, she also says, "Why, of course, I did, child," but if you ask her whether he rode on a goat in those days, she says she never heard of his having a goat. Perhaps she has forgotten, just as she sometimes forgets your name and calls you Mildred, which is your mother's name. Still, she could hardly forget such an important thing as the goat. Therefore there was no goat when your grandmother was a little girl. This shows that, in telling the story of Peter Pan, to begin with the goat (as most people do) is as silly as to put on your jacket before your vest.

Of course, it also shows that Peter is ever so old, but he is really always the same age, so that does not matter in the least. His age is one week, and though he was born so long ago he has never had a birthday, nor is there the slightest chance of his ever having one. The reason is that he escaped from being a human when he was seven days old; he escaped by the window and flew back to the Kensington Gardens.

If you think he was the only baby who ever wanted to escape, it shows how completely you have forgotten your own young days. When David heard this story first he was quite certain that he had never tried to escape, but I told him to think back hard, pressing his hands to his temples, and when he had done this hard, and even harder, he distinctly remembered a youthful desire to return to the tree-tops, and with that memory came others, as that he had lain in bed planning to escape as soon as his mother was asleep, and how she had once caught him half-way up the chimney. All children could have such recollections if they would press their hands hard to their temples, for, having been birds before they were human, they are naturally a little wild during the first few weeks, and very itchy at the shoulders, where their wings used to be. So David tells me.

I ought to mention here that the following is our way with a story: First, I tell it to him, and then he tells it to me, the understanding being that it is quite a different story; and then I retell it with his additions, and so we go on until no one could say whether it is more his story or mine. In this story of Peter Pan, for instance, the bald narrative and most of the moral reflections are mine, though not all, for this boy can be a stern moralist, but the interesting bits about the ways and customs of babies in the bird-stage are mostly reminiscences of David's, recalled by pressing his hands to his temples and thinking hard.

Well, Peter Pan got out by the window, which had no bars. Standing on the ledge he could see trees far away, which were doubtless the Kensington Gardens, and the moment he saw them he entirely forgot that he was now a little boy in a night-gown, and away he flew, right over the houses to the Gardens. It is wonderful that he could fly without wings, but the place itched tremendously, and perhaps we could all fly if we were as dead-confident-sure of our capacity to do it as was bold Peter Pan that evening.

He alighted gaily on the open sward, between the Baby's Palace and the Serpentine, and the first thing he did was to lie on his back and kick. He was quite unaware already that he had ever been human, and thought he was a bird, even in appearance, just the same as in his early days, and when he tried to catch a fly he did not understand that the reason he missed it was because he had attempted to seize it with his hand, which, of course, a bird never does. He saw, however, that it must be past Lock-out Time, for there were a good many fairies about, all too busy to notice him; they were getting breakfast ready, milking their cows, drawing water, and so on, and the sight of the water-pails made him thirsty, so he flew over to the Round Pond to have a drink. He stooped, and dipped his beak in the pond; he thought it was his beak, but, of course, it was only his nose, and, therefore, very little water came up, and that not so refreshing as usual, so next he tried a puddle, and he fell flop into it. When a real bird falls in flop, he spreads out his feathers and pecks them dry, but Peter could not remember what was the thing to do, and he decided, rather sulkily, to go to sleep on the weeping beech in the Baby Walk.

At first he found some difficulty in balancing himself on a branch, but presently he remembered the way, and fell asleep. He awoke long before morning, shivering, and saying to himself, "I never was out in such a cold night"; he had really been out in colder nights when he was a bird, but, of course, as everybody knows, what seems a warm night to a bird is a cold night to a boy in a night-gown. Peter also felt strangely uncomfortable, as if his head was stuffy; he heard loud noises that made him look round sharply, though they were really himself sneezing. There was something he wanted very much, but, though he knew he wanted it, he could not think what it was. What he wanted so much was his mother to blow his nose, but that never struck him, so he decided to appeal to the fairies for enlightenment. They are reputed to know a good deal.

There were two of them strolling along the Baby Walk, with their arms round each other's waists, and he hopped down to address them. The fairies have their tiffs with the birds, but they usually give a civil answer to a civil question, and he was quite angry when these two ran away the moment they saw him. Another was lolling on a garden-chair, reading a postage-stamp which some human had let fall, and when he heard Peter's voice he popped in alarm behind a tulip.

To Peter's bewilderment he discovered that every fairy he met fled from him. A band of workmen, who were sawing down a toadstool, rushed away, leaving their tools behind them. A milkmaid turned her pail upside down and hid in it. Soon the Gardens were in an uproar. Crowds of fairies were running this way and that, asking each other stoutly, who was afraid; lights were extinguished, doors barricaded, and from the grounds of Queen Mab's palace came the rubadub of drums, showing that the royal guard had been called out. A regiment of Lancers came charging down the Broad Walk, armed with holly-leaves, with which they jog the enemy horribly in passing. Peter heard the little people crying everywhere that there was a human in the Gardens after Lock-out Time, but he never thought for a moment that he was the human. He was feeling stuffier and stuffier, and more and more wistful to learn what he wanted done to his nose, but he pursued them with the vital question in vain; the timid creatures ran from him, and even the Lancers, when he approached them up the Hump, turned swiftly into a side-walk, on the pretence that they saw him there.

Despairing of the fairies, he resolved to consult the birds, but now he remembered, as an odd thing, that all the birds on the weeping beech had flown away when he alighted on it, and though that had not troubled him at the time, he saw its meaning now. Every living thing was shunning him. Poor little Peter Pan, he sat down and cried, and even then he did not know that, for a bird, he was sitting on his wrong part. It is a blessing that he did not know, for otherwise he would have lost faith in his power to fly, and the moment you doubt whether you can fly, you cease for ever to be able to do it. The reason birds can fly and we can't is simply that they have perfect faith, for to have faith is to have wings.

Now, except by flying, no one can reach the island in the Serpentine, for the boats of humans are forbidden to land there, and there are stakes round it, standing up in the water, on each of which a bird-sentinel sits by day and night. It was to the island that Peter now flew to put his strange case before old Solomon Caw, and he alighted on it with relief, much heartened to find himself at last at home, as the birds call the island. All of them were asleep, including the sentinels, except Solomon, who was wide awake on one side, and he listened quietly to Peter's adventures, and then told him their true meaning.

"Look at your night-gown, if you don't believe me," Solomon said, and with staring eyes Peter looked at his night-gown, and then at the sleeping birds. Not one of them wore anything.

"How many of your toes are thumbs?" said Solomon a little cruelly, and Peter saw, to his consternation, that all his toes were fingers. The shock was so great that it drove away his cold.

"Ruffle your feathers," said that grim old Solomon, and Peter tried most desperately hard to ruffle his feathers, but he had none. Then he rose up, quaking, and for the first time since he stood on the window-ledge, he remembered a lady who had been very fond of him.

"I think I shall go back to mother," he said timidly.

"Good-bye," replied Solomon Caw with a queer look.

But Peter hesitated. "Why don't you go?" the old one asked politely.

"I suppose," said Peter huskily, "I suppose I can still fly?"

You see, he had lost faith.

"Poor little half-and-half," said Solomon, who was not really hard-hearted, "you will never be able to fly again, not even on windy days. You must live here on the island always."

"And never even go to the Kensington Gardens?" Peter asked tragically.

"How could you get across?" said Solomon. He promised very kindly, however, to teach Peter as many of the bird ways as could be learned by one of such an awkward shape.

"Then I sha'n't be exactly a human?" Peter asked.

"No."

"Nor exactly a bird?"

"No."

"What shall I be?"

"You will be a Betwixt-and-Between," Solomon said, and certainly he was a wise old fellow, for that is exactly how it turned out.

The birds on the island never got used to him. His oddities tickled them every day, as if they were quite new, though it was really the birds that were new. They came out of the eggs daily, and laughed at him at once, then off they soon flew to be humans, and other birds came out of other eggs, and so it went on for ever. The crafty mother-birds, when they tired of sitting on their eggs, used to get the young ones to break their shells a day before the right time by whispering to them that now was their chance to see Peter washing or drinking or eating. Thousands gathered round him daily to watch him do these things, just as you watch the peacocks, and they screamed with delight when he lifted the crusts they flung him with his hands instead of in the usual way with the mouth. All his food was brought to him from the Gardens at Solomon's orders by the birds.

He would not eat worms or insects (which they thought very silly of him), so they brought him bread in their beaks. Thus, when you cry out, "Greedy! Greedy!" to the bird that flies away with the big crust, you know now that you ought not to do this, for he is very likely taking it to Peter Pan.

Peter wore no night-gown now. You see, the birds were always begging him for bits of it to line their nests with, and, being very good-natured, he could not refuse, so by Solomon's advice he had hidden what was left of it. But though he was now quite naked, you must not think that he was cold or unhappy. He was usually very happy and gay, and the reason was that Solomon had kept his promise and taught him many of the bird ways. To be easily pleased, for instance, and always to be really doing something, and to think that whatever he was doing was a thing of vast importance. Peter became very clever at helping the birds to build their nests; soon he could build better than a wood-pigeon, and nearly as well as a blackbird, though never did he satisfy the finches, and he made nice little water-troughs near the nests and dug up worms for the young ones with his fingers. He also became very learned in bird-lore, and knew an east-wind from a west-wind by its smell, and he could see the grass growing and hear the insects walking about inside the tree-trunks. But the best thing Solomon had done was to teach him to have a glad heart. All birds have glad hearts unless you rob their nests, and so as they were the only kind of heart Solomon knew about, it was easy to him to teach Peter how to have one.

Peter's heart was so glad that he felt he must sing all day long, just as the birds sing for joy, but, being partly human, he needed an instrument, so he made a pipe of reeds, and he used to sit by the shore of the island of an evening, practising the sough of the wind and the ripple of the water, and catching handfuls of the shine of the moon, and he put them all in his pipe and played them so beautifully that even the birds were deceived, and they would say to each other, "Was that a fish leaping in the water or was it Peter playing leaping fish on his pipe?" and sometimes he played the birth of birds, and then the mothers would turn round in their nests to see whether they had laid an egg. If you are a child of the Gardens you must know the chestnut-tree near the bridge, which comes out in flower first of all the chestnuts, but perhaps you have not heard why this tree leads the way. It is because Peter wearies for summer and plays that it has come, and the chestnut, being so near, hears him and is cheated.

But as Peter sat by the shore tootling divinely on his pipe he some-times fell into sad thoughts, and then the music became sad also, and the reason of all this sadness was that he could not reach the Gardens, though he could see them through the arch of the bridge. He knew he could never be a real human again, and scarcely wanted to be one, but oh, how he longed to play as other children play, and of course there is no such lovely place to play in as the Gardens. The birds brought him news of how boys and girls play, and wistful tears started in Peter's eyes.

Perhaps you wonder why he did not swim across. The reason was that he could not swim. He wanted to know how to swim, but no one on the island knew the way except the ducks, and they are so stupid. They were quite willing to teach him, but all they could say about it was, "You sit down on the top of the water in this way, and then you kick out like that." Peter tried it often, but always before he could kick out he sank. What he really needed to know was how you sit on the water without sinking, and they said it was quite impossible to explain such an easy thing as that. Occasionally swans touched on the island, and he would give them all his day's food and then ask them how they sat on the water, but as soon as he had no more to give them the hateful things hissed at him and sailed away.

Once he really thought he had discovered a way of reaching the Gardens. A wonderful white thing, like a runaway newspaper, floated high over the island and then tumbled, rolling over and over after the manner of a bird that has broken its wing. Peter was so frightened that he hid, but the birds told him it was only a kite, and what a kite is, and that it must have tugged its string out of a boy's hand, and soared away. After that they laughed at Peter for being so fond of the kite; he loved it so much that he even slept with one hand on it, and I think this was pathetic and pretty, for the reason he loved it was because it had belonged to a real boy.

To the birds this was a very poor reason, but the older ones felt grateful to him at this time because he had nursed a number of fledg-lings through the German measles, and they offered to show him how birds fly a kite. So six of them took the end of the string in their beaks and flew away with it; and to his amazement it flew after them and went even higher than they.

Peter screamed out, "Do it again!" and with great good-nature they did it several times, and always instead of thanking them he cried, "Do it again!" which shows that even now he had not quite forgotten what it was to be a boy.

At last, with a grand design burning within his brave heart, he begged them to do it once more with him clinging to the tail, and now a hundred flew off with the string, and Peter clung to the tail, meaning to drop off when he was over the Gardens. But the kite broke to pieces in the air, and he would have drowned in the Serpentine had he not caught hold of two indignant swans and made them carry him to the island. After this the birds said that they would help him no more in his mad enterprise.

Nevertheless, Peter did reach the Gardens at last by the help of Shelley's boat, as I am now to tell you.

The Thrush's Nest

Shelley was a young gentleman and as grown-up as he need ever expect to be. He was a poet; and they are never exactly grown-up. They are people who despise money except what you need for to-day, and he had all that and five pounds over. So, when he was walking in the Kensington Gardens, he made a paper boat of his bank-note, and sent it sailing on the Serpentine.

It reached the island at night; and the look-out brought it to Solomon Caw, who thought at first that it was the usual thing, a message from a lady, saying she would be obliged if he could let her have a good one. They always ask for the best one he has, and if he likes the letter he sends one from Class A; but if it ruffles him he sends very funny ones indeed. Sometimes he sends none at all, and at another time he sends a nestful; it all depends on the mood you catch him in. He likes you to leave it all to him, and if you mention particularly that you hope he will see his way to making it *a boy this time,* he is almost sure to send another girl. And whether you are a lady or only a little boy who wants a baby-sister, always take pains to write your address clearly. You can't think what a lot of babies Solomon has sent to the wrong house.

Shelley's boat, when opened, completely puzzled Solomon, and he took counsel of his assistants, who having walked over it twice, first with their toes pointed out, and then with their toes pointed in, decided that it came from some greedy person who wanted five. They thought this because there was a large five printed on it. "Preposterous!" cried Solomon in a rage, and he presented it to Peter; anything useless which drifted upon the island was usually given to Peter as a plaything.

But he did not play with his precious bank-note, for he knew what it was at once, having been very observant during the week when he was an ordinary boy. With so much money, he reflected, he could surely at last contrive to reach the Gardens, and he considered all the possible ways, and decided (wisely, I think) to choose the best way. But, first, he had to tell the birds of the value of Shelley's boat; and though they were too honest to demand it back, he saw that they were galled, and they cast such black looks at Solomon, who was rather vain of his cleverness, that he flew away to the end of the island, and sat there very depressed with his head buried in his wings. Now Peter knew that unless Solomon was on your side, you never got anything done for you in the island, so he followed him and tried to hearten him.

Nor was this all that Peter did to gain the powerful old fellow's good-will. You must know that Solomon had no intention of remaining in office all his life. He looked forward to retiring by-and-by, and devoting his green old age to a life of pleasure on a certain yew-stump in the Figs which had taken his fancy, and for years he had been quietly filling his stocking. It was a stocking belonging to some bathing person which had been cast upon the island, and at the time I speak of it contained a hundred and eighty crumbs, thirty-four nuts, sixteen crusts, a pen-wiper and a boot-lace. When his stocking was full, Solomon calculated that he would be able to retire on a competency. Peter now gave him a pound. He cut it off his bank-note with a sharp stick.

This made Solomon his friend for ever, and after the two had consulted together they called a meeting of the thrushes. You will see presently why thrushes only were invited.

The scheme to be put before them was really Peter's, but Solomon did most of the talking, because he soon became irritable if other people talked. He began by saying that he had been much impressed by the superior ingenuity shown by the thrushes in nest-building, and this put them into good-humour at once, as it was meant to do; for all the quarrels between birds are about the best way of building nests.

Other birds, said Solomon, omitted to line their nests with mud, and as a result they did not hold water. Here he cocked his head as if he had used an unanswerable argument; but, unfortunately, a Mrs. Finch had come to the meeting uninvited, and she squeaked out, "We don't build nests to hold water, but to hold eggs," and then the thrushes stopped cheering, and Solomon was so perplexed that he took several sips of water.

"Consider," he said at last, "how warm the mud makes the nest."

"Consider," cried Mrs. Finch, "that when water gets into the nest it remains there and your little ones are drowned."

The thrushes begged Solomon with a look to say something crushing in reply to this, but again he was perplexed.

"Try another drink," suggested Mrs. Finch pertly. Kate was her name, and all Kates are saucy.

Solomon did try another drink, and it inspired him. "If," said he, "a finch's nest is placed on the Serpentine it fills and breaks to pieces, but a thrush's nest is still as dry as the cup of a swan's back."

How the thrushes applauded! Now they knew why they lined their nests with mud, and when Mrs. Finch called out, "We don't place our nests on the Serpentine," they did what they should have done at first: chased her from the meeting. After this it was most orderly. What they had been brought together to hear, said Solomon, was this: their young friend, Peter Pan, as they well knew, wanted very much to be able to cross to the Gardens, and he now proposed, with their help, to build a boat.

At this the thrushes began to fidget, which made Peter tremble for his scheme.

Solomon explained hastily that what he meant was not one of the cumbrous boats that humans use; the proposed boat was to be simply a thrush's nest large enough to hold Peter.

But still, to Peter's agony, the thrushes were sulky. "We are very busy people," they grumbled, "and this would be a big job."

"Quite so," said Solomon, "and, of course, Peter would not allow you to work for nothing. You must remember that he is now in comfortable circumstances, and he will pay you such wages as you have never been paid before. Peter Pan authorises me to say that you shall all be paid sixpence a day."

Then all the thrushes hopped for joy, and that very day was begun the celebrated Building of the Boat. All their ordinary business fell into arrears. It was the time of year when they should have been pairing, but not a thrush's nest was built except this big one, and so Solomon soon ran short of thrushes with which to supply the demand from the mainland. The stout, rather greedy children, who look so well in perambulators but get puffed easily when they walk, were all young thrushes once, and ladies often ask specially for them. What do you think Solomon did? He sent over to the house-tops for a lot of sparrows and ordered them to lay their eggs in old thrushes' nests and sent their young to the ladies and swore they were all thrushes! It was known afterward on the island as the Sparrows' Year, and so, when you meet, as you doubtless sometimes do, grown-up people who puff and blow as if they thought themselves bigger than they are, very likely they belong to that year. You ask them.

Peter was a just master, and paid his work-people every evening. They stood in rows on the branches, waiting politely while he cut the paper sixpences out of his bank-note, and presently he called the roll, and then each bird, as the names were mentioned, flew down and got sixpence. It must have been a fine sight.

And at last, after months of labor, the boat was finished. Oh, the deportment of Peter as he saw it growing more and more like a great thrush's nest! From the very beginning of the building of it he slept by its side, and often woke up to say sweet things to it, and after it was lined with mud and the mud had dried he always slept in it. He sleeps in his nest still, and has a fascinating way of curling round in it, for it is just large enough to hold him comfortably when he curls round like a kitten. It is brown inside, of course, but outside it is mostly green, being woven of grass and twigs, and when these wither or snap, the walls are thatched afresh. There are also a few feathers here and there, which came off the thrushes while they were building.

The other birds were extremely jealous and said that the boat would not balance on the water, but it lay most beautifully steady; they said the water would come into it, but no water came into it. Next they said that Peter had no oars, and this caused the thrushes to look at each other in dismay, but Peter replied that he had no need of oars, for he had a sail, and with such a proud, happy face he produced a sail which he had fashioned out of his night-gown, and though it was still rather like a night-gown it made a lovely sail. And that night, the moon being full, and all the birds asleep, he did enter his coracle (as Master Francis Pretty would have said) and depart out of the island. And first, he knew not why, he looked upward, with his hands clasped, and from that moment his eyes were pinned to the west.

He had promised the thrushes to begin by making short voyages, with them to be his guides, but far away he saw the Kensington Gardens beckoning to him beneath the bridge, and he could not wait. His face was flushed, but he never looked back; there was an exultation in his little breast that drove out fear. Was Peter the least gallant of the English mariners who have sailed westward to meet the Unknown?

At first, his boat turned round and round, and he was driven back to the place of his starting, whereupon he shortened sail, by removing one of the sleeves, and was forthwith carried backward by a contrary breeze, to his no small peril. He now let go the sail, with the result that he was drifted toward the far shore, where are black shadows he knew not the dangers of, but suspected them, and so once more hoisted his night-gown and went roomer of the shadows until he caught a favouring wind, which bore him westward, but at so great a speed that he was like to be broke against the bridge. Which having avoided, he passed under the bridge and came, to his great rejoicing, within full sight of the delectable Gardens. But having tried to cast anchor, which was a stone at the end of a piece of the kite-string, he found no bottom, and was fain to hold off, seeking for moorage, and, feeling his way, he buffeted against a sunken reef that cast him overboard by the greatness of the shock, and he was near to being drowned, but clambered back into the vessel. There now arose a mighty storm, accompanied by roaring of waters, such as he had never heard the like, and he was tossed this way and that, and his hands so numbed with the cold that he could not close them. Having escaped the danger of which, he was mercifully carried into a small bay, where his boat rode at peace.

Nevertheless, he was not yet in safety; for, on pretending to disembark, he found a multitude of small people drawn up on the shore to contest his landing, and shouting shrilly to him to be off, for it was long past Lock-out Time. This, with much brandishing of their holly-leaves, and also a company of them carried an arrow which some boy had left in the Gardens, and this they were prepared to use as a battering-ram.

Then Peter, who knew them for the fairies, called out that he was not an ordinary human and had no desire to do them displeasure, but to be their friend; nevertheless, having found a jolly harbour, he was in no temper to draw off therefrom, and he warned them if they sought to mischief him to stand to their harms.

So saying, he boldly leapt ashore, and they gathered around him with intent to slay him, but there then arose a great cry among the women, and it was because they had now observed that his sail was a baby's night-gown. Whereupon, they straightway loved him, and grieved that their laps were too small, the which I cannot explain, except by saying that such is the way of women. The men-fairies now sheathed their weapons on observing the behaviour of their women, on whose intelligence they set great store, and they led him civilly to their Queen, who conferred upon him the courtesy of the Gardens after Lock-out Time, and henceforth Peter could go whither he chose, and the fairies had orders to put him in comfort.

Such was his first voyage to the Gardens, and you may gather from the antiquity of the language that it took place a long time ago. But Peter never grows any older, and if we could be watching for him under the bridge tonight (but, of course, we can't), I daresay we should see him hoisting his night-gown and sailing or paddling toward us in the Thrush's Nest. When he sails, he sits down, but he stands up to paddle. I shall tell you presently how he got his paddle.

Long before the time for the opening of the gates comes he steals back to the island, for people must not see him (he is not so human as all that), but this gives him hours for play, and he plays exactly as real children play. At least he thinks so, and it is one of the pathetic things about him that he often plays quite wrongly.

You see, he had no one to tell him how children really play, for the fairies were all more or less in hiding until dusk, and so know nothing, and though the birds pretended that they could tell him a great deal, when the time for telling came, it was wonderful how little they really knew. They told him the truth about hide-and-seek, and he often plays it by himself, but even the ducks on the Round Pond could not explain to him what it is that makes the pond so fascinating to boys. Every night the ducks have forgotten all the events of the day, except the number of pieces of cake thrown to them. They are gloomy creatures, and say that cake is not what it was in their young days.

So Peter had to find out many things for himself. He often played ships at the Round Pond, but his ship was only a hoop which he had found on the grass. Of course, he had never seen a hoop, and he wondered what you play at with them, and decided that you play at pretending they are boats. This hoop always sank at once, but he waded in for it, and sometimes he dragged it gleefully round the rim of the pond, and he was quite proud to think that he had discovered what boys do with hoops.

Another time, when he found a child's pail, he thought it was for sitting in, and he sat so hard in it that he could scarcely get out of it. Also he found a balloon. It was bobbing about on the Hump, quite as if it was having a game by itself, and he caught it after an exciting chase. But he thought it was a ball, and Jenny Wren had told him that boys kick balls, so he kicked it; and after that he could not find it anywhere.

Perhaps the most surprising thing he found was a perambulator. It was under a lime-tree, near the entrance to the Fairy Queen's Winter Palace (which is within the circle of the seven Spanish chestnuts), and Peter approached it warily, for the birds had never mentioned such things to him. Lest it was alive, he addressed it politely, and then, as it gave no answer, he went nearer and felt it cautiously. He gave it a little push, and it ran from him, which made him think it must be alive after all; but, as it had run from him, he was not afraid. So he stretched out his hand to pull it to him, but this time it ran at him, and he was so alarmed that he leapt the railing and scudded away to his boat. You must not think, however, that he was a coward, for he came back next night with a crust in one hand and a stick in the other, but the perambulator had gone, and he never saw another one. I have promised to tell you also about his paddle. It was a child's spade which he had found near St. Govor's Well, and he thought it was a paddle.

Do you pity Peter Pan for making these mistakes? If so, I think it rather silly of you. What I mean is that, of course, one must pity him now and then, but to pity him all the time would be impertinence. He thought he had the most splendid time in the Gardens, and to think you have it is almost quite as good as really to have it. He played without ceasing, while you often waste time by being mad-dog or Mary-Annish. He could be neither of these things, for he had never heard of them, but do you think he is to be pitied for that?

Oh, he was merry. He was as much merrier than you, for instance, as you are merrier than your father. Sometimes he fell, like a spinning-top, from sheer merriment. Have you seen a greyhound leaping the fences of the Gardens? That is how Peter leaps them.

And think of the music of his pipe. Gentlemen who walk home at night write to the papers to say they heard a nightingale in the Gardens, but it is really Peter's pipe they hear. O course, he had no mother—at least what use was she to him? You can be sorry for him for that, but don't be too sorry, for the next thing I mean to tell you is how he revisited her. It was the fairies who gave him the chance.

Lock-out Time

It is frightfully difficult to know much about the fairies, and almost the only thing known for certain is that there are fairies wherever there are children. Long ago children were forbidden the Gardens, and at that time there was not a fairy in the place; then the children were admitted, and the fairies came trooping in that very evening. They can't resist following the children, but you seldom see them, partly because they live in the daytime behind the railings, where you are not allowed to go, and also partly because they are so cunning. They are not a bit cunning after Lock-out, but until Lock-out, my word!

When you were a bird you knew the fairies pretty well, and you remember a good deal about them in your babyhood, which it is a great pity you can't write down, for gradually you forget, and I have heard of children who declared that they had never once seen a fairy. Very likely if they said this in the Kensington Gardens, they were standing looking at a fairy all the time. The reason they were cheated was that she pretended to be something else. This is one of their best tricks. They usually pretend to be flowers, because the court sits in the Fairies' Basin, and there are so many flowers there, and all along the Baby Walk, that a flower is the thing least likely to attract attention. They dress exactly like flowers, and change with the seasons, putting on white when lilies are in and blue for blue-bells, and so on. They like crocus and hyacinth time best of all, as they are partial to a bit of colour, but tulips (except white ones, which are the fairy-cradles) they consider garish, and they sometimes put off dressing like tulips for days, so that the beginning of the tulip weeks is almost the best time to catch them.

When they think you are not looking they skip along pretty lively, but if you look and they fear there is no time to hide, they stand quite still, pretending to be flowers. Then, after you have passed without knowing that they were fairies, they rush home and tell their mothers they have had such an adventure. The Fairy Basin, you remember, is all covered with ground-ivy (from which they make their castor-oil), with flowers growing in it here and there. Most of them really are flowers, but some of them are fairies. You never can be sure of them, but a good plan is to walk by looking the other way, and then turn round sharply. Another good plan, which David and I sometimes follow, is to stare them down. After a long time they can't help winking, and then you know for certain that they are fairies.

There are also numbers of them along the Baby Walk, which is a famous gentle place, as spots frequented by fairies are called. Once twenty-four of them had an extraordinary adventure. They were a girls' school out for a walk with the governess, and all wearing hyacinth gowns, when she suddenly put her finger to her mouth, and then they all stood still on an empty bed and pretended to be hyacinths. Unfortunately, what the governess had heard was two gardeners coming to plant new flowers in that very bed. They were wheeling a handcart with the flowers in it, and were quite surprised to find the bed occupied. "Pity to lift them hyacinths," said the one man. "Duke's orders," replied the other, and, having emptied the cart, they dug up the boarding-school and put the poor, terrified things in it in five rows. Of course, neither the governess nor the girls dare let on that they were fairies, so they were carted far away to a potting-shed, out of which they escaped in the night without their shoes, but there was a great row about it among the parents, and the school was ruined.

As for their houses, it is no use looking for them, because they are the exact opposite of our houses. You can see our houses by day, but you can't see them by dark. Well, you can see their houses by dark, but you can't see them by day, for they are the colour of night, and I never heard of any one yet who could see night in the daytime. This does not mean that they are black, for night has its colours just as day has, but ever so much brighter. Their blues and reds and greens are like ours with a light behind them. The palace is entirely built of many-coloured glasses, and is quite the loveliest of all royal residences, but the Queen sometimes complains because the common people will peep in to see what she is doing. They are very inquisitive folk, and press quite hard against the glass, and that is why their noses are mostly snubby. The streets are miles long and very twisty, and have paths on each side made of bright worsted. The birds used to steal the worsted for their nests, but a policeman has been appointed to hold on at the other end.

One of the great differences between the fairies and us is that they never do anything useful. When the first baby laughed for the first time, his laugh broke into a million pieces, and they all went skipping about. That was the beginning of fairies. They look tremendously busy, you know, as if they had not a moment to spare, but if you were to ask them what they are doing, they could not tell you in the least. They are frightfully ignorant, and everything they do is make-believe. They have a postman, but he never calls except at Christmas with his little box, and though they have beautiful schools, nothing is taught in them; the youngest child being chief person is always elected mistress, and when she has called the roll, they all go out for a walk and never come back. It is a very noticeable thing that, in fairy families, the youngest is always chief person, and usually becomes a prince or princess; and children remember this, and think it must be so among humans also, and that is why they are often made uneasy when they come upon their mother furtively putting new frills on the bassinette.

You have probably observed that your baby-sister wants to do all sorts of things that your mother and her nurse want her not to do: to stand up at sitting-down time, and to sit down at standing-up time, for instance, or to wake up when she should fall asleep, or to crawl on the floor when she is wearing her best frock, and so on, and perhaps you put this down to naughtiness. But it is not; it simply means that she is doing as she has seen the fairies do; she begins by following their ways, and it takes about two years to get her into the human ways. Her fits of passion, which are awful to behold, and are usually called teething, are no such thing; they are her natural exasperation, because we don't understand her, though she is talking an intelligible language. She is talking fairy. The reason mothers and nurses know what her remarks mean, before other people know, as that "Guch" means "Give it to me at once," while "Wa" is "Why do you wear such a funny hat?" is because, mixing so much with babies, they have picked up a little of the fairy language.

Of late David has been thinking back hard about the fairy tongue, with his hands clutching his temples, and he has remembered a number of their phrases which I shall tell you some day if I don't forget.

He had heard them in the days when he was a thrush, and though I suggested to him that perhaps it is really bird language he is remembering, he says not, for these phrases are about fun and adventures, and the birds talked of nothing but nest-building. He distinctly remembers that the birds used to go from spot to spot like ladies at shop-windows, looking at the different nests and saying, "Not my colour, my dear," and "How would that do with a soft lining?" and "But will it wear?" and "What hideous trimming!" and so on.

The fairies are exquisite dancers, and that is why one of the first things the baby does is to sign to you to dance to him and then to cry when you do it. They hold their great balls in the open air, in what is called a fairy-ring. For weeks afterward you can see the ring on the grass. It is not there when they begin, but they make it by waltzing round and round. Sometimes you will find mushrooms inside the ring, and these are fairy-chairs that the servants have forgotten to clear away. The chairs and the rings are the only tell-tale marks these little people leave behind them, and they would remove even these were they not so fond of dancing that they toe it till the very moment of the opening of the gates. David and I once found a fairy-ring quite warm.

But there is also a way of finding out about the ball before it takes place. You know the boards which tell at what time the Gardens are to close to-day. Well, these tricky fairies sometimes slyly change the board on a ball night, so that it says the Gardens are to close at six-thirty for instance, instead of at seven. This enables them to get begun half an hour earlier.

If on such a night we could remain behind in the Gardens, as the famous Maimie Mannering did, we might see delicious sights, hundreds of lovely fairies hastening to the ball, the married ones wearing their wedding-rings round their waists, the gentlemen, all in uniform, holding up the ladies' trains, and linkmen running in front carrying winter cherries, which are the fairy-lanterns, the cloak-room where they put on their silver slippers and get a ticket for their wraps, the flowers streaming up from the Baby Walk to look on, and always welcome because they can lend a pin, the supper-table, with Queen Mab at the head of it, and behind her chair the Lord Chamberlain, who carries a dandelion on which he blows when Her Majesty wants to know the time.

The table-cloth varies according to the seasons, and in May it is made of chestnut-blossom. The way the fairy-servants do is this: The men, scores of them, climb up the trees and shake the branches, and the blossom falls like snow. Then the lady servants sweep it together by whisking their skirts until it is exactly like a table-cloth, and that is how they get their table-cloth.

They have real glasses and real wine of three kinds, namely, blackthorn wine, berberis wine, and cowslip wine, and the Queen pours out, but the bottles are so heavy that she just pretends to pour out. There is bread and butter to begin with, of the size of a threepenny bit; and cakes to end with, and they are so small that they have no crumbs. The fairies sit round on mushrooms, and at first they are very well-behaved and always cough off the table, and so on, but after a bit they are not so well-behaved and stick their fingers into the butter, which is got from the roots of old trees, and the really horrid ones crawl over the table-cloth chasing sugar or other delicacies with their tongues. When the Queen sees them doing this she signs to the servants to wash up and put away, and then everybody adjourns to the dance, the Queen walking in front while the Lord Chamberlain walks behind her, carrying two little pots, one of which contains the juice of wall-flower and the other the juice of Solomon's Seals. Wall-flower juice is good for reviving dancers who fall to the ground in a fit, and Solomon's Seals juice is for bruises. They bruise very easily, and when Peter plays faster and faster they foot it till they fall down in fits. For, as you know without my telling you, Peter Pan is the fairies' orchestra. He sits in the middle of the ring, and they would never dream of having a smart dance nowadays without him. "P. P." is written on the corner of the invitation-cards sent out by all really good families. They are grateful little people, too, and at the princess's coming-of-age ball (they come of age on their second birthday and have a birthday every month) they gave him the wish of his heart.

The way it was done was this. The Queen ordered him to kneel, and then said that for playing so beautifully she would give him the wish of his heart. Then they all gathered round Peter to hear what was the wish of his heart, but for a long time he hesitated, not being certain what it was himself.

"If I chose to go back to mother," he asked at last, "could you give me that wish?"

Now this question vexed them, for were he to return to his mother they should lose his music, so the Queen tilted her nose contemptuously and said, "Pooh, ask for a much bigger wish than that."

"Is that quite a little wish?" he inquired.

"As little as this," the Queen answered, putting her hands near each other.

"What size is a big wish?" he asked.

She measured it off on her skirt and it was a very handsome length.

Then Peter reflected and said, "Well, then, I think I shall have two little wishes instead of one big one."

Of course, the fairies had to agree, though his cleverness rather shocked them, and he said that his first wish was to go to his mother, but with the right to return to the Gardens if he found her disappointing. His second wish he would hold in reserve.

They tried to dissuade him, and even put obstacles in the way.

"I can give you the power to fly to her house," the Queen said, "but I can't open the door for you."

"The window I flew out at will be open," Peter said confidently. "Mother always keeps it open in the hope that I may fly back."

"How do you know?" they asked, quite surprised, and, really, Peter could not explain how he knew.

"I just do know," he said.

So as he persisted in his wish, they had to grant it. The way they gave him power to fly was this: They all tickled him on the shoulder, and soon he felt a funny itching in that part, and then up he rose higher and higher and flew away out of the Gardens and over the house-tops.

It was so delicious that instead of flying straight to his old home he skimmed away over St. Paul's to the Crystal Palace and back by the river and Regent's Park, and by the time he reached his mother's window he had quite made up his mind that his second wish should be to become a bird.

The window was wide open, just as he knew it would be, and in he fluttered, and there was his mother lying asleep. Peter alighted softly on the wooden rail at the foot of the bed and had a good look at her. She lay with her head on her hand, and the hollow in the pillow was like a nest lined with her brown wavy hair. He remembered, though he had long forgotten it, that she always gave her hair a holiday at night. How sweet the frills of her night-gown were. He was very glad she was such a pretty mother.

But she looked sad, and he knew why she looked sad. One of her arms moved as if it wanted to go round something, and he knew what it wanted to go round.

"Oh, mother," said Peter to himself, "if you just knew who is sitting on the rail at the foot of the bed."

Very gently he patted the little mound that her feet made, and he could see by her face that she liked it. He knew he had but to say "Mother" ever so softly, and she would wake up. They always wake up at once if it is you that says their name. Then she would give such a joyous cry and squeeze him tight. How nice that would be to him, but oh, how exquisitely delicious it would be to her! That I am afraid is how Peter regarded it. In returning to his mother he never doubted that he was giving her the greatest treat a woman can have. Nothing can be more splendid, he thought, than to have a little boy of your own. How proud of him they are; and very right and proper, too.

But why does Peter sit so long on the rail, why does he not tell his mother that he has come back?

I quite shrink from the truth, which is that he sat there in two minds. Sometimes he looked longingly at his mother, and sometimes he looked longingly at the window. Certainly it would be pleasant to be her boy again, but, on the other hand, what times those had been in the Gardens! Was he so sure that he would enjoy wearing clothes again? He popped off the bed and opened some drawers to have a look at his old garments. They were still there, but he could not remember how you put them on. The socks, for instance, were they worn on the hands or on the feet? He was about to try one of them on his hand, when he had a great adventure. Perhaps the drawer had creaked; at any rate, his mother woke up, for he heard her say "Peter," as if it was the most lovely word in the language. He remained sitting on the floor and held his breath, wondering how she knew that he had come back. If she said "Peter" again, he meant to cry "Mother" and run to her. But she spoke no more, she made little moans only, and when next he peeped at her she was once more asleep, with tears on her face.

It made Peter very miserable, and what do you think was the first thing he did? Sitting on the rail at the foot of the bed, he played a beautiful lullaby to his mother on his pipe. He had made it up himself out of the way she said "Peter," and he never stopped playing until she looked happy.

He thought this so clever of him that he could scarcely resist wakening her to hear her say, "Oh, Peter, how exquisitely you play." However, as she now seemed comfortable, he again cast looks at the window. You must not think that he meditated flying away and never coming back. He had quite decided to be his mother's boy, but hesitated about beginning to-night. It was the second wish which troubled him. He no longer meant to make it a wish to be a bird, but not to ask for a second wish seemed wasteful, and, of course, he could not ask for it without returning to the fairies. Also, if he put off asking for his wish too long it might go bad. He asked himself if he had not been hard-hearted to fly away without saying good-bye to Solomon. "I should like awfully to sail in my boat just once more," he said wistfully to his sleeping mother. He quite argued with her as if she could hear him. "It would be so splendid to tell the birds of this adventure," he said coaxingly. "I promise to come back," he said solemnly and meant it, too.

And in the end, you know, he flew away. Twice he came back from the window, wanting to kiss his mother, but he feared the delight of it might waken her, so at last he played her a lovely kiss on his pipe, and then he flew back to the Gardens.

Many nights and even months passed before he asked the fairies for his second wish; and I am not sure that I quite know why he delayed so long. One reason was that he had so many good-byes to say, not only to his particular friends, but to a hundred favourite spots. Then he had his last sail, and his very last sail, and his last sail of all, and so on. Again, a number of farewell feasts were given in his honour; and another comfortable reason was that, after all, there was no hurry, for his mother would never weary of waiting for him. This last reason displeased old Solomon, for it was an encouragement to the birds to procrastinate. Solomon had several excellent mottoes for keeping them at their work, such as "Never put off laying to-day because you can lay to-morrow," and "In this world there are no second chances," and yet here was Peter gaily putting off and none the worse for it. The birds pointed this out to each other, and fell into lazy habits.

But, mind you, though Peter was so slow in going back to his mother, he was quite decided to go back. The best proof of this was his caution with the fairies. They were most anxious that he should remain in the Gardens to play to them, and to bring this to pass they tried to trick him into making such a remark as "I wish the grass was not so wet," and some of them danced out of time in the hope that he might cry, "I do wish you would keep time!" Then they would have said that this was his second wish. But he smoked their design, and though on occasions he began, "I wish——" he always stopped in time. So when at last he said to them bravely, "I wish now to go back to mother for ever and always," they had to tickle his shoulders and let him go.

He went in a hurry in the end because he had dreamt that his mother was crying, and he knew what was the great thing she cried for, and that a hug from her splendid Peter would quickly make her to smile. Oh, he felt sure of it, and so eager was he to be nestling in her arms that this time he flew straight to the window, which was always to be open for him.

But the window was closed, and there were iron bars on it, and peering inside he saw his mother sleeping peacefully with her arm round another little boy.

Peter called, "Mother! mother!" but she heard him not; in vain he beat his little limbs against the iron bars. He had to fly back, sobbing, to the Gardens, and he never saw his dear again. What a glorious boy he had meant to be to her. Ah, Peter, we who have made the great mistake, how differently we should all act at the second chance. But Solomon was right; there is no second chance, not for most of us. When we reach the window it is Lock-out Time. The iron bars are up for life.

The Mouse Festival

Johannes Bobrowski

Johannes Bobrowski (1917–1965) was born in Tilsit, East Prussia (now part of the Soviet Union. He became a German soldier in 1939, and was released from a Russian prison camp in 1949. In "The Mouse Festival," a fragile piece that explores the evil within, a Jewish shopkeeper, the Moon, a young German soldier, and many mice spend time in an empty store in the early days of the German invasion. The story's title is a play on the old line "When the cat's away, the mice will play" (German: tanzen). German literature has a tradition of moonlight as the realm of the supernatural, and here the supernatural is a source of repressed information. It is interesting to compare the moonlight in this story to the water in James Tiptree's story (pp.389–405).

Moise Trumpeter sits on the little chair in the corner of the shop. The shop is small and it is empty. Most likely because the Sun, which always comes into the shop, needs room, and the Moon too. The Moon always stops in when he passes by. The Moon came in through the door, and the bell on the door barely stirred, and perhaps only because of mice running and dancing on the thin floorboards. So the Moon came in and Moise said, Good evening, Moon! And now the two of them watch the mice.

It is different every time with these mice. Sometimes they dance one way and sometimes another, and all that with four legs, a pointed head, and a thin little tail.

But dear Moon, says Moise, that isn't all. They have those little bodies and everything inside! But you probably can't understand. And besides, it isn't always different. Rather it is always the same. And precisely that is why it is so curious. It is more likely that you would be every day different, though you always come in through the same door and it is always dark before you take your place here. But be quiet now and pay attention.

You see, it's always the same.

Moise had dropped a bread crust before by his feet and now the mice scurry closer, one step after another, a few standing on their hind legs sniffing the air. You see, so is it. Always the same.

There sit the two old friends and are happy, and at first they don't even notice that the door to the shop has been opened. Only the mice heard it immediately and have gone. Competely gone and so fast that one couldn't even begin to say where they went to.

In the doorway stands a soldier, a German. Moise has good eyes and he sees: a young person, a schoolboy who really doesn't know what he wants here now that he stands on the threshold.

Go see how the Jewish folk live, he would have thought outside. But now the old Jew sits on his little chair and the shop is bright with moonlight. If you like, come in, Mr. Lieutenant, says Moise.

The boy shuts the door. He doesn't even stop to wonder how the Jew knows German, he stands there so. And as Moise gets up and says: Come here sir, I don't have another chair, he says: Thank you, I can stand, but he takes a few steps toward the middle of the room and a few more toward the chair. And after Moise offers him a seat again, he sits down.

Now you are very quiet, says Moise and leans against the wall.

The bread crust is still there on the floor and, you see, here come the mice again. Just like before and not a bit slower. Exactly like before, one step, another step, up on hind legs sniffing and even a tiny pant that Moise hears and maybe the Moon too. Exactly like before.

And now they've found the crust again. A mouse festival in a small frame, nothing special, but not really an everyday occurrence either.

One sits there and watches. The war is already a few days old. The land is called Poland. It is very flat and sandy. The streets are bad and there are many children here. What else is there to say? The Germans have come, uncountably many. One of them sits here in this Jewish shop, a very young one with the faintest hint of a moustache on his upper lip. He has a mother in Germany, and a father in Germany too, and two little sisters. One gets around in the world, he will think. Now one is in Poland, and maybe later one travels to England. And this Poland is very Polish.

The old Jew leans against the wall. The mice are still assembled around the crust. When the crust is smaller an old mother mouse will take the crust home with her and the other mice will run after her.

You know, says the Moon to Moise, I've really got to be moving along. And Moise knows already that the Moon is uncomfortable with this German sitting around. What does he want here anyway? So Moise says only: Why don't you stay awhile, boy?

But the soldier gets up now. The mice run away so fast that one doesn't know where they could have gone. He wonders if he should say good-bye, and stands there in the shop for a moment and then simply leaves.

Moise says nothing and waits for the Moon to speak. The mice are gone. They disappeared. Mice can do that.

That was a German, says the Moon. You know what's going on with these Germans. And as Moise leans against the wall, as before, and says nothing, the Moon continues urgently: You don't want to run away, you don't want to hide yourself. Oh, Moise. That was a German, you saw that. Just don't tell me that the boy isn't one, or at least not a bad one. That doesn't make a difference anymore. When they've come through Poland, how will it go for your people?

I heard you, says Moise.

It is now very white in the shop. The light fills the room all the way to the door in the back wall. Where Moise leans it is very white, and one imagines that he is becoming one with the wall with every word that he says. I know, says Moise, you are quite right there. I will become angry with my God.

TRANSLATED BY KATHRYN CRAMER

A Proper Santa Claus

Anne McCaffrey

Anne McCaffrey is one of the most popular contemporary science fiction writers for her stories of the dragons of the planet Pern, and is often mis-called a fantasy writer. And she objects, citing the publication of the first dragon stories in Analog SF *magazine, edited by John W. Campbell, the most rigorous of SF editors, and the real scientific background supporting the wonderful adventures. This, however, is a fantasy story about the death of the imagination, lightly told but powerful in its impact. Here we have pure McCaffrey, who can cut deeply into the human psyche and not flinch. Since it is a story about art, privacy and authority, it is ironic that "A Proper Santa Claus" was first published with an altered, artificially happy ending, tacked on at the insistence of an editor named Elwood, rather than the logical ending (as originally written) as it appears here. It is interesting to compare this story to Lucy Clifford's "Wooden Tony" (pp.58–70).*

Jeremy was painting. He used his fingers instead of the brush because he liked the feel of paint. Blue was soothing to the touch, red was silky, and orange had a gritty texture. Also he could tell when a color was "proper" if he mixed it with his fingers. He could hear his mother singing to herself, not quite on pitch, but it was a pleasant background noise. It went with the rhythm of his fingers stroking color onto the paper.

He shaped a cookie and put raisins on it, big, plump raisins. He attempted a sugar frosting but the white kind of disappeared into the orange of the cookie. So he globbed up chocolate brown and made an icing. Then he picked the cookie out of the paper and ate it. That left a hole in the center of the paper. It was an excellent cookie, though it made his throat very dry.

Critically he eyed the remaining unused space. Yes, there was room enough, so he painted a glass of Coke. He had trouble representing the bubbles that're supposed to bounce up from the bottom of the glass. That's why the Coke tasted flat when he drank it.

It was disappointing. He'd been able to make the cookie taste so good, why couldn't he succeed with the Coke? Maybe if he drew the bubbles in first . . . he was running out of paper.

"Momma, Momma?"

"What is it, honey?"

"Can I have more paper? Please?"

"Honest, Jeremy, you use up more paper . . . Still, it does keep you quiet and out of my hair . . . why, whatever have you done with your paper? What are those holes?"

Jeremy pointed to the round one. "That was a cookie with raisins and choc'late icing. And that was a Coke only I couldn't make the bubbles bounce."

His mother gave him "the look," so he subsided.

"Jeremy North, you use more paper than—than a . . ."

"Newspaperman?" he suggested, grinning up at her. Momma liked happy faces best.

"Than a newspaperman."

"Can you paint on newspaper?"

His mother blinked. "I don't see why not. And there's pictures already. You can color them in." She obligingly rummaged in the trash and came up with several discarded papers. "There you are, love. Enough supplies to keep you in business a while. I hope."

Well, Jeremy hadn't planned on any business, and newsprint proved less than satisfactory. There wasn't enough white spaces to draw *his* paintings on, and the newspaper soaked up his paints when he tried to follow the already-pictures. So he carefully put the paints away, washed his hands, and went outside to play.

For his sixth birthday Jeremy North got a real school-type easel with a huge pad of paper that fastened onto it at the top and could be torn off, sheet by sheet. There was a rack of holes for his poster paint pots and a rack for his crayons and chalk and eraser. It was exactly what he wanted. He nearly cried for joy. He hugged his mother, and he climbed into his father's lap and kissed him despite his prickly beard.

"Okay, okay, da Vinci," his father laughed. "Go paint us a masterpiece."

Jeremy did. But he was so eager that he couldn't wait until the paint had completely dried. It smeared and blurred, brushing against his body as he hurried to find his dad. So the effect wasn't quite what Jeremy intended.

"Say, that's pretty good," said his father, casting a judicious eye on the proffered artwork. "What's it supposed to be?"

"Just what you wanted." Jeremy couldn't keep the disappointment out of his voice.

"I guess you're beyond me, young feller me lad. I can dig Andy Warhol when he paints tomato soup, but you're in Picasso's school." His father tousled his hair affectionately and even swung him up high so that, despite his disappointment, Jeremy was obliged to giggle and squeal in delight.

Then his father told him to take his painting back to his room.

"But it's your masterpiece, Daddy. I can fix it . . ."

"No, son. You painted it. You understand it." And his father went about some Sunday errand or other.

Jeremy did understand his painting. Even with the smears he could plainly see the car, just like the Admonsens', which Daddy had admired the previous week. It *had* been a proper car. If only Daddy had *seen* it . . .

His grandmother came, around lunchtime, and brought him a set of pastel crayons with special pastel paper and a simply superior picture book of North American animals and birds.

"Of course, he'll break every one of the pastels in the next hour," he heard his grandmother saying to his mother, "but you said he wants only drawing things."

"I like the book, too, Gramma," Jeremy said politely, but his fingers closed possessively around the pastels.

Gramma glanced at him and then went right on talking. "But I think it's about time he found out what animals really look like instead of those monstrosities he's forever drawing. His teacher's going to wonder about his home life when she sees those nightmares."

"Oh, c'mon, Mother. There's nothing abnormal about Jeremy. I'd far rather he daubed himself all over with paint than ran around like the Reckoffs' kids, slinging mud and sand everywhere."

"If you'd only *make* Jeremy . . ."

"Mother, you can't *make* Jeremy do anything. He slides away from you like . . . like a squeeze of paint."

Jeremy lost interest in the adults. As usual, they ignored his presence, despite the fact that he was the subject of their conversation. He began to leaf through the book of birds and animals. The pictures weren't proper. That brown wasn't a bird-brown. And the red of the robin had too much orange, not enough gray. He kept his criticism to himself, but by the time he'd catalogued the anatomical faults in the sketch of the mustang, he was thoroughly bored with the book. His animals might *look* like nightmares, but they were proper ones for all of that. They worked.

His mother and grandmother were engrossed in discussing the fixative that would have have made the pictures "permanent." Gramma said she hadn't bought it because it would be dangerous for him to breathe the fumes. They continued to ignore him. Which was as well. He picked up the pastels and began to experiment. A green horse with pink mane and tail, however anatomically perfect, would arouse considerable controversy.

He didn't break a single one of the precious pastels. He even blew away the rainbow dust from the tray. But he didn't let the horse off the pad until after Gramma and his mother had wandered into the kitchen for lunch.

"I wish . . ."

The horse was lovely.

"I *wish* I had some . . ." Jeremy said.

The horse went cantering around the room, pink tail streaming out behind him and pink mane flying.

". . . Fixative, Green Horse!" But it didn't work. Jeremy knew it took more than just *wishing* to do it proper.

He watched regretfully as Green Horse pranced too close to a wall and brushed himself out of existence.

Miss Bradley, his first-grade teacher, evidently didn't find anything untoward about his drawings, for she constantly displayed them on the bulletin boards. She had a habit of pouncing on him when he had just about finished a drawing so that after all his effort, he hadn't much chance to see if he'd done it "proper" after all. Once or twice he managed to reclaim one from the board and use it, but Miss Bradley created so much fuss about the missing artwork that he diplomatically ceased to repossess his efforts.

On the whole he liked Miss Bradley, but about the first week in October she developed the distressing habit of making him draw to order: "class assignments," she called it. Well, that was all right for the ones who never knew what to draw anyhow, but "assignments" just did not suit Jeremy. While part of him wanted to do hobgoblins, and witches, and pumpkin moons, the other part obstinately refused.

"I'd really looked forward to *your* interpretations of Hallowe'en, Jeremy," Miss Bradley said sadly when he proffered another pedantic landscape with nothing but ticky-tacky houses. "This is very beautiful, Jeremy, but it isn't the assigned project. Now, look at Cynthia's witch and Mark's hobgoblin. I'm certain you could do something just as original."

Jeremy dutifully regarded Cynthia's elongated witch on an outsized broomstick apparently made from *2 x 4s instead of broom reeds, and the hobgoblin Mark had created by splashing paint on the paper and folding, thus blotting the wet paint. Neither creation had any chance of working properly; surely Miss Bradley could see that. So he was obliged to tell her that his landscape was original, particularly if she would look at it* properly.

"You're not getting the point, Jeremy," Miss Bradley said with unaccustomed sternness.

She wasn't either, but Jeremy thought he might better not say that. So he was the only student in the class who had no Hallowe'en picture for parents to admire on Back-to-School Night.

His parents were a bit miffed since they'd heard that Jeremy's paintings were usually prominently displayed.

"The assignment was Hallowe'en and Jeremy simply refused to produce something acceptable," Miss Bradley said with a slightly forced smile.

"Perhaps that's just as well," his mother said, a trifle sourly. "He used to draw the most frightening nightmares and say he 'saw' them."

"He's got a definite talent. Are either of you or Mr. North artistically inclined?"

"Not like he is," Mr. North replied, thinking that if he himself were artistically inclined he would use Miss Bradley as a model. "Probably he's used up all his Hallowe'en inspiration."

"Probably," Miss Bradley said with a laugh.

Actually Jeremy hadn't. Although he dutifully set out trick-or-treating, he came home early. His mother made him sort out his candy, apples, and money for UNICEF, and permitted him to stay up long past his regular bedtime to answer the door for other beggars. But, once safely in his room, he dove for his easel and drew frenetically, slathering black and blue poster paint across clean paper, dashing globs of luminescence for horrific accents. The proper ones took off or crawled obscenely around the room, squeaking and groaning until he released them into the night air for such gambols and aerial maneuvers as they were capable of. Jeremy was impressed. He hung over the windowsill, cheering them on by moonlight. (Around three o'clock there was a sudden shower. All the water solubles melted into the ground.)

For a while after that, Jeremy was not tempted to approach the easel at all, either in school or at home. At first, Miss Bradley was sincerely concerned lest she had inhibited her budding artist by arbitrary assignments. But he was only busy with a chemical garden, lumps of coal and bluing and ammonia and all that. Then she got the class involved in making candles out of plastic milk cartons for Thanksgiving, and Jeremy entered into the project with such enthusiasm that she was reassured.

She ought not to have been.

Three-dimensionality and a malleable substance fascinated Jeremy. He went in search of anything remotely pliable. He started with butter (his mother had a fit about a whole pound melted on his furry rug; he'd left the creature he'd created prancing around his room, but then the heat came up in the radiators). Then he tried mud (which set his mother screaming at him). She surrendered to the inevitable by supplying him with Play-Doh. However, now his creations thwarted him because as soon as the substance out of which the proper ones had been created hardened, they lost their mobility. He hadn't minded the ephemeral quality of his drawings, but he'd begun to count on the fact that sculpture lasted a while.

Miss Bradley introduced him to plasticine. And Christmas.

Success with three-dimensional figures, the availability of plasticine, and the sudden influx of all sorts of Christmas mail order catalogues spurred Jeremy to unusual efforts. This time he did not resist the class assignment of a centerpiece to deck the Christmas festive tables. Actually, Jeremy scarcely heard what Miss Bradley was saying past her opening words.

"Here's a chance for you to create your very own Santa Claus and reindeer, or a sleigh full of presents . . ."

Dancer, Prancer, Donner, Blitzen, and Dasher and Comet and Rudolph of the red nose took form under his flying fingers. Santa's sack was crammed with full-color advertisements clipped from mail order wish-books. Indeed, the sleigh threatened to crumble on its runners from paper weight. He saved Santa Claus till the last. And once he had the fat and jolly gentleman seated in his sleigh, whip in hand, ready to urge his harnessed team, Jeremy was good and ready to make them proper.

Only they weren't; they remained obdurately immobile. Disconsolate, Jeremy moped for nearly a week, examining and re-examining his handiwork for the inhibiting flaw.

Miss Bradley had been enthusiastically complimentary and the other children sullenly envious of his success when the finished group was displayed on a special table, all red and white, with Ivory Snow snow and little evergreens in proportion to the size of the figures. There was even a convenient chimney for the good Santa to descend. Only Jeremy knew that that was not *his* Santa's goal.

In fact Jeremy quite lost interest in the whole Christmas routine. He refused to visit the Santa on tap at the big shopping center, although his mother suspected that his heart had been set on the Masterpiece Oil Painting Set with its enticing assortment of brushes and every known pigment in life-long-lasting color.

Miss Bradley, too, lost all patience with him and became quite stern with his inattentiveness, to the delight of his classmates.

As so often happens when people concentrate too hard on a problem, Jeremy almost missed the solution, inadvertently provided by the pert Cynthia, now basking in Miss Bradley's favor.

"He's naked, that's what. He's naked and ugly. Everyone knows Santa is red and white. And reindeers aren't gray-yecht. They're brown and soft and have fuzzy tails."

Jeremy had, of course, meticulously detailed the clothing on Santa and the harness on the animals, but they were still plasticine. It hadn't mattered with his other creations that they were the dull gray-brown of plasticene because that's how he'd envisaged them, being products of his imagination. But Santa wasn't, or so he thought.

To conform to a necessary convention was obviously, to Jeremy, the requirement that had prevented his Santa from being a proper one. He fabricated harness of string for the reindeer. And a new sleigh of balsa wood with runners of laboriously straightened bobby pins took some time and looked real tough. A judicious coat of paint smartened both reindeer and sleigh. However, the design and manufacture of the red Santa suit proved far more difficult and occupied every spare moment of Jeremy's time. He had to do it in the privacy of his room at home because, when Cynthia saw him putting harness on the reindeer, she twitted him so unmercifully that he couldn't work in peace at school.

He had had little practice with needle and thread, so he actually had to perfect a new skill in order to complete his project. Christmas was only a few days away before he was satisfied with his Santa suit.

He raced to school so he could dress Santa and make him proper. He was just as startled as Miss Bradley when he slithered to a stop inside his classroom door and found her tying small gifts to the branches of the class tree. They stared at each other for a long moment, and then Miss Bradley smiled. She'd been so hard on poor Jeremy lately.

"You're awfully early, Jeremy. Would you like to help me . . . Oh! How adorable!" She spotted the Santa suit which he hadn't had the presence of mind to hide from her. "And you did them yourself? Jeremy, you never cease to amaze me." She took the jacket and pants and little hat from his unresisting hand, and examined them carefully. "They are simply beautiful. Just beautiful. But honestly, Jeremy, your Santa is lovely just as he is. No need to gild the lily."

"He isn't a proper Santa without a proper Santa suit."

Miss Bradley looked at him gravely, and then put her hands on his shoulders, making him look up at her.

"A *proper* Santa Claus is the one we have in our own hearts at this time of year, Jeremy. Not the ones in the department stores or on the street corners or on TV. They're just his helpers." You never knew which of your first-graders still did believe in Santa Claus in this cynical age, Miss Bradley thought. "A proper Santa Claus is the spirit of giving and sharing, of good fellowship. Don't let anyone tell you that there isn't a Santa Claus. The proper Santa Claus belongs to all of us."

Then, pleased with her eloquence and restraint, she handed him back the Santa suit and patted his shoulder encouragingly.

Jeremy was thunderstruck. *His* Santa Claus had only been made for

Jeremy. But poor Miss Bradley's words rang in his ears. Miss Bradley couldn't know that she had improperly understood Jeremy's dilemma. Once again the blight of high-minded interpretation and ladylike good intentions withered primitive magic.

The little reindeer in their shrinking coats of paint would have pulled the sleigh only to Jeremy's house so that Santa could descend only Jeremy's chimney with the little gifts all bearing Jeremy's name.

There was no one there to tell him that it's proper for little boys and girls of his age to be selfish and acquisitive, to regard Santa as an exclusive property.

Jeremy took the garments and let Miss Bradley push him gently toward the table on which his figures were displayed.

She'd put tinsel about the scene, and glitter, but they didn't shine or glisten in the dull gray light filtering through the classroom windows. They weren't proper snow and icicles anyway.

Critically, he saw only string and the silver cake ornaments instead of harness and sleigh bells. He could see the ripples now in the unbent bobby pins which wouldn't ever draw the sleigh smoothly, even over Ivory Snow snow. Dully, he reached for the figure of his Santa Claus.

Getting on the clothes, he dented the plasticene a bit, but it scarcely mattered now. After he'd clasped Santa's malleable paw around the whip, the toothpick with a bright, thick, nylon thread attached to the top with glue, he stood back and stared.

A proper Santa Claus is the spirit of giving and sharing.

So overwhelming was Jeremy's sense of failure, so crushing his remorse for making a selfish Santa Claus instead of the one that belonged to everyone, that he couldn't imagine ever creating anything properly again.

Inside Out

Rudy Rucker

Rudy Rucker is a mathematician who writes books of popular science and science fiction. His SF swings widely and freely into the surreal and metaphysical upon occasion. In this story, his future is a fantasy land and his science is transformed by metaphor. In direct rebellion against the tradition of fantasy world-building, Rucker doesn't just paint the world of the story with a broad brush; he paints it with a broom. He simultaneously denies the necessity of rationalizing the world of the story while invoking the standard scientific technique of oversimplifying for the sake of mathematical argument (in this case involving topology—an interesting contrast to R. A Lafferty's story (pp.375–88). Fast and loose, wild-and-crazy fantastic, that's Rudy Rucker.

You might think of Killeville as a town where every building is a Pizza Hut. Street after street of Pizza Huts, each with the same ten toppings and the same mock mansard roof—the same shiny zero repeated over and over like same tiles in a pavement, same pixels in a grid, same blank neurons in an imbecile's brain.

The Killevillers—the men and women on either side of the Pizza Hut counters—see nothing odd about the boredom, the dodecaduplication. They are ugly people, cheap and odd as K-Mart dolls. The Killeville gene pool is a dreg from which all fine vapors evaporate, a dreg so small that some highly recessive genes have found expression. Killeville is like New Zealand with its weirdly unique fauna.

Walking down a Killeville street, you might see the same hideous platypus face three times in ten minutes.

Of course a platypus is beautiful . . . to another platypus. The sound that drifts out of Killeville's country clubs and cocktail parties is smug and well-pleased. It's a sound like locusts, or like feasting geese. "This is good food," they say, "Have you tried the spinach?" The words don't actually matter; the nasal buzzing honk of the vowels conveys it all: *We're the same. We're the same.*

Unless you were born there, Killeville is a horrible place to live. Especially in August. In August the sky is a featureless gray pizza. The unpaved parts of the outdoors are choked with thorns and poison ivy. Inside the houses, mold grows on every surface, and fleas seethe in the wall-to-wall carpeting. In the wet grayness, time seems to have stopped. How to kill it?

One can watch TV, go to a restaurant, see a movie, or drink in a bar—though none of these pastimes is fun in Killeville. The TV channels are crowded with evangelists so stupid that it isn't even funny. All the restaurants are, of course, Pizza Huts. And if all the restaurants are Pizza Huts, then all the movie theaters are showing Rambo and the Care Bears movie. MADD is very active in Killeville, and drinking in bars is risky. Sober, vigilant law-enforcement officers patrol the streets at every hour.

For all this, stodgy, nasty Killeville is as interesting a place as can be found in our universe. For whatever reason, it's a place where strange things keep happening . . . *very* strange things. Look at what happened to Rex and Candy Redman in August, 198–.

Rex and Candy Redman: married twelve years, with two children aged eight and eleven. Rex was dark and skinny; Candy was a plump, fairskinned redhead with blue eyes. She taught English at Killeville Middle School. Rex had lost his job at GE back in April. Rex had been a CB radio specialist at the Killeville GE plant—the job was the reason the Redmans had moved to Killeville in the first place. When Rex got laid off, he went a little crazy. Instead of selling the house and moving—which is what he should have done—he got a second mortgage on their house and started a business of his own: Redman Novelties & Magic, Wholesale & Retail. So far it hadn't clicked. Far from it. The Redmans were broke and stuck in wretched Killeville. They avoided each other in the daytime, and in the evenings they read magazines.

Rex ran his business out of a run-down building downtown, a building abandoned by its former tenants, a sheet music sales corporation called, of all things, Bongo Fury. Bongo Fury had gotten some federal money to renovate the building next door, and were letting Rex's building moulder as some kind of tax dodge. Rex had the whole second floor for fifty dollars a month. There was a girl artist who rented a room downstairs; she called it her studio. Her name was Marjorie. She thought Rex was cute. Candy didn't like the situation.

"How was *Marjorie* today?" Candy asked, suddenly looking up from her copy of *People*. It was a glum Wednesday night.

"Look, Candy, she's just a person. I do not have the slightest sexual interest in Marjorie. Even if I did, do you think I'd be stupid enough to start something with her? She'd be upstairs bothering me all the time. You'd find out right away . . . life would be even more of a nightmare."

"It just seems funny," said Candy, a hard glint in her eye. "It seems funny, that admiring young girl alone with you in an abandoned building all day. It *stinks!* Put yourself in my shoes! How would *you* like it?"

Rex went out to the kitchen for a glass of water. "Candy," he said, coming back into the living room. "Just because you're bored is no reason to start getting mean. Why can't you be a little more rational?"

"Yeah?" said Candy. She threw her magazine to the floor. "Yeah? Well I've got a question for *you*. Why don't you get a JOB?"

"I'm trying, hon, you know that." Rex ran his fingers through his thinning hair. "And you know I just sent the catalogs out. The orders'll be pouring in soon."

"BULL!" Candy was escalating fast. "GET A JOB!"

"Ah, go to hell, ya goddamn naggin . . ." Rex moved rapidly out of the room as he said this.

"THAT'S RIGHT, GET OUT OF HERE!"

He grabbed his Kools pack and stepped out on the front stoop. A little breeze tonight; it was better than it had been. Good night to take a walk, have a cigarette, bring home a Dr. Pepper, and fool around in his little basement workshop. He had a new effect he was working on. Candy would be asleep on the couch before long; it was her new dodge to avoid going to bed with him.

Walking towards the 7-Eleven, Rex thought about his new trick. It was a box called Reverso that was supposed to turn things into their opposites. A left glove into a right glove, a saltshaker into a pepper grinder, a deck of cards into a Bible, a Barbie doll into a Ken doll. Reverso could even move a coffee cup's handle to its inside. Of course all the Reverso action could be done by sleight of hand—the idea was to sell the trapdoored Reverso box with before-and-after props. But now, walking along, Rex remembered his math and tried to work out what it would be like if Reverso were for real. What if it were possible, for instance, to turn things inside out by inverting in a sphere, turning each radius vector around on itself, sending a tennis ball's fuzz to its inside, for instance. Given the right dimensional flow, it could be done. . . .

As Rex calmed himself with thoughts of math, his senses opened and took in the night. The trees looked nice, nice and black against the citylit gray sky. The leaves whispered on a rising note. Storm coming; there was heat lightning in the distance and thundermutter. *Buddaboombabububu.* The wind picked up all of a sudden; fat rain started spitting; and then KCRAAACK! there was a blast to Rex's right like a bomb going off! Somehow he'd felt it coming, and he jerked just the right way at just the right time. Things crashed all around him—what seemed like a whole tree. Sudden deaf silence and the crackling of flames.

Lightning had struck a big elm tree across the street from him; struck it and split it right down the middle. Half the tree had fallen down all around Rex, with heavy limbs just missing him on either side.

Shaky and elated, Rex picked his way over the wood to look at the exposed flaming heart of the tree. Something funny about the flame. Something very strange indeed. The flames were in the shape of a little person, a woman with red eyes and trailing limbs.

"Please help me, sir," said the flame girl, her voice rough and skippy as an old LP. "I am of the folk, come down on the bolt. I need a flow to live on. When this fire goes out, I'm gone."

"I," said Rex. "You." He thought of Moses and the burning bush. "Are you a spirit?"

Tinkling laughter. "The folk are information patterns. I drift through the levels doing this and that. Can you lend me a body or two? I'll make it worth your while."

The rain was picking up, and the fire was dying out. A siren approached. The little figure's hot perfect face stared at Rex. She reached out towards him beseechingly.

"I have an idea," said Rex. "I'll put you in Candy . . . my wife. Just for a little while. Right now she's probably asleep, so she won't notice anyway. I live just over there. . . ."

"Carry me in a coal," hissed the little voice.

Rex tried to pick up part of the burning heartwood, but it was all one piece. On a sudden inspiration, he drew out a Kool and lit it by holding it against the dying flames. He puffed once, getting it lit, and the elfgirl entered him.

It felt good, it felt tingly, it felt like being alive. Quick thin fractal pathways grew down his arms and legs, spidering out from his chest, where the girl—

"My name is Zee."

—had settled in.

"It's nice in here," said Zee, her voice subvocal in Rex's throat. "No need to introduce yourself, Rex, I'm reading your mind. I'm going to keep your body and give Candy to Alf." Rex's lips moved slightly as Zee spoke. The reality of this hit Rex—he was possessed! He began a howl of surprise, but Zee cut him off toot sweet. She took over his motor reflexes and began marching him home. Rex's nerves felt thick, coated, crustacean.

"Sorry to do this to you, Rex," said the voice, "but I really don't have a choice. It's the only way I can get rid of Alf, the little spirit who possesses me. He's been insisting I get him a human body. But I like you, so we'll put him in your wife instead of you."

Candy was stretched out on the couch, softly snoring. Rex put the Kool in his mouth and leaned over Candy so that the ash end was just inside her mouth. He blew as she inhaled. A tiny figure of smoke—a little man much, much smaller than Zee—twisted off the cigarette tip and disappeared into Candy's chest. *Gazzzunk.* She snorted and sat up, eyes unnaturally bright.

"So you're Rex?" It was Candy's voice, but huskier, and with a different pronunciation.

"Rex Redman. And you're in my wife Candy. We're both possessed, me by little Zee and she by smaller who? Who are you? You haven't *hurt* Candy have you?"

"Hi Zee. Tell him shut up, Candy's here asleep, and I'm Alf. Let's shake this meat, Zee." Candy/Alf stretched her arms and pushed out her chest. "Hmm." She undid her blouse and bra and examined her breasts with interest. Her motions were pert and youthful, and her features had a new tautness. "Do you want to make love?"

"Yeah," said Rex/Zee. "Sure."

Up in their second-floor bedroom, the sex was more fun than it had been in quite a while. The only reason Candy kept bugging Rex about Marjorie was, Rex felt, because Candy wanted to be unfaithful herself. Lately she'd been sick of him. Pumping in and out, Rex wondered if *this* was adultery. It *was* Candy's body, but Candy's mind was asleep, or on hold, and, for his part, Zee was calling the shots so good Rex wanted them all: come shots, smack shots, booze shots in the sweaty night. Eventually Candy woke up halfway and was happy. It became almost a fourway scene.

The way Zee told it, flaked out on the mattress there, she came from a race of discorporated beings consisting of pure patterns of information. The folk. They could live at any size scale or, ideally, at several size scales at once. Each of the folk had a physically real ancestor on some level or another, but the originals were long lost in the endless mindgaming and switching of hosts. Before entering Rex's nervous system, Zee had been a pattern of air turbulence up in the sky, a pattern that had wafted out from the leaves of a virus-infested bamboo grove in Thailand. The virus—which had been Zee —had evolved out of a self-replicating crystalline clay structure in the ground, which had been Zee too.

Alf was a kind of parasite who'd just entered Zee recently. There were folk throughout the universe, and Alf had arrived in the form of a shower of cosmic rays. He'd latched right onto Zee. It had been his idea to get Zee to come down and possess a person—the folk didn't usually like to do that. Alf had gotten Zee to possess Rex so Rex would help put Alf into a person too. Zee was glad to get Alf out of her—she didn't like him.

Lying there spent, fondling Candy and listening to Zee in the dark, Rex began to think he was dreaming. Dreaming a factual dream of the folk who live in the world's patterns—live as clouds, as fires, as trees, as brooks, as people, as cells, as genes, as superstrings from dimension Z. Any type of ongoing process at all would do. *Fractal;* the word kept coming back. It meant something that is endlessly complex at every level—like a coastline, with its spits within inlets within bays; like a high-tree habitat where the thick branches keep merging to thicker ones, and the thin ones split and split.

"Would you really have died if I'd let your fire go out?" Rex asked. It was dawn and this was no dream.

"No," laughed Zee. "I'm a terrible liar. I would have gone down into the wood's grain-patterns, and then into the sugars of the sap. But I just had to get rid of Alf. And I like you, Rex. I was *aiming* for you when I rode the lightning down. You smelled interesting and . . . thick like extra space."

"You could smell me all the way up in the sky?"

"It's not really *smelling*. For us nothing's so far away, you know. Your whole notion of space and distances is . . . a kind of flat picture? The folk are much realer than that. We live in full fractal Hilbert space. You think like a flat picture, but the paper, if you'll just look, is all bumpy like a moonscape of bristlebushes covered with fuzzy fleas. There's no fixed dimensions at all. Does it feel good when Alf and I do this?"

"Yes."

Candy's wordless smiling daze ended when the first rays of the sun came angling in the window. She jerked, rubbed her eyes, and groaned. "Rex, what have you been *doing* to me? I dreamed. . . ." She tried to sit up and Alf wouldn't let her. Her eyes rolled. "There *are* things in us, Rex, it's real, I'm scared, I'm SCARED *SCARED* oooo—"

Her skin seemed to ridge up as Alf's tendrils clamped down. Her mouth snapped shut and then her face smoothed into an icky pixie grin. She got out of bed and dressed awkwardly. Rex didn't usually pay much attention to what women wore, but Candy's outfit today definitely did not look right. A cocktail dress tucked into a pair of jeans. Where did she think she was going so early?

"I'll call in sick," said Alf through Candy. "Just a minute." She went to the phone and tried to call the school where she worked. Alf didn't seem to realize it was summer vacation.

"Mommy's up!" shouted Griff, hearing the call.

"Where's breakfast?" demanded little Leda.

"LOOK OUT, KIDS!" shouted Rex. "MOMMY AND I HAVE BEEN TAKEN OVER BY—" Zee's clampdown hit him like a shot of animal tranquilizer.

"Just kidding," called Zee/Rex. The kids laughed. Daddy was wild. Zee/Rex went into the kitchen to look for food and Leda asked for breakfast again. "Feed yourself, grubber," mouthed Rex. Hungry. Zee had him brush past Griff and Leda and fill a bowl with milk, sugar, and three raw eggs. Zee/Rex leaned over the bowl and lapped the contents up.

"Daddy, you are eating like a pig!" laughed Leda. She fixed herself a bowl of milk and sugar and tried lapping it up like Daddy. The bowl slid off the table and onto the floor. Griff, upset by the disorder, grabbed some bread and headed out the door to play with the dog. Leda cleaned up halfheartedly until she realized that Daddy didn't care, and then she went to watch cable TV.

"Do you want to fuck your wife some more?" said Zee. The voice was subvocal.

"Uh, no," said Rex, beginning to wonder what he'd gotten his family into. "Not right now. Do you remember saying that you'd make it worth my while if I gave the use of our bodies, Zee? What kind of payment do the folk give?"

"As a rule, none," said Zee, making Rex nibble on a stick of butter. "I told you I'm a terrible liar. Isn't having me in you payment enough? Don't you like being part of the Zee fractal?" Rex didn't understand, but Zee helped him and then he did. Folk like Zee were long thin vortices in the fractal soup of all that is. Or like a necklace strung with diverse beads. Rex was a Zee-bead now, and Candy was an Alf-bead. Alf's thread passed up through Zee, too, and up through Zee to who knew where.

It was dizzying to think about: the endlessness and the weird geometry of it all. To hear Zee tell it, every size scale was equally central, each object just another crotch in the transdimensional fractal worldtree. Zee and Alf were in them, above them, and maybe below them now, too: in their genes and in their memes. Rex's thoughts felt no longer quite his.

He'd made a terrible mistake picking Zee up. He kept remembering the desperate expression on Candy's face as Alf made her stop yelling. And the puzzled looks the children had given their terribly altered Dad.

"Can't you and Alf move on, Zee? Leave your fractal trail in us, but move on down into the atoms? Can I drive you anywhere?"

"No. It's ugly here in Killeville. I just came down because of you. When I'm through eating, I want to get back in bed with Candy and Alf." Rex watched himself open the fridge, hunker down, and begin using a stick of celery to dig peanut butter out of the jar. Crunch off some celery each time. It tasted good. Whenever he relaxed, the nerve-tingle of Zee's possession started to feel good. That was bad.

"What was it about me that attracted you so much, Zee?"

"I said I could smell you. You were thinking about your magic box called Reverso. It makes your flat space get thick, and it spins things over themselves. I told you the higher dimensions are real; you can build up to them with fractals. I bet I could make Reverso really work. I could do *that* for you, dear Rex."

"Well, all right." Rex went back in the bedroom and talked things over with Candy, who was busy putting on a different set of clothes. "I think I'll drive down to my office, Candy," said Rex. "Zee says she can help me get the Reverso working. And maybe then they'll leave."

"I'm going to stay in bed all day," said Candy, making that pixie face. She had taken all her clothes back off, and one of her hands was busy down in her crotch. "I love this body." Her voice was husky and strange. Rex felt very uneasy.

"Maybe I shouldn't leave you like this, Candy."

"Go on, go downtown to your Marjorie. I won't be lonely, Rex. You can count on that."

"Do you mean—"

Zee cut him off and marched him out of the bedroom and back down the stairs.

"And take the kids," called Candy in something like her normal voice. She sounded scared. "Get the poor children out of here!"

"Right."

Rex rounded up the children and took them over to the Carrandines' house. Luanne Carrandine was a little surprised when Rex asked her to babysit, but after the usual heavy flirting, she agreed to help out. She was a charming blonde woman with a small jaded face. Some of the suggestions which Zee forced out of Rex's mouth made Luanne laugh out loud. If her husband Garvey hadn't been upstairs, Rex and Zee might have stayed on, but as it was, they headed downtown.

Last night's storm had left Killeville gray and steamy. Kudzu writhed up the walls of the abandoned building Rex rented space in. The other renter—the famous Marjorie—didn't usually show up till ten. Rex/Zee's footsteps echoed in the empty space. He walked her up the filthy stairs to his little office. There on his desk sat the Reverso: a silver-painted, wood box with a hidden trapdoor in the bottom.

Rex felt foolish showing his crummy trick to a truly magical spirit like Zee. But she insisted, and he ran through the patter.

"This is a handy little box that turns things into their opposites," said Rex, putting a right-handed leather glove in the chamber. "Suppose that you have two pairs of gloves, but you lose the left glove to each pair. No problem with Reverso!" He lifted the box up and shook it (meanwhile sneaking a hand in through the trapdoor to turn the special glove inside out). He set the Reverso back down. "Open it up, Zee. You see! Right into left." He took out the left glove and put in a fake saltshaker. "But that's not all. Reverso changes all kinds of opposites. What if you have salt but no pepper?" He shook the chamber again. (A hidden curtain inside the "saltshaker" slid down, changing its sides from white to black.) "Open the chamber, Zee— salt into pepper! Now what if you're short on shelf space and your coffee cups' handles keep bumping into each other?" He drew out a (special) coffee cup and placed it in the chamber. "Simple! We use Reverso to turn inside to out and put the handle on the inside for storage!" (He opened the chamber, moving the suctioned-on cup-handle to the cup's inside as he drew it out.) "See!"

"I know a way to do the first and last tricks without cheating," said Zee. "I know how to really turn things inside out. Look." Rex's hand picked up a pencil and drew a picture of two concentric circles. "See the annular ring between the circles? Think of lots of little radial arrows in the ring, all leading from the inner circle to the outer circle." His hand sketched rapidly. "Think of the ring part as something solid. To turn it inside out means to flip each of the arrows over." Zee stopped drawing and ran a kind of animation on Rex's retina. He seemed to see the ring's radial arrows rotating up out of the paper to point inwards. All of them turning together made a trail shaped like a torus. "Yes, a torus, whose intersection with the plane looks like two circles. Think of a smoke-ring, a torus whose inner circle keeps moving out—like a tornado biting its own tail. A planecutting toroidal vortex ring turns flat objects inside out. What we need for your real Reverso is a hypertorus whose intersection with your space looks like two spheres, a big one and a little one. I know where to get 'em, Rex, closer than you know. These hypertoruses have a fuzzy fractal surface and a built-in vortex flow. You won't *believe* where. . . ."

"Talking to yourself, Rex?" It was Marjorie, come up the stairs to say hi. Rex and Zee, in the throes of scientific rapture, had failed to hear her come in.

Marjorie was a thin young woman who smiled a lot. She wore her hair very short, and she smoked Gauloises—which took some doing in a chain-store town like Killeville. "I'm making coffee for us, and I wondered if you remembered to bring milk and sugar."

"Uh, no. Yes, I guess I am talking to myself. This Reverso trick, you know." Suddenly Zee seized control of Rex's tongue. "Do you want to make love?"

Marjorie laughed and gave Rex a gentle butt with her head. "I never thought you'd ask. Sex *now?*"

"No time now," cried Rex, taking back over. "Shut up, Zee!"

Majorie stepped back to the door and gave Rex a considering look. "Are you high, Rex? Or what? You have some for me?"

"I have to work," said Rex. "Stay quiet, Zee."

"I can make you feel like Rex," said Zee through Rex's mouth. "With an Alf. Come back here, honey."

"Meanwhile on planet Earth," said Marjorie, and disappeared down the stairs, shaking her head.

"Stop it, Zee, and let's get to work. Where are we supposed to find that hypertoroidal vortex ring you were talking about?"

"Space's dimensionality depends on the size scale you look at, Rex. From a distance a tree seems like a pattern of one-D lines. Get closer and the bark looks like a warpy two-D surface. Land on the surface and it's a fissured three-D world. Down and down. Hypertoroidal vortex rings are common at the atomic scale. They're called quarks."

"Quarks!"

"A quark is a toroidal loop of superstring. Now just hold still while I reach down and yank—"

There was a sinking feeling in Rex's chest. Zee was moving down through him, descending into the dimensional depths. With her bright "growth tip" gone from him, Rex felt more fully himself than he had since last night. Zee's fractal trail was still in him, but her active self was down somewhere in his atoms. He sighed and sank down into his armchair.

Interesting how receptive Marjorie had been to that suggestion of Zee's . . . but no. The peace of his neutral isolation was too sweet to compromise. *But what was Candy up to right now? What was Alf getting her to do?*

Rex's nervous gaze strayed to the shelves of the little novelties that he was ready to mail, once the orders started coming in. He tried to calm himself by thinking about business. *Boy's Life* might be a good place to advertise, maybe he should write them for their rates. Or—

"Wuugh!" Zee's heavy catch swelled and stung in Rex's rising gorge and he gagged again, harder. A flickering fur sphere flopped out of his mouth and plopped onto the floor in front of him. It had an aura of frenzied activity, but it didn't seem to be going anyplace. It just lay there on the pine boards, its surface flowing this way and that.

"I'm back," murmured Zee with Rex's mouth.

Rex nudged the sphere with his foot. It shrank from his touch.

"If you're rough with it, it shrinks," said Zee. "And if you pat it, it gets bigger. Try."

Rex leaned forward and placed his hands lightly on the sphere's equator. It wasn't exactly fur-covered after all. Velcro was more like it. Zee had him rub his hands back and forth caressingly, and then move them apart. The sphere bulged along with his hands, out and out till it was four feet across. Rex felt like a tailor fitting a fat man for a suit. He pushed back his chair and got up to take a better look at the thing.

At any instant, its surface was fractally rough: cracked and fissured, with cracks in its cracks, and with a tufty overlay of slippery fuzz that branched and rebranched. In its richness of structure, it was a bit like an incredibly detailed scale model of some alien planet.

What made the fuzzball doubly strange was that its surface was in constant flux. If it was like the model of a planet, it was a dynamic model, with speeded-up time. As if to the rhythm of unseen seasons, patches of the fuzzball's stubble would grow dark red, flatten out to eroded yellow badlands, glaze over with blue crackle, and then blossom back into pale red growth.

"A quark is this complex?" Rex asked unbelievingly. "And you say this is really a hypertorus? Where's the inner sphere? And how can anything ever get inside it?"

"It's the hyperflow that makes it impervious," said Zee. "And you valve that down with a twist like this." She made Rex grab the sphere and twist it clockwise about its vertical axis It turned as grudgingly as a stiff faucet. "If you give it a half-turn, the hyperflow stops." Sure enough, as Zee/Rex's hands rotated the sphere it stopped its flickering. It was static now, with a big red patch near Rex. Frozen still like this, the sphere was filmy and transparent. Peering into it, Rex could see a small sphere in the middle with a green patch matching the outer sphere's red patch.

"You can still make it change size when it's stopped like this," said Zee, urging Rex's reluctant hands forward. "But now, even better, you can push right through it. Even though it still resists shear, it's gone matter-transparent."

The outer sphere was insubstantial as a curtain of water; the central sphere was, too. It had been the hyperflow, now halted, that gave the spheres their seeming solidity. Zee now demonstrated that if Rex jabbed or caressed the barely palpable inner sphere, it grew and shrank just as willingly as did the outer sphere. The two could be adjusted to bound concentric shells of any size.

The region between the spheres felt tingly with leashed energies. Rex could begin to see what would happen if the hyperflow started back up. Everything would turn over. The inside would go out, and the outside would go in. He jerked his hands back.

"And of course you restart it by turning it the other way," said Zee. Rex dug into the sphere's yeilding surface and twisted it counterclockwise. Insubstantial though it was, the sphere resisted this axial rotation as strongly as before. Slowly it gave and unvalved. The hyperflow started back up. The big outer patch near Rex shifted shades from red through orange to yellow to green to blue to violet. Rex watched for a while and then stopped the flow the next time a green outer patch appeared. Peered in. Yes, now the inner patch was red. They'd traded places. The stuff of the outer sphere had flowed up through hyperspace and back down to the inner sphere. It was just the same as the way the stuff of a donut-shape's outer equator can flow up over the donut's top and down to its inner equator. Like a sea cucumber, the big quark lived to evert.

"Let's call it a cumberquark," said Rex.

"Fine," said Zee. "Wonderful. I'm glad I showed it to you. Aren't you going to try it out?"

Rex's eye lit on a glass jar of rubber cement. He halted the cumberquark's flow, jabbed the central sphere down to the size of a BB, squeezed the outer sphere down to the size of a small cantaloupe, and then adjusted the temporarily matter-transparent sphere so that the inner one was inside his jar of rubber cement. The outer sphere included the whole jar and a small disk-section of Rex's desktop. With one quick motion, Rex unvalved the cumberquark just enough

for the green patch to turn red, twisted the hyperflow back off, and shoved the cumberquark aside to see what it had wrought. Thud floop. A moundy puddle of rubber cement resting in a crater on his desk. Wedged into the hole was an odd-shaped glass object. Rex picked it up. A jar, it was the rubber cement jar, but with the label inside, and rattling around inside it was—
"That hard little thing is the disk of desk the jar was sitting on." The jar's lid was on the top, but facing inwards. Rex pushed on its underside and got it untwisted. As he untwisted it, compressed air hissed out: all the air that had been between the jar and the cumberquark's outer sphere was squeezed in there. The lid clattered into the jar's dry inside. Peeking in, Rex could see that the RUBBER CEMENT label had mirror-flipped to TИƎMƎⱭ ЯƎᙠᙠUЯ. Check. He jiggled the jar and spilled the shrunken bit of desk out into his hand. Neat. It was a tiny sphere, with a BB-sized craterlet where the cumberquark's inner sphere had nestled. A small gobbet of uneverted rubber cement clung to this dimple.

Quick youthful footsteps ascended the steps to Rex's office. Marjorie, back for today's Round Two.

"I want you to meet Kissycat. Kissycat, this is Rex." Marjorie had a sinewy black cat nestled against her flattish chest. She pressed forward and placed the cat on Rex's shoulder. It dug its claws in. Rex sneezed. He was allergic to cats. He had some trouble getting the neurotic beast off his shoulder and onto the desktop. He had a wonderful, awful, Grinchy idea.

"Will you sell me that cat, Marjorie?"

"No, but you can babysit him. I'm going down to the sub shop. Want anything?"

"Just a Coke. I'm going to meet Candy for lunch." He'd been away too long already.

"La dee da. Where?"

"Oh, just at home." Rex ran his shaky fingers through his hair, wondering if Candy was still in bed. But dammit, this was more important than Candy's crazy threats. The cat. In just a minute he would be alone with the cat.

Kissycat nosed daintily around Rex's desktop and began sniffing at the cumberquark.

"Rad," said Marjorie, noticing it. "Is that a magic trick?"

"It's a cumberquark. I just invented it."

"What does it do?"

"Maybe I'll show you when you get back. Sure, Kissycat can stay here. That's fine. Here's seventy-five cents for the Coke."

As soon as she'd left the building, Rex dilated the cumberquark to pumpkin size and began stalking Kissycat. Sensing Rex's mood—a mixture of prickly ailurophobia and psychotic glee—the beast kept well away from him. Fortunately he'd closed his office door and windows. Kissycat wedged himself under Rex's armchair. Rex thumped the chair over and lunged. The cat yowled, spit, and slapped four nasty scratches across Rex's left hand.

"You want me to kill you *first?*" Rex snarled, snatching up the heavy rod that he used to prop his window open. Candy had him all upset. "You want me to crush your head before I turn you inside out, you god—"

His voice broke and sweetened. Zee taking over. He'd forgotten all about her.

"Niceums kitty. Dere he is. All thcared of nassy man? Oobie doobie purr purr purr." Zee made Rex rummage in his trashcan till he found a crust of yesterday's tuna sandwich. "Nummy nums for Mr. Tissytat! Oobie doobie purr purr purr." This humiliating performance went on for longer than Rex liked, but finally Kissycat was stretched out on the canvas seat of the director's chair next to Rex's desk, shedding hair and licking his feet. Rex halted the cumberquark's flow and moved gingerly forward. "Niceums!"

Kissycat seemed not to notice as the gossamer outer sphere passed through his body. Cooing and peering in, Rex manipulated the sphere till its BB-sized center was inside the cat, hopefully inside its stomach. With a harsh cackle, Rex unvalved the sphere, let it flow through a flip, and turned it back off. There was a circle of canvas missing from the chair seat now, and the everted cat dropped through the hole to the floor, passing right through the temporarily matter-transparent cumberquark.

Kissycat was a goodsized pink ball with two holes in it. Rex had managed to get the middle sphere bang on in the cat's stomach. The crust he'd just fed Kissycat was lying right there next to the stomach. The stomach twitched and jerked. It had two sphincterish holes in it —holes that presumably tunneled to Kissycat's mouth and anus. Rex gave the ball a little kick and it made a muffled mewing noise.

"A little *strange* in there is it, hand-scratcher?"

"Rex," came Zee's subvocal voice. "Don't be mean. Isn't he going to suffocate?" She was like a goddamn good conscience. If only Alf had been good, too. *He couldn't let himself think about Candy!*

Rex forced his attention back to the matter at hand. "Kissycat won't suffocate for a few minutes. Look how big he is. There's a lot of air in there with him. He's like a balloon!" The ball shuddered and mewed again, more faintly than before. "I'm just surprised the flip didn't break his neck or something."

"No, that's safe enough. Space is kind of rubbery, you know. But listen, Rex, his air is running out fast. Turn him back."

"I don't want to. I want to show him to—" Rex was struck by an idea. Moving quickly, he took the tubular housing of a ballpoint pen and pushed it deep into one of the stomach holes. Kissycat's esophagus. Stale air came rushing out in a gassy yowl. The pink ball shrank to catsize. After a few moments of confused struggle, the ball began pulsing steadily, pumping breaths in and out of the pen-tube.

There was noise downstairs. Marjorie! Rex turned the cumberquark back into a brightflowing little fuzzball, then put it and the everted cat inside his briefcase. He pounded down the stairs and got his Coke. "Thanks, Marjorie! Sorry to run, I just realized how late it is."

"Where's Kissycat?"

"Uh . . . I'm not sure. Inside or outside or something." Rex's briefcase was making a faint hissing noise.

"Some babysitter *you* are," said Marjorie, cocking her head in kittenish pique. "What's that *noise?* Do you—"

Rex lunged for the door, but now Zee had to put her two-cents worth in. "Look," cried Rex's mouth as his arms dumped the contents of his briefcase out onto the dirty hallway floor.

Marjorie screamed. "You've killed him! You're crazy! Help!"

Zee relinquished control of Rex and hunkered somewhere inside him, snickering. Rex could hear her laughter like elfin bells. He snatched up his cumberquark and made as if to run for it, but Marjorie's tearful face won his sudden sympathy. She was a pest, and a kid, but still—

"Stop screaming, dammit. I can turn him back."

"You killed my cat!"

"He scratched my hand. And he's not dead anyway. He's just inside out. I wanted to borrow him to show Candy. I wasn't going to hurt him any. Honest. I turned him inside out with my cumberquark, and I can turn him back."

"You can? What's that plastic tube?"

"He's breathing through it. Now look. Let's get something that can go in his stomach without making him sick. Uh . . . how about a sheet of newspaper. Yeah." Moving quickly, Rex spread out a sheet of old newspaper and set the everted cat on it. Marjorie watched him with wide, frightened eyes. "Don't look at me that way, dammit. Come here and pick up the paper, Marjorie, hold it stretched tight out in front of you." She obeyed, and Rex got the cumberquark halted and in position, more or less. He reached in and took out the pen-tube, then readjusted the cumberquark. Marjorie was shaking. If Rex did the flip with the inner sphere intersecting Kissycat's flesh, this was going to be gross.

"Hold real still." He steadied himself and unvalved the cumberquark for a half turn, then tightened it back.

Mrrraaaow! Kissycat landed on his feet, right on the circle of cloth that had been part of Rex's chairseat upstairs. Marjorie stared down through the hole in her newspaper at him and cried out his name. Spotting Rex, the cat took off down the hall, heading for the dark recesses of the basement.

Everything was OK for a moment there, but then Zee had to speak back up. "I was thinking, Marjorie, about a wild new way to have sex. I could put the cumberquark's central sphere in your womb and turn you inside out and—"

With a major effort of will, Rex got himself out the door and on the street before Zee could finish her suggestion. Marjorie watched him leave, too stunned to react.

The three-mile drive home seemed to take a very long time. As the hot summer air beat in through the open car window, Rex kept thinking about inside out. What was the very innermost of all—the one/many language of quantum logic? And what, finally, was outermost of all—dead Aristotle's Empyrean? Zee knew, or maybe she didn't. Though Zee was not so scalebound as Rex, she was still finite, and her levels reached only so far, both up and down. There's a sense in which zero is as far away as infinity: you can keep halving your size or keep doubling, but you never get to zero or infinity.

Rex's thoughts grew less abstract. His perceptions were so loosened by the morning's play that he kept seeing things inside out. Passing through Killeville, he could hear the bored platypus honking inside the offices, outside the tense exchanges in the Pizza Hut kitchens, inside the slow rustlings in the black people's small shops, outside the redundant empty Killeville churches, inside the funeral homes with secret stinks, outside the huge "fine homes" with only a widow home, inside a supermarket office with the manager holding a plain teenage girl clerk on his gray-clad knees, outside a plastic gallon of milk. Entering his neighborhood, Rex could see into his neighbor's hearts, see the wheels of worry and pain; and finally he could understand how little anyone else's problems connected to his own. No one cared about him, nobody but Candy.

There were four strange cars in front of his house. A rusty pickup, a beetle, an MG, and a Jap pickup. Rex knew the MG was Roland Brody's, but who the hell were those other people?

There was a man sitting on Rex's porch steps, a redneck who worked at the gas station. He smiled thinly and patted the spot on the porch next to him.

"Hydee. Ah'm Jody. And Ah believe yore her old man. Poor son. Hee hee."

"This isn't right."

Another man hollered out the front door, a banker platypus in his white undershirt and flipperlength black socks. "Get some brew, Jodih, and we'll *all* go back for seconds! She goin' strong!"

Laughter drifted down from the second floor. The phone was ringing.

Rex staggered about on the sidewalk there, in the hot sun, reeling under the impact of all this nightmare. What could he do? Candy had flipped, she was doing it with every guy she vaguely even knew! A Plymouth van full of teenage boys pulled into Rex's drive. He recognized the driver from church, but the boy didn't recognize Rex.

"Is old lady Redman still up there putting out?" asked the callow, lightly mustached youth.

Rex put his briefcase down on the ground and took out the cumberquark. "You better get out of here, kid. I'm Mr. Redman."

The van backed up rapidly and drove off. Rex could hear the excited boys whooping and laughing. Jody smiled down at him from the porch. Standing there in the high-noon moment, Rex could hear moans from upstairs. His wife; his wife having an orgasm with another man. This was just so—

"Poor Rex," said Zee. "That Alf is awful. He's not even from Earth."

"Shut up, you bitch," said Rex, starting up the steps.

"You gonna try and whup me?" Jody's hands were large and callused. He was ready for a fight. In Jody's trailerpark circles, fighting went with sex.

Rex spread the cumberquark out to the size of a washing machine, and cut off its rotation. There was a lot of noise in his head: thumps and jabber. Jody rose up into a crouch. Rex lunged forward, spreading the cumberquark just a bit wider. For a frozen second there, the outer sphere surrounded Jody, and Rex cut the hyperflow on.

The surface was opaque fractal fuzz. You wouldn't have known someone was inside, if it hadn't been for the wah-wah-wah sound of Jody's screams, chopped into pulses by the hyperflow. The cumberquark rested solidly on the hole it had cut into the porch steps.

"You're next, man," Rex yelled to the platypus man looking out the front door. "I'm going to kill you, you preppy bastard!" With rapid movements of his bill and flippers, the banker got in his black Toyota truck and left. Rex turned Jody off to see what was what.

Not right. Edge-on to all normal dimensions, Jody was an annular cut-out, a slice of Halloween pumpkin. Rex eased him through another quarter turn and Jody was back on the steps. The cumberquark had stayed good and steady through all this—everything was back where it had started.

"How did it look, Jody?" Rex's teeth were chattering.

"Unh." For gasping Jody, Rex was no longer a person but rather a force of nature. Jody moved slowly down the steps talking to himself. "No nothin' all inside out mah haid up mah butt just for snatch mah god—"

Rex shrank the cumberquark down a bit as Jody drove off. The VW and the MG were still there. How could Roland have done this to him? And who was the fourth guy?

The fourth guy was the real one, the lover a husband never sees. As Rex entered his house, the fourth man ran out the back door, looped around the house, and took off in his bug. Let him go. Rex went upstairs. Roland Brody was sitting on the edge of Rex and Candy's bed looking chipper.

"Damn, Rex! I didn't know Candy had it in her. I mean to tell you!" Roland fished his underpants off the floor and pulled them on. He was an old friend, an utterly charming man, tall and twitchy and with a profile like Thomas Jefferson on the nickel. A true Virginia gentleman. He had a deprecating way of turning everything into a joke. Even now, it was hard to be angry with him. The VW's popping faded, and Rex sank down into a chair. He was trembling all over. The cumberquark nestled soothingly in his lap.

Candy had the sheet pulled all the way up to her nose. Her big blue eyes peered over the top. "Don't leave, Roland, I'm scared of what he'll do. Can you forgive me, Rex? Alf made me do it."

"Who's this *Alf* fellow?" asked Roland, tucking the tail of his button-down shirt into his black pants. "Was he the guy in the VW?"

"You're a bastard to have done it too, Roland," said Rex.

"Hell, Rex. Wouldn't you?"

The room reeked of sex. The jabbering was still in Rex's head—a sound like a woman talking fast. All of a sudden he didn't know what he was doing. He stretched the cumberquark out big and stopped and started it, turning big chunks of the room inside out. Part of the chair, circles of the floor, Candy's dresser-top, a big piece of mattress. Roland tried to grab Rex, and Rex turned Roland's forearm into pulp that fell to the floor. Candy was screaming bloody murder. Rex advanced on her, chunking the cumberquark on and off like a holepuncher, eating up their defiled bed. The womanvoice in his head was coming through Rex's mouth.

"Better get out of her, Alf, better get out or your bod is gone, you crooked hiss from outspace, Alf, I'll chunk you down, man, better split Alf, better go or—"

"Stop!" yelled Candy. "Rex please stop!" Rex made the cumberquark go matter-transparent, and he slid it up over her legs. Candy's face got that pixie look and Alf spoke.

"I'm only having fun," he said. "Leave me alone, jerk, I'm your wife. I'm in here to stay."

Then Rex knew what to do, he knew it like a math problem. He thought it fast with Zee, and she said yes.

Rex shrank the cumberquark real small and put it in his pocket. Poor Roland had collapsed on the floor. He was bleeding to death. Rex tied off Roland's armstub with his necktie.

"Sorry, Roland. I'll drive you to the hospital, man."

"Damn, Rex, damn. Hurry."

"That's right," said Alf/Candy. "Get out of here and leave me alone."

The hospital wasn't far. Rex dropped Roland at the emergency door and went back home. Instead of going in the front door he went in the basement door to sit in his study. There was no use talking to Candy before he got rid of Alf.

He took the cumberquark out of his pocket and set it down on his desk. Small, fast, flowy. He leaned over it and breathed. Hot bright Zee rode his breath out of his body and into the cumberquark. She could live there as well as in Rex. The little sphere lifted off Rex's desk and buzzed around the study like a housefly. Zee had a way of pulsing its flow off and on to convert some of its four-D momentum into antigravity. Now she stopped the quark's flow entirely and inflated it out through Rex so that it held all of him except his feet. Rex hopped into the air, up into the big light bubble. It stuttered on when he was all in.

Rex's sense inputs became a flicker. His room, his body, his room, his body, his room, his body. . . . In between the two three-D views were two prospects on hyperspace: *ana* and *kata,* black and white, heaven and hell. Room, *ana,* body, *kata,* room. . . . The four images were shuffled together seamlessly, but only the room view mattered right now.

Zee shrank the cumberquark down to fly-size again. Rex felt the antigravity force as a jet from his spine. Thanks to the way Zee was pulsing the hyperflow, there was plenty of fresh air. They looped the loop, got a fix on things, and space-curved their way upstairs.

Candy/Alf didn't notice them at first. She was lying still, staring at the ceiling. Rex/Zee hovered over her and then, before the woman could react, they zoomed down at her, shrinking small enough to enter her nose.

Pink cavern with blonde hairs, a dark tunnel at the back, rush of wind, onward. No light in here, but Rex/Zee could see by the quark-light of quantum strangeness. Oh Candy it's nice in you. Me, *kata,* you, *ana,* me, *kata* you. . . .

There was an evil glow in one of Candy's lungs: Alf. He looked like a goblin, crouched there with pointed nose and ears. Rex/Zee bored right into him, wrapping his fibers around and around them, knotting him into their complex join.

And zoomed back out Candy's nose, and got big again, and stopped.

Rex was standing in his bedroom. The ball that was Zee and Alf dipped in salute and sailed out the window.

Candy stood up and hugged Rex. They were still in love.

That winter Rex would get a new job, and they would leave Killeville, taking with them the children, a van of furniture, and the memory of this strange summer day.

The Facts Concerning the Recent Carnival of Crime in Connecticut

Mark Twain

Here Mark Twain, the great American writer, performs one of his character-istic inversions, on the old allegorical tradition embodied in this moral tale of a man confronted by the living personification of his conscience. The result is a masterpiece of having one's cake and eating it too. Twain makes a moral point with an immoral tale.

I was feeling blithe, almost jocund. I put a match to my cigar, and just then the morning's mail was handed in. The first superscription I glanced at was in a handwriting that sent a thrill of pleasure through and through me. It was Aunt Mary's; and she was the person I loved and honored most in all the world, outside of my own household. She had been my boyhood's idol; maturity, which is fatal to so many enchantments, had not been able to dislodge her from her pedestal; no, it had only justified her right to be there, and placed her de-thronement permanently among the impossibilities. To show how strong her influence over me was, I will observe that long after every-body else's *"do*-stop-smoking" had ceased to affect me in the slightest degree, Aunt Mary could still stir my torpid conscience into faint signs of life when she touched upon the matter. But all things have their limit, in this world. A happy day came at last, when even Aunt Mary's words could no longer move me. I was not merely glad to see that day arrive; I was more than glad—I was grateful; for when its sun had set, the one alloy that was able to mar my enjoyment of my aunt's society was gone. The remainder of her stay with us that winter was in every way a delight. Of course she pleaded with me just as earnestly as ever, after that blessed day, to quit my pernicious habit, but to no purpose whatever; the moment she opened the subject I at once became calmly, peacefully, contentedly indifferent—absolutely, adamantinely indifferent. Consequently the closing weeks of that memorable visit melted away as pleasantly as a dream, they were so freighted, for me, with tranquil satisfaction. I could not have enjoyed my pet vice more if my gentle tormentor had been a smoker herself, and an advocate of the practice. Well, the sight of her handwriting reminded me that I was getting very hungry to see her again. I easily guessed what I should find in her letter. I opened it. Good! just as I expected; she was coming! Coming this very day, too, and by the morning train; I might expect her any moment.

I said to myself, "I am thoroughly happy and content, now. If my most pitiless enemy could appear before me at this moment, I would freely right any wrong I may have done him."

Straightway the door opened, and a shrivelled, shabby dwarf entered. He was not more than two feet high. He seemed to be about forty years old. Every feature and every inch of him was a trifle out of shape; and so, while one could not put his finger upon any particular part and say, "This is a conspicuous deformity," the spectator perceived that this little person was a deformity as a whole—a vague, general, evenly blended, nicely adjusted deformity. There was a fox-like cunning in the face and the sharp little eyes, and also alertness and malice. And yet, this vile bit of human rubbish seemed to bear a sort of remote and ill-defined resemblance to me! It was dully perceptible in the mean form, the countenance, and even the clothes, gestures, manner, and attitudes of the creature. He was a far-fetched, dim suggestion of a burlesque upon me, a caricature of me in little. One thing about him struck me forcibly, and most unpleasantly: he was covered all over with a fuzzy, greenish mould, such as one sometimes sees upon mildewed bread. The sight of it was nauseating.

He stepped along with a chipper air, and flung himself into a doll's chair in a very free and easy way, without waiting to be asked. He tossed his hat into the waste basket. He picked up my old chalk pipe from the floor, gave the stem a wipe or two on his knee, filled the bowl from the tobacco-box at his side, and said to me in a tone of pert command—

"Gimme a match!"

I blushed to the roots of my hair; partly with indignation, but mainly because it somehow seemed to me that this whole performance was very like an exaggeration of conduct which I myself had sometimes been guilty of in my intercourse with familiar friends—but never, never with strangers, I observed to myself. I wanted to kick the pygmy into the fire, but some incomprehensible sense of being legally and legitimately under his authority forced me to obey his order. He applied the match to the pipe, took a contemplative whiff or two, and remarked, in an irritatingly familiar way—

"Seems to me it's devilish odd weather for this time of year."

I flushed again, and in anger and humiliation as before; for the language was hardly an exaggeration of some that I have uttered in my day, and moreover was delivered in a tone of voice and with an exasperating drawl that had the seeming of a deliberate travesty of my style. Now there is nothing I am quite so sensitive about as a mocking imitation of my drawling infirmity of speech. I spoke up sharply and said—

"Look here, you miserable ash-cat! you will have to give a little more attention to your manners, or I will throw you out of the window!"

The manikin smiled a smile of malicious content and security, puffed a whiff of smoke contemptuously toward me, and said, with a still more elaborate drawl—

"Come—go gently, now; don't put on *too* many airs with your betters."

This cool snub rasped me all over, but it seemed to subjugate me, too, for a moment. The pygmy contemplated me awhile with his weasel eyes, and then said, in a peculiarly sneering way—

"You turned a tramp away from your door this morning."

I said crustily—

"Perhaps I did, perhaps I didn't. How do *you* know?"

"Well, I know. It isn't any matter *how* I know."

"Very well. Suppose I *did* turn a tramp away from the door—what of it?"

"Oh, nothing; nothing in particular. Only you lied to him."

"I *didn't!* That is, I—"

"Yes, but you did; you lied to him."

I felt a guilty pang,—in truth I had felt it forty times before that tramp had travelled a block from my door—but still I resolved to make a show of feeling slandered; so I said—

"This is a baseless impertinence. I said to the tramp—"

"There—wait. You were about to lie again. *I* know what you said to him. You said the cook was gone down town and there was nothing left from breakfast. Two lies. You knew the cook was behind the door, and plenty of provisions behind *her*."

This astonishing accuracy silenced me; and it filled me with wondering speculations, too, as to how this cub could have got his information. Of course he could have culled the conversation from the tramp, but by what sort of magic had he contrived to find out about the concealed cook? Now the dwarf spoke again:

"It was rather pitiful, rather small, in you to refuse to read that poor young woman's manuscript the other day, and give her an opinion as to its literary value; and she had come so far, too, and *so* hopefully. Now *wasn't it?*"

I felt like a cur! And I had felt so every time the thing had recurred to my mind, I may as well confess. I flushed hotly and said—

"Look here, have you nothing better to do than prowl around prying into other people's business? Did that girl tell you that?"

"Never mind whether she did or not. The main thing is, you did that contemptible thing. And you felt ashamed of it afterwards. Aha! you feel ashamed of it *now!*"

This with a sort of devilish glee. With fiery earnestness I responded—

"I told that girl, in the kindest, gentlest way, that I could not consent to deliver judgment upon *any* one's manuscript, because an individual's verdict was worthless. It might underrate a work of high merit and lose it to the world, or it might overrate a trashy production and so open the way for its infliction upon the world. I said that the great public was the only tribunal competent to sit in judgment upon a literary effort, and therefore it must be best to lay it before that tribunal in the outset, since in the end it must stand or fall by that mighty court's decision any way."

"Yes, you said all that. So you did, you juggling, small-souled shuffler! And yet when the happy hopefulness faded out of that poor girl's face, when you saw her furtively slip beneath her shawl the scroll she had so patiently and honestly scribbled at—so ashamed of her darling now, so proud of it before—when you saw the gladness go out of her eyes and the tears come there, when she crept away so humbly who had come so—"

"Oh, peace! peace! peace! Blister your merciless tongue, haven't all these thoughts tortured me enough, without *your* coming here to fetch them back again?"

Remorse! remorse! It seemed to me that it would eat the very heart out of me! And yet that small fiend only sat there leering at me with joy and contempt, and placidly chuckling. Presently he began to speak again. Every sentence was an accusation, and every accusation a truth. Every clause was freighted with sarcasm and derision, every slow-dropping word burned like vitriol. The dwarf reminded me of times when I had flown at my children in anger and punished them for faults which a little inquiry would have taught me that others, and not they, had committed. He reminded me of how I had disloyally allowed old friends to be traduced in my hearing, and been too craven to utter a word in their defence. He reminded me of many dishonest things which I had done; of many which I had procured to be done by children and other irresponsible persons; of some which I had planned, thought upon, and longed to do, and been kept from the performance by fear of consequences only. With exquisite cruelty he recalled to my mind, item by item, wrongs and unkindnesses I had inflicted and humiliations I had put upon friends since dead, "who died thinking of those injuries, maybe, and grieving over them," he added, by way of poison to the stab.

"For instance," said he, "take the case of your younger brother, when you two were boys together, many a long year ago. He always lovingly trusted in you with a fidelity that your manifold treacheries were not able to shake. He followed you about like a dog, content to suffer wrong and abuse if he might only be with you; patient under these injuries so long as it was your hand that inflicted them. The latest picture you have of him in health and strength must be such a comfort to you! You pledged your honor that if he would let you blindfold him no harm should come to him; and then, giggling and choking over the rare fun of the joke, you led him to a brook thinly glazed with ice, and pushed him in; and how you did laugh! Man, you will never forget the gentle, reproachful look he gave you as he struggled shivering out, if you live a thousand years! Oho! you see it now, you see it *now!*"

"Beast, I have seen it a million times, and shall see it a million more! and may you rot away piecemeal, and suffer till doomsday what I suffer now, for bringing it back to me again!"

The dwarf chuckled contentedly, and went on with his accusing history of my career. I dropped into a moody, vengeful state, and suffered in silence under the merciless lash. At last this remark of his gave me a sudden rouse:

"Two months ago, on a Tuesday, you woke up, away in the night, and fell to thinking, with shame, about a peculiarly mean and pitiful act of yours toward a poor ignorant Indian in the wilds of the Rocky Mountains in the winter of eighteen hundred and—"

"Stop a moment, devil! Stop! Do you mean to tell me that even my very *thoughts* are not hidden from you?"

"It seems to look like that. Didn't you think the thoughts I have just mentioned?"

"If I didn't, I wish I may never breathe again! Look here, friend—look me in the eye. Who *are* you?"

"Well, who do you think?"

"I think you are Satan himself. I think you are the devil."

"No."

"No? Then who *can* you be?"

"Would you really like to know?"

"*Indeed* I would."

"Well, I am your *Conscience!*"

In an instant I was in a blaze of joy and exultation. I sprang at the creature, roaring—

"Curse you, I have wished a hundred million times that you were tangible, and that I could get my hands on your throat once! Oh, but I will wreak a deadly vengeance on—"

Folly! Lightning does not move more quickly than my Conscience did! He darted aloft so suddenly that in the moment my fingers clutched the empty air he was already perched on the top of the high book-case, with his thumb at his nose in token of derision. I flung the poker at him, and missed. I fired the bootjack. In a blind rage I flew from place to place, and snatched and hurled any missile that came handy; the storm of books, inkstands, and chunks of coal gloomed the air and beat about the manikin's perch relentlessly, but all to no purpose; the nimble figure dodged every shot; and not only that, but burst into a cackle of sarcastic and triumphant laughter as I sat down exhausted. While I puffed and gasped with fatigue and excitement, my Conscience talked to this effect:

"My good slave, you are curiously witless—no, I mean characteristically so. In truth, you are always consistent, always yourself, always an ass. Otherwise it must have occurred to you that if you attempted this murder with a sad heart and a heavy conscience, I would droop under the burdening influence instantly. Fool, I should have weighed a ton, and could not have budged from the floor; but instead, you are so cheerfully anxious to kill me that your conscience is as light as a feather; hence I am away up here out of your reach. I can almost respect a mere ordinary sort of fool; but *you*—pah!"

I would have given anything, then, to be heavy-hearted, so that I could get this person down from there and take his life, but I could no more be heavy-hearted over such a desire than I could have sorrowed over its accomplishment. So I could only look longingly up at my master, and rave at the ill-luck that denied me a heavy conscience the one only time that I had ever wanted such a thing in my life. By and by I got to musing over the hour's strange adventure, and of course my human curiosity began to work. I set myself to framing in my mind some questions for this fiend to answer. Just then one of my boys entered, leaving the door open behind him, and exclaimed—

"My! what *has* been going on, here? The bookcase is all one riddle of—"

I sprang up in consternation, and shouted—

"Out of this! Hurry! Jump! Fly! Shut the door! Quick, or my Conscience will get away!"

The door slammed to, and I locked it. I glanced up and was grateful, to the bottom of my heart, to see that my owner was still my prisoner. I said—

"Hang you, I might have lost you! Children are the heedlessest creatures. But look here, friend, the boy did not seem to notice you at all; how is that?"

"For a very good reason. I am invisible to all but you."

I made mental note of that piece of information with a good deal of satisfaction. I could kill this miscreant now, if I got a chance, and no one would know it. But this very reflection made me so light-hearted that my Conscience could hardly keep his seat, but was like to float aloft toward the ceiling like a toy balloon. I said, presently—

"Come, my Conscience, let us be friendly. Let us fly a flag of truce for a while. I am suffering to ask you some questions."

"Very well. Begin."

"Well, then, in the first place, why were you never visible to me before?"

"Because you never asked to see me before; that is, you never asked in the right spirit and the proper form before. You were just in the right spirit this time, and when you called for your most pitiless enemy I was that person by a very large majority, though you did not suspect it."

"Well, did that remark of mine turn you into flesh and blood?"

"No. It only made me visible to you. I am unsubstantial, just as other spirits are."

This remark prodded me with a sharp misgiving. If he was unsubstantial, how was I going to kill him? But I dissembled, and said persuasively—

"Conscience, it isn't sociable of you to keep at such a distance. Come down and take another smoke."

This was answered with a look that was full of derision, and with this observation added:

"Come where you can get at me and kill me? The invitation is declined with thanks."

"All right," said I to myself; "so it seems a spirit *can* be killed, after all; there will be one spirit lacking in this world, presently, or I lose my guess." Then I said aloud—

"Friend—"

"There; wait a bit. I am not your friend, I am your enemy; I am not your equal, I am your master. Call me 'my lord,' if you please. You are too familiar."

"I don't like such titles. I am willing to call you *sir.* That is as far as—"

"We will have no argument about this. Just obey; that is all. Go on with your chatter."

"Very well, my lord—since nothing but my lord will suit you—I was going to ask you how long you will be visible to me?"

"Always!"

I broke out with strong indignation: "This is simply an outrage. That is what I think of it. You have dogged, and dogged, and *dogged* me, all the days of my life, invisible. That was misery enough; now to have such a looking thing as you tagging after me like another shadow all the rest of my days is an intolerable prospect. You have my opinion, my lord; make the most of it."

"My lad, there was never so pleased a conscience in this world as I was when you made me visible. It gives me an inconceivable advantage. *Now,* I can look you straight in the eye, and call you names, and leer at you, jeer at you, sneer at you; and *you* know what eloquence there is in visible gesture and expression, more especially when the effect is heightened by audible speech. I shall always address you henceforth in your o-w-n s-n-i-v-e-l-l-i-n-g d-r-a-w-l—baby!"

I let fly with the coal-hod. No result. My lord said—

"Come, come! Remember the flag of truce!"

"Ah, I forgot that. I will try to be civil; and *you* try it, too, for a novelty. The idea of a *civil* conscience! It is a good joke; an excellent joke. All the consciences *I* have ever heard of were nagging, badgering, fault-finding, execrable savages! Yes; and always in a sweat about some poor little insignificant trifle or other—destruction catch the lot of them, *I* say! I would trade mine for the small-pox and seven kinds of consumption, and be glad of the chance. Now tell me, why *is* it that a conscience can't haul a man over the coals once, for an offence, and then let him alone? Why is it that it wants to keep on pegging at him, day and night and night and day, week in and week out, forever and ever, about the same old thing? There is no sense in that, and no reason in it. I think a conscience that will act like that is meaner than the very dirt itself."

"Well, *we* like it; that suffices."

"Do you do it with the honest intent to improve a man?"

That question produced a sarcastic smile, and this reply:

"No, sir. Excuse me. We do it simply because it is 'business.' It is our trade. The *purpose* of it *is* to improve the man, but *we* are merely disinterested agents. We are appointed by authority, and haven't anything to say in the matter. We obey orders and leave the consequences where they belong. But I am willing to admit this much: we *do* crowd the orders a trifle when we get a chance, which is most of the time. We enjoy it. We are instructed to remind a man a few times of an error; and I don't mind acknowledging that we try to give pretty good measure. And when we get hold of a man of a peculiarly sensitive nature, oh, but we do haze him! I have known consciences to come all the way from China and Russia to see a person of that kind put through his paces, on a special occasion. Why, I knew a man of that sort who had accidentally crippled a mulatto baby; the news went abroad, and I wish you may never commit another sin if the consciences didn't flock from all over the earth to enjoy the fun and help his master exercise him. That man walked the floor in torture for forty-eight hours, without eating or sleeping, and then blew his brains out. The child was perfectly well again in three weeks."

"Well, you are a precious crew, not to put it too strong. I think I begin to see, now, why you have always been a trifle inconsistent with me. In your anxiety to get all the juice you can out of a sin, you make a man repent of it in three or four different ways. For instance, you found fault with me for lying to that tramp, and I suffered over that. But it was only yesterday that I told a tramp the square truth, to wit, that, it being regarded as bad citizenship to encourage vagrancy, I would give him nothing. What did you do *then?* Why, you made me say to myself, 'Ah, it would have been so much kinder and more blameless to ease him off with a little white lie, and send him away feeling that if he could not have bread, the gentle treatment was at least something to be grateful for!' Well, I suffered all day about *that.* Three days before, I had fed a tramp, and fed him freely, supposing it a virtuous act. Straight off you said, 'O false citizen, to have fed a tramp!' and I suffered as usual. I gave a tramp work; you objected to it—*after* the contract was made, of course; you never speak up beforehand. Next, I *refused* a tramp work; you objected to *that.* Next, I proposed to kill a tramp; you kept me awake all night, oozing remorse at every pore. Sure I was going to be right *this* time, I sent the next tramp away with my benediction; and I wish you may live as long as I do, if you didn't make me smart all night again because I didn't kill him. Is there *any* way of satisfying that malignant invention which is called a conscience?"

"Ha, ha! this is luxury! Go on!"

"But come, now, answer me that question. *Is* there any way?"

"Well, none that I propose to tell *you,* my son. Ass! I don't care *what* act you may turn your hand to, I can straightway whisper a word in your ear and make you think you have committed a dreadful meanness. It is my *business*—and my joy—to make you repent of *every*thing you do. If I have fooled away any opportunities it was not intentional; I beg to assure you it was not intentional!"

"Don't worry; you haven't missed a trick that *I* know of. I never did a thing in all my life, virtuous or otherwise, that I didn't repent of within twenty-four hours. In church last Sunday I listened to a charity sermon. My first impulse was to give three hundred and fifty dollars; I repented of that and reduced it a hundred; repented of that and reduced it another hundred; repented of that and reduced it another hundred; repented of that and reduced the remaining fifty to twenty-five; repented of that and came down to fifteen; repented of that and dropped to two dollars and a half; when the plate came around at last, I repented once more and contributed ten cents. Well, when I got home, I did wish to goodness I had that ten cents back again! You never *did* let me get through a charity sermon without having something to sweat about."

"Oh, and I never shall, I never shall. You can always depend on me."

"I think so. Many and many's the restless night I've wanted to take you by the neck. If I could only get hold of you now!"

"Yes, no doubt. But I am not an ass; I am only the saddle of an ass. But go on, go on. You entertain me more than I like to confess."

"I am glad of that. (You will not mind my lying a little, to keep in practice.) Look here; not to be too personal, I think you are about the shabbiest and most contemptible little shrivelled-up reptile that can be imagined. I am grateful enough that you are invisible to other people, for I should die with shame to be seen with such a mildewed monkey of a conscience as *you* are. Now if you were five or six feet high, and—"

"Oh, come! who is to blame?"

"*I* don't know."

"Why, you are; nobody else."

"Confound you, I wasn't consulted about your personal appearance."

"I don't care, you had a good deal to do with it, nevertheless. When you were eight or nine years old, I was seven feet high, and as pretty as a picture."

"I wish you had died young! So you have grown the wrong way, have you?"

"Some of us grow one way and some the other. You had a large conscience once; if you've a small conscience now, I reckon there are reasons for it. However, both of us are to blame, you and I. You see, you used to be conscientious about a great many things; morbidly so, I may say. It was a great many years ago. You probably do not remember it, now. Well, I took a great interest in my work, and I so enjoyed the anguish which certain pet sins of yours afflicted you with, that I kept pelting at you until I rather overdid the matter. You began to rebel. Of course I began to lose ground, then, and shrivel a little— diminish in stature, get mouldy, and grow deformed. The more I weakened, the more stubbornly you fastened on to those particular sins; till at last the places on my person that represent those vices became as callous as shark skin. Take smoking, for instance. I played that card a little too long, and I lost. When people plead with you at this late day to quit that vice, that old callous place seems to enlarge and cover me all over like a shirt of mail. It exerts a mysterious, smothering effect; and presently I, your faithful hater, your devoted Conscience, go sound asleep! Sound? It is no name for it. I couldn't hear it thunder at such a time. You have some few other vices—perhaps eighty, or maybe ninety—that affect me in much the same way."

"This is flattering; you must be asleep a good part of your time."

"Yes, of late years. I should be asleep *all* the time, but for the help I get."

"Who helps you?"

"Other consciences. Whenever a person whose conscience I am acquainted with tries to plead with you about the vices you are callous to, I get my friend to give his client a pang concerning some villany of his own, and that shuts off his meddling and starts him off to hunt personal consolation. My field of usefulness is about trimmed down to tramps; budding authoresses, and that line of goods, now; but don't you worry—I'll harry you on *them* while they last! Just you put your trust in me."

"I think I can. But if you had only been good enough to mention these facts some thirty years ago, I should have turned my particular attention to sin, and I think that by this time I should not only have had you pretty permanently asleep on the entire list of human vices, but reduced to the size of a homoeopathic pill, at that. That is about the style of conscience *I* am pining for. If I only had you shrunk down to a homoeopathic pill, and could get my hands on you, would I put you in a glass case for a keepsake? No, sir. I would give you to a yellow dog! That is where *you* ought to be—you and all your tribe. You are not fit to be in society, in my opinion. Now another question. Do you know a good many consciences in this section?"

"Plenty of them."

"I would give anything to see some of them! Could you bring them here? And would they be visible to me?"

"Certainly not."

"I suppose I ought to have known that, without asking. But no matter, you can describe them. Tell me about my neighbor Thompson's conscience, please."

"Very well. I know him intimately; have known him many years. I knew him when he was eleven feet high and of a faultless figure. But he is very rusty and tough and misshapen, now, and hardly ever interests himself about anything. As to his present size—well, he sleeps in a cigar box."

"Likely enough. There are few smaller, meaner men in this region than Hugh Thompson. Do you know Robinson's conscience?"

"Yes. He is a shade under four and a half feet high; used to be a blonde; is a brunette, now, but still shapely and comely."

"Well, Robinson is a good fellow. Do you know Tom Smith's conscience?"

"I have known him from childhood. He was thirteen inches high, and rather sluggish, when he was two years old—as nearly all of us are, at that age. He is thirty-seven feet high, now, and the stateliest figure in America. His legs are still racked with growing-pains, but he has a good time, nevertheless. Never sleeps. He is the most active and energetic member of the New England Conscience Club; is president of it. Night and day you can find him pegging away at Smith, panting with his labor, sleeves rolled up, countenance all alive with enjoyment. He has got his victim splendidly dragooned, now. He can make poor Smith imagine that the most innocent little thing he does is an odious sin; and then he sets to work and almost tortures the soul out of him about it."

"Smith is the noblest man in all this section, and the purest; and yet is always breaking his heart because he cannot be good! Only a conscience *could* find pleasure in heaping agony upon a spirit like that. Do you know my aunt Mary's conscience?"

"I have seen her at a distance, but am not acquainted with her. She lives in the open air altogether, because no door is large enough to admit her."

"I can believe that. Let me see. Do you know the conscience of that publisher who once stole some sketches of mine for a 'series' of his, and then left me to pay the law expenses I had to incur in order to choke him off?"

"Yes. He has a wide fame. He was exhibited, a month ago, with some other antiquities, for the benefit of a recent Member of the Cabinet's conscience, that was starving in exile. Tickets and fares were high, but I travelled for nothing by pretending to be the conscience of an editor, and got in for half price by representing myself to be the conscience of a clergyman. However, the publisher's conscience, which was to have been the main feature of the entertainment, was a failure—as an exhibition. He was there, but what of that? The management had provided a microscope with a magnifying power of only thirty thousand diameters, and so nobody got to see him, after all. There was great and general dissatisfaction, of course, but—"

Just here there was an eager footstep on the stair; I opened the door, and my aunt Mary burst into the room. It was a joyful meeting, and a cheery bombardment of questions and answers concerning family matters ensued. By and by my aunt said—

"But I am going to abuse you a little now. You promised me, the day I saw you last, that you would look after the needs of the poor family around the corner as faithfully as I had done it myself. Well, I found out by accident that you failed your promise. *Was* that right?"

In simple truth, I never had thought of that family a second time! And now such a splintering pang of guilt shot through me! I glanced up at my Conscience. Plainly, my heavy heart was affecting him. His body was drooping forward; he seemed about to fall from the bookcase. My aunt continued:

"And think how you have neglected my poor *protégée* at the almshouse, you dear, hard-hearted promise-breaker!" I blushed scarlet, and my tongue was tied. As the sense of my guilty negligence waxed sharper and stronger, my Conscience began to sway heavily back and forth; and when my aunt, after a little pause, said in a grieved tone, 'Since you never once went to see her, maybe it will not distress you now to know that that poor child died, months ago, utterly friendless and forsaken!' my Conscience could no longer bear up under the weight of my sufferings, but tumbled headlong from his high perch and struck the floor with a dull, leaden thump. He lay there writhing with pain and quaking with apprehension, but straining every muscle in frantic efforts to get up. In a fever of expectancy I sprang to the door, locked it, placed my back against it, and bent a watchful gaze upon my struggling master. Already my fingers were itching to begin their murderous work.

"Oh, what *can* be the matter!" exclaimed my aunt, shrinking from me, and following with her frightened eyes the direction of mine. My breath was coming in short, quick gasps now, and my excitement was almost uncontrollable. My aunt cried out—

"Oh, do not look so! You appall me! Oh, what can the matter be?

What is it you see? Why do you stare so? Why do you work your fingers like that?"

"Peace, woman!" I said, in a hoarse whisper. "Look elsewhere; pay no attention to me; it is nothing—nothing. I am often this way. It will pass in a moment. It comes from smoking too much."

My injured lord was up, wild-eyed with terror, and trying to hobble toward the door. I could hardly breathe, I was so wrought up. My aunt wrung her hands, and said—

"Oh, I knew how it would be; I knew it would come to this at last! Oh, I implore you to crush out that fatal habit while it may yet be time! You must not, you shall not be deaf to my supplications longer!" My struggling Conscience showed sudden signs of weariness! "Oh, promise me you will throw off this hateful slavery of tobacco!" My Conscience began to reel drowsily, and grope with his hands—enchanting spectacle! "I beg you, I beseech you, I implore you! Your reason is deserting you! There is madness in your eye! It flames with frenzy! Oh, hear me, hear me, and be saved! See, I plead with you on my very knees!" As she sank before me my Conscience reeled again, and then drooped languidly to the floor, blinking toward me a last supplication for mercy, with heavy eyes. "Oh, promise, or you are lost! Promise, and be redeemed! Promise! Promise and live!" With a long-drawn sigh my conquered Conscience closed his eyes and fell fast asleep!

With an exultant shout I sprang past my aunt, and in an instant I had my life-long foe by the throat. After so many years of waiting and longing, he was mine at last. I tore him to shreds and fragments. I rent the fragments to bits. I cast the bleeding rubbish into the fire, and drew into my nostrils the grateful incense of my burnt-offering. At last, and forever, my Conscience was dead!

I was a free man! I turned upon my poor aunt, who was almost petrified with terror, and shouted—

"Out of this with your paupers, your charities, your reforms, your pestilent morals! You behold before you a man whose life-conflict is done, whose soul is at peace; a man whose heart is dead to sorrow, dead to suffering, dead to remorse; a man WITHOUT A CONSCIENCE! In my joy I spare you, though I could throttle you and never feel a pang! Fly!"

She fled. Since that day my life is all bliss Bliss, unalloyed bliss. Nothing in all the world could persuade me to have a conscience again. I settled all my old outstanding scores, and began the world anew. I killed thirty-eight persons during the first two weeks—all of them on account of ancient grudges. I burned a dwelling that interrupted my view. I swindled a widow and some orphans out of their last cow, which is a very good one, though not thoroughbred, I believe. I have also committed scores of crimes, of various kinds, and have enjoyed my work exceedingly, whereas it would formerly have broken my heart and turned my hair gray, I have no doubt.

In conclusion I wish to state, by way of advertisement, that medical colleges desiring assorted tramps for scientific purposes, either by the gross, by cord measurement, or per ton, will do well to examine the lot in my cellar before purchasing elsewhere, as these were all selected and prepared by myself, and can be had at a low rate, because I wish to clear out my stock and get ready for the spring trade.

The Woman
Who Thought
She Could Read

Avram Davidson

Avram Davidson's ironic fantasies are treasures. He is a modern master, author of such novels as The Phoenix and the Mirror *and the classic chronicles of Dr. Ezsterhazy. His stories have been praised by such luminaries as fantasy authors Peter S. Beagle and Damon Knight for being perhaps the best of all contemporary fantasies. He characteristically juxtaposes the supernatural or the magical with the naturalistic and gritty reality of contemporary life. This is a story about losing magic but it is still, somehow, an affirmation of wonder. One wants magic to redeem us. But the world stacks the deck against us and the magic is sometimes inadequate to the task in the face of common ignorance. This story offers an interesting contrast to Anne McCaffrey's "A Proper Santa Claus" (pp.183–91).*

About a hundred years ago a man named Vanderhorn built the little house. He built it one and a half stories high, with attached and detached sheds snuggling around it as usual; and he covered it with clapboards cut at his own mill—he had a small sawmill down at the creek, Mr. Vanderhorn did. After that he lived in the little house with his daughter and her husband (being a widower man) and one day he died there. So the daughter and son-in-law, a Mr. Hooten or Wooten or whatever it was, they came into his money which he made out of musket stocks for the Civil War, and they built a big new house next to the old one, only further back from the street. This Mr. Wooten or

Hooten or something like that, *he* didn't have any sons, either; and *his* son-in-law turned the sawmill into a buggy factory. Well, you know what happened to *that* business! Finally, a man named Carmichael, who made milk wagons and baggage carts and piewagons, he bought the whole Vanderhorn estate. He fixed up the big house and put in apartments, and finally he sold it to my father and went out of business. Moved away somewhere.

I was just a little boy when we moved in. My sister was a lot older. The *old* Vanderhorn house wasn't part of the property any more. A lady named Mrs. Grummick was living there and Mr. Carmichael had sold her all the property the width of her house from the street on back to the next lot which faced the street behind ours. I heard my father say it was one of the narrowest lots in the city, and it was separated from ours by a picket fence. In the front of the old house was an old weeping willow tree and a big lilac bush like a small tree. In back were a truck garden and a few flowerbeds. Mrs. Grummick's house was so near to our property that I could look right into her window, and one day I did, and she was sorting beans.

Mrs. Grummick looked out and smiled at me. She had one of those broad faces with high cheekbones, and when she smiled her little bright black eyes almost disappeared.

"Liddle boy, hello!" she said. I said Hello and went right on staring, and she went right on sorting her beans. On her head was a kerchief (you have to remember that this was before they became fashionable) and there was a tiny gold earring in each plump earlobe. The beans were in two crocks on the table and in a pile in front of her. She was moving them around and sorting them into little groups. There were more crocks on the shelves, and glass jars, and bundles of herbs and strings of onions and peppers and bunches of garlic all hanging around the room. I looked through the room and out the window facing the street and there was a sign in front of the little house, hanging on a sort of one-armed gallows. *Anastasia Grummick, Midwife,* it said.

"What's a midwife?" I asked her.

"Me," she said. And she went on pushing the beans around, lining them up in rows, taking some from one place and putting them in another.

"Have you got any children, Mrs. Grimmick?"

"One. I god one boy. *Big* boy." She laughed.

"Where is he?"

"I think he come home today. I *know* he come home today." Her head bobbed.

"How do you know?"

"I know because I know. He come home and I make a bean soup for him. You want go errand for me?"

"All right." She stood up and pulled a little change purse out of her apron pocket, and counted out some money and handed it to me out of the window.

'Tell butcher Mrs. Grummick want him to cut some meat for a bean soup. He knows. Mr. Schloutz. And you ged iche-cream comb with nickel, for you."

I started to go, but she gave me another nickel. "Ged *two* iche-cream combs. I ead one, too." She laughed. "One, too. One, two three—Oh, Englisht languish!" Then she went back to the table, put part of the beans back in the crocks, and swept the rest of them into her apron. I got the meat for her and ate my French vanilla and then went off to play.

A few hours later a taxicab stopped in front of the little gray house and a man got out of it. A big fellow. Of course, to a kid, all grown-ups are real big, but he was *very* big—tremendous, he was, across, but not so tall. Mrs. Grummick came to the door.

"Eddie!" she said. And they hugged and kissed, so I decided this was her son, even before he called her "Mom."

"Mom," he said, "do I smell bean soup?"

"Just for you I make it," she said.

He laughed. "You knew I was coming, huh? You been reading them old beans again, Mom?" And they went into the house to-gether.

I went home, thinking. My mother was doing something over the washtub with a ball of bluing. "Mama," I said, "can a person read beans?"

"Did you take your milk of magnesia?" my mother asked. Just as if I hadn't spoken. "Did you?"

I decided to bluff it out. "Uh-huh," I said.

"Oh *no* you didn't. Get me a spoon."

"Well, why do you ask if you ain't going to believe me?"

"Open up," she ordered. "More. Swallow it. Take the rest. All of it. If you could see your face! Suppose it froze and stayed like that? Go and wash the spoon off."

Next morning Eddie was down in the far end of the garden with a hoe. He had his shirt off. Talk about shoulders! Talk about arms! Talk about a chest! My mother was out in front of our house, which made her near Eddie's mother out in back of hers. Of course my mother had to know everybody's business.

"That your son, Mrs. Grummick?"

"My son, yes."

"What does he do for a living?"

"Rachel."

"No, I mean your *son* . . . what does he do. . . ."

"He rachel. All over country. I show you."

She showed us a picture of a man in trunks with a hood over his head. "The Masked Marvel! Wrestling's Greatest Mystery!" The shoulders, arms, and chest—they could only have been Eddie's. There were other pictures of him in bulging poses, with names like, oh, The Slav Slayer, Chief Thunderwing, Young Kehoe, and so on. Every month Eddie Grummick sent his mother another photograph. It was the only kind of letter he sent because she didn't know how to read English. Or any other language, for that matter.

Back in the vegetable patch Eddie started singing a very popular song at that time, called "I Faw Down And Go *Boom!*"

It was a hot summer that year, a long hot summer, and September was just as hot as July. One shimmering, blazing day Mrs. Grummick called my father over. He had his shirt off and was sitting under our tree in his BVD top. We were drinking lemonade.

"When I was a kid," he said, "we used to make lemonade with brown sugar and sell it in the streets. We used to call out

> Brown lemonade
> Mixed in the shade
> Stirred by an old maid.

"People used to think that was pretty funny."

Mrs. Grummick called out: "Hoo-hoo! Mister! Hoo-hoo!"

"Guess she wants *me*," my father said. He went across the lawn. "Yes ma'am . . ." he was saying. "Yes ma'am."

She asked, "You buy coal yed, mister?"

"*Coal?* Why, no-o-o . . . not *yet*. Looks like a pretty mild winter ahead, wouldn't you say?"

She pressed her lips together, closed her eyes and shook her head.

"No! Bedder you buy soon coal. Lots coal. Comes very soon bad wedder. Bad!"

My father scratched his head. "Why, you sound pretty certain, Mrs. Grummick, but—uh—"

"I *know*, mister. If I say id, if I tell you, I *know*."

Then I piped up and asked, "Did you read it in the beans, Mrs. Grummick?"

"Hey!" She looked at me, surprised. "How you know, liddle boy?"

My father said, "You mean you can tell a bad winter is coming from the *beans?*"

"Iss true. I know. I read id."

"*Well*, now, that's very interesting. Where I come from, used to be a man—a weather prophet, they called him—*he* used to predict the weather by studying skunk stripes. Said his grandfather'd learned it from the Indians. How wide this year, how wide last year. Never failed. So you use beans?"

So I pushed my oar in and I said, "I guess you don't have the kind of beans that the man gave Jack for the cow and he planted them and they were all different colors. Well, a beanstalk grew way way up and he climbed—"

Father said, "Now don't bother Mrs. Grummick, sonny," but she leaned over the fence and picked me up and set me down on her side of it.

"You, liddle boy, come in house and tell me. You, mister: buy coal."

Mrs. Grummick gave me a glass of milk from the nanny goat who lived in one of the sheds, and a piece of gingerbread, and I told her the story of Jack and the beanstalk. Here's a funny thing—she believed it. I'm sure she did. It wasn't even what the kids call Making Believe, it was just a pure and simple belief. Then she told *me* a story. This happened on the other side, in some backwoods section of Europe where she came from. In this place they used to teach the boys to read, but not the girls. They figured, what did they need it for? So one day there was this little girl, her brothers were all off in school and she was left at home sorting beans. She was supposed to pick out all the bad beans and the worms, and when she thought about it and about everything, she began to cry.

Suddenly the little girl looked up and there was this old woman.

She asked the kid how come she was crying. Because all the boys can learn to read, but not me. Is *that* all? the old lady asked.

Don't cry, she said. *I'll* teach you how to read, only not in books, the old lady said. Let the *men* read books, books are new things, people could read before there were books. Books tell you what *was*, but you'll be able to tell you what's *going* to be. And this old lady taught the little girl how to read the beans instead of the books. And I kind of have a notion that Mrs. Grummick said something about how they once used to read *bones*, but maybe it was just her accent and she meant beans. . . .

And you know, it's a funny thing, but, now, if you look at dried beans, you'll notice how each one is maybe a little different shape or maybe the wrinkles are a little different. But I was thinking that, after all, an "A" is an "A" even if it's big or small or twisted or. . . .

But that was the story Mrs. Grummick told me. So it isn't remarkable, if she could believe *that* story, she could easily believe the Jack and the Beanstalk one. But the funny thing was, all that hot weather just vanished one day suddenly, and from October until almost April we had what you might call an ironbound winter. Terrible blizzards one right after another. The rivers were frozen and the canals were frozen and even the railroads weren't running and the roads were blocked more than they were open. And coal? Why, you just couldn't *get* coal. People were freezing to death right and left. But Mrs. Grummick's little house was always warm and it smelled real nice with all those herbs and dried flowers and stuff hanging around in it.

A few years later my sister got married. And after that, in the summertime, she and her husband Jim used to come back and visit with us. Jim and I used to play ball and we had a fine time—they didn't have any children, so they made much of me. I'll always remember those happy summers.

Well, you know, each summer, a few of the churches used to get together and charter a boat and run an excursion. All the young couples used to go, but my sister always made some excuse. See, she was always afraid of the water. This particular summer the same thing happened, but her friends urged her to come. My brother-in-law, he didn't care one way or the other. And then, with all the joking, someone said, Let's ask Mrs. Grummick to read it in the beans for us. It had gotten known, you see. Everybody laughed, and more for the fun of it than anything else, I suppose, they went over and spoke to her. She said that Sister and Jim could come inside, but there wasn't room for anybody else. So we watched through the window.

Mrs. Grummick spread her beans on the table and began to shove them around here and there with her fingers. Some she put to one side and the rest she little by little lined up in rows. Then she took from one row and added to another row and changed some around from one spot to another. And meanwhile, mind you, she was muttering to herself, for all the world like one of these old people who reads by putting his finger on each word and mumbling it. And what was the answer?

"Don't go by the water."

And that was all. Well, like I say, my sister was just looking for any excuse at all, and Jim didn't care. So the day of the excursion they went off on a picnic by car. I'd like to have gone, but I guess they sort of wanted to be by themselves a bit and Jim gave me a quarter and I went to the movies and bought ice-cream and soda.

I came out and the first thing I saw was a boy my own age, by the name of Bill Baumgardner, running down the street crying. His shirt was out and his nose was running and he kept up an awful grinding kind of howl. I called to him but he paid no attention. I still don't know where he was running from or where to and I guess maybe he didn't know either. Because he'd been told, by some old fool who should've known better, that the excursion boat had caught on fire, with his parents on it. The news swept through town and almost everybody with folks on the boat was soon in as bad a state as poor Billy.

First they said everybody was burned or drowned or trampled. Later on it turned out to be not that bad—but it was bad enough.

Oh, my folks were shook up, sure enough, but it's easier to be calm when you know it's not your own flesh and blood. I recall hearing the church clock striking six and my mother saying, "I'll never laugh at Mrs. Grummick again as long as I live." Well, she never did.

Almost everyone who had people on the boat went up the river to where it had finally been run ashore, or else they waited by the police station for news. There was a deaf lady on our street, I guess her daughter got tired of its being so dull at home and she'd lied to her mother, told her she was going riding in the country with a friend. So when the policeman came and told her—shouted at her they'd pulled out the girl's body, she didn't know what he was talking about. And when she finally understood she began to scream and scream and scream.

The policeman came over toward us and my mother said, "I'd better get over there," and she started out. He was just a young policeman and his face was pale. He held up his hand and shook his head. Mother stopped and he came over. I could hear how hard he was breathing. Then he mentioned Jim's name.

"Oh, no," my mother said, very quickly. "They didn't *go* on the boat." He started to say something and she interrupted him and said, "But I tell you, they didn't *go*—" and she looked around, kind of frantically, as if wishing someone would come and send the policeman away.

But no one did. We had to hear him out. It was Sister and Jim, all right. A big truck had gotten out of control ("—but they didn't go on the boat," my mother kept repeating, kind of stupidly. "They had this warning and so—") and smashed into their car. It fell off the road into the canal. The police were called right away and they came and pulled it out. ("Oh, *oh!* Then they're all *right!*" my mother cried. *Then* she was willing to understand.) But they weren't all right. They'd been drowned.

So we forgot about the deaf neighbor lady because my mother, poor thing, *she* got hysterical. My father and the policeman helped her inside and after a while she just lay there on the couch, kind of moaning. The door opened and in tiptoed Mrs. Grummick. She had her lower lip tucked in under her teeth and her eyes were wide and she was kind of rocking her head from side to side. In each hand she held a little bottle—smelling salts, maybe, and some kind of cordial. I was glad to see her and I think my father was. I *know* the policeman was, because he blew out his cheeks, nodded very quickly to my father, and went away.

Mother said, in a weak, thin voice: "They didn't go on the boat. They didn't go because they had a warning. That's why—" Then she saw Mrs. Grummick. The color came back to her face and she just leaped off the couch and tried to hit Mrs. Grummick, and she yelled at her in a hoarse voice I'd never heard and called her names—the kind of names I was just beginning to find out what they meant. I was, I think, more shocked and stunned to hear my mother use them than I was at the news that Sister and Jim were dead.

Well, my father threw his arms around her and kept her from

reaching Mrs. Grummick and I remember I grabbed hold of one hand and how it tried to get away from me.

"You *knew!*" my mother shouted, struggling, her hair coming loose. "*You* knew! You read it there, you witch! And you didn't tell! You didn't tell! She'd be alive now if she'd gone on the boat. They weren't all killed, on the boat— But you didn't say a *word!*"

Mrs. Grummick's mouth opened and she started to speak. She was so mixed up, I guess, that she spoke in her own language, and my mother screamed at her.

My father turned his head around and said, "You'd better get out."

Mrs. Grummick made a funny kind of noise in her throat. Then she said, "But, Lady—mister—no—I tell you only what I see—I read there, *'Don't go by the water.'* I only can say what I see in front of me, only what I read. Nothing else. Maybe it mean one thing or maybe another. I only can read it. Please, lady—"

But we knew we'd lost them, and it was because of her.

"They ask *me*," Mrs. Grummick said. "They *ask* me to read."

My mother kind of collapsed, sobbing. Father said, "Just get out of here. Just turn around and get out."

I heard a kid's voice saying, high, and kind of trembling, "We don't want you here, you old witch! *We hate you!*"

Well, it was *my* voice. And then her shoulders sagged and she looked for the first time like a real old woman. She turned around and shuffled away. At the door she stopped and half faced us. "I read no more," she said. "I never read more. Better not to know at all." And she went out.

Not long after the funeral we woke up one morning and the little house was empty. We never heard where the Grummicks went and it's only now that I begin to wonder about it and to think of it once again.

The Third Level

Jack Finney

Jack Finney was one of the premier fantasists of the 1950s. His stories appeared in all the leading magazines and the best were collected into two volumes, The Third Level *and* I Love Galesburg in the Springtime. *His novel* The Body Snatchers *was made twice into films called* Invasion of the Body Snatchers. *His finest novel,* Time and Again, *was published in the 1960s, and his novels still appear, but he has ceased writing short fiction in recent decades. Time and nostalgia are recurring interests in his fiction, and "The Third Level" is quintessential Finney, yearning for a utopia in the past and finding it in the midst of, at the center of, the contemporary world.*

The presidents of the New York Central and the New York, New Haven and Hartford railroads will swear on a stack of timetables that there are only two. But I say there are three, because I've *been* on the third level at Grand Central Station. Yes, I've taken the obvious step: I talked to a psychiatrist friend of mine, among others. I told him about the third level at Grand Central Station, and he said it was a waking-dream wish fulfillment. He said I was unhappy. That made my wife kind of mad, but he explained that he meant the modern world is full of insecurity, fear, war, worry and all the rest of it, and that I just want to escape. Well, hell, who doesn't? Everybody I know wants to escape, but they don't wander down into any third level at Grand Central Station.

But that's the reason, he said, and my friends all agreed. Everything points to it, they claimed. My stamp collecting, for example; that's a "temporary refuge from reality." Well, maybe, but my grandfather didn't need any refuge from reality; things were pretty nice and peaceful in his day, from all I hear, and he started my collection. It's a nice collection, too, blocks of four of practically every U. S. issue, first-day covers, and so on. President Roosevelt collected stamps, too, you know.

Anyway, here's what happened at Grand Central. One night last summer I worked late at the office. I was in a hurry to get uptown to my apartment so I decided to take the subway from Grand Central because it's faster than the bus.

Now, I don't know why this should have happened to me. I'm just an ordinary guy named Charley, thirty-one years old, and I was wearing a tan gabardine suit and a straw hat with a fancy band; I passed a dozen men who looked just like me. And I wasn't trying to escape from anything; I just wanted to get home to Louisa, my wife.

I turned into Grand Central from Vanderbilt Avenue, and went down the steps to the first level, where you take trains like the Twentieth Century. Then I walked down another flight to the second level, where the suburban trains leave from, ducked into an arched doorway heading for the subway—and got lost. That's easy to do. I've been in and out of Grand Central hundreds of times, but I'm always bumping into new doorways and stairs and corridors. Once I got into a tunnel about a mile long and came out in the lobby of the Roosevelt Hotel. Another time I came up in an office building on Forty-sixth Street, three blocks away.

Sometimes I think Grand Central is growing like a tree, pushing out new corridors and staircases like roots. There's probably a long tunnel that nobody knows about feeling its way under the city right now, on its way to Times Square, and maybe another to Central Park. And maybe—because for so many people through the years Grand Central *has* been an exit, a way of escape—maybe that's how the tunnel I got into . . . But I never told my psychiatrist friend about that idea.

The corridor I was in began angling left and slanting downward and I thought that was wrong, but I kept on walking. All I could hear was the empty sound of my own footsteps and I didn't pass a soul. Then I heard that sort of hollow roar ahead that means open space and people talking. The tunnel turned sharp left; I went down a short

flight of stairs and came out on the third level at Grand Central
Station. For just a moment I thought I was back on the second level,
but I saw the room was smaller, there were fewer ticket windows and
train gates, and the information booth in the center was wood and
old-looking. And the man in the booth wore a green eyeshade and
long black sleeve protectors. The lights were dim and sort of flickering. Then I saw why; they were open-flame gaslights.

There were brass spittoons on the floor, and across the station a
glint of light caught my eye; a man was pulling a gold watch from his
vest pocket. He snapped open the cover, glanced at his watch, and
frowned. He wore a derby hat, a black four-button suit with tiny
lapels, and he had a big, black, handle-bar mustache. Then I looked
around and saw that everyone in the station was dressed like eight-
een-ninety-something; I never saw so many beards, sideburns and
fancy mustaches in my life. A woman walked in through the train
gate; she wore a dress with leg-of-mutton sleeves and skirts to the top
of her high-buttoned shoes. Back of her, out on the tracks, I caught a
glimpse of a locomotive, a very small Currier & Ives locomotive with
a funnel-shaped stack. And then I knew.

To make sure, I walked over to a newsboy and glanced at the stack
of papers at his feet. It was The *World;* and The *World* hasn't been
published for years. The lead story said something about President
Cleveland. I've found that front page since, in the Public Library
files, and it was printed June 11, 1894.

I turned toward the ticket windows knowing that here—on the
third level at Grand Central—I could buy tickets that would take
Louisa and me anywhere in the United States we wanted to go. In the
year 1894. And I wanted two tickets to Galesburg, Illinois.

Have you ever been there? It's a wonderful town still, with big old
frame houses, huge lawns and tremendous trees whose branches
meet overhead and roof the streets. And in 1894, summer evenings
were twice as long, and people sat out on their lawns, the men smoking cigars and talking quietly, the women waving palm-leaf fans, with
the fireflies all around, in a peaceful world. To be back there with the
First World War still twenty years off, and World War II over forty
years in the future . . . I wanted two tickets for that.

The clerk figured the fare—he glanced at my fancy hatband, but he
figured the fare—and I had enough for two coach tickets, one way.
But when I counted out the money and looked up, the clerk was
staring at me. He nodded at the bills. "That ain't money, mister," he

said, "and if you're trying to skin me you won't get very far," and he glanced at the cash drawer beside him. Of course the money in his drawer was old-style bills, half again as big as the money we use nowadays, and different-looking. I turned away and got out fast. There's nothing nice about jail, even in 1894.

And that was that. I left the same way I came, I suppose. Next day, during lunch hour, I drew three hundred dollars out of the bank, nearly all we had, and bought old-style currency (that *really* worried my psychiatrist friend). You can buy old money at almost any coin dealer's but you have to pay a premium. My three hundred dollars bought less than two hundred in old-style bills, but I didn't care; eggs were thirteen cents a dozen in 1894.

But I've never again found the corridor that leads to the third level at Grand Central Station, although I've tried often enough.

Louisa was pretty worried when I told her all this, and didn't want me to look for the third level any more, and after a while I stopped; I went back to my stamps. But now we're *both* looking, every week end, because now we have proof that the third level is still there. My friend Sam Weiner disappeared! Nobody knew where, but I sort of suspected because Sam's a city boy, and I used to tell him about Galesburg—I went to school there—and he always said he liked the sound of the place. And that's where he is, all right. In 1894.

Because one night, fussing with my stamp collection, I found—well, do you know what a first-day cover is? When a new stamp is issued, stamp collectors buy some and use them to mail envelopes to themselves on the very first day of sale; and the postmark proves the date. The envelope is called a first-day cover. They're never opened; you just put blank paper in the envelope.

That night, among my oldest first-day covers, I found one that shouldn't have been there. But there it was. It was there because someone had mailed it to my grandfather at his home in Galesburg; that's what the address on the envelope said. And it had been there since July 18, 1894—the postmark showed that—yet I didn't remember it at all. The stamp was a six-cent, dull brown, with a picture of President Garfield. Naturally, when the envelope came to Granddad in the mail, it went right into his collection and stayed there—till I took it out and opened it.

The paper inside wasn't blank. It read:

> *941 Willard Street*
> *Galesburg, Illinois*
> *July 18, 1894*

Charley:

I got to wishing that you were right. Then I got to believing you were right. And, Charley, it's true; I found the third level! I've been here two weeks, and right now, down the street at the Daly's, someone is playing a piano, and they're all out on the front porch singing, "Seeing Nellie home." And I'm invited over for lemonade. Come on back, Charley and Louisa. Keep looking till you find the third level! It's worth it, believe me!

The note was signed *Sam.*

At the stamp and coin store I go to, I found out that Sam bought eight hundred dollars' worth of old-style currency. That ought to set him up in a nice little hay, feed and grain business; he always said that's what he really wished he could do, and he certainly can't go back to his old business. Not in Galesburg, Illinois, in 1894. His old business? Why, Sam was my psychiatrist.

Creatures

Stories of strange and unusual
beasts and entities

The Griffin and the
Minor Canon

Frank R. Stockton

Frank R. Stockton (1834–1902) was one of the first popular American writers to collect his fantasy stories in a volume for adults (The Bee-Man of Orn). *Although the tales had initially been published in* St. Nicholas, *the best children's magazine of its time, Stockton chose to present them to adults in book form, thus participating in the evolution of fantasy fiction, out of the nursery forms into the adult fictions of our century. "The Griffin and the Minor Canon" is perhaps Stockton's masterpiece of fantasy, a charming, witty invention reminiscent of some pretty grim folktales. The fable has a moral force that is organic and does not seem in any way tacked on. And the griffin is not cute.*

Over the great door of an old, old church which stood in a quiet town of a far-away land there was carved in stone the figure of a large griffin. The old-time sculptor had done his work with great care, but the image he had made was not a pleasant one to look at. It had a large head, with enormous open mouth and savage teeth; from its back arose great wings, armed with sharp hooks and prongs; it had stout legs in front, with projecting claws; but there were no legs behind—the body running out into a long and powerful tail, finished off at the end with a barbed point. This tail was coiled up under him, the end sticking up just back of his wings.

The sculptor, or the people who had ordered this stone figure, had evidently been very much pleased with it, for little copies of it, also in stone, had been placed here and there along the sides of the church, not very far from the ground, so that people could easily look at them, and ponder on their curious forms. There were a great many other sculptures on the outside of this church—saints, martyrs, grotesque heads of men, beasts, and birds, as well as those of other creatures which cannot be named, because nobody knows exactly what they were; but none were so curious and interesting as the great griffin over the door, and the little griffins on the sides of the church.

A long, long distance from the town, in the midst of dreadful wilds scarcely known to man, there dwelt the Griffin whose image had been put up over the church-door. In some way or other, the old-time sculptor had seen him, and afterward, to the best of his memory, had copied his figure in stone. The Griffin had never known this, until, hundreds of years afterward, he heard from a bird, from a wild animal, or in some manner which it is not now easy to find out, that there was a likeness of him on the old church in the distant town. Now, this Griffin had no idea how he looked. He had never seen a mirror, and the streams where he lived were so turbulent and violent that a quiet piece of water, which would reflect the image of any thing looking into it, could not be found. Being, as far as could be ascertained, the very last of his race, he had never seen another griffin. Therefore it was, that, when he heard of this stone image of himself, he became very anxious to know what he looked like, and at last he determined to go to the old church, and see for himself what manner of being he was. So he started off from the dreadful wilds, and flew on and on until he came to the countries inhabited by men, where his appearance in the air created great consternation; but he alighted nowhere, keeping up a steady flight until he reached the suburbs of the town which had his image on its church. Here, late in the afternoon, he alighted in a green meadow by the side of a brook, and stretched himself on the grass to rest. His great wings were tired, for he had not made such a long flight in a century, or more.

The news of his coming spread quickly over the town, and the people, frightened nearly out of their wits by the arrival of so extraordinary a visitor, fled into their houses, and shut themselves up. The Griffin called loudly for some one to come to him, but the more he called, the more afraid the people were to show themselves. At length he saw two laborers hurrying to their homes through the fields, and in a terrible voice he commanded them to stop. Not daring to disobey, the men stood, trembling.

"What is the matter with you all?" cried the Griffin. "Is there not a man in your town who is brave enough to speak to me?"

"I think," said one of the laborers, his voice shaking so that his words could hardly be understood, "that—perhaps—the Minor Canon—would come."

"Go, call him, then!" said the Griffin; "I want to see him."

The Minor Canon, who filled a subordinate position in the old church, had just finished the afternoon services, and was coming out of a side door, with three aged women who had formed the week-day congregation. He was a young man with a kind disposition, and very anxious to do good to the people of the town. Apart from his duties in the church, where he conducted services every week-day, he visited the sick and the poor, counselled and assisted persons who were in trouble, and taught a school composed entirely of the bad children in the town with whom nobody else would have any thing to do. Whenever the people wanted something difficult done for them, they always went to the Minor Canon. Thus it was that the laborer thought of the young priest when he found that some one must come and speak to the Griffin.

The Minor Canon had not heard of the strange event, which was known to the whole town except himself and the three old women, and when he was informed of it, and was told that the Griffin had asked to see him, he was greatly amazed, and frightened.

"Me!" he exclaimed. "He has never heard of me! What should he want with *me?*"

"Oh! you must go instantly!" cried the two men. "He is very angry now because he has been kept waiting so long; and nobody knows what may happen if you don't hurry to him."

The poor Minor Canon would rather have had his hand cut off than go out to meet an angry griffin; but he felt that it was his duty to go, for it would be a woeful thing if injury should come to the people of the town because he was not brave enough to obey the summons of the Griffin. So, pale and frightened, he started off.

"Well," said the Griffin, as soon as the young man came near, "I am glad to see that there is some one who has the courage to come to me."

The Minor Canon did not feel very courageous, but he bowed his head.

"Is this the town," said the Griffin, "where there is a church with a likeness of myself over one of the doors?"

The Minor Canon looked at the frightful creature before him and saw that it was, without doubt, exactly like the stone image on the church. "Yes," he said, "you are right."

"Well, then," said the Griffin, "will you take me to it? I wish very much to see it."

The Minor Canon instantly thought that if the Griffin entered the town without the people knowing what he came for, some of them would probably be frightened to death, and so he sought to gain time to prepare their minds.

"It is growing dark, now," he said, very much afraid, as he spoke, that his words might enrage the Griffin, "and objects on the front of the church can not be seen clearly. It will be better to wait until morning, if you wish to get a good view of the stone image of yourself."

"That will suit me very well," said the Griffin. "I see you are a man of good sense. I am tired, and I will take a nap here on this soft grass, while I cool my tail in the little stream that runs near me. The end of my tail gets red-hot when I am angry or excited, and it is quite warm now. So you may go, but be sure and come early to-morrow morning, and show me the way to the church."

The Minor Canon was glad enough to take his leave, and hurried into the town. In front of the church he found a great many people assembled to hear his report of his interview with the Griffin. When they found that he had not come to spread ruin and devastation, but simply to see his stony likeness on the church, they showed neither relief nor gratification, but began to upbraid the Minor Canon for consenting to conduct the creature into the town.

"What could I do?" cried the young man. "If I should not bring him he would come himself and, perhaps, end by setting fire to the town with his red-hot tail."

Still the people were not satisfied, and a great many plans were proposed to prevent the Griffin from coming into the town. Some elderly persons urged that the young men should go out and kill him; but the young men scoffed at such a ridiculous idea. Then some one said that it would be a good thing to destroy the stone image so that the Griffin would have no excuse for entering the town; and this proposal was received with such favor that many of the people ran for hammers, chisels, and crowbars, with which to tear down and break up the stone griffin. But the Minor Canon resisted this plan with all the strength of his mind and body. He assured the people that this action would enrage the Griffin beyond measure, for it would be impossible to conceal from him that his image had been destroyed during the night. But the people were so determined to break up the stone griffin that the Minor Canon saw that there was nothing for him to do but to stay there and protect it. All night he walked up and down in front of the church-door, keeping away the men who brought ladders, by which they might mount to the great stone griffin, and knock it to pieces with their hammers and crowbars. After many hours the people were obliged to give up their attempts, and went home to sleep; but the Minor Canon remained at his post till early morning, and then he hurried away to the field where he had left the Griffin.

The monster had just awakened, and rising to his fore-legs and shaking himself, he said that he was ready to go into the town. The Minor Canon, therefore, walked back, the Griffin flying slowly through the air, at a short distance above the head of his guide. Not a person was to be seen in the streets, and they proceeded directly to the front of the church, where the Minor Canon pointed out the stone griffin.

The real Griffin settled down in the little square before the church and gazed earnestly at his sculptured likeness. For a long time he looked at it. First he put his head on one side, and then he put it on the other; then he shut his right eye and gazed with his left, after which he shut his left eye and gazed with his right. Then he moved a little to one side and looked at the image, then he moved the other way. After a while he said to the Minor Canon, who had been standing by all this time:

"It is, it must be, an excellent likeness! That breadth between the eyes, that expansive forehead, those massive jaws! I feel that it must resemble me. If there is any fault to find with it, it is that the neck seems a little stiff. But that is nothing. It is an admirable likeness—admirable!"

The Griffin sat looking at his image all the morning and all the afternoon. The Minor Canon had been afraid to go away and leave him, and had hoped all through the day that he would soon be satisfied with his inspection and fly away home. But by evening the poor young man was utterly exhausted, and felt that he must eat and sleep. He frankly admitted this fact to the Griffin, and asked him if he would not like something to eat. He said this because he felt obliged in politeness to do so, but as soon as he had spoken the words, he was seized with dread lest the monster should demand half a dozen babies, or some tempting repast of that kind.

"Oh, no," said the Griffin, "I never eat between the equinoxes. At the vernal and at the autumnal equinox I take a good meal, and that lasts me for half a year. I am extremely regular in my habits, and do not think it healthful to eat at odd times. But if you need food, go and get it, and I will return to the soft grass where I slept last night and take another nap."

The next day the Griffin came again to the little square before the church, and remained there until evening, steadfastly regarding the stone griffin over the door. The Minor Canon came once or twice to look at him, and the Griffin seemed very glad to see him; but the young clergyman could not stay as he had done before, for he had many duties to perform. Nobody went to the church, but the people came to the Minor Canon's house, and anxiously asked him how long the Griffin was going to stay.

"I do not know," he answered, "but I think he will soon be satisfied with regarding his stone likeness, and then he will go away."

But the Griffin did not go away. Morning after morning he came to the church, but after a time he did not stay there all day. He seemed to have taken a great fancy to the Minor Canon, and followed him about as he pursued his various avocations. He would wait for him at the side door of the church, for the Minor Canon held services every day, morning and evening, though nobody came now. "If any one should come," he said to himself, "I must be found at my post." When the young man came out, the Griffin would accompany him in his visits to the sick and the poor, and would often look into the windows of the school-house where the Minor Canon was teaching his unruly scholars. All the other schools were closed, but the parents of the Minor Canon's scholars forced them to go to school, because they were so bad they could not endure them all day at home—griffin or no griffin. But it must be said they generally behaved very well when that great monster sat up on his tail and looked in at the school-room window.

When it was perceived that the Griffin showed no sign of going away, all the people who were able to do so left the town. The canons and the higher officers of the church had fled away during the first day of the Griffin's visit, leaving behind only the Minor Canon and some of the men who opened the doors and swept the church. All the citizens who could afford it shut up their houses and travelled to distant parts, and only the working people and the poor were left behind. After some days these ventured to go about and attend to their business, for if they did not work they would starve. They were getting a little used to seeing the Griffin, and having been told that he did not eat between equinoxes, they did not feel so much afraid of him as before.

Day by day the Griffin became more and more attached to the Minor Canon. He kept near him a great part of the time, and often spent the night in front of the little house where the young clergyman lived alone. This strange companionship was often burdensome to the Minor Canon; but, on the other hand, he could not deny that he derived a great deal of benefit and instruction from it. The Griffin had lived for hundreds of years, and had seen much; and he told the Minor Canon many wonderful things.

"It is like reading an old book," said the young clergyman to himself; "but how many books I would have had to read before I would have found out what the Griffin has told me about the earth, the air, the water, about minerals, and metals, and growing things, and all the wonders of the world!"

Thus the summer went on, and drew toward its close. And now the people of the town began to be very much troubled again.

"It will not be long," they said, "before the autumnal equinox is here, and then that monster will want to eat. He will be dreadfully hungry, for he has taken so much exercise since his last meal. He will devour our children. Without doubt, he will eat them all. What is to be done?"

To this question no one could give an answer, but all agreed that the Griffin must not be allowed to remain until the approaching equinox. After talking over the matter a great deal, a crowd of the people went to the Minor Canon, at a time when the Griffin was not with him.

"It is all your fault," they said, "that that monster is among us. You brought him here, and you ought to see that he goes away. It is only on your account that he stays here at all, for, although he visits his image every day, he is with you the greater part of the time. If you were not here, he would not stay. It is your duty to go away and then he will follow you, and we shall be free from the dreadful danger which hangs over us."

"Go away!" cried the Minor Canon, greatly grieved at being spoken to in such a way. "Where shall I go? If I go to some other town, shall I not take this trouble there? Have I a right to do that?"

"No," said the people, "you must not go to any other town. There is no town far enough away. You must go to the dreadful wilds where the Griffin lives; and then he will follow you and stay there."

They did not say whether or not they expected the Minor Canon to stay there also, and he did not ask them any thing about it. He bowed his head, and went into his house, to think. The more he thought, the more clear it became to his mind that it was his duty to go away, and thus free the town from the presence of the Griffin.

That evening he packed a leathern bag full of bread and meat, and early the next morning he set out on his journey to the dreadful wilds. It was a long, weary, and doleful journey, especially after he had gone beyond the habitations of men, but the Minor Canon kept on bravely, and never faltered. The way was longer than he had expected, and his provisions soon grew so scanty that he was obliged to eat but a little every day, but he kept up his courage, and pressed on, and, after many days of toilsome travel, he reached the dreadful wilds.

When the Griffin found that the Minor Canon had left the town he seemed sorry, but showed no disposition to go and look for him. After a few days had passed, he became much annoyed, and asked some of the people where the Minor Canon had gone. But, although the citizens had been so anxious that the young clergyman should go to the dreadful wilds, thinking that the Griffin would immediately follow him, they were now afraid to mention the Minor Canon's destination, for the monster seemed angry already, and, if he should suspect their trick he would, doubtless, become very much enraged. So every one said he did not know, and the Griffin wandered about disconsolate. One morning he looked into the Minor Canon's schoolhouse, which was always empty now, and thought that it was a shame that every thing should suffer on account of the young man's absence.

"It does not matter so much about the church," he said, "for nobody went there; but it is a pity about the school. I think I will teach it myself until he returns."

It was the hour for opening the school, and the Griffin went inside and pulled the rope which rang the school-bell. Some of the children who heard the bell ran in to see what was the matter, supposing it to be a joke of one of their companions; but when they saw the Griffin they stood astonished, and scared.

"Go tell the other scholars," said the monster, "that school is about to open, and that if they are not all here in ten minutes, I shall come after them."

In seven minutes every scholar was in place.

Never was seen such an orderly school. Not a boy or girl moved, or uttered a whisper. The Griffin climbed into the master's seat, his wide wings spread on each side of him, because he could not lean back in his chair while they stuck out behind, and his great tail coiled around, in front of the desk, the barbed end sticking up, ready to tap any boy or girl who might misbehave. The Griffin now addressed the scholars, telling them that he intended to teach them while their master was away. In speaking he endeavored to imitate, as far as possible, the mild and gentle tones of the Minor Canon, but it must be admitted that in this he was not very successful. He had paid a good deal of attention to the studies of the school, and he determined not to attempt to teach them any thing new, but to review them in what they had been studying; so he called up the various classes, and questioned them upon their previous lessons. The children racked their brains to remember what they had learned. They were so afraid of the Griffin's displeasure that they recited as they had never recited before. One of the boys, far down in his class, answered so well that the Griffin was astonished.

"I should think you would be at the head," said he. "I am sure you have never been in the habit of reciting so well. Why is this?"

"Because I did not choose to take the trouble," said the boy, trembling in his boots. He felt obliged to speak the truth, for all the children thought that the great eyes of the Griffin could see right through them, and that he would know when they told a falsehood.

"You ought to be ashamed of yourself," said the Griffin. "Go down to the very tail of the class, and if you are not at the head in two days, I shall know the reason why."

The next afternoon this boy was number one.

It was astonishing how much these children now learned of what they had been studying. It was as if they had been educated over again. The Griffin used no severity toward them, but there was a look about him which made them unwilling to go to bed until they were sure they knew their lessons for the next day.

The Griffin now thought that he ought to visit the sick and the poor; and he began to go about the town for this purpose. The effect upon the sick was miraculous. All, expect those who were very ill indeed, jumped from their beds when they heard he was coming, and declared themselves quite well. To those who could not get up, he gave herbs and roots, which none of them had ever before thought of as medicines, but which the Griffin had seen used in various parts of the world; and most of them recovered. But, for all that, they afterward said that no matter what happened to them, they hoped that they should never again have such a doctor coming to their bed-sides, feeling their pulses and looking at their tongues.

As for the poor, they seemed to have utterly disappeared. All those who had depended upon charity for their daily bread were now at work in some way or other; many of them offering to do odd jobs for their neighbors just for the sake of their meals—a thing which before had been seldom heard of in the town. The Griffin could find no one who needed his assistance.

The summer had now passed, and the autumnal equinox was rapidly approaching. The citizens were in a state of great alarm and anxiety. The Griffin showed no signs of going away, but seemed to have settled himself permanently among them. In a short time, the day for his semi-annual meal would arrive, and then what would happen? The monster would certainly be very hungry, and would devour all their children.

Now they greatly regretted and lamented that they had sent away the Minor Canon; he was the only one on whom they could have depended in this trouble, for he could talk freely with the Griffin, and so find out what could be done. But it would not do to be inactive. Some step must be taken immediately. A meeting of the citizens was called, and two old men were appointed to go and talk to the Griffin. They were instructed to offer to prepare a splendid dinner for him on equinox day—one which would entirely satisfy his hunger. They would offer him the fattest mutton, the most tender beef, fish, and game of various sorts, and any thing of the kind that he might fancy. If none of these suited, they were to mention that there was an orphan asylum in the next town.

"Any thing would be better," said the citizens, "than to have our dear children devoured."

The old men went to the Griffin, but their propositions were not received with favor.

"From what I have seen of the people of this town," said the monster, "I do not think I could relish any thing which was prepared by them. They appear to be all cowards, and, therefore, mean and selfish. As for eating one of them, old or young, I could not think of it for a moment. In fact, there was only one creature in the whole place for whom I could have had any appetite, and that is the Minor Canon, who had gone away. He was brave, and good, and honest, and I think I should have relished him."

"Ah!" said one of the old men very politely, "in that case I wish we had not sent him to the dreadful wilds!"

"What!" cried the Griffin. "What do you mean? Explain instantly what you are talking about!"

The old man, terribly frightened at what he had said, was obliged to tell how the Minor Canon had been sent away by the people, in the hope that the Griffin might be induced to follow him.

When the monster heard this, he became furiously angry. He dashed away from the old men and, spreading his wings, flew backward and forward over the town. He was so much excited that his tail became red-hot, and glowed like a meteor against the evening sky. When at last he settled down in the little field where he usually rested, and thrust his tail into the brook, the steam arose like a cloud, and the water of the stream ran hot through the town. The citizens were greatly frightened, and bitterly blamed the old man for telling about the Minor Canon.

"It is plain," they said, "that the Griffin intended at last to go and look for him, and we should have been saved. Now who can tell what misery you have brought upon us."

The Griffin did not remain long in the little field. As soon as his tail was cool he flew to the town-hall and rang the bell. The citizens knew that they were expected to come there, and although they were afraid to go, they were still more afraid to stay away; and they crowded into the hall. The Griffin was on the platform at one end, flapping his wings and walking up and down, and the end of his tail was still so warm that it slightly scorched the boards as he dragged it after him.

When everybody who was able to come was there, the Griffin stood still and addressed the meeting.

"I have had a contemptible opinion of you," he said, "ever since I discovered what cowards you are, but I had no idea that you were so ungrateful, selfish, and cruel, as I now find you to be. Here was your Minor Canon, who labored day and night for your good, and thought of nothing else but how he might benefit you and make you happy;

and as soon as you imagine yourselves threatened with a danger—for well I know you are dreadfully afraid of me—you send him off, caring not whether he returns or perishes, hoping thereby to save yourselves. Now, I had conceived a great liking for that young man, and had intended, in a day or two, to go and look him up. But I have changed my mind about him. I shall go and find him, but I shall send him back here to live among you, and I intend that he shall enjoy the reward of his labor and his sacrifices. Go, some of you, to the officers of the church, who so cowardly ran away when I first came here, and tell them never to return to this town under penalty of death. And if, when your Minor Canon comes back to you, you do not bow yourselves before him, put him in the highest place among you, and serve and honor him all his life, beware of my terrible vengeance! There were only two good things in this town: the Minor Canon and the stone image of myself over your church-door. One of these you have sent away, and the other I shall carry away myself."

With these words he dismissed the meeting, and it was time, for the end of his tail had become so hot that there was danger of its setting fire to the building.

The next morning, the Griffin came to the church, and tearing the stone image of himself from its fastenings over the great door, he grasped it with his powerful fore-legs and flew up into the air. Then, after hovering over the town for a moment, he gave his tail an angry shake and took up his flight to the dreadful wilds. When he reached this desolate region, he set the stone Griffin upon a ledge of a rock which rose in front of the dismal cave he called his home. There the image occupied a position somewhat similar to that it had had over the church-door; and the Griffin, panting with the exertion of carrying such an enormous load to so great a distance, lay down upon the ground, and regarded it with much satisfaction. When he felt somewhat rested he went to look for the Minor Canon. He found the young man, weak and half starved, lying under the shadow of a rock. After picking him up and carrying him to his cave, the Griffin flew away to a distant marsh, where he procured some roots and herbs which he well knew were strengthening and beneficial to man, though he had never tasted them himself. After eating these the Minor Canon was greatly revived, and sat up and listened while the Griffin told him what had happened in the town.

"Do you know," said the monster, when he had finished, "that I have had, and still have, a great liking for you?"

"I am very glad to hear it," said the Minor Canon, with his usual politeness.

"I am not at all sure that you would be," said the Griffin, "if you thoroughly understood the state of the case, but we will not consider that now. If some things were different, other things would be otherwise. I have been so enraged by discovering the manner in which you have been treated that I have determined that you shall at last enjoy the rewards and honors to which you are entitled. Lie down and have a good sleep, and then I will take you back to the town."

As he heard these words, a look of trouble came over the young man's face.

"You need not give yourself any anxiety," said the Griffin, "about my return to the town. I shall not remain there. Now that I have that admirable likeness of myself in front of my cave, where I can sit at my leisure, and gaze upon its noble features and magnificent proportions, I have no wish to see that abode of cowardly and selfish people."

The Minor Canon, relieved from his fears, lay back, and dropped into a doze; and when he was sound asleep the Griffin took him up, and carried him back to the town. He arrived just before day-break, and putting the young man gently on the grass in the little field where he himself used to rest, the monster, without having been seen by any of the people, flew back to his home.

When the Minor Canon made his appearance in the morning among the citizens, the enthusiasm and cordiality with which he was received were truly wonderful. He was taken to a house which had been occupied by one of the banished high officers of the place, and every one was anxious to do all that could be done for his health and comfort. The people crowded into the church when he held services, so that the three old women who used to be his week-day congregation could not get to the best seats, which they had always been in the habit of taking; and the parents of the bad children determined to reform them at home, in order that he might be spared the trouble of keeping up his former school. The Minor Canon was appointed to the highest office of the old church, and before he died, he became a bishop.

During the first years after his return from the dreadful wilds, the people of the town looked up to him as a man to whom they were bound to do honor and reverence; but they often, also, looked up to the sky to see if there were any signs of the Griffin coming back. However, in the course of time, they learned to honor and reverence their former Minor Canon without the fear of being punished if they did not do so.

But they need never have been afraid of the Griffin. The autumnal equinox day came round, and the monster ate nothing. If he could not have the Minor Canon, he did not care for any thing. So, lying down, with his eyes fixed upon the great stone griffin, he gradually declined, and died. It was a good thing for some of the people of the town that they did not know this.

If you should ever visit the old town, you would still see the little griffins on the sides of the church; but the great stone griffin that was over the door is gone.

The Man Who Sold Rope to the Gnoles

Margaret St. Clair

Margaret St. Clair, who has written many fine stories, published this piece originally under her pseudonym, Idris Seabright, in the Magazine of Fantasy & Science Fiction *in the 1950s. She borrowed strange creatures from Lord Dunsany, one of the great fantasy writers, who invented the gnoles at the turn of the century. They are dark creatures from the imagination, not from any folk tradition. This is a moral tale about a bad man who is punished horribly. Perhaps it is also a parody of the classical idea of the tragic flaw. It is, for certain, grim humor.*

The Gnoles had a bad reputation, and Mortensen was quite aware of this. But he reasoned, correctly enough, that cordage must be something for which the gnoles had a long unsatisfied want, and he saw no reason why he should not be the one to sell it to them. What a triumph such a sale would be! The district sales manager might single out Mortensen for special mention at the annual sales-force dinner. It would help his sales quota enormously. And, after all, it was none of his business what the gnoles used cordage for.

Mortensen decided to call on the gnoles on Thursday morning. On Wednesday night he went through his *Manual of Modern Salesmanship,* underscoring things.

"The mental states through which the mind passes in making a purchase," he read, "have been catalogued as 1) arousal of interest 2) increase of knowledge 3) adjustment to needs . . . " There were seven mental states listed, and Mortensen underscored all of them. Then he went back and double-scored No.1, arousal of interest, No.4, appreciation of suitability, and No.7, decision to purchase. He turned the page.

"Two qualities are of exceptional importance to a salesman," he read. "They are adaptability and knowledge of merchandise." Mortensen underlined the qualities. "Other highly desirable attributes are physical fitness, and high ethical standard, charm of manner, a dogged persistence, and unfailing courtesy." Mortensen underlined these too. But he read on to the end of the paragraph without underscoring anything more, and it may be that his failure to put "tact and keen power of observation" on a footing with the other attributes of a salesman was responsible for what happened to him.

The gnoles live on the very edge of Terra Cognita, on the far side of a wood which all authorities unite in describing as dubious. Their house is narrow and high, in architecture a blend of Victorian Gothic and Swiss chalet. Though the house needs paint, it is kept in good repair. Thither on Thursday morning, sample case in hand, Mortensen took his way.

No path leads to the house of the gnoles, and it is always dark in that dubious wood. But Mortensen, remembering what he had learned at his mother's knee concerning the odor of gnoles, found the house quite easily. For a moment he stood hesitating before it. His lips moved as he repeated, "Good morning, I have come to supply your cordage requirements," to himself. The words were the beginning of his sales talk. Then he went up and rapped on the door.

The gnoles were watching him through holes they had bored in the trunks of trees; it is an artful custom of theirs to which the prime authority on gnoles attests. Mortensen's knock almost threw them into confusion, it was so long since anyone had knocked at their door. Then the senior gnole, the one who never leaves the house, went flitting up from the cellars and opened it.

The senior gnole is a little like a Jerusalem artichoke made of India rubber, and he has small red eyes which are faceted in the same way that gemstone are. Mortensen had been expecting something unusual, and when the gnole opened the door he bowed politely, took off his hat, and smiled. He had got past the sentence about cordage requirements and into an enumeration of the different types of cordage his firm manufactured when the gnole, by turning his head to the side, showed him that he had no ears. Nor was there anything on his head which could take their place in the conduction of sound. Then the gnole opened his little fanged mouth and let Mortensen look at his narrow, ribbony tongue. As a tongue it was no more fit for human speech than was a serpent's. Judging from his appearance, the gnole could not safely be assigned to any of the four physio-characterological types mentioned in the *Manual;* and for the first time Mortensen felt a definite qualm.

Nonetheless, he followed the gnole unhesitantly when the creature motioned him within. Adaptability, he told himself, adaptability must be his watchword. Enough adaptability, and his knees might even lose their tendency to shakiness.

It was the parlor the gnole led him to. Mortensen's eyes widened as he looked around it. There were whatnots in the corner, and cabinets of curiosities, and on the fretwork table an album with gilded hasps; who knows whose pictures were in it? All around the walls in brackets, where in lesser houses the people display ornamental plates, were emeralds as big as your head. The gnoles set great store by their emeralds. All the light in the dim room came from them.

Mortensen went through the phrases of his sales talk mentally. It distressed him that that was the only way he could go through them. Still, adaptability! The gnole's interest was already aroused, or he would never have asked Mortensen into the parlor; and as soon as the gnole saw the various cordages the sample case contained he would no doubt proceed of his own accord through "appreciation of suitability" to "desire to possess."

Mortensen sat down in the chair the gnole indicated and opened his sample case. He got out henequen cable-laid rope, an assortment of ply and yarn goods, and some superlative slender abaca fiber rope. He even showed the gnole a few soft yarns and twines made of cotton and jute.

On the back of an envelope he wrote prices for hanks and cheeses of the twines, and for fifty- and hundred-foot lengths of the ropes. Laboriously he added details about the strength, durability, and resistance to climatic conditions of each sort of cord. The senior gnole watched him intently, putting his little feet on the top rung of his chair and poking at the facets of his left eye now and then with a tentacle. In the cellars from time to time someone would scream.

Mortensen began to demonstrate his wares. He showed the gnole the slip and resilience of one rope, the tenacity and stubborn strength of another. He cut a tarred hemp rope in two and laid a five foot piece on the parlor floor to show the gnole how absolutely "neutral" it was, with no tendency to untwist of its own accord. He even showed the gnole how nicely some of the cotton twines made up a square knotwork.

They settled at last on two ropes of abaca fiber, 3/16 and 5/8 inch in diameter. The gnole wanted an enormous quantity. Mortensen's comment on those ropes, "unlimited strength and durability," seemed to have attracted him.

Soberly Mortensen wrote the particulars down in his order book, but ambition was setting his brain on fire. The gnoles, it seemed, would be regular customers; and after the gnoles, why should he not try the gibbelins? They too must have a need for rope.

Mortensen closed his order book. On the back of the same envelope he wrote, for the gnole to see, that delivery would be made within ten days. Terms were 30 per cent with order, balance upon receipt of goods.

The senior gnole hesitated. Shyly he looked at Mortensen with his little red eyes. Then he got down the smallest of the emeralds from the wall and handed it to him.

The sales representative stood weighing it in his hands. It was the smallest of the gnoles' emeralds, but it was as clear as water, as green as grass. In the outside world it would have ransomed a Rockefeller or a whole family of Guggenheims; a legitimate profit from a transaction was one thing, but this was another; "a high ethical standard"— any kind of ethical standard—would forbid Mortensen to keep it. He weighed it a moment longer. Then with a deep, deep sigh he gave the emerald back.

He cast a glance around the room to see if he could find something which would be more negotiable. And in an evil moment he fixed on the senior gnole's auxiliary eyes.

The senior gnole keeps his extra pair of optics on the third shelf of the curiosity cabinet with the glass doors. They look like fine dark emeralds about the size of the end of your thumb. And if the gnoles in general set store by their gems, it is nothing at all compared to the senior gnole's emotions about his extra eyes. The concern good Christian folk should feel for their soul's welfare is a shadow, a figment, a nothing, compared to what the thoroughly heathen gnole feels for those eyes. He would rather, I think, choose to be a mere miserable human being than that some vandal should lay hands upon them.

If Mortensen had not been elated by his success to the point of anaesthesia, he would have seen the gnole stiffen, he would have heard him hiss, when he went over to the cabinet. All innocent, Mortensen opened the glass door, took the twin eyes out, and juggled them sacrilegiously in his hand; the gnole could feel them clink Smiling to evince the charm of manner advised in the *Manual,* and raising his brows as one who says, "Thank you, these will do nicely," Mortensen dropped the eyes into his pocket.

The gnole growled.

The growl awoke Mortensen from his trance of euphoria. It was a growl whose meaning no one could mistake. This was clearly no time to be doggedly persistent. Mortensen made a break for the door.

The senior gnole was there before him, his network of tentacles outstretched. He caught Mortensen in them easily and wound them, flat as bandages, around his ankles and his hands. The best abaca fiber is no stronger than those tentacles; though the gnoles would find rope a convenience, they get along very well without it. Would you, dear reader, go naked if zippers should cease to be made? Growling indignantly, the gnole fished his ravished eyes from Mortensen's pockets, and then carried him down to the cellar to the fattening pens.

But great are the virtues of legitimate commerce. Though they fattened Mortensen sedulously, and, later, roasted and sauced him and ate him with real appetite, the gnoles slaughtered him in quite a humane manner and never once thought of torturing him. That is unusual, for gnoles. And they ornamented the plank on which they served him with a beautiful border of fancy knotwork made of cotton cord from his own sample case.

The Dragons

Murilo Rubião

Murilo Rubião is a Brazilian writer whose approach to fantasy is through the school of magic realism. This story from his collection The Ex-magician and Other Stories, *which contains several fantastic tales, is about our inability to appreciate the truly wonderful in the world when we find it, our inability to truly see. Dragons, in the past, were often not distinguished from devils, especially by medieval Christians. Thus, in this story, the vicar has problems with them. At times the dragons seem to be noble savages fallen upon hard times; at others, simply alien beings with their own agenda. But whatever they are, we can try to civilize them only at the risk of losing their essence.*

> I am a brother to dragons, and a companion to owls.
> Job, XXX:29

The first dragons to appear in our city suffered a great deal due to the backwardness of our customs. They received precarious training at best, and their moral instruction was compromised dreadfully by absurd discussions which their arrival had somehow prompted.

Very few of us were able to understand them, and the general confusion was such that, until we saw to their education, we were hopelessly lost in contradictory speculation as to their race and country of origin.

The initial dispute was the fault of the vicar. Convinced that—in spite of their docile, almost pleasant exterior—they were still messengers of the Devil, he refused to allow me to begin to instruct them. Instead, he gave orders to have them confined to an old house, which was to be first exorcised and to which no one was permitted access. By the time he repented of his mistake, the controversy had already widened, with one elderly grammarian denying them the quality of dragons: "an Asiatic thing, of European importation." Another reader of newspapers, a highschool dropout with vaguely scientific ideas, spoke of "antediluvian monsters." Still others, making the sign of the cross, suggested headless mules and werewolves.

Only the children, who secretly played with our guests, understood that their new companions were simple dragons. To them, however, no one bothered to listen.

Exhaustion and time overcame the obstinacy of many. Even those who still maintained their convictions at least avoided the subject.

Nevertheless, the polemic resurfaced after a brief respite. The pretext was a suggestion for utilizing dragons as a means of transportation. Everyone agreed that the idea was excellent, but quarreling broke out as to the specific distribution of the animals, whose number was far less than those who hoped to make use of them.

To put an end to the discussion, which threatened to drag on indefinitely and to no practical purpose, the vicar subscribed to the following proposal: the dragons should be baptized, given proper names, and taught to read and write.

Until that moment I had acted with discretion, so as to avoid contributing to the general aggravation of tempers. And if, for an instant, I seemed to lack my usual composure, or proper respect for the good father, I must blame the prevailing foolishness. I was utterly irritated and gave vent to my disapproval:

"They are dragons! They have no need of baptism or any proper names!"

Shocked at my attitude, which normally conformed to that of the community at large, His Reverence gave ample display of his humility by withdrawing the idea of baptism. I returned the gesture, by acceding to his demand for proper names.

I comprehended the extent of my responsibility when, rescued from the neglect they had fallen into, they were finally brought to me for instruction. The majority had contracted various unknown maladies, as a result of which they slowly died. Only two had still survived, unfortunately the most corrupt of the lot. Endowed with even greater cunning than their brothers, they would sneak away from the old mansion at night, to go drinking at a local tavern. Since the bartender enjoyed watching them get tipsy, he didn't charge for the liquor he served. Eventually the identical scene, month after month, ceased to amuse him, and he refused to give them any more drinks. In order to sustain their vice, they decided to resort to petty thefts.

In the meantime, I still clung to the possibility of reeducating them and thereby vindicating the success of my undertaking in the eyes of the incredulous. I took advantage of my friendship with the police commissioner in order to have them released from jail, where they were constantly remanded on the same charges: petty larceny, drunken disorder.

Since I had never taught dragons before, I spent a great deal of time inquiring about their past, their families and pedagogical methods in their own homeland. The successive interrogations to which they were subjected provided me with little information. Particularly since, having come to our city while fairly young, they remembered everything rather confusedly, including the death of their mother, who had fallen off a precipice just after the ascent of the first mountain. And to further complicate my task, the already weak memory of my pupils was beclouded with constant ill-humor, occasioned by poor sleep and continual hangovers.

The ingrained habits of teaching, coupled with a lack of my own offspring, contributed to my eventually bestowing a certain paternal regard upon them. Moreover, a gentle candor that sometimes radiated from their eyes induced me to pardon faults in them which I should never have forgiven in my other students.

Odorico, the oldest of the dragons, caused me the greatest problems. At once disastrously mischievous and completely engaging, he was transported at the mere sight of a skirt. Because of that habit and, even more, out of some inborn tendency toward degeneracy, he was constantly truant from classes. Women somehow found him attractive, and there was one who became so impassioned, she left her husband to go live with him.

I did everything to terminate the sinful alliance, but never managed to separate them. They refused my appeals with a voiceless, impenetrable defiance. My words never reached them: Odorico would smile at Raquel, and, reassured, she would once again bend over the laundry she was washing.

Sometime later they found her crying next to her lover's body. His death was attributed to an accidental shot, probably by some hunter with a poor aim. Her husband, however, told another story.

With the death of Odorico, my wife and I transferred our affections to the last of the dragons. We took upon ourselves his complete rehabilitation and finally managed, after considerable effort, to wean him from alcoholism. Perhaps having a son of our own would not have approached what we accomplished with such loving persistence. Gentle in his behavior, João applied himself to his studies, helped Joana with the housework, carried groceries home from the market. After dinner, we would sit on the porch and watch him play happily with the neighborhood children, giving them rides, and practicing somersaults.

Upon my return home one evening from the monthly meeting with parents, I found my wife quite disturbed: João had just vomited fire. I felt apprehensive also, realizing he had reached his majority.

The event itself, far from making him fearful, increased his popularity with the local girls and boys. He spent most of his time surrounded by lively crowds begging him to spit fire. The adulation of some, coupled with invitations and presents from others, slowly kindled his vanity. No party was successful without his attendance. Even the vicar considered his presence indispensable for animating the booths at the fair on our patron saint's day.

Three months before the great flood devastated the whole county, a traveling circus livened up our city, thrilling us with daring acrobats, merry clowns, trained lions, and a man who could swallow live coals. Toward the end of the juggler's act, several youths interrupted the show with rhythmic shouts and hand-clapping:

"We've got something better! We've got something better!"

Judging it to be some boyish prank, the ringmaster immediately accepted the challenge:

"Let's see something better, then!"

To the dismay of the circus personnel and the applause of the spectators, João made his way to the ring and performed his customary feat of vomiting fire.

By the following afternoon he had received several invitations to join the circus, but refused: it would have been difficult to surpass the prestige he already enjoyed in our own community. He even cherished the ambition of one day becoming mayor.

This, however, was not to happen. Instead, João's disappearance was confirmed, just days after the departure of the circus troop.

Fanciful accounts were given of his flight: that he fell passionately in love with one of the trapezists, who had been hired to seduce him; that he took up gambling and lapsed back into heavy drinking.

Whatever the reason, so many dragons have traveled along our highways since then. . . . Yet, no matter how vigorously I and my students—posted at the city gates—press them to stay with us, they refuse to answer. Huddled together in long lines, on their way to distant places, they seem indifferent to our cries.

On the Downhill Side

Harlan Ellison

Harlan Ellison is a dark fantasist (Stephen King, in **Danse Macabre,** *says he's the best of them) whose short fiction has earned him wide popularity. Prolific, controversial, energetic, he is a writer whose work is characterized by extreme and colorful effects, as if the volume were turned up on a big and expensive stereo system. "On the Downhill Side" is an unusually delicate, almost fragile ghost story, atypical, but one of his most enduring. It is also one of the very few contemporary fantasies to use the image of the unicorn well, putting it into the company of Theodore Sturgeon's "The Silken Swift" and Peter S. Beagle's* **The Last Unicorn.** *In every love relationship the tendency is for one party to do most of the emotional work—and get used up. This is a story about balance, and the sacrifice necessary to attain it.*

"In love, there is always one who kisses and one who offers the cheek."

—French proverb

I knew she was a virgin because she was able to ruffle the silken mane of my unicorn. Named Lizette, she was a Grecian temple in which no sacrifice had ever been made. Vestal virgin of New Orleans, found walking without shadow in the thankgod coolness of cockroach-crawling Louisiana night. My unicorn whinnied, inclined his head, and she stroked the ivory spiral of his horn.

Much of this took place in what is called the Irish Channel, a strip of street in old New Orleans where the lace curtain micks had settled decades before; now the Irish were gone and the Cubans had taken over the Channel. Now the Cubans were sleeping, recovering from the muggy today that held within its hours the *déjà vu* of muggy yesterday, the *déjà rêvé* of intolerable tomorrow. Now the crippled bricks of side streets off Magazine had given up their nightly ghosts, and one such phantom had come to me, calling my unicorn to her—thus, clearly, a virgin—and I stood waiting.

Had it been Sutton Place, had it been a Manhattan evening, and had we met, she would have kneeled to pet my dog. And I would have waited. Had it been Puerto Vallarta, had it been 20°36' N, 105° 13' W, and had we met, she would have crouched to run her fingertips over the oil-slick hide of my iguana. And I would have waited. Meeting in streets requires ritual. One must wait and not breathe too loud, if one is to enjoy the congress of the nightly ghosts.

She looked across the fine head of my unicorn and smiled at me. Her eyes were a shade of gray between onyx and miscalculation. "Is it a bit chilly for you?" I asked.

"When I was thirteen," she said, linking my arm, taking a tentative two steps that led me with her, up the street, "or perhaps I was twelve, well no matter, when I was that approximate age, I had a marvelous shawl of Belgian lace. I could look through it and see the mysteries of the sun and the other stars unriddled. I'm sure someone important and very nice has purchased that shawl from an antique dealer, and paid handsomely for it."

It seemed not a terribly responsive reply to a simple question.

"A queen of the Mardi Gras Ball doesn't get chilly," she added, unasked. I walked along beside her, the cool evasiveness of her arm binding us, my mind a welter of answer choices, none satisfactory.

Behind us, my unicorn followed silently. Well, not entirely silently. His platinum hoofs clattered on the bricks. I'm afraid I felt a straight pin of jealousy. Perfection does that to me.

"When were you queen of the Ball?"

The date she gave me was one hundred and thirteen years before. It must have been brutally cold down there in the stones.

There is a little book they sell, a guide to manners and dining in New Orleans: I've looked: nowhere in the book do they indicate the proper responses to a ghost. But then, it says nothing about the wonderful cemeteries of New Orleans' West Bank, or Metairie. Or the gourmet dining at such locations. One seeks, in vain, through the mutable, mercurial universe, for the compleat guide. To everything. And, failing in the search, one makes do the best one can. And suffers the frustration, suffers the ennui.

Perfection does that to me.

We walked for some time, and grew to know each other, as best we'd allow. These are some of the high points. They lack continuity. I don't apologize, I merely point it out, adding with some truth, I feel, that *most* liaisons lack continuity. We find ourselves in odd places at various times, and for a brief span we link our lives to others—even as Lizette had linked her arm with mine—and then, our time elapsed, we move apart. Through a haze of pain occasionally; usually through a veil of memory that clings, then passes; sometimes as though we have never touched.

"My name is Paul Ordahl," I told her. "And the most awful thing that ever happened to me was my first wife, Bernice. I don't know how else to put it—even if it sounds melodramatic, it's simply what happened—she went insane, and I divorced her, and her mother had her committed to a private mental home."

"When I was eighteen," Lizette said, "my family gave me my coming-out party. We were living in the Garden District, on Prytania Street. The house was a lovely white Plantation—they call them antebellum now—with Grecian pillars. We had a persimmon-green gazebo in the rear gardens, directly beside a weeping willow. It was six-sided. Octagonal. Or is that hexagonal? It was the loveliest party. And while it was going on, I sneaked away with a boy . . . I don't remember his name . . . and we went into the gazebo, and I let him touch my breasts. I don't remember his name."

We were on Decatur Street, walking toward the French Quarter; the Mississippi was on our right, dark but making its presence known.

"Her mother was the one had her committed, you see. I only heard from them twice after the divorce. It had been four stinking years and I really didn't want any more of it. Once, after I'd started making some money, the mother called and said Bernice had to be put in the state asylum. There wasn't enough money to pay for the private home any more. I sent a little; not much. I suppose I could have sent more, but I was remarried, there was a child from her previous marriage. I didn't want to send any more. I told the mother not to call me again. There was only once after that . . . it was the most terrible thing that ever happened to me."

We walked around Jackson Square, looking in at the very black grass, reading the plaques bolted to the spear-topped fence, plaques telling how New Orleans had once belonged to the French. We sat on one of the benches in the street. The street had been closed to traffic, and we sat on one of the benches.

"Our name was Charbonnet. Can you say that?"

I said it, with a good accent.

"I married a very wealthy man. He was in real estate. At one time he owned the entire block where the *Vieux Carré* now stands, on Bourbon Street. He admired me greatly. He came and sought my hand, and my *maman* had to strike the bargain because my father was too weak to do it; he drank. I can admit that now. But it didn't matter, I'd already found out how my suitor was set financially. He wasn't common, but he wasn't quality, either. But he was wealthy and I married him. He gave me presents. I did what I had to do. But I refused to let him make love to me after he became friends with that awful Jew who built the Metairie Cemetery over the race track because they wouldn't let him race his Jew horses. My husband's name was Dunbar. Claude Dunbar, you may have heard the name? Our parties were *de rigueur*."

"Would you like some coffee and *beignets* at Du Monde?"

She stared at me for a moment, as though she wanted me to say something more, then she nodded and smiled.

We walked around the Square. My unicorn was waiting at the curb. I scratched his rainbow flank and he struck a spark off the cobblestone with his right front hoof. "I know," I said to him, "we'll soon start the downhill side. But not just yet. Be patient. I won't forget you."

Lizette and I went inside the Café Du Monde and I ordered two coffees with warm milk and two orders of *beignets* from a waiter who was originally from New Jersey but had lived most of his life only a few miles from College Station, Texas.

There was a coolness coming off the levee.

"I was in New York," I said. "I was receiving an award at an architects' convention—did I mention I was an architect—yes, that's what I was at the time, an architect—and I did a television interview. The mother saw me on the program, and checked the newspapers to find out what hotel we were using for the convention, and she got my room number and called me. I had been out quite late after the banquet where I'd gotten my award, quite late. I was sitting on the side of the bed, taking off my shoes, my tuxedo tie hanging from my unbuttoned collar, getting ready just to throw clothes on the floor and sink away, when the phone rang. It was the mother. She was a terrible person, one of the worst I ever knew, a shrike, a terrible, just a terrible person. She started telling me about Bernice in the asylum. How they had her in this little room and how she stared out the window most of the time. She'd reverted to childhood, and most of the time she couldn't even recognize the mother; but when she did, she'd say something like, 'Don't let them hurt me, Mommy, don't let them hurt me.' So I asked her what she wanted me to do, did she want money for Bernice or what . . . Did she want me to go see her since I was in New York . . . and she said God no. And then she did an awful thing to me. She said the last time she'd been to see Bernice, my ex-wife had turned around and put her finger to her lips and said, 'Shhh, we have to be very quiet. Paul is working.' And I swear, a snake uncoiled in my stomach. It was the most terrible thing I'd ever heard. No matter how secure you are that you honest to God had *not* sent someone to a madhouse, there's always that little core of doubt, and saying what she'd said just burned out my head. I couldn't even think about it, couldn't even really *hear* it, or it would have collapsed me. So down came these iron walls and I just kept on talking, and after a while she hung up.

"It wasn't till two years later that I allowed myself to think about it, and then I cried; it had been a long time since I'd cried. Oh, not because I believed that nonsense about a man isn't supposed to cry, but just because I guess there hadn't been anything that important to cry *about*. But when I let myself hear what she'd said, I started crying, and just went on and on till I finally went in and looked into the bathroom mirror and I asked myself, face-to-face, if I'd done that, if I'd ever made her be quiet so I could work on blueprints or drawings . . .

"And after a while I saw myself shaking my head no, and it was easier. That was perhaps three years before I died."

She licked the powdered sugar from the *beignets* off her fingers, and launched into a long story about a lover she had taken. She didn't remember his name.

It was sometime after midnight. I'd thought midnight would signal the start of the downhill side, but the hour had passed, and we were still together, and she didn't seem ready to vanish. We left the Café Du Monde and walked into the Quarter.

I despise Bourbon Street. The strip joints, with the pasties over nipples, the smell of need, the dwarfed souls of men attuned only to flesh. The noise.

We walked through it like art connoisseurs at a showing of motel room paintings. She continued to talk about her life, about the men she had known, about the way they had loved her, the ways in which she had spurned them, and about the trivia of her past existence. I continued to talk about my loves, about all the women I had held dear in my heart for however long each had been linked with me. We talked across each other, our conversation at right angles, only meeting in the intersections of silence at story's end.

She wanted a julep and I took her to the Royal Orleans Hotel and we sat in silence as she drank. I watched her, studying that phantom face, seeking for even the smallest flicker of light off the ice in her eyes, hoping for an indication that glacial melting could be forthcoming. But there was nothing, and I burned to say correct words that might cause heat. She drank and reminisced about evenings with young men in similar hotels, a hundred years before.

We went to a night club where a Flamenco dancer and his two-woman troupe performed on a stage of unpolished woods, their star-shining black shoes setting up resonances in me that I chose to ignore.

Then I realized there were only three couples in the club, and that the extremely pretty Flamenco dancer was playing to Lizette. He gripped the lapels of his bolero jacket and clattered his heels against the stage like a man driving nails. She watched him, and her tongue made a wholly obvious flirtatious trip around the rim of her liquor glass. There was a two-drink minimum, and as I have never liked the taste of alcohol, she was more than willing to prevent waste by drinking mine as well as her own. Whether she was getting drunk or simply indulging herself, I do not know. It didn't matter. I became blind with jealousy, and dragons took possession of my eyes.

When the dancer was finished, when his half hour show was concluded, he came to our table. His suit was skintight and the color of Arctic lakes. His hair was curly and moist from his exertions, and his prettiness infuriated me. There was a scene. He asked her name, I interposed a comment, he tried to be polite, sensing my ugly mood, she overrode my comment, he tried again in Castilian, *th*-ing his *esses*, she answered, I rose and shoved him, there was a scuffle. We were asked to leave.

Once outside, she walked away from me.

My unicorn was at the curb, eating from a porcelain *Sèvres* soup plate filled with *flan*. I watched her walk unsteadily up the street toward Jackson Square. I scratched my unicorn's neck and he stopped eating the egg custard. He looked at me for a long moment. Ice crystals were sparkling in his mane.

We were on the downhill side.

"Soon, old friend," I said.

He dipped his elegant head toward the plate. "I see you've been to the Las Americas. When you return the plate, give my best to *Señor* Pena."

I followed her up the street. She was walking rapidly toward the Square. I called to her, but she wouldn't stop. She began dragging her left hand along the steel bars of the fence enclosing the Square. Her fingertips thudded softly from bar to bar, and once I heard the chitinous *clak* of a manicured nail.

"Lizette!"

She walked faster, dragging her hand across the dark metal bars.

"Lizette! Damn it!"

I was reluctant to run after her; it was somehow terribly demeaning. But she was getting farther and farther away. There were bums in the Square, sitting slouched on the benches, their arms out along the backs. Itinerants, kids with beards and knapsacks. I was suddenly frightened for her. Impossible. She had been dead for a hundred years. There was no reason for it . . . I was afraid for her!

I started running, the sound of my footsteps echoing up and around the Square. I caught her at the corner and dragged her around. She tried to slap me, and I caught her hand. She kept trying to hit me, to scratch my face with the manicured nails. I held her and swung her away from me, swung her around, and around, dizzyingly, trying to keep her off-balance. She swung wildly, crying out and saying things inarticulately. Finally, she stumbled and I pulled her in to me and held her tight against my body.

"Stop it! Stop, Lizette! I . . . *Stop it!*" She went limp against me and I felt her crying against my chest. I took her into the shadows and my unicorn came down Decatur Street and stood under a streetlamp, waiting.

The chimera winds rose. I heard them, and knew we were well on

the downhill side, that time was growing short. I held her close and
smelled the woodsmoke scent of her hair. "Listen to me," I said,
softly, close to her. "Listen to me, Lizette. Our time's almost gone.
This is our last chance. You've lived in stone for a hundred years; I've
heard you cry. I've come there, to that place, night after night, and
I've heard you cry. You've paid enough, God knows. So have I. We
can *do* it. We've got one more chance, and we can make it, if you'll
try. That's all I ask. Try."

She pushed away from me, tossing her head so the auburn hair
swirled away from her face. Her eyes were dry. Ghosts can do that.
Cry without making tears. Tears are denied us. Other things; I won't
talk of them here.

"I lied to you," she said.

I touched the side of her face. The high cheekbone just at the
hairline. "I know. My unicorn would never have let you touch him if
you weren't pure. I'm not, but he has no choice with me. He was
assigned to me. He's my familiar and he puts up with me. We're
friends."

"No. Other lies. My life was a lie. I've told them all to you. We
can't make it. You have to let me go."

I didn't know exactly where, but I knew how it would happen. I
argued with her, trying to convince her there was a way for us. But
she couldn't believe it, hadn't the strength or the will or the faith.
Finally, I let her go.

She put her arms around my neck and drew my face down to hers,
and she held me that way for a few moments. Then the winds rose,
and there were sounds in the night, the sounds of calling, and she left
me there, in the shadows.

I sat down on the curb and thought about the years since I'd died.
Years without much music. Light leached out. Wandering. Nothing
to pace me but memories and the unicorn. How sad I was for *him;*
assigned to me till I got my chance. And now it had come and I'd
taken my best go, and failed.

Lizette and I were the two sides of the same coin; devalued and
impossible to spend. Legal tender of nations long since vanished, no
longer even names on the cracked papyrus of cartographers' maps.
We had been snatched away from final rest, had been set adrift to
roam for our crimes, and only once between death and eternity
would we receive a chance. This night . . . this nothing-special
night . . . this was our chance.

My unicorn came to me, then, and brushed his muzzle against my shoulder. I reached up and scratched around the base of his spiral horn, his favorite place. He gave a long, silvery sigh, and in that sound I heard the sentence I was serving on him, as well as myself. We had been linked, too. Assigned to one another by the one who had ordained this night's chance. But if I lost out, so did my unicorn; he who had wandered with me through all the soundless, lightless years.

I stood up. I was by no means ready to do battle, but at least I could stay in for the full ride . . . all the way on the downhill side. "Do you know where they are?"

My unicorn started off down the street.

I followed, hopelessness warring with frustration. Dusk to dawn is the full ride, the final chance. After midnight is the downhill side. Time was short, and when time ran out there would be nothing for Lizette or me or my unicorn *but* time. Forever.

When we passed the Royal Orleans Hotel I knew where we were going. The sound of the Quarter had already faded. It was getting on toward dawn. The human lice had finally crawled into their fleshmounds to sleep off the night of revelry. Though I had never experienced directly the New Orleans in which Lizette had grown up, I longed for the power to blot out the cancerous blight that Bourbon Street and the Quarter had become, with its tourist filth and screaming neon, to restore it to the colorful yet healthy state in which it had thrived a hundred years before. But I was only a ghost, not one of the gods with such powers, and at that moment I was almost at the end of the line held by one of those gods.

My unicorn turned down dark streets, heading always in the same general direction, and when I saw the first black shapes of the tombstones against the night sky, the *lightening* night sky, I knew I'd been correct in my assumption of destination.

The Saint Louis Cemetery.

Oh, how I sorrow for anyone who has never seen the world-famous Saint Louis Cemetery in New Orleans. It is the perfect graveyard, the complete graveyard, the finest graveyard in the universe. (There is a perfection in some designs that informs the function totally. There are Danish chairs that could be nothing *but* chairs, are so totally and completely *chair* that if the world as we know it ended, and a billion years from now the New Orleans horsy cockroaches became the dominant species, and they dug down through the alluvial layers, and found one of those chairs, even if they themselves did not use chairs, were not constructed physically for the use of chairs, had never seen a chair, *still* they would know it for what it had been made to be: a chair. Because it would be the essence of *chairness.* And from it, they could reconstruct the human race in replica. *That* is the kind of graveyard one means when one refers to the world-famous Saint Louis Cemetery.)

The Saint Louis Cemetery is ancient. It sighs with shadows and the comfortable bones and their afterimages of deaths that became great merely because those who died went to be interred in the Saint Louis Cemetery. The water table lies just eighteen inches below New Orleans—there are no graves in the earth for that reason. Bodies are entombed aboveground in crypts, in sepulchers, vaults, mausoleums. The gravestones are all different, no two alike, each one a testament to the stonecutter's art. Only secondarily testaments to those who lie beneath the markers.

We had reached the moment of final nightness. That ultimate moment before day began. Dawn had yet to fill the eastern sky, yet there was a warming of tone to the night; it was the last of the downhill side of my chance. Of Lizette's chance.

We approached the cemetery, my unicorn and I. From deep in the center of the skyline of stones beyond the fence I could see the ice-chill glow of a pulsing blue light. The light one finds in a refrigerator, cold and flat and brittle.

I mounted my unicorn, leaned close along his neck, clinging to his mane with both hands, knees tight to his silken sides, now rippling with light and color, and I gave a little hiss of approval, a little sound of go.

My unicorn sailed over the fence, into the world-famous Saint Louis Cemetery.

I dismounted and thanked him. We began threading our way between the tombstones, the sepulchers, the crypts.

The blue glow grew more distinct. And now I could hear the chimera winds rising, whirling, coming in off alien seas. The pulsing of the light, the wail of the winds, the night dying. My unicorn stayed close. Even we of the spirit world know when to be afraid.

After all, I was only operating off a chance; I was under no god's protection. Naked, even in death.

There is no fog in New Orleans.

Mist began to form around us.

Except sometimes in the winter, there is no fog in New Orleans.

I remembered the daybreak of the night I'd died. There had been mist. I had been a suicide.

My third wife had left me. She had gone away during the night, while I'd been at a business meeting with a client; I had been engaged to design a church in Baton Rouge. All that day I'd steamed the old wallpaper off the apartment we'd rented. It was to have been our first home together, paid for by the commission. I'd done the steaming myself, with a tall ladder and a steam condenser and two flat pans with steam holes. Up near the ceiling the heat had been so awful I'd almost fainted. She'd brought me lemonade, freshly squeezed. Then I'd showered and changed and gone to my meeting. When I'd returned, she was gone. No note.

Lizette and I were two sides of the same coin, cast off after death for the opposite extremes of the same crime. She had never loved. I had loved too much. Overindulgence in something as delicate as love is to be found monstrously offensive in the eyes of the God of Love. And some of us—who have never understood the salvation in the Golden Mean—some of us are cast adrift with but one chance. It can happen.

Mist formed around us, and my unicorn crept close to me, somehow smaller, almost timid. We were moving into realms he did not understand, where his limited magics were useless. These were realms of potency so utterly beyond even the limbo creatures—such as my unicorn—so completely alien to even the intermediary zone wanderers—Lizette and myself—that we were as helpless and without understanding as those who live. We had only one advantage over living, breathing, as yet undead humans: we *knew* for certain that the realms on the other side existed.

Above, beyond, deeper: where the gods live. Where the one who had given me my chance, had given Lizette *her* chance, where He lived. Undoubtedly watching.

The mist swirled up around us, as chill and final as the dust of pharaohs' tombs.

We moved through it, toward the pulsing heart of blue light. And as we came into the penultimate circle, we stopped. We were in the outer ring of potency, and we saw the claiming things that had come for Lizette. She lay out on an altar of crystal, naked and trembling. They stood around her, enormously tall and transparent. Man shapes without faces. Within their transparent forms a strange, silvery fog swirled, like smoke from holy censers. Where eyes should have been on a man or a ghost, there were only dull flickering firefly glowings, inside, hanging in the smoke, moving, changing shape and position. No eyes at all. And tall, very tall, towering over Lizette and the altar.

For me, overcommitted to love, when dawn came without salvation, there was only an eternity of wandering, with my unicorn as sole companion. Ghost forevermore. Incense chimera viewed as dust-devil on the horizon, chilling as I passed in city streets, forever gone, invisible, lost, empty, helpless, wandering.

But for her, empty vessel, the fate was something else entirely. The God of Love had allowed her the time of wandering, trapped by day in stones, freed at night to wander. He had allowed her the final chance. And having failed to take it, her fate was with these claiming creatures, gods themselves . . . of another order . . . higher or lower I had no idea. But terrible.

"Lagniappe!" I screamed the word. The old Creole word they use in New Orleans when they want a little extra; a bonus of *croissants,* a few additional carrots dumped into the shopping bag, a baker's dozen, a larger portion of clams or crabs or shrimp. "*Lagniappe!* Lizette, take a little more! Try for the extra! Try . . . demand it . . . there's time . . . you have it coming to you . . . you've paid . . . I've paid . . . it's ours . . . *try!*"

She sat up, her naked body lit by lambent fires of chill blue cold from the other side. She sat up and looked across the inner circle to me, and I stood there with my arms out, trying desperately to break through the outer circle to her. But it was solid and I could not pass. Only virgins could pass.

And they would not let her go. They had been promised a feed, and they were there to claim. I began to cry, as I had cried when I finally heard what the mother had said, when I finally came home to the empty apartment and knew I had spent my life loving too much, demanding too much, myself a feeder at a board that *could* be depleted and emptied and serve up no more. She wanted to come to me, I could *see* she wanted to come to me. But they would have their meal.

Then I felt the muzzle of my unicorn at my neck, and in a step he had moved through the barrier that was impenetrable to me, and he moved across the circle and stood waiting. Lizette leaped from the altar and ran to me.

It all happened at the same time. I felt Lizette's body anchor in to mine, and *we* saw my unicorn standing over there on the other side, and for a moment *we* could not summon up the necessary reactions, the correct sounds. We knew for the first time in either our lives or our deaths what it was to be paralyzed. Then reactions began washing over me, we, us in wave after wave: cascading joy that Lizette had come to . . . us; utter love for this Paul ghost creature; realization that instinctively part of us was falling into the same pattern again; fear that that part would love too much at this mystic juncture; resolve to temper our love; and then anguish at the sight of our unicorn standing there, waiting to be claimed . . .

We called to him . . . using his secret name, one we had never spoken aloud. We could barely speak. Weight pulled at his throat, our throats. "Old friend . . ." We took a step toward him but could not pass the barrier. Lizette clung to me, Paul held me tight as I trembled with terror and the cold of that inner circle still frosting my flesh.

The great transparent claimers stood silently, watching, waiting, as if content to allow us our moments of final decision. But their impatience could be felt in the air, a soft purring, like the death rattle always in the throat of a cat. "Come back! Not for me . . . don't do it for me . . . it's not fair!"

Paul's unicorn turned his head and looked at us.

My friend of starless nights, when we had gone sailing together through the darkness. My friend who had walked with me on endless tours of empty places. My friend of gentle nature and constant companionship. Until Lizette, my friend, my only friend, my familiar assigned to an onerous task, who had come to love me and to whom I had belonged, even as he had belonged to me.

I could not bear the hurt that grew in my chest, in my stomach; my head was on fire, my eyes burned with tears first for Paul, and now for the sweetest creature a god had ever sent to temper a man's anguish . . . and for myself. I could not bear the thought of never knowing—as Paul had known it—the silent company of that gentle, magical beast.

But he turned back, and moved to them, and they took that as final decision, and the great transparent claimers moved in around him, and their quickglass hands reached down to touch him, and for an instant they seemed to hesitate, and I called out, "Don't be afraid . . ." and my unicorn turned his head to look across the mist of potency for the last time, and I saw he *was* afraid, but not as much as he would have been if I had not been there.

Then the first of them touched his smooth, silvery flank and he gave a trembling sigh of pain. A ripple ran down his hide. Not the quick flesh movement of ridding himself of a fly, but a completely alien, unnatural tremor, containing in its swiftness all the agony and loss of eternities. A sigh went out from Paul's unicorn, though he had not uttered it.

We could feel the pain, the loneliness. My unicorn with no time left to him. Ending. All was now a final ending; he had stayed with me, walked with me, and had grown to care for me, until that time when he would be released from his duty by that special God; but now freedom was to be denied him; an ending.

The great transparent claimers all touched him, their ice fingers caressing his warm hide as we watched, helpless, Lizette's face buried in Paul's chest. Colors surged across my unicorn's body, as if by becoming more intense the chill touch of the claimers could be beaten off. Pulsing waves of rainbow color that lived in his hide for moments, then dimmed, brightened again and were bled off. Then the colors leaked away one by one, chroma weakening: purple-blue, manganese violet, discord, cobalt blue, doubt, affection, chrome green, chrome yellow, raw sienna, contemplation, alizarin crimson, irony, silver, severity, compassion, cadmium red, white.

They emptied him . . . he did not fight them . . . going colder and colder . . . flickers of yellow, a whisper of blue, pale as white . . . the tremors blending into one constant shudder . . . the wonderful golden eyes rolled in torment, went flat, brightness dulled, flat metal . . . the platinum hoofs caked with rust . . . and he stood, did not try to escape, gave himself for us . . . and he was emptied. Of everything. Then, like the claimers, we could see through him. Vapors swirled within the transparent husk, a fogged glass, shimmering . . . then nothing. And then they absorbed even the husk.

The chill blue light faded, and the claimers grew indistinct in our sight. The smoke within them seemed thicker, moved more slowly, horribly, as though they had fed and were sluggish and would go away, back across the line to that dark place where they waited, always waited, till their hunger was aroused again. And my unicorn was gone. I was alone with Lizette. I was alone with Paul. The mist died away, and the claimers were gone, and once more it was merely a cemetery as the first rays of the morning sun came easing through the tumble and disarray of headstones.

We stood together as one, her naked body white and virginal in my weary arms; and as the light of the sun struck us we began to fade, to merge, to mingle our bodies and our wandering spirits one into the other; forming one spirit that would neither love too much, nor too little, having taken our chance on the downhill side.

We faded and were lifted invisibly on the scented breath of that good God who had owned us, and were taken away from there. To be born again as one spirit, in some other human form, man or woman we did not know which. Nor would we remember. Nor did it matter.

This time, love would not destroy us. This time out, we would have luck.

The luck of silken mane and rainbow colors, platinum hoofs and spiral horn.

The Parrot

Isaac Bashevis Singer

Winner of the Nobel Prize for Literature, Isaac Bashevis Singer is simply one of the great contemporary writers. His stories are translated from Yiddish into English, and he writes often of the Eastern European settings from which his rich heritage derives. The fantastic is a common strain in his work, particularly the fantastic traditions of Jewish culture. Here is a story of men in prison, grimy and filled with suppressed violence, who hear the tale of a confessed murderer, of his passion and his love, of madness and the supernatural, quiet, intense, ironic, chilling.

Outside, the moon was shining, but in the prison cell it was almost dark. Although the single window was barred and screened, enough light filtered in to disclose parts of faces. New snow had fallen and gave a violet glow to the speck of sky which came through the window as through a sieve. By midnight it had become as cold as in the street and the prisoners had covered themselves with all the rags they had: cotton vests, jackets, overcoats. They slept in their caps, with rags stuffed in their shoes. In summer the chamber pot had given off a stench, but now the winter wind came in and blew away the odor. It had begun to get dark at half past three in the afternoon, and by six Stach the watchman put out the kerosene lamp. The prisoners went on talking for a little while until they fell asleep. Their snoring kept up till about one o'clock, when they began to wake.

The first one to awake was Leibele the thief, a married man, a father of daughters. He yawned like a bell. Mottele Roiskes woke up with a belch; then Berele Zakelkover sat up and went to urinate. The three had been there for months and had told one another all their stories. But this morning there was a new prisoner, a giant of a man with a snub nose, a straight neck, thick mustaches the color of beer, dressed in a new jacket, tight high boots, and a cap lined with fur. He had brought a padded blanket and an additional pair of new boots which hung over his shoulders. He seemed like a big shot who had influence with the police. In the beginning they thought him a Gentile. They even spoke about him in thieves' jargon. But he proved to be a Jew, a silent man, a recluse. When they spoke to him, he scarcely answered. He stretched out on the bench and lay there for hours without a word. Stach brought him a bowl of kasha and a piece of black bread, but he was in no hurry to eat. Leibele asked him, "A word from you is like a gold coin, eh?"

To which he answered, "Two coins."

They couldn't get any more out of him.

"Well, he'll soften up, the snob," Mottele Roiskes said.

If this new inmate had been a weaker fellow, the others would have known what to do with him, but he had the shoulders and hands of a fighter. Such a man might have a hidden knife. As long as there was light, Leibele, Mottele Roiskes, and Berele Zakelkover played Sixty-six with a pack of marked cards. Then they went to sleep with heavy hearts. In prison it's not good when a man thinks too highly of himself. But sooner or later he has to break down.

Presently all three of them were silent and listened to the stranger. Since he didn't snore, it was hard to know if he was asleep or awake. The few words which he had spoken he pronounced with hard *r*"s, a sign that he was not from around Lublin. He must have come from Great Poland, on the other side of the Vistula. Then what was he doing in the prison at Yanev? They seldom sent anyone from so far away. Mottele Roiskes was the first to talk. "What time can it be?" Nobody answered. "What happened to the rooster?" he continued. "He stopped crowing."

"Maybe it's too cold for him to crow," Berele Zakelkover answered.

"Too cold? They get warm from crowing. There was a teacher in our town, Reb Itchele, who said that when a rooster crows he burns behind his wings. That's the reason he flaps his wings—to cool off."

"What nonsense," Leibele growled.

"It's probably written in a holy book."

"A holy book can also say silly things."

"It's probably from the Gemara."

"How does the Gemara know what's happening behind a rooster's wings? They sit in the study house and they invent things."

"They know some things. A preacher came to us and he said that all the philosophers wanted to know how long a snake is pregnant and nobody knew. But they asked a tanna and he said seven years."

"So long?"

They became quiet; conversation petered out. Berele Zakelkover began to scratch his foot. He suffered from eczema. He scratched and hissed softly at the same time. Suddenly the stranger said in a deep voice, "A snake is not pregnant seven years, perhaps not even seven months."

All became tense. All became cheerful.

"How do you know how long a snake is pregnant?" Leibele asked. "Do you breed snakes?"

"No creature is pregnant seven years. How long does a snake live?"

"There are all kinds of snakes."

"How can the Gemara know? To know you have to keep two snakes in the house, a he and a she, and let them mate."

"Perhaps God told him."

"Yes."

They became quiet again. The stranger was now sitting up. One could barely see his silhouette but his eyes reflected the gold of the moon. After a little while he said, "God says nothing. God is silent."

"He spoke to Moses."

"I wasn't there."

"An unbeliever, eh?"

"How can you know what God said to Moses?" the stranger argued. "It's written in the Pentateuch, but who wrote the Pentateuch? With a pen you can write anything. I come from Kalisch, where there are two rabbis. When one pronounced a thing kosher, the other said unkosher. Before Passover the miller asked one of them to make the mill kosher. So the other one got angry that he hadn't received ten rubles and he said the Passover flour was unkosher. Does all this come from God?"

Mottele Roiskes was about to answer, but Leibele interrupted. "If you are from Kalisch, what are you doing here?"

"That's a different matter."

"What do you mean?"

The stranger gave no reply. The stillness became heavy and tense.

"Do you have a smoke?" the stranger asked.

"We're all out."

"I can do without food, but I have to have a smoke. Can you get it from the watchman?"

"We have no money."

"I have some."

"With money you can buy anything. Even in the clink," Leibele answered. "But not now. Wait until morning."

"The winter nights are rough," Berele Zakelkover began to say. "You go to sleep with the chickens, and by twelve o'clock you're already slept out. You lie in the dark and all kinds of thoughts come into your mind. Here you've got to talk or you'll go crazy."

"What is there to talk about?" the stranger asked. "There's a proverb: man spouts, God flouts. I'm not an unbeliever, but God sits in the seventh heaven and snaps his fingers at everything."

"Why did they put you in this cage?" Leibele asked.

"For singing psalms."

"No, I'm serious."

The stranger was silent.

"A big pile, eh?"

"No pile at all. I'm not a thief and I don't like anyone to steal from me. If somebody tries it, I break him in pieces. That's the reason I'm here now."

"In what yeshiva did they keep you before?"

"First in Kielc and then in Lublin."

"Did you polish off someone?"

"Yes, that's exactly what I did."

2

The stranger stretched out on the bench again. Berele Zakelkover went to scratching his foot. Mottele Roiskes asked, "Are you going to stay here?"

"They'll probably send me to Siberia."

Leibele walked over to the window. "A blizzard."

"It's a sin to let out a dog in weather like this," Mottele Roiskes said.

"I'd like to be the dog," Berele joked.

The stranger sat up again. He leaned his back against the wall and supported his chin on his knees. Broken moon rays reflected on his shiny boot tops. He said, "So what if they let you out? In half a year you'd be sitting here again."

"A half a year isn't anything to sneeze at."

"This is the last time for me," Leibele said, both to himself and to the stranger. "I've eaten enough half-baked bread. I have a wife and children."

"That's the usual song they all sing," remarked the stranger. "Where do you all come from? From Piask?"

"You're a thief yourself."

"I'm not a thief, and till now I wasn't a murderer. I could always swap blows, but for many years I've never touched anyone, not even a fly."

"So what happened all of a sudden?" Leibele asked.

The stranger hesitated. "It was fated."

"Who did you finish off? A merchant?"

"A woman."

"Your own wife?"

"No. She wasn't my wife."

"Did you catch her red-handed?"

The stranger gave no answer. He seemed to doze off while sitting there. Suddenly he said, "It all happened because of a bird."

"A bird? No kidding."

"It's the truth."

"What kind of a bird?"

"A parrot."

"Tell us about it. If you hold it in, you'll lose your mind."

"That wouldn't be so bad, but you can't choose when to lose your mind. I'm a horse dealer, or, rather, that's what I was. They knew me in Kalisch as Simon the horse trader. My father also dealt in horses; my grandfather too. When the horse thieves in Kalisch tried to sell me bargains, I sent them packing. I didn't need stolen goods. Sometimes I used to buy a half-dead nag, but under my care it recovered. I love animals, all animals. We're a family of horse traders. My wife died two years after our marriage and for thirteen years I was alone. I loved her and I couldn't forget her. We had no child. I had a house,

stables; I kept a Gentile maid—not a young shiksa, an older woman.
And not for what you think either. I lived, as they say, respectably.
The matchmakers proposed all kinds of women, but I didn't like any
of them. I'm one of those men who must love, and if I don't love a
woman I can't live with her. It's as simple as that."

"Aha."

"I like animals. For me a horse is not just a horse. When I sold a
horse, I wanted to know to whom I was selling it. There was a coachman in our town who used to whip the horses, and I refused to sell to
him. For sixteen years I traded in horses and I never lifted a whip to
one. You can get anything out of an animal with good treatment. It's
the same with a horse, a dog, or a cat. Animals understand what you
say to them; they even guess your thoughts. Animals see in the dark
and have a better memory than men. Many times I've lost my way
and my horses have led me to the right spot. The snow might be
knee-deep, but my horses would take me to the peasant's hut and stop
in front of it. Sometimes my horse would even turn his head, as
though to say, 'Here it is, boss.'

"If you're alone, you have time to observe these creatures. Besides
horses, I had dogs, cats, rabbits, a cow, a goat. I lived in the suburbs
because in the city you can't keep a big stable, and can't take a horse
to pasture. Oats and hay are good in winter, but in summer a horse
needs fresh grass, green grass with flowers, and all the rest. The
peasants hobble their horses and leave them all night in the pasture,
but a hobbled animal is like a hobbled human being. Is it good to be
in prison? I made a fence around my pasture, and the peasants
laughed at me. It doesn't pay to build a fence around six acres of
land, they told me, but I didn't want to hobble my horses, or let them
stray into strange fields and get beaten. That's how I used to be
before I became a murderer."

"What about the bird?"

"Wait. I'm coming to that. I kept fowl, and birds too. In the beginning, they weren't in my house but under the roof and in the granary.
Storks used to come after Passover from the warm countries and
build nests on my roof. They didn't have to build new ones, they just
mended last year's nests after the rain and snow. Under the eaves,
starlings had built theirs. People believe that crows bring bad luck,
but actually crows are clever birds. I also had pigeon cotes. Some
people eat squabs but I never tasted one. How much meat is there in
a squab?"

"You seem to be a regular saint."

"I'm not a saint, but when you live in the suburbs you see all sorts of things. A bird flies in with a broken wing. A dog comes in limping. I'm not softhearted, but when you see a bird tottering on the ground and not able to lift itself up, you want to help it. I once took such a bird into my house and kept it until its wing was healed. I bandaged it like a doctor. Of course, the Jews laughed at me, but what do Jews know about animals? Some Gentiles understood. In summer my windows are wide open. As long as a bird wants to, it can stay and get its seed. When it's healthy again, it flies away. Once a bird returned to me, not alone, but with a wife. I was sitting on a stool fixing a saddle and suddenly two birds flew in. I recognized the male immediately because he had a scar on his leg. They stood on a shelf and sang me a good morning. It was like a dream.

"Matchmakers used to come to me and propose all kinds of arrangements, but when I looked over the merchandise she never pleased me. One was ugly, the other fat, the third one talked too much—I can't stand chatterboxes. Animals are silent; that's why I love them."

"A parrot talks."

"Yes."

"Well, what else?"

"Nothing. The years go by. One day it's my wife's first anniversary, then the second, then the eighth. Other horse dealers became rich, but I just made a living. I didn't fool the customer. I decided how much profit I wanted and that was all. I got used to being alone."

"What did you do when you needed a female?"

"What do you do?"

"In a prison you have no choice."

"If you don't like anyone, it's like being in a prison. There were whores in Kalisch, but when I looked at them I felt like vomiting. You could get a peasant girl or even a woman, but they were all lousy. Mine was a clean one. Each night she combed her hair. In the summer we bathed in a pond. She died from a lump in her breast. They cut it out but it grew again. Such suffering I don't wish my worst enemy."

"Was she beautiful?"

"A princess."

3

"Well, what about the parrot?"

"Wait. Where can I begin? I'm not a grandmother and I don't tell grandmothers' tales. Gypsies used to come to me to sell horses, but I never bought them. First of all, they're thieves. Second, their horses are seldom healthy and, if you're not an expert, you find the defect later. But I see everything the first minute. The gypsies knew that they couldn't put anything over on me.

"Once I was sitting and eating breakfast, millet with milk. I used to eat the same thing every morning. I always had a sack full of it for myself and for the birds. As I sat there, I saw a gypsy woman, a fat black one with large earrings and many strings of beads around her neck. She came in and said, 'Master, show me your hand.' I had never been to a fortune-teller; I didn't believe in it. Besides, what is the good of knowing things in advance? What must happen will happen. But, for some reason, I gave her my hand and she looked at my right palm and clucked in dismay. Then she asked for my left hand. 'Why do you need my left hand?' I asked. She said, 'The right one shows your fortune and the left one the fortune of your wife.' 'But I have no wife,' I said. 'My wife died.' And she said, 'There will be a second one.' 'When will she come?' I asked. 'She will fly into your window like a bird.' 'Will she have wings?' I asked. She smiled and showed her white teeth. I gave her a few groschen and a slice of bread, and she left. I paid no attention to her talk. Who cares about the babble of gypsies? But somehow the words were stored in my head and I remembered them and thought about them. Sometimes an idea ticks in your mind and you can't get rid of it.

"Now listen to what happened. They had just called me into a village to buy horses and I stayed overnight. The next day I came riding home with four horses, one my own mare and three which I had bought from a peasant. I walked into my house and there was a parrot. I didn't believe my own eyes. Local birds flew in and out, but where did a parrot come from? Parrots are not of this country. He stood on my wardrobe and looked at me as though he had been expecting me. He was as green as an unripe lemon but on his wings he had dark spots and his neck was yellow. He was not a large parrot; in fact, he seemed a young one. I gave him some millet and he ate it. I held out a saucer of water and he drank. I stretched out a finger to him and he perched on it like an old friend. I forgot all my business. I loved him immediately like my own child. In the beginning I wanted to close the window, because he could fly out as easily as he flew in. But it was summer, and besides, I thought, if he's destined to stay here, he'll stay.

"He didn't fly away. I bought him a cage, put in a saucer of millet, a dish of water, vegetables, a little mirror, and whatever else a bird needs. I named him Metzotze and the name stuck. In the beginning he didn't talk; he just clucked and cawed. Then suddenly he began to speak in a strange language. It must have been gypsy talk because it wasn't Polish or Russian or Yiddish. He must have escaped from the gypsies.

"The moment he came I knew that what the gypsy foretold would come true. Somehow I felt that this would happen. The summer was over and winter was coming on. I closed the windows to keep the house warm. He began to talk Yiddish and call me Simon, and when the Gentiles spoke in Polish he imitated them. The moment I entered the room he would fly up to my shoulder. When I went to the stable he stayed sitting there. He put his beak to my ear and played with my earlobe, telling me secrets in bird language. In the beginning I didn't know if he was a he or a she, but a magician passed by and told me it was a he. I began to look for a wife for him and at the same time I knew I would find my intended."

"A strange story," Mottele Roiskes interrupted.

"Just wait. Once I had to go to an estate to deliver horses, but since I loved my Metzotze so much, it was hard for me to leave him. But— how do they say it?—making a living is like waging a war. I took my horses and went to the estate. I told my maid—Tekla was her name— that she should watch the parrot like the eyes in her head. I didn't have to tell her—she was attached to the bird herself, as was my stable man. In a word, he was not among strangers. I sold my horses for a good price and everything went as smoothly as on greased wheels. I wanted to go home, but new business came up. The bird had brought me luck. I had to spend the night at an inn and the moment I entered I saw a woman: small, dark, with black eyes, a short nose. She looked at me and smiled familiarly as though I were an old friend. Outside, there was a blizzard, much as today, and we were the only guests. The landlady heated a samovar for us, but I said, 'Perhaps you have some vodka?' I'm not a drunkard but in business you sometimes have to drink. When the deal is finished, the buyer and the seller strike their palms together and have a drink. The landlady brought us a bottle and a bowl of pretzels. I asked the woman, 'Perhaps you want to taste some?' and she answered, 'Why not? I'm still able to enjoy life.' I poured a full glass for her and she tossed it off as if it were nothing at all. She didn't even take a pretzel afterwards. I saw that she could pour it down. When the landlady went to see a peasant about a cow, we were left alone. I took a glass, she took a glass. I don't get drunk quickly—I can pour down a large bottle and still stay sober. I was afraid she would get fuddled but she sat there and smiled, and we just became more cheerful and familiar. We talked like old cronies. She told me her name was Esther and she came from somewhere in Volhynia. 'What is a young woman doing alone in an inn?' I asked her.

" 'I'm waiting for a smuggler.'

" 'What do you need a smuggler for?' I asked, and she told me she was going to America. 'What's wrong with this country?'

"She told me she had had an affair and the man left her. She learned that he had a wife. He was a traveling salesman, one of those skirt chasers who think tricking a woman is something to boast about. 'Well,' she said, 'I played and lost. I couldn't show my face at home any more.' It came out that she had had a husband and had divorced him. Her father was a pious man and it was below his dignity. In short, she had to leave. Some smuggler was going to lead her to the German border.

" 'What will you do in faraway America?' I said. And she answered, 'Sew blouses. If you do something silly, you have to pay for it.' I poured her a fourth glass, a fifth glass. She said, 'Why didn't I meet you before? A man like you would make a good husband for me.' 'It's never too late,' I said. Why should I drag it out? By the time the landlady came back from the peasant, everything was settled between us. I was drawn to her as to a magnet and she felt the same way. We held hands, kissed, and her kissing drove you crazy. She wasn't a female, she was a piece of fire. I didn't want the landlady to know what was going on and I went to sleep in my room, but I lay there in a fever. She slept right next door and I heard through the thin wall how she tossed on her bed. At dawn I fell asleep and in the morning I had to leave. We had already decided that she was going with me. The whole business of America was out. She didn't need a smuggler any more.

"I came out of my room and found my woman already packed and ready. She smiled at me and her eyes shone. When the landlady heard that she was going with me, she understood what had happened, but what did I care? My heart was with Esther. I took her in my sleigh and she sat near me on the driver's seat. She was afraid of falling and she held on to me and excited me all over again. Riding along, we decided to get married. We didn't need any special ceremonies. I was a widower and she a divorcee. We would go to Getzel, the assistant rabbi, and he would lead us under a canopy. I told her about the bird and she said, 'I will be a mother to him.' We spoke about him as though he would be our child."

"Did you really marry her?" Leibele asked.

"No."

"Why not?"

"Because she was divorced and I was a Cohen. I had forgotten the law."

"Who reminded you? The assistant rabbi?"

"Who else?"

"What a story!"

4.

"When Rabbi Getzel told me that we couldn't marry, I wanted to tear him to pieces, but was it his fault? I never went to pray except at Rosh Hashanah and Yom Kippur. Suddenly I was a Cohen, descended from a priestly line! I took Esther and went home with her. 'Let's pretended that I'm a Catholic priest and you're my housekeeper.' I lived far from the city and nobody would look through the keyhole. At first she was disappointed. What should she write to her family? But we were both so much in love that we could barely wait till night. Metzotze immediately became pals with her. The moment she entered, he perched on her shoulder and she kissed him on the beak and he kissed back. I said to her, 'He's our matchmaker,' and I told her the story of the gypsy and the rest of it.

"In the beginning everything went well. We lived like two doves. They gossiped about us in the city, but who cared? So what if Simon the horse dealer isn't pious? So they won't call me up to the reading of the scroll. Well, but Esther wanted a baby and that was bad. It would mean that the baby would be a bastard. Some student from the study house told me that such a baby is not exactly a bastard but is called by some other name. But it's bad just the same. Esther had written to her parents that she got married and they wanted to visit us. Now the complications began. I was satisfied to be alone with her. Esther and Metzotze were enough for me. But she only wanted to go to town. She asked me if I had friends, wanted to invite guests to show off her cooking and baking. Her cooking was fit for a king. She could bake a cake which you couldn't match in the best bakeries. She dressed nicely too, but for whom? In the fields she wore a corset. She tried to persuade me to go with her to America. I wish I had listened to her, but I had no desire to travel thousands of miles. I had a house, stables, grounds. If you have to sell all this, you get almost nothing in return. What could I do in America? Press pants? Besides, I was so attached to the bird that I couldn't leave him. And it's not so easy to drag a parrot over borders and oceans. I was attached to my mare too. And where could I leave her? She wasn't young any more and if she fell into the hands of a coachman he would whip her to pieces. I said to Esther, 'We love each other, let's live quietly. Who cares about what people babble about?' But she was only drawn to people. She went to the city, made acquaintances, entangled herself with low characters and the devil knows what. I let her persuade me to invite a few horse dealers to a party, but in the years when I was a widower I had kept away from everybody and no one wanted to come to the suburbs. Those who came did us a great favor. After they left, Esther burst into tears and cried until daybreak.

"Why drag it out? We began to quarrel. I mean, she quarreled. She scolded, she cursed, she cried and screamed that I had trapped her. Why didn't I tell her I was a Cohen? I didn't remember that I was a Cohen any more than you remember what you ate in your mother's belly. She lay beside me at night and kept talking as though possessed by a dybbuk. One moment she laughed; the next moment she cried. She was putting on an act, but for whom? She talked to herself and did such strange things that you wouldn't believe that it was the same Esther. She called me names that you don't hear in my part of the country. Suddenly she began to be hostile to the bird. He screamed too much, he dirtied the house, he didn't let her sleep at night. She was jealous too, complaining that I loved him more than I did her.

"When this began I knew that it would have a bad ending. Was it Metzotze's fault? He was as good as an angel. At night he was quiet, but in the morning a bird doesn't lie under a quilt and snore. A bird begins to sing at daybreak. Esther, however, went to sleep at two o'clock in the morning, and at eleven at night she might begin to wash her hair or bake a cake. I saw I was in a mess, but what could I do? One minute she was sane, the next minute crazy. There's a teahouse in Kalisch where all the scum gather together. She kept on dragging me there. I sat and drank tea while she made friends with all the roughnecks. She met some strange nobody and told him all our secrets. I must have been stronger than iron not to bury myself from shame. She could be clever, but when she wanted she could act like the worst fool. It was all from spite, but what did I do to deserve it? Another man in my place would take her by the hair and throw her out, but I get used to a person. Also, I have pity.

"I can tell you, it became worse from day to day. I never knew what Gehenna was, but I had Gehenna in my own house. She picked quarrels with the maid, the Gentile, and made her leave. I had never touched her, but Esther suspected the worst. She was only looking for excuses to make trouble. She also began to pick fights with the stable boy. For years both had worked for me with devotion. Now they had to run away, and in my business you need help. You can't do everything by yourself. Horses have to be scrubbed and groomed. There are imps that come into the stables at night. Don't laugh at me. I didn't believe it either until I saw it with my own eyes. I would buy a horse and put him in the stable. I'd come in the morning and he was bathed in sweat as though he had been driven all night long over hills and ditches. He was foaming at the mouth. I would look at the mane and it would be in pigtails. Who would come at night to braid pigtails on a horse? It happened not once but ten times. These imps can torture a horse to death. I had to go down at night and keep watch. But when the groom left, I had to do his work too. In short, it was bad. When I talked she flared up; when I was silent she complained that I ignored her. She was only looking for something to pick on. I couldn't write, and she tried to teach me. She gave me one lesson and that was it. We played cards just to kill time, but she cheated. Why did she have to cheat? I gave her enough money."

"For such a piece of merchandise there is only one remedy," said Leibele. "A good swat in the kisser."

"Just what I wanted to say," Mottele Roiskes chimed in.

"I tried that too. But I have a heavy hand and when I give a blow I can cripple someone. If I touched her I had to pay the doctor. She also threatened to denounce me. But what was there to denounce? I didn't make counterfeit money. She was far from religious, but if she felt like it she could become pious. To make a fire on the Sabbath was all right, but to pour out the slops was forbidden. She changed the rules whenever it suited her. The women in the city knew of my misfortune and laughed in my face.

"It happened two years ago in the winter. I don't know how it was here, but around Kalisch there were terrible frosts. Old men couldn't remember such cold, and heating the stoves didn't help. The wind blew and broke the trees. On my place, the wind tore off a piece of the fence. Usually it's warm in the stable, but I was afraid for my horses, for when a horse catches cold it's the end. To this day I don't remember what we quarreled about that evening, but then, when didn't we quarrel? It was one long war. Sometimes at night we made peace for a few minutes, but later we didn't even do this. She slept in the bed and I on a bench. When I had to get up, she went to sleep. I'm a light sleeper—it's easy to disturb me. She crept around, boiled tea, moved chairs; she began to say the Shema and suddenly she burst out laughing like mad. She wasn't mad—she did it to spite me. She knew that I loved the parrot and she had it in for him. A parrot comes from a warm climate and if he catches a draft he's finished. But she opened the doors and let the wind blow in. He could have flown away, because he was an animal, not a man with understanding. I told her clearly, 'If anything happens to Metzotze, it's all over with you.' And she screamed, 'Go and marry him. A Cohen is allowed to marry a parrot.' I know now that it was all predestined. It's written on a man's palm or on his forehead: he will live this long; he will do this and that. But what did she have against me? I didn't stop her from going to America. I was even ready to pay her expenses.

"Where am I? Oh. Yes, I warned her, 'You can do with me whatever you want, but don't take it out on Metzotze.' Nonetheless, she screamed at him and scolded him as though he were a man. 'He's scabby, lousy, a demon's in him,' and so on. You know, a bird needs to have darkness at night. When a lamp is lit, he thinks it's day. She kept on lighting the candles, and the bird couldn't stand light at night and tucked his head under his wing. What does a bird need? A few grains of seed and a little sleep. How can a man torture a bird? One night I heard noises in the stable. I took my lantern and went to look at the horses. As I stepped over the threshold I somehow knew there would be misfortune."

For a while all was silent. Then Leibele asked, "What did she do? Chase out the parrot?"

The stranger began to murmur and to clear his throat. "Yes, in the middle of the night, in a burning frost."

"He wasn't found, huh?"

"He flew away."

"And you finished her, huh?"

The stranger paused.

"As I came back from the stable and I saw that the parrot wasn't there, I went over to her and said, 'Esther, it's your end.' I grabbed her by the hair, took her outside, and threw her into the well."

"She didn't fight back?"

"No, she went quietly."

"Still, one has to be a murderer to do something like that," Mottele Roiskes remarked.

"I am a murderer."

"What else?"

"Nothing. I went to the police and said, 'This is what I did. Take me.' "

"In the middle of the night?"

"It was already beginning to get light."

"Did they let you go to the funeral?"

"No funeral."

"They say that a Cohen is an angry man," Berele Zakelkover threw in.

"It looks that way."

"How much did they give you?"

"Eight years."

"Well, you got off easy."

"I'll never get out," the stranger said.

For a long while all were quiet. Then the stranger said, "Metzotze is still around."

"What do you mean?"

"You'll think I'm crazy, but what do I care?"

"What do you mean, around?"

"He comes to me. He perches on my shoulder."

"Are you dreaming?"

"No, it's the truth."

"You imagine it."

"He speaks. I hear his voice."

"In that case you're a little touched."

"He sleeps on my forehead."

"Well, you're out of your mind."

"A parrot has a soul."

"Nonsense," Leibele said. "If a parrot has a soul, so has a chicken. If all the chickens, geese, and ducks had souls, the world would be full of souls."

"All I know is that Metzotze visits me."

"It's because you miss him so much."

"He comes, he kisses me on the mouth. He flutters his tail against my ear."

"Will he come here too?"

"Perhaps."

"And how will he know that they sent you to Yanev?"

"He knows everything."

"Nonsense. Tell it to the doctor. They'll send you to the nuthouse. It's easy to run away from there. What about Esther? Does she visit you too?"

"No, she doesn't."

"Fantasies. The dead are dead. Men as well as animals."

The stranger stretched out on the bench again. "I know the truth."

TRANSLATED BY RUTH WHITMAN

The Gray Wolf

George MacDonald

George MacDonald is one of the greatest fantasists in the language. His fantasies for children are classics and his fantasy novels for adults, such as Lilith and Phantastes, have influenced such later masters as C. S. Lewis and J. R. R. Tolkien. Here is a little-known tale, dark and fierce, with an unusual vision of a conventional fantasy creature. Inevitably, one must compare it to Peter S. Beagle's "Lila the Werewolf" (pp.332–52). This is a fable of the dangers of women to a young man.

One evening-twilight in spring, a young English student, who had wandered northwards as far as the outlying fragments of Scotland called the Orkney and Shetland Islands, found himself on a small island of the latter group, caught in a storm of wind and hail, which had come on suddenly. It was in vain to look about for any shelter; for not only did the storm entirely obscure the landscape, but there was nothing around him save a desert moss.

At length, however, as he walked on for mere walking's sake, he found himself on the verge of a cliff, and saw, over the brow of it, a few feet below him, a ledge of rock, where he might find some shelter from the blast, which blew from behind. Letting himself down by his hands, he alighted upon something that crunched beneath his tread, and found the bones of many small animals scattered about in front of a little cave in the rock, offering the refuge he sought. He went in, and sat upon a stone. The storm increased in violence, and as the darkness grew he became uneasy, for he did not relish the thought of spending the night in the cave. He had parted from his companions on the opposite side of the island, and it added to his uneasiness that they must be full of apprehension about him. At last there came a lull in the storm, and the same instant he heard a footfall, stealthy and light as that of a wild beast, upon the bones at the mouth of the cave. He started up in some fear, though the least thought might have satisfied him that there could be no very dangerous animals upon the island. Before he had time to think, however, the face of a woman appeared in the opening. Eagerly the wanderer spoke. She started at the sound of his voice. He could not see her well, because she was turned towards the darkness of the cave.

"Will you tell me how to find my way across the moor to Shielness?" he asked.

"You cannot find it to-night," she answered, in a sweet tone, and with a smile that bewitched him, revealing the whitest of teeth.

"What am I to do, then?"

"My mother will give you shelter, but that is all she has to offer."

"And that is far more than I expected a minute ago," he replied. "I shall be most grateful."

She turned in silence and left the cave. The youth followed.

She was barefooted, and her pretty brown feet went catlike over the sharp stones, as she led the way down a rocky path to the shore. Her garments were scanty and torn, and her hair blew tangled in the wind. She seemed about five and twenty, lithe and small. Her long fingers kept clutching and pulling nervously at her skirts as she went. Her face was very gray in complexion, and very worn, but delicately formed, and smooth-skinned. Her thin nostrils were tremulous as eyelids, and her lips, whose curves were faultless, had no colour to give sign of indwelling blood. What her eyes were like he could not see, for she had never lifted the delicate films of her eyelids.

At the foot of the cliff they came upon a little hut leaning against it, and having for its inner apartment a natural hollow within. Smoke was spreading over the face of the rock, and the grateful odour of food gave hope to the hungry student. His guide opened the door of the cottage; he followed her in, and saw a woman bending over a fire in the middle of the floor. On the fire lay a large fish broiling. The daughter spoke a few words, and the mother turned and welcomed the stranger. She had an old and very wrinkled but honest face, and looked troubled. She dusted the only chair in the cottage, and placed it for him by the side of the fire, opposite the one window, whence he saw a little patch of yellow sand over which the spent waves spread themselves out listlessly. Under this window there was a bench, upon which the daughter threw herself in an unusual posture, resting her chin upon her hand. A moment after, the youth caught the first glimpse of her blue eyes. They were fixed upon him with a strange look of greed, amounting to craving, but, as if aware that they belied or betrayed her, she dropped them instantly. the moment she veiled them, her face, notwithstanding its colourless complexion, was almost beautiful.

When the fish was ready, the old woman wiped the deal table, steadied it upon the uneven floor, and covered it with a piece of fine table-linen. She then laid the fish on a wooden platter, and invited the guest to help himself. Seeing no other provision, he pulled from his pocket a hunting knife, and divided a portion from the fish, offering it to the mother first.

"Come, my lamb," said the old woman; and the daughter approached the table. But her nostrils and mouth quivered with disgust.

The next moment she turned and hurried from the hut.

"She doesn't like fish," said the old woman, "and I haven't anything else to give her."

"She does not seem in good health," he rejoined.

The woman answered only with a sigh, and they ate their fish with the help of a little rye bread. As they finished their supper, the youth heard the sound as of the pattering of a dog's feet upon the sand close to the door; but ere he had time to look out of the window, the door opened, and the young woman entered. She looked better, perhaps from having just washed her face. She drew a stool to the corner of the fire opposite him. But as she sat down, to his bewilderment, and even horror, the student spied a single drop of blood on her white skin within her torn dress. The woman brought out a jar of whisky, put a rusty old kettle on the fire, and took her place in front of it. As soon as the water boiled, she proceeded to make some toddy in a wooden bowl.

Meantime the youth could not take his eyes off the young woman, so that at length he found himself fascinated, or rather bewitched. She kept her eyes for the most part veiled with the loveliest eyelids fringed with darkest lashes, and he gazed entranced; for the red glow of the little oil-lamp covered all the strangeness of her complexion.

But as soon as he met a stolen glance out of those eyes unveiled, his soul shuddered within him. Lovely face and craving eyes alternated fascination and repulsion.

The mother placed the bowl in his hands. He drank sparingly, and passed it to the girl. She lifted it to her lips, and as she tasted—only tasted it—looked at him. He thought the drink must have been drugged and have affected his brain. Her hair smoothed itself back, and drew her forehead backwards with it; while the lower part of her face projected towards the bowl, revealing, ere she sipped, her dazzling teeth in strange prominence. But the same moment the vision vanished; she returned the vessel to her mother, and rising, hurried out of the cottage.

Then the old woman pointed to a bed of heather in one corner with a murmured apology; and the student, wearied both with the fatigues of the day and the strangeness of the night, threw himself upon it, wrapped in his cloak. The moment he lay down, the storm began afresh, and the wind blew so keenly through the crannies of the hut, that it was only by drawing his cloak over his head that he could protect himself from its currents. Unable to sleep, he lay listening to the uproar which grew in violence, till the spray was dashing against the window. At length the door opened, and the young woman came in, made up the fire, drew the bench before it, and lay down in the same strange posture, with her chin propped on her hand and elbow, and her face turned towards the youth. He moved a little; she dropped her head, and lay on her face, with her arms crossed beneath her forehead. The mother had disappeared.

Drowsiness crept over him. A movement of the bench roused him, and he fancied he saw some four-footed creature as tall as a large dog trot quietly out of the door. He was sure he felt a rush of cold wind. Gazing fixedly through the darkness, he thought he saw the eyes of the damsel encountering his, but a glow from the falling together of the remnants of the fire revealed clearly enough that the bench was vacant. Wondering what could have made her go out in such a storm, he fell fast asleep.

In the middle of the night he felt a pain in his shoulder, came broad awake, and saw the gleaming eyes and grinning teeth of some animal close to his face. Its claws were in his shoulder, and its mouth in the act of seeking his throat. Before it had fixed its fangs, however, he had its throat in one hand, and sought his knife with the other. A terrrible struggle followed; but regardless of the tearing claws, he found and opened his knife. He had made one futile stab, and was drawing it for a surer, when, with a spring of the whole body, and one wildly contorted effort, the creature twisted its neck from his hold, and with something betwixt a scream and a howl, darted from him. Again he heard the door open; again the wind blew in upon him, and it continued blowing; a sheet of spray dashed across the floor, and over his face. He sprung from his couch and bounded to the door.

It was a wild night—dark, but for the flash of whiteness from the waves as they broke within a few yards of the cottage; the wind was raving, and the rain pouring down the air. A gruesome sound as of mingled weeping and howling came from somewhere in the dark. He turned again into the hut and closed the door, but could find no way of securing it.

The lamp was nearly out, and he could not be certain whether the form of the young woman was upon the bench or not. Overcoming a strong repugnance, he approached it, and put out his hands—there was nothing there. He sat down and waited for the daylight: he dared not sleep any more.

When the day dawned at length, he went out yet again, and looked around. The morning was dim and gusty and gray. The wind had fallen, but the waves were tossing wildly. He wandered up and down the little strand, longing for more light.

At length he heard a movement in the cottage. By and by the voice of the old woman called to him from the door.

"You're up early, sir. I doubt you didn't sleep well."

"Not very well," he answered. "But where is your daughter?"

"She's not awake yet," said the mother. "I'm afraid I have but a poor breakfast for you. But you'll take a dram and a bit of fish. It's all I've got."

Unwilling to hurt her, though hardly in good appetite, he sat down at the table. While they were eating, the daughter came in, but turned her face away and went to the farther end of the hut. When she came forward after a minute or two, the youth saw that her hair was drenched, and her face whiter than before. She looked ill and faint, and when she raised her eyes, all their fierceness had vanished, and sadness had taken its place. Her neck was now covered with a cotton handkerchief. She was modestly attentive to him, and no longer shunned his gaze. He was gradually yielding to the temptation of braving another night in the hut, and seeing what would follow, when the old woman spoke.

"The weather will be broken all day, sir," she said. "You had better be going, or your friends will leave without you."

Ere he could answer, he saw such a beseeching glance on the face of the girl, that he hesitated, confused. Glancing at the mother, he saw the flash of wrath in her face. She rose and approached her daughter, with her hand lifted to strike her. The young woman stooped her head with a cry. He darted round the table to interpose between them. But the mother had caught hold of her; the hand kerchief had fallen from her neck; and the youth saw five blue bruises on her lovely throat—the marks of the four fingers and the thumb of a left hand. With a cry of horror he darted from the house, but as he reached the door he turned. His hostess was lying motionless on the floor, and a huge gray wolf came bounding after him.

There was no weapon at hand; and if there had been, his inborn chivalry would never have allowed him to harm a woman even under the guise of a wolf. Instinctively, he set himself firm, leaning a little forward, with half outstretched arms, and hands curved ready to clutch again at the throat upon which he had left those pitiful marks. But the creature as she sprung eluded his grasp, and just as he expected to feel her fangs, he found a woman weeping on his bosom, with her arms around his neck. The next instant, the gray wolf broke from him, and bounded howling up the cliff. Recovering himself as he best might, the youth followed, for it was the only way to the moor above, across which he must now make his way to find his companions.

All at once he heard the sound of a crunching of bones—not as if a creature was eating them, but as if they were ground by the teeth of rage and disappointment; looking up, he saw close above him the mouth of the little cavern in which he had taken refuge the day before. Summoning all his resolution, he passed it slowly and softly. From within came the sounds of a mingled moaning and growling.

Having reached the top, he ran at full speed for some distance across the moor before venturing to look behind him. When at length he did so, he saw, against the sky, the girl standing on the edge of the cliff, wringing her hands. One solitary wail crossed the space between. She made no attempt to follow him, and he reached the opposite shore in safety.

The Harrowing of the Dragon of Hoarsbreath

Patricia A. McKillip

Winner of the first World Fantasy Award *for best novel (1975), for* The Forgotten Beasts of Eld, *Patricia McKillip went on to write the popular "Riddle-Master of Hed" trilogy, as well as a number of books for younger readers. She rarely writes short stories. This one, however, is an interesting science fantasy about dragon-killing on another planet (a tradition that goes back to E. R. Eddison's fantasies set on the planet Mercury, especially* The Worm Ouroboros*). Beware of sincere young men who offer salvation: The solution they have may well be worse than the problem.*

Once, on the top of a world, there existed the ring of an island named Hoarsbreath, made out of gold and snow. It was all mountain, a grim, briny, yellowing ice-world covered with winter twelve months out of thirteen. For one month, when the twin suns crossed each other at the world's cap, the snow melted from the peak of Hoarsbreath. The hardly trees shrugged the snow off their boughs, and sucked in light and mellow air, pulling themselves toward the suns. Snow and icicles melted off the roofs of the miners' village; the snow-tunnels they had dug from house to tavern to storage barn to mineshaft sagged to the ground; the dead-white river flowing down from the mountain to the sea turned blue and began to move again. Then the miners gathered the gold they had dug by firelight out of the chill, harsh darkness of the deep mountain, and took it downriver, across the sea to the mainland, to trade for food and furs, tools and a liquid fire called worm-spoor, because it was gold and bitter, like the leavings of dragons. After three swallows of it, in a busy city with a harbor frozen only part of the year, with people who wore rich furs, kept horses and sleds to ride in during winter, and who knew the patterns of the winter stars since they weren't buried alive by the snow, the miners swore they would never return to Hoarsbreath. But the gold waiting in the dark, secret places of the mountain-island drew at them in their dreaming, lured them back.

For two hundred years after the naming of Hoarsbreath, winter followed winter, and the miners lived rich isolated, precarious lives on the pinnacle of ice and granite, cursing the cold and loving it, for it kept lesser folk away. They mined, drank, spun tales, raised children who were sent to the mainland when they were half-grown, to receive their education, and find easier, respectable lives. But always a few children found their way back, born with a gnawing in their hearts for fire, ice, stone, and the solitary pursuit of gold in the dark.

Then, two miners' children came back from the great world and destroyed the island.

They had no intention of doing that. The younger of them was Peka Krao. After spending five years on the mainland, boring herself with schooling, she came back to Hoarsbreath to mine. At seventeen, she was good-natured and sturdy, with dark eyes, and dark, braided hair. She loved every part of Hoarsbreath, even its chill, damp shafts at midwinter and the bone-jarring work of hewing through darkness and stone to unbury its gold. Her instincts for gold were uncanny: she seemed to sense it through her fingertips touching bare rock. The miners called her their good luck. She could make wormspoor, too, one of the few useful things she had learned on the mainland. It lost its bitterness, somehow, when she made it: it aged into a rich, smokey gold that made the miners forget their sore muscles, and inspired marvellous tales out of them that whittled away at the endless winter.

She met the Dragon-Harrower one evening at a cross-section of tunnel between her mother's house and the tavern. She knew all the things to fear in her world: a rumble in the mountain, a guttering torch in the mines, a crevice in the snow, a crack of ice underfoot. There was little else she couldn't handle with a soft word or her own right arm. Even when he loomed out of the darkness unexpectedly into her taper-light, she wasn't afraid. But he made her stop instinctively, like an animal might stop, faced with something that puzzled its senses.

His hair was dead-white, with strands bright as wormspoor running through it; his eyes were the light, hard blue of dawn during suns-crossing. Rich colors flashed out of him everywhere in her light: from a gold knife-hilt and a brass pack buckle; from the red ties of his cloak that were weighted with ivory, and the blue and silver threads in his gloves. His heavy fur cloak was closed, but she felt that if he shifted, other colors would escape from it into the cold, dark air. At first she thought he must be ancient: the taper-fire showed her a face that was shadowed and scarred, remote with strange experience, but no more than a dozen years older than hers.

"Who are you?" she breathed. Nothing on Hoarsbreath glittered like that in midwinter; its colors were few and simple: snow, damp fur and leather, fire, gold.

"I can't find my father," he said. "Lule Yarrow."

She stared at him, amazed that his colors had their beginnings on Hoarsbreath. "He's dead." His eyes widened slightly, losing some of their hardness. "He fell in a crevice. They chipped him out of the ice at suns-crossing, and buried him six years ago."

He looked away from her a moment, down at the icy ridges of tramped snow. "Winter." He broke the word in two, like an icicle. Then he shifted his pack, sighing. "Do they still have wormspoor on this ice-tooth?"

"Of course. Who are you?"

"Ryd Yarrow. Who are you?"

"Peka Krao."

"Peka. I remember. You were squalling in somebody's arms when I left."

"You look a hundred years older than that," she commented, still puzzling, holding him in her light, though she was beginning to feel the cold. "Seventeen years you've been gone. How could you stand it, being away from Hoarsbreath so long? I couldn't stand five years of it. There are so many people whose names you don't know, trying to tell you about things that don't matter, and the flat earth and the blank sky are everywhere. Did you come back to mine?"

He glanced up at the grey-white ceiling of the snow-tunnel, barely an inch above his head. "The sky is full of stars, and the gold wake of dragon-flights," he said softly. "I am a Dragon-Harrower. I am trained and hired to trouble dragons out of their lairs. That's why I came back here."

"Here. There are no dragons on Hoarsbreath."

His smile touched his eyes like a reflection of fire across ice. "Hoarsbreath is a dragon's heart."

She shifted, her own heart suddenly chilled. She said tolerantly. "That sounds like a marvellous tale to me."

"It's no tale. I know. I followed this dragon through centuries, through ancient writings, through legends, through rumors of terror and deaths. It is here, sleeping, coiled around the treasures of Hoarsbreath. If you on Hoarsbreath rouse it, you are dead. If I rouse it, I will end your endless winter."

"I like winter." Her protest sounded very small, muted within the thick snow-walls, but he heard it. He lifted his hand, held it lightly against the low ceiling above his head.

"You might like the sky beyond this. At night it is a mine of lights and hidden knowledge."

She shook her head. "I like close places, full of fire and darkness. And faces I know. And tales spun out of wormspoor. If you come with me to the tavern, they'll tell you where your father is buried, and give you lodgings, and then you can leave."

"I'll come to the tavern. With a tale."

Her taper was nearly burned down, and she was beginning to shiver. "A dragon." She turned away from him. "No one will believe you anyway."

"You do."

She listened to him silently, warming herself with wormspoor, as he spoke to the circle of rough, fire-washed faces in the tavern. Even in the light, he bore little resemblance to his father, except for his broad cheekbones and the threads of gold in his hair. Under his bulky cloak, he was dressed as plainly as any miner, but stray bits of color still glinted from him, suggesting wealth and distant places.

"A dragon," he told them, "is creating your winter. Have you ever asked yourselves why winter on this island is nearly twice as long as winter on the mainland twenty miles away? You live in dragon's breath, in the icy mist of its bowels, hoar-frost cold, that grips your land in winter the way another dragon's breath might burn it to flinders. One month out of the year, in the warmth of suns-crossing, it looses its ring-grip on your island, slides into the sea, and goes to mate. Its ice-kingdom begins to melt. It returns, loops its length around its mountain of ice and gold. Its breath freezes the air once more, locks the river into its bed, you into your houses, the gold into its mountain, and you curse the cold and drink until the next dragon-mating." He paused. There was not a sound around him. "I've been to strange places in this world, places even colder than this, where the suns never cross, and I have seen such monsters. They are ancient as rock, white as old ice, and their skin is like iron. They breed winter and they cannot be killed. But they can be driven away, into far corners of the world where they are dangerous to no one. I'm trained for this. I can rid you of your winter. Harrowing is dangerous work, and usually I am highly paid. But I've been looking for this ice-dragon for many years, through its spoor of legend and destruction. I tracked it here, one of the oldest of its kind, to the place where I was born. All I ask from you is a guide."

He stopped, waiting. Peka, her hands frozen around her glass, heard someone swallow. A voice rose and faded from the tavern-kitchen; sap hissed in the fire. A couple of the miners were smiling; the others looked satisfied and vaguely expectant, wanting the tale to continue. When it didn't, Kor Flynt, who had mined Hoarsbreath for fifty years, spat wormspoor into the fire. The flame turned a baleful gold, and then subsided. "Suns-crossing," he said politely, reminding a scholar of a scrap of knowledge children acquired with their first set of teeth, "cause the seasons."

"Not here," Ryd said. "Not on Hoarsbreath. I've seen. I know."

Peka's mother Ambris leaned forward. "Why," she asked curi-ously, "would a miner's son become a dragon harrower?" She had a pleasant, craggy face; her dark hair and her slow, musing voice were like Peka's. Peka saw the Dragon-Harrower ride between two an-swers in his mind. Meeting Ambris' eyes, he made a choice, and his own eyes strayed to the fire.

"I left Hoarsbreath when I was twelve. When I was fifteen, I saw a dragon in the mountains east of the city. Until then, I had intended to come back and mine. I began to learn about dragons. The first one I saw burned red and gold under the suns' fire; it swallowed small hills with its shadow. I wanted to call it, like a hawk. I wanted to fly with it. I kept studying, meeting other people who studied them, seeing other dragons. I saw a night-black dragon in the northern deserts; it scales were dusted with silver, and the flame that came out of it was silver. I saw people die in that flame, and I watched the harrowing of that dragon. It lives now on the underside of the world, in shadow.

We keep watch on all known dragons. In the green mid-world belt, rich with rivers and mines, forests and farmland, I saw a whole mining town burned to the ground by a dragon so bright I thought at first it was sun-fire arching down to the ground. Someone I loved had the task of tracking that one to its cave, deep beneath the mine-shafts. I watched her die, there. I nearly died. The dragon is sealed into the bottom of the mountain, by stone and by words. That is the dragon which harrowed me." He paused to sip wormspoor. His eyes lifted, not to Ambris, but to Peka. "Now do you understand what danger you live in? What if one year the dragon sleeps through its mating-time, with the soft heat of the suns making it sluggish from dreaming? You don't know it's there, wrapped around your world. It doesn't know you're there, stealing its gold. What if you sail your boats full of gold downriver and find the great white bulk of it sprawled like a wall across your passage? Or worse, you find its eye opening like a third, dead sun to see your hands full of its gold? It would slide its length around the mountain, coil upward and crush you all, then breathe over the whole of the island, and turn it dead-white as its heart, and it would never sleep again."

There was another silence. Peka felt something play along her spine like the thin, quavering, arthritic fingers of wind. "It's getting better," she said, "your tale." She took a deep swallow of wormspoor and added, "I love sitting in a warm, friendly place listening to tales I don't have to believe."

Kor Flynt shrugged. "It rings true, lass."

"It is true," Ryd said.

"Maybe so," she said. "And it may be better if you just let the dragon sleep."

"And if it wakes unexpectedly? The winter killed my father. The dragon at the heart of winter could destroy you all."

"There are other dangers. Rock falls, sudden floods, freezing winds. A dragon is simply one more danger to live with."

He studied her. "I saw a dragon once with wings as softly blue as a spring sky. Have you ever felt spring on Hoarsbreath? It could come."

She drank again. "You love them," she said. "Your voice loves them and hates them, Dragon-Harrower."

"I hate them," he said flatly. "Will you guide me down the mountain?"

"No. I have work to do."

He shifted, and the colors rippled from him again, red, gold, silver, spring-blue. She finished the wormspoor, felt it burn in her like liquid gold. "It's only a tale. All your dragons are just colors in our heads. Let the dragon sleep. If you wake it, you'll destroy the night."

"No," he said. "You will see the night. That's what you're afraid of."

Kor Flynt shrugged. "There probably is no dragon, anyway."

"Spring, though," Ambris said; her face had softened. "Sometimes I can smell it from the mainland, and, and I always wonder . . . Still, after a hard day's work, sitting beside a roaring fire sipping dragon-spit, you can believe anything. Especially this." She looked into her glass at the glowering liquid. "Is this some of yours, Peka? What did you put into it?"

"Gold." The expression in Ryd's eyes made her swallow sudden tears of frustration. She refilled her glass. "Fire, stone, dark, woodsmoke, night air smelling like cold tree-bark. You don't care, Ryd Yarrow."

"I do care," he said imperturbably. "It's the best wormspoor I've ever tasted."

"And I put a dragon's heart into it." She saw him start slightly; ice and hoar-frost shimmered from him. "If that's what Hoarsbreath is." A dragon beat into her mind, its wings of rime, its breath smoldering with ice, the guardian of winter. She drew breath, feeling the vast bulk of it looped around them all, dreaming its private dreams. Her bones seemed suddenly fragile as kindling, and the gold wormspoor in her hands a guilty secret. "I don't believe it," she said, lifting her glass. "It's a tale."

"Oh, go with him, lass," her mother said tolerantly. "There may be no dragon, but we can't have him swallowed up in the ice like his father. Besides, it may be a chance for spring."

"Spring is for flatlanders. There are things that shouldn't be wakened. I know."

"How?" Ryd asked.

She groped, wishing for the first time for a flatlander's skill with words. She said finally, "I feel it," and he smiled. She sat back in her chair, irritated and vaguely frightened. "Oh, all right, Ryd Yarrow, since you'll go with or without me. I'll lead you down to the shores in the morning. Maybe by then you'll listen to me."

"You can't see beyond your snow-world," he said implacably. "It is morning."

They followed one of the deepest mine-shafts, and clambered out of it to stand in the snow half-way down the mountain. The sky was lead grey; across the mists ringing the island's shores, they could see the ocean, a swirl of white, motionless ice. The mainland harbor was locked. Peka wondered if the ships were stuck like birds in the ice. The world looked empty and somber.

"At least in the dark mountain there is fire and gold. Here, there isn't even a sun." She took out a skin of wormspoor, sipped it to warm her bones. She held it out to Ryd, but he shook his head.

"I need all my wits. So do you, or we'll both end up preserved in ice at the bottom of a crevice."

"I know. I'll keep you safe." She corked the skin and added, "In case you were wondering."

But he looked at her, startled out of his remoteness. "I wasn't. Do you feel that strongly?"

"Yes."

"So did I, when I was your age. Now I feel very little." He moved again. She stared after him, wondering how he kept her smoldering and on edge. She said abruptly, catching up with him,

"Ryd Yarrow."

"Yes."

"You have two names. Ryd Yarrow, and Dragon-Harrower. One is a plain name this mountain gave you. The other you got from the world, the name that gives you color. One name I can talk to, the other is the tale at the bottom of a bottle of wormspoor. Maybe you could understand me if you hadn't brought your past back to Hoarsbreath."

"I do understand you," he said absently. "You want to sit in the dark all your life and drink wormspoor."

She drew breath and held it. "You talk but you don't listen," she said finally. "Just like all the other flatlanders." He didn't answer. They walked in silence awhile, following the empty bed of an old river. The world looked dead, but she could tell by the air, which was not even freezing spangles of breath on her hood-fur, that the winter was drawing to an end. "Suns-crossing must be only two months away," she commented surprisedly.

"Besides, I'm not a flatlander," he said abruptly, surprising her again. "I do care about the miners, about Hoarsbreath. It's because I care that I want to challenge that ice-dragon with all the skill I possess. Is it better to let you live surrounded by danger, in bitter cold, carving half-lives out of snow and stone, so that you can come fully alive for one month of the year?"

"You could have asked us."

"I did ask you."

She sighed. "Where will it live, if you drive it away from Hoarsbreath?"

He didn't answer for a few paces. In the still day, he loosed no colors, though Peka thought she saw shadows of them around his pack. His head was bowed; his eyes were burning back at a memory. "It will find some strange, remote places where there is no gold, only rock; it can ring itself around emptiness and dream of its past. I came across an ice-dragon unexpectedly once, in a land of ice. The bones of its wings seemed almost translucent. I could have sworn it cast a white shadow."

"Did you want to kill it?"

"No. I loved it."

"Then why do you—" But he turned at her suddenly, almost angrily, waking out of a dream.

"I came here because you've built your lives on top of a terrible danger, and I asked for a guide, not a gad-fly."

"You wanted me," she said flatly. "And you don't care about Hoarsbreath. All you want is that dragon. Your voice is full of it. What's a gad-fly?"

"Go ask a cow. Or a horse. Or anything else that can't live on this forsaken, frostbitten lump of ice."

"Why should you care, anyway? You've got the whole great world to roam in. Why do you care about one dragon wrapped around the tiny island on the top of nowhere?"

"Because it's beautiful and deadly and wrapped around my heartland. And I don't know—I don't know at the end of things which of us will be left on Hoarsbreath." She stared at him. He met her eyes fully. "I'm very skilled. But that is one very powerful dragon."

She whirled, fanning snow. "I'm going back. Find your own way to your harrowing. I hope it swallows you."

His voice stopped her. "You'll always wonder. You'll sit in the dark, drinking wormspoor twelve months out of thirteen, wondering what happened to me. What an ice-dragon looks like, on a winter's day, in full flight."

She hovered between two steps. Then, furiously, she followed him.

They climbed deeper into mist, and then into darkness. They camped at night, ate dried meat and drank wormspoor beside a fire in the snow. The night-sky was sullen and starless as the day. They woke to grey mists and travelled on. The cold breathed up around them; walls of ice, yellow as old ivory, loomed over them. They smelled the chill, sweaty smell of the sea. The dead riverbed came to an end over an impassible cliff. They shifted ground, followed a frozen stream downward. The ice-walls broke up into great jewels of ice, blue, green, gold, massed about them like a giant's treasure hoard. Peka stopped to stare at them. Ryd said with soft, bitter satisfaction, "Wormspoor."

She drew breath. "Wormspoor." Her voice sounded small, absorbed by cold. "Ice-jewels, fallen stars. Down here you could tell me anything and I might believe it. I feel very strange." She uncorked the wormspoor and took a healthy swig. Ryd reached for it, but he only rinsed his mouth and spat. His face was pale; his eyes red-rimmed, tired.

"How far down do you think we are?"

"Close. There's no dragon. Just mist." She shuddered suddenly at the soundlessness. "The air is dead. Like stone. We should reach the ocean soon."

"We'll reach the dragon first."

They descended hillocks of frozen jewels. The stream they followed fanned into a wide, skeletal filigree of ice and rock. The mist poured around them, so painfully cold it burned their lungs. Peka pushed fur over her mouth, breathed through it. The mist or wormspoor she had drunk was forming shadows around her, flickerings of faces and enormous wings. Her heart felt heavy; her feet dragged like boulders when she lifted them. Ryd was coughing mist; he moved doggedly, as if into a hard wind. The stream fanned again, going very wide before it met the sea. They stumbled down into a bone-searing flow of mist. Ryd disappeared; Peka found him again, bumping into him, for he had stopped. The threads of mist untangled above them, and she saw a strange black sun, hodded with a silvery web. As she blinked at it, puzzled, the web rolled up. The dark sun gazed back at her. She became aware then of her own heartbeat, of a rhythm in the mists, of a faint, echoing pulse all around her: the icy heartbeat of Hoarsbreath.

She drew a hiccup of a breath, stunned. There was a mountain-cave ahead of them, from which the mists breathed and eddied. Icicles dropped like bars between its grainy-white surfaces. Within it rose stones or teeth as milky white as quartz. A wall of white stretched beyond the mists, vast, earthworm round, solid as stone. She couldn't tell in the blur and welter of mist, where winter ended and the dragon began.

She made a sound. The vast, silvery eyelid drooped like a parchment unrolled, then lifted again. From the depths of the cave came a faint, rumbling, a vague, drowsy waking question: Who?

She heard Ryd's breath finally. "Look at the scar under its eye," he said softly. She saw a jagged track beneath the black sun. "I can name the Harrower who put that there three hundred years ago. And the broken eyetooth. It razed a marble fortress with its wings and jaws; I know the word that shattered that tooth, then. Look at its wing-scales. Rimed with silver. It's old. Old as the world." He turned finally, to look at her. His white hair, slick with mists, made him seem old as winter. "You can go back now. You won't be safe here."

"I won't be safe up there, either," she whispered. "Let's both go back. Listen to its heart."

"Its blood is gold. Only one Harrower ever saw that and lived."

"Please." She tugged at him, at his pack. Colors shivered into the air: sulphur, malachite, opal. The deep rumble came again; a shadow quickened in the dragon's eye. Ryd moved quickly, caught her hands. "Let it sleep. It belongs here on Hoarsbreath. Why can't you see that? Why can't you see? It's a thing made of gold, snow, darkness—" But he wasn't seeing her; his eyes, remote and alien as the black sun, were full of memories and calculations. Behind him, a single curved claw lay like a crescent moon half-buried in the snow.

Peka stepped back from the Harrower, envisioning a bloody moon through his heart, and the dragon roused to fury, coiling upward around Hoarsbreath, crushing the life out of it. "Ryd Yarrow," she whispered. "Ryd Yarrow. Please." But he did not hear his name.

He began to speak, startling echoes against the solid ice around them. "Dragon of Hoarsbreath, whose wings are of hoarfrost, whose blood is gold—" The backbone of the hoar-dragon rippled slightly, shaking away snow. "I have followed your path of destruction from your beginnings in a land without time and without seasons. You have slept one night too long on this island. Hoarsbreath is not your dragon's dream; it belongs to the living, and I, trained and titled Dragon-Harrower, challenge you for its freedom." More snow shook away from the dragon, baring a rippling of scale, and the glistening of its nostrils. The rhythm of its mist was changing. "I know you," Ryd continued, his voice growing husky, strained against the silence. "You were the white death of the fishing-island Klonos, of ten Harrowers in Ynyme, of the winter palace of the ancient lord of Zuirsh. I have harried nine ice-dragons—perhaps your children—out of the known world. I have been searching for you many years, and I came back to the place where I was born to find you here. I stand before you armed with knowledge, experience, and the dark wisdom of necessity. Leave Hoarsbreath, go back to your birthplace forever, or I will harry you down to the frozen shadow of the world."

The dragon gazed at him motionlessly, an immeasurable ring of ice looped about him. The mist out of its mouth was for a moment suspended. Then its jaws crashed together, spitting splinters of ice. It shuddered, wrenched itself loose from the ice. Its white head reared high, higher, ice booming and cracking around it. Twin black suns stared down at Ryd from the grey mist of the sky. Before it roared, Peka moved.

She found herself on a ledge above Ryd's head, without remembering how she got there. Ryd vanished in a flood of mist. The mist turned fiery; Ryd loomed out of them like a red shadow, dispersing them. Seven crescents lifted out of the snow, slashed down at him scarring the air. A strange voice shouted Ryd's name. He flung back his head and cried a word. Somehow the claw missed him, wedged deep into the ice.

Peka sat back. She was clutching the skin of wormspoor against her heart; she could feel her heartbeat shaking it. Her throat felt raw; the strange voice had been hers. She uncorked the skin, took a deep swallow, and another. Fire licked down her veins. A cloud of ice billowed at Ryd. He said something else, and suddenly he was ten feet away from it, watching a rock where he had stood freeze and snap into pieces.

Peka crouched closer to the wall of ice behind her. From her high point she could see the briny, frozen snarl of the sea. It flickered green, then an eerie orange. Bands of color pinioned the dragon briefly like a rainbow, arching across its wings. A scale caught fire; a small bone the size of Ryd's forearm snapped. Then the cold wind of the dragon's breath froze and shattered the rainbow. A claw slapped at Ryd; he moved a fraction of a moment too slowly. The tip of a talon caught his pack. It burst open with an explosion of glittering colors. The dragon hooded its eyes; Peka hid hers under her hands.

She heard Ryd cry out in pain. Then he was beside her instead of in several pieces, prying the wormspoor out of her hands.

He uncorked it, his hands shaking. One of them was seared silver.

"What are they?" she breathed. He poured wormspoor on his burned hand, then thrust it into the snow. The colors were beginning to die down.

"Flame," he panted. "Dragon-flame. I wasn't prepared to handle it."

"You carry it in your pack?"

"Caught in crystals, in fire-leaves. It will be more difficult than I anticipated."

Peka felt language she had never used before clamor in her throat. "It's all right," she said dourly. "I'll wait."

For a moment, as he looked at her, there was a memory of fear in his eyes. "You can walk across the ice to the mainland from here."

"You can walk to the mainland," she retorted. "This is my home. I have to live with or without that dragon. Right now, there's no living with it. You woke it out of its sleep. You burnt its wing. You broke its bone. You told it there are people on its island. You are going to destroy Hoarsbreath."

"No. This will be my greatest harrowing." He left her suddenly, and appeared flaming like a torch on the dragon's skull, just between its eyes. His hair and his hands spattered silver. Word after word came out of him, smoldering, flashing, melting in the air. The dragon's voice thundered; its skin rippled and shook. Its claw ripped at ice, dug chasms out of it. The air clapped nearby, as if its invisible tail had lifted and slapped at the ground. Then it heaved its head, flung Ryd at the wall of mountain. Peka shut her eyes. But he fell lightly, caught up a crystal as he rose, and sent a shaft of piercing gold light at the upraised scales of its underside, burrowing towards its heart.

Peka got unsteadily to her feet, her throat closing with a sudden whimper. But the dragon's tail, flickering out of the mist behind Ryd, slapped him into a snowdrift twenty feet away. It gave a cold, terrible hiss; mist bubbled over everything, so that for a few minutes Peka could see nothing beyond the lip of the ledge. She drank to stop her shivering. Finally a green fire blazed within the white swirl. She sat down again slowly, waited.

Night rolled in from the sea. But Ryd's fires shot in raw, dazzling streaks across the darkness, illuminating the hoary, scarred bulk of dragon in front of him. Once, he shouted endless poetry at the dragon, lulling it until its mist-breath was faint and slow from its maw. It nearly put Peka to sleep, but Ryd's imperceptible steps closer and closer to the dragon kept her watching. The tale was evidently an old one to the dragon; it didn't wait for an ending. Its head lunged and snapped unexpectedly, but a moment too soon. Ryd leaped for shelter in the dark, while the dragon's teeth ground painfully on nothingness. Later, Ryd sang to it, a whining, eerie song that showered icicles around Peka's head. One of the dragon's teeth cracked, and it made an odd, high-pitched noise. A vast webbed wing shifted free to fly, unfolding endlessly over the sea. But the dragon stayed, sending mist at Ryd to set him coughing. A foul ashy-grey miasma followed it, blurring over them. Peka hid her face in her arms. Sounds like the heaving of boulders and the spattering of fire came from beneath her. She heard the dragon's dry roar, like stones dragged against one another. There was a smack, a musical shower of breaking icicles, and a sharp, anguished curse. Ryd appeared out of the turmoil of light and air, sprawled on the ledge beside Peka.

His face was cut, with ice she supposed, and there was blood in his white hair. He looked at her with vague amazement.

"You're still here."

"Where else would I be? Are you winning or losing?"

He scooped up snow, held it against his face. "I feel as if I've been fighting for a thousand years . . . Sometimes, I think I tangle in its memories, as it thinks of other harrowers, old dragon-battles, distant places. It doesn't remember what I am, only that I will not let it sleep . . . Did you *see* its wingspan? I fought a red dragon once with such a span. Its wings turned to flame in the sunlight. You'll see this one in flight by dawn."

She stared at him numbly, huddled against herself. "Are you so sure?"

"It's old and slow. And it can't bear the gold fire." He paused, then dropped the snow in his hand with a sigh, and leaned his face against the ice-wall. "I'm tired, too. I have one empty crystal, to capture the essence of its mist, its heart's breath. After that's done, the battle will be short." He lifted his head at her silence, as if he could hear her thoughts. "What?"

"You'll go on to other dragons. But all I've ever had is this one."

"You never know—"

"It doesn't matter that I never knew it. I know now. It was coiled all around us in the winter, while we lived in warm darkness and firelight. It kept out the world. Is that such a terrible thing? Is there so much wisdom in the flatlands that we can't live without?"

He was silent again, frowning a little, either in pain or faint confusion. "It's a dangerous thing, a destroyer."

"So is winter. So is the mountain, sometimes. But they're also beautiful. You are full of so much knowledge and experience that you forgot how to see simple things. Ryd Yarrow, miner's son. You must have loved Hoarsbreath once."

"I was a child, then."

She sighed. "I'm sorry I brought you down here. I wish I were up there with the miners, in the last peaceful night."

"There will be peace again," he said, but she shook her head wearily.

"I don't feel it." She expected him to smile, but his frown deepened. He touched her face suddenly with his burned hand.

"Sometimes I almost hear what you're trying to tell me. And then it fades against all my knowledge and experience. I'm glad you stayed. If I die, I'll leave you facing one maddened dragon. But still, I'm glad."

A black moon rose high over his shoulder and she jumped. Ryd rolled off the ledge, into the mists. Peka hid her face from the peering black glare. Blue lights smouldered through the mist, the moon rolled suddenly out of the sky and she could breathe again.

Streaks of dispersing gold lit the dawn-sky like the sunrises she saw one month out of the year. Peka, in a cold daze on the ledge, saw Ryd for the first time in an hour. He was facing the dragon, his silver hand outstretched. In his palm lay a crystal so cold and deathly white that Peka, blinking at it, felt its icy stare into her heart.

She shuddered. Her bones turned to ice; mist seemed to flow through her veins. She breathed bitter, frozen air as heavy as water. She reached for the wormspoor; her arm moved sluggishly, and her fingers unfolded with brittle movements. The dragon was breathing in short, harsh spurts. The silvery hoods were over its eyes. Its unfolded wing lay across the ice like a limp sail. Its jaws were open, hissing faintly, but its head was reared back, away from Ryd's hand. Its heartbeat, in the silence, was slow, slow.

Peka dragged herself up, icicle by icicle. In the clear wintry dawn, she saw the beginning and the end of the enormous ring around Hoarsbreath. The dragon's tail lifted wearily behind Ryd, then fell again, barely making a sound. Ryd stood still; his eyes, relentless, spring-blue, were his only color. As Peka watched, swaying on the edge, the world fragmented into simple things: the edges of silver on the dragon's scales, Ryd's silver fingers, his old-man's hair, the pure white of the dragon's hide. They face one another, two powerful creatures born out of the same winter, harrowing one another. The dragon rippled along its bulk; its head reared farther back, giving Peka a dizzying glimpse of its open jaws. She saw the cracked tooth, crumbled like a jewel she might have battered inadvertently with her pick, and winced. Seeing her, it hissed, a tired, angry sigh.

She stared down at it; her eyes seemed numb, incapable of sorrow. The wing on the ice was beginning to stir. Ryd's head lifted. He looked bone-pale, his face expressionless with exhaustion. But the faint, icy smile of triumph in his eyes struck her as deeply as the stare from the death-eye in his palm.

She drew in mist like the dragon, knowing that Ryd was not harrowing an old, tired ice-dragon, but one out of his memories who never seemed to yield. "You bone-brained dragon," she shouted, "how can you give up Hoarsbreath so easily? And to a Dragon-Harrower whose winter is colder and more terrible than yours." Her heart seemed trapped in the weary, sluggish pace of its heart. She knelt down, wondering if it could understand her words, or only feel them. "Think of Hoarsbreath," she pleaded, and searched for words to warm them both. "Fire. Gold. Night. Warm dreams, winter tales, silence—" Mist billowed at her and she coughed until tears froze on her cheeks. She heard Ryd call her name on a curious, inflexible note that panicked her. She uncorked the wormspoor with trembling fingers, took a great gulp, and coughed again as the blood shocked through her. "Don't you have any fire at all in you? Any winter flame?" Then a vision of gold shook her: the gold within the dragon's heart, the warm gold of wormspoor, the bitter gold of dragon's blood. Ryd said her name again, his voice clear as breaking ice. She shut her eyes against him, her hands rising through a chill, dark dream. As he called the third time, she dropped the wormspoor down the dragon's throat.

The hoods over its eyes rose; they grew wide, white-rimmed. She heard a convulsive swallow. Its head snapped down; it made a sound between a bellow and a whimper. Then its jaws opened again and it raked the air with gold flame.

Ryd, his hair and eyebrows scored suddenly with gold, dove into the snow. The dragon hissed at him again. The stream beyond him turned fiery, ran towards the sea. The great tail pounded furiously; dark cracks tore through the ice. The frozen cliffs began to sweat under the fire; pillars of ice sagged down, broke against the ground. The ledge Peka stood on crumbled at a wave of gold. She fell with it in a small avalanche of ice-rubble. The enormous white ring of dragon began to move, blurring endlessly past her eyes as the dragon gathered itself. A wing arched up toward the sky, then another. The dragon hissed at the mountain, then roared desperately, but only flame came out of its bowels, where once it had secreted winter. The chasms and walls of ice began breaking apart. Peka, struggling out of the snow, felt a lurch under her feet. A wind sucked at her her hair, pulled at her heavy coat. Then it drove down at her, thundering, and she sat in the snow. The dragon, aloft, its wingspan the span of half the island, breathed fire at the ocean, and its husk of ice began to melt.

Ryd pulled her out of the snow. The ground was breaking up under their feet. He said nothing; she thought he was scowling, though he looked strange with singed eyebrows. He pushed at her, flung her toward the sea. Fire sputtered around them. Ice slid under her; she slipped and clutched at the jagged rim of it. Brine splashed in her face. The ice whirled, as chunks of the mountain fell into the sea around them. The dragon was circling the mountain, melting huge peaks and cliffs. They struck the water hard, heaving the ice-floes farther from the island. The mountain itself began to break up, as ice tore away from it, leaving only a bare peak riddled with mine-shafts.

Peka began to cry. "Look what I've done. Look at it." Ryd only grunted. She thought she could see figures high on the top of the peak, staring down at the vanishing island. The ocean, churning, spun the ice-floe toward the mainland. The river was flowing again, a blue-white streak spiralling down from the peak. The dragon was over the mainland now, billowing fire at the harbor, and ships without crews or cargo were floating free.

"Wormspoor," Ryd muttered. A wave ten feet high caught up with them, spilled, and shoved them into the middle of the channel. Peka saw the first of the boats taking the swift, swollen current down from the top of the island. Ryd spat out seawater, and took a firmer grip of the ice. "I lost every crystal, every dragon's fire I possessed. They're at the bottom of the sea. Thanks to you. Do you realize how much work, how many years—"

"Look at the sky." It spun above her, a pale, impossible mass of nothing. "How can I live under that? Where will I ever find dark, quiet places full of gold?"

"I held that dragon. It was just about to leave quietly, without taking half of Hoarsbreath with it."

"How will we live on the island again? All its secrets are gone."

"For fourteen years I studied dragons, their lore, their flights, their fires, the patterns of their lives and their destructions. I had all the knowledge I thought possible for me to acquire. No one—"

"Look at all that dreary flatland—"

"No one," he said, his voice rising, "ever told me you could harrow a dragon by pouring wormspoor down its throat!"

"Well, no one told me, either!" She slumped beside him, too despondent for anger. She watched more boats carrying miners, young children, her mother, down to the mainland. Then the dragon caught her eye, pale against the winter sky, somehow fragile, beautifully crafted, flying into the wake of its own flame.

It touched her mourning heart with the fire she had given it. Beside her, she felt Ryd grow quiet. His face, tired and battered, held a young, forgotten wonder, as he watched the dragon blaze across the world's cap like a star, searching for its winter. He drew a soft, incredulous breath.

"What did you put into that wormspoor?"

"Everything."

He looked at her, then turned his face toward Hoarsbreath. The sight made him wince. "I don't think we left even my father's bones at peace," he said hollowly, looking for a moment less Dragon-Harrower than a harrowed miner's son.

"I know," she whispered.

"No, you don't," he sighed. "You feel. The dragon's heart. My heart. It's not a lack of knowledge or experiences that destroyed Hoarsbreath, but something else I lost sight of: you told me that. The dark necessity of wisdom."

She gazed at him, suddenly uneasy for he was seeing her. "I'm not wise. Just lucky—or unlucky."

"Wisdom is a flatlander's word for your kind of feeling. You put your heart into everything—wormspoor, dragons, gold—and they become a kind of magic."

"I do not. I don't understand what you're talking about Ryd Yarrow. I'm a miner; I'm going to find another mine—"

"You have a gold-mine in your heart. There are other things you can do with yourself. Not harrow dragons, but become a Watcher. You love the same things they love."

"Yes. Peace and quiet and private places—"

"I could show you dragons in their beautiful, private places all over the world. You could speak their language."

"I can't even speak my own. And I hate the flatland." She gripped the ice, watching it come.

"The world is only another tiny island, ringed with a great dragon of stars and night."

She shook her head, not daring to meet his eyes. "No. I'm not listening to you anymore. Look what happened the last time I listened to your tales."

"It's always yourself you are listening to," he said. The grey ocean swirled the ice under them, casting her back to the bewildering shores of the world. She was still trying to argue when the ice moored itself against the scorched pilings of the harbor.

The Last
of the Dragons

Edith Nesbit

Edith Nesbit was one of the greatest of the Victorian children's story writers, a turn-of-the-century contemporary of H. G. Wells and G. B. Shaw, and the author of a number of novels and several volumes of fantasy stories. The best of her works, such as this story, have an ironic attitude toward the usual fantasy images, of which even children are tired after a while. One should note that the character of the dragon is working-class British, yet loyal to the noble princess. This is a story about treating your inferiors well, and at the same time a story about a vanishing breed, worthy of comparison to Mark Twain's story, earlier (pp.213–28).

Of course you know that dragons were once as common as motor-omnibuses are now, and almost as dangerous. But as every well-brought-up prince was expected to kill a dragon, and rescue a princess, the dragons grew fewer and fewer till it was often quite hard for a princess to find a dragon to be rescued from. And at last there were no more dragons in France and no more dragons in Germany, or Spain, or Italy, or Russia. There were some left in China, and are still, but they are cold and bronzy, and there were never any, of course, in America. But the last real live dragon left was in England, and of course that was a very long time ago, before what you call English History began. This dragon lived in Cornwall in the big caves amidst the rocks, and a very fine dragon it was, quite seventy feet long from

the tip of its fearful snout to the end of its terrible tail. It breathed fire
and smoke, and rattled when it walked, because its scales were made
of iron. Its wings were like half-umbrellas—or like bat's wings, only
several thousand times bigger. Everyone was very frightened of it,
and well they might be.

Now the King of Cornwall had one daughter, and when she was
sixteen, of course she would have to go and face the dragon: such
tales are always told in royal nurseries at twilight, so the Princess
knew what she had to expect. The dragon would not eat her, of
course—because the prince would come and rescue her. But the
Princess could not help thinking it would be much pleasanter to have
nothing to do with the dragon at all—not even to be rescued from
him. "All the princes I know are such very silly little boys," she told
her father. "Why must I be rescued by a prince?"

"It's always done, my dear," said the King, taking his crown off
and putting it on the grass, for they were alone in the garden, and
even kings must unbend sometimes.

"Father, darling?" said the Princess presently, when she had made
a daisy chain and put it on the King's head, where the crown ought to
have been. "Father, darling, couldn't we tie up one of the silly little
princes for the dragon to look at—and then *I* could go and kill the
dragon and rescue the prince? I fence much better than any of the
princes we know."

"What an unladylike idea!" said the King, and put his crown on
again, for he saw the Prime Minister coming with a basket of new-
laid Bills for him to sign. "Dismiss the thought, my child. I rescued
your mother from a dragon, and you don't want to set yourself up
above her, I should hope?"

"But this is the *last* dragon. It is different from all other dragons."

"How?" asked the King.

"Because he *is* the last," said the Princess, and went off to her
fencing lessons, with which she took great pains. She took great pains
with all her lessons—for she could not give up the idea of fighting the
dragon. She took such pains that she became the strongest and
boldest and most skilful and most sensible princess in Europe. She
had always been the prettiest and nicest.

And the days and years went on, till at last the day came which was
the day before the Princess was to be rescued from the dragon. The
Prince who was to do this deed of valour was a pale prince, with large
eyes and a head full of mathematics and philosophy, but he had un-

fortunately neglected his fencing lessons. He was to stay the night at the palace, and there was a banquet.

After supper the Princess sent her pet parrot to the Prince with a note. It said:

Please, Prince, come on to the terrace. I want to talk to you without anybody else hearing.—The Princess.

So, of course, he went—and he saw her gown of silver a long way off shining among the shadows of the trees like water in starlight. And when he came quite close to her he said: "Princess, at your service," and bent his cloth-of-gold-covered knee and put his hand on his cloth-of-gold-covered heart.

"Do you think," said the Princess earnestly, "that you will be able to kill the dragon?"

"I will kill the dragon," said the Prince firmly, "or perish in the attempt."

"It's no use your perishing," said the Princess.

"It's the least I can do," said the Prince.

"What I'm afraid of is that it'll be the most you can do," said the Princess.

"It's the only thing I can do," said he, "unless I kill the dragon."

"Why you should do anything for me is what I can't see," said she.

"But I want to," he said. "You must know that I love you better than anything in the world."

When he said that he looked so kind that the Princess began to like him a little.

"Look here," she said, "no one else will go out tomorrow. You know they tie me to a rock and leave me—and then everybody scurries home and puts up the shutters and keeps them shut till you ride through the town in triumph shouting that you've killed the dragon, and I ride on the horse behind you weeping for joy."

"I've heard that that is how it is done," said he.

"Well, do you love me well enough to come very quickly and set me free—and we'll fight the dragon together?"

"It wouldn't be safe for you."

"Much safer for both of us for me to be free, with a sword in my hand, than tied up and helpless. *Do* agree?"

He could refuse her nothing. So he agreed. And the next day everything happened as she had said.

When he had cut the cords that tied her to the rock they stood on the lonely mountain-side looking at each other.

"It seems to me," said the Prince, "that this ceremony could have been arranged without the dragon."

"Yes," said the Princess, "but since it has been arranged with the dragon—"

"It seems such a pity to kill the dragon—the last in the world," said the Prince.

"Well then, don't let's," said the Princess; "let's tame it not to eat princesses but to eat out of their hands. They say everything can be tamed by kindness."

"Taming by kindness means giving them things to eat," said the Prince. "Have you got anything to eat?"

She hadn't, but the Prince owned that he had a few biscuits. "Breakfast was so very early," said he, "and I thought you might have felt faint after the fight."

"How clever," said the Princess, and they took a biscuit in each hand. And they looked here, and they looked there, but never a dragon could they see.

"But here's its tail," said the Prince, and pointed to where the rock was scarred and scratched so as to make a track leading to a dark cave. It was like cart-ruts in a Sussex road, mixed with the marks of sea-gull's feet on the sea-sand. "Look, that's where it's dragged its brass tail and planted its steel claws."

"Don't let's think how hard its tail and its claws are," said the Princess, "or I shall begin to be frightened—and I know you can't tame anything, even by kindness, if you're frightened of it. Come on. Now or never."

She caught the Prince's hand in hers and they ran along the path towards the dark mouth of the cave. But they did not run into it. It really was so very *dark*.

So they stood outside, and the Prince shouted: "What ho! Dragon there! What ho within!" And from the cave they heard an answering voice and great clattering and creaking. It sounded as though a rather large cotton-mill were stretching itself and waking up out of its sleep.

The Prince and Princess trembled, but they stood firm.

"Dragon—I say, dragon!" said the Princess, "do come out and talk to us. We've brought you a present."

"Oh yes—I know your presents," growled the dragon in a huge rumbling voice. "One of those precious princesses, I suppose? And

I've got to come out and fight for her. Well, I tell you straight, I'm
not going to do it. A fair fight I wouldn't say no to—a fair fight and
no favour—but one of those put-up fights where you've got to lose—
no! So I tell you. If I wanted a princess I'd come and take her, in my
own time—but I don't. What do you suppose I'd do with her, if I'd
got her?"

"Eat her, wouldn't you?" said the Princess, in a voice that trembled a little.

"Eat a fiddle-stick end," said the dragon very rudely. "I wouldn't
touch the horrid thing."

The Princess's voice grew firmer.

"Do you like biscuits?" she said.

"No," growled the dragon.

"Not the nice little expensive ones with sugar on the top?"

"No," growled the dragon.

"Then what *do* you like?" asked the Prince.

"You go away and don't bother me," growled the dragon, and
they could hear it turn over, and the clang and clatter of its turning
echoed in the cave like the sound of the steam-hammers in the Arse-
nal at Woolwich.

The Prince and Princess looked at each other. What *were* they to
do? Of course it was no use going home and telling the King that the
dragon didn't want princesses—because His Majesty was very old-
fashioned and would never have believed that a new-fashioned
dragon could ever be at all different from an old-fashioned dragon.
They could not go into the cave and kill the dragon. Indeed, unless
he attacked the Princess it did not seem fair to kill him at all.

"He must like something," whispered the Princess, and she called
out in a voice as sweet as honey and sugar-cane:

"Dragon! Dragon dear!"

"WHAT?" shouted the dragon. "Say that again!" and they could
hear the dragon coming towards them through the darkness of the
cave. The Princess shivered, and said in a very small voice:

"Dragon—Dragon dear!"

And then the dragon came out. The Prince drew his sword, and
the Princess drew hers—the beautiful silver-handled one that the
Prince had brought in his motor-car. But they did not attack; they
moved slowly back as the dragon came out, all the vast scaly length of
him, and lay along the rock—his great wings halfspread and his silvery sheen gleaming like diamonds in the sun. At last they could

retreat no further—the dark rock behind them stopped their way—
and with their backs to the rock they stood swords in hand and
waited.

The dragon drew nearer and nearer—and now they could see that
he was not breathing fire and smoke as they had expected—he came
crawling slowly towards them wriggling a little as a puppy does when
it wants to play and isn't quite sure whether you're not cross with it.

And then they saw that great tears were coursing down its brazen
cheek.

"Whatever's the matter?" said the Prince.

"Nobody," sobbed the dragon, "ever called me 'dear' before!"

"Don't cry, dragon dear," said the Princess. "We'll call you 'dear'
as often as you like. We want to tame you."

"I *am* tame," said the dragon—"that's just it. That's what nobody
but you has ever found out. I'm so tame that I'd eat out of your
hands."

"Eat what, dragon dear?" said the Princess. "Not biscuits?" The
dragon slowly shook his heavy head.

"Not biscuits?" said the Princess tenderly. "What, then, dragon
dear?"

"Your kindness quite undragons me," it said. "No one has ever
asked any of us what we like to eat—always offering us princesses,
and then rescuing them—and never once, 'What'll you take to drink
the King's health in?' Cruel hard I call it," and it wept again.

"But what would you like to drink our health in?" said the Prince.
"We're going to be married today, aren't we, Princess?"

She said that she supposed so.

"What'll I take to drink your health in?" asked the dragon. "Ah,
you're something like a gentleman, you are, sir. I don't mind if I do,
sir. I'll be proud to drink your and your good lady's health in a tiny
drop of"—its voice faltered—"to think of you asking me so friendly
like," it said. "Yes, sir, just a tiny drop of puppuppuppuppupetrol—
tha-that's what does a dragon good, sir—"

"I've lots in the car," said the Prince, and was off down the mountain like a flash. He was a good judge of character and knew that with
this dragon the Princess would be safe.

"If I might make so bold," said the dragon, "while the gentleman's
away—p'raps just to pass the time you'd be so kind as to call me Dear
again, and if you'd shake claws with a poor old dragon that's never

been anybody's enemy but his own—well, the last of the dragons'll be the proudest dragon that's ever been since the first of them."

It held out an enormous paw, and the great steel hooks that were its claws closed over the Princess's hand as softly as the claws of the Himalayan bear will close over the bit of bun you hand it through the bars at the Zoo.

And so the Prince and Princess went back to the palace in triumph, the dragon following them like a pet dog. And all through the wedding festivities no one drank more earnestly to the happiness of the bride and bridegroom than the Princess's pet dragon—whom she had at once named Fido.

And when the happy pair were settled in their own kingdom, Fido came to them and begged to be allowed to make himself useful.

"There must be some little thing I can do," he said, rattling his wings and stretching his claws. "My wings and claws and so on ought to be turned to some account—to say nothing of my grateful heart."

So the Prince had a special saddle or howdah made for him—very long it was—like the tops of many tramcars fitted together. One hundred and fifty seats were fitted to this, and the dragon, whose greatest pleasure was now to give pleasure to others, delighted in taking parties of children to the seaside. It flew through the air quite easily with its hundred and fifty little passengers—and would lie on the sand patiently waiting till they were ready to return. The children were very fond of it, and used to call it Dear, a word which never failed to bring tears of affection and gratitude to its eyes. So it lived, useful and respected, till quite the other day—when someone happened to say, in his hearing, that dragons were out-of-date, now so much new machinery had come in. This so distressed him that he asked the King to change him into something less old-fashioned, and the kindly monarch at once changed him into a mechanical contrivance. The dragon, indeed, became the first aeroplane.

Lila the Werewolf

Peter S. Beagle

The author of A Fine and Private Place *and* The Last Unicorn, *a pair of the very best fantasy novels of our time, Peter S. Beagle has written only two fantasy short stories of which "Lila the Werewolf" is the best, a contemporary classic. Beagle is a musician, a script writer, and a literary descendant of the fantasist Robert Nathan. Like Avram Davidson, he is an urban fantasist of wit and perception; a lover of animals who knows their personalities; a writer with a flair for characterization that raises him to the very top rank of contemporary writers who choose the fantastic as their métier. And his New York setting vibrates with authenticity, though it has been twenty years since dogs have been so common in the city. This is not a story about love.*

Lila Braun had been living with Farrell for three weeks before he found out she was a werewolf. They had met at a party when the moon was a few nights past the full, and by the time it had withered to the shape of a lemon Lila had moved her suitcase, her guitar, and her Ewan MacColl records two blocks north and four blocks west to Farrell's apartment on Ninety-eighth Street. Girls sometimes happened to Farrell like that.

One evening Lila wasn't in when Farrell came home from work at the bookstore. She had left a note on the table, under a can of tunafish. The note said that she had gone up to the Bronx to have dinner with her mother, and would probably be spending the night there. The coleslaw in the refrigerator should be finished up before it went bad.

Farrell ate the tunafish and gave the coleslaw to Grunewald. Grunewald was a half-grown Russian wolfhound, the color of sour milk. He looked like a goat, and had no outside interests except shoes. Farrell was taking care of him for a girl who was away in Europe for the summer. She sent Grunewald a tape recording of her voice every week.

Farrell went to a movie with a friend, and to the West End afterward for beer. Then he walked home alone under the full moon, which was red and yellow. He reheated the morning coffee, played a record, read through a week-old "News of the Week in Review" section of the Sunday *Times,* and finally took Grunewald up to the roof for the night, as he always did. The dog had been accustomed to sleep in the same bed with his mistress, and the point was not negotiable. Grunewald mooed and scrabbled and butted all the way, but Farrell pushed him out among the looming chimneys and ventilators and slammed the door. Then he came back downstairs and went to bed.

He slept very badly. Grunewald's baying woke him twice; and there was something else that brought him half out of bed, thirsty and lonely, with his sinuses full and the night swaying like a curtain as the figures of his dream scurried offstage. Grunewald seemed to have gone off the air—perhaps it was the silence that had awakened him. Whatever the reason, he never really got back to sleep.

He was lying on his back, watching a chair with his clothes on it becoming a chair again, when the wolf came in through the open window. It landed lightly in the middle of the room and stood there for a moment, breathing quickly, with its ears back. There was blood on the wolf's teeth and tongue, and blood on its chest.

Farrell, whose true gift was for acceptance, especially in the morning, accepted the idea that there was a wolf in his bedroom and lay quite still, closing his eyes as the grim, black-lipped head swung toward him. Having once worked at a zoo, he was able to recognize the beast as a Central European subspecies—smaller and lighter-boned than the northern timber wolf variety, lacking the thick, ruffy mane at the shoulders, and having a more pointed nose and ears. His own pedantry always delighted him, even at the worst moments.

Blunt claws clicking on the linoleum, then silent on the throw rug by the bed. Something warm and slow splashed down on his shoul-

der, but he never moved. The wild smell of the wolf was over him,
and that did frighten him at last—to be in the same room with that
smell and the Miró prints on the walls. Then he felt the sunlight on
his eyelids, and at the same moment he heard the wolf moan softly
and deeply. The sound was not repeated, but the breath on his face
was suddenly sweet and smoky, dizzyingly familiar after the other.
He opened his eyes and saw Lila. She was sitting naked on the edge
of the bed, smiling, with her hair down.

"Hello, baby," she said. "Move over, baby. I came home."

Farrell's gift was for acceptance. He was perfectly willing to believe
that he had dreamed the wolf; to believe Lila's story of boiled chicken
and bitter arguments and sleeplessness on Tremont Avenue; and to
forget that her first caress had been to bite him on the shoulder; hard
enough so that the blood crusting there as he got up and made breakfast might very well be his own. But then he left the coffee perking
and went up to the roof to get Grunewald. He found the dog
sprawled in a grove of TV antennas, looking more like a goat than
ever, with his throat torn out. Farrell had never actually seen an
animal with its throat torn out.

The coffeepot was still chuckling when he came back into the apartment, which struck him as very odd. You could have either werewolves or Pyrex nine-cup percolators in the world, but not both,
surely. He told Lila, watching her face. She was a small girl, not really
pretty, but with good eyes and a lovely mouth, and with a curious
sullen gracefulness that had been the first thing to speak to Farrell at
the party. When he told her how Grunewald had looked, she shivered all over, once.

"Ugh!" she said, wrinkling her lips back from her neat white teeth.
"Oh baby, how awful. Poor Grunewald. Oh, poor Barbara." Barbara
was Grunewald's owner.

"Yeah," Farrell said. "Poor Barbara, making her little tapes in
Saint-Tropez." He could not look away from Lila's face.

She said, "Wild dogs. Not really wild, I mean, but with owners.
You hear about it sometimes, how a pack of them get together and
attack children and things, running through the streets. Then they go
home and eat their Dog Yummies. The scary thing is that they probably live right around here. Everybody on the block seems to have a
dog. God, that's scary. Poor Grunewald."

"They didn't tear him up much," Farrell said. "It must have been just for the fun of it. And the blood. I didn't know dogs killed for the blood. He didn't have any blood left."

The tip of Lila's tongue appeared between her lips, in the unknowing reflex of a fondled cat. As evidence, it wouldn't have stood up even in old Salem; but Farrell knew the truth then, beyond laziness or rationalization, and went on buttering toast for Lila. Farrell had nothing against werewolves, and he had never liked Grunewald.

He told his friend Ben Kassoy about Lila when they met in the Automat for lunch. He had to shout it over the clicking and rattling all around them, but the people sitting six inches away on either hand never looked up. New Yorkers never eavesdrop. They hear only what they simply cannot help hearing.

Ben said, "I told you about Bronx girls. You better come stay at my place for a few days."

Farrell shook his head. "No, that's silly. I mean, it's only Lila. If she were going to hurt me, she could have done it last night. Besides, it won't happen again for a month. There has to be a full moon."

His friend stared at him. "So what? What's that got to do with anything? You going to go on home as though nothing had happened?"

"Not as though nothing had happened," Farrell said lamely. "The thing is, it's still only Lila, not Lon Chaney or somebody. Look, she goes to her psychiatrist three afternoons a week, and she's got her guitar lesson one night a week, and her pottery class one night, and she cooks eggplant maybe twice a week. She calls her mother every Friday night, and one night a month she turns into a wolf. You see what I'm getting at? It's still Lila, whatever she does, and I just can't get terribly shook about it. A little bit, sure, because what the hell. But I don't know. Anyway, there's no mad rush about it. I'll talk to her when the thing comes up in the conversation, just naturally. It's okay."

Ben said, "God damn. You see why nobody has any respect for liberals anymore? Farrell, I know you. You're just scared of hurting her feelings."

"Well, it's that too," Farrell agreed, a little embarrassed. "I hate confrontations. If I break up with her now, she'll think I'm doing it because she's a werewolf. It's awkward, it feels nasty and middle-class. I should have broken up with her the first time I met her mother, or the second time she served the eggplant. Her mother, boy, there's the real werewolf, there's somebody I'd wear wolfbane against, that woman. Damn, I wish I hadn't found out. I don't think I've ever found out anything about people that I was the better for knowing."

Ben walked all the way back to the bookstore with him, arguing. It touched Farrell, because Ben hated to walk. Before they parted, Ben suggested, "At least you could try some of that stuff you were talking about, the wolfbane. There's garlic, too—you put some in a little bag and wear it around your neck. Don't laugh, man. If there's such a thing as werewolves, the other stuff must be real too. Cold iron, silver, oak, running water—"

"I'm not laughing at you," Farrell said, but he was still grinning. "Lila's shrink says she has a rejection thing, very deep-seated, take us years to break through all that scar tissue. Now if I start walking around wearing amulets and mumbling in Latin every time she looks at me, who knows how far it'll set her back? Listen, I've done some things I'm not proud of, but I don't want to mess up anyone's analysis. That's the sin against God." He sighed and slapped Ben lightly on the arm. "Don't worry about it. We'll work it out, I'll talk to her."

But between that night and the next full moon, he found no good, casual way of bringing the subject up. Admittedly, he did not try as hard as he might have: it was true that he feared confrontations more than he feared werewolves, and he would have found it almost as difficult to talk to Lila about her guitar playing, or her pots, or the political arguments she got into at parties. "The thing is," he said to Ben, "it's sort of one more little weakness not to take advantage of. In a way."

They made love often that month. The smell of Lila flowered in the bedroom, where the smell of the wolf still lingered almost visibly, and both of them were wild, heavy zoo smells, warm and raw and fearful, the sweeter for being savage. Farrell held Lila in his arms and knew what she was, and he was always frightened; but he would not have let her go if she had turned into a wolf again as he held her. It was a relief to peer at her while she slept and see how stubby and childish her fingernails were, or that the skin around her mouth was rashy because she had been snacking on chocolate. She loved secret sweets, but they always betrayed her.

It's only Lila after all, he would think as he drowsed off. Her mother used to hide the candy, but Lila always found it. Now she's a big girl, neither married nor in a graduate school, but living in sin with an Irish musician, and she can have all the candy she wants.

What kind of a werewolf is that. Poor Lila, practicing *Who killed Davey Moore? Why did he die?* . . .

The note said that she would be working late at the magazine, on layout, and might have to be there all night. Farrell put on about four feet of Telemann laced with Django Reinhardt, took down *The Golden Bough,* and settled into a chair by the window. The moon shone in at him, bright and thin and sharp as the lid of a tin can, and it did not seem to move at all as he dozed and woke.

Lila's mother called several times during the night, which was interesting. Lila still picked up her mail and most messages at her old apartment, and her two roommates covered for her when necessary, but Farrell was absolutely certain that her mother knew she was living with him. Farrell was an expert on mothers. Mrs. Braun called him Joe each time she called and that made him wonder, for he knew she hated him. Does she suspect that we share a secret? Ah, poor Lila.

The last time the telephone woke him, it was still dark in the room, but the traffic lights no longer glittered through rings of mist, and the cars made a different sound on the warming pavement A man was saying clearly in the street, "Well, *I*'d shoot'm. *I*'d shoot'm." Farrell let the telephone ring ten times before he picked it up.

"Let me talk to Lila," Mrs. Braun said.

"She isn't here." What if the sun catches her, what if she turns back to herself in front of a cop, or a bus driver, or a couple of nuns going to early Mass? "Lila isn't here, Mrs. Braun."

"I have reason to believe that's not true." The fretful, muscular voice had dropped all pretense of warmth. "I want to talk to Lila."

Farrell was suddenly dry-mouthed and shivering with fury. It was her choice of words that did it. "Well, I have reason to believe you're a suffocating old bitch and a bourgeois Stalinist. How do you like them apples, Mrs. B?" As though his anger had summoned her, the wolf was standing two feet away from him. Her coat was dark and lank with sweat, and yellow saliva was mixed with the blood that strung from her jaws. She looked at Farrell and growled far away in her throat.

"Just a minute," he said. He covered the receiver with his palm. "It's for you," he said to the wolf. "It's your mother."

The wolf made a pitiful sound, almost inaudible, and scuffed at the floor. She was plainly exhausted. Mrs. Braun pinged in Farrell's ear like a bug against a lighted window. "What, what? Hello, what is this? Listen, you put Lila on the phone right now. Hello? I want to talk to Lila. I know she's there."

Farrell hung up just as the sun touched a corner of the window. The wolf became Lila. As before, she only made one sound. The phone rang again, and she picked it up without a glance at Farrell. "Bernice?" Lila always called her mother by her first name. "Yes— no, no—yeah, I'm fine. I'm all right, I just forgot to call. No, I'm all right, will you listen? Bernice, there's no law that says you have to get hysterical. Yes, you are." She dropped down on the bed, groping under her pillow for cigarettes. Farrell got up and began to make coffee.

"Well, there was a little trouble," Lila was saying. "See, I went to the zoo, because I couldn't find—Bernice, I know, I *know*, but that was, what, three months ago. The thing is, I didn't think that they'd have their horns so soon. Bernice, I had to, that's all. There'd only been a couple of cats and a—well, sure they chased me, but I—well, Momma, Bernice, what did you want me to do? Just what did you want me to do? You're always so dramatic—why do I shout? I shout because I can't get you to listen to me any other way. You remember what Dr. Schechtman said—what? No, I told you, I just forgot to call. No, that is the reason, that's the real and only reason. Well, whose fault is that? What? Oh, Bernice. Jesus Christ, Bernice. All right, *how* is it Dad's fault?"

She didn't want the coffee, or any breakfast, but she sat at the table in his bathrobe and drank milk greedily. It was the first time he had ever seen her drink milk. Her face was sandy pale, and her eyes were red. Talking to her mother left her looking as though she had actually gone ten rounds with the woman. Farrell asked, "How long has it been happening?"

"Nine years," Lila said. "Since I hit puberty. First day, cramps; the second day, this. My introduction to womanhood." She snickered and spilled her milk. "I want some more," she said. "Got to get rid of that taste."

"Who knows about it?" he asked. "Pat and Janet?" They were the two girls she had been rooming with.

"God, no. I'd never tell them. I've never told a girl. Bernice knows, of course, and Dr. Schechtman—he's my head doctor. And you now. That's all." Farrell waited. She was a bad liar, and only did it to heighten the effect of the truth. "Well, there was Mickey," she said. "The guy I told you about the first night, you remember? It doesn't matter. He's an acidhead in Vancouver, of all the places. He'll never tell anybody."

He thought: I wonder if any girl has ever talked about me in that sort of voice. I doubt it, offhand. Lila said, "It wasn't too hard to keep it secret. I missed a lot of things. Like I never could go to the riding camp, and I still want to. And the senior play, when I was in high school. They picked me to play the girl in *Liliom,* but then they changed the evening, and I had to say I was sick. And the winter's bad, because the sun sets so early. But actually, it's been a lot less trouble than my goddamn allergies." She made a laugh, but Farrell did not respond.

"Dr. Schechtman says it's a sex thing," she offered. "He says it'll take years and years to cure it. Bernice thinks I should go to someone else, but I don't want to be one of those women who runs around changing shrinks like hair colors. Pat went through five of them in a month one time. Joe, I wish you'd say something. Or just go away."

"Is it only dogs?" he asked. Lila's face did not change, but her chair rattled, and the milk went over again. Farrell said, "Answer me. Do you only kill dogs, and cats, and zoo animals?"

The tears began to come, heavy and slow, bright as knives in the morning sunlight. She could not look at him, and when she tried to speak she could only make creaking, cartilaginous sounds in her throat. "You don't know," she whispered at last. "You don't have any idea what it's like."

"That's true," he answered. He was always very fair about that particular point.

He took her hand, and then she really began to cry. Her sobs were horrible to hear, much more frightening to Farrell than any wolf noises. When he held her, she rolled in his arms like a stranded ship with the waves slamming into her. I always get the criers, he thought sadly. My girls always cry, sooner or later. But never for me.

"Don't leave me!" she wept. "I don't know why I came to live with you—I knew it wouldn't work—but don't leave me! There's just Bernice and Dr. Schechtman, and it's so lonely. I want somebody else, I get so lonely. Don't leave me, Joe. I love you, Joe. I love you."

She was patting his face as though she were blind. Farrell stroked her hair and kneaded the back of her neck, wishing that her mother would call again. He felt skilled and weary, and without desire. I'm doing it again, he thought.

"I love you," Lila said. And he answered her, thinking, I'm doing it again. That's the great advantage of making the same mistake a lot of times. You come to know it, and you can study it and get inside it, really make it yours. It's the same good old mistake, except this time the girl's hang-up is different. But it's the same thing. I'm doing it again.

The building superintendent was thirty or fifty: dark, thin, quick, and shivering. A Lithuanian or a Latvian, he spoke very little English. He smelled of black friction tape and stale water, and he was strong in the twisting way that a small, lean animal is strong. His eyes were almost purple, and they bulged a little, straining out—the terrible eyes of a herald angel stricken dumb. He roamed in the basement all day, banging on pipes and taking the elevator apart.

The superintendent met Lila only a few hours after Farrell did: on that first night, when she came home with him. At the sight of her the little man jumped back, dropping the two-legged chair he was carrying. He promptly fell over it, and did not try to get up, but cowered there, clucking and gulping, trying to cross himself and make the sign of the horns at the same time. Farrell started to help him up, but he screamed. They could hardly hear the sound.

It would have been merely funny and embarrassing, except for the fact that Lila was equally as frightened of the superintendent from that moment. She would not go down to the basement for any reason, nor would she enter or leave the house until she was satisfied that he was nowhere near. Farrell had thought then that she took the superintendent for a lunatic.

"I don't know how he knows," he said to Ben. "I guess if you believe in werewolves and vampires, you probably recognize them right away. I don't believe in them at all, and I live with one."

He lived with Lila all through the autumn and the winter. They went out together and came home, and her cooking improved slightly, and she gave up the guitar and got a kitten named Theodora. Sometimes she wept, but not often. She turned out not to be a real crier.

She told Dr. Schechtman about Farrell, and he said that it would probably be a very beneficial relationship for her. It wasn't, but it wasn't a particularly bad one either. Their lovemaking was usually good, though it bothered Farrell to suspect that it was the sense and smell of the Other that excited him. For the rest, they came near being friends. Farrell had known that he did not love Lila before he found out that she was a werewolf, and this made him feel a great deal easier about being bored with her.

"It'll break up by itself in the spring," he said, "like ice."

Ben asked, "What if it doesn't?" They were having lunch in the Automat again. "What'll you do if it just goes on?"

"It's not that easy." Farrell looked away from his friend and began to explore the mysterious, swampy innards of his beef pie. He said, "The trouble is that I know her. That was the real mistake. You shouldn't get to know people if you know you're not going to stay with them, one way or another. It's all right if you come and go in ignorance, but you shouldn't know them."

A week or so before the full moon, she would start to become nervous and strident, and this would continue until the day preceding her transformation. On that day, she was invariably loving, in the tender, desperate manner of someone who is going away; but the next day would see her silent, speaking only when she had to. She always had a cold on the last day, and looked gray and patchy and sick, but she usually went to work anyway.

Farrell was sure, though she never talked about it, that the change into wolf shape was actually peaceful for her, though the returning hurt. Just before moonrise she would take off her clothes and take the pins out of her hair and stand waiting. Farrell never managed not to close his eyes when she dropped heavily down on all fours; but there was a moment before that when her face would grow a look that he never saw at any other time, except when they were making love. Each time he saw it, it struck him as a look of wondrous joy at not being Lila any more.

"See, I know her," he tried to explain to Ben. "She only likes to go to color movies, because wolves can't see color. She can't stand the Modern Jazz Quartet, but that's all she plays the first couple of days afterward. Stupid things like that. Never gets high at parties, because she's afraid she'll start talking. It's hard to walk away, that's all. Taking what I know with me."

Ben asked, "Is she still scared of the super?"

"Oh, God," Farrell said. "She got his dog last time. It was a Dalmatian—good-looking animal. She didn't know it was his. He doesn't hide when he sees her now, he just gives her a look like a stake through the heart. That man is a really classy hater, a natural. I'm scared of him myself." He stood up and began to pull on his overcoat. "I wish he'd get turned on to her mother. Get some practical use out of him. Did I tell you she wants me to call her Bernice?"

Ben said, "Farrell, if I were you, I'd leave the country. I would."

They went out into the February drizzle that sniffled back and forth between snow and rain. Farrell did not speak until they reached the corner where he turned toward the bookstore. Then he said very softly, "Damn, you have to be so careful. Who wants to know what people turn into?"

May came, and a night when Lila once again stood naked at the window, waiting for the moon. Farrell fussed with dishes and garbage bags and fed the cat. These moments were always awkward. He had just asked her, "You want to save what's left of the rice?" when the telephone rang.

It was Lila's mother. She called two and three times a week now. "This is Bernice. How's my Irisher this evening?"

"I'm fine, Bernice," Farrell said. Lila suddenly threw back her head and drew a heavy, whining breath. The cat hissed silently and ran into the bathroom.

"I called to inveigle you two uptown this Friday," Mrs. Braun said. "A couple of old friends are coming over, and I know if I don't get some young people in we'll just sit around and talk about what went wrong with the Progressive Party. The Old Left. So if you could sort of sweet-talk our girl into spending an evening in Squaresville—"

"I'll have to check with Lila." She's *doing* it, he thought, that terrible woman. Every time I talk to her, I sound married. I see what she's doing, but she goes right ahead anyway. He said, "I'll talk to her in the morning." Lila struggled in the moonlight, between dancing and drowning.

"Oh," Mrs. Braun said. "Yes, of course. Have her call me back." She sighed. "It's such a comfort to me to know you're there. Ask her if I should fix a fondue."

Lila made a handsome wolf: tall and broad-chested for a female, moving as easily as water sliding over stone. Her coat was dark brown, showing red in the proper light, and there were white places on her breast. She had pale green eyes, the color of the sky when a hurricane is coming.

Usually she was gone as soon as the changing was over, for she never cared for him to see her in her wolf form. But tonight she came slowly toward him, walking in a strange way, with her hindquarters almost dragging. She was making a high, soft sound, and her eyes were not focusing on him.

"What is it?" he asked foolishly. The wolf whined and skulked under the table, rubbing against the leg. Then she lay on her belly and rolled, and as she did so the sound grew in her throat until it became an odd, sad, thin cry, not a hunting howl, but a shiver of longing turned into breath.

"Jesus, don't do that!" Farrell gasped. But she sat up and howled again, and a dog answered her from somewhere near the river. She wagged her tail and whimpered.

Farrell said, "The super'll be up here in two minutes flat. What's the matter with you?" He heard footsteps and low frightened voices in the apartment above them. Another dog howled, this one nearby, and the wolf wriggled a little way toward the window on her haunches, like a baby, scooting. She looked at him over her shoulder, shuddering violently. On an impulse, he picked up the phone and called her mother.

Watching the wolf as she rocked and slithered and moaned, he described her actions to Mrs. Braun. "I've never seen her like this," he said. "I don't know what's the matter with her."

"Oh, my God," Mrs. Braun whispered, She told him.

When he was silent, she began to speak very rapidly. "It hasn't happened for such a long time. Schechtman gives her pills, but she must have run out and forgotten—she's always been like that, since she was little. All the thermos bottles she used to leave on the school bus, and every week her piano music—"

"I wish you'd told me before," he said. He was edging very cautiously toward the open window. The pupils of the wolf's eyes were pulsing with her quick breaths.

"It isn't a thing you tell people!" Lila's mother wailed in his ears. "How do you think it was for me when she brought her first little boyfriend—" Farrell dropped the phone and sprang for the window. He had the inside track, and he might have made it, but she turned her head and snarled so wildly that he fell back. When he reached the window, she was already two fire escape landings below, and there was eager yelping waiting for her in the street.

Dangling and turning just above the floor, Mrs. Braun heard Farrell's distant yell, followed immediately by a heavy thumping on the door. A strange, tattered voice was shouting unintelligibly beyond the knocking. Footsteps crashed by the receiver and the door opened.

"My dog, my dog!" the strange voice mourned. "My dog, my dog, my dog!"

"I'm sorry about your dog," Farrell said. "Look, please go away. I've got work to do."

"I got work," the voice said. "I know my work." It climbed and spilled into another language, out of which English words jutted like broken bones. "Where is she? Where is she? She kill my dog."

"She's not here." Farrell's own voice changed on the last word. It seemed a long time before he said, "You'd better put that away."

Mrs. Braun heard the howl as clearly as though the wolf were running beneath her own window—lonely and insatiable, with a kind of gasping laughter in it. The other voice began to scream. Mrs. Braun caught the phrase *silver bullet* several times. The door slammed, then opened and slammed again.

Farrell was the only man of his own acquaintance who was able to play back his dreams while he was having them: to stop them in midflight, no matter how fearful they might be—or how lovely—and run them over and over studying them in his sleep, until the most terrifying reel became at once utterly harmless and unbearably familiar. This night that he spent running after Lila was like that.

He would find them congregated under the marquee of an apartment house, or romping around the moonscape of a construction site: ten or fifteen males of all races, creeds, colors, and previous conditions of servitude; whining and yapping, pissing against tires, inhaling indiscriminately each other and the lean, grinning bitch they surrounded. She frightened them, for she growled more wickedly than coyness demanded, and where she snapped, even in play, bone showed. Still they tumbled on her and over her, biting her neck and ears in their turn; and she snarled but she did not run away.

Never, at least, until Farrell came charging upon them, shrieking like any cuckold, kicking at the snuffling lovers. Then she would turn and race off into the spring dark, with her thin, dreamy howl floating behind her like the train of a smoky gown. The dogs followed, and so did Farrell, calling and cursing. They always lost him quickly, that jubilant marriage procession, leaving him stumbling down rusty iron ladders into places where he fell over garbage cans. Yet he would come upon them as inevitably in time, loping along Broadway or trotting across Columbus Avenue toward the park; he would hear them in the tennis courts near the river, breaking down the nets over Lila and her moment's Ares. There were dozens of them now, coming from all directions. They stank of their joy, and he threw stones at them and shouted, and they ran.

And the wolf ran at their head, on sidewalks and on wet grass, her tail waving contentedly, but her eyes still hungry, and her howl growing ever more warning than wistful. Farrell knew that she must have blood before sunrise, and that it was both useless and dangerous to follow her. But the night wound and unwound itself, and he knew the same things over and over, and ran down the same streets, and saw the same couples walk wide of him, thinking he was drunk.

Mrs. Braun kept leaping out of a taxi that pulled up next to him, usually at corners where the dogs had just piled by, knocking over the crates stacked in market doorways and spilling the newspapers at the subway kiosks. Standing in broccoli, in black taffeta, with a front like a ferryboat—yet as lean in the hips as her wolf-daughter—with her plum-colored hair all loose, one arm lifted, and her orange mouth pursed in a bellow, she was no longer Bernice but a wronged fertility goddess getting set to blast the harvest. "We've got to split up!" she would roar at Farrell, and each time it sounded like a sound idea. Yet he looked for her whenever he lost Lila's trail, because she never did.

The superintendent kept turning up too, darting after Farrell out of alleys or cellar entrances, or popping from the freight elevators that load through the sidewalk. Farrell would hear his numberless passkeys clicking on the flat piece of wood tucked into his belt.

"You see her? You see her, the wolf, kill my dog?" Under the fat, ugly moon, the army .45 glittered and trembled like his own mad eyes.

"Mark with a cross." He would pat the barrel of the gun and shake it under Farrell's nose like a maraca. "Mark with a cross, bless by a priest. Three silver bullets. She kill my dog."

Lila's voice would come sailing to them then, from up in Harlem or away near Lincoln Center, and the little man would whirl and dash down into the earth, disappearing into the crack between two slabs of sidewalk. Farrell understood quite clearly that the superintendent was hunting Lila underground, using the keys that only superintendents have to take elevators down to the black sub-sub-basements, far below the bicycle rooms and the wet, shaking laundry rooms, and below the furnace rooms, below the passages walled with electricity meters and roofed with burly steam pipes; down to the realms where the great dim water mains roll like whales, and the gas lines hump and preen, down where the roots of the apartment houses fade together; and so along under the city, scrabbling through secret ways with silver bullets, and his keys rapping against the piece of wood. He never saw Lila, but he was never very far behind her.

Cutting across parking lots, pole-vaulting between locked bumpers, edging and dancing his way through fluorescent gaggles of haughty children; leaping uptown like a salmon against the current of the theater crowds; walking quickly past the random killing faces that floated down the night tide like unexploded mines, and especially avoiding the crazy faces that wanted to tell him what it was like to be crazy—so Farrell pursued Lila Braun, of Tremont Avenue and CCNY, in the city all night long. Nobody offered to help him, or tried to head off the dangerous-looking bitch bounding along with the delirious raggle of admirers streaming after her; but then, the dogs had to fight through the same clenched legs and vengeful bodies that Farrell did. The crowds slowed Lila down, but he felt relieved whenever she turned toward the emptier streets. *She must have blood soon, somewhere.*

Farrell's dreams eventually lost their clear edge after he played them back a certain number of times, and so it was with the night. The full moon skidded down the sky, thinning like a tatter of butter in a skillet, and remembered scenes began to fold sloppily into each other. The sound of Lila and the dogs grew fainter whichever way he followed. Mrs. Braun blinked on and off at longer intervals; and in dark doorways and under subway gratings, the superintendent burned like a corposant, making the barrel of his pistol run rainbow. At last he lost Lila for good, and with that it seemed that he woke.

It was still night, but not dark, and he was walking slowly home on Riverside Drive through a cool, grainy fog. The moon had set, but the river was strangely bright—glittering gray as far up as the bridge, where headlights left shiny, wet paths like snails. There was no one else on the street.

"Dumb broad," he said aloud. "The hell with it. She wants to mess around, let her mess around." He wondered whether werewolves could have cubs, and what sort of cubs they might be. Lila must have turned on the dogs by now, for the blood. Poor dogs, he thought. They were all so dirty and innocent and happy with her.

"A moral lesson for all of us," he announced sententiously. "Don't fool with strange, eager ladies, they'll kill you." He was a little hysterical. Then, two blocks ahead of him, he saw the gaunt shape in the gray light of the river, alone now, and hurrying. Farrell did not call to her, but as soon as he began to run, the wolf wheeled and faced him. Even at that distance, her eyes were stained and streaked and wild. She showed all the teeth on one side of her mouth, and she growled like fire.

Farrell trotted steadily toward her, crying, "Go home, go home! Lila, you dummy, get on home, it's morning!" She growled terribly, but when Farrell was less than a block away she turned again and dashed across the street, heading for West End Avenue. Farrell said, "Good girl, that's it," and limped after her.

In the hours before sunrise on West End Avenue, many people came out to walk their dogs. Farrell had done it often enough with poor Grunewald to know many of the dawn walkers by sight, and some to talk to. A fair number of them were whores and homosexuals, both of whom always seem to have dogs in New York. Quietly, almost always alone, they drifted up and down the Nineties, piloted by their small, fussy beasts, but moving in a kind of fugitive truce with the city and the night that was ending. Farrell sometimes fancied that they were all asleep, and that this hour was the only true rest they ever got.

He recognized Robie by his two dogs, Scone and Crumpet. Robie lived in the apartment directly below Farrell's, usually unhappily. The dogs were horrifying little homebrews of Chihuahua and Yorkshire terrier, but Robie loved them.

Crumpet, the male, saw Lila first. He gave a delighted yap of welcome and proposition (according to Robie, Scone bored him, and he liked big girls anyway) and sprang to meet her, yanking his leash through Robie's slack hand. The wolf was almost upon him before he realized his fatal misunderstanding and scuttled desperately in retreat, meowing with utter terror.

Robie wailed, and Farrell ran as fast as he could, but Lila knocked Crumpet off his feet and slashed his throat while he was still in the air. Then she crouched on the body, nuzzling it in a dreadful way.

Robie actually came within a step of leaping upon Lila and trying to drag her away from his dead dog. Instead, he turned on Farrell as he came panting up, and began hitting him with a good deal of strength and accuracy. "Damn you, damn you!" he sobbed. Little Scone ran away around the corner, screaming like a mandrake.

Farrell put up his arms and went with the punches, all the while yelling at Lila until his voice ripped. But the blood frenzy had her, and Farrell had never imagined what she must be like at those times.

Somehow she had spared the dogs who had loved her all night, but she was nothing but thirst now. She pushed and kneaded Crumpet's body as though she were nursing.

All along the avenue, the morning dogs were barking like trumpets. Farrell ducked away from Robie's soft fists and saw them coming, tripping over their trailing leashes, running too fast for their stubby legs. They were small, spoiled beasts, most of them, overweight and short-winded, and many were not young. Their owners cried unmanly pet names after them, but they waddled gallantly toward their deaths, barking promises far bigger than themselves, and none of them looked back.

She looked up with her muzzle red to the eyes. The dogs did falter then, for they knew murder when they smelled it, and even their silly, nearsighted eyes understood vaguely what creature faced them. But they knew the smell of love too, and they were all gentlemen.

She killed the first two to reach to her—a spitz and a cocker spaniel —with two snaps of her jaws. But before she could settle down to her meal, three Pekes were scrambling up to her, though they would have had to stand on each others' shoulders. Lila whirled without a sound, and they fell away, rolling and yelling but unhurt. As soon as she turned, the Pekes were at her again, joined now by a couple of valiant poodles. Lila got one of the poodles when she turned again.

Robie had stopped beating on Farrell, and was leaning against a traffic light, being sick. But other people were running up now: a middle-aged black man, crying; a plump youth in a plastic car coat and bedroom slippers, who kept whimpering, "Oh God, she's eating them, look at her, she's really eating them!"; two lean, ageless girls in slacks, both with foamy beige hair. They all called wildly to their unheeding dogs, and they all grabbed at Farrell and shouted in his face. Cars began to stop.

The sky was thin and cool, rising pale gold, but Lila paid no attention to it. She was ramping under the swarm of little dogs, rearing and spinning in circles, snarling blood. The dogs were terrified and bewildered, but they never swerved from their labor. The smell of love told them that they were welcome, however ungraciously she seemed to receive them. Lila shook herself, and a pair of squealing dachshunds, hobbled in a double harness, tumbled across the sidewalk to end at Farrell's feet. They scrambled up and immediately towed themselves back into the maelstrom. Lila bit one of them almost in half, but the other dachshund went on trying to climb her hindquarters, dragging his ripped comrade with him. Farrell began to laugh.

The black man said, "You think it's funny?" and hit him. Farrell sat down, still laughing. The man stood over him, embarrassed, offering Farrell his handkerchief. "I'm sorry, I shouldn't have done that," he said. "But your dog killed my dog."

"She isn't my dog," Farrell said. He moved to let a man pass between them, and then saw that it was the superintendent, holding his pistol with both hands. Nobody noticed him until he fired; but Farrell pushed one of the foamy-haired girls, and she stumbled against the superintendent as the gun went off. The silver bullet broke a window in a parked car.

The superintendent fired again while the echoes of the first shot were still clapping back and forth between the houses. A Pomeranian screamed that time, and a woman cried out, "Oh, my God, he shot Borgy!" But the crowd was crumbling away, breaking into its individual components like pills on television. The watching cars had sped off at the sight of the gun, and the faces that had been peering down from windows disappeared. Except for Farrell, the few people who remained were scattered halfway down the block. The sky was brightening swiftly now.

"For God's sake, don't let him!" the same woman called from the shelter of a doorway. But two men made shushing gestures at her, saying, "It's all right, he knows how to use that thing. Go ahead, buddy."

The shots had at last frightened the little dogs away from Lila. She crouched among the twitching splotches of fur, with her muzzle wrinkled back and her eyes more black than green. Farrell saw a plaid rag that had been a dog jacket protruding from under her body. The superintendent stooped and squinted over the gun barrel, aiming with grotesque care, while the men cried to him to shoot. He was too far from the werewolf for her to reach him before he fired the last silver bullet, though he would surely die before she died. His lips were moving as he took aim.

Two long steps would have brought Farrell up and behind the superintendent. Later he told himself that he had been afraid of the pistol, because that was easier than remembering how he had felt when he looked at Lila. Her tongue never stopped lapping around her dark jaws, and even as she set herself to spring, she lifted a bloody paw to her mouth. Farrell thought of her padding in the bedroom, breathing on his face. The superintendent grunted and Farrell closed his eyes. Yet even then he expected to find himself doing something.

Then he heard Mrs. Braun's unmistakable voice. *"Don't you dare!"* She was standing between Lila and the superintendent—one shoe gone, and the heel off the other one; her knit dress torn at the shoulder, and her face tired and smudgy. But she pointed a finger at the startled superintendent, and he stepped quickly back, as though she had a pistol too.

"Lady, that's a wolf," he protested nervously. "Lady, you please get, get out of the way. That's a wolf, I go shoot her now."

"I want to see your license for that gun." Mrs. Braun held out her hand. The superintendent blinked at her, muttering in despair. She said, "Do you know that you can be sent to prison for twenty years for carrying a concealed weapon in this state? Do you know what the fine is for having a gun without a license? The fine is Five. Thousand. Dollars." The men down the street were shouting at her, but she swung around to face the creature snarling among the little dead dogs.

"Come on, Lila," she said. "Come on home with Bernice. I'll make tea and we'll talk. It's been a long time since we've really talked, you know? We used to have nice long talks when you were little, but we don't anymore." The wolf had stopped growling, but she was crouching even lower, and her ears were still flat against her head. Mrs. Braun said, "Come on, baby. Listen, I know what—you'll call in sick at the office and stay for a few days. You'll get a good rest, and maybe we'll even look around a little for a new doctor, what do you say? Schechtman hasn't done a thing for you, I never liked him. Come on home, honey. Momma's here, Bernice knows." She took a step toward the silent wolf, holding out her hand.

The superintendent gave a desperate, wordless cry and pumped forward, clumsily shoving Mrs. Braun to one side. He leveled the pistol point-blank, wailing, "My dog, my dog!" Lila was in the air when the gun went off, and her shadow sprang after her, for the sun had risen. She crumpled down across a couple of dead Pekes. Their blood dabbled her breasts and her pale throat.

Mrs. Braun screamed like a lunch whistle. She knocked the superintendent into the street and sprawled over Lila, hiding her completely from Farrell's sight. "Lila, Lila," she keened her daughter, "poor baby, you never had a chance. He killed you because you were different, the way they kill everything different." Farrell approached her and stooped down, but she pushed him against a wall without looking up. "Lila, Lila, poor baby, poor darling, maybe it's better, maybe you're happy now. You never had a chance, poor Lila."

The dog owners were edging slowly back, and the surviving dogs were running to them. The superintendent squatted on the curb with his head in his arms. A weary, muffled voice said, "For God's sake, Bernice, would you get up off me? You don't have to stop yelling, just get off."

When she stood up, the cars began to stop in the street again. It made it very difficult for the police to get through.

Nobody pressed charges, because there was no one to lodge them against. The killer dog—or wolf, as some insisted—was gone, and if she had an owner, he could not be found. As for the people who had actually seen the wolf turn into a young girl when the sunlight touched her; most of them managed not to have seen it, though they never really forgot. There were a few who knew quite well what they had seen, and never forgot it either, but they never said anything. They did, however, chip in to pay the superintendent's fine for possessing an unlicensed handgun. Farrell gave what he could.

Lila vanished out of Farrell's life before sunset. She did not go uptown with her mother, but packed her things and went to stay with friends in the village. Later he heard that she was living on Christopher Street, and later still, that she had moved to Berkeley and gone back to school. He never saw her again.

"It had to be like that," he told Ben once. "We got to know too much about each other. See, there's another side to knowing. She couldn't look at me."

"You mean because you saw her with all those dogs? Or because she knew you'd have let that little nut shoot her?" Farrell shook his head.

"It was that, I guess, but it was more something else, something I know. When she sprang, just as he shot at her that last time, she wasn't leaping at him. She was going straight for her mother. She'd have got her too, if it hadn't been sunrise."

Ben whistled softly. "I wonder if her old lady knows."

"Bernice knows everything about Lila," Farrell said.

"Mrs. Braun called him nearly two years later to tell him that Lila was getting married. It must have cost her a good deal of money and ingenuity to find him (where Farrell was living then, the telephone line was open for four hours a day), but he knew by the spitefulness in the static that she considered it money well spent.

"He's at Stanford," she crackled. "A research psychologist. They're going to Japan for their honeymoon."

"That's fine," Farrell said. "I'm really happy foɪ her, Bernice." He hesitated before he asked, "Does he know about Lila? I mean, about what happens?—"

"Does he know?" she cried. "He's proud of it—he thinks it's wonderful! It's his field!"

"That's great. That's fine. Good-bye, Bernice. I really am glad."

And he was glad, and a little wistful, thinking about it. The girl he was living with here had a really strange hang-up.

AFTERWORD BY PETER S. BEAGLE: "This story was written very long ago, in another world, by a young man to whom the idea of equating womanhood with lycanthropy, sexual desire with blood and death and humiliation, seemed no more at the time than a casual grisly joke. I would write 'Lila the Werewolf' today, but not for that reason, and not in that way."

The Drowned Giant

J. G. Ballard

J. G. Ballard whose fictionalized autobiography The Empire of the Sun *was made into a popular film in recent years, is an English writer whose initial fame came from his startlingly original science fiction stories, which led him to be the model for the 1960s "new wave" in SF. In stories such as this one, first published in the experimental magazine* New Worlds, *Ballard joins the international company of such contemporary writers as Jorge Luis Borges, Italo Calvino and Stanislaw Lem, who use fantastic images to illuminate the real. The story takes place in a city by the sea reduced to Lilliputian scale by a beached corpse. No one, even the scientist who tells the tale, is ever struck by the wonder of it all. "The Drowned Giant" is meant to disturb and unsettle the reader's sense of the normal through the use of clinical detail and detached tone. Brrrr.*

On the morning after the storm the body of a drowned giant was washed ashore on the beach five miles to the northwest of the city. The first news of its arrival was brought by a nearby farmer and subsequently confirmed by the local newspaper reporters and the police. Despite this the majority of people, I among them, remained skeptical, but the return of more and more eyewitnesses attesting to the vast size of the giant was finally too much for our curiosity. The library where my colleagues and I were carrying out our research was almost deserted when we set off for the coast shortly after two o'clock, and throughout the day people continued to leave their offices and shops as accounts of the giant circulated around the city.

By the time we reached the dunes above the beach, a substantial crowd had gathered, and we could see the body lying in the shallow water two hundred yards away. At first the estimates of its size seemed greatly exaggerated. It was then at low tide, and almost all the giant's body was exposed, but he appeared to be little larger than a basking shark. He lay on his back with his arms at his sides, in an attitude of repose, as if asleep on the mirror of wet sand, the reflection of his blanched skin fading as the water receded. In the clear sunlight his body glistened like the white plumage of a seabird.

Puzzled by this spectacle and dissatisfied with the matter-of-fact explanations of the crowd, my friends and I stepped down from the dunes onto the shingle. Everyone seemed reluctant to approach the giant, but half an hour later two fishermen in wading boots walked out across the sand. As their diminutive figures neared the recumbent body, a sudden hubbub of conversation broke out among the spectators. The two men were completely dwarfed by the giant. Although his heels were partly submerged in the sand, the feet rose to at least twice the fishermen's height, and we immediately realized that this drowned leviathan had the mass and dimensions of the largest sperm whale.

Three fishing smacks had arrived on the scene and with keels raised remained a quarter of a mile offshore, the crews watching from the bows. Their discretion deterred the spectators on the shore from wading out across the sand. Impatiently everyone stepped down from the dunes and waited on the single slopes, eager for a closer view. Around the margins of the figure the sand had been washed away, forming a hollow, as if the giant had fallen out of the sky. The two fishermen were standing between the immense plinths of the feet, waving to us like tourists among the columns of some water-lapped temple on the Nile. For a moment I feared that the giant was merely asleep and might suddenly stir and clap his heels together, but his glazed eyes stared skyward, unaware of the minuscule replicas of himself between his feet.

The fishermen then began a circuit of the corpse, strolling past the long white flanks of the legs. After a pause to examine the fingers of the supine hand, they disappeared from sight between the arm and chest, then reemerged to survey the head, shielding their eyes as they gazed up at its Grecian profile. The shallow forehead, straight high-bridged nose, and curling lips reminded me of a Roman copy of Praxiteles, and the elegantly formed cartouches of the nostrils emphasized the resemblance to sculpture.

Abruptly there was a shout from the crowd, and a hundred arms pointed to the sea. With a start I saw that one of the fishermen had climbed onto the giant's chest and was now strolling about and signaling to the shore. There was a roar of surprise and triumph from the crowd, lost in a rushing avalanche of shingle as everyone surged forward across the sand.

As we approached the recumbent figure, which was lying in a pool of water the size of a field, our excited chatter fell away again, subdued by the huge physical dimensions of this dead colossus. He was stretched out at a slight angle to the shore, his legs carried nearer the beach, and this foreshortening had disguised his true length. Despite the two fishermen standing on his abdomen, the crowd formed itself into a wide circle, groups of people tentatively advancing toward the hands and feet.

My companions and I walked around the seaward side of the giant, whose hips and thorax towered above us like the hull of a stranded ship. His pearl-colored skin, distended by immersion in saltwater, masked the contours of the enormous muscles and tendons. We passed below the left knee, which was flexed slightly, threads of damp seaweed clinging to its sides. Draped loosely across the midriff, and preserving a tenuous propriety, was a shawl of heavy open-weave material, bleached to a pale yellow by the water. A strong odor of brine came from the garment as it steamed in the sun, mingled with the sweet, potent scent of the giant's skin.

We stopped by his shoulder and gazed up at the motionless profile. The lips were parted slightly, the open eye cloudy and occluded, as if injected with some blue milky liquid, but the delicate arches of the nostrils and eyebrows invested the face with an ornate charm that belied the brutish power of the chest and shoulders.

The ear was suspended in midair over our heads like a sculptured doorway. As I raised my hand to touch the pendulous lobe, someone appeared over the edge of the forehead and shouted down at me. Startled by this apparition, I stepped back, and then saw that a group of youths had climbed up onto the face and were jostling each other in and out of the orbits.

People were now clambering all over the giant, whose reclining arms provided a double stairway. From the palms they walked along the forearms to the elbows and then crawled over the distended belly of the biceps to the flat promenade of the pectoral muscles which covered the upper half of the smooth hairless chest. From here they climbed up onto the face, hand over hand along the lips and nose, or forayed down the abdomen to meet others who had straddled the ankles and were patrolling the twin columns of the thighs.

We continued our circuit through the crowd and stopped to examine the outstretched right hand. A small pool of water lay in the palm, like the residue of another world, now being kicked away by the people ascending the arm. I tried to read the palm lines that grooved the skin, searching for some clue to the giant's character, but the distention of the tissues had almost obliterated them, carrying away all trace of the giant's identity and his last tragic predicament. The huge muscles and wristbones of the hand seemed to deny any sensitivity to their owner, but the delicate flection of the fingers and the well-tended nails, each cut symmetrically to within six inches of the quick, argued a certain refinement of temperament, illustrated in the Grecian features of the face, on which the townsfolk were now sitting like flies.

One youth was even standing, arms waving at his sides, on the very tip of the nose, shouting down at his companions, but the face of the giant still retained its massive composure.

Returning to the shore, we sat down on the shingle and watched the continuous stream of people arriving from the city. Some six or seven fishing boats had collected offshore, and their crews waded in through the shallow water for a closer look at this enormous storm catch. Later a party of police appeared and made a halfhearted attempt to cordon off the beach, but after walking up to the recumbent figure, any such thoughts left their minds, and they went off together with bemused backward glances.

An hour later there were a thousand people present on the beach, at least two hundred of them standing or sitting on the giant, crowded along his arms and legs or circulating in a ceaseless melee across his chest and stomach. A large gang of youths occupied the head, toppling each other off the cheeks and sliding down the smooth planes of the jaw. Two or three straddled the nose, and another crawled into one of the nostrils, from which he emitted barking noises like a demented dog.

That afternoon the police returned and cleared a way through the crowd for a party of scientific experts—authorities on gross anatomy and marine biology—from the university. The gang of youths and most of the people on the giant climbed down, leaving behind a few hardy spirits perched on the tips of the toes and on the forehead. The experts strode around the giant, heads nodding in vigorous consultation, preceded by the policemen who pushed back the press of spectators. When they reached the outstretched hand, the experts hastily demurred.

After they returned to the shore, the crowd once more climbed onto the giant, and was in full possession when we left at five o'clock, covering the arms and legs like a dense flock of gulls sitting on the corpse of a large fish.

I next visited the beach three days later. My friends at the library had returned to their work, and delegated to me the task of keeping the giant under observation and preparing a report. Perhaps they sensed my particular interest in the case, and it was certainly true that I was eager to return to the beach. There was nothing necrophilic about this, for to all intents the giant was still alive for me, indeed more alive than many of the people watching him. What I found so fascinating was partly his immense scale, the huge volumes of space occupied by his arms and legs, which seemed to confirm the identity of my own miniature limbs, but above all, the mere categorical fact of his existence. Whatever else in our lives might be open to doubt, the giant, dead or alive, existed in an absolute sense, providing a glimpse into a world of similar absolutes of which we spectators on the beach were such imperfect and puny copies.

When I arrived at the beach the crowd was considerably smaller, and some two or three hundred people sat on the shingle, picnicking and watching the groups of visitors who walked out across the sand. The successive tides had carried the giant nearer the shore, swinging his head and shoulders toward the beach, so that he seemed doubly to gain in size, his huge body dwarfing the fishing boats beached beside his feet. The uneven contours of the beach had pushed his spine into a slight arch, expanding his chest and tilting back the head, forcing him into a more expressly heroic posture. The combined effects of seawater and the tumefaction of the tissues had given the face a sleeker and less youthful look. Although the vast proportions of the features made it impossible to assess the age and character of the giant, on my previous visit his classically modeled mouth and nose suggested that he had been a young man of discreet and modest temper. Now, however, he appeared to be at least in early middle age. The puffy cheeks, thicker nose and temples, and narrowing eyes gave him a look of well-fed maturity that even now hinted at a growing corruption to come.

This accelerated postmortem development of the giant's character, as if the latent elements of his personality had gained sufficient momentum during his life to discharge themselves in a brief final résumé continued to fascinate me. It marked the beginning of the giant's surrender to that all-demanding system of time in which the rest of humanity finds itself, and of which, like the million twisted ripples of a fragmented whirlpool, our finite lives are the concluding products. I took up my position on the shingle directly opposite the giant's head, from where I could see the new arrivals and the children clambering over the legs and arms.

Among the morning's visitors were a number of men in leather jackets and cloth caps, who peered up critically at the giant with a professional eye, pacing out his dimensions and making rough calculations in the sand with spars of driftwood. I assumed them to be from the public works department and other municipal bodies, no doubt wondering how to dispose of this monster.

Several rather more smartly attired individuals, circus proprietors and the like, also appeared on the scene, and strolled slowly around the giant, hands in the pockets of their long overcoats, saying nothing to one another. Evidently its bulk was too great even for their matchless enterprise. After they had gone, the children continued to run up and down the arms and legs, and the youths wrestled with each other over the supine face, the damp sand from their feet covering the white skin.

The following day I deliberately postponed my visit until the late afternoon, and when I arrived there were fewer than fifty or sixty people sitting on the shingle. The giant had been carried still closer to the shore, and was now little more than seventy-five yards away, his feet crushing the palisade of a rotting breakwater. The slope of the firmer sand tilted his body toward the sea, the bruised, swollen face averted in an almost conscious gesture. I sat down on a large metal winch which had been shackled to a concrete caisson above the shingle, and looked down at the recumbent figure.

His blanched skin had now lost its pearly translucence and was spattered with dirty sand which replaced that washed away by the night tide. Clumps of seaweed filled the intervals between the fingers and a collection of litter and cuttlebones lay in the crevices below the hips and knees. But despite this, and the continuous thickening of his features, the giant still retained his magnificent Homeric stature. The enormous breadth of the shoulders, and the huge columns of the arms and legs, still carried the figure into another dimension, and the giant seemed a more authentic image of one of the drowned Argonauts or heroes of the *Odyssey* than the conventional portrait previously in my mind.

I stepped down onto the sand, and walked between the pools of water toward the giant. Two small boys were sitting in the well of the ear, and at the far end a solitary youth stood perched high on one of the toes, surveying me as I approached. As I had hoped when delaying my visit, no one else paid any attention to me, and the people on the shore remained huddled beneath their coats.

The giant's supine right hand was covered with broken shells and sand, in which a score of footprints were visible. The rounded bulk of the hip towered above me, cutting off all sight of the sea. The sweetly acrid odor I had noticed before was now more pungent, and through the opaque skin I could see the serpentine coils of congealed blood vessels. However repellent it seemed, this ceaseless metamorphosis, a macabre life-in-death, alone permitted me to set foot on the corpse.

Using the jutting thumb as a stair rail, I climbed up onto the palm and began my ascent. The skin was harder than I expected, barely yielding to my weight. Quickly I walked up the sloping forearm and the bulging balloon of the biceps. The face of the drowned giant loomed to my right, the cavernous nostrils and huge flanks of the cheeks like the cone of some freakish volcano.

Safely rounding the shoulder, I stepped out onto the broad promenade of the chest, across which the bony ridges of the rib cage lay like huge rafters. The white skin was dappled by the darkening bruises of countless footprints, in which the patterns of individual heel marks were clearly visible. Someone had built a small sand castle on the center of the sternum, and I climbed onto this partly demolished structure to get a better view of the face.

The two children had now scaled the ear and were pulling themselves into the right orbit, whose blue globe, completely occluded by some milk-colored fluid, gazed sightlessly past their miniature forms. Seen obliquely from below, the face was devoid of all grace and repose, the drawn mouth and raised chin propped up by gigantic slings of muscles resembling the torn prow of a colossal wreck. For the first time I became aware of the extremity of this last physical agony of the giant, no less painful for his unawareness of the collapsing musculature and tissues. The absolute isolation of the ruined figure, cast like an abandoned ship upon the empty shore, almost out of sound of the waves, transformed his face into a mask of exhaustion and helplessness.

As I stepped forward, my foot sank into a trough of soft tissue, and a gust of fetid gas blew through an aperture between the ribs. Retreating from the fouled air, which hung like a cloud over my head, I turned toward the sea to clear my lungs. To my surprise I saw that the giant's left hand had been amputated.

I stared with shocked bewilderment at the blackening stump, while the solitary youth reclining on his aerial perch a hundred feet away surveyed me with a sanguinary eye.

This was only the first of a sequence of depredations. I spent the following two days in the library, for some reason reluctant to visit the shore, aware that I had probably witnessed the approaching end of a magnificent illusion. When I next crossed the dunes and set foot on the shingle, the giant was little more than twenty yards away, and with this close proximity to the rough pebbles all traces had vanished of the magic which once surrounded his distant wave-washed form. Despite his immense size, the bruises and dirt that covered his body made him appear merely human in scale, his vast dimensions only increasing his vulnerability.

His right hand and foot had been removed, dragged up the slope, and trundled away by cart. After questioning the small group of people huddled by the breakwater, I gathered that a fertilizer company and a cattlefood manufacturer were responsible.

The giant's remaining foot rose into the air, a steel hawser fixed to the large toe, evidently in preparation for the following day. The surrounding beach had been disturbed by a score of workmen, and deep ruts marked the ground where the hands and foot had been hauled away. A dark brackish fluid leaked from the stumps, and stained the sand and the white cones of the cuttlefish. As I walked down the shingle I noticed that a number of jocular slogans, swastikas, and other signs had been cut into the gray skin, as if the mutilation of this motionless colossus had released a sudden flood of repressed spite. The lobe of one of the ears was pierced by a spear of timber, and a small fire had burned out in the center of the chest, blackening the surrounding skin. The fine wood ash was still being scattered by the wind.

A foul smell enveloped the cadaver, the undisguisable signature of putrefaction, which had at last driven away the usual gathering of youths. I returned to the shingle and climbed up onto the winch. The giant's swollen cheeks had now almost closed his eyes, drawing the lips back in a monumental gape. The once straight Grecian nose had been twisted and flattened, stamped into the ballooning face by countless heels.

When I visited the beach the following day I found, almost with relief, that the head had been removed.

Some weeks elapsed before I made my next journey to the beach, and by then the human likeness I had noticed earlier had vanished again. On close inspection the recumbent thorax and abdomen were unmistakably manlike, but as each of the limbs was chopped off, first at the knee and elbow, and then at shoulder and thigh, the carcass resembled that of any headless sea animal—whale or whale shark. With this loss of identity, and the few traces of personality that had clung tenuously to the figure, the interest of the spectators expired, and the foreshore was deserted except for an elderly beachcomber and the watchman sitting in the doorway of the contractor's hut.

A loose wooden scaffolding had been erected around the carcass, from which a dozen ladders swung in the wind, and the surrounding sand was littered with coils of rope, long metal-handled knives, and grappling irons, the pebbles oily with blood and pieces of bone and skin.

I nodded to the watchman, who regarded me dourly over his brazier of burning coke. The whole area was pervaded by the pungent smell of huge squares of blubber being simmered in a vat behind the hut.

Both the thighbones had been removed, with the assistance of a small crane draped in the gauzelike fabric which had once covered the waist of the giant, and the open sockets gaped like barn doors. The upper arms, collarbones, and pudenda had likewise been dispatched. What remained of the skin over the thorax and abdomen had been marked out in parallel strips with a tarbrush, and the first five or six sections had been pared away from the midriff, revealing the great arch of the rib cage.

As I left, a flock of gulls wheeled down from the sky and alighted on the beach, picking at the stained sand with ferocious cries.

Several months later, when the news of his arrival had been generally forgotten, various pieces of the body of the dismembered giant began to reappear all over the city. Most of these were bones, which the fertilizer manufacturers had found too difficult to crush, and their massive size, and the huge tendons and disks of cartilage attached to their joints, immediately identified them. For some reason, these disembodied fragments seemed better to convey the essence of the giant's original magnificence than the bloated appendages that had been subsequently amputated. As I looked across the road at the premises of the largest wholesale merchants in the meat market, I recognized the two enormous thighbones on either side of the doorway. They towered over the porters' heads like the threatening megaliths of some primitive druidical religion, and I had a sudden vision of the giant climbing to his knees upon these bare bones and striding away through the streets of the city, picking up the scattered fragments of himself on his return journey to the sea.

A few days later I saw the left humerus lying in the entrance to one of the shipyards. In the same week the mummified right hand was exhibited on a carnival float during the annual pageant of the guilds.

The lower jaw, typically, found its way to the museum of natural history. The remainder of the skull has disappeared, but is probably still lurking in the waste grounds or private gardens of the city—quite recently, while sailing down the river, I noticed two ribs of the giant forming a decorative arch in a waterside garden, possibly confused with the jawbones of a whale. A large square of tanned and tattooed skin, the size of an Indian blanket, forms a back cloth to the dolls and masks in a novelty shop near the amusement park, and I have no doubt that elsewhere in the city, in the hotels or golf clubs, the mummified nose or ears of the giant hang from the wall above a fireplace. As for the immense pizzle, this ends its days in the freak museum of a circus which travels up and down the Northwest. This monumental apparatus, stunning in its proportions and sometime potency, occupies a complete booth to itself. The irony is that it is wrongly identified as that of a whale, and indeed most people, even those who first saw him cast up on the shore after the storm, now remember the giant, if at all, as a large sea beast.

The remainder of the skeleton, stripped of all flesh, still rests on the seashore, the clutter of bleached ribs like the timbers of a derelict ship. The contractor's hut, the crane, and scaffolding have been removed, and the sand being driven into the bay along the coast has buried the pelvis and backbone. In the winter the high curved bones are deserted, battered by the breaking waves, but in the summer they provide an excellent perch for the sea-wearying gulls.

Worlds

*Stories of other places,
where wonders abide*

The Enchanted Buffalo

L. Frank Baum

L. Frank Baum, the creator of Oz, set out to use American settings and creatures in his fairy tales in an attempt to foster the growth of a national fantasy literature in the United States. At least in his own works he succeeded admirably, but his Oz stories have so dominated his reputation that his many other fine tales are somewhat neglected. Here, from his book Animal Fairy Tales, *is one of his most successful efforts in this vein, which deserves a wider audience. A tale of betrayal and revenge among the rulers of the greatest buffalo tribe, it is starkly moral and rich with feeling for its setting. "The prairie is vast. It is lonely, as well." Somehow, Baum brings something of vast scope into this short piece. It is a delight.*

This is a tale of the Royal Tribe of Okolom—those mighty buffaloes that once dominated all the Western prairies. Seven hundred strong were the Okolom—great, shaggy creatures herding together and defying all enemies. Their range was well known to the Indians, to lesser herds of bisons and to all the wild animals that roamed in the open; but none cared to molest or interfere with the Royal Tribe.

Dakt was the first King of the Okolom. By odds the fiercest and most intelligent of his race, he founded the Tribe, made the Laws that directed their actions and led his subjects through wars and dangers until they were acknowledged masters of the prairie.

Dakt had enemies, of course; even in the Royal Tribe. As he grew old it was whispered he was in league with Pagshat, the Evil Genius of the prairies; yet few really believed the lying tale, and those who did but feared King Dakt the more.

The days of this monarch were prosperous days for the Okolom. In Summer their feeding grounds were ever rich in succulent grasses; in Winter Dakt led them to fertile valleys in the shelter of the mountains.

But in time the great leader grew old and gray. He ceased quarreling and fighting and began to love peace—a sure sign that his days were numbered. Sometimes he would stand motionless for hours, apparently in deep thought. His dignity relaxed; he became peevish; his eye, once shrewd and compelling, grew dim and glazed.

Many of the younger bulls, who coveted his Kingship, waited for Dakt to die; some patiently, and some impatiently. Throughout the herd there was an undercurrent of excitement. Then, one bright Spring morning, as the Tribe wandered in single file toward new feeding grounds, the old King lagged behind. They missed him, presently, and sent Barrag the Bull back over the hills to look for him. It was an hour before this messenger returned, coming into view above the swell of the prairie.

"The King is dead," said Barrag the Bull, as he walked calmly into the midst of the tribe. "Old age has at last overtaken him."

The members of the Okolom looked upon him curiously. Then one said: "There is blood upon your horns, Barrag. You did not wipe them well upon the grass."

Barrag turned fiercely. "The old King is dead," he repeated. "Hereafter, I am the King!"

No one answered in words; but, as the Tribe pressed backward into a dense mass, four young bulls remained standing before Barrag, quietly facing the would-be King. He looked upon them sternly. He had expected to contend for his royal office. It was the Law that any of the Tribe might fight for the right to rule the Okolom. But it surprised him to find there were four who dared dispute his assertion that he was King.

Barrag the Bull had doubtless been guilty of a cowardly act in goring the feeble old King to his death. But he could fight; and fight he did. One after another the powerful young bulls were overthrown, while every member of the Tribe watched the great tournament with eager interest. Barrag was not popular with them, but they could not fail to marvel at his prowess. To the onlookers he seemed inspired by unseen powers that lent him a strength fairly miraculous. They murmured together in awed tones, and the name of the dread Pagshat was whispered more than once.

As the last of the four bulls—the pride of half the Tribe—lay at the feet of the triumphant Barrag, the victor turned and cried aloud: "I am King of the Okolom! Who dares dispute my right to rule?"

For a moment there was silence. Then a fresh young voice exclaimed: "I dare!" and a handsome bull calf marched slowly into the space before Barrag and proudly faced him. A muttered protest swelled from the assemblage until it became a roar. Before it had subsided the young one's mother rushed to his side with a wail of mingled love and fear.

"No, no, Oknu!" she pleaded, desperately. "Do not fight, my child. It is death! See—Barrag is twice thy size. Let him rule the Okolom!"

"But I myself am the son of Dakt the King, and fit to rule in his place," answered Oknu, tossing his head with pride. "This Barrag is an interloper! There is no drop of royal blood in his veins."

"But he is nearly twice thy size!" moaned the mother, nearly frantic with terror. "He is leagued with the Evil Genius. To fight him means defeat and death!"

"He is a murderer!" returned the young bull, glaring upon Barrag. "He has killed his King, my father!"

"Enough!" roared the accused. "I am ready to silence this king's cub. Let us fight."

"No!" said an old bull, advancing from the herd. "Oknu shall not fight to-day. He is too young to face the mighty Barrag. But he will grow, both in size and strength; and then, when he is equal to the contest, he may fight for his father's place among the Okolom. In the meantime we acknowledge Barrag our King!"

A shout of approval went up from all the Tribe, and in the confusion that followed the old Queen thrust her bold son out of sight amidst the throng.

Barrag was King. Proudly he accepted the acclaims of the Okolom —the most powerful tribe in his race. His ambition was at last fulfilled; his plotting had met with success. The unnatural strength he had displayed had vanquished every opponent. Barrag was King.

Yet as the new ruler led his followers away from the field of conflict and into fresh pastures, his heart was heavy within him. He had not thought of Prince Oknu, the son of the terrible old King he had

assisted to meet death. Oknu was a mere youth, half-grown and un-
tried. Yet the look in his dark eyes as he had faced his father's murderer filled Barrag with a vague uneasiness. The youth would grow,
and bade fair to become as powerful in time as old Dakt himself. And
when he was grown he would fight for the leadership of the Okolom.

Barrag had not reckoned upon that.

When the moon came up, and the prairie was dotted with the
reclining forms of the hosts of the Royal Tribe, the new King rose
softly to his feet and moved away with silent tread. His pace was slow
and stealthy until he had crossed the first rolling swell of prairie; then
he set off at a brisk trot that covered many leagues within the next
two hours.

At length Barrag reached a huge rock that towered above the
plain. It was jagged and full of rents and fissures, and after a moment's hesitation the King selected an opening and stalked fearlessly
into the black shadows. Presently the rift became a tunnel; but Barrag
kept on, feeling his way in the darkness with his fore feet. Then a tiny
light glimmered ahead, guiding him, and soon after he came into a
vast cave hollowed in the centre of the rock. The rough walls were
black as ink, yet glistened with an unseen light that shed its mellow
but awesome rays throughout the cavern.

Here Barrag paused, saying in a loud voice:

"To thee, O Pagshat, Evil Genius of the Prairies, I give greeting!
All has occurred as thou didst predict. The great Dakt is dead, and I,
Barrag the Bull, am ruler of the Tribe of Okolom."

For a moment after he ceased the stillness was intense. Then a
Voice, grave and deep, answered in the language of the buffaloes: "It
is well!"

"But all difficulties are not yet swept aside," continued Barrag.
"The old King left a son, an audacious young bull not half grown,
who wished to fight me. But the patriarchs of the Tribe bade him wait
until he had size and strength. Tell me, can the young Prince Oknu
defeat me then?"

"He can," responded the Voice.

"Then what shall I do?" demanded the King. "Thou hast promised
to make me secure in my power."

"I promised only to make you King of the Tribe—and you are
King. Farther than that, you must protect yourself," the Voice of the
Evil Genius made answer. "But, since you are hereafter my slave, I

will grant you one more favor—the power to remove your enemy by enchantment."

"And how may I do that?" asked Barrag, eagerly.

"I will give you the means," was the reply. "Bow low thine head, and between the horns I will sprinkle a magical powder."

Barrag obeyed. "And now?" said he, inquiringly.

"Now," responded the unseen Voice, "mark well my injunctions. You must enchant the young Prince and transform him from a buffalo into some small and insignificant animal. Therefore, to-morrow you must choose a spring, and before any of the Tribe has drunk therein, shake well your head above the water, that the powder may sift down into the spring. At the same time centre your thoughts intently upon the animal into which you wish the Prince transformed. Then let him drink of the water in the spring, and the transformation on the instant will be accomplished."

"That is very simple," said Barrag. "Is the powder between my horns?"

"It is," answered the Voice.

"Then farewell, O Pagshat!"

From the cavern of the Evil Genius the King felt his way through the passages until he emerged upon the prairie. Then, softly—that he might not disturb the powder of enchantment—he trotted back to the sleeping herd.

Just before he reached it a panther, slender, lithe and black as coal, bounded across his path, and with a quick blow of his hoof Barrag crushed in the animal's skull. "Panthers are miserable creatures," mused the King, as he sought his place among the slumbering buffaloes. "I think I shall transform young Oknu into a black panther."

Secure in his great strength, he forgot that a full-grown panther is the most terrible foe known to his race.

At sunrise the King led the Royal Tribe of Okolom to a tiny spring that welled clear and refreshing from the centre of a fertile valley.

It is the King's right to drink first, but after bending his head above the spring and shaking it vigorously Barrag drew back and turned to the others.

"Come! I will prove that I bear no ill will," said he, treacherously. "Prince Oknu is the eldest son of our dead but venerated King Dakt. It is not for me to usurp his right. Prince Oknu shall drink first."

Hearing this, the patriarchs looked upon one another in surprise. It was not like Barrag the Bull to give way to another. But the Queen-mother was delighted at the favor shown her son, and eagerly pushed him forward. So Oknu advanced proudly to the spring and drank, while Barrag bent his thought intently upon the black panther.

An instant later a roar of horror and consternation came from the Royal Tribe; for the form of Prince Oknu had vanished, and in its place crouched the dark form of a trembling, terrified panther.

Barrag sprang forward. "Death to the vermin!" he cried, and raised his cloven hoof to crush in the panther's skull.

A sudden spring, a flash through the air, and the black panther alighted upon Barrag's shoulders. Then its powerful jaws closed over the buffalo's neck, pressing the sharp teeth far into the flesh.

With a cry of pain and terror the King reared upright, striving to shake off his tormentor; but the panther held fast. Again Barrag reared, whirling this way and that, his eyes staring, his breath quick and short, his great body trembling convulsively.

The others looked on fearfully. They saw the King kneel and roll upon the grass; they saw him arise with his foe still clinging to his back with claw and tooth; they heard the moan of despair that burst from their stricken leader, and the next instant Barrag was speeding away across the prairie like an arrow fresh from a bow, and his bellows of terror grew gradually fainter as he passed from their sight.

The prairie is vast. It is lonely, as well. A vulture, resting on outstretched wings, watched anxiously the flight of Barrag the Bull as hour by hour he sped away to the southward—the one moving thing on all that great expanse.

The sun sank low and buried itself in the prairie's edge. Twilight succeeded, and faded into night. And still a black shadow, leap by leap, sprang madly through the gloom. The jackals paused, listening to the short, quick pants of breath—the irregular hoof-beats of the galloping bull. But while they hesitated the buffalo passed on, with the silent panther still crouched upon its shoulders.

In the black night Barrag suddenly lifted up his voice. "Come to me, O Pagshat—Evil Genius that thou art—come to my rescue!" he cried.

And presently it seemed that another dark form rushed along beside his own.

"Save me, Pagshat!" he moaned. "Crush thou mine enemy, and set me free!"

A cold whisper reached him in reply: "I cannot!"

"Change him again into his own form," panted Barrag; "hark ye, Pagshat: 'tis the King's son—the cub—the weakling! Disenchant him, ere he proves my death!"

Again came the calm reply, like a breath of Winter sending a chill to his very bones: "I cannot."

Barrag groaned, dashing onward—ever onward.

"When you are dead," continued the Voice, "Prince Oknu will resume his own form. But not before."

"Did we not make a compact?" questioned Barrag, in despairing tone.

"We did," said the Evil Genius, "and I have kept my pact. But you have still to fulfill a pledge to me."

"At my death—only at my death, Pagshat!" cried the bull, trembling violently.

A cruel laugh was the only response. The moon broke through a rift in the clouds, flooding the prairie with silver light. The Evil Genius had disappeared, and the form of the solitary buffalo, with its clinging, silent foe, stumbled blindly across the endless plains.

Barrag had bargained with the Evil One for strength, and the strength of ten bulls was his. The legends do not say how many days and nights the great buffalo fled across the prairies with the black panther upon his shoulders. We know that the Utes saw him, and the Apaches, for their legends tell of it. Far to the south, hundreds of miles away, lived the tribe of the Comanches; and those Indians for many years told their children of Barrag the Bull, and how the Evil Genius of the Prairies, having tempted him to sin, betrayed the self-made King and abandoned him to the vengeance of the Black Panther, who was the enchanted son of the murdered King Dakt.

The strength of ten bulls was in Barrag; but even that could not endure forever. The end of the wild run came at last, and as Barrag fell lifeless upon the prairie the black panther relaxed its hold and was transformed into its original shape. For the enchantment of the Evil Genius was broken, and, restored to his own proper form, Prince Oknu cast one last glance upon his fallen enemy and then turned his head to the north.

It would be many moons before he could rejoin the Royal Tribe of the Okolom.

Since King Barrag had left them in his mad dash to the southward the Royal Tribe had wandered without a leader. They knew Oknu, as the black panther, would never relax his hold on his father's murderer; but how the strange adventure might end all were unable to guess.

So they remained in their well-known feeding grounds and patiently awaited news of the absent ones.

A full year had passed when a buffalo bull was discovered one day crossing the prairie in the direction of the Okolom. Dignity and pride was in his step; his glance was fearless, but full of wisdom. As he stalked majestically to the very centre of the herd his gigantic form towered far above that of any buffalo among them.

A stillness fraught with awe settled upon the Royal Tribe.

"It is old King Dakt, come to life again!" finally exclaimed one of the patriarchs.

"Not so," answered the newcomer, in a clear voice; "but it is the son of Dakt—who has avenged his father's death. Look upon me! I am Oknu, King of the Royal Tribe of Okolom. Dares any dispute my right to rule?"

No voice answered the challenge. Instead, every head of the seven hundred was bowed in silent homage to Oknu, the son of Dakt, the first King of the Okolom.

Narrow Valley

R. A. Lafferty

R. A. Lafferty is an extraordinary fantasist whose major novels, such as The
Devil is Dead *and* Arrive at Easterwine, *dominate the tradition of Christian fantasy in our time, although he is most often identified as a science
fiction writer. His many uniquely characteristic short stories were a hallmark
of the* 1960s *and* 1970s *in the genre magazines, and his collections, which
include* 900 Grandmothers *and* Does Anyone Else Have Something Further to Add?, *are filled with gems. This story is a piece of secular fantasy set
in the American West. It owes something to the tall-tale tradition but is, upon
reflection, pure vintage Lafferty, a wild and silly piece that uses topology as a
kind of scientification of an Indian curse.*

In the year 1893, land allotments in severalty were made to the remaining eight hundred and twenty-one Pawnee Indians. Each would
receive one hundred and sixty acres of land and no more, and thereafter the Pawnees would be expected to pay taxes on their land, the
same as the White-Eyes did.

"Kitkehahke!" Clarence Big-Saddle cussed. "You can't kick a dog
around proper on a hundred and sixty acres. And I sure am not hear
before about this pay taxes on land."

Clarence Big-Saddle selected a nice green valley for his allotment.
It was one of the half dozen plots he had always regarded as his own.

He sodded around the summer lodge that he had there and made it an all-season home. But he sure didn't intend to pay taxes on it.

So he burned leaves and bark and made a speech:

"That my valley be always wide and flourish and green and such stuff as that!" he orated in Pawnee chant style, "but that it be narrow if an intruder come."

He didn't have any balsam bark to burn. He threw on a little cedar bark instead. He didn't have any elder leaves. He used a handful of jack-oak leaves. And he forgot the word. How you going to work it if you forget the word?

"Petahauerat!" he howled out with the confidence he hoped would fool the fates.

"That's the same long of a word," he said in a low aside to himself. But he was doubtful. "What am I, a White Man, a burr-tailed jack, a new kind of nut to think it will work?" he asked. "I have to laugh at me. Oh well, we see."

He threw the rest of the bark and the leaves on the fire, and he hollered the wrong word out again.

And he was answered by a dazzling sheet of summer lightning.

"Skidi!" Clarence Big-Saddle swore. "It worked. I didn't think it would."

Clarence Big-Saddle lived on his land for many years, and he paid no taxes. Intruders were unable to come down to his place. The land was sold for taxes three times, but nobody ever came down to claim it. Finally, it was carried as open land on the books. Homesteaders filed on it several times, but none of them fulfilled the qualification of living on the land.

Half a century went by. Clarence Big-Saddle called his son.

"I've had it, boy," he said. "I think I'll just go in the house and die."

"Okay, Dad," the son Clarence Little-Saddle said. "I'm going in to town to shoot a few games of pool with the boys. I'll bury you when I get back this evening."

So the son Clarence Little-Saddle inherited. He also lived on the land for many years without paying taxes.

There was a disturbance in the courthouse one day. The place seemed to be invaded in force, but actually there were but one man, one woman, and five children. "I'm Robert Rampart," said the man, "and we want the Land Office."

"I'm Robert Rampart Junior," said a nine-year-old gangler, "and we want it pretty blamed quick."

"I don't think we have anything like that," the girl at the desk said. "Isn't that something they had a long time ago?"

"Ignorance is no excuse for inefficiency, my dear," said Mary Mabel Rampart, an eight year old who could easily pass for eight and a half. "After I make my report, I wonder who will be sitting at your desk tomorrow."

"You people are either in the wrong state or the wrong century," the girl said.

"The Homestead Act still obtains," Robert Rampart insisted. "There is one tract of land carried as open in this county. I want to file on it."

Cecilia Rampart answered the knowing wink of a beefy man at a distant desk. "Hi," she breathed as she slinked over. "I'm Cecilia Rampart, but my stage name is Cecilia San Juan. Do you think that seven is too young to play ingenue roles?"

"Not for you," the man said. "Tell your folks to come over here."

"Do you know where the Land Office is?" Cecilia asked.

"Sure. It's the fourth left-hand drawer of my desk. The smallest office we got in the whole courthouse. We don't use it much any more."

The Ramparts gathered around. The beefy man started to make out the papers.

"This is the land description," Robert Rampart began. "Why, you've got it down already. How did you know?"

"I've been around here a long time," the man answered.

They did the paper work, and Robert Rampart filed on the land.

"You won't be able to come onto the land itself, though," the man said.

"Why won't I?" Rampart demanded. "Isn't the land description accurate?"

"Oh, I suppose so. But nobody's ever been able to get to the land. It's become a sort of joke."

"Well, I intend to get to the bottom of that joke," Rampart insisted. "I will occupy the land, or I will find out why not."

"I'm not sure about that," the beefy man said. "The last man to file on the land, about a dozen years ago, wasn't able to occupy the land. And he wasn't able to say why he couldn't. It's kind of interesting, the look on their faces after they try it for a day or two, and then give it up."

The Ramparts left the courthouse, loaded into their camper, and drove out to find their land. They stopped at the house of a cattle and wheat farmer named Charley Dublin. Dublin met them with a grin which indicated he had been tipped off.

"Come along if you want to, folks," Dublin said. "The easiest way is on foot across my short pasture here. Your land's directly west of mine."

They walked the short distance to the border.

"My name is Tom Rampart, Mr. Dublin." Six-year-old Tom made conversation as they walked. "But my name is really Ramires, and not Tom. I am the issue of an indiscretion of my mother in Mexico several years ago."

"The boy is a kidder, Mr. Dublin," said the mother Nina Rampart, defending herself. "I have never been in Mexico, but sometimes I have the urge to disappear there forever."

"Ah yes, Mrs. Rampart. And what is the name of the youngest boy here?" Charles Dublin asked.

"Fatty," said Fatty Rampart.

"But surely that is not your given name?"

"Audifax," said five-year-old Fatty.

"Ah well, Audifax, Fatty, are you a kidder too?"

"He's getting better at it, Mr. Dublin," Mary Mabel said. "He was a twin till last week. His twin was named Skinny. Mama left Skinny unguarded while she was out tippling, and there were wild dogs in the neighborhood. When mama got back, do you know what was left of Skinny? Two neck bones and an ankle bone. That was all."

"Poor Skinny," Dublin said. "Well, Rampart, this is the fence and the end of my land. Yours is just beyond."

"Is that ditch on my land?" Rampart asked.

"That ditch *is* your land."

"I'll have it filled in. It's a dangerous deep cut even if it is narrow. And the other fence looks like a good one, and I sure have a pretty plot of land beyond it."

"No, Rampart, the land beyond the second fence belongs to Holister Hyde," Charley Dublin said. "That second fence is the *end* of your land."

"Now, just wait a minute, Dublin! There's something wrong here.

My land is one hundred and sixty acres, which would be a half mile on a side. Where's my half mile width?"

"Between the two fences."

"That's not eight feet."

"Doesn't look like it, does it, Rampart? Tell you what—there's plenty of throwing-sized rocks around. Try to throw one across it."

"I'm not interested in any such boys' games," Rampart exploded. "I want my land."

But the Rampart children *were* interested in such games. They got with it with those throwing rocks. They winged them out over the little gully. The stones acted funny. They hung in the air, as it were, and diminished in size. And they were small as pebbles when they dropped down, down into the gully. None of them could throw a stone across that ditch, and they were throwing kids.

"You and your neighbor have conspired to fence open land for your own use," Rampart charged.

"No such thing, Rampart," Dublin said cheerfully. "My land checks perfectly. So does Hyde's. So does yours, if we knew how to check it. It's like one of those trick topological drawings. It really is a half mile from here to there, but the eye gets lost somewhere. It's your land. Crawl through the fence and figure it out."

Rampart crawled through the fence, and drew himself up to jump the gully. Then he hesitated. He got a glimpse of just how deep that gully was. Still, it wasn't five feet across.

There was a heavy fence post on the ground, designed for use as a corner post. Rampart up-ended it with some effort. Then he shoved it to fall and bridge the gully. But it fell short, and it shouldn't have. An eight foot post should bridge a five foot gully.

The post fell into the gully, and rolled and rolled and rolled. It spun as though it were rolling outward, but it made no progress except vertically. The post came to rest on a ledge of the gully, so close that Rampart could almost reach out and touch it, but it now appeared no bigger than a match stick.

"There is something wrong with that fence post, or with the world, or with my eyes," Robert Rampart said. "I wish I felt dizzy so I could blame it on that."

"There's a little game that I sometimes play with my neighbor Hyde when we're both out," Dublin said. "I've a heavy rifle and I train it on the middle of his forehead as he stands on the other side of the ditch apparently eight feet away. I fire it off then (I'm a good shot), and I hear it whine across. It'd kill him dead if things were as they seem. But Hyde's in no danger. The shot always bangs into that little scuff of rocks and boulders about thirty feet below him. I can see it kick up the rock dust there, and the sound of it rattling into those little boulders comes back to me in about two and a half seconds."

A bull-bat (poor people call it the night-hawk) raveled around in the air and zoomed out over the narrow ditch, but it did not reach the other side. The bird dropped below ground level and could be seen against the background of the other side of the ditch. It grew smaller and hazier as though at a distance of three or four hundred yards. The white bars on its wings could no longer be discerned; then the bird itself could hardly be discerned; but it was far short of the other side of the five foot ditch.

A man identified by Charley Dublin as the neighbor Holister Hyde had appeared on the other side of the little ditch. Hyde grinned and waved. He shouted something, but could not be heard.

"Hyde and I both read mouth," Dublin said, "so we can talk across the ditch easy enough. Which kid wants to play chicken? Hyde will barrel a good-sized rock right at your head, and if you duck or flinch you're chicken."

"Me! Me!" Audifax Rampart challenged. And Hyde, a big man with big hands, did barrel a fearsome jagged rock right at the head of the boy. It would have killed him if things had been as they appeared. But the rock diminished to nothing and disappeared into the ditch. Here was a phenomenon—things seemed real-sized on either side of the ditch, but they diminished coming out over the ditch either way.

"Everybody game for it?" Robert Rampart Junior asked.

"We won't get down there by standing here," Mary Mabel said.

"Nothing wenchered, nothing gained," said Cecilia. "I got that from an ad for a sex comedy."

Then the five Rampart kids ran down into the gully. Ran *down* is right. It was almost as if they ran down the vertical face of a cliff. They couldn't do that. The gully was no wider than the stride of the biggest kids. But the gully diminished those children, it ate them alive. They were doll-sized. They were acorn-sized. They were running for minute after minute across a ditch that was only five feet across. They were going, deeper in it, and getting smaller. Robert Rampart was roaring his alarm, and his wife Nina was screaming. Then she stopped. "What am I carrying on so loud about?" she asked herself. "It looks like fun. I'll do it too."

She plunged into the gully, diminished in size as the children had done, and ran at a pace to carry her a hundred yards away across a gully only five feet wide.

That Robert Rampart stirred things up for a while then. He got the sheriff there, and the highway patrolmen. A ditch had stolen his wife and five children, he said, and maybe had killed them. And if anybody laughs, there may be another killing. He got the colonel of the State National Guard there, and a command post set up. He got a couple of airplane pilots. Robert Rampart had one quality: when he hollered, people came.

He got the newsmen out from T-Town, and the eminent scientists, Dr. Velikof Vonk, Arpad Arkabaranan, and Willy McGilly. That bunch turns up every time you get on a good one. They just happen to be in that part of the country where something interesting is going on.

They attacked the thing from all four sides and the top, and by inner and outer theory. If a thing measures a half mile on each side, and the sides are straight, there just has to be something in the middle of it. They took pictures from the air, and they turned out perfect. They proved that Robert Rampart had the prettiest hundred and sixty acres in the country, the larger part of it being a lush green valley, and all of it being a half mile on a side, and situated just where it should be. They took ground-level photos then, and it showed a beautiful half mile stretch of land between the boundaries of Charley Dublin and Holister Hyde. But a man isn't a camera. None of them could see that beautiful spread with the eyes in their heads. Where was it?

Down in the valley itself everything was normal. It really was a half mile wide and no more than eighty feet deep with a very gentle slope. It was warm and sweet, and beautiful with grass and grain.

Nina and the kids loved it, and they rushed to see what squatter had built that little house on their land. A house, or a shack. It had never known paint, but paint would have spoiled it. It was built of split timbers dressed near smooth with axe and draw knife, chinked with white clay, and sodded up to about half its height. And there was an interloper standing by the little lodge.

"Here, here, what are you doing on our land?" Robert Rampart Junior demanded of the man. "Now you just shamble off again wherever you came from. I'll bet you're a thief too, and those cattle are stolen."

"Only the black-and-white calf," Clarence Little-Saddle said. "I couldn't resist him, but the rest are mine. I guess I'll just stay around and see that you folks get settled all right."

"Is there any wild Indians around here?" Fatty Rampart asked.

"No, not really. I go on a bender about every three months and get a little bit wild, and there's a couple Osage boys from Gray Horse that get noisy sometimes, but that's about all," Clarence Little-Saddle said.

"You certainly don't intend to palm yourself off on us as an Indian," Mary Mabel challenged. "You'll find us a little too knowledgeable for that."

"Little girl, you might as well tell this cow there's no room for her to be a cow since you're so knowledgeable. She thinks she's a shorthorn cow named Sweet Virginia. I think I'm a Pawnee Indian named Clarence. Break it to us real gentle if we're not."

"If you're an Indian where's your war bonnet? There's not a feather on you anywhere."

"How you be sure? There's a story that we got feathers instead of hair on— Aw, I can't tell a joke like that to a little girl! How come you're not wearing the Iron Crown of Lombardy if you're a white girl? How you expect me to believe you're a little white girl and your folks came from Europe a couple hundred years ago if you don't wear it? There were six hundred tribes, and only one of them, the Oglala Sioux, had the war bonnet, and only the big leaders, never more than two or three of them alive at one time, wore it."

"Your analogy is a little strained," Mary Mabel said. "Those Indians we saw in Florida and the ones at Atlantic City had war bonnets, and they couldn't very well have been the kind of Sioux you said. And just last night on the TV in the motel, those Massachusetts Indians put a war bonnet on the President and called him the Great White Father. You mean to tell me that they were all phonies? Hey, who's laughing at who here?"

"If you're an Indian where's your bow and arrow?" Tom Rampart interrupted. "I bet you can't even shoot one."

"You're sure right there," Clarence admitted. "I never shot one of those things but once in my life. They used to have an archery range in Boulder Park over in T-Town, and you could rent the things and shoot at targets tied to hay bales. Hey, I barked my whole forearm and nearly broke my thumb when the bow-string thwacked home. I couldn't shoot that thing at all. I don't see how anybody ever could shoot one of them."

"Okay, kids," Nina Rampart called to her brood. "Let's start pitching this junk out of the shack so we can move in. Is there any way we can drive our camper down here, Clarence?"

"Sure, there's a pretty good dirt road, and it's a lot wider than it looks from the top. I got a bunch of green bills in an old night charley in the shack. Let me get them, and then I'll clear out for a while. The shack hasn't been cleaned out for seven years, since the last time this happened. I'll show you the road to the top, and you can bring your car down it."

"Hey, you old Indian, you lied!" Cecilia Rampart shrilled from the doorway of the shack. "You *do* have a war bonnet. Can I have it?"

"I didn't mean to lie, I forgot about that thing," Clarence Little-Saddle said. "My son Clarence Bare-Back sent that to me from Japan for a joke a long time ago. Sure, you can have it."

All the children were assigned tasks carrying the junk out of the shack and setting fire to it. Nina Rampart and Clarence Little-Saddle ambled up to the rim of the valley by the vehicle road that was wider than it looked from the top.

"Nina, you're back! I thought you were gone forever," Robert Rampart jittered at seeing her again. "What—where are the children?"

"Why, I left them down in the valley, Robert. That is, ah, down in that little ditch right there. Now you've got me worried again. I'm going to drive the camper down there and unload it. You'd better go on down and lend a hand too, Robert, and quit talking to all these funny-looking men here."

And Nina went back to Dublin's place for the camper.

"It would be easier for a camel to go through the eye of a needle than for that intrepid woman to drive a car down into that narrow ditch," the eminent scientist Dr. Velikof Vonk said.

"You know how that camel does it?" Clarence Little-Saddle offered, appearing of a sudden from nowhere. "He just closes one of his own eyes and flops back his ears and plunges right through. A camel is mighty narrow when he closes one eye and flops back his ears. Besides, they use a big-eye needle in the act."

"Where'd this crazy man come from?" Robert Rampart demanded, jumping three feet in the air. "Things are coming out of the ground now. I want my land! I want my children! I want my wife!

Whoops, here she comes driving it. Nina, you can't drive a loaded camper into a little ditch like that! You'll be killed or collapsed!"

Nina Rampart drove the loaded camper into the little ditch at a pretty good rate of speed. The best of belief is that she just closed one eye and plunged right through. The car diminished and dropped, and it was smaller than a toy car. But it raised a pretty good cloud of dust as it bumped for several hundred yards across a ditch that was only five feet wide.

"Rampart, it's akin to the phenomenon known as looming, only in reverse," the eminent scientist Arpad Arkabaranan explained as he attempted to throw a rock across the narrow ditch. The rock rose very high in the air, seemed to hang at its apex while it diminished to the size of a grain of sand, and then fell into the ditch not six inches of the way across. There isn't anybody going to throw across a half mile valley even if it looks five feet. "Look at a rising moon sometime, Rampart. It appears very large, as though covering a great sector of the horizon, but it only covers one half of a degree. It is hard to believe that you could set seven hundred and twenty of such large moons side by side around the horizon, or that it would take one hundred and eighty of the big things to reach from the horizon to a point overhead. It is also hard to believe that your valley is five hundred times as wide as it appears, but it has been surveyed, and it is."

"I want my land. I want my children. I want my wife," Robert chanted dully. "Damn, I let her get away again."

"I tell you, Rampy," Clarence Little-Saddle squared on him, "a man that lets his wife get away twice doesn't deserve to keep her. I give you till nightfall; then you forfeit. I've taken a liking to the brood. One of us is going to be down there tonight."

After a while a bunch of them were off in that little tavern on the road between Cleveland and Osage. It was only a half mile away. If the valley had run in the other direction, it would have been only six feet away.

"It is a psychic nexus in the form of an elongated dome," said the eminent scientist Dr. Velikof Vonk. "It is maintained subconsciously by the concatenation of at least two minds, the stronger of them belonging to a man dead for many years. It has apparently existed for a little less than a hundred years, and in another hundred years it will be considerably weakened. We know from our checking out of folk tales of Europe as well as Cambodia that these ensorceled areas seldom survive for more than two hundred and fifty years. The person who first set such a thing in being will usually lose interest in it, and in all worldly things, within a hundred years of his own death. This is a simple thanatopsychic limitation. As a short-term device, the thing has been used several times as a military tactic.

"This psychic nexus, as long as it maintains itself, causes group illusion, but it is really a simple thing. It doesn't fool birds or rabbits or cattle or cameras, only humans. There is nothing meteorological about it. It is strictly psychological. I'm glad I was able to give a scientific explanation to it or it would have worried me."

"It is continental fault coinciding with a noospheric fault," said the eminent scientist Arpal Arkabaranan. "The valley really is a half mile wide, and at the same time it really is only five feet wide. If we measured correctly, we would get these dual measurements. Of course it is meteorological! Everything including dreams is meteorological. It is the animals and cameras which are fooled, as lacking a true dimension; it is only humans who see the true duality. The phenomenon should be common along the whole continental fault where the earth gains or loses a half mile that has to go somewhere. Likely it extends through the whole sweep of the Cross Timbers. Many of those trees appear twice, and many do not appear at all. A man in the proper state of mind could farm that land or raise cattle on it, but it doesn't really exist. There is a clear parallel in the Luftspiegelungthal sector in the Black Forest of Germany which exists, or does not exist, according to the circumstances and to the attitude of the beholder. Then we have the case of Mad Mountain in Morgan County, Tennessee, which isn't there all the time, and also the Little Lobo Mirage south of Presidio, Texas, from which twenty thousand barrels of water were pumped in one two-and-a-half year period before the mirage reverted to mirage status. I'm glad I was able to give a scientific explanation to this or it would have worried me."

"I just don't understand how he worked it," said the eminent scientist Willy McGilly. "Cedar bark, jack-oak leaves, and the word 'Petahauerat.' The thing's impossible! When I was a boy and we wanted to make a hideout, we used bark from the skunk-spruce tree, the leaves of a box-elder, and the word was 'Boadicea.' All three elements are wrong here. I cannot find a scientific explanation for it, and it does worry me."

They went back to Narrow Valley. Robert Rampart was still chanting dully: "I want my land. I want my children. I want my wife."

Nina Rampart came chugging up out of the narrow ditch in the camper and emerged through that little gate a few yards down the fence row.

"Supper's ready and we're tired of waiting for you, Robert," she said. "A fine homesteader you are! Afraid to come onto your own land! Come along now; I'm tired of waiting for you."

"I want my land! I want my children! I want my wife!" Robert Rampart still chanted. "Oh, there you are, Nina. You stay here this time. I want my land! I want my children! I want an answer to this terrible thing."

"It is time we decided who wears the pants in this family," Nina said stoutly. She picked up her husband, slung him over her shoulder, carried him to the camper and dumped him in, slammed (as it seemed) a dozen doors at once, and drove furiously down into Narrow Valley, which already seemed wider.

Why, that place was getting normaler and normaler by the minute! Pretty soon it looked almost as wide as it was supposed to be. The psychic nexus in the form of an elongated dome had collapsed. The continental fault that coincided with the noospheric fault had faced facts and decided to conform. The Ramparts were in effective possession of their homestead, and Narrow Valley was as normal as any place anywhere.

"I have lost my land," Clarence Little-Saddle moaned. "It was the land of my father Clarence Big-Saddle, and I meant it to be the land of my son Clarence Bare-Back. It looked so narrow that people did not notice how wide it was, and people did not try to enter it. Now I have lost it."

Clarence Little-Saddle and the eminent scientist Willy McGilly were standing on the edge of Narrow Valley, which now appeared its true half-mile extent. The moon was just rising, so big that it filled a third of the sky. Who would have imagined that it would take a hundred and eighty of such monstrous things to reach from the horizon to a point overhead, and yet you could sight it with sighters and figure it so.

"I had the little bear-cat by the tail and I let go," Clarence groaned. "I had a fine valley for free, and I have lost it. I am like that hard-luck guy in the funny-paper or Job in the Bible. Destitution is my lot."

Willy McGilly looked around furtively. They were alone on the edge of the half mile wide valley.

"Let's give it a booster shot," Willy McGilly said.

Hey, those two got with it! They started a snapping fire and began to throw the stuff onto it. Bark from the dog-elm tree—how do you know it won't work?

It *was* working! Already the other side of the valley seemed a hundred yards closer, and there were alarmed noises coming up from the people in the valley.

Leaves from a black locust tree—and the valley narrowed still more! There was, moreover, terrified screaming of both children and big people from the depths of Narrow Valley, and the happy voice of Mary Mabel Rampart chanting "Earthquake! Earthquake!"

"That my valley be always wide and flourish and such stuff, and green with money and grass!" Clarence Little-Saddle orated in Pawnee chant style, "but that it be narrow if intruders come, smash them like bugs!"

People, that valley wasn't over a hundred feet wide now, and the screaming of the people in the bottom of the valley had been joined by the hysterical coughing of the camper car starting up.

Willy and Clarence threw everything that was left on the fire. But the word? The word? Who remembers the word?

"Corsicanatexas!" Clarence Little-Saddle howled out with confidence he hoped would fool the fates.

He was answered not only by a dazzling sheet of summer lightning, but also by thunder and raindrops.

"Chahiksi!" Clarence Little-Saddle swore. "It worked. I didn't think it would. It will be all right now. I can use the rain."

The valley was again a ditch only five feet wide.

The camper car struggled out of Narrow Valley through the little gate. It was smashed flat as a sheet of paper, and the screaming kids and people in it had only one dimension.

"It's closing in! It's closing in!" Robert Rampart roared, and he was no thicker than if he had been made out of cardboard.

"We're smashed like bugs," the Rampart boys intoned. "We're thin like paper."

"Mort, ruine, ecrasement!" spoke-acted Cecilia Rampart like the great tragedienne she was.

"Help! Help!" Nina Rampart croaked, but she winked at Willy and Clarence as they rolled by. "This homesteading jag always did leave me a little flat."

"Don't throw those paper dolls away. They might be the Ramparts," Mary Mabel called.

The camper car coughed again and bumped along on level ground. This couldn't last forever. The car was widening out as it bumped along.

"Did we overdo it, Clarence?" Willy McGilly asked. "What did one flat-lander say to the other?"

"Dimension of us never got around," Clarence said. "No, I don't think we overdid it, Willy. That car must be eighteen inches wide already, and they all ought to be normal by the time they reach the main road. The next time I do it, I think I'll throw wood-grain plastic on the fire to see who's kidding who."

Beyond the Dead Reef

James Tiptree, Jr.

James Tiptree, Jr., was the pseudonym of Alice Sheldon of Maclean, Va., ex-CIA employee and a giant of science fiction. Tiptree was in many ways the characteristic SF writers of the 1970s. In the last years of her life, she wrote a series of stories which were collected in 1987, the year of her death, as Tales of the Quintana Roo *(winner of the World Fantasy Award for best collection). These dark fantastic tales, including "Beyond the Dead Reef," were among her few forays into fantasy fiction. This story, with its ecological horror, is almost SF, but not quite. It expresses one of the most common fears of travelers, that nothing here is as it seems. Note that all the fantasy takes place underwater, submerged, rather like the fantastic images of the unconscious mind welling up, disturbing, unreliable, threatening, powerful. This is a story about fantasy.*

A love that is not sated
Calls from a poisoned bed;
Where monsters half-created
writhe, unliving and undead.
None knows for what they're fated;
None knows on what they've fed.

My informant was, of course, spectacularly unreliable.

The only character reference I have for him comes from the intangible nuances of a small restaurant-owner's remarks, and the only confirmation of his tale lies in the fact that an illiterate fishing-guide appears to believe it. If I were to recount all the reasons why no sane mind should take it seriously, we could never begin. So I will only report the fact that today I found myself shuddering with terror when a perfectly innocent sheet of seaworn plastic came slithering over my snorkelling-reef, as dozens have done for years—and get on with the story.

I met him one evening in December at the Cozumel *Buzo,* on my first annual supply trip. As usual, the *Buzo's* outer rooms were jammed with tourist divers and their retinues and gear. That's standard. *El Buzo* means, roughly, The Diving, and the *Buzo* is their place. Marcial's big sign in the window reads "DIVVERS UELCOME! BRING YR FISH WE COK WITH CAR. FIRST DRINK FREE!"

Until he went in for the "Divvers," Marcial's had been a small quiet place where certain delicacies like stone-crab could be at least semi-legally obtained. Now he did a roaring trade in snappers and groupers cooked to order at outrageous fees, with a flourishing sideline in fresh fish sales to the neighborhood each morning.

The "roaring" was quite literal. I threaded my way through a crush of burly giants and giantesses of all degrees of nakedness, hairiness, age, proficiency, and inebriation—all eager to share their experiences and plans in voices powered by scuba-deafened ears and Marcial's free drink, beneath which the sound-system could scarcely be heard at full blast. (Marcial's only real expense lay in first-drink liquor so strong that few could recall whether what they ultimately ate bore any resemblance to what they had given him to cook.) Only a handful were sitting down yet and the amount of gear underfoot and on the walls would have stocked three sports shops. This was not mere exhibitionism; on an island chronically short of washers, valves and other spare parts, the diver who lets his gear out of his sight is apt to find it missing in some vital.

I paused to allow a young lady to complete her massage of the neck of a youth across the aisle who was deep in talk with three others, and had time to notice the extraordinary number of heavy spear-guns racked about. Oklahomans, I judged, or perhaps South Florida. But then I caught clipped New England from the center group. Too bad; the killing mania seems to be spreading yearly, and the armament growing ever more menacing and efficient. When I inspected their platters, however, I saw the usual array of lavishly garnished lobsters and common fish. At least they had not yet discovered what to eat.

The mermaiden blocking me completed her task—unthanked—and I continued on my way in the little inner sanctum Marcial keeps for his old clientele. As the heavy doors cut off the uproar, I saw that this room was full too—three tables of dark-suited Mexican business-men and a decorous family of eight, all quietly intent on their plates. A lone customer sat at the small table by the kitchen door, leaving an empty seat and a child's chair. He was a tall, slightly balding Anglo some years younger than I, in a very decent sports jacket. I recalled having seen him about now and then on my banking and shopping trips to the island.

Marcial telegraphed me a go-ahead nod as he passed through laden with more drinks, so I approached.

"Mind if I join you?"

He looked up from his stone-crab and gave me a slow, owlish smile.

"Welcome. A *diverse* welcome," he enunciated carefully. The accent was vaguely British, yet agreeable. I also perceived that he was extremely drunk, but in no common way.

"Thanks."

As I sat down I saw that he was a diver too, but his gear was stowed so unobtrusively I hadn't noticed it. I tried to stack my own modest snorkel outfit as neatly, pleased to note that, like me, he seemed to carry no spear-guns. He watched me attentively, blinking once or twice, and then returned to an exquisitely exact dissection of his crab.

When Marcial brought my own platter of crab—unasked—we engaged in our ritual converse. Marcial's English is several orders of magnitude better than my Spanish, but he always does me the delicate courtesy of allowing me to use his tongue. How did I find my rented casita on the coco ranch this year? Fine. How goes the tourist business this year? Fine. I learn from Marcial: the slight pause before his answer with a certain tone, meant that in fact the tourist business was lousy so far, but would hopefully pick up; I used the same to convey that in fact my casa was in horrible shape but reparable. I tried to cheer him by saying that I thought the *Buzo* would do better than the general *turismo,* because the diving enthusiasm was spreading in the States. "True," he conceded. "So long as they don't discover other places—like Bélize." Here he flicked a glance at my companion, who gave his solemn blink. I remarked that my country's politics were in disastrous disarray, and he conceded the same for his; the Presidente and his pals had just made off with much of the nation's treasury. And I expressed the hope that Mexico's new oil would soon prove a great boon. "Ah, but it will be a long time before it gets to the little people like us," said Marcial, with so much more than his normal acerbity that I refrained from my usual joke about his having a Swiss bank account. The uproar from the outer rooms had risen several decibels but just before Marcial had to leave he paused and said in a totally different voice, "My grandson Antonito Vincente has four teeth!"

His emotion was so profound that I seized his free hand and shook it lightly, congratulating him in English. And then he was gone, taking on his "Mexican waiter" persona quite visibly as he passed the inner doors.

As we resumed our attention to the succulence before us, my companion said in his low, careful voice, "Nice chap, Marcial. He likes you."

"It's mutual," I told him between delicate mouthfuls. Stone-crab is not to be gulped. "Perhaps because I'm old enough to respect the limits where friendship ends and the necessities of life take over."

"I say, that's rather good," my companion chuckled, "Respect for the limits where friendship ends and the necessities of life take over, eh? Very few Yanks do, you know. At least the ones we see down here."

His speech was almost unslurred, and there were no drinks before him on the table. We chatted idly a bit more. It was becoming apparent that we would finish simultaneously and be faced with the prospect of leaving together, which could be awkward, if he, like me, had no definite plans for the evening.

The dilemma was solved when my companion excused himself momentarily just as Marcial happened by.

I nodded to his empty chair. "Is he one of your old customers, Senor Marcial?"

As always Marcial understood the situation at once. "One of the oldest," he told me, and added low-voiced, *"muy buena gente*—a really good guy. *Un poco de dificultaes*—" he made an almost imperceptible gesture of drinking—"But *controlado*. And he has also *negocios*—I do not know all, but some are important for his country. —So you really like the crab?" he concluded in his normal voice. "We are honoured."

My companion was emerging from the rather dubious regions that held the *excusado.*

Marcial's recommendation was good enough for me. Only one puzzle remained: what was his country? As we both refused *dulces* and coffee, I suggested that he might care to stroll down to the marina with me and watch the sunset.

"Good thought."

We paid up Marcial's outrageous bills, and made our way through the exterior bedlam, carrying our gear. One of the customers was brandishing his spear-gun as he protested his bill. Marcial seemed to have lost all his English except the word "Police," and cooler heads were attempting to calm the irate one. "All in a night's work," my companion commented as we emerged into a blaze of golden light.

The marina to our left was a simple L-shaped *muelle,* or pier, still used by everything from dinghies to commercial fishermen and baby yachts. It will be a pity when and if the town decides to separate the sports tourist trade from the more interesting working craft. As we walked out toward the pier in the last spectacular color of the tropic sunset over the mainland, the rigging lights of a cruise ship standing out in the channel came on, a fairyland illusion over the all-too-dreary reality.

"They'll be dumping and cleaning out their used bunkers tonight," my companion said, slurring a trifle now. He had a congenial walking gait, long-strided but leisurely. I had the impression that his drunkenness had returned slightly; perhaps the fresh air. "Damn crime."

"I couldn't agree more," I told him. "I remember when we used to start snorkelling and scuba-diving right off the shore here—you could almost wade out to untouched reefs. And now—"

There was no need to look; one could smell it. The effluvia of half a dozen hotels and the town behind ran out of pipes that were barely covered at low tide; only a few parrot-fish, who can stand anything, remained by the hotel-side restaurants to feed on the crusts the tourists threw them from their tables. And only the very ignorant would try out—once—the renters of dilapidated Sunfish and water-skis who plied the small stretches of beach between hotels.

We sat down on one of the near benches to watch a commercial trawler haul net. I had been for some time aware that my companion, while of largely British culture, was not completely Caucasian. There was a minute softness to the voice, a something not quite dusky about hair and fingernails—not so much as to be what in my youth was called "a touch of the tarbrush," but nothing that originated in Yorkshire, either. Nor was it the obvious Hispano-Indian. I recollected Marcial's earlier speech and enlightenment came.

"Would I be correct in taking Marcial's allusions to mean that you are a British Honduran—forgive me, I mean a Bélizian, or Belizan?"

"Nothing to forgive, old chap. We haven't existed long enough to get our adjectives straight."

"May god send you do." I was referring to the hungry maws of Guatemala and Honduras, the little country's big neighbors, who had the worst of intentions toward her. "I happen to be quite a fan of your country. I had some small dealings there after independence which involved getting all my worldly goods out of your customs on a national holiday, and people couldn't have been finer to me."

"Ah yes. Bélize the blessed, where sixteen nationalities live in perfect racial harmony. The odd thing is, they do."

"I could see that. But I couldn't quite count all sixteen."

"My own grandmother was a Burmese—so called. I think it was the closest grandfather could come to Black. Although the mix *is* extraordinary."

"My factor there was a very dark Hindu with red hair and a Scottish accent, named Robinson. I had to hire him in seven minutes. He was a miracle of efficiency. I hope he's still going."

"Robinson . . . Used to work for customs?"

"Why, yes, now you recall it."

"He's fine . . . Of course, we felt it when the British left. Among other things, half the WCs in the hotels broke down the first month. But there are more important things in life than plumbing."

"That I believe . . . But you know, I've never been sure how much help the British would have been to you. Two years before your independence I called the British Embassy with a question about your immigration laws, and believe it or not I couldn't find one soul who even knew there *was* a British Honduras, let alone that they owned it. One child finally denied it flatly and hung up. And this was their main embassy in Washington, D.C. I realized then that Britain was not only sick, but crazy."

"Actually denied our existence, eh?" My companion's voice held a depth and timbre of sadness such as I have heard only from victims of better-known world wrongs. Absently his hand went under his jacket, and he pulled out something gleaming.

"Forgive me." It was a silver flask, exquisitely plain. He uncapped and drank, a mere swallow, but, I suspected, something of no ordinary power. He licked his lips as he recapped it, and sat up straighter while he put it away.

"Shall we move along out to the point?"

"With pleasure."

We strolled on, passing a few late sports-boats disgorging hungry divers.

"I'm going to do some modest exploring tomorrow," I told him. "A guide named Jorge"—in Spanish it's pronounced Hor-hay— "Jorge Chuc is taking me out to the end of the North reef. He says there's a pretty little untouched spot there. I hope so. Today I went South, it was so badly shot over I almost wept. Cripples—and of course shark everywhere. Would you believe I found a big she-turtle, trying to live with a steel bolt through her neck? I managed to catch her, but all I could do for her was pull it out. I hope she makes it."

"Bad . . . Turtles are tough, though. If it wasn't vital you may have saved her. But did you say that Jorge Chuc is taking you to the end of the North reef?"

"Yes, why. Isn't it any good?"

"Oh, there is one pretty spot. But there's some very bad stuff there too. If you don't mind my advice, don't go far from the boat. I mean, a couple of metres. And don't follow anything. And above all be very sure it *is* Jorge's boat."

His voice had become quite different, with almost military authority.

"A couple of metres!" I expostulated. "But—"

"I know, I know. What I don't know is why Chuc is taking you there at all." He thought for a moment. "You haven't by any chance offended him, have you? In any way?"

"Why no—we were out for a long go yesterday, and had a nice chat on the way back. Yes . . . although he is a trifle changeable, isn't he? I put it down to fatigue, and gave him some extra dinero for being only one party."

My companion made an untranslatable sound, compounded of dubiety, speculation, possible enlightenment, and strong suspicion.

"Did he tell you the name of that part of the reef? Or that it's out of sight of land?"

"Yes, he said it was far out. And that part of it was so poor it's called dead."

"And you chatted—forgive me, but was your talk entirely in Spanish?"

I chuckled deprecatingly. "Well, yes—I know my Spanish is pretty horrible, but he seemed to get the drift."

"Did you mention his family?"

"Oh yes—I could draw you the whole Chuc family tree."

"H'mmm. . . ." My companion's eyes had been searching the pier-side where the incoming boats were being secured for the night. "Ah. There's Chuc now. This is none of my business, you understand—but do I have your permission for a short word with Jorge?"

"Why yes. If you think it necessary."

"I do, my friend. I most certainly do."

"Carry on."

His long-legged stride had already carried him to Chuc's big skiff, the *Estrellita.* Chuc was covering his motors. I had raised my hand in greeting, but he was apparently too busy to respond. Now he greeted my companion briefly, but did not turn when he clambered into the boat uninvited. I could not hear the interchange. But presently the two men were standing, faces somewhat averted from each other as they conversed. My companion made rather a long speech, ending with questions. There was little response from Chuc, until a sudden outburst from him took me by surprise. The odd dialog went on for some time after that; Chuc seemed to calm down. Then the tall Bélizian waved me over.

"Will you say exactly what I tell you to say!"

"Why, yes, if you think it's important."

"It is. Can you say in Spanish, 'I ask your pardon, Mr. Chuc. I mistook myself in your language. I did not say anything of what you thought I said. Please forgive my error. And please let us be friends again.' "

"I'll try."

I stumbled through the speech, which I will not try to reproduce here, as I repeated several phrases with what I thought was better accent, and I'm sure I threw several verbs into the conditional future. Before I was through, Chuc was beginning to grin. When I came to the "friends" part he had relaxed, and after a short pause, said in very tolerable English, "I see, so I accept your apology. We will indeed be friends. It was a regrettable error . . . And I advise you, do not again speak in Spanish."

We shook on it.

"Good," said my companion. "And he'll take you out tomorrow, but not to the dead reef. And keep your hands off your wallet tonight, but I suggest liberality tomorrow eve."

We left Chuc to finish up, and paced down to a bench at the very end of the *muelle*. The last colors of evening, peaches and rose shot with unearthly green, were set off by a few low-lying clouds already in grey shadow, like sharks of the sky passing beneath a sentimental vision of bliss.

"Now what was all *that* about!" I demanded of my new friend. He was just tucking the flask away again, and shuddered lightly.

"I don't wish to seem overbearing but *that* probably saved your harmless life, my friend. I repeat Jorge's advice—stay away from that Spanish of yours unless you are absolutely sure of being understood."

"I know it's ghastly."

"That's not actually the problem. The problem is that it isn't ghastly enough. Your pronunciation is quite fair, and you've mastered some good idioms, so people who don't know you think you speak much more fluently than you do. In this case the trouble came from your damned rolled rrrs. Would you mind saying the words for 'but' and 'dog'?"

"Pero . . . perro. Why?"

"The difference between a rolled and a single r, particularly in Maya Spanish, is very slight. The upshot of it was that you not only insulted his boat in various ways, but you ended by referring to his mother as a dog . . . He was going to take you out beyond the Dead Reef and leave you there."

"What?"

"Yes. And if it hadn't been I who asked—he knows I know the story—you'd never have understood a thing. Until you turned up as a statistic."

"Oh Jesus Christ. . . ."

"Yes," he said dryly.

"I guess some thanks are in order," I said finally. "But words seem a shade inadequate. Have you any suggestions?"

My companion suddenly turned and gave me a highly concentrated look.

"You were in World War Two, weren't you? And afterwards you

worked around a bit." He wasn't asking me, so I kept quiet. "Right now, I don't see anything," he went on. "But just possibly I might be calling on you," he grinned, "with something you may not like."

"If it's anything I can do from a wheelchair, I won't forget."

"Fair enough. We'll say no more about it now."

"Oh yes we will," I countered. "You may not know it, but you owe *me* something. I can smell a story when one smacks me in the face. What I want from you is the story behind this Dead Reef business, and how it is that Jorge knows you know something special about it. If I'm not asking too much? I'd really like to end our evening with your tale of the Dead Reef."

"Oh. My error—I'd forgotten Marcial telling me you wrote . . . Well, I can't say I enjoy reliving it, but maybe it'll have a salutary effect on your future dealings in Spanish. The fact is, I was the one it happened to, and Jorge was driving a certain boat. You realize, though, there's not a shred of proof except my own word? And my own word—" he tapped the pocket holding his flask "—is only as good as you happen to think it is."

"It's good enough for me."

"Very well then. Very well," he said slowly, leaning back. "It happened about three, no four years back—by god, you know this is hard to tell, though there's not much to it." He fished in another pocket, and took out, not a flask, but the first cigaret I'd seen him smoke, a *Petit Caporal.* "I was still up to a long day's scuba then, and, like you, I wanted to explore North. I'd run into this nice, strong, young couple who wanted the same thing. Their gear was good, they seemed experienced and sensible. So we got a third tank apiece, and hired a trustable boatman—not Jorge, Victor Camul—to take us North over the worst of the reef. It wasn't so bad then, you know.

"We would be swimming North with the current until a certain point, where if you turn East, you run into a long reverse eddy that makes it a lot easier to swim back to Cozumel. And just to be extra safe, Victor was to start out up the eddy in two hours sharp to meet us and bring us home. I hadn't one qualm about the arrangements. Even the weather cooperated—not a cloud, and the forecast perfect. Of course, if you miss up around here, the next stop is four hundred miles to Cuba, but you know that; one gets used to it . . . By the way, have you heard they're still looking for that girl who's been gone two days on a Sunfish with no water?"

I said nothing.

"Sorry." He cleared his throat. "Well, Victor put us out well in sight of shore. We checked watches and compasses and lights. The plan was for the lad Harry to lead, Ann to follow, and me to bring up the rear. Harry had dayglo-red shorts you could see a mile, and Ann was white-skinned with long black hair and a brilliant neon-blue and orange bathing suit on her little rump—you could have seen her in a mine at midnight. Even I got some yellow water safety tape and tied it around my arse and tanks.

"The one thing we didn't have then was a radio. At the time they didn't seem worth the crazy cost, and were unreliable besides. I had no way of guessing I'd soon give my life for one—and very nearly did.

"Well, when Victor let us out and we got organized and started North single file over the dead part of the reef, we almost surfaced and yelled for him to take us back right then. It was purely awful. But we knew there was better stuff ahead, so we stuck it out and flippered doggedly along—actually doing pretty damn fair time, with the current—and trying not to look too closely at what lay below.

"Not only was the coral dead, you understand—that's where the name got started. We think now it's from oil and chemical wash, such as that pretty ship out there is about to contribute—but there was tons and tons of litter, *basura* of all description, crusted there. It's everywhere, of course—you've seen what washes onto the mainland beach—but here the current and the reef produce a particularly visible concentration. Even quite large heavy things—bedsprings, an auto chassis—in addition to things you'd expect, like wrecked skiffs. Cozumel, *Basurera del Caribe!*"

He gave a short laugh, mocking the Gem-of-the-Caribbean ads, as he lit up another Caporal. The most polite translation of *basurera* is garbage can.

"A great deal of the older stuff was covered with that evil killer algae—you know, the big coarse red-brown hairy kind, which means that nothing else can ever grow there again. But some of the heaps were too new.

"I ended by getting fascinated and swimming lower to look, always keeping one eye on that blue-and-orange rump above me with her white legs and black flippers. And the stuff—I don't mean just Clorox and *detergente* bottles, beer cans and netting—but weird things like about ten square metres of butchered pink plastic baby-dolls—arms and legs wiggling, and rose-bud mouths—it looked like a babies' slaughter-house. Syringes, hypos galore. Fluorescent tubes on end, waving like drowned orchestra conductors. A great big red sofa with a skeletonized banana-stem or *something* sitting in it—when I saw that, I went back up and followed right behind Ann.

"And then the sun dimmed unexpectedly, so I surfaced for a look. The shoreline was fine, we had plenty of time, and the cloud was just one of a dozen little thermals that form on a hot afternoon like that. When I went back down, Ann was looking at me, so I gave her the All's fair sign. And with that we swam over a pair of broken dories and found ourselves in a different world—the beauty patch we'd been looking for.

"The reef was live here—whatever had killed the coral hadn't reached yet, and the damned *basura* had quit or been deflected, aside from a beer bottle or two. There was life everywhere; anemones, sponges, conches, fans, stars—and fish, oh my! No one ever came here, you see. In fact, there didn't seem to have been any spearing, the fish were as tame as they used to be years back.

"Well, we began zigzagging back and forth, just revelling in it. And every time we'd meet head on we'd make the gesture of putting our fingers to our lips, meaning Don't tell anyone about this, ever!

The formation of the reef was charming, too. It broadened into a sort of big stadium, with allées and cliffs and secret pockets, and there were at least eight different kinds of coral. And most of it was shallow enough so the sunlight brought out the glorious colors—those little black and yellow fish—butterflies, or I forget their proper name—were dazzling. I kept having to brush them off my mask, they wanted to look in.

"The two ahead seemed to be in ecstasies; I expect they hadn't seen much like this before. They swam on and on, investigating it all —and I soon realized there was real danger of losing them in some coral pass. So I stuck tight to Ann. But time was passing. Presently I surfaced again to investigate—and, my god, the shoreline was damn near invisible and the line-up we had selected for our turn marker was all but passed! Moreover, a faint hazy overcast was rising from the West.

"So I cut down again, intending to grab Ann and start, which Harry would have to see. So I set off after the girl. I used to be a fair sprint-swimmer, but I was amazed how long it took me to catch her. I recall vaguely noticing that the reef was going a bit bad again, dead coral here and there. Finally I came right over her, signed to her to halt, and kicked up in front of her nose for another look.

"To my horror, the shoreline was gone and the overcast had overtaken the sun. We would have to swim East by compass, and swim hard. I took a moment to hitch my compass around where I could see it well—it was the old-fashioned kind—and then I went back down for Ann. And the damn fool girl wasn't there. It took me a minute to locate that blue bottom and white legs; I assumed she'd gone after Harry, having clearly no idea of the urgency of our predicament.

"I confess the thought crossed my mind that I could cut out of there, and come back for them later with Victor, but this was playing a rather iffy game with someone else's lives. And if they were truly unaware, it would be fairly rotten to take off without even warning them. So I went after Ann again—my god, I can still see that blue tail and the white limbs and black feet and hair with the light getting worse every minute and the bottom now gone really rotten again. And as bad luck would have it she was going in just the worst line— north-north-west.

"Well I swam and I swam and I *swam*. You know how a chase takes you, and somehow being unable to overtake a mere girl made it worse. But I was gaining, age and all, until just as I got close enough to sense something was wrong, she turned sidewise above two automobile tires—and I saw it wasn't a girl at all.

"I had been following a god-damned great fish—a fish with a bright blue and orange band around its belly, and a thin white body ending in a black, flipperlike tail. Even its head and nape were black, like her hair and mask. It had a repulsive catfish-like mouth, with barbels.

"The thing goggled at me, and then swam awkwardly away, just as the light went worse yet. But there was enough for me to see that it was no normal fish, either, but a queer archaic thing that looked more tacked together than grown. This I can't swear to, because I was looking elsewhere by then, but it was my strong impression that as it went out of my line of sight its whole tail broke off.

"But, as I say, I was looking elsewhere. I had turned my light on, although I was not deep but only dim, because I had to read my watch and compass. It had just dawned on me that I was very probably a dead man. My only chance, if you can call it that, was to swim East as long as I could, hoping for that eddy and Victor. And when my light came on, the first thing I saw was the girl, stark naked and obviously stone cold dead, lying in a tangle of nets and horrid stuff on the bottom ahead.

"Of Harry or anything human there was no sign at all. But there was a kind of shining, like a pool of moonlight, around her, which was so much stronger than my lamp that I clicked it off and swam slowly toward her, through the nastiest mess of *basura* I had yet seen. The very water seemed vile. It took longer to reach her than I had expected, and soon I saw why.

"They speak of one's blood running cold with horror, y'know. Or people becoming numb with horror piled on horrors. I believe I experienced both those effects. It isn't pleasant, even now." He lit a third Caporal, and I could see that the smoke column trembled. Twilight had fallen while he'd been speaking. A lone mercury lamp came on at the shore end of the pier; the one near us was apparently out, but we sat in what would ordinarily have been a pleasant tropic evening, sparkling with many moving lights—whites, reds and green, of late-moving incomers and the rainbow lighting from the jewel-lit cruise ship ahead, all cheerfully reflected in the unusually calm waters.

"Again I was mistaken, you see. It wasn't Ann at all; but the rather more distant figure of a young woman, of truly enormous size. All in this great ridge of graveyard luminosity, of garbage in phosphorescent decay. The current was carrying me slowly, inexorably, right toward her—as it had carried all that was there now. And perhaps I was also a bit hypnotized. She grew in my sight metre by metre as I neared her. I think six metres—eighteen feet—was about it, at the end . . . I make that guess later, you understand, as an exercise in containing the unbearable—by recalling the size of known items in the junkpile she lay on. One knee, for example, lay alongside an oil drum. At the time she simply filled my world. I had no doubt she was dead, and very beautiful. One of her legs seemed to writhe gently.

"The next stage of horror came when I realized that she was not a gigantic woman at all—or rather, like the fish, she was a woman-shaped construction. The realization came to me first, I think, when I could no longer fail to recognize that her 'breasts' were two of those great net buoys with the blue knobs for nipples.

"After that it all came with a rush—that she was a made-up body— all sorts of pieces of plastic, rope, styrofoam, netting, crates and bolts —much of it clothed with that torn translucent white polyethylene for skin. Her hair was a dreadful tangle of something, and her crotch was explicit and unspeakable. One hand was a torn, inflated rubber glove, and her face—well, I won't go into it except that one eye was a traffic reflector and her mouth was partly a rusted can.

"Now you might think this discovery would have brought some relief, but quite the opposite. Because simultaneously I had realized the very worst thing of all—

"She was alive."

He took a long drag on his cigaret.

"You know how things are moved passively in water? Plants waving, a board seesawing and so on? Sometimes enough almost to give an illusion of mobile life. What I saw was nothing of this sort.

"It wasn't merely that as I floated over, her horrible eyes 'opened' and looked at me, and her rusted-can mouth *smiled.* Oh, no.

"What I mean is that as she smiled, first one whole arm, shedding junk, stretched up and reached for me *against the current,* and then the other did the same.

"And when I proved to be out of reach, this terrifying figure, or creature, or unliving life, actually sat up, again *against the current,* and reached up toward me with both arms at full extension.

"And as she did so, one of her 'breasts'—the right one—came loose and dangled by some sort of tenuous thready stuff.

"All this seemed to pass in slow motion—I even had time to see that there were other unalive yet living things moving near her on the pile. Not fish, but more what I should have taken, on land, for rats or vermin—and I distinctly recall the paper-flat skeleton of something like a chicken, running and pecking. And other moving things like nothing in this world. I have remembered all this very carefully, y'see, from what must have been quick glimpses, because in actual fact I was apparently kicking like mad in a frenzied effort to get away from those dreadful, reaching arms.

"It was not 'til I shot to the surface with a mighty splash that I came somewhere near my senses. Below and behind me I could still see faint cold light. Above was twilight and the darkness of an oncoming small storm.

"At that moment the air in my last tank gave out—or rather that splendid Yank warning buzz, which means you have just time to get out of your harness, sounded off.

"I had, thank god, practiced the drill. Despite being a terror-paralysed madman, habit got me out of the harness before the tanks turned into lethal deadweight. In my panic of course, the headlight went down too. I was left unencumbered in the night, free to swim toward Cuba, or Cozumel, and to drown as slow or fast as fate willed. "The little storm had left the horizon stars free. I recall that pure habit made me take a sight on what seemed to be Canopus, which should be over Cozumel. I began to swim in that direction. I was appallingly tired, and as the adrenaline of terror which had brought me this far began to fade out of my system, I realized I would soon be merely drifting, and would surely die in the next day's sun if I survived 'til then. Nevertheless it seemed best to swim whilst I could.

"I rather resented it when some time later a boat motor passed nearby. It forced me to attempt to yell and wave, nearly sinking myself. I was perfectly content when the boat passed on. But someone had seen—a spotlight wheeled blindingly, motors reversed, I was forcibly pulled from my grave and voices from what I take to be your Texas demanded, roaring with laughter,"—here he gave quite a creditable imitation—" 'Whacha doin' out hyar, boy, this time of night? Ain't no pussy out hyar, less'n ya'll got a date with a mermaid.' They had been trolling for god knows what, mostly beer.

"The driver of that boat claimed me as a friend and later took me home for the night, where I told to him—and to him alone—the whole story. He was *Jorge* Chuc.

"Next day I found that the young couple, Harry and Ann, had taken only a brief look at the charming unspoiled area, and then started East, exactly according to plan, with me—or something very much like me—following behind them all the way. They had been a trifle surprised at my passivity and uncommunicativeness, and more so when, on meeting Victor, I was no longer to be found. But they had taken immediate action, even set a full-scale search in progress— approximately seventy kilometers from where I then was. As soon as I came to myself I had to concoct a wild series of lies about cramps and heart trouble to get them in the clear and set their minds at ease. Needless to say, my version included no mention of diver-imitating fishlife."

He tossed the spark of his cigaret over the rail before us.

"So now, my friend, you know the story of all I know of what is to be found beyond the Dead Reef. It may be that others know of other happenings and . . . developments there. Or of similar traps elsewhere. The sea is large . . . Or it may be that the whole yarn comes from neurons long abused by stuff like this."

I had not seen him extract his flask, but he now took two deep, shuddering swallows.

I sighed involuntarily, and then sighed again. I seemed to have been breathing rather inadequately during the end of his account.

"Ordinary thanks don't seem quite appropriate here," I finally said. "Though I do thank you. Instead I am going to make two guesses. The second is that you might prefer to sit quietly here alone, enjoying the evening, and defer the mild entertainment I was about to offer you to some other time. I'd be glad to be proved wrong . . . ?"

"No. You're very perceptive, I welcome the diverse—the deferred offer." His tongue stumbled a bit now, more from fatigue than anything he'd drunk. "But what was your first guess?"

I rose and slowly paced a few metres to and fro, remembering to pick up my absurd snorkel bag. Then I turned and gazed out to the sea.

"I can't put it into words. It has something to do with the idea that the sea is still, well, strong. It lived before we did, it once had life of a different sort, before the oxygen came. Perhaps it can take revenge? No, that's too simple. I don't know. I have only a feeling that our ordinary ideas of what may be coming on us may be—oh—not deep, or broad enough. I put this poorly. But perhaps the sea, or nature, will not die passively at our hands, . . . perhaps death itself may turn or return in horrible life upon us, besides the more mechanical dooms. . . ."

"Our thoughts are not so far apart," the tall Bélizian said. "I welcome them to my night's agenda."

"To which I now leave you, unless you've changed your mind?"

He shook his head. I hoisted his bag to the seat beside him. "Don't forget this. I almost left mine."

"Thanks. And don't you forget about dogs and mothers," he grinned faintly.

"Goodnight."

My footsteps echoed on the now deserted *muelle* as I left him sitting there. I was quite sure he was no longer smiling.

Nor was I.

The King's Bride

A Fairy Tale After Nature

E. T. A. Hoffmann

If any one writer can be assigned credit for the invention of the literary genre of adult fantasy fiction, it is E. T. A. Hoffmann, who is as well a crucial figure in the evolution of the prose fiction form of the short story. In the early years of the nineteenth century in Germany he wrote several volumes of tales which were to have enormous popularity and influence throughout Europe. His use of the supernatural in many of his most famous stories, such as the classic "The Sandman," and his combination of science, the occult, and folk superstition make him perhaps the dominant fantasist of the nineteenth century, and his influence can still be widely seen. "The King's Bride," a fairy tale filled with wonders, is an antecedent of W. S. Gilbert's and Jack Vance's diverse stories and even L. Frank Baum's The Wizard of Oz. *It is an energetic stylistic tour de force about a romance between a Zabelthau and a Nebelstern, a lady gardener and a nice young man who is a bad poet, which is interrupted by the arrival of an extraordinary supernatural rival whose advent is signaled by a ring-bearing carrot.*

CHAPTER ONE

in which information is given regarding various persons and their relationships, and the way is prepared in pleasant fashion for all the astonishing and most marvellous things contained in subsequent chapters.

It was a bountiful year. In the fields wheat and barley, oats and rye sprouted and blossomed magnificently, the country lads went among the peas and the cattle among the clover; the trees were so weighted down with cherries that the whole host of sparrows, despite their ardent wish to gobble up everything, had to leave half the fruit untouched to provide food for others. All things ate their fill day after day at Nature's hospitable table. More than all else, however, the vegetables in Herr Dapsul von Zabelthau's kitchen garden did so surpassingly well that it was no wonder Fräulein Ännchen was quite beside herself with joy.

Some explanation must at once be given concerning the identity of this Herr Dapsul von Zabelthau and Fräulein Ännchen.

It is possible that at some time in your travels, dear reader, you have entered the lovely region through which flows the friendly Main. Balmy morning winds were breathing their scented breath over the meadow shimmering in the golden glitter of the risen sun. You could not bear to remain in the confinement of your carriage, you alighted and wandered through the little wood beyond which, once you began to descend into the valley, you discerned a small village. Suddenly you saw approaching you through this wood a tall, gaunt man whose strange attire riveted your gaze. He was wearing a little grey felt cap perched on a jet-black wig, clothes that were all of grey: coat, waistcoat and trousers, grey stockings and shoes, indeed even his very long stick was painted grey. The man came towards you with long strides, staring at you with big, deep-set eyes and yet seeming not to notice you at all. "Good morning, good sir," you cried out to him as he almost ran into you. Then he started, as though woken abruptly from a deep dream, raised his cap, and spoke in a hollow, tearful voice. "Good morning? O good sir, how glad we can be that we have a good morning—we poor inhabitants of Santa Cruz—two earthquakes have only just taken place and now the rain is pouring down in torrents!" You were at a loss, dear reader, as to what to answer this strange man, but while you were still thinking it over he had already gently touched your brow and gazed into the palm of your hand with a "By your leave, good sir!" In a voice as hollow and tearful as before, he then said, "Heaven bless you, good sir, your stars are auspicious," and strode on.

This singular man was none other than that Herr Dapsul von Zabelthau, whose one and only meagre inheritance was the little

village of Dapsulheim, which lay before you in the most charming
and smiling landscape, and which you were about to enter. You
wanted breakfast, but things looked dismal in the inn. All its provisions had been consumed during the *kermis,* and since you were not
prepared to content yourself with nothing but milk, you were directed to the manor house, where the gracious Fräulein Anna would
kindly regale you with whatever she had to offer. You lost no time in
making your way thither.

There is really no more to be said about this manor house than that
it had windows and doors like those of the former castle of Baron von
Tondertonktonk in Westphalia. Over the front door hung the arms of
the Zabelthau family carved in wood in the New Zealand style. The
house had an odd look, however, through the fact that the north side
came into direct contact with the encircling wall of an ancient ruined
castle, in such a way that the back door was the old castle gate and
opened straight into the castle forecourt, in the centre of which the
tall, circular watch-tower stood completely intact. From out of the
front door surmounted by the armorial bearings there stepped a red-
cheeked young girl, who could be considered quite pretty with her
clear blue eyes and fair hair and a figure that was perhaps just a trifle
too buxom and robust. Friendliness itself, she pressed you to come
into the house and, as soon as she realized your need, plied you with
the most excellent milk, a substantial slice of bread and butter, ham
that appeared to you to have been cured in Bayonne, and a small
glass of beetroot brandy. As she did so, the girl, who was none other
than Fräulein Anna von Zabelthau, spoke gaily and freely of everything appertaining to agriculture, of which she exhibited no small
knowledge.

But suddenly there rang out, as though from the air, a loud and
terrible voice: "Anna—Anna! Anna!" You started with fright, but
Fräulein Anna remarked quite amiably: "Papa has come back from
his walk and is calling for breakfast from his study." "Calling—from
his study?" you asked in amazement. "Yes," replied Fräulein Anna,
or Fräulein Ännchen as people called her, "yes, Papa's study is up
there in the tower and he is calling through the tube." And then,
beloved reader, you saw Ännchen open the narrow door of the tower
and run up the stairs with the same early lunch you yourself had just
enjoyed, that is to say a good solid helping of ham and bread accompanied by beetroot brandy.

She was with you again in a twinkling, however, and took you round the splendid kitchen garden, talking so much about curly kale, rampion, English turnips, little green-head montrue, great mogul, yellow prince's head, and so forth that you must have been quite staggered, especially if you did not know that all these grand names referred to nothing more than various species of cabbage and other vegetables.

I imagine that the brief visit which you, dear reader, paid to Dapsulheim will have given you an idea of what life was like in the house of which I am about to relate all sorts of strange and wellnigh unbelievable things. During his youth Herr Dapsul von Zabelthau rarely left the castle of his parents, who owned considerable property. His tutor, after instructing him in foreign, and especially Oriental, languages, encouraged his interest in mysticism, or rather hocuspocus. The tutor died and left young Dapsul a whole library of books on the occult sciences, in which he became absorbed. His parents also died, and now young Dapsul set off on journeys to distant places; impelled by the desires implanted in him by his tutor, he made his way to Egypt and India. When he returned, after many years, he found that the cousin to whom he had entrusted his fortune had administered it with such zeal that there was nothing left of it but the little village of Dapsulheim. Herr Dapsul von Zabelthau was too intent upon the sun-born gold of a loftier world to have much use for earthly wealth; hence he was profoundly grateful to his cousin for having preserved for him the cheerful village of Dapsulheim with the beautiful high watch-tower, which seemed built for astrological operations and at the very top of which Herr Dapsul von Zabelthau immediately installed his study.

The prudent cousin then persuaded Herr Dapsul von Zabelthau that he ought to marry. Dapsul saw the necessity and at once married the young lady his cousin chose for him. The lady left the house as quickly as she had entered it. She died, after bearing him a daughter. The cousin saw to wedding, baptism, and funeral, so that Dapsul, in his tower, noticed very little of it all, especially since just at this time a very remarkable comet appeared in the sky, with whose conjunctions the melancholy Dapsul, always forecasting disaster, believed his destiny to be entwined. To the great joy of the old great-aunt responsible for her upbringing, his little daughter developed a liking for agriculture. Fräulein Ännchen had to rise from the ranks, as the saying goes. She worked her way up from goose girl, through maid, upper maid, and housekeeper, to lady of the house, so that theory was clarified and consolidated by beneficial practice.

She was quite unusually fond of geese and ducks, chickens and pigeons, cattle and sheep; even the rearing of well-shaped little piglets by no means left her indifferent, although she did not deck out a little white piglet with a ribbon and bell and make a lap animal of it, as one young lady is said to have done somewhere. Above all, and far above fruit-growing, however, she liked the vegetable garden. Benefiting from her great-aunt's agricultural erudition, Fräulein Ännchen, as the gentle reader will have observed, had in fact acquired a pretty good theoretical knowledge of vegetable growing; while the soil was being dug over, the seed scattered, and plants set, Fräulein Ännchen did not merely stand and watch, but took an active part. Fräulein Ännchen was handy with a spade, there was no denying that. Thus, while Herr Dapsul von Zabelthau was absorbed in his astrological observations and other mystic matters, Fräulein Ännchen, once her aged great-aunt was dead, ran the estate; while Dapsul was studying heavenly affairs, Ännchen saw with industry and skill to those of the earth.

As we have said, it was no wonder Ännchen was almost beside herself with joy at the magnificent burgeoning of the kitchen garden that year. One bed of carrots, however, surpassed everything else in luxuriant growth and promised a quite exceptional crop.

"Oh, my lovely, dear carrots!" cried Fräulein Ännchen time and again, clapping her hands, jumping up and down, dancing around and generally behaving like a child who has received a generous profusion of Christmas presents. And it really seemed as though the carrot children in the earth rejoiced over Ännchen's joy, for the thin laughter that rang out clearly rose from the soil. Ännchen paid no particular attention to it, but ran to meet the farmhand, who, holding up a letter, cried out: "For you, Fräulein Ännchen, Gottlieb brought it with him from the town." Ännchen immediately recognized from the address that the letter was from none other than young Herr Amandus von Nebelstern, the only son of a neighbouring landowner, who was at the university. While still living in his father's village, Amandus had paid daily visits to Dapsulheim and had become convinced that never in his whole life could he love anyone but Fräulein Ännchen. Equally, Fräulein Ännchen knew for sure that she could never feel the slightest affection for anyone but Amandus with the curly brown hair. Hence both of them, Ännchen and Amandus, had agreed that they would marry, and the sooner the better, and that they would be the happiest married couple in the whole wide world.

Amandus, in the normal way, was a gay and carefree youth, but at the university he fell into the hands of some person unknown who not only persuaded him that he was a world-shaking poetic genius but also led him to wallow in sentimentality. He did this so successfully, that in a short time he had hoisted himself up above everything which the drearily prosaic call sense and reason and which they erroneously assert can perfectly well exist side by side with the most active imagination. As we have said, the letter which Fräulein Ännchen now received was from young Herr Amandus von Nebelstern. Opening it joyfully, she read:

Heavenly maid,

Can you see, can you feel, can you picture your Amandus, himself a flower, enveloped by the orange-blossom breath of the scented evening, lying on his back in the grass and gazing aloft with eyes full of pious love and reverent yearning! Thyme and lavender, roses and carnations, as well as yellow-eyed narcissi and modest violets, he weaves into a garland. And the flowers are thoughts of love, thoughts of you, O Anna! But is sober prose a fitting language for the lips of passion? Hear, oh hear, how I can love and speak of my love only in the form of a sonnet.

> Upon a myriad thirsty suns love flares,
>   Seeking its joy within another's heart;
>   Down from the dark sky stars do dart
>   And mirrored are in springs of loving tears.
>
> Tremendous rapture thrills and tears
>   The sweet fruit born of bitter seed apart
>   And longing calls its distant counterpart;
>   My being melts away in lover's cares.
>
> In waves of fire the storm-tossed waters roar;
>   The fearless swimmer girds his loins and leaps
>   Into the turmoil of the surf below.
>
> A hyacinth blooms upon the other shore;
>   The true heart opens like a bud, out seeps
>   Warm blood, in which the roots of love best grow.

O Anna, when you read this sonnet of sonnets, may you be pervaded by all the heavenly delight in which my whole being dissolved as I wrote it and afterwards read it aloud with divine enthusiasm to like-minded friends, people with a feeling for the highest things in life. Think, oh, think, sweet maid, of your faithful, enraptured Amandus von Nebelstern.

P. S. When you reply, O lofty virgin, do not forget to send me a pound of the Virginian tobacco you grow yourself. It burns well and tastes better than the Porto Rico the lads smoke here when they go visiting taverns.

Fräulein Ännchen pressed the letter to her lips and then said: "Oh, how sweet, how beautiful! And the lovely verses that rhyme so prettily! Oh, if only I were clever enough to understand it all, but I suppose only a student can do that. I wonder what he means about the roots of love. Oh, I'm sure he must be referring to the long red English carrots or even the rampion, the dear fellow!"

That very day Fräulein Ännchen made it her business to pack up the tobacco and hand over twelve of the finest goose quills to the schoolmaster, so that he could cut them carefully. Fräulein Ännchen resolved to sit down the same day and begin her answer to the exquisite letter. Once again a very audible laugh followed her as she ran from the kitchen garden, and if Ännchen had paid only the slightest attention she could not have failed to hear the thin voice that called: "Pull me out, pull me out—I am ripe—ripe—ripe!" But as we have said, she paid no attention to it.

CHAPTER TWO

which contains an account of the first miraculous happening and other things worth reading about, without which the promised fairy tale could not develop.

Herr Dapsul von Zabelthau generally descended from his astronomic tower at midday to share with his daughter a frugal meal that lasted a very short time and passed almost in silence, since Dapsul was not fond of conversation. Ännchen did not bother him by talking herself, all the less because she knew that if her Papa were to start speaking at all he would come out with a farrago of queer, incomprehensible stuff that would make her head spin. Today, however, her mind was in such a turmoil over the blossoming of the kitchen garden and the letter from her beloved Amandus that she talked incessantly of both jumbled together. In the end Herr Dapsul von Zabelthau dropped his knife and fork, covered both ears with his hands, and cried: "Oh, what vapid, drab and muddled babble!" But when Fräulein Ännchen lapsed into a dismayed silence he said in his characteristic drawling, tearful tone: "As regards the vegetables, my dear daughter, I have long known that the conjunction of the stars this year is particularly propitious to such fruits, and earthly man will doubtless enjoy cabbages and radishes and lettuces so that his terrestrial substance may multiply and withstand the fire of the World Spirit like a well-kneaded pot. The gnomic principle will resist the assaults of the salamander, and I look forward to eating parsnips, which you cook so excellently. As to young Herr Amandus von Nebelstern, I have not the slightest objection to your marrying him as soon as he returns from the university. Just send word to me through Gottlieb when you are going to your wedding with your bridegroom, so that I may escort you to the church."

Herr Dapsul remained silent for a few moments and then, without looking at Ännchen, whose face was glowing all over with joy, he continued, smiling and tapping his glass with his fork (two actions which he always liked to combine, though he rarely had an opportunity): "Your Amandus is someone who should and must be, I mean a gerund, and I will admit, my dear Ännchen, that I long ago worked out this gerund's horoscope. The conjunctions of the planets are all quite auspicious. He has Jupiter in the ascending node, which Venus looks upon in the sextile aspect. Only the orbit of Sirius intersects it, and precisely at the point of intersection there stands a great danger, from which he will save his bride. The danger itself is inexplicable, since there enters the picture a strange being that seems to baffle all astrological science. It is, however, apparent that Amandus will save you with that singular state of mind which men call madness or lunacy. O my daughter"—here Herr Dapsul relapsed into his usual tearful tone—"O my daughter, let no sinister power cunningly concealed from my clairvoyant eyes step suddenly into your path, let not young Herr Amandus von Nebelstern have need to save you from any other danger than that of becoming an old maid!" Herr Dapsul heaved a series of deep sighs, then he went on: "But once this danger has passed, the orbit of Sirius is suddenly interrupted, and Venus and Jupiter, previously far apart, are reunited and reconciled."

It was years since Herr Dapsul von Zabelthau had spoken so much as he had that day. Quite exhausted, he rose and climbed his tower again.

Early the following day Ännchen was ready with her answer to
Herr Amandus von Nebelstern. It read:

My dearly beloved Amandus,

*You have no idea what joy your letter gave me. I told Papa about it and he
promised to escort us to the church for the wedding. Do hurry and come back
from the university. Oh, if only I could quite understand your dearest verses
which rhyme so prettily! When I read them aloud to myself it all sounds so
wonderful and I imagine I understand every word, then it all slips away and
I feel as though I had simply been reading disconnected words. The schoolmaster says it's supposed to be that way, that is the new refined speech, but I—
oh!—I'm a silly, simple thing! Write and tell me if I can't perhaps become a
student for a time, without neglecting my domestic duties? No, that's impossible? Then I shall have to wait till we are man and wife, then perhaps I shall
pick up some of your learning and the new refined speech. I'm sending you the
Virginian tobacco, my darling Amandchen. I have stuffed my hatbox absolutely full—so much wanted to go in—and placed my straw hat for the time
being on Charlemagne, who stands in our guest room, though without legs
because he is, as you know, only a bust. Don't laugh at me, Amandchen, I
have also written a few lines of verse and they rhyme quite well. Do write and
tell me how it is that one knows so well what rhymes without being taught.
Now listen:*

> I love you though you now be far away
> And long with all my heart your wife to be.
> The sky above my head, blue like the sea,
> At night is bright with golden stars that play.
> Love me always, dear, and never leave me,
> O sweetheart promise you will ne'er deceive me.
> Virginian tobacco I send you now in haste
> And wish you much enjoyment from its taste!

*Take the will for the deed; when I understand refined speech I shall do
better. The yellow stone-head has done splendidly this year, and the broad
beans have made a fine start, but my dachshund, little Feldmann, gave the big
gander a terrible bite in the leg yesterday. Well, we can't have everything
perfect in this world. A hundred kisses in thought, my dearest Amandus, your
faithful bride, Anna von Zabelthau.*

*P. S. I have written in a great hurry, that's why the letters are a bit
crooked in places.*

P. S. You mustn't hold that against me, even if I write a bit crooked my heart is straight and I am always your faithful Anna.

P. S. Good gracious, I nearly forgot, scatterbrain that I am. Papa sends his best wishes and told me to tell you that you are one who should and must be and will one day save me from a great danger. I am very pleased about this and am once more your ever-loving, ever-faithful Anna von Zabelthau.

Fräulein Ännchen felt much relieved when she had finished this letter, which had been a great effort to write. She became completely light-hearted and gay when she had also prepared the envelope, sealed it without burning either the paper or her fingers, and given the letter and the tobacco box, on which she had painted distinctly with a brush the letters A. v. N., to Gottlieb, who was to take them both to the town by the mail coach.

After seeing to the poultry in the yard, Fräulein Anna ran quickly to her favourite spot, the kitchen garden. When she came to the carrot bed she thought to herself that it was now obviously time to provide for the gourmets in town and pull up the first carrots. The maid was called to help her with the work. Fräulein Anna stepped carefully into the middle of the bed and seized hold of a magnificent tuft of carrot leaves. But the moment she pulled a strange sound made itself heard. The reader must not think of the mandrake root and the horrible whimpering and whining that rends the human heart as it is pulled out of the earth. No, the sound that seemed to come from the earth resembled a thin, joyful laugh. Nevertheless, Fräulein Ännchen let go of the tuft of leaves and exclaimed in some dismay: "Why, who is that laughing at me?" But since there was no further sound, she took a fresh grip on the tuft of leaves, which seemed taller and more luxuriant than any of the others, gave it a hearty tug, disregarding the laughter that rang out again, and pulled out of the soil the finest and tenderest of carrots. But the moment Fräulein Ännchen looked at the carrot she uttered a shout of mingled joy and terror, so that the maid rushed over to her and, like Fräulein Anna, cried out aloud at the pretty wonder she perceived. Firmly encircling the carrot there was a magnificent gold ring with a fierily sparkling topaz. "Ah," cried the maid, "that is meant for you, Fräulein Ännchen, that is your wedding ring, you must put it on immediately." "What nonsense you are talking," replied Fräulein Ännchen, "I must receive my wedding ring from Herr Amandus von Nebelstern, not from a carrot!"

The longer Fräulein Ännchen looked at the ring, the better she

liked it. The workmanship was so fine and delicate that it seemed to
surpass anything ever produced by human art. The band was formed
of hundreds and hundreds of tiny little figures, entwined in the most
diverse groups, which it was impossible to distinguish at the first
glance with the naked eye, but which, on looking at the ring longer
and more intently, seemed to grow in size, to come to life and to
dance in graceful rows. And then the gem had such a special fire that
it would have been difficult to match it even among the topazes in the
Green Vault of the Royal Palace at Dresden.

"Who knows," said the maid, "how long the beautiful ring may
have been lying deep in the earth, and then it was raised by the spade
and the carrot grew through it."

Fräulein Ännchen now pulled the ring off the carrot, and strangely
enough the latter slipped through her fingers and vanished into the
soil. Neither the maid nor Fräulein Ännchen paid much heed to this,
however; they were too profoundly absorbed in contemplation of the
magnificent ring, which Fräulein Ännchen, without more ado, now
placed on the little finger of her right hand. As she did so, a stabbing
pain ran from the root of her finger to the tip, but ceased as quickly as
it began.

At midday, of course, she gave Herr Dapsul von Zabelthau an
account of the strange thing that had happened to her in the carrot
bed, and showed him the beautiful ring the carrot had been wearing.
She tried to pull the ring off her finger so that her Papa could examine it more closely. But she felt the same stabbing pain she had felt
when she put the ring on, and this pain continued as long as she
tugged at the ring, till finally it became so unbearable that she had to
let go. Herr Dapsul scrutinized the ring on her finger with close
attention, made Anna describe a variety of circles with outstretched
finger towards all the points of the compass, sank into profound medi-
tation, and then climbed the tower without uttering another word.
Fräulein Anna heard her Papa sighing and groaning loudly as he
mounted the stairs.

The following morning, while Fräulein Ännchen was out in the
yard chasing the big cock which got up to all sorts of mischief and in
particular quarrelled with the pigeons, Herr Dapsul von Zabelthau
wailed so terrifyingly down the speaking-tube that Ännchen was
quite shaken and shouted up through her cupped hand: "Why do you
howl so mercilessly, dearest Papa, it's driving the fowls crazy!"

Thereupon Herr Dapsul yelled down the speaking-tube: "Anna, my daughter Anna, come up to me at once."

Fräulein Ännchen was greatly surprised by this command, for her Papa had never before ordered her to come into the tower; on the contrary, he had kept the gate carefully locked. She was seized with a certain trepidation as she mounted the narrow spiral stairs and opened the heavy door that led into the tower's one and only room. Herr Dapsul von Zabelthau was sitting in a large armchair of peculiar shape, surrounded by all kinds of strange instruments and dusty books. In front of him was a stand bearing a sheet of paper stretched in a frame with various lines drawn on it. He was wearing a tall, pointed, grey cap on his head and a wide cloak of grey callimanco and had a long white beard on his chin. Because of the false beard, Fräulein Ännchen did not at first recognize her Papa and looked anxiously around to see if he wasn't in one of the corners of the room; when she realized that the man with the beard was really Papa she laughed heartily and asked whether it was already Christmas and Papa was dressed up as Father Christmas.

Paying no heed to Ännchen's talk, Herr Dapsul von Zabelthau picked up a small piece of iron, touched Ännchen's forehead with it, and then stroked her right arm several times from the shoulder down to the tip of the little ring finger. After this she had to sit in the armchair, which Herr Dapsul had vacated, and place her little be-ringed finger against the paper in the frame in such a way that the topaz come in contact with the focal point upon which all the lines converged. Immediately yellow rays spurted from the gem in all directions, until the whole sheet of paper had turned dark yellow. Then the lines jiggled up and down and it was as if the little men on the band of the ring were hopping merrily all over the sheet. Herr Dapsul, keeping his eyes glued to the paper, had meanwhile picked up a thin metal plate; he held it high in the air with both hands and was about to press it down on the paper, when he slipped on the smooth stone floor and fell very un-gently on his hindquarters, while the metal plate; which he had instinctively dropped in an attempt to break his fall and preserve his coccyx, fell to the floor with a clinking noise. Fräulein Ännchen awoke with a soft "Oh!" from the strange, dreamy state into which she had sunk. Herr Dapsul rose to his feet with an effort, put back the grey sugar-loaf hat that had fallen from his head, and sat down facing Fräulein Ännchen on a pile of folio-volumes.

"My daughter," he said then, "my daughter Anna, what was your state of mind just now? What did you think, what did you feel? What shapes did you see with the eye of the spirit within you?"

"Oh," replied Fräulein Ännchen, "I felt wonderful, more wonderful than I have ever felt before. Then I thought of Herr Amandus von Nebelstern. I saw him clearly before my eyes, but he was even handsomer than usual, and he was smoking a pipe of the Virginian leaves I sent him, which suited him extremely well. Then I suddenly had a tremendous appetite for young carrots and little sausages and was quite delighted when the dish stood in front of me. I was about to set to, when I awoke from the dream with a sudden painful jerk."

"—Amandus von Nebelstern—Virginian canaster—carrots—sausages!" Thus spoke Herr Dapsul von Zabelthau very thoughtfully and signed to his daughter, who was about to leave, that she should stay.

"Happy, ingenuous child," he began in a tone that was far more tearful than ever before, "happy not to have been initiated into the deep mysteries of the universe, not to know the dangers that threaten you from all sides. You know nothing of the supernatural science of the sacred Cabbala. It is true that on that account you will never share in the heavenly pleasure of the wise, who, once they have reached the highest stage, need neither eat nor drink except for pleasure, and remain unaffected by all human considerations; but in compensation you are not subject to the fear that comes on the way up to this stage, like your unhappy father, who is seized by far too much human vertigo and in whom what he laboriously discovers by research arouses only horror and dismay, and who is still compelled to eat and drink and—everything else—from pure earthly necessity. Know, my lovely and happily ignorant child, that the deep earth, the air, water, and fire are full of spiritual beings of a higher yet more limited nature than man. It seems unnecessary to explain to you, my little stupid one, the peculiar nature of the gnomes, salamanders, sylphs, and undines, you would not be able to grasp it. To indicate the danger in which you may possibly be, it will be sufficient to tell you that these beings strive for union with mortals, and since they know that mortals normally fight shy of such a union, the aforesaid spirits employ all sorts of cunning devices to entice the human beings upon whom they have bestowed their favour. They may use a twig, a flower, a glass of water, a flash of fire, or any other apparently insignificant thing as a means of attaining their aim. It is correct to say that such a union often turns out very advantageous, as was the case with two priests, of whom the Prince of Mirandola relates that they lived for forty years in happy wedlock with one such spirit. It is also correct that the greatest sages sprang from unions between a human being and a spirit of the elements. Thus the great Zoroaster was the son of the salamander Oromasis, thus great Apollonius, wise Merlin, the brave Count of Cleve, and the great Cabbalist Ben Sira, were the offspring of such unions, while according to the statement of Paracelsus the beautiful Melusine was nothing else than a sylph. But in spite of these possible advantages, the danger of such a union is too great, for apart from the fact that the elemental spirits demand that the brightest light of the profoundest wisdom shall blaze forth upon those on whom they bestow their favour, they are also extremely sensitive and wreak terrible vengeance for any slight. Thus it once came about that when a sylph who was united with a philosopher heard him speak with his friends a trifle too enthusiastically of a beautiful woman she immediately displayed her snow-white and beautifully shaped leg in the air, as though to convince his friends of her beauty, and then killed the poor philosopher on the spot. But why should I speak of others? Why do I not speak of myself? I know that for twelve years a sylph has loved me, but she is shy and bashful, and I am tormented by thoughts of the danger of trying to enslave her by Cabbalistic means, because I am still far too dependent upon earthly needs, and hence lack the necessary wisdom. Every morning I resolve to fast and happily allow breakfast to pass, but when midday comes—O Anna, my daughter Anna—you know well—I guzzle terribly!"

Herr Dapsul von Zabelthau uttered these words almost in a howl, while the bitterest tears ran down over his emaciated, hollow cheeks; then he continued more calmly: "But I take care to behave with the greatest refinement, the most exquisite gallantry towards the elemental spirit that bears me affection. I never venture to smoke a pipe of tobacco without observing the appropriate Cabbalistic precautions, since I do not know whether my gentle spirit of the air likes the brand and might not be sensitive to the pollution of her element, for which reason those who smoke hunter's canaster or shag can never grow wise and enjoy the love of a sylph. I take the same precautions every time I cut a hazel wand, pick a flower, eat fruit, or strike fire, for I make every possible effort to avoid coming into conflict with any spirit of the elements. And yet—you see that nutshell on which I slipped and, falling over backwards, spoiled the whole experiment that would have revealed to me the secret of the ring in its entirety? I do not remember ever having eaten nuts in this room that is dedicated exclusively to the pursuit of knowledge (you know now why I always lunch on the stairs), and it is therefore all the clearer that there was a little gnome hidden in this shell, perhaps for the purpose of lodging with me and listening in to my experiments. For the spirits of the elements love human sciences, especially such as uninitiated people, if they do not call them foolish and insane, at least consider beyond the power of the human mind and therefore dangerous. Hence they often slip in to observe divine magnetic operations. In particular, the gnomes, who are incorrigible jokers, make a practice of finding some magnetizer who has not yet attained the stage of wisdom which I described to you just now and is still too dependent upon earthly needs, and substituting an infatuated child of the earth at the moment when he believes that he is embracing a sylph in totally pure and clarified air.

"When I trod on the little student's head he grew angry and threw me down. But the gnome doubtless had a deeper reason for preventing me from uncovering the mystery of the ring. Anna!—my daughter Anna!—hear me—I should have disclosed that a gnome had bestowed his favor upon you, one who, to judge by the construction of the ring, must be a wealthy, distinguished, and at the same time extremely refined man. But, my precious Anna, my dearly beloved little stupid, how can you enter into a union with one of these elemental spirits without running the most terrible risk? If you had read Cassiodorus Remus you could retort that according to his true account the famous Magdalena de la Cruz, abbess of a convent at Gordova in Spain, lived in agreeable matrimony with a little gnome for thirty years, that the same thing happened with a male sylph and young Gertrude, who was a nun in the convent of Nazareth at Cologne; but think of the learned preoccupations of those spiritual ladies and of your own. What a difference! Instead of reading in wise books, you very often feed chickens, geese, ducks, and other creatures that are a source of irritation to every Cabbalist; instead of observing the sky, the course of the stars, you dig the earth; instead of following the track of the future in artistic horoscopical diagrams, you churn milk into butter and pickle *sauerkraut* to meet the base needs of winter, though I myself should not like to go without this dish. Tell me, can all that continue for long to please a sensitive philosophical spirit of the elements? For, O Anna, through you Dapsulheim flourishes and your spirit never may and never can escape from this earthly vocation. And yet you felt concerning the ring, even though it caused you sudden violent pain, an unrestrained and thoughtless joy! For your salvation I wished by this operation to break the power of the ring, to free you utterly from the gnome who is pursuing you. The ritual failed through the cunning of the little student in the nutshell. And yet I feel a courageous readiness to combat the elemental spirit such as I have never before experienced! You are my child—whom I did not beget with a sylph, a female salamander, or any other elemental spirit, but with that poor country maid from the best family, whom wicked neighbours mockingly referred to as the Lady of the Goats, on account of her idyllic nature, which induced her to pasture a small flock of pretty white goats on the green hills every day all by herself, while I, at that time an infatuated fool, blew the shawm on my tower. You are and remain my child, my blood! I shall save you; this mystic file here shall free you from the baneful ring!"

So saying, Herr Dapsul von Zabelthau picked up a small file and began to file the ring. But no sooner had he scraped the file this way and that a few times than Fräulein Ännchen cried out in pain: "Papa —Papa, you're filing my finger off!" And as she cried, thick, dark blood did indeed well up from under the ring. Thereupon, Herr Dapsul von Zabelthau dropped the file, sank half-fainting into the armchair, and cried out: "Oh!—oh!—oh!—I'm done for! Perhaps this very hour the gnome will come and bite through my throat, if the sylph does not save me!—O Anna—Anna—go—flee!"

Fräulein Ännchen, who had wished herself miles away as soon as her Papa began his strange outburst, raced downstairs with the speed of the wind.

CHAPTER THREE

in which an account is given of the arrival of a remarkable man in Dapsulheim and further events are described.

Herr Dapsul Von Zabelthau had just embraced his daughter with many tears and was about to ascend the tower, where he dreaded to be visited at any moment by the irate gnome, when the clear and merry notes of a horn were heard and a little rider of rather curious and droll appearance galloped into the courtyard. The yellow horse was not at all large, consequently the little man, in spite of his big, shapeless head, did not look so very dwarflike, but towered above the horse's head. This was solely due to the length of his body, however, for the legs and feet dangling from the saddle were so small as to be scarcely worth taking into account. For the rest, the little man wore a very pleasant riding habit of golden-yellow satin, a tall hat of the same material with a splendid bunch of grass-green feathers and riding boots of highly polished mahogany wood. With a penetrating "Whoa!" the rider pulled up his mount directly in front of Herr Dapsul von Zabelthau. He seemed about to dismount, then slid down with the speed of lightning under the belly of his horse, flung himself up on the other side two, three times in succession twelve ells high in the air, in such a way that at each ell he turned six somersaults, and ended by standing on his head on the pommel of his saddle. In this position he galloped forwards, backwards, sideways in all sorts of astonishing twists and turns, while his little feet beat trochees, Pyrrhics, dactyls, and so on in the air. When the elegant gymnast and equestrian finally stood still and uttered a polite greeting there could be seen on the soil of the courtyard the words: "Cordial greetings to you and your lady daughter, honoured Herr Dapsul von Zabelthau!" He had ridden these words into the earthly element in beautiful roman uncial letters. After this, the little man jumped off his horse, turned three cartwheels, and then said that he had been instructed to present to Herr Dapsul von Zabelthau the compliments of his gracious master, Baron Porphyrio von Ockerodastes, called Corduanspitz, and if Herr Dapsul von Zabelthau had no objection, the Baron would like to pay him a friendly visit for a few days, since he hoped in the future to become his closest neighbour.

Herr Dapsul von Zabelthau looked more like a dead man than a living one, so pale and rigid was he as he stood there leaning on his daughter. Scarcely had the words "It—will—be—a—great—pleasure" with difficulty passed his lips, than the little rider made off at lightning speed, after the same ceremonial he had performed on arrival.

"Oh, my daughter," now cried Herr Dapsul von Zabelthau, wailing and sobbing, "oh, my daughter, my poor unhappy daughter, it is only too evident that it is the gnome who is coming to abduct you and wring my neck! But we will summon the last ounce of courage that remains to us! Perhaps it will be possible to placate the enraged elemental spirit, we must behave towards him with all the propriety we can muster. I shall immediately read to you, my precious child, a few chapters from Lactantius or Thomas Aquinas on how to deal with elemental spirits, so that you shall not commit any terrible *faux pas*. . . ."

But before Herr Dapsul von Zabelthau had time to fetch Lactantius, Thomas Aquinas, or any other authority on elemental spirits, there rang out from quite close by the sort of music that is performed by musical children at Christmas. Then a fine long column wound its way up the road. In the front came some sixty or seventy little riders on small yellow horses, all dressed like the emissary in yellow riding habits, pointed caps, and boots of polished mahogany. They were followed by a coach of purest crystal drawn by eight yellow horses, which again was followed by about forty other, less sumptuous, coaches, some drawn by six and some by four horses. Alongside the column swarmed a multitude of pages, runners, and other servants decked out in glittering clothes, so that the whole *cortège* presented a picture as gay as it was singular. Fräulein Ännchen, who had never before guessed that there could be such pretty little things in the whole world as these tiny horses and people, was beside herself and forgot everything, even to shut her mouth, which she had opened wide in joyful exclamation.

The coach drawn by eight horses stopped just in front of Herr Dapsul von Zabelthau. Riders jumped down from their horses, pages and servants hurried forward, the coachdoor was opened, and he who now gracefully descended from the coach and out of the arms of his servants was none other than Baron Porphyrio von Ockerodastes, called Corduanspitz. In stature, the Baron was far from being an Apollo of the Belvedere, in fact he wasn't even to be compared with the dying warrior. For apart from the fact that he was less than three feet tall, a third part of this small body consisted of the obviously too large, fat head, which, moreover, was embellished by a big, long, hooked nose and a pair of large, round, bulging eyes. Since the body was also somewhat long, only some four inches were left for the legs. This small space was well utilized, however, for in themselves the baronial legs were the daintiest one could possibly see. Of course, they appeared too weak to bear the dignified head; the Baron had a tottering walk and frequently tripped and fell; but he was on his feet again in a trice, like a corktumbler, so that his falls looked more like the attractive capers of a dance. The Baron wore a close-fitting habit of gleaming gold material and a little cap almost like a crown, topped by an enormous bush of many plant-green feathers.

As soon as the Baron was standing on the ground, he rushed up to Herr Dapsul von Zabelthau, grasped him with both hands, bounded up to his neck, which he clasped, and cried in a voice that boomed far more loudly than one would have expected from his small stature: "O my Dapsul von Zabelthau—my dearly beloved Father!"

Having said this, the Baron swung himself down from Herr Dapsul's neck as agilely and adroitly as he had gone up, jumped or rather hurled himself at Fräulein Ännchen, seized the hand of the beringed finger, smothered it with noisy, smacking kisses, and boomed as loudly as before: "O my most beautiful Fräulein Anna von Zabelthau, my best beloved bride!"

Thereupon the Baron clapped his hands, and immediately the shrill children's music struck up again and more than a hundred tiny gentlemen sprang out of the coaches and down from the horses, and danced as the courier had done—now on their heads, now on their feet—the most elegant trochees, spondees, iambics, Pyrrhics, anapests, tribrachs, bachs, antibachs, choriambics, and dactyls, so that it was a joy to behold. While this rejoicing was going on, however, Fräulein Ännchen recovered from the great shock caused by the terms in which the little Baron had addressed her and became preoccupied by all sorts of well-founded domestic qualms. "How," she thought, "can our small house lodge all these little people? Should I be forgiven if, out of necessity, I bedded at least the servants in the big barn, and would there be room for them even there? And what shall I do with the nobles, who have come in coaches and are undoubtedly used to sleeping in soft beds in fine rooms? Must the two plough-horses also be turned out of their stable, and even if I were so unmerciful as to drive lame old Fox out to grass, would there be enough room then for all these little beasts of horses the ugly Baron has brought with him? And it's the same with the hundred coaches! But then comes the worst thing of all—will our whole year's stock of provisions be sufficient to satisfy all these little creatures for as long as two days?"

This last worry was the worst of all. Fräulein Ännchen could see everything being gobbled up, all the new vegetables, the flock of sheep, the poultry, the salt meat, even the beetroot brandy, and this brought the sparkling tears to her eyes. It seemed to her as though just at this moment Baron Corduanspitz made a thoroughly impudent and malicious face; this gave her the courage, while his retinue was still dancing with all their might, to tell him in plain words that, much as her father esteemed his visit, a stay at Dapsulheim of more than two hours was out of the question; since space and everything else necessary to the proper reception and appropriate entertainment of such a fine and wealthy gentleman with his numerous attendants was totally lacking. At this, little Corduanspitz suddenly looked as sweet and tender as a marzipan loaf and, pressing Fräulein Ännchen's rather rough and none too white hand to his lips with closed eyes, assured her that nothing could be farther from his wishes than to cause the dear Papa and the loveliest daughter even the very slightest inconvenience. Everything demanded by kitchen and cellar he had brought with him, but as regards a lodging he asked no more than a patch of ground and the open sky above, so that his people could erect the usual travelling palace, in which he and his whole retinue and all their animals would lodge.

Fräulein Ännchen was so delighted by Baron Porphyrio von Ockerodastes's words that, to show she did not in the least mind parting with her titbits, she was on the point of offering the little man doughnuts she had saved from the last *kermis* and a glass of beetroot brandy —unless he preferred double-bitter, which the upper maid had brought from the town and recommended as beneficial to the stomach. But at this moment Corduanspitz added that he had chosen the vegetable garden for the erection of his palace, and Ännchen's joy was at an end!

While the retinue, to celebrate their master's arrival in Dapsulheim, continued their Olympic Games, butting one another in their pointed stomachs with their fat heads and turning back-somersaults, flinging themselves up into the air, playing games of skittles in which they themselves took the part of skittles, ball, and skittlers, and the like, little Baron Porphyrio von Ockerodastes plunged into a conversation with Herr Dapsul von Zabelthau that seemed to grow more and more weighty, till the two of them went off hand in hand and mounted the astronomic tower.

Terrified at the thought of what she might find, Fräulein Ännchen now ran as fast as she could to the vegetable garden, to save what could still be saved. The upper maid was already standing in the field staring open-mouthed in front of her, motionless, as though she had been changed into a pillar of salt like Lot's wife. Fräulein Ännchen went equally rigid beside her. Finally, both of them yelled so that their words echoed far and wide: "Merciful heavens, what a disaster!"

They found the whole beautiful vegetable garden transformed into a desert. There was not a green plant, not a shrub, nothing but a barren, desolate field. "No," cried the enraged maid, "there is no other possibility, that must have been done by the accursed little creatures who have just arrived. They came in coaches? They want to pass themselves off as people of breeding? Ha, ha! They are goblins, believe me, Fräulein Ännchen, nothing but an unChristian witches' brood, and if only I had a piece of crosswort with me you would see a miracle. But just let them come, the little beasts, I'll strike them dead with this spade!" So saying, the upper maid swung her fearsome weapon aloft, while Fräulein Ännchen wept loudly.

In the meantime four gentlemen from Herr Corduanspitz's retinue approached with such pleasant, elegant mien and courtly bows, and looking at the same time so extremely strange, that the upper maid, instead of striking out as she had intended, let the spade slowly sink, and Fräulein Ännchen ceased her weeping.

The gentlemen announced themselves as the closest friends of Baron Porphyrio von Ockerodastes, called Corduanspitz; they belonged, as their clothes symbolically indicated, to four different nations, and gave their names as Pan Kapustowicz from Poland, Herr von Schwarzrettig from Pomerania, Signor di Broccoli from Italy, and Monsieur de Roccambolle from France. They assured Ännchen in mellifluous tones that in no time at all the builders would come and give the beautiful young lady the great pleasure of watching a lovely palace of pure silk go up in the twinkling of an eye.

"What good is a silken palace to me?" cried Fräulein Ännchen, weeping loudly in profound grief. "What is your Baron Corduanspitz to me anyway, since you wicked people have destroyed all my lovely vegetables and all my joy is gone?" But the courteous gentlemen consoled Ännchen, assuring her that they were not responsible for the devastation of her vegetable garden, that, on the contrary, it would soon be a picture of luxuriant growth such as Fräulein Ännchen had never seen here or in any other vegetable garden in the world.

The little builders came indeed, and such a wild and confused turmoil broke out in the field that both Fräulein Ännchen and the upper maid ran away in terror to the shelter of a bush, from where they watched to see what would happen.

Although they could not understand how such a thing could take place by natural means, in a few minutes a sumptuous and lofty tent of golden-yellow material, decorated with multi-coloured garlands and feathers, went up before their eyes; it occupied the whole of the big vegetable garden, and its guy-ropes passed right over the village to the nearby forest, where they were attached to large trees.

No sooner was the tent ready than Baron von Ockerodastes came down with Herr Dapsul von Zabelthau from the astronomic tower, and after repeated embraces climbed into his coach and drove with all his followers, in the same order in which they had come to Dapsulheim, into the silken palace, which closed behind the last man.

Fräulein Ännchen had never seen her Papa as he was now. All trace of the grief that normally plagued him had vanished from his face, he seemed almost to be smiling, and at the same time there was a transfigured look in his eyes that seemed to indicate some great and unexpected stroke of luck. Without a word, Herr Dapsul von Zabelthau took his daughter's hand, led her into the house, embraced her three times in succession, and at last burst out: "Happy Anna— immensely happy child!—happy father! O daughter, all worry, all distress, all grief of the heart is now past! You have been vouchsafed a destiny that rarely comes to mortals! Know that this Baron Porphyrio von Ockerodastes is no malignant gnome, although he is descended from one of these spirits of the elements, but one who succeeded in purifying himself and developing his higher nature through the instruction of the salamander Oromasis. From this purifying fire there sprang love for a mortal woman, with whom he was united, becoming the ancestor of the most illustrious family whose name ever embellished parchment. I believe that I have already told you, beloved daughter Anna, that the pupil of the great salamander Oromasis, the noble gnome Tsilmenech—a Chaldean name meaning Dunderhead —fell in love with Magdalena de la Cruz, abbess of a convent at Cordova in Spain, and lived with her for thirty years in happy and agreeable wedlock. Now, the dear Baron Porphyrio von Ockerodastes—who has assumed the surname Corduanspitz, from Cordovan or Spanish leather, to indicate his origin in Cordova and also to distinguish himself from a prouder, but fundamentally less worthy collateral line that bears the surname Saffian, from Saffian or Moroccan leather—is a scion of the sublime family of supernatural beings that developed from this union. The fact that Spitz, meaning lace, was added to the Corduan must have some elemental, astrological explanation; I have not yet reflected upon this point. Following the example of his great forefather, the gnome Tsilmenech, who loved Magdalena de la Cruz ever since her twelfth year, the excellent Ockerodastes bestowed his love upon you when you were only twelve. He was happy to receive a little gold ring from you, and now you have also put on his ring, so that you have irrevocably become his betrothed!"

"What," cried Fräulein Ännchen, full of terror and dismay, "what? —his bride? I'm to marry that repulsive little goblin? Have I not long been the betrothed of Herr Amandus von Nebelstern? No—I shall never take the ugly sorcerer for a husband, even if he is made a thousand times of cordovan or saffian!"

"There!" replied Herr Dapsul von Zabelthau, growing more serious, "I see to my regret how little heavenly wisdom is able to penetrate your stubborn earthly mind! You call the noble, elemental Porphyrio von Ockerodastes ugly and repulsive, perhaps because he is only three feet tall and apart from his head carries little that is impressive in the way of torso, arms and legs, and other irrelevant features, while the legs of the sort of earthly dandy you have in mind cannot be long enough, because of his coat tails. O my daughter, into what a heinous error you have fallen! All beauty lies in wisdom, all wisdom in thought, and the physical symbol of thought is the head! The more head, the more beauty and wisdom, and if man could cast off all his other limbs as noxious luxuries and sources of evil he would have attained the loftiest ideal form! Whence come all diseases, all affliction, all discord, all dispute, in short all the corruption of the earthly realm, but from the damned luxuriance of the limbs? Oh, what peace, what tranquillity, what bliss on earth, if mankind existed without belly, rump, arms, or legs, if it consisted solely of the bust! Happy, therefore, is the artists' idea of portraying great statesmen or great scholars as busts, in order to indicate symbolically the higher nature that must dwell in them by virtue of their responsibilities or their books! Well, then, my daughter Anna, no more talk of ugliness, repulsiveness, or other denigratory comments upon the noblest of the spirits, the magnificent Porphyrio von Ockerodastes, whose betrothed you are and will remain. Know that through him your father will shortly attain to the highest degree of happiness, after which he has so long striven in vain. Porphyrio von Ockerodastes is informed that the sylph Nehahilah (Syrian, meaning Pointed Nose) loves me and he will aid me with all his powers to become worthy of union

with this being of a higher spiritual nature. I am sure you will be
pleased with your future step-mother. May kind fate so dispose that
our two weddings may be celebrated at the same happy hour!'' With
this, Herr Dapsul von Zabelthau dramatically left the room, casting
his daughter one more meaning glance.

Fräulein Ännchen's heart was heavy as she recalled that long ago,
when she was still a child, a small gold ring had inexplicably slipped
from her finger. Now she was sure that the repulsive little sorcerer
had lured her into his snare, leaving her small chance of escape. The
thought plunged her into the deepest grief. She had to unburden her
oppressed heart, and this she did with the aid of a goose quill, with
which she swiftly wrote as follows to Herr Amandus von Nebelstern.

My best beloved Amandus,

*Everything is finished, I am the unhappiest person in the whole world and
sob and weep so bitterly for sorrow that even the domestic animals have pity
and compassion on me, and how much more deeply will you be moved. As a
matter of fact, the disaster affects you as much as it does me, and you will be
equally filled with grief. You know that we love one another as warmly as any
couple can love and that I am your betrothed and that Papa was going to
escort us to church? Well, a horrid little yellow man has suddenly come along
in a coach and eight and claims that I have exchanged rings with him and
that we are bride and bridegroom! And just think how terrible it is! Papa also
says I must marry the little monster, because he comes of a very distinguished
family. That may be, to judge by the retinue and the gorgeous clothes they
wear, but the man has such a ghastly name that for this reason alone I never
want to be his wife. At the same time, he is also called Corduanspitz, and that
is his family name. Write and tell me whether the Corduanspitzes are really so
noble and distinguished; they will know that in the town. I can't understand
what has come over Papa in his old age, he wants to marry as well, and the
horrible Corduanspitz is to couple him off with a woman who floats in the air.
God protect us! The upper maid shrugs her shoulders and says she doesn't
think much of mistresses that fly in the air and float on water and that she
would give notice at once and that she hopes for my sake that my step-mama
will break her neck at the next witches' ride on Walpurgis Night. These are
nice goings on, I can tell you. But you are my one and only hope. I know that
you are the one who should and must, and will save me from great danger.
The danger is here, come quick and save*

Your mortally afflicted, but
ever faithful betrothed,
Anna von Zabelthau.

P.S. Couldn't you challenge the little yellow Corduanspitz to a duel? You would be bound to win, because he is rather weak in the legs.

P.S. I beg you once more, put on your clothes at once and hurry to your unhappy, but, as I said above, ever faithful betrothed, Anna von Zabelthau.

CHAPTER FOUR

which describes the court of a powerful king, but first reports a bloody duel and other strange happenings.

Fräulein Ännchen felt as if paralysed in every limb by dejection. She sat at the window with arms folded and stared out, paying no heed to the clucking, crowing, quacking, and squawking of the poultry, which, as dusk was falling, wanted to be put to rest by her. Indeed, with the greatest indifference she allowed this task to be carried out by the maid and did not even protest when the latter struck the rooster—who resented this change in routine and rose in revolt against the substitute—a violent blow with the whip. The love pains that rent her own breast robbed her of all feeling for the suffering of the favourite pupil of her sweetest hours, which she devoted to his education.

Corduanspitz had not put in an appearance the whole day, but had remained with Herr Dapsul von Zabelthau in the tower, where important operations were no doubt being performed. Now, however, Fräulein Ännchen observed the little man tottering across the courtyard in the glow of the setting sun. In his bright yellow habit he looked to her more repulsive than ever, and the droll way in which he hopped this way and that, seeming at every instant to trip and fall and bounce up again—at which anyone else would have laughed himself sick—only caused her more chagrin. Finally, indeed, she put both hands over her face to shut out the sight of the loathsome buffoon. Then suddenly she felt a tug at her apron. "Down, Feldmann," she cried, thinking it was the dog tugging at her. But it was not the dog; when Fräulein Ännchen took her hands from her face she saw Baron Porphyrio von Ockerodastes, who bounded with unparalleled nimbleness on to her lap and threw both arms around her neck. Fräulein Ännchen screamed loudly with terror and disgust and jumped up from her chair. But Corduanspitz hung on to her neck and seemed all of a sudden to weigh at least twenty hundredweight, so that he pulled poor Ännchen down with the speed of an arrow into the chair in which she had been sitting. Now, however, Corduanspitz slipped down off Ännchen's lap, dropped as elegantly and politely as his lack of balance would allow on to his little right knee, and said in a clear, rather curious, but not unpleasant voice: "Adored Fräulein Anna von Zabelthau, most excellent lady, chosen bride, do not be angry, I beg, I beseech you! Do not be angry, do not be angry! I know you think my people have laid waste your beautiful vegetable garden in order to build my palace. O powers of the universe! If only you could look into my small body and see my heart that is jumping with love and generous impulses! If you could discover all the cardinal virtues gathered in my breast beneath this yellow satin! Oh, how far removed I am from that deed of horrid violence which you ascribe to me! How could a gentle prince possibly harm his own sub . . . but no, stop, what are words, what are speeches?! You must see for yourself, my betrothed, all the splendours that await you! You must come with me to my palace, where a joyful people await the adored mistress of their lord!"

It is easy to imagine how horrified Fräulein Ännchen was by Corduanspitz's demand, how she struggled against moving one step to follow the terrifying buffoon. But Corduanspitz continued to describe in such emphatic terms the extraordinary beauty, the boundless wealth of the vegetable garden that was really his palace that she finally decided at least to peep into the tent, which could do her no harm at all. The little man turned at least a dozen cartwheels in succession for joy and delight, then took Fräulein Ännchen very tenderly by the hand and led her through the garden to his silken palace.

Fräulein Ännchen stopped dead as though rooted in the soil, with a loud "Oh!," as the entrance curtains were drawn aside to reveal the prospect of an endless kitchen garden more splendid than she had ever seen in her loveliest dreams of vegetable luxuriance. Every kind of green and root vegetable, of salad, pea and bean, flourished there in a radiant splendour beyond the power of words to describe. The music of pipes and drums and cymbals rang out with redoubled vigour, and the four courtly gentlemen whom Fräulein Ännchen had already met, to wit Herr von Schwarzrettig, Monsieur de Roccambolle, Signor di Broccoli, and Pan Kapustowicz, approached with many ceremonious bows.

"My chamberlains," said Porphyrio von Ockerodastes with a smile as, preceded by these gentlemen, he led Fräulein Ännchen through the double rank formed by the guard of English red carrots to the centre of the field, where stood a sumptuous high throne. Round this throne the great ones of the kingdom were gathered, the lettuce princes with the bean princesses, the cucumber counts with the melon dukes at their head, the cabbage ministers, the onion and beetroot generals, the kale ladies, and so on, all in the most magnificent attire appropriate to their rank and estate. And among them a hundred or so of the dearest lavender and fennel pages ran about spreading sweet odours. As Ockerodastes mounted the throne with Fräulein Ännchen, the Lord High Chamberlain Turnip waved his long staff, and immediately the music ceased and everyone listened in silent reverence. Then Ockerodastes raised his voice and, speaking very solemnly, said: "My faithful and beloved subjects, behold here at my side the noble Fräulein Anna von Zabelthau, whom I have chosen as my consort. Richly endowed as she is with beauty and virtue, she has long looked upon you with the eyes of mother-love and has provided and tended a soft and fertile bed for you. She will always be and remain a true and worthy mother of our country. Now show your dutiful approval and orderly jubilation at the act of benevolence which I am about to perform towards you!"

At a second sign from the Lord High Chamberlain Turnip a thousand-voiced roar of jubilation went up, the bulb artillery fired their salvo, and the band of the Carrot Guards struck up the well-known anthem "Lettuce, lettuce and green parsley."

It was a sublime moment that drew tears of rapture from the great ones of the kingdom, and especially the kale ladies. Fräulein Ännchen was thoroughly bemused, when suddenly she noticed that the little man beside her had a crown sparkling with diamonds on his head and a golden sceptre in his hand. "Oh, oh!" she cried, clapping her hands together in astonishment. "Heaven preserve us! You are much more than you seem, are you not, my dear Herr von Corduanspitz?"

"Adored Anna," replied Ockerodastes very gently, "the stars compelled me to appear to your respected father under a borrowed name. Know, my dearest child, that I am one of the mightiest kings and rule an empire whose frontiers cannot be traced, because cartographers have forgotten to mark them on their maps. It is the King of the Vegetables, Daucus Carota I, who is offering you, O sweetest Anna, his hand and his throne. All the vegetable princes are my vassals, and only on one day a year, in accordance with ancient tradition, does the Bean King reign."

"Then I am to be a queen and possess this splendid and magnificent vegetable garden?" cried Fräulein Ännchen joyfully.

King Daucus Carota assured her once again that such was the case, and added that all vegetables which sprouted from the soil would be subject to his and her dominion. Fräulein Ännchen had not expected anything like this, and she considered that from the moment little Corduanspitz had turned into King Daucus Carota I he had become far less ugly than before and that the crown and sceptre and the royal cloak suited him exceedingly well. When Fräulein Ännchen also took account of his pleasant manner and the riches that would come to her through union with him, she could not escape the conviction that no young country maid could hope to make a better match than she, who in the twinkling of an eye had become a king's bride. Fräulein Ännchen was therefore delighted beyond measure and asked her royal bridegroom whether she could not remain in the beautiful palace there and then, and whether the wedding could not be celebrated the following day. King Daucus replied that, charmed as he was by the ardour of his adored bride, he must postpone his happiness on account of certain conjunctions of the planets. For one thing, it was imperative that Herr Dapsul von Zabelthau should not learn of his son-in-law's royal estate, because otherwise the operations destined to effect the desired union with the sylph Nehahilah might be disturbed. For another, he had promised Herr Dapsul von Zabelthau that both weddings should be celebrated on the same day. Fräulein Ännchen had to promise solemnly that she would not let slip a syllable to Herr Dapsul von Zabelthau concerning what had happened to her; she then left the silken palace to the accompaniment of loud and clamorous jubilation from the populace, who were completely enraptured by her beauty and her courteous and affable behaviour.

In her dreams she saw the kingdom of the entrancing King Daucus Carota again and dissolved in bliss.

The letter she had sent to Herr Amandus von Nebelstern had affected the poor lad most terribly. It was not long before Fräulein Ännchen received the following reply:

Idol of my heart, celestial Anna,
The words of your letter were daggers, sharp-pointed, red-hot, poisoned, murderous daggers that transpierced my breast. O Anna! Are you to be torn from me? What a thought! I can't understand why I didn't go mad on the spot and kick up some frightful, savage rumpus! But, outraged by my dreadful

destiny, I fled from men, and immediately after supper, instead of playing billiards as usual, I rushed out into the forest, where I wrung my hands and cried out your name a thousand times! It began to rain terribly hard and I happened to be wearing a brand new cap of red velvet with a gorgeous golden tassel on top. People say no cap has ever suited me so well as this one. The rain was liable to ruin this superbly tasteful article of dress, but what does amorous despair care for caps, for velvet and gold! I wandered around until I was soaked through, frozen stiff, and assailed by a terrible belly-ache. This drove me to the nearby tavern, where I had some excellent mulled wine prepared and smoked a pipe of your heavenly Virginia with it. I soon felt myself possessed by divine inspiration, I whipped out my notebook and hastily scribbled down a dozen splendid poems, and—such is the wondrous power of poesy!—both amorous despair and belly-ache were gone. I shall communicate to you only the last of these poems and you, O ornament of virgins, will be filled, like me, with joyful hope!

> Shroud me in my grief,
> Candles of love are out
> Within my empty heart
> Raided by a thief.
> Yet the spirit lives,
> Word and rhyme it gives.
> When the poem's down,
> My face has lost its frown.
> Once more within my heart
> Love's candles brightly burn,
> Gone is all my grief,
> Forgotten is the thief.

Yes, my sweet Anna, I shall soon hasten to your aid, a guardian knight, and wrest you from the scoundrel who seeks to rob me of you! So that in the meantime you shall not despair, I am writing you a few divine, consoling aphorisms from my Treasury of Masterpieces, from which you may draw comfort.

> The breast expands, the spirit takes on wings?
> Be gay like Owlglass, heart, who always jests and sings!
> · · · · ·
> Love may feel for love a bitter hate,
> And time itself may sometimes be too late.
> · · · · ·

Love is the scent of flowers, existence without let.
O youth, wash thou the fur, but do not get it wet!
   • • • • •
Say you in winter that a cold wind blows?
Fur coats are warm, friend, as every man knows!

What divine, sublime, pregnant maxims! And how simply, how unassumingly, how concisely expressed! Once more, then, my sweetest maid! Be consoled, carry me in your heart as always. I shall come, I shall save you, I shall press you to my breast shaken by passion's storm,

Your ever true
Amandus von Nebelstern.

P.S. Whatever happens I cannot challenge Herr von Corduanspitz to a duel. For, O Anna, every drop of blood that might flow from your Amandus at the hostile onslaught of a foolhardy adversary is glorious poet's blood, the ichor of the gods, which may not be spilt. The world is justly entitled to claim that a spirit such as mine shall be preserved by every possible means. The poet's weapon is the word, the song. I shall have at my rival with Tyrtaeic battle songs, strike him down with pointed epigrams, beat him to the ground with dithyrambs full of amorous frenzy—these are the weapons of the true poet which, ever victorious, secure him against any attack, and thus armed and accoutred, I shall appear and win your hand in battle, O Anna!

Farewell, once more I press thee to my breast! You may hope everything from my love and especially from my heroic courage, which will shrink from no peril to set you free from the shameful net into which, by all appearances, a demonic monster has lured you!

Fräulein Ännchen received this letter just as she was playing tig with her future bridegroom, King Daucus Carota I, in the meadow beyond the garden, deriving great amusement from ducking quickly down while running at full speed, so that the little king shot straight over her head. Contrary to her usual practice, she slipped her beloved's letter into her pocket without reading it, and we shall see in a minute that it had come too late.

Herr Dapsul von Zabelthau was completely at a loss to understand why Fräulein Ännchen had suddenly changed her mind and fallen in love with Herr Porphyrio von Ockerodastes, whom she had previously found so repulsive. He sought an explanation from the stars, but when the latter gave him no satisfactory answer he was forced to conclude that the human mind was more impenetrable than all the mysteries of the cosmos and not to be understood by any conjunction of the planets. He could not suppose that the bridegroom's higher nature had swayed Ännchen's affections in spite of his obvious lack of all physical beauty. Although, as the gentle reader has already heard, Herr Dapsul von Zabelthau's conception of beauty was infinitely far removed from that held by young ladies, he had at least sufficient worldly experience to know that the said young ladies regard understanding, wit, intelligence, and feeling as desirable tenants only when they occupy a fine house, and that man upon whom a fashionable frock coat does not sit well—even if he be in other respects a Shakespeare, a Goethe, a Tieck, or a Friedrich Richter—runs the risk of being driven from the field by any tolerably well-built hussar in the state uniform the moment he takes it into his head to march against a young girl. Things had turned out differently with Fräulein Ännchen; it was not a question either of beauty or understanding, however, but simply that a poor country maid does not often have a chance of becoming a queen. Herr Dapsul von Zabelthau was unaware of this, however; especially since on this point, too, the stars had let him down.

As may well be imagined, these three people—Herr Porphyrio von Ockerodastes, Herr Dapsul von Zabelthau, and Fräulein Ännchen—were one heart and one soul. Things went so far that Herr Dapsul von Zabelthau left his tower more often than ever before in order to chat with his esteemed son-in-law about all sorts of entertaining subjects; in particular, he now regularly took his lunch down in the house. At this time of day Herr Porphyrio von Ockerodastes also emerged from his silken palace and allowed himself to be fed by Fräulein Ännchen with bread and butter.

"Oh, oh," Fräulein Ännchen frequently giggled into his ear, "oh, oh, if Papa knew that you are really a king, best Corduanspitz."

"Contain yourself, dear heart," replied Daucus Carota I, "contain yourself, dear heart, do not dissolve in rapture. Near, near is your day of joy!"

It happened that the schoolmaster presented Fräulein Ännchen with a bunch of the most magnificent radishes from his garden. Fräulein Ännchen was delighted, because Herr Dapsul von Zabelthau was very fond of radishes, but Ännchen could not take anything from the vegetable garden over which the palace had been built. Moreover, it now occurred to her that among the various leaf and root plants in the palace she had seen everything except radishes.

Fräulein Ännchen quickly cleaned the gift radishes and took them to her father for breakfast. Herr Dapsul von Zabelthau had already mercilessly cut off the crown of leaves from several of them, dipped them in the salt-cellar, and eaten them with relish, when Corduanspitz entered. "O Ockerodastes, my friend, have some radishes," Herr Dapsul von Zabelthau cried out to him. There was still one large, exceptionally fine radish on the plate. Corduanspitz had no sooner caught sight of it than his eyes began to blaze and he shouted in a terrifyingly booming voice: "What, unworthy duke, you still dare to appear before my eyes and even to force your way with atrocious impertinence into a house that is protected by my power? Did I not banish you for ever, you who sought to contest my lawful throne? Away with you, traitorous vassal!"

Two little legs suddenly grew under the fat head of the radish, and with them he quickly jumped off the plate. He then took up a position close in front of Corduanspitz and spoke as follows: "Cruel Daucus Carota I who sought in vain to destroy my clan! Did ever one of your race have such a big head as I and my relatives? Understanding, wisdom, sagacity, we are gifted with all that, and while you frequent kitchens and stables and are of some value only at the height of your youth, so that it is the *diable de la jeunesse* alone that affords your brief, ephemeral joy, we enjoy social intercourse with persons of rank and eminence and are greeted with jubilation the moment we raise our green heads! But I challenge you, O Daucus Carota, even if you are a clumsy great oaf like all your kind! Let us see which of us is the stronger!"

So saying, the Radish Duke brandished a long whip and without more ado set upon King Daucus Carota I. But the latter swiftly drew his little dagger and defended himself bravely. The two little men chased one another about the room in a series of the most astonishing and fantastic leaps, until Daucus Carota had the Radish Duke in such straits that he was forced to make a bold leap out of the open window and take to his heels. Daucus Carota, with whose exceptional agility the gentle reader is already familiar, bounded after him and pursued the Radish Duke across the field.

Herr Dapsul von Zabelthau had watched the frightful hand-to-hand combat in mute, dumbfounded dismay. Now he burst out weeping and wailing: "O daughter Anna! O my poor, unhappy daughter Anna! We are lost—you—I—we are both lost!" And with these words he ran out of the room and climbed as quickly as he could up into his astronomic tower.

Fräulein Ännchen had no idea what on earth had cast her father into a state of such boundless distress all at once. The whole incident had given her exceptional pleasure, and she was joyful at heart to have observed that her bridegroom possessed not only rank and wealth but also courage, for there is probably no girl in the world who can love a coward. Now that she had been convinced of King Daucus Carota's courage she felt very resentful of Herr Amandus von Nebelstern's unwillingness to fight him.

Had she still been in doubt whether to sacrifice Herr Amandus to King Daucus Carota I, she would now have made up her mind to do so, since all her bridegroom's magnificence had been revealed to her. She instantly sat down and wrote the following letter:

My dear Amandus,

"Everything in the world may change, everything passes," says the school-master, and he is quite right. You too, my dear Amandus, are far too wise and learned a student not to agree with the schoolmaster or to be in the least surprised when I tell you that there has also been a slight change in my mind and heart. You can believe me when I say that I am still very fond of you and can well imagine how fine you must look in the red velvet cap with the gold tassel, but as to marriage—you know, dear Amandus, clever as you are and pretty as are the little verses you write, you will never, never become a king, and—do not jump out of your skin, dearest—little Herr von Corduanspitz is not Herr von Corduanspitz, but a mighty king named Daucus Carota I who rules the whole great realm of vegetables and has chosen me for his queen! Since the day my dear little king cast off his incognito he has also grown much better looking, and I can now see how right Papa was when he asserted that the head is a man's crowning glory and hence cannot be too big. At the same time Daucus Carota I—you see how well I can remember and write his beautiful name, now that it seems quite familiar to me—I was going to say, at the same time my little royal bridegroom behaves in such a pleasant and endearing manner that it is quite indescribable. And what courage, what audacity the man has! Before my eyes he put to flight the Radish Duke, who seems to be an ill-mannered, refractory fellow, and you should have seen how Daucus jumped out of the window after him! Nor do I think my Daucus Carota would bother much about your verses; he seems to be a man of fortitude upon whom verses, be they ever so fine and pointed, would have little effect. Well, dear Amandus, accept your destiny like a pious man and do not take it amiss that I am going to become a queen, instead of your wife. But be consoled, I shall always remain your affectionate friend, and if in the future you wish

to be appointed to the Carrot Guard or, since you prefer knowledge to weapons, to the Parsnip Academy or the Ministry of Pumpkins, you have only to say the word and your fortune will be made.

Farewell and do not be angry with your

former betrothed but now
affectionate friend and future queen,
Anna von Zabelthau
(soon to be no longer von Zabelthau, but simply Anna).

P.S. You shall also be kept regularly supplied with the finest Virginian leaves, you can firmly rely on that. Although I am inclined to think that there will be no smoking at my court, a few beds not far from the throne shall immediately be planted out with Virginian tobacco under my special supervision. This will promote culture and morality, and my little Daucus shall have a special law written on the matter.

CHAPTER FIVE

in which news is given of a frightful disaster and the further course of events is reported.

Fräulein Ännchen had just sent off her letter to Herr Amandus von Nebelstern, when Herr Dapsul von Zabelthau came into the room and said in the tearful tone of utter despondency: "O my daughter Anna, how shamefully we have both been betrayed! That infamous scoundrel who lured you into his snare, who made me believe he was Baron Porphyrio von Ockerodastes, called Corduanspitz, a scion of the illustrious family founded by the gnome Tsilmenech in alliance with the noble Cordovan abbess, this infamous scoundrel—learn, and fall in a swoon!—is himself a gnome, but of the lowest order, that which tends vegetables! The gnome Tsilmenech belonged to the noblest order, that entrusted with the care of diamonds. Then comes the order of those who prepare metals in the realm of the Metal King. Then follow the flower gnomes, who are not so high in rank because they are dependent upon the sylphs. The basest and least noble, however, are the vegetable gnomes, and not merely is the deceitful Corduanspitz such a gnome—no, he is actually the king of this race and is called Daucus Carota!"

Instead of swooning, or showing the slightest sign of dismay, Fräulein Ännchen gave her lamenting Papa a friendly smile; the gentle reader already knows why! But when Herr Dapsul von Zabelthau showed great amazement at this and insisted upon trying to bring home to Fräulein Ännchen the enormity of her fate and making her grieve over it, Fräulein Ännchen felt that she could no longer keep the secret entrusted to her. She told Herr Dapsul von Zabelthau that the so-called Baron von Corduanspitz had long since disclosed his true rank to her himself and had thereafter appeared to her so lovable that she desired no other husband. She then went on to describe all the wondrous beauties of the vegetable kingdom into which King Daucus Carota I had introduced her, not forgetting to pay fitting tribute to the strange charm of all the manifold inhabitants of this great realm.

Herr Dapsul von Zabelthau struck his hands together time after time and wept bitterly at the sly malice of the gnome king, who had employed the most ingenious means, which were also the most dangerous to himself, in order to drag the unhappy Anna down into his gloomy demoniac empire.

Splendid and beneficial as the union of any ordinary elemental spirit with a human principle might be, Herr Dapsul von Zabelthau now explained to his attentive daughter—citing as an example the marriage between the gnome Tsilmenech and Magdalena de la Cruz, the success of which was the reason why the treacherous Daucus Carota claimed to be a scion of this family—the position was quite different in the case of the kings and princes of these races of spirits. Whereas the salamander kings were merely irascible, the sylph kings merely haughty, the undine queens merely very infatuated and jealous, the gnome kings, on the contrary, were sly, malicious, and cruel; for no other reason than to avenge themselves upon the children of the earth, who abducted their vassals, they would seek to entice one of them; the victim was then entirely divested of his or her human form—becoming just as misshapen as the gnomes themselves—and forced to descend into the earth, never to reappear.

Fräulein Ännchen seemed unwilling to believe all the evil which Herr Dapsul von Zabelthau imputed to her beloved Daucus; on the contrary, she began once more to enumerate all the wonders of the vegetable kingdom over which she would soon be ruling.

"Blind and foolish child!" cried the enraged Herr Dapsul von Zabelthau. "Do you not credit your father with sufficient Cabbalistic wisdom to know that everything the infamous Daucus Carota has shown you is nothing but a snare and a delusion? No, you do not believe me; to save you I must convince you, and to do this I must employ the most desperate means. Come with me!"

For the second time, Fräulein Ännchen had now to ascend with her father into the astronomic tower. From a large box Herr Dapsul von Zabelthau took out a quantity of yellow, red, white, and green ribbons and, to the accompaniment of a curious ceremonial, wrapped Fräulein Ännchen in them from head to toe. He did the same with himself and then the two of them, Fräulein Ännchen and Herr Dapsul von Zabelthau, cautiously approached the silken palace of King Daucus Carota I. On her father's orders, Fräulein Ännchen slit open a seam with a pair of scissors she had brought with her and looked inside.

Heaven preserve us, what did she see instead of the beautiful vegetable garden, instead of the Carrot Guard, the kale ladies, the lavender pages, the lettuce princes, and everything that had seemed to her so magnificent? She looked down into a deep puddle that appeared to be filled with colourless, nauseating mud. And in this mud there wriggled and squiggled all kinds of horrible creatures from the womb of the earth. Fat-rain worms writhed slowly in tangled masses, while beetle-like creatures stretched out their short legs and crawled laboriously away. On their backs they carried large onions that had ugly human faces and grinned and squinted at one another with murky yellow eyes and tried to grasp each other's long, crooked noses with the little claws that grew just under their ears, and drag one another down into the slime, while long, naked slugs slowly weltered in a seething mass and stretched up their long horns out of the depths. Fräulein Ännchen almost swooned with horror at this loathsome sight. She put both hands over her face and ran away as fast as her legs would carry her.

"Now do you see," Herr Dapsul von Zabelthau said to her, "how shamefully the detestable Daucus Carota deceived you, by showing you a magnificence that lasts only for a brief moment? He had his vassals don gala dress and his guards the uniform of the state in order to entice you with their dazzling splendour! But now you have seen the kingdom over which you would rule in its négligé, and once you were the horrible Daucus Carota's wife you would be forced to remain in the subterranean realm and never emerge again upon the surface of the earth! And if . . . oh . . . oh . . . what do I see, unhappiest of fathers!"

Herr Dapsul von Zabelthau now lapsed into such a state of frantic distress that Fräulein Ännchen was left in no doubt that some fresh disaster must have descended upon them. Fearfully, she asked the cause of her Papa's heart-rending laments; but he was sobbing so bitterly he could only stammer: "O—daugh-ter—just—look—at—yourself!" Fräulein Ännchen ran into the house, looked at herself in the mirror, and started back in mortal terror.

She had good cause to be terrified. The situation was this: just as Herr Dapsul von Zabelthau was trying to open the eyes of King Daucus Carota's bride to the risk she was running of gradually losing her appearance and shape and changing bit by bit into the true image of a gnome queen, he perceived something terrible already taking place. Fräulein Ännchen's head had grown much fatter and her skin had turned saffron-yellow, making her look quite horrible. Although Fräulein Ännchen was not particularly vain, she was nevertheless girl enough to realize that to become ugly was the most terrible misfortune that could befall one here on earth. How often had she pictured the glorious joy she would feel, when, as a queen, she drove to church beside her royal husband in the coach and eight with a crown on her head, dressed in satin and decked out with diamond and gold necklaces and rings, amazing all the women, not excluding the schoolmaster's wife, and imposing respect even upon the proud gentry of the village to whose diocese Dapsulheim belonged; yes—how often had she indulged in these and other bizarre dreams! Fräulein Ännchen burst into tears!

"Anna—my daughter Anna, come up to me at once!" Thus Herr Dapsul von Zabelthau called down through the speaking-tube.

Fräulein Ännchen found her Papa dressed in a kind of miner's outfit. Speaking with composure, he said: "When need is greatest, help is often nearest at hand. I have just ascertained that Daucus Carota will not leave his palace today or, indeed, until tomorrow noon. He has assembled the princes of the house, the ministers, and the other great ones of the land in order to confer on the subject of the future crop of winter cabbage. The meeting is an important one and may last so long that we get no winter cabbage at all this year. I intend to employ this time, when Daucus Carota is so absorbed by matters of state that he does not notice me and my activities, to devise a weapon by means of which I can perhaps combat and defeat the base gnome, so that he is compelled to flee and leave you your freedom. While I am at work, gaze fixedly through this tube at the tent and tell me at once if you see anyone looking out or actually emerging from it."

Fräulein Ännchen did as she was bid, but the tent remained closed. In spite of the fact that Herr Dapsul von Zabelthau was hammering away hard at metal plates a few paces behind her, however, she frequently heard wild shouting that seemed to come from the tent and then loud slapping sounds, as though someone's ears were being boxed. She reported this to Herr Dapsul von Zabelthau, who was delighted and said that the more violently they quarrelled inside, the less likely they were to notice what was being forged to their ruin outside.

Fräulein Ännchen was no little surprised when she saw that Herr Dapsul von Zabelthau had hammered out of copper a few absolutely charming saucepans and equally delightful frying-pans. Looking at them with an expert eye, she could see that the tinning was exceptionally well done and that her Papa had fully conformed with all the laws governing the work of coppersmiths; she asked whether she might not take the fine utensils and use them in the kitchen.

At this, Herr Dapsul von Zabelthau smiled mysteriously and merely replied: "All in good time, my daughter Anna, all in good time, now go downstairs and wait and see what happens in our house tomorrow."

Herr Dapsul von Zabelthau had smiled, and it was this which gave the unhappy Ännchen hope and confidence.

The following day, as noon approached, Herr Dapsul von Zabelthau came down with his saucepans and frying-pans, went into the kitchen, and requested Fräulein Ännchen and the maid to leave, as he wished to prepare the midday meal on his own today. He particularly exhorted Fräulein Ännchen to be as amiable and affectionate as possible towards Corduanspitz, who would no doubt shortly make his appearance.

Corduanspitz, or rather King Daucus Carota I, did indeed soon appear, and if he had previously acted as though deeply in love, today he was the very embodiment of delight and rapture. To her horror, Fräulein Ännchen noticed that she had already grown so small that Daucus had no difficulty in jumping up on to her lap and hugging and kissing her, which the unhappy girl had to endure in spite of her profound aversion to the horrid little monster.

At last Herr Dapsul von Zabelthau entered and said: "O excellent Porphyrio von Ockerodastes, will you not accompany my daughter and myself into the kitchen and see how neatly and hospitably your future wife has arranged everything there?''

Fräulein Ännchen had never before seen in her father's face the sly, malicious expression it wore as he took little Daucus by the arm and dragged him almost forcibly out of the room into the kitchen. At a sign from her father, Fräulein Ännchen followed them.

Fräulein Ännchen's heart leapt when she saw the splendidly crackling fire, the glowing coals, and the pretty copper saucepans and frying-pans on the stove. As Herr Dapsul von Zabelthau led Corduanspitz close to the stove, the hissing and bubbling in the saucepans and frying-pans grew louder and louder. Then the hissing and bubbling turned into frightened whimpering and groaning, and from one of the saucepans a voice wailed: "O Daucus Carota, O my king, save thy faithful vassals, save us poor carrots! Cut in pieces, flung into injurious water, painfully stuffed with butter and salt, we languish in unspeakable suffering which noble parsley youths share with us!" And from a frying-pan came the lament: "O Daucus Carota, O my king, save thy faithful vassals, save us poor carrots! We are frying in hell and we have been given so little water that terrible thirst compels us to drink our own heart's blood." And from another saucepan a voice whimpered: "O Daucus Carota, O my king, save thy vassals, save us poor carrots! A brutal cook has hollowed us out, chopped up our inside and stuffed it back in again mixed with all sorts of foreign matter, with eggs, cream, and butter, so that all our senses and powers of understanding are in confusion and we ourselves no longer know what we are thinking!" Then a babble of voices screamed and cried from all the saucepans and frying-pans: "O Daucus Carota, mighty king, save, oh save thy faithful vassals, save us poor carrots!"

Thereupon Corduanspitz screeched loudly, "Damned, idiotic foolishness!", bounded with his usual agility up on to the stove, looked into one of the saucepans, lost his balance, and fell in. Herr Dapsul von Zabelthau quickly sprang towards him and tried to close the lid of the saucepan, exclaiming jubilantly: "Caught!" But Corduanspitz sprang out of the saucepan with the force of a spring and struck Herr Dapsul von Zabelthau several cracking blows across the mouth, crying: "Impertinent simpleton of a Cabbalist, you shall pay for that! Out, boys, all together, out!"

At this, a sound came from all the pots and pans like the onrush of Wotan's Host, and hundreds and hundreds of horrible little fellows the length of a finger hooked themselves firmly all over Herr Dapsul von Zabelthau's body and hurled him backwards into a large basin and prepared him for cooking by pouring over him the scalding contents of all the vessels and sprinkling him with chopped eggs, mace, and grated wheaten rolls. Then Daucus Carota bounded out of the window and his subjects did likewise.

Fräulein Ännchen sank down in horror before the basin in which her poor father lay ready to be cooked; she took him to be dead, since he did not give the slightest sign of life. She began to lament: "Oh, my poor Papa—oh, now you are dead and nothing can save me from the fiendish Daucus!" At this, however, Herr Dapsul von Zabelthau opened his eyes, leapt with renewed energy out of the basin, and yelled in a terrifying voice Fräulein Ännchen had never heard him use before: "Ha, despicable Daucus Carota, my powers are not yet exhausted! You will soon see what the impertinent simpleton of a Cabbalist can do!"

Fräulein Ännchen quickly brushed off the chopped eggs, mace, and grated wheaten rolls with the kitchen broom. Then Herr Dapsul seized a copper saucepan, set it on his head like a helmet, took a frying-pan in his left hand and a big iron ladle in his right, and, thus armed and accoutred, rushed out of the house. Fräulein Ännchen saw Herr Dapsul von Zabelthau running at full speed towards Corduanspitz's tent and yet not moving from the spot. She fell senseless at the sight.

When she came to, Herr Dapsul von Zabelthau had vanished, and she fell into a state of terrible anxiety when he did not return in the evening, during the night, or even the following morning. She could not help surmising that some fresh enterprise had come to a still more disastrous end.

CHAPTER SIX

which is the last and at the same time the most edifying of all.

Fräulein Ännchen was sitting alone in her room, plunged in profound grief, when the door opened and who should come in but Herr Amandus von Nebelstern? Overcome with shame and regret, Fräulein Ännchen let loose a flood of tears and begged in the most doleful tones: "O my best beloved Amandus, forgive what I wrote you in my blindness! But I was bewitched and probably still am. Save me, save me, my Amandus! I look yellow and repulsive, woe is me, but I have kept my faithful heart and do not want to be a queen!"

"I don't know what you are complaining about, my dear young lady," replied Amandus von Nebelstern, "since the finest, most splendid lot has fallen to you."

"Oh, do not mock me," cried Fräulein Ännchen. "I have been punished severely enough for my stupid pride in wanting to become a queen!"

"I really don't understand you, my dear young lady," continued Herr Amandus von Nebelstern. "If I am to be honest, I must admit that your last letter put me in a state of rage and despair. I beat the serving lad, then the poodle, smashed a few glasses—and, you know, there's no joking with a student who is breathing vengeance! But once I had worked off my rage, I decided to hurry here and see with my own eyes why and to whom I had lost my beloved bride. Love knows neither rank nor estate, I wanted to question King Daucus Carota himself and ask him whether he really was going to marry my betrothed or not. But everything worked out differently when I got here. As I was passing the fine tent that has been set up outside, King Daucus Carota stepped out and I soon perceived that I had before me the most amiable of all possible princes, although I have never seen one before; just imagine, my dear young lady, he immediately sensed in me the sublime poet, lauded to the skies my verses which he has not yet read, and offered me the post of court poet in his service. Such a position has long been the splendid goal of my most ardent desires, and I therefore accepted his offer with delight. O my dear young lady, with what inspiration I shall sing your praises! A poet can be in love with queens and princesses, or rather it is part of his duties to choose such an exalted personage as the lady of his heart, and if this renders him slightly mad it produces the divine delirium without which there can be no poetry, and nobody should be surprised at the poet's rather strange behaviour; they should think of the great Tasso, who also suffered a certain clouding of his common sense as a result of falling in love with the Princess Leonora d'Este. Yes, my dear young lady, though you will soon be a queen, you shall yet remain the lady of my heart, whom I shall raise to the lofty stars in the most sublime and godly verses!"

"What, you have seen the knavish goblin and he . . ." Fräulein Ännchen burst out in amazement; but at this moment the object of her wrath, the little gnomic king, entered in person and said in tender tones: "O my dear, sweet bride, idol of my heart, have no fear that I am angry on account of Herr Dapsul von Zabelthau's little slip. No—and all the less because it actually furthered my happiness and as a result of it my solemn wedding to you, my most lovely one, can already be celebrated tomorrow, something I had not previously been able to hope for. You will be glad to know that I have chosen Herr Amandus von Nebelstern to be our court poet, and I should like him at once to afford us a specimen of his talent and sing us something now. But let us go to the arbour, for I love the open air; I shall sit on your lap and you, dearest bride, can scratch my head a little during the song, which is something I enjoy on such occasions!"

Petrified with fear and horror, Fräulein Ännchen meekly obeyed. Daucus Carota sat on her lap in the arbour, she scratched his head, and Herr Amandus von Nebelstern, accompanying himself on the guitar, began the first of the twelve dozen songs which he had himself written and set to music and bound together in a thick tome.

It is a pity that these songs are not written down in the Chronicle of Dapsulheim, from which the whole of this story is taken; there is merely a remark to the effect that passing peasants stopped and inquired curiously who was suffering such agonies in Herr Dapsul von Zabelthau's arbour that he had to give vent to these fearful cries of pain.

Daucus Carota twisted and turned on Fräulein Ännchen's lap and groaned and whimpered more and more bitterly, as though he were suffering from a terrible colic. Fräulein Ännchen observed to her astonishment that while Amandus was singing, Corduanspitz was growing smaller and smaller. Finally, Herr Amandus von Nebelstern sang the following sublime lines (the only song that is actually recorded in the Chronicle):

> List how the singer sings his lay!
> The scent of flowers and shining dreams
> Drift through rosy realms of space
> Towards some golden far-away,
> Blessed, heavenly far-away!
> Where iridescent rainbow gleams,
> Flower petals hang in veils like lace.
> O childish heart, so full of love,
> You long to be like turtle dove,
> To bill and coo and peck and patter

Where no one sees and 'tis no matter.
All this is in the singer's lay.
He sings the blissful far-away,
And drifts with his dreams through heavenly space
Where starlight knits its golden lace.
Eternal longing fills his breast,
He sings his song at love's behest.
The flames of love that blaze within
Set his poor, heated brain a-spin.
Out of the world and out of time
He puts his burning thoughts in rhyme
And . . .

Daucus Carota, who had shrunk to a tiny little carrot, uttered a loud screech, slipped down from Ännchen's lap and into the earth, so that in a moment he had completely disappeared. Thereupon the grey toadstool that seemed to have grown up during the night beside the grassy bank, shot up into the air; but the toadstool was in fact Herr Dapsul von Zabelthau's grey felt cap, and he himself was underneath it and flung himself upon Herr Amandus von Nebelstern's chest and cried ecstatically: "O my dearest, best beloved Herr Amandus von Nebelstern! With your powerful poem of conjuration you have outdone all my Cabbalistic wisdom. What the most profound magic art, what the reckless courage of the despairing philosopher was unable to achieve, your verses have done, entering into the body of the treacherous Daucus Carota like the strongest poison, so that despite his gnomic nature he would have perished miserably of the colic if he had not escaped fast enough into his own kingdom! My daughter Anna is set free, and I am set free from the terrible spell that held me here in the shape of an obnoxious toadstool, in danger of being slain by the hands of my own daughter! For the good girl mercilessly removes all toadstools from garden and field with a sharp spade, if they do not at once prove their noble character like mushrooms. Thanks, my warmest and most heartfelt thanks and—is it not so, most esteemed Herr Amandus von Nebelstern, everything will remain as it was with regard to my daughter? It is true, woe is me, that she has been cheated of her pretty appearance by the villainy of the malignant gnome, but you are far too much of a philosopher to . . ."

"O Papa, my best Papa," exulted Fräulein Ännchen, "just look there, just look there, the silken palace has disappeared. He has gone, the ugly monster, along with his train of lettuce princes and pumpkin ministers and all the rest!"

With these words, Fräulein Ännchen raced off to the vegetable garden. Herr Dapsul von Zabelthau ran after his daughter as fast as he could go, and Herr Amandus von Nebelstern followed, grumbling into his beard: "I really don't know what to make of all this, but I can say for sure that the horrid little carrot fellow is an impudent prosaic clown and no poetic king, otherwise he would not have got the colic and crawled into the ground on hearing my sublimest song!"

As Fräulein Ännchen stood in the vegetable garden, where there was not a blade of green to be seen, she felt an atrocious pain in the finger on which she was wearing the fatal ring. At the same time a heart-rending cry rose from the depths and the tip of a carrot peeped forth. Correctly guided by her intuition, Fräulein Ännchen quickly and easily slipped off the ring, which hitherto she had been unable to remove from her finger, and set it on the carrot; the latter vanished and the lament ceased. But, oh wonder, Fräulein Ännchen was all at once as pretty as before, well proportioned, and as white as can be expected of any country maid. Both Fräulein Ännchen and Herr Dapsul von Zabelthau rejoiced vociferously, while Herr Amandus von Nebelstern stood there utterly bewildered and still not knowing what to make of it all.

Fräulein Ännchen took the spade from the hand of the maid, who had come running up, and swung it in the air with a jubilant cry of "Now let us work"; but as bad luck would have it she struck Herr Amandus von Nebelstern hard on the head (just on the spot where the "bump of common sense" is said to be located), so that he fell down as though dead. Fräulein Ännchen flung the murderous instrument far from her, threw herself down beside her beloved, and burst into desperate wails of anguish, while the maid poured a whole jug of water over him and Herr Dapsul von Zabelthau quickly ascended his astronomic tower, to inquire of the stars as fast as he could whether Herr Amandus von Nebelstern was really dead. It was not long before the latter reopened his eyes, jumped up, wet as he was, took Fräulein Ännchen in his arms, and cried with all the rapture of love: "O my best, my dearest Ännchen! Now we have each other again!"

The very remarkable, almost incredible effect of this incident on the lovers was soon apparent. The minds of both were curiously changed.

Fräulein Ännchen had acquired an aversion to handling the spade and really ruled like a true queen over the vegetable kingdom, which she cared for lovingly, making sure that her subjects were properly hoed and weeded, but without taking any part herself in the work, which she left to faithful maids. Herr Amandus von Nebelstern, on the other hand, came to regard everything he had written and his whole ambition to be a poet as extremely silly and pretentious, and instead devoted himself to studying the works of the great, true poets of the past and present; in this way his whole inner being was filled with a beneficial enthusiasm that left no place for thoughts of his own ego. He became convinced that a poem must be something other than the muddled jumble of words produced by a sober delirium, and after he had thrown into the fire all the versifyings with which he had previously given himself airs in a spirit of boastful self-approval, he became once more a sensible young man, lucid in mind and heart, as he had been before.

One morning Herr Dapsul von Zabelthau really did come down from his astronomic tower and escort Fräulein Ännchen and Herr Amandus von Nebelstern to the church to be married.

Thereafter they lived a happy and contented married life; but as to whether anything finally came of Herr Dapsul's wedlock with the sylph Nehahilah, the Chronicle of Dapsulheim is silent.

TRANSLATED BY MICHAEL BULLOCK

Under the Garden

Graham Greene

Graham Greene is one of the great contemporary writers in the English language, universally respected for his novels such as The Heart of the Matter *and admired for such entertainments as* Our Man in Havana. *His fiction often deals with figures in spiritual crisis. This strange story of a world underground seems strikingly original and at the same time uncannily familiar. Seeking some relief from the literal fact of his mortality, a man returns to the summer place of his childhood, in search of the one true wonder he has experienced in his life. Did it really happen, or was it a dream? He desperately needs the wonder, the belief, now.*

PART ONE

I

It was only when the doctor said to him, "Of course the fact that you don't smoke is in your favour," Wilditch realized what it was he had been trying to convey with such tact. Dr. Cave had lined up along one wall a series of X-ray photographs, the whorls of which reminded the patient of those pictures of the earth's surface taken from a great height that he had pored over at one period during the war, trying to detect the tiny grey seed of a launching ramp.

Dr. Cave had explained, "I want you clearly to understand my problem." It was very similar to an intelligence briefing of such "top secret" importance that only one officer could be entrusted with the information. Wilditch felt gratified that the choice had fallen on him, and he tried to express his interest and enthusiasm, leaning forward and examining more closely than ever the photographs of his own interior.

"Beginning at this end," Dr. Cave said, "let me see April, May, June, three months ago, the scar left by the pneumonia is quite obvi-- ous. You can see it here."

"Yes, sir," Wilditch said absent-mindedly. Dr. Cave gave him a puzzled look.

"Now if we leave out the intervening photographs for the moment and come straight to yesterday's, you will observe that this latest one is almost entirely clear, you can only just detect . . ."

"Good," Wilditch said. The doctor's finger moved over what might have been tumuli or traces of prehistoric agriculture.

"But not entirely, I'm afraid. If you look now along the whole series you will notice how very slow the progress has been. Really by this stage the photographs should have shown no trace."

"I'm sorry," Wilditch said. A sense of guilt had taken the place of gratification.

"If we had looked at the last plate in isolation I would have said there was no cause for alarm." The doctor tolled the last three words like a bell. Wilditch thought, Is he suggesting tuberculosis?

"It's only in relation to the others, the slowness . . . it suggests the possibility of an obstruction."

"Obstruction?"

"The chances are that it's nothing, nothing at all. Only I wouldn't be *quite* happy if I let you go without a deep examination. Not *quite* happy." Dr. Cave left the photographs and sat down behind his desk. The long pause seemed to Wilditch like an appeal to his friendship.

"Of course," he said, "if it would make you happy . . ."

It was then the doctor used those revealing words, "Of course the fact that you don't smoke is in your favour."

"Oh"

"I think we'll ask Sir Nigel Sampson to make the examination. In case there is something there, we couldn't have a better surgeon . . . for the operation."

Wilditch came down from Wimpole Street into Cavendish Square looking for a taxi. It was one of those summer days which he never remembered in childhood: grey and dripping. Taxis drew up outside the tall liver-coloured buildings partitioned by dentists and were immediately caught by the commissionaires for the victims released. Gusts of wind barely warmed by July drove the rain aslant across the blank eastern gaze of Epstein's virgin and dripped down the body of her fabulous son. "But it hurt," the child's voice said behind him. "You make a fuss about nothing," a mother—or a governess—replied.

2

This could not have been said of the examination Wilditch endured a week later, but he made no fuss at all, which perhaps aggravated his case in the eyes of the doctors who took his calm for lack of vitality. For the unprofessional to enter a hospital or to enter the services has very much the same effect; there is a sense of relief and indifference; one is placed quite helplessly on a conveyor-belt with no responsibility any more for anything. Wilditch felt himself protected by an organization, while the English summer dripped outside on the coupés of the parked cars. He had not felt such freedom since the war ended.

The examination was over—a bronchoscopy; and there remained a nightmare memory, which survived through the cloud of the anaesthetic, of a great truncheon forced down his throat into the chest and then slowly withdrawn; he woke next morning bruised and raw so that even the act of excretion was a pain. But that, the nurse told him, would pass in one day or two; now he could dress and go home. He was disappointed at the abruptness with which they were thrusting him off the belt into the world of choice again.

"Was everything satisfactory?" he asked, and saw from the nurse's expression that he had shown indecent curiosity.

"I couldn't say, I'm sure," the nurse said. "Sir Nigel will look in, in his own good time."

Wilditch was sitting on the end of the bed tying his tie when Sir Nigel Sampson entered. It was the first time Wilditch had been conscious of seeing him: before he had been a voice addressing him politely out of sight as the anaesthetic took over. It was the beginning of the week-end and Sir Nigel was dressed for the country in an old tweed jacket. He had tousled white hair and he looked at Wilditch with a far-away attention as though he were a float bobbing in mid-stream.

"Ah, feeling better," Sir Nigel said incontrovertibly.

"Perhaps."

"Not very agreeable," Sir Nigel said, "but you know we couldn't let you go, could we, without taking a look?"

"Did you see anything?"

Sir Nigel gave the impression of abruptly moving downstream to a quieter reach and casting his line again.

"Don't let me stop you dressing, my dear fellow." He looked vaguely around the room before choosing a strictly upright chair, then lowered himself on to it as though it were a tuffet which might "give." He began feeling in one of his large pockets—for a sandwich?

"Any news for me?"

"I expect Dr. Cave will be along in a few minutes. He was caught by a rather garrulous patient." He drew a large silver watch out of his pocket—for some reason it was tangled up in a piece of string. "Have to meet my wife at Liverpool Street. Are *you* married?"

"No."

"Oh well, one care the less. Children can be a great responsibility."

"I have a child—but she lives a long way off."

"A long way off? I see."

"We haven't seen much of each other."

"Doesn't care for England?"

"The colour-bar makes it difficult for her." He realized how childish he sounded directly he had spoken, as though he had been trying to draw attention to himself by a bizarre confession, without even the satisfaction of success.

"Ah yes," Sir Nigel said. "Any brothers or sisters? You, I mean."

"An elder brother. Why?"

"Oh well, I suppose it's all on the record," Sir Nigel said, rolling in his line. He got up and made for the door. Wilditch sat on the bed with the tie over his knee. The door opened and Dr. Nigel said, "Ah, here's Dr. Cave. Must run along now. I was just telling Mr. Wilditch that I'll be seeing him again. You'll fix it, won't you?" and he was gone.

"Why should I see him again?" Wilditch asked and then, from Dr. Cave's embarrassment, he saw the stupidity of the question. "Oh, yes, of course, you did find something?"

"It's really very lucky. If caught in time . . . ."

"There's sometimes hope?"

"Oh, there's always hope."

So, after all, Wilditch thought, I am—if I so choose—on the conveyor-belt again.

Dr. Cave took an engagement-book out of his pocket and said briskly, "Sir Nigel has given me a few dates. The tenth is difficult for the clinic, but the fifteenth—Sir Nigel doesn't think we should delay longer than the fifteen."

"Is he a great fisherman?"

"Fisherman? Sir Nigel? I have no idea." Dr. Cave looked aggrieved, as though he were being shown an incorrect chart. "Shall we say the fifteenth?"

"Perhaps I could tell you after the week-end. You see, I have not made up my mind to stay as long as that in England."

"I'm afraid I haven't properly conveyed to you that this is serious, really serious. Your only chance—I repeat your only chance," he spoke like a telegram, "is to have the obstruction removed in time."

"And then, I suppose, life can go on for a few more years."

"It's impossible to guarantee . . . but there have been complete cures."

"I don't want to appear dialectical," Wilditch said, "but I do have to decide, don't I, whether I want my particular kind of life prolonged."

"It's the only one we have," Dr. Cave said.

"I see you are not a religious man—oh, please don't misunderstand me, nor am I. I have no curiosity at all about the future."

3

The past was another matter. Wilditch remembered a leader in the Civil War who rode from an undecided battle mortally wounded. He revisited the house where he was born, the house in which he was married, greeted a few retainers who did not recognize his condition, seeing him only as a tired man upon a horse, and finally—but Wilditch could not recollect how the biography had ended: he saw only a figure of exhaustion slumped over the saddle, as he also took, like Sir Nigel Sampson, a train from Liverpool Street. At Colchester he changed onto the branch line to Winton, and suddenly summer began, the kind of summer he always remembered as one of the conditions of life at Winton. Days had become so much shorter since then. They no longer began at six in the morning before the world was awake.

Winton Hall had belonged, when Wilditch was a child, to his uncle, who had never married, and every summer he lent the house to Wilditch's mother. Winton Hall had been virtually Wilditch's, until school cut the period short, from late June to early September. In memory his mother and brother were shadowy background figures. They were less established even than the machine upon the platform of "the halt" from which he bought Fry's chocolates for a penny a bar: than the oak tree spreading over the green in front of the red-brick wall—under its shade as a child he had distributed apples to soldiers halted there in the hot August of 1914: the group of silver birches on the Winton lawn and the broken fountain, green with slime. In his memory he did not share the house with others: he owned it.

Nevertheless the house had been left to his brother not to him; he was far away when his uncle died and he had never returned since. His brother married, had children (for them the fountain had been mended), the paddock behind the vegetable garden and the orchard, where he used to ride the donkey, had been sold (so his brother had written to him) for building council-houses, but the hall and the garden which he had so scrupulously remembered nothing could change.

Why then go back now and see it in other hands? Was it that at the approach of death one must get rid of everything? If he had accumulated money he would now have been in the mood to distribute it. Perhaps the man who had ridden the horse around the countryside had not been saying goodbye, as his biographer imagined, to what he valued most: he had been ridding himself of illusions by seeing them again with clear and moribund eyes, so that he might be quite bankrupt when death came. He had the will to possess at that absolute moment nothing but his wound.

His brother, Wilditch knew, would be faintly surprised by this visit. He had become accustomed to the fact that Wilditch never came to Winton; they would meet at long intervals at his brother's club in London, for George was a widower by this time, living alone. He always talked to others of Wilditch as a man unhappy in the country, who needed a longer range and stranger people. It was lucky, he would indicate, that the house had been left to him, for Wilditch would probably have sold it in order to travel further. A restless man, never long in one place, no wife, no children, unless the rumours were true that in Africa . . . or it might have been in the

East . . . Wilditch was well aware of how his brother spoke of him. His brother was the proud owner of the lawn, the goldfish pond, the mended fountain, the laurel-path which they had known when they were children as the Dark Walk, the lake, the island . . . Wilditch looked out at the flat hard East Anglian countryside, the meagre hedges and the stubbly grass, which had always seemed to him barren from the salt of Danish blood. All these years his brother had been in occupation, and yet he had no idea of what might lie underneath the garden.

4

The chocolate-machine had gone from Winton Halt, and the halt had been promoted—during the years of nationalization—to a station; the chimneys of a cement-factory smoked along the horizon and council-houses now stood three deep along the line.

Wilditch's brother waited in a Humber at the exit. Some familiar smell of coal-dust and varnish had gone from the waiting-room and it was a mere boy who took his ticket instead of a stooped and greying porter. In childhood nearly all the world is older than oneself.

"Hullo, George," he said in remote greeting to the stranger at the wheel.

"How are things, William?" George asked as they ground on their way—it was part of his character as a countryman that he had never learnt how to drive a car well.

The long chalky slope of a small hill—the highest point before the Ural mountains he had once been told—led down to the village between the bristly hedges. On the left was an abandoned chalk-pit—it had been just as abandoned forty years ago, when he had climbed all over it looking for treasure, in the form of brown nuggets of iron pyrites which when broken showed an interior of starred silver.

"Do you remember hunting for treasure?"

"Treasure?" George said. "Oh, you mean that iron stuff."

Was it the long summer afternoons in the chalk-pit which had made him dream—or so vividly imagine—the discovery of a real treasure? If it was a dream it was the only dream he remembered from those years, or, if it was a story which he had elaborated at night in bed, it must have been the final effort of a poetic imagination that afterwards had been rigidly controlled. In the various services which had over the years taken him from one part of the world to another, imagination was usually a quality to be suppressed. One's job was to provide

facts, to a company (import and export), a newspaper, a government
department. Speculation was discouraged. Now the dreaming child
was dying of the same disease as the man. He was so different from
the child that it was odd to think the child would not outlive him and
go on to quite a different destiny.

George said, "You'll notice some changes, William. When I had
the new bathroom added, I found I had to disconnect the pipes from
the fountain. Something to do with pressure. After all there are no
children now to enjoy it."

"It never played in my time either."

"I had the tennis-lawn dug up during the war, and it hardly seemed
worth while to put it back."

"I'd forgotten that there was a tennis-lawn."

"Don't you remember it, between the pond and goldfish-tank?"

"The pond? Oh, you mean the lake and the island."

"Not much of a lake. You could jump on to the island with a short
run."

"I thought of it as much bigger."

But all measurements had changed. Only for a dwarf does the
world remain the same size. Even the red-brick wall which separated
the garden from the village was lower than he remembered—a mere
five feet, but in order to look over it in those days he had always to
scramble to the top of some old stumps covered deep with ivy and
dusty spiders' webs. There was no sign of these when they drove in:
everything was very tidy everywhere, and a handsome piece of iron-
mongery had taken the place of the swing-gate which they had ruined
as children.

"You keep the place up very well," he said.

"I couldn't manage it without the market-garden. That enables me
to put the gardener's wages down as a professional expense. I have a
very good accountant."

He was put into his mother's room with a view of the lawn and the
silver birches; George slept in what had been his uncle's. The little
bedroom next door which had once been his was now converted into
a tiled bathroom—only the prospect was unchanged. He could see
the laurel bushes where the Dark Walk began, but they were smaller
too. Had the dying horseman found as many changes?

Sitting that night over coffee and brandy, during the long family
pauses Wilditch wondered whether as a child he could possibly have
been so secretive as never to have spoken of his dream, his game,

whatever it was. In his memory the adventure had lasted for several days. At the end of it he had found his way home in the early morning when everyone was asleep: there had been a dog called Joe who bounded towards him and sent him sprawling in the heavy dew of the lawn. Surely there must have been some basis of fact on which the legend had been built. Perhaps he had run away, perhaps he had been out all night—on the island in the lake or hidden in the Dark Walk—and during those hours he had invented the whole story.

Wilditch took a second glass of brandy and asked tentatively, "Do you remember much of those summers when we were children here?" He was aware of something unconvincing in the question: the apparently harmless opening gambit of a wartime interrogation.

"I never cared for the place much in those days," George said surprisingly. "You were a secretive little bastard."

"Secretive?"

"And uncooperative. I had a great sense of duty towards you, but you never realized that. In a year or two you were going to follow me to school. I tried to teach you the rudiments of cricket. You weren't interested. God knows what you were interested in."

"Exploring?" Wilditch suggested, he thought with cunning.

"There wasn't much to explore in fourteen acres. You know, I had such plans for this place when it became mine. A swimming-pool where the tennis-lawn was—it's mainly potatoes now. I meant to drain the pond too—it breeds mosquitoes. Well, I've added two bathrooms and modernized the kitchen, and even that has cost me four acres of pasture. At the back of the house now you can hear the children caterwauling from the council houses. It's all been a bit of a disappointment."

"At least I'm glad you haven't drained the lake."

"My dear chap, why go on calling it the lake? Have a look at it in the morning and you'll see the absurdity. The water's nowhere more than two feet deep." He added, "Oh well, the place won't outlive me. My children aren't interested, and the factories are beginning to come out this way. They'll get a reasonably good price for the land— I haven't much else to leave them." He put some more sugar in his coffee. "Unless, of course, you'd like to take it on when I am gone?"

"I haven't the money and anyway there's no cause to believe that I won't be dead first."

"Mother was against my accepting the inheritance," George said. "She never liked the place."

"I thought she loved her summers here." The great gap between their memories astonished him. They seemed to be talking about different places and different people.

"It was terribly inconvenient, and she was always in trouble with the gardener. You remember Ernest? She said she had to wring every vegetable out of him. (By the way he's still alive, though retired of course—you ought to look him up in the morning. It would please him. He still feels he owns the place.) And then, you know, she always thought it would have been better for us if we could have gone to the seaside. She had an idea that she was robbing us of a heritage—buckets and spades and sea-water-bathing. Poor mother, she couldn't afford to turn down Uncle Henry's hospitality. I think in her heart she blamed father for dying when he did without providing for holidays at the sea."

"Did you talk it over with her in those days?"

"Oh no, not then. Naturally she had to keep a front before the children. But when I inherited the place—you were in Africa—she warned Mary and me about the difficulties. She had very decided views, you know, about any mysteries, and that turned her against the garden. Too much shrubbery, she said. She wanted everything to be very clear. Early Fabian training, I daresay."

"It's odd. I don't seem to have known her very well."

"You had a passion for hide-and-seek. She never liked that. Mystery again. She thought it a bit morbid. There was a time when we couldn't find you. You were away for hours."

"Are you sure it was hours? Not a whole night?"

"I don't remember it at all myself. Mother told me." They drank their brandy for a while in silence. Then George said, "She asked Uncle Henry to have the Dark Walk cleared away. She thought it was unhealthy with all the spiders' webs, but he never did anything about it."

"I'm surprised *you* didn't."

"Oh, it was on my list, but other things had priority, and now it doesn't seem worth while to make more changes." He yawned and stretched. "I'm used to early bed. I hope you don't mind. Breakfast at 8:30?"

"Don't make any changes for me."

"There's just one thing I forgot to show you. The flush is tricky in your bathroom."

George led the way upstairs. He said, "The local plumber didn't do a very good job. Now, when you've pulled this knob, you'll find the flush never quite finishes. You have to do it a second time—sharply like this."

Wilditch stood at the window looking out. Beyond the Dark Walk and the space where the lake must be, he could see the splinters of light given off by the council-houses; through one gap in the laurels there was even a street-light visible, and he could hear the faint sound of television-sets joining together different programmes like the discordant murmur of a mob.

He said, "That view would have pleased mother. A lot of the mystery gone."

"I rather like it this way myself," George said, "on a winter's evening. It's a kind of companionship. As one gets older one doesn't want to feel quite alone on a sinking ship. Not being a churchgoer myself . . ." he added, leaving the sentence lying like a torso on its side.

"At least we haven't shocked mother in that way, either of us."

"Sometimes I wish I'd pleased her, though, about the Dark Walk. And the pond—how she hated that pond too."

"Why?"

"Perhaps because you liked to hide on the island. Secrecy and mystery again. Wasn't there something you wrote about it once? A story?"

"Me? A story? Surely not."

"I don't remember the circumstances. I thought—in a school magazine? Yes, I'm sure of it now. She was very angry indeed and she wrote rude remarks in the margin with a blue pencil. I saw them somewhere once. Poor mother."

George led the way into the bedroom. He said, "I'm sorry there's no bedside light. It was smashed last week, and I haven't been into town since."

"It's all right. I don't read in bed."

"I've got some good detective-stories downstairs if you wanted one."

"Mysteries?"

"Oh, mother never minded those. They came under the heading of puzzles. Because there was always an answer."

Beside the bed was a small bookcase. He said, "I brought some of mother's books here when she died and put them in her room. Just the ones that she had liked and no bookseller would take." Wilditch made out a title, *My Apprenticeship* by Beatrice Webb. "Sentimental, I suppose, but I didn't want actually to *throw away* her favourite books. Good night." He repeated, "I'm sorry about the light."

"It really doesn't matter."

George lingered at the door. He said, "I'm glad to see you here, William. There were times when I thought you were avoiding the place."

"Why should I?"

"Well, you know how it is. I never go to Harrods now because I was there with Mary a few days before she died."

"Nobody has died here. Except Uncle Henry, I suppose."

"No, of course not. But why did you, suddenly, decide to come?"

"A whim," Wilditch said.

"I suppose you'll be going abroad again soon?"

"I suppose so."

"Well, good night." He closed the door.

Wilditch undressed, and then, because he felt sleep too far away, he sat down on the bed under the poor centrelight and looked along the rows of shabby books. He opened Mrs. Beatrice Webb at some account of a trade union congress and put it back. (The foundations of the future Welfare State were being truly and uninterestingly laid.) There were a number of Fabian pamphlets heavily scored with the blue pencil which George had remembered. In one place Mrs. Wilditch had detected an error of one decimal point in some statistics dealing with agricultural imports. What passionate concentration must have gone to that discovery. Perhaps because his own life was coming to an end, he thought how little of this, in the almost impossible event of a future, she would have carried with her. A fairy-story in such an event would be a more valuable asset than a Fabian graph, but his mother had not approved of fairy-stories. The only children's book on these shelves was a history of England. Against an enthusiastic account of the battle of Agincourt she had pencilled furiously,

> And what good came of it at last?
> Said little Peterkin.

The fact that his mother had quoted a poem was in itself remarkable.

The storm which he had left behind in London had travelled east in his wake and now overtook him in short gusts of wind and wet that slapped at the pane. He thought, for no reason, It will be a rough night on the island. He had been disappointed to discover from George that the origin of the dream which had travelled with him round the world was probably no more than a story invented for a school-magazine and forgotten again, and just as that thought occurred to him, he saw a bound volume called *The Warburian* on the shelf.

He took it out, wondering why his mother had preserved it, and found a page turned down. It was the account of a cricket-match against Lancing and Mrs. Wilditch had scored the margin: "Wilditch One did good work in deep field." Another turned-down leaf produced a passage under the heading Debating Society: "Wilditch One spoke succinctly to the motion." The motion was "That this House has no belief in the social policies of His Majesty's Government." So George in those days had been a Fabian too.

He opened the book at random this time and a letter fell out. It had a printed heading, Dean's House, Warbury, and it read, "Dear Mrs. Wilditch, I was sorry to receive your letter of the 3rd and to learn that you were displeased with the little fantasy published by your younger son in *The Warburian.* I think you take a rather extreme view of the tale which strikes me as quite a good imaginative exercise for a boy of thirteen. Obviously he has been influenced by the term's reading of *The Golden Age*—which after all, fanciful though it may be, was written by a governor of the Bank of England." (Mrs. Wilditch had made several blue exclamation marks in the margin—perhaps representing her view of the Bank.) "Last term's *Treasure Island* too may have contributed. It is always our intention at Warbury to foster the imagination—which I think you rather harshly denigrate when you write of 'silly fancies.' We have scrupulously kept our side of the bargain, knowing how strongly you feel, and the boy is not 'subjected,' as you put it, to any religious instruction at all. Quite frankly, Mrs. Wilditch, I cannot see any trace of religious feeling in this little fancy—I have read it through a second time before writing to you— indeed the treasure, I'm afraid, is only too material, and quite at the mercy of those 'who break in and steal.' "

Wilditch tried to find the place from which the letter had fallen, working back from the date of the letter. Eventually he found it: "The Treasure on the Island" by W.W.

Wilditch began to read.

5

*"In the middle of the garden there was a great lake and in the middle of the
lake an island with a wood. Not everybody knew about the lake, for to reach it
you had to find your way down a long dark walk, and not many people's
nerves were strong enough to reach the end. Tom knew that he was likely to be
undisturbed in that frightening region, and so it was there that he constructed
a raft out of old packing cases, and one drear wet day when he knew that
everybody would be shut in the house, he dragged the raft to the lake and
paddled it across to the island. As far as he knew he was the first to land there
for centuries.*

*"It was all overgrown on the island, but from a map he had found in an
ancient sea-chest in the attic he made his measurements, three paces north from
the tall umbrella pine in the middle and then two paces to the right. There
seemed to be nothing but scrub, but he had brought with him a pick and a
spade and with the dint of almost superhuman exertions he uncovered an iron
ring sunk in the grass. As first he thought it would be impossible to move, but
by inserting the point of the pick and levering it he raised a kind of stone lid
and there below, going into the darkness, was a long narrow passage.*

*"Tom had more than the usual share of courage, but even he would not
have ventured further if it had not been for the parlous state of the family
fortunes since his father had died. His elder brother wanted to go to Oxford
but for lack of money he would probably have to sail before the mast, and the
house itself, of which his mother was passionately fond, was mortgaged to the
hilt to a man in the City called Sir Silas Dedham whose name did not belie his
nature."*

Wilditch nearly gave up reading. He could not reconcile this childish story with the dream which he remembered. Only the "drear wet
night" seemed true as the bushes rustled and dripped and the birches
swayed outside. A writer, so he had always understood, was supposed
to order and enrich the experience which was the source of his story,
but in that case it was plain that the young Wilditch's talents had not
been for literature. He read with growing irritation, wanting to ex-
claim again and again to this thirteen-year-old ancestor of his, "But
why did you leave that out? Why did you alter this?"

*"This passage opened out into a great cave stacked from floor to ceiling with
gold bars and chests overflowing with pieces of eight. There was a jewelled
crucifix"*—Mrs. Wilditch has underlined the word in blue—*"set with
precious stones which had once graced the chapel of a Spanish galleon and on
a marble table were goblets of precious metal."*

But, as he remembered, it was an old kitchen-dresser, and there were no pieces of eight, no crucifix, and as for the Spanish galleon . . .

"Tom thanked the kindly Providence which had led him first to the map in the attic" (but there had been no map. Wilditch wanted to correct the story, page by page, much as his mother had done with her blue pencil) *"and then to this rich treasure trove"* (his mother had written in the margin, referring to the kindly Providence, "No trace of religious feeling!!"). *"He filled his pockets with the pieces of eight and taking one bar under each arm, he made his way back along the passage. He intended to keep his discovery secret and slowly day by day to transfer the treasures to the cupboard in his room, thus surprising his mother at the end of the holidays with all this sudden wealth. He got safely home unseen by anyone and that night in bed he counted over his new riches while outside it rained and rained. Never had he heard such a storm. It was as though the wicked spirit of his old pirate ancestor raged against him"* (Mrs. Wilditch had written, "Eternal punishment I suppose!") *"and indeed the next day, when he returned to the island in the lake, whole trees had been uprooted and now lay across the entrance to the passage. Worse still there had been a landslide, and now the cavern must lie hidden forever below the waters of the lake. However,"* the young Wilditch had added briefly forty years ago, *"the treasure already recovered was sufficient to save the family home and send his brother to Oxford."*

Wilditch undressed and got into bed, then lay on his back listening to the storm. What a trivial conventional day-dream W.W. had constructed—out of what? There had been no attic-room—probably no raft: these were preliminaries which did not matter, but why had W.W. so falsified the adventure itself? Where was the man with the beard? The old squawling woman? Of course it had all been a dream, it could have been nothing else but a dream, but a dream too was an experience, the images of a dream had their own integrity, and he felt professional anger at this false report just as his mother had felt at the mistake in the Fabian statistics.

All the same, while he lay there in his mother's bed and thought of her rigid interrogation of W.W.'s story, another theory of the falsifications came to him, perhaps a juster one. He remembered that agents parachuted into France during the bad years after 1940 had been made to memorize a cover-story which they could give, in case of torture, with enough truth in it to be checked. Perhaps forty years ago the pressure to tell had been almost as great on W.W., so that he had been forced to find relief in fantasy. Well, an agent dropped into occupied territory was always given a time-limit after capture. "Keep the interrogators at bay with silence or lies for just so long, and then you may tell all." The time-limit had surely been passed in his case a long time ago, his mother was beyond the possibility of hurt, and Wilditch for the first time deliberately indulged his passion to remember.

He got out of bed and, after finding some notepaper stamped, presumably for income-tax purposes, Winton Small Holdings Limited, in the drawer of the desk, he began to write an account of what he had found—or dreamed that he found—under the garden of Winton Hall. The summer night was nosing wetly around the window just as it had done fifty years ago, but, as he wrote, it began to turn grey and recede; the trees of the garden became visible, so that, when he looked up after some hours from his writing, he could see the shape of the broken fountain and what he supposed were the laurels in the Dark Walk, looking like old men humped against the weather.

PART TWO

I

Never mind how I came to the island in the lake, never mind whether in fact, as my brother says, it is a shallow pond with water only two feet deep (I suppose a raft can be launched on two feet of water, and certainly I must have always come to the lake by way of the Dark Walk, so that it is not at all unlikely that I built my raft there). Never mind what hour it was—I think it was evening, and I had hidden, as I remember it, in the Dark Walk because George had not got the courage to search for me there. The evening turned to rain, just as it's raining now, and George must have been summoned into the house for shelter. He would have told my mother that he couldn't find me and she must have called from the upstairs windows, front and back—perhaps it was the occasion George spoke about tonight. I am not sure of these facts, they are plausible only, I can't yet *see* what I'm describing. But I know that I was not to find George and my mother again for many days . . . it cannot, whatever George says, have been less than three days and nights that I spent below the ground. Could he really have forgotten so inexplicable an experience?

And here I am already checking my story as though it were something which had really happened, for what possible relevance has George's memory to the events of a dream?

I dreamed that I crossed the lake, I dreamed . . . that is the only certain fact and I must cling to it, the fact that I dreamed. How my poor mother would grieve if she could know that, even for a moment, I had begun to think of these events as true . . . but, of course, if it were possible for her to know what I am thinking now, there would be no limit to the area of possibility. I dreamed then that I crossed the water (either by swimming—I could already swim at seven years old—or by wading if the lake is really as small as George makes out, or by paddling a raft) and scrambled up the slope of the island. I can remember grass, scrub, brush-wood, and at last a wood. I would describe it as a forest if I had not already seen, in the height of the garden-wall, how age diminishes size. I don't remember the umbrella-pine which W.W. described—I suspect he stole the sentinel-tree from *Treasure Island,* but I do know that when I got into the wood I was completely hidden from the house and the trees were close enough together to protect me from the rain. Quite soon I was lost, and yet how could I have been lost if the lake were no bigger than a pond, and the island therefore not much larger than the top of a kitchen-table?

Again I find myself checking my memories as though they were facts. A dream does not take account of size. A puddle can contain a continent, and a clump of trees stretch in sleep to the world's edge. I dreamed, I *dreamed* that I was lost and that night began to fall. I was not frightened. It was as though even at seven I was accustomed to travel. All the rough journeys of the future were already in me then, like a muscle which had only to develop. I curled up among the roots of the trees and slept. When I woke I could still hear the pit-pat of the rain in the upper branches and the steady zing of an insect near by. All these noises come as clearly back to me now as the sound of the rain on the parked cars outside the clinic in Wimpole Street, the music of yesterday.

The moon had risen and I could see more easily around me. I was determined to explore further before the morning came, for then an expedition would certainly be sent in search of me. I knew, from the many books of exploration George had read to me, of the danger to a person lost of walking in circles until eventually he dies of thirst or hunger, so I cut a cross in the bark of the tree (I had brought a knife

with me that contained several blades, a small saw and an instrument
for removing pebbles from horses' hooves). For the sake of future
reference I named the place where I had slept Camp Hope. I had no
fear of hunger, for I had apples in both pockets, and as for thirst I had
only to continue in a straight line and would come eventually to the
lake again where the water was sweet, or at worst a little brackish. I
go into all these details, which W.W. unaccountably omitted, to test
my memory. I had forgotten until now how far or how deeply it
extended. Had W.W. forgotten or was he afraid to remember?

I had gone a little more than three hundred yards—I paced the
distances and marked every hundred paces or so on a tree—it was the
best I could do, without proper surveying instruments, for the map I
already planned to draw—when I reached a great oak of apparently
enormous age with roots that coiled away above the surface of the
ground. (I was reminded of those roots once in Africa where they
formed a kind of shrine for a fetish—a seated human figure made out
of a gourd and palm fronds and unidentifiable vegetable matter gone
rotten in the rains and a great penis of bamboo. Coming on it suddenly, I was frightened, or was it the memory that it brought back
which scared me?) Under one of these roots the earth had been
disturbed; somebody had shaken a mound of charred tobacco from a
pipe and a sequin glistened like a snail in the moist moonlight. I
struck a match to examine the ground closer and saw the imprint of a
foot in a patch of loose earth—it was pointing at the tree from a few
inches away and it was as solitary as the print Crusoe found on the
sands of another island. It was as though a one-legged man had taken
a leap out of the bushes straight at the tree.

Pirate ancestor! What nonsense W.W. had written, or had he converted the memory of that stark frightening footprint into some comforting thought of the kindly scoundrel, Long John Silver, and his
wooden leg?

I stood astride the imprint and stared up the tree, half expecting to
see a one-legged man perched like a vulture among the branches. I
listened and there was no sound except last night's rain dripping from
leaf to leaf. Then—I don't know why—I went down on my knees and
peered among the roots. There was no iron ring, but one of the roots
formed an arch more than two feet high like the entrance to a cave. I
put my head inside and lit another match—I couldn't see the back of
the cave.

It's difficult to remember that I was only seven years old. To the self we remain always the same age. I was afraid at first to venture further, but so would any grown man have been, any of the explorers I thought of as my peers. My brother had been reading aloud to me a month before from a book called *The Romance of Australian Exploration*—my own powers of reading had not advanced quite as far as that, but my memory was green and retentive and I carried in my head all kinds of new images and evocative words—aboriginal, sextant, Murumbidgee, Stony Desert, and the points of the compass with their big capital letters E.S.E. and N.N.W. had an excitement they have never quite lost. They were like the figure on a watch which at last comes round to pointing the important hour. I was comforted by the thought that Sturt had been sometimes daunted and that Burke's bluster often hid his fear. Now, kneeling by the cave, I remembered a cavern which George Grey, another hero of mine, had entered and how suddenly he had come on the figure of a man ten feet high painted on the wall, clothed from the chin down to the ankles in a red garment. I don't know why, but I was more afraid of that painting than I was of the aborigines who killed Burke, and the fact that the feet and hands which protruded from the garment were said to be badly executed added to the terror. A foot which looked like a foot was only human, but my imagination could play endlessly with the faults of the painter—a club-foot, the worm-like toes of a bird. Now I associated this strange footprint with the ill-executed painting, and I hesitated a long time before I got the courage to crawl into the cave under the root. Before doing so, in reference to the footprint, I gave the spot the name of Friday's Cave.

2

For some yards I could not even get upon my knees, the roof grated my hair, and it was impossible for me in that position to strike another match. I could only inch along like a worm, making an ideograph in the dust. I didn't notice for a while in the darkness that I was crawling down a long slope, but I could feel on either side of me roots rubbing my shoulders like the banisters of a staircase. I was creeping through the branches of an underground tree in a mole's world. Then the impediments were passed—I was out the other side; I banged my head again on the earth-wall and found that I could rise to my knees. But I nearly toppled down again, for I had not realized how steeply the ground sloped. I was more than a man's height below ground and, when I struck a match, I could see no finish to the long gradient going down. I cannot help feeling a little proud that I continued on my way, on my knees this time, though I suppose it is arguable whether one can really show courage in a dream.

I was halted again by a turn in the path, and this time I found I could rise to my feet after I had struck another match. The track had flattened out and ran horizontally. The air was stuffy with an odd disagreeable smell like cabbage cooking, and I wanted to go back. I remembered how miners carried canaries with them in cages to test the freshness of the air, and I wished I had thought of bringing our own canary with me which had accompanied us to Winton Hall—it would have been company too in that dark tunnel with its tiny song. There was something, I remembered, called coal-damp which caused explosions, and this passage was certainly damp enough. I must be nearly under the lake by this time, and I thought to myself that, if there was an explosion, the waters of the lake would pour in and drown me.

I blew out my match at the idea, but all the same I continued on my way in the hope that I might come on an exit a little easier than the long crawl back through the roots of the trees.

Suddenly ahead of me something whistled, only it was less like a whistle than a hiss: it was like the noise a kettle makes when it is on the boil. I thought of snakes and wondered whether some giant serpent had made its nest in the tunnel. There was something fatal to man called a Black Mamba . . . I stood stock-still and held my breath, while the whistling went on and on for a long while, before it whined out into nothing. I would have given anything then to have been safe back in bed in the room next to my mother's, with the electric-light switch close to my hand and the firm bed-end at my feet. There was a strange clanking sound and a duck-like quack. I couldn't bear the darkness any more and I lit another match, reckless of coal-damp. It shone on a pile of old newspapers and nothing else—it was strange to find I had not been the first person here. I called out "Hullo!" and my voice went on in diminishing echoes down the long passage. Nobody answered, and when I picked up one of the papers I saw it was no proof of a human presence. It was the *East Anglian Observer* for April 5th 1885—"with which is incorporated the *Colchester Guardian.*" It's funny how even the date remains in my mind and the Victorian Gothic type of the titling. There was a faint fishy smell about it as though—oh, eons ago—it had been wrapped around a bit of prehistoric cod. The match burnt my fingers and went out. Perhaps I was the first to come here for all those years, but suppose whoever had brought those papers were lying somewhere dead in the tunnel . . .

Then I had an idea. I made a torch of the paper in my hand, tucked the others under my arm to serve me later, and with the stronger light advanced more boldly down the passage. After all wild beasts— so George had read to me—and serpents too in all likelihood—were afraid of fire, and my fear of an explosion had been driven out by the greater terror of what I might find in the dark. But it was not a snake or a leopard or a tiger or any other cavern-haunting animal that I saw when I turned the second corner. Scrawled with the simplicity of ancient man upon the left-hand wall of the passage—done with a sharp tool like a chisel—was the outline of a gigantic fish. I held up my paper-torch higher and saw the remains of lettering either half-obliterated or in a language I didn't know.

$$\zeta \cdot r \eta \quad \gamma r \quad c \, k \, \cdot_{| \nearrow}$$

I was trying to make sense of the symbols when a hoarse voice out of sight called, "Maria, Maria."

I stood very still and the newspaper burned down in my hand. "Is that you, Maria?" the voice said. It sounded to me very angry. "What kind of a trick are you playing? What's the clock say? Surely it's time for my broth." And then I heard again that strange quacking sound which I had heard before. There was a long whispering and after that silence.

3

I suppose I was relieved that there were human beings and not wild beasts down the passage, but what kind of human beings could they be except criminals hiding from justice or gypsies who are notorious for stealing children? I was afraid to think what they might do to anyone who discovered their secret. It was also possible, of course, that I had come on the home of some aboriginal tribe . . . I stood there unable to make up my mind whether to go on or turn back. It was not a problem which my Australian peers could help me to solve, for they had sometimes found the aboriginals friendly folk who gave them fish (I thought of the fish on the wall) and sometimes enemies who attacked with spears. In any case—whether these were criminals or gypsies or aboriginals—I had only a pocket-knife for my defence. I think it showed the true spirit of an explorer that in spite of my fears I thought of the map I must one day draw if I survived and so named this spot Camp Indecision.

My indecision was solved for me. An old woman appeared suddenly and noiselessly around the corner of the passage. She wore an old blue dress which came down to her ankles covered with sequins, and her hair was grey and straggly and she was going bald on top. She was every bit as surprised as I was. She stood there gaping at me and then she opened her mouth and squawked. I learned later that she had no roof to her mouth and was probably saying, "Who are you?" but then I thought it was some foreign tongue she spoke—perhaps aboriginee—and I replied with an attempt at assurance, "I'm English."

The hoarse voice out of sight said, "Bring him along here, Maria."

The old woman took a step towards me, but I couldn't bear the thought of being touched by her hands, which were old and curved like a bird's and covered with the brown patches that Ernest, the gardener, had told me were "gravemarks"; her nails were very long and filled with dirt. Her dress was dirty too and I thought of the sequin I'd seen outside and imagined her scrabbling home through the roots of the tree. I backed up against the side of the passage and somehow squeezed around her. She quacked after me, but I went on. Round a second—or perhaps a third—corner I found myself in a great cave some eight feet high. On what I thought was a throne, but I later realized was an old lavatory-seat, sat a big old man with a white beard yellowing round the mouth from what I suppose now to have been nicotine. He had one good leg, but the right trouser was sewn up and looked stuffed like a bolster. I could see him quite well because an oil-lamp stood on a kitchen-table, beside a carving-knife and two cabbages, and his face came vividly back to me the other day when I was reading Darwin's description of a carrier-pigeon: "Greatly elongated eyelids, very large external orifices to the nostrils, and a wide gape of mouth."

He said, "And who would you be and what are you doing here and why are you burning my newspaper?"

The old woman came squawking around the corner and then stood still behind me, barring my retreat.

I said, "My name's William Wilditch, and I come from Winton Hall."

"And where's Winton Hall?" he asked, never stirring from his lavatory-seat.

"Up there," I said and pointed at the roof of the cave.

"That means precious little," he said. "Why, everything is up there, China and all America too and the Sandwich Islands."

"I suppose so," I said. There was a kind of reason in most of what he said, as I came to realize later.

"But down here there's only us. We are exclusive," he said, "Maria and me."

I was less frightened of him now. He spoke English. He was a fellow-countryman. I said, "If you'll tell me the way out I'll be going on my way."

"What's that you've got under your arm?" he asked me sharply. "More newspapers?"

"I found them in the passage . . ."

"Finding's not keeping here," he said, "whatever it may be up there in China. You'll soon discover that. Why, that's the lot of papers Maria brought in. What would we have for reading if we let you go and pinch them?"

"I didn't mean . . ."

"Can you read?" he asked, not listening to my excuses.

"If the words aren't too long."

"Maria can read, but she can't see very well any more than I can, and she can't articulate much."

Maria went kwahk, kwahk behind me, like a bull-frog it seems to me now, and I jumped. If that was how she read I wondered how he could understand a single word. He said, "Try a piece."

"What do you mean?"

"Can't you understand plain English? You'll have to work for your supper down here."

"But it's not supper-time. It's still early in the morning," I said.

"What o'clock is it, Maria?"

"Kwahk," she said.

"Six. That's supper-time."

"But it's six in the morning, not the evening."

"How do you know? Where's the light? There aren't such things as mornings and evenings here."

"Then how do you ever wake up?" I asked. His beard shook as he laughed. "What a shrewd little shaver he is," he exclaimed. "Did you hear that, Maria? How do you ever wake up? he said. All the same

you'll find that life here isn't all beer and skittles and who's your
Uncle Joe. If you are clever, you'll learn and if you are not clever
. . ." He brooded morosely. "We are deeper here than any grave
was ever dug to bury secrets in. Under the earth or over the earth,
it's there you'll find all that matters." He added angrily, "Why aren't
you reading a piece as I told you to? If you are to stay with us, you've
got to jump to it."

"I don't want to stay."

"You think you can just take a peek, is that it? and go away. You
are wrong—but take all the peek you want and then get on with it."

I didn't like the way he spoke, but all the same I did as he suggested. There was an old chocolate-stained chest of drawers, a tall
kitchen-cupboard, a screen covered with scraps and transfers, and a
wooden crate which perhaps served Maria for a chair, and another
larger one for a table. There was a cooking-stove with a kettle pushed
to one side, steaming yet. That would have caused the whistle I had
heard in the passage. I could see no sign of any bed, unless a heap of
potato-sacks against the wall served that purpose. There were a lot of
breadcrumbs on the earth-floor and a few bones had been swept into
a corner as though awaiting interment.

"And now," he said, "show your young paces. I've yet to see
whether you are worth your keep."

"But I don't want to be kept," I said. "I really don't. It's time I
went home."

"Home's where a man lies down," he said, "and this is where
you'll lie from now on. Now take the first page that comes and read
to me. I want to hear the news."

"But the paper's nearly fifty years old," I said. "There's no news in
it."

"News is news however old it is." I began to notice a way he had
of talking in general statements like a lecturer or a prophet. He
seemed to be less interested in conversation than in the recital of
some articles of belief, odd crazy ones, perhaps, yet somehow I could
never put my finger convincingly on an error. "A cat's a cat even
when it's a dead cat. We get rid of it when it's smelly, but news never
smells, however long it's dead. News keeps, and it comes round
again when you least expect. Like thunder."

I opened the paper at random and read: "Garden fête at the
Grange. The fête at the Grange, Long Wilson, in aid of Distressed
Gentlewomen was opened by Lady (Isobel) Montgomery." I was a

bit put out by the long words coming so quickly, but I acquitted myself with fair credit. He sat on the lavatory-seat with his head sunk a little, listening with attention. "The Vicar presided at the White Elephant Stall."

The old man said with satisfaction, "They are royal beasts."

"But these were not really elephants," I said.

"A stall is part of a stable, isn't it? What do you want a stable for if they aren't real? Go on. Was it a good fate or an evil fate?"

"It's not that kind of fate either," I said.

"There's no other kind," he said. "It's your fate to read to me. It's *her* fate to talk like a frog, and mine to listen because my eyesight's bad. This is an underground fate we suffer from here, and that was a garden fate—but it all comes to the same fate in the end." It was useless to argue with him and I read on: "Unfortunately the festivities were brought to an untimely close by a heavy rainstorm."

Maria gave a kwahk that sounded like a malicious laugh, and "You see," the old man said, as though what I had read proved somehow he was right, "that's fate for you."

"The evening's events had to be transferred indoors, including the Morris dancing and the Treasure Hunt."

"Treasure Hunt?" the old man asked sharply.

"That's what it says here."

"The impudence of it," he said. "The sheer impudence. Maria, did you hear that?"

She kwahked—this time, I thought, angrily.

"It's time for my broth," he said with deep gloom, as though he were saying, "It's time for my death."

"It happened a long time ago," I said trying to soothe him.

"Time," he exclaimed, "you can — time," using a word quite unfamiliar to me which I guessed—I don't know how—was one that I could not with safety use myself when I returned home. Maria had gone behind the screen—there must have been other cupboards there, for I heard her opening and shutting doors and clanking pots and pans.

I whispered to him quickly, "Is she your luba?"

"Sister, wife, mother, daughter," he said, "what difference does it make? Take your choice. She's a woman, isn't she?" He brooded there on the lavatory-seat like a king on a throne. "There are two sexes," he said. "Don't try to make more than two with definitions." The statement sank into my mind with the same heavy mathematical

certainty with which later on at school I learned the rule of Euclid
about the sides of an isosceles triangle. There was a long silence.

"I think I'd better be going," I said, shifting up and down. Maria
came in. She carried a dish marked Fido filled with hot broth. Her
husband, her brother, whatever he was, nursed it on his lap a long
while before he drank it. He seemed to be lost in thought again, and
I hesitated to disturb him. All the same, after a while, I tried again.

"They'll be expecting me at home."

"Home?"

"Yes."

"You couldn't have a better home than this," he said. "You'll see.
In a bit of time—a year or two—you'll settle down well enough."

I tried my best to be polite. "It's very nice here, I'm sure,
but . ."

"It's no use your being restless. I didn't ask you to come, did I, but
now you are here, you'll stay. Maria's a great hand with cabbage. You
won't suffer any hardship."

"But I can't stay. My mother . . ."

"Forget your mother and your father too. If you need anything
from up there Maria will fetch it down for you."

"But I can't stay here."

"*Can't*'s not a word that you can use to the likes of me."

"But you haven't any right to keep me . . ."

"And what right had you to come busting in like a thief, getting
Maria all disturbed when she was boiling my broth?"

"I couldn't stay here with you. It's not—sanitary." I don't know
how I managed to get that word out. "I'd die . . ."

"There's no need to talk of dying down here. No one's ever died
here, and you've no reason to believe that anyone ever will. We
aren't dead, are we, and we've lived a long long time, Maria and me.
You don't know how lucky you are. There's treasure here beyond all
the riches of Asia. One day, if you don't go disturbing Maria, I'll
show you. You know what a millionaire is?" I nodded. "They aren't
one quarter as rich as Maria and me. And they die too, and where's
their treasure then? Rockefeller's gone and Fred's gone and Columbus. I sit here and just read about dying—it's an entertainment that's
all. You'll find in all those papers what they call an obituary—there's
one about a Lady Caroline Winterbottom that made Maria laugh and
me. It's summerbottoms we have here, I said, all the year round,
sitting by the stove."

Maria kwahked in the background, and I began to cry more as a way of interrupting him than because I was really frightened.

It's extraordinary how vividly after all these years I can remember that man and the words he spoke. If they were to dig down now on the island below the roots of the tree, I would half expect to find him sitting there still on the old lavatory-seat which seemed to be detached from any pipes or drainage and serve no useful purpose, and yet, if he had really existed, he must have passed his century a long time ago. There was something of a monarch about him and something, as I said, of a prophet and something of the gardener my mother disliked and of a policeman in the next village; his expressions were often countrylike and coarse, but his ideas seemed to move on a deeper level, like roots spreading below a layer of compost. I could sit here now in this room for hours remembering the things he said—I haven't made out the sense of them all yet: they are stored in my memory like a code uncracked which waits for a clue or an inspiration.

He said to me sharply, "We don't need salt here. There's too much as it is. You taste any bit of earth and you'll find it salt. We live in salt. We are pickled, you might say, in it. Look at Maria's hands, and you'll see the salt in the cracks."

I stopped crying at once and looked (my attention could always be caught by bits of irrelevant information), and true enough, there seemed to be grey-white seams running between her knuckles.

"You'll turn salty too in time," he said encouragingly and drank his broth with a good deal of noise.

I said, "But I really am going, Mr. . . ."

"You can call me Javitt," he said, "but only because it's not my real name. You don't believe I'd give you that, do you? And Maria's not Maria—it's just a sound she answers to, you understand me, like Jupiter."

"No."

"If you had a dog called Jupiter, you wouldn't believe he was really Jupiter, would you?"

"I've got a dog called Joe."

"The same applies," he said and drank his soup. Sometimes I think that in no conversation since have I found the interest I discovered in those inconsequent sentences of his to which I listened during the days (I don't know how many) that I spent below the garden. Because, of course, I didn't leave that day. Javitt had his way.

He might be said to have talked me into staying, though if I had proved obstinate I have no doubt at all that Maria would have blocked my retreat, and certainly I would not have fancied struggling to escape through the musty folds of her clothes. That was the strange balance—to and fro—of those days; half the time I was frightened as though I were caged in a nightmare and half the time I only wanted to laugh freely and happily at the strangeness of his speech and the novelty of his ideas. It was as if, for those hours or days, the only important things in life were two, laughter and fear. (Perhaps the same ambivalence was there when I first began to know a woman.) There are people whose laughter has always a sense of superiority, but it was Javitt who taught me that laughter is more often a sign of equality, of pleasure and not of malice. He sat there on his lavatory-seat and he said, "I shit dead stuff every day, do I? How wrong you are." (I was already laughing because that was a word I knew to be obscene and I had never heard it spoken before.) "Everything that comes out of me is alive, I tell you. It's squirming around there, germs and bacilli and the like, and it goes into the ground like a womb, and it comes out somewhere, I daresay, like my daughter did —I forgot I haven't told you about her."

"Is she here?" I said with a look at the curtain, wondering what monstrous woman would next emerge.

"Oh, no, she went upstairs a long time ago."

"Perhaps I could take her a message from you," I said cunningly.

He looked at me with contempt. "What kind of a message," he asked, "could the likes of you take to the likes of her?" He must have seen the motive behind my offer, for he reverted to the fact of my imprisonment. "I'm not unreasonable," he said, "I'm not one to make hailstorms in harvest time, but if you went back up there you'd talk about me and Maria and the treasure we've got, and people would come digging."

"I swear I'd say nothing," (and at least I have kept that promise, whatever others I have broken, through all the years).

"You talk in your sleep maybe. A boy's never alone. You've got a brother, I daresay, and soon you'll be going to school and hinting at things to make you seem important. There are plenty of ways of keeping an oath and breaking it in the same moment. Do you know what I'd do then? If they came searching? I'd go further in."

Maria khahk-kwahked her agreement where she listened from somewhere behind the curtains.

"What do you mean?"

"Give me a hand to get off this seat," he said. He pressed his hands down on my shoulder and it was like a mountain heaving. I looked at the lavatory-seat and I could see that it had been placed exactly to cover a hole which went down down down out of sight. "A moit of the treasure's down there already," he said, "but I wouldn't let the bastards enjoy what they could find here. There's a little matter of subsidence I've got fixed up so that they'd never see the light of day again."

"But what would you do below there for food?"

"We've got tins enough for another century or two," he said. "You'd be surprised at what Maria's stored away there. We don't use tins up here because there's always broth and cabbage and that's more healthy and keeps the scurvy off, but we've no more teeth to lose and our gums are fallen as it is, so if we had to fall back on tins we would. Why, there's hams and chickens and red salmon's eggs and butter and steak-and-kidney pies and caviar, venison too and marrow-bones. I'm forgetting the fish—cods' roe and sole in white wine, langouste legs, sardines, bloaters, and herrings in tomato-sauce, and all the fruits that ever grew, apples, pears, strawberries, figs, raspberries, plums and greengages and passion fruit, mangoes, grapefruit, loganberries and cherries, mulberries too and sweet things from Japan, not to speak of vegetables. Indian corn and taties, salsify and spinach and that thing they call endive asparagus, peas and the hearts of bamboo, and I've left out our old friend the tomato." He lowered himself heavily back on to his seat above the great hole going down.

"You must have enough for two lifetimes," I said.

"There's means of getting more," he added darkly, so that I pictured other channels delved through the undersoil of the garden like the section of an ant's nest, and I remembered the sequin on the island and the single footprint.

Perhaps all this talk of food had reminded Maria of her duties because she came quacking out from behind her dusty curtain, carrying two bowls of broth, one medium size for me and one almost as small as an egg-cup for herself. I tried politely to take the small one, but she snatched it away from me.

"You don't have to bother about Maria," the old man said. "She's been eating food for more years than you've got weeks. She knows her appetite."

"What do you cook with?" I asked.

"Calor," he said.

That was an odd thing about this adventure or rather this dream: fantastic though it was, it kept coming back to ordinary life with simple facts like that. The man could never, if I really thought it out, have existed all those years below the earth, and yet the cooking, as I seem to remember it, was done on a cylinder of calor-gas.

The broth was quite tasty and I drank it to the end. When I had finished I fidgeted about on the wooden box they had given me for a seat—nature was demanding something for which I was too embarrassed to ask aid.

"What's the matter with you?" Javitt said. "Chair not comfortable?"

"Oh, it's very comfortable," I said.

"Perhaps you want to lie down and sleep?"

"No."

"I'll show you something which will give you dreams," he said. "A picture of my daughter."

"I want to do number one," I blurted out.

"Oh, is that all?" Javitt said. He called to Maria, who was still clattering around behind the curtain, "The boy wants to piss. Fetch him the golden po." Perhaps my eyes showed interest, for he added to me diminishingly, with the wave of a hand, "It's the least of my treasures."

All the same it was remarkable enough in my eyes, and I can remember it still, a veritable chamber-pot of gold. Even the young dauphin of France on that long road back from Varennes with his father had only a silver cup at his service. I would have been more embarrassed, doing what I called number one in front of the old man Javitt, if I had not been so impressed by the pot. It lent the everyday affair the importance of a ceremony, almost of a sacrament. I can remember the tinkle in the pot like faraway chimes as though a gold surface resounded differently from china or base metal.

Javitt reached behind him to a shelf stacked with old papers and picked one out. He said, "Now you look at that and tell me what you think."

It was a kind of magazine I'd never seen before—full of pictures which are now called cheese-cake. I have no earlier memory of a woman's unclothed body, or as nearly unclothed as made no difference to me then, in the skintight black costume. One whole page was given up to a Miss Ramsgate, shot from all angles. She was the favourite contestant for something called Miss England and might later go on, if she were successful, to compete for the title of Miss Europe, Miss World and after that Miss Universe. I stared at her as though I wanted to memorize her for ever. And that is exactly what I did.

"That's our daughter," Javitt said.

"And did she become . . ."

"She was launched," he said with pride and mystery, as though he were speaking of some moon-rocket which had at last after many disappointments risen from the pad and soared to outer space. I looked at the photograph, at the wise eyes and the inexplicable body, and I thought, with all the ignorance children have of age and generations, I never want to marry anybody but her. Maria put her hand through the curtains and quacked, and I thought, she would be my mother then, but not a hoot did I care. With that girl for my wife I could take anything, even school and growing up and life. And perhaps I could have taken them, if I had ever succeeded in finding her.

Again my thoughts are interrupted. For if I am remembering a vivid dream—and dreams do stay in all their detail far longer than we realize—how would I have known at that age about such absurdities as beauty-contests? A dream can only contain what one has experienced, or, if you have sufficient faith in Jung, what our ancestors have experienced. But calor-gas and the Ramsgate Beauty Queen? . . . They are not ancestral memories, nor the memories of a child of seven. Certainly my mother did not allow us to buy with our meagre pocket-money—sixpence a week?—such papers as that. And yet the image is there, caught once and for all, not only the expression of the eyes, but the expression of the body too, the particular tilt of the breasts, the shallow scoop of the navel like something carved in sand, the little trim buttocks—the dividing line swung between them close and regular like the single sweep of a pencil. Can a child of seven fall in love for life with a body? And there is a further mystery which did not occur to me then: how could a couple as old as Javitt and Maria have had a daughter so young in the period when such contests were the vogue?

"She's a beauty," Javitt said, "you'll never see her like where your folks live. Things grow differently underground, like a mole's coat. I ask you where there's softness softer than that?" I'm not sure whether he was referring to the skin of his daughter or the coat of the mole.

I sat on the golden po and looked at the photograph and listened to

Javitt as I would have listened to my own father if I had possessed
one. His sayings are fixed in my memory like the photograph. Gross
some of them seem now, but they did not appear gross to me then
when even the graffiti on walls were innocent. Except when he called
me "boy" or "snapper" or something of the kind he seemed unaware
of my age: it was not that he talked to me as an equal but as someone
from miles away, looking down from his old lavatory-seat to my
golden po, from so far away that he couldn't distinguish my age, or
perhaps he was so old that anyone under a century or so seemed
much alike to him. All that I write here was not said at that moment.
There must have been many days or nights of conversation—you
couldn't down there tell the difference—and now I dredge the sentences up, in no particular order, just as they come to mind, sitting at
my mother's desk so many years later.

4

"You laugh at Maria and me. You think we look ugly. I tell you she
could have been painted if she had chosen by some of the greatest—
there's one that painted women with three eyes—she'd have suited
him. But she knew how to tunnel in the earth like me, when to
appear and when not to appear. It's a long time now that we've been
alone down here. It gets more dangerous all the time—if you can
speak of time—on the upper floor. But don't think it hasn't happened
before. But when I remember . . ." But what he remembered has
gone from my head, except only his concluding phrase and a sense of
desolation: "Looking round at all those palaces and towers, you'd
have thought they'd been made like a child's castle of the desert-sand.

"In the beginning you had a name only the man or woman knew
who pulled you out of your mother. Then there was a name for the
tribe to call you by. That was of little account, but of more account all
the same than the name you had with strangers; and there was a name
used in the family—by your pa and ma if it's those terms you call
them by nowadays. The only name without any power at all was the
name you used to strangers. That's why I call myself Javitt to you, but
the name the man who pulled me out knew—that was so secret I had
to keep him as a friend for life; so that he wouldn't even tell me
because of the responsibility it would bring—I might let it slip before
a stranger. Up where you come from they've begun to forget the
power of the name. I wouldn't be surprised if you only had the one
name and what's the good of a name everyone knows? Do you sup-

pose even I feel secure here with my treasure and all—because, you see, as it turned out, I got to know the first name of all. He told it me before he died, before I could stop him, with a hand over his mouth. I doubt if there's anyone in the world but me who knows his first name. It's an awful temptation to speak it out loud—introduce it casually into the conversation like you might say by Jove, by George, for Christ's sake. Or whisper it when I think no one's attentive.

"When I was born, time had a different pace to what it has now. Now you walk from one wall to another, and it takes you twenty steps—or twenty miles—who cares?—between the towns. But when I was young we took a leisurely way. Don't bother me with 'I must be gone now' or 'I've been away so long.' I can't talk to you in terms of time—your time and my time are different. Javitt isn't my usual name either even with strangers. It's one I thought up fresh for you, so that you'll have no power at all. I'll change it right away if you escape. I warn you that.

"You get a sense of what I mean when you make love with a girl. The time isn't measured by clocks. Time is fast or slow or it stops for a while altogether. One minute is different to every other minute. When you make love it's a pulse in a man's part which measures time and when you spill yourself there's no time at all. That's how time comes and goes, not by an alarm-clock made by a man with a magnifying glass in his eye. Haven't you ever heard them say, 'It's — time' up there?" and he used again the word which I guessed was forbidden like his name, perhaps because it had power too.

"I daresay you are wondering how Maria and me could make a beautiful girl like that one. That's an illusion people have about beauty. Beauty doesn't come from beauty. All that beauty can produce is prettiness. Have you never looked around upstairs and counted the beautiful women with their pretty daughters? Beauty diminishes all the time, it's the law of diminishing returns, and only when you get back to zero, to the real ugly base of things, there's a chance to start again free and independent. Painters who paint what they call ugly things know that. I can still see that little head with its cap of blonde hair coming out from between Maria's thighs and how she leapt out of Maria in a spasm (there wasn't any doctor down here or midwife to give her a name and rob her of power—and she's Miss Ramsgate to you and to the whole world upstairs). Ugliness and beauty; you see it in war too; when there's nothing left of a house but a couple of pillars against the sky, the beauty of it starts all over again like before the builder ruined it. Perhaps when Maria and I go up there next, there'll only be pillars left, sticking up around the flattened world like it was fucking time." (The word had become familiar to me by this time and no longer had the power to shock.)

"Do you know, boy, that when they make those maps of the universe you are looking at the map of something that looked like that six thousand million years ago? You can't be much more out of date than that, I'll swear. Why, if they've got pictures up there of us taken yesterday, they'll see the world all covered with ice—if their photos are a bit more up to date than ours, that is. Otherwise we won't be there at all, maybe, and it might just as well be a photo of the future. To catch a star while it's alive you have to be as nippy as if you were snatching at a racehorse as it goes by.

"You are a bit scared still of Maria and me because you've never seen anyone like us before. And you'd be scared to see our daughter too, there's no other like her in whatever country she is now, and what good would a scared man be to her? Do you know what a rogue-plant is? And do you know that white cats with blue eyes are deaf? People who keep nursery-gardens look around all the time at the seedlings and they throw away any oddities like weeds. They call them rogues. You won't find many white cats with blue eyes and that's the reason. But sometimes you find someone who wants things different, who's tired of all the plus signs and wants to find zero, and he starts breeding away with the differences. Maria and I are both rogues and we are born of generations of rogues. Do you think I lost this leg in an accident? I was born that way just like Maria with her squawk. Generations of us uglier and uglier, and suddenly out of Maria comes our daughter, who's Miss Ramsgate to you. I don't speak her name even when I'm asleep. We're unique like the Red Grouse. You ask anybody if they can tell you where the Red Grouse came from.

"You are still wondering why we are unique. It's because for generations we haven't been thrown away. Man kills or throws away what he doesn't want. Somebody once in Greece kept the wrong child and exposed the right one, and then one rogue at least was safe and it only needed another. Why, in Tierra del Fuego in starvation years they kill and eat their old women because the dogs are of more value. It's the hardest thing in the world for a rogue to survive. For hundreds of years now we've been living underground and we'll have the laugh of you yet, coming up above for keeps in a dead world. Except I'll bet you your golden po that Miss Ramsgate will be there somewhere—her beauty's rogue too. We have long lives, we— Javitts to you. We've kept our ugliness all those years and why shouldn't she keep her beauty? Like a cat does. A cat is as beautiful the last day as the first. And it keeps its spittle. Not like a dog.

"I can see your eye light up whenever I say Miss Ramsgate, and you still wonder how it comes Maria and I have a child like that in spite of all I'm telling you. Elephants go on breeding till they are ninety years old, don't they, and do you suppose a rogue like Javitt (which isn't my real name) can't go on longer than a beast so stupid it lets itself be harnessed and draw logs? There's another thing we have in common with elephants. No one sees us dead.

"We know the sex-taste of female birds better than we know the sex-taste of women. Only the most beautiful in the hen's eyes survives, so when you admire a peacock you know you have the same taste as a pea-hen. But women are more mysterious than birds. You've heard of beauty and the beast, haven't you? They have rogue-tastes. Just look at me and my leg. You won't find Miss Ramsgate by going round the world preening yourself like a peacock to attract a beautiful woman—she's our daughter and she has rogue-tastes too. She isn't for someone who wants a beautiful wife at his dinner-table to satisfy his vanity, and an understanding wife in bed who'll treat him just the same number of times as he was accustomed to at school —so many times a day or a week. She went away, our daughter did, with a want looking for a want—and not a want you can measure in inches either or calculate in numbers by the week. They say that in the northern countries people make love for their health, so it won't be any good looking for her in the north. You might have to go as far as Africa or China. And talking of China . . ."

5

Sometimes I think that I learned more from Javitt—this man who never existed—than from all my schoolmasters. He talked to me while I sat there on the po or lay upon the sacks as no one had ever done before or has ever done since. I could not have expected my mother to take time away from the Fabian pamphlets to say, "Men are like monkeys—they don't have any season in love, and the monkeys aren't worried by this notion of dying. They tell us from pulpits we're

immortal and then they try to frighten us with death. I'm more a
monkey than a man. To the monkeys death's an accident. The gorillas
don't bury their dead with hearses and crowns of flowers, thinking
one day it's going to happen to them and they better put on a show if
they want one for themselves too. If one of them dies, it's a special
case, and so they can leave it in the ditch. I feel like them. But I'm not
a special case yet. I keep clear of hackney-carriages and railway-trains,
you won't find horses, wild dogs or machinery down here. I love life
and I survive. Up there they talk about natural death, but it's natural
death that's unnatural. If we lived for a thousand years—and there's
no reason we shouldn't—there'd always be a smash, a bomb, tripping
over your left foot—those are the natural deaths. All we need to live
is a bit of effort, but nature sows booby-traps in our way.

"Do you believe those skulls monks have in their cells are set there
for contemplation? Not on your life. They don't believe in death any
more than I do. The skulls are there for the same reason you'll see a
queen's portrait in an embassy—they're just part of the official furniture. Do you believe an ambassador ever looks at that face on the
wall with a diamond and tiara and an empty smile?

"Be disloyal. It's your duty to the human race. The human race
needs to survive and it's the loyal man who dies first from anxiety or a
bullet or overwork. If you have to earn a living, boy, and the price
they make you pay is loyalty, be a double agent—and never let either
of the two sides know your real name. The same applies to women
and God. They both respect a man they don't own, and they'll go on
raising the price they are willing to offer. Didn't Christ say that very
thing? Was the prodigal son loyal or the lost shilling or the strayed
sheep? The obedient flock didn't give the shepherd any satisfaction
or the loyal son interest his father.

"People are afraid of bringing May blossom into the house. They
say it's unlucky. The real reason is it smells strong of sex and they are
afraid of sex. Why aren't they afraid of fish then, you may rightly ask?
Because when they smell fish they smell a holiday ahead and they feel
safe from breeding for a short while."

I remember Javitt's words far more clearly than the passage of
time; certainly I must have slept at least twice on the bed of sacks, but
I cannot remember Javitt sleeping until the very end—perhaps he
slept like a horse or a god, upright. And the broth—that came at
regular intervals, so far as I could tell, though there was no sign
anywhere of a clock, and once I think they opened for me a tin of

sardines from their store (it had a very Victorian label on it of two bearded sailors and a seal, but the sardines tasted good).

I think Javitt was glad to have me there. Surely he could not have been talking quite so amply over the years to Maria who could only quack in response, and several times he made me read to him from one of the newspapers. The nearest to our time I ever found was a local account of the celebrations for the relief of Mafeking. ("Riots," Javitt said, "purge like a dose of salts.")

Once he told me to pick up the oil-lamp and we would go for a walk together, and I was able to see how agile he could be on his one leg. When he stood upright he looked like a rough carving from a tree-trunk where the sculptor had not bothered to separate the legs, or perhaps, as with the image on the cave, they were "badly executed." He put one hand on each wall and hopped gigantically in front of me, and when he paused to speak (like many old people he seemed unable to speak and move at the same time) he seemed to be propping up the whole passage with his arms as thick as pit-beams. At one point he paused to tell me that we were now directly under the lake. "How many tons of water lie up there?" he asked me—I had never thought of water in tons before that, only in gallons, but he had the exact figure ready, I can't remember it now. Further on, where the passage sloped upwards, he paused again and said, "Listen," and I heard a kind of rumbling that passed overhead and after that a rattling as little cakes of mud fell around us. "That's a motor-car," he said, as an explorer might have said, "That's an elephant."

I asked him whether perhaps there was a way out near there since we were so close to the surface, and he made his answer, even to that direct question, ambiguous and general like a proverb. "A wise man has only one door to his house," he said.

What a boring old man he would have been to an adult mind, but a child has a hunger to learn which makes him sometimes hang on the lips of the dullest schoolmaster. I thought I was learning about the world and the universe from Javitt, and still to this day I wonder how it was that a child could have invented these details, or have they accumulated year by year, like coral, in the sea of the unconscious around the original dream?

There were times when he was in a bad humour for no apparent reason, or at any rate for no adequate reason. An example: for all his freedom of speech and range of thought, I found there were tiny rules which had to be obeyed, else the thunder of his invective broke

—the way I had to arrange the spoon in the empty broth-bowl, the method of folding a newspaper after it had been read, even the arrangement of my limbs on the bed of sacks.

"I'll cut you off," he cried once and I pictured him lopping off one of my legs to resemble him. "I'll starve you, I'll set you alight like a candle for a warning. Haven't I given you a kingdom here of all the treasures of the earth and all the fruits of it, tin by tin, where time can't get in to destroy you and there's no day or night, and you go and defy me with a spoon laid down longways in a saucer? You come of an ungrateful generation." His arms waved about and cast shadows like wolves on the wall behind the oil-lamp, while Maria sat squatting behind a cylinder of calor-gas in an attitude of terror.

"I haven't even seen your wonderful treasure," I said with feeble defiance.

"Nor you won't," he said, "nor any lawbreaker like you. You lay last night on your back grunting like a small swine, but did I curse you as you deserved? Javitt's patient. He forgives and he forgives seventy times seven, but then you go and lay your spoon longways . . ." He gave a great sigh like a wave withdrawing. He said, "I forgive even that. There's no fool like an old fool and you will search a long way before you find anything as old as I am—even among the tortoises, the parrots and the elephants. One day I'll show you the treasure, but not now. I'm not in the right mood now. Let time pass. Let time heal."

I had found the way, however, on an earlier occasion to set him in a good humour and that was to talk to him about his daughter. It came quite easily to me, for I found myself to be passionately in love, as perhaps one can only be at an age when all one wants is to give and the thought of taking is very far removed. I asked him whether he was sad when she left him to go "upstairs" as he liked to put it.

"I knew it had to come," he said. "It was for that she was born. One day she'll be back and the three of us will be together for keeps."

"Perhaps I'll see her then," I said.

"You won't live to see that day," he said, as though it was I who was the old man, not he.

"Do you think she's married?" I asked anxiously.

"She isn't the kind to marry," he said. "Didn't I tell you she's a rogue like Maria and me? She has her roots down here."

"I thought Maria and you were married," I said anxiously.

He gave a sharp crunching laugh like a nut-cracker closing. "There's no marrying in the ground," he said. "Where would you find the witnesses? Marriage is public. Maria and me, we just grew into each other, that's all, and then she sprouted."

I sat silent for a long while, brooding on that vegetable picture. Then I said with all the firmness I could muster, "I'm going to find her when I get out of here."

"If you get out of here," he said, "you'd have to live a very long time and travel a very long way to find her."

"I'll do just that," I replied.

He looked at me with a trace of humour. "You'll have to take a look at Africa," he said, "and Asia—and then there's America, North and South, and Australia—you might leave out the Arctic and the other Pole—she was always a warm girl." And it occurs to me now when I think of the life I have led since, that I have been in most of those regions—except Australia where I have only twice touched down between planes.

"I will go to them all," I said, "and I'll find her." It was as though the purpose of life had suddenly come to me as it must have come often enough to some future explorer when he noticed on a map for the first time an empty space in the heart of a continent.

"You'll need a lot of money," Javitt jeered at me.

"I'll work my passage," I said, "before the mast." Perhaps it was a reflection of that intention which made the young author W.W. menace his elder brother with such a fate before preserving him for Oxford of all places. The mast was to be a career sacred to me—it was not for George.

"It'll take a long time," Javitt warned me.

"I'm young," I said.

I don't know why it is that when I think of this conversation with Javitt the doctor's voice comes back to me saying hopelessly, "There's always hope." There's hope perhaps, but there isn't so much time left now as there was then to fulfil a destiny.

That night, when I lay down on the sacks, I had the impression that Javitt had begun to take a favourable view of my case. I woke once in the night and saw him sitting there on what is popularly called a throne, watching me. He closed one eye in a wink and it was like a star going out.

Next morning after my bowl of broth, he suddenly spoke up. "Today," he said, "you are going to see my treasure."

6

It was a day heavy with the sense of something fateful coming nearer—I call it a day but for all I could have told down there it might have been a night. And I can only compare it in my later experience with those slow hours I have sometimes experienced before I have gone to meet a woman with whom for the first time the act of love is likely to come about. The fuse has been lit, and who can tell the extent of the explosion? A few cups broken or a house in ruins?

For hours Javitt made no further reference to the subject, but after the second cup of broth (or was it perhaps, on that occasion, the tin of sardines?) Maria disappeared behind the screen and when she reappeared she wore a hat. Once, years ago perhaps, it had been a grand hat, a hat for the races, a great black straw affair; now it was full of holes like a colander decorated with one drooping scarlet flower which had been stitched and restitched and stitched again. I wondered when I saw her dressed like that whether we were about to go "upstairs." But we made no move. Instead she put a kettle upon the stove, warmed a pot and dropped in two spoonfuls of tea. Then she and Javitt sat and watched the kettle like a couple of soothsayers bent over the steaming entrails of a kid, waiting for a revelation. The kettle gave a thin preliminary whine and Javitt nodded and the tea was made. He alone took a cup, sipping it slowly, with his eyes on me, as though he were considering and perhaps revising his decision.

On the edge of his cup, I remember, was a tea-leaf. He took it on his nail and placed it on the back of my hand. I knew very well what that meant. A hard stalk of tea indicated a man upon the way and the soft leaf a woman; this was a soft leaf. I began to strike it with the palm of my other hand counting as I did so, "One, two, three." It lay flat, adhering to my hand. "Four, five." It was on my fingers now and I said, triumphantly, "In five days," thinking of Javitt's daughter in the world above.

Javitt shook his head. "You don't count time like that with us," he said. "That's five decades of years." I accepted his correction—he must know his own country best, and it's only now that I find myself calculating, if every day down there were ten years long, what age in our reckoning could Javitt have claimed?

I have no idea what he had learned from the ceremony of the tea, but at least he seemed satisfied. He rose on his one leg, and now that he had his arms stretched out to either wall, he reminded me of a gigantic crucifix, and the crucifix moved in great hops down the way we had taken the day before. Maria gave me a little push from behind and I followed. The oil lamp in Maria's hand cast long shadows ahead of us.

First we came under the lake and I remembered the tons of water hanging over us like a frozen falls, and after that we reached the spot where we had halted before, and again a car went rumbling past on the road above. But this time we continued our shuffling march. I calculated that now we had crossed the road which led to Winton Halt; we must be somewhere under the inn called The Three Keys, which was kept by our gardener's uncle, and after that we should have arrived below the Long Meadow, a field with a small minnowy stream along its northern border owned by a farmer called Howell. I had not given up all idea of escape and I noted our route carefully and the distance we had gone. I had hoped for some side-passage which might indicate that there was another entrance to the tunnel, but there seemed to be none and I was disappointed to find that before we travelled below the inn we descended quite steeply, perhaps in order to avoid the cellars—indeed at one moment I heard a groaning and a turbulence as though the gardener's uncle were taking delivery of some new barrels of beer.

We must have gone nearly half a mile before the passage came to an end in a kind of egg-shaped hall. Facing us was a kitchen-dresser of unstained wood, very similar to the one in which my mother kept her stores of jam, sultanas, raisins and the like.

"Open up, Maria," Javitt said, and Maria shuffled by me, clanking a bunch of keys and quacking with excitement, while the lamp swung to and fro like a censer.

"She's heated up," Javitt said. "It's many days since she saw the treasure last." I do not know which kind of time he was referring to then, but judging from her excitement I think the days must really have represented decades—she had even forgotten which key fitted the lock and she tried them all and failed and tried again before the tumbler turned.

I was disappointed when I first saw the interior—I had expected gold bricks and a flow of Maria Theresa dollars spilling on the floor, and there were only a lot of shabby cardboard-boxes on the upper shelves and the lower shelves were empty. I think Javitt noted my disappointment and was stung by it. "I told you," he said, "the moit's down below for safety." But I wasn't to stay disappointed very long. He took down one of the biggest boxes off the top shelf and shook the contents on to the earth at my feet, as though defying me to belittle *that*.

And *that* was a sparkling mass of jewellery such as I had never seen before—I was going to say in all the colours of the rainbow, but the colours of stones have not that pale girlish simplicity. There were reds almost as deep as raw liver, stormy blues, greens like the underside of a wave, yellow sunset colours, greys like a shadow on snow, and stones without colour at all that sparkled brighter than all the rest. I say I'd seen nothing like it: it is the scepticism of middle-age which leads me now to compare that treasure-trove with the caskets overflowing with artificial jewellery which you sometimes see in the shop-windows of Italian tourist-resorts.

And there again I find myself adjusting a dream to the kind of criticism I ought to reserve for some agent's report on the import or export value of coloured glass. If this was a dream, these were real stones. Absolute reality belongs to dreams and not to life. The gold of dreams is not the diluted gold of even the best goldsmith, there are no diamonds in dreams made of paste—what seems is. "Who seems most kingly is the king."

I went down on my knees and bathed my hands in the treasure, and while I knelt there Javitt opened box after box and poured the contents upon the ground. There is no avarice in a child. I didn't concern myself with the value of this horde: it was simply a treasure, and a treasure is to be valued for its own sake and not for what it will buy. It was only years later, after a deal of literature and learning and knowledge at second hand, that W.W. wrote of the treasure as something with which he could save the family fortunes. I was nearer to the jackdaw in my dream, caring only for the glitter and the sparkle.

"It's nothing to what lies below out of sight," Javitt remarked with pride.

There were necklaces and bracelets, lockets and bangles, pins and rings and pendants and buttons. There were quantities of those little gold objects which girls like to hang on their bracelets: the Vendôme column and the Eiffel Tower and a Lion of St. Mark's, a champagne bottle and a tiny booklet with leaves of gold inscribed with the names of places important perhaps to a pair of lovers—Paris, Brighton, Rome, Assisi and Moreton-in-Marsh. There were gold coins too—some with the heads of Roman emperors and others of Victoria and

George IV and Frederick Barbarossa. There were birds made out of precious stone with diamond-eyes, and buckles for shoes and belts, hairpins too with the rubies turned into roses, and vinaigrettes. There were toothpicks of gold, and swizzle-sticks, and little spoons to dig the wax out of your ears of gold too, and cigarette-holders studded with diamonds, and small boxes of gold for pastilles and snuff, horse-shoes for the ties of hunting men, and emerald-hounds for the lapels of hunting women: fishes were there too and little carrots of ruby for luck, diamond stars which had perhaps decorated generals or states-men, golden key-rings with emerald-initials, and sea-shells picked out with pearls, and a portrait of a dancing-girl in gold and enamel, with Haidee inscribed in what I suppose were rubies.

"Enough's enough," Javitt said, and I had to drag myself away, as it seemed to me, from all the riches of the world, its pursuits and enjoyments. Maria would have packed everything that lay there back into the cardboard-boxes, but Javitt said with his lordliest voice, "Let them lie," and back we went in silence the way we had come, in the same order, our shadows going ahead. It was as if the sight of the treasure had exhausted me. I lay down on the sacks without waiting for my broth and fell at once asleep. In my dream within a dream somebody laughed and wept.

7

I have said that I can't remember how many days and nights I spent below the garden. The number of times I slept is really no guide, for I slept simply when I had the inclination or when Javitt commanded me to lie down, there being no light or darkness save what the oil-lamp determined, but I am almost sure it was after this sleep of ex-haustion that I woke with the full intention somehow to reach home again. Up till now I had acquiesced in my captivity with little com-plaint; perhaps the meals of broth were palling on me, though I doubt if that was the reason, for I have fed for longer, with as little variety and less appetite, in Africa; perhaps the sight of Javitt's trea-sure had been a climax which robbed my story of any further interest; perhaps, and I think this is the most likely reason, I wanted to begin my search for Miss Ramsgate.

Whatever the motive, I came awake determined from my deep sleep, as suddenly as I had fallen into it. The wick was burning low in the oil-lamp and I could hardly distinguish Javitt's features and Maria was out of sight somewhere behind the curtain. To my astonishment Javitt's eyes were closed—it had never occurred to me before that there were moments when these two might sleep. Very quietly, with my eyes on Javitt, I slipped off my shoes—it was now or never. When I had got them off with less sound than a mouse makes, an idea came to me and I withdrew the laces—I can still hear the sharp ting of the metal tag ringing on the gold po beside my sacks. I thought I had been too clever by half, for Javitt stirred—but then he was still again and I slipped off my makeshift bed and crawled over to him where he sat on the lavatory-seat. I knew that, unfamiliar as I was with the tunnel, I could never outpace Javitt, but I was taken aback when I realized that it was impossible to bind together the ankles of a one-legged man.

But neither could a one-legged man travel without the help of his hands—the hands which lay now conveniently folded like a statue's on his lap. One of the things my brother had taught me was to make a slipknot. I made one now with the laces joined and very gently, millimetre by millimetre, passed it over Javitt's hands and wrists, then pulled it tight.

I had expected him to wake the howl of rage and even in my fear felt some of the pride Jack must have experienced at outwitting the giant. I was ready to flee at once, taking the lamp with me, but his very silence detained me. He only opened one eye, so that again I had the impression that he was winking at me. He tried to move his hands, felt the knot, and then acquiesced in their imprisonment. I expected him to call for Maria, but he did nothing of the kind, just watching me with his one open eye.

Suddenly I felt ashamed of myself. "I'm sorry," I said.

"Ha, ha," he said, "my prodigal, the strayed sheep, you're learning fast."

"I promise not to tell a soul."

"They wouldn't believe you if you did," he said.

"I'll be going now," I whispered with regret, lingering there absurdly, as though with half of myself I would have been content to stay for always.

"You better," he said. "Maria might have different views from me." He tried his hands again. "You tie a good knot."

"I'm going to find your daughter," I said, "whatever you may think."

"Good luck to you then," Javitt said. "You'll have to travel a long way; you'll have to forget all your schoolmasters try to teach you; you must lie like a horsetrader and not be tied up with loyalties any more than you are here, and who knows? I doubt it, but you might, you just might."

I turned away to take the lamp, and then he spoke again. "Take your golden po as a souvenir," he said. "Tell them you found it in an old cupboard. You've got to have something when you start a search to give you substance."

"Thank you," I said, "I will. You've been very kind." I began—absurdly in view of, his bound wrists—to hold out my hand like a departing guest; then I stooped to pick up the po just as Maria, woken perhaps by our voices, came through the curtain. She took the situation in as quick as a breath and squeaked at me—what I don't know—and made a dive with her bird-like hand.

I had the start of her down the passage and the advantage of the light, and I was a few feet ahead when I reached Camp Indecision, but at that point, what with the wind of my passage and the failing wick, the lamp went out. I dropped it on the earth and groped on in the dark. I could hear the scratch and whimper of Maria's sequin dress, and my nerves leapt when her feet set the lamp rolling on my tracks. I don't remember much after that. Soon I was crawling upwards, making better speed on my knees than she could do in her skirt, and a little later I saw a grey light where the roots of the tree parted. When I came up into the open it was much the same early morning hour as the one when I had entered the cave. I could hear kwahk, kwahk, kwahk, come up from below the ground—I don't know if it was a curse or a menace or just a farewell, but for many nights afterwards I lay in bed afraid that the door would open and Maria would come in to fetch me, when the house was silent and asleep. Yet strangely enough I felt no fear of Javitt, then or later.

Perhaps—I can't remember—I dropped the gold po at the entrance of the tunnel as a propitiation to Maria; certainly I didn't have it with me when I rafted across the lake or when Joe, our dog, came leaping out of the house at me and sent me sprawling on my back in the dew of the lawn by the green broken fountain.

PART THREE

I

Wilditch stopped writing and looked up from the paper. The night had passed and with it the rain and the wet wind. Out of the window he could see thin rivers of blue sky winding between the banks of cloud, and the sun as it slanted in gleamed weakly on the cap of his pen. He read the last sentence which he had written and saw how again at the end of his account he had described his adventure as though it were one which had really happened and not something that he had dreamed during the course of a night's truancy or invented a few years later for the school-magazine. Somebody, early though it was, trundled a wheelbarrow down the gravel-path beyond the fountain. The sound, like the dream, belonged to childhood.

He went downstairs and unlocked the front door. There unchanged was the broken fountain and the path which led to the Dark Walk, and he was hardly surprised when he saw Ernest, his uncle's gardener, coming towards him behind the wheelbarrow. Ernest must have been a young man in the days of the dream and he was an old man now, but to a child a man in the twenties approaches middle-age and so he seemed much as Wilditch remembered him. There was something of Javitt about him, though he had a big moustache and not a beard—perhaps it was only a brooding and scrutinizing look and that air of authority and possession which had angered Mrs. Wilditch when she approached him for vegetables.

"Why, Ernest," Wilditch said, "I thought you had retired?"

Ernest put down the handle of the wheelbarrow and regarded Wilditch with reserve. "It's Master William, isn't it?"

"Yes. George said—"

"Master George was right in a way, but I have to lend a hand still. There's a thing in this garden others don't know about." Perhaps he *had* been the model for Javitt, for there was something in his way of speech that suggested the same ambiguity.

"Such as . . ."

"It's not everyone can grow asparagus in chalky soil," he said, making a general statement out of the particular in the same way Javitt had done.

"You've been away a long time, Master William."

"I've travelled a lot."

"We heard one time you was in Africa and another time in Chinese parts. Do you like a black skin, Master William?"

"I suppose at one time or another I've been fond of a black skin."

"I wouldn't have thought they'd win a beauty prize," Ernest said.

"Do you know Ramsgate, Ernest?"

"A gardener travels far enough in a day's work," he said. The wheelbarrow was full of fallen leaves after the night's storm. "Are the Chinese as yellow as people say?"

"No."

There *was* a difference, Wilditch thought: Javitt never asked for information, he gave it: the weight of water, the age of the earth, the sexual habits of a monkey. "Are there many changes in the garden," he asked, "since I was here?"

"You'll have heard the pasture was sold?"

"Yes. I was thinking of taking a walk before breakfast—down the Dark Walk perhaps to the lake and the island."

"Ah."

"Did you ever hear any story of a tunnel under the lake?"

"There's no tunnel there. For what would there be a tunnel?"

"No reason that I know. I suppose it was something I dreamed."

"As a boy you was always fond of that island. Used to hide there from the missus."

"Do you remember a time when I ran away?"

"You was always running away. The missus used to tell me to go and find you. I'd say to her right out, straight as I'm talking to you, I've got enough to do digging the potatoes you are always asking for. I've never known a woman get through potatoes like she did. You'd have thought she ate them. She could have been living on potatoes and not the fat of the land."

"Do you think I was treasure-hunting? Boys do."

"You was hunting for something. That's what I said to the folk round here when you were away in those savage parts—not even coming back here for your uncle's funeral. 'You take my word,' I said to them, 'he hasn't changed, he's off hunting for something, like he always did, though I doubt if he knows what he's after,' I said to them. 'The next we hear,' I said, 'he'll be standing on his head in Australia.'"

Wilditch remarked with regret, "Somehow I never looked there";

he was surprised that he had spoken aloud. "And The Three Keys, is it still in existence?"

"Oh, it's there all right, but the brewers bought it when my uncle died and it's not a free house any more."

"Did they alter it much?"

"You'd hardly know it was the same house with all the pipes and tubes. They put in what they call pressure, so you can't get an honest bit of beer without a bubble in it. My uncle was content to go down to the cellar for a barrel, but it's all machinery now."

"When they made all those changes you didn't hear any talk of a tunnel under the cellar?"

"Tunnel again. What's got you thinking of tunnels? The only tunnel I know is the railway tunnel at Bugham and that's five miles off."

"Well, I'll be walking on, Ernest, or it will be breakfast time before I've seen the garden."

"And I suppose now you'll be off again to foreign parts. What's it to be this time? Australia?"

"It's too late for Australia now."

Ernest shook his brindled head at Wilditch with an air of sober disapproval. "When I was born," he said, "time had a different pace to what it seems to have now," and, lifting the handle of the wheel-barrow, he was on his way towards the new iron gate before Wilditch had time to realize he had used almost the very words of Javitt. The world was the world he knew.

2

The Dark Walk was small and not very dark—perhaps the laurels had thinned with the passing of time, but the cobwebs were there as in his childhood to brush his face as he went by. At the end of the walk there was the wooden gate on to the green which had always in his day been locked—he had never known why that route out of the garden was forbidden him, but he had discovered a way of opening the gate with the rim of a halfpenny. Now he could find no halfpennies in his pocket.

When he saw the lake he realized how right George had been. It was only a small pond, and a few feet from the margin there was an island the size of the room in which last night they had dined. There *were* a few bushes growing there, and even a few trees, one taller and larger than the others, but certainly it was neither the sentinel-pine of

W.W.'s story nor the great oak of his memory. He took a few steps
back from the margin of the pond and jumped.

He hadn't quite made the island, but the water in which he landed
was only a few inches deep. Was any of the water deep enough to
float a raft? He doubted it. He sloshed ashore, the water not even
penetrating his shoes. So this little spot of earth had contained Camp
Hope and Friday's Cave. He wished that he had the cynicism to laugh
at the half-expectation which had brought him to the island.

The bushes came only to his waist and he easily pushed through
them towards the largest tree. It was difficult to believe that even a
small child could have been lost here. He was in the world that
George saw every day, making his round of a not very remarkable
garden. For perhaps a minute, as he pushed his way through the
bushes, it seemed to him that his whole life had been wasted, much as
a man who has been betrayed by a woman wipes out of his mind even
the happy years with her. If it had not been for his dream of the
tunnel and the bearded man and the hidden treasure, couldn't he
have made a less restless life for himself, as George in fact had done,
with marriage, children, a home? He tried to persuade himself that
he was exaggerating the importance of a dream. His lot had probably
been decided months before that when George was reading him *The
Romance of Australian Exploration.* If a child's experience does really
form his future life, surely he had been formed, not by Javitt, but by
Grey and Burke. It was his pride that at least he had never taken his
various professions seriously: he had been loyal to no one—not even
to the girl in Africa (Javitt would have approved his disloyalty). Now
he stood beside the ignoble tree that had no roots above the ground
which could possibly have formed the entrance to a cave and he
looked back at the house: it was so close that he could see George at
the window of the bathroom lathering his face. Soon the bell would
be going for breakfast and they would be sitting opposite each other
exchanging the morning small talk. There was a good train back to
London at 10:25. He supposed that it was the effect of his disease that
he was so tired—not sleepy but achingly tired as though at the end of
a long journey.

After he had pushed his way a few feet through the bushes he came
on the blackened remains of an oak; it had been split by lightning
probably and then sawed close to the ground for logs. It could easily
have been the source of his dream. He tripped on the old roots
hidden in the grass, and squatting down on the ground he laid his ear

close to the earth. He had an absurd desire to hear from somewhere far below the kwahk, kwahk from a roofless mouth and the deep rumbling of Javitt's voice saying, "We are hairless, you and I," shaking his beard at him, "so's the hippopotamus and the elephant and the dugong—you wouldn't know, I suppose, what a dugong is. We survive the longest, the hairless ones."

But, of course, he could hear nothing except the emptiness you hear when a telephone rings in an empty house. Something tickled his ear, and he almost hoped to find a sequin which had survived the years under the grass, but it was only an ant staggering with a load towards its tunnel.

Wilditch got to his feet. As he levered himself upright, his hand was scraped by the sharp rim of some metal object in the earth. He kicked the object free and found it was an old tin chamber-pot. It had lost all colour in the ground except that inside the handle there adhered a few flakes of yellow paint.

3

How long he had been sitting there with the pot between his knees he could not tell; the house was out of sight: he was as small now as he had been then—he couldn't see over the tops of the bushes, and he was back in Javitt's time. He turned the pot over and over; it was certainly not a golden po, but that proved nothing either way; a child might have mistaken it for one when it was newly painted. Had he then really dropped this in his flight—which meant that somewhere underneath him now Javitt sat on his lavatory-seat and Maria quacked beside the calor-gas . . . ? There was no certainty; perhaps years ago, when the paint was fresh, he had discovered the pot, just as he had done this day, and founded a whole afternoon-legend around it. Then why had W.W. omitted it from his story?

Wilditch shook the loose earth out of the po, and it rang on a pebble just as it had rung against the tag of his shoelace fifty years ago. He had a sense that there was a decision he had to make all over again. Curiosity was growing inside him like the cancer. Across the pond the bell rang for breakfast and he thought, "Poor mother—she had reason to fear," turning the tin chamber-pot on his lap.

Adventures

*Stories of heroes, quests,
battles, in fantastic lands*

The Things
That Are Gods

John Brunner

*John Brunner is a Hugo award–winning SF writer. It is traditional for
writers in the SF field since the days of John W. Campbell (who edited not
only the great SF magazine* Astounding *but also the innovative fantasy
magazine* Unknown *in the late 1930s and early 1940s) to stray occasionally
over the boundaries into fantasy, especially as a recreation and in homage to
another writer. Fritz Leiber, Theodore Sturgeon, and even Robert A. Heinlein
and many others did so toward the beginning of their careers. Such is the case
here, with Brunner's stories of the Traveller in Black, written in the late
1960s and early 1970s in the manner of James Branch Cabell, with perhaps
a touch of Jack Vance. This story, the last of the series, is a tour de force filled
with amusing twists and the play of language. Like John M. Ford's "Green Is
the Color," it is complex and logical and a high-water mark in contemporary
fantasy.*

Lo how smothe and curvit be these rocks that in the creacion weren
jaggit, for that they haf ben straikit by myriades of thickheidit folk
hither ycommen in peregrinage, beggarlie criand after *Miracula*. And
I say one at the leste wis granted 'em. Was't not a marvel and a
wonder, pass and credence, that they helden dull ston for more puis-

saunt than your quicke man, the which mought brethe and dreme and
soffre and fede wormes?

—*A Lytel Boke Againste Folie*

I

Tipping back the hood of his black cloak, leaning on his staff of
curdled light, the traveler contemplated the land where he had incar-
cerated the elemental called Litorgos. That being hated both salt and
silt; accordingly, here had been a most appropriate choice.

Half a day's walk from the edge of the sea the land reared up to
form a monstrous irregular battlemented cliff twenty times the height
of a tall man, notched where a river cascaded over the rim of the
plateau above. Thence it spilled across a wedge-shaped plain of its
own making and developed into a narrow delta, following sometimes
this and sometimes that main channel. In principle such land should
have been fertile. Opposite the river's multiple mouths, however, a
dragon-backed island created a swinge, such that at spring tide ocean
water flooded ankle-deep over the soil, permeating it with salt.
Therefore, only hardy and resistant crops could be grown there, and
in a bad year they might be overtaken by the salty inundation before
they were ready to harvest.

This had not prevented the establishment of cities. One had been
founded close to the waterfall, and flourished awhile on trade with
the plateau above. A crude staircase had been carved out of the living
rock, up which slaves daily toiled bearing salt, dried fish and baskets
of edible seaweed, to return with grain and fruit and sunflower oil.
Then the elemental slumbering below stretched to test the firmness
of his intangible bonds; they held him, but the staircase crumbled and
the city disappeared.

More recently a port had been built on wooden piles at the mouth
of the main channel; the island opposite was thickly forested. With
the clearance of the woodland, marble was discovered. Cutting and
polishing it, exporting it on rafts poled along the coastal shallows, the
inhabitants grew rich enough to deck their own homes with marble
and with colorful tiles in patterns, each of which constituted a charm
against ill fortune. But now the marble was exhausted, and so was
most of the timber, and the city Stanguray, which had once been
famous, was reduced to a village. Its present occupants lived in the
attics and lofts of the old town, and as they lay down to sleep could

listen to the chuckle of water rippling within the lower part of their homes. To get from one surviving building to another even toddlers deftly walked along flimsy rope bridges, while the needs of the elderly and better-off—for there were still rich and poor in Stanguray—were met by bearers of reed-mat palankeens, adept at striding down the waterways and across the mudflats on stilts taller than themselves. This mode of transport had no counterpart elsewhere.

And it was entirely fitting, the traveler reflected, that this should be so. For once the river, which here met the ocean, had run under the ramparts of Acromel, and was known as Metamorphia. No longer did it instantly change whatever fell or swam in its waters, it having been decreed that after a certain span of altering the nature of other things, it must amend its own. Yet and still a trace of what had gone before remained, and would forever in the work of all rivers: they would erode mountains, create plains, cause the foundation and destruction of countless cities.

Moreover, in all the settlements along it, including those around Lake Taxhling on the plateau above—the first earnest of the inevitable change in the river's nature, for there it spread out and grew sluggish and reed-fringed before it ultimately spilled over the cliffs and became the opposite, violent and fast and sparkling—the residual magic of Metamorphia had led to schools of enchantment. Of no very great import, admittedly, nothing to compare with the traditions of Ryovora or Barbizond or the Notorious Magisters of Alken Cromlech, but dowered nonetheless with a certain potency.

Such matters being of the keenest interest to him, the traveler set forth along riverside paths toward this paradoxical village of marble columns and tiled pilasters. It was dawn; the clouds in the east were flushing scarlet and rose and vermilion, and fisherfolk were chanting melodiously as they carried their night's catch ashore in reed baskets and spilled them into marble troughs, once destined for the watering of noblemen's horses, where women and children busily gutted them. The smell of blood carried on the wind. It was acute in the traveler's nostrils when he was still a quarter-hour's walk distant.

And then it occurred to him that in fact there was only a slight breeze, and that it was at his back: blowing off the land, toward the sea.

Moreover he perceived of a sudden that it was not just the light of dawn which was tinting pink the water in the channels at either side of the crude causeway he was following.

There must have been an astonishing slaughter.

The traveler sighed. Last time he had seen a river literally running red in this manner, it had been because of a battle: one of dozens, all indecisive, in the constant war between Kanishmen and Kulyamen. But that matter was regulated pretty well to his satisfaction, and in any case this was not human blood.

If it were a precedented event, the inhabitants of Stanguray would presumably be able to inform him concerning this tainting of their river. The ground being impregnated with salt, one could not sink a sweet-water well; rainfall, moreover, was exiguous and seasonal hereabouts. Consequently folk were much dependent on the river's cleanliness.

More disturbed by the situation than seemed reasonable, the traveler lengthened his strides.

II

When the fish guts had been thrown to the gulls, the people of Stanguray went their various ways: the poorest to the beach, where they made fires of twigs and scorched a few of the smaller fish, sardines and pilchards, and gobbled them down with a crust of bread left over from yesterday's baking; the most prosperous, including naturally all those who owned an entire fishing smack with a reliable charm on it, to their homes where breakfast awaited them; and the middling sort to the town's only cookshop, where they handed over a coin or a portion of their catch against the privilege of having their repast grilled on the public fire. Fuel was very short in Stanguray.

The said cookshop was the upper part of what had formerly been a temple, extended under the sky by a platform of creaky scantlings, water-worn and boreworm-pierced, salvaged from a wreck or a building long submerged.

Here a thin-faced, sharp-nosed, sharp-tongued young woman in a russet gown and a long apron supervised a fire on a block of slate whose visible sides were engraved with curlicues and runes. It would have been the altar when the temple's cult still thrived. Presiding over it like any priestess, she deigned to dispense hunks of griddle cake and char or stew vegetables brought by those lucky enough to own a farmable patch of ground, as well as cooking fish, while a hunchbacked boy who never moved fast enough to please her meted out rations of pickled onions, vinegar and verjuice to add a quicker relish to the oily food.

A public fire, plainly, was a profitable operation, for everything about the shop was better appointed than one might have predicted. Though the external platform was fragile, though the variety of the food was wholly dependent on who brought what, nonetheless the woman's gown was of excellent quality, and the walls were ornamented with numerous precious relics, such as one would rather have expected to find in the homes of wealthy fishing-boat owners. Also, at least for those who paid in money, not only beer but even wine was to be had. The hunchback, lashed on by the woman's shouted order, rushed them by the mugful to the customers.

It was clear that at least one more waiter was not only affordable, but urgently needed.

However, that—to the traveler's way of thinking—was not the most curious aspect of this cookshop.

Having sated their bellies, the homeless poor plodded up from the beach carrying clay jars, which they had filled at the point where the estuary water turned from brackish to drinkable . . . or should have. Not long after, a string of children bearing by ones and twos full leathern buckets they could scarcely stand under the weight of also assembled.

The woman in charge seemed not to notice them for a long while. The delay grated on the patience of one girl, some twelve or thirteen years old, and finally she called out:

"Crancina, don't you know it's a foul-water day?"

"What of it?" the woman retorted, rescuing a roasted turnip from the flames, not quite in time.

"We had salt eels this morning, and we're clemmed!"

"Tell your mother to learn better," was the brusque reply, and Crancina went on serving her other customers.

Finally, several minutes later, she stood back from the fire and dusted her hands. Instantly the people waiting rushed toward her. The poorer got there first, being adult and desperate; nonetheless they contrived to offer at least a copper coin, which she took, bit, and dropped in the pocket of her apron, while pronouncing a cantrip over their water jugs. Forced to the rear by those larger and stronger, the children from wealthier homes had no lack of cash, but they cautiously tasted the water after the spell had been spoken, as though fearing that much repetition might weaken it. All satisfied, they wended homeward.

"Are you curious concerning what you see, sir?" a thin voice said at the traveler's elbow. He had taken pains, as ever, not to be conspicuous, but it was time now to make more direct inquiries.

Turning, he found the hunchbacked boy perched on a table, for all the world like a giant frog about to take a leap. His sly dark eyes peered from under a fringe of black hair.

"I own that I'm intrigued," the traveler said.

"I thought you would be, seeing as I don't recall noticing you before. A pilgrim, are you? Cast ashore by some rascally sea captain because contrary winds made it too expensive to carry you all the way to the shrine you booked your passage for?" The boy grinned hugely, making his face as well as his body resemble a frog.

"Do you meet many castaway pilgrims here, then?"

A crooked shrug. "Never! But even that would vary the monotony of my existence. Every day is more or less the same for all of us. Why otherwise would this enchanting of water be so remarkable?"

"Ah, then magic is at work."

"What else? Crancina has a sweet-water spell from granny, all she left when she died, and so whenever the water pinkens they all come here. It's making a nice little pile for her, naturally."

"She charges everybody?"

"Indeed, yes! She claims that performing the rite tires her out, so she must be recompensed."

"What of those—for there must be some such—who have no money to pay for her services?"

"Why, she says they may wait for rain!" The boy essayed a laugh, which became more of a croak immediately.

"I deduce you are Crancina's brother," the traveler said after a pause.

"How so?" The boy blinked.

"You spoke of 'granny,' as though you shared her."

A grimace. "Well, half-brother. I often wonder whether it was granny's curse that twisted me, for I know she disapproved of our mother's second marriage. . . . However that may be!" His tone took on sudden urgency. "Will not you instruct me to bring you something, if only a hunk of bread? For I should by now have cooked and brought her the choicest of last night's catch, rich with oil and fragrant with herbs, and grilled to perfection on the best of our scant supply of logs. Any moment now she will tongue-lash me until it stings like a physical castigation—at which, I may say, she is even more adept! Would you inspect my bruises?"

"There seems to be little love lost between you," the traveler observed.

"Love?" The hunchback cackled. "She wouldn't know the meaning of the word! So long as my father survived, and before our mother became bedridden, I made the most of life despite my deformity. Now that she's my sole commander, mine's a weary lot! I wish with all my heart that someday I may find means to break free of her tyranny and make my own way in the world, against all odds!"

Prompt to his prediction, Crancina shouted, "Jospil, why have you not set my breakfast on the embers? There's costly wood going up in smoke and all the customers are served!"

Her shrill reprimand quite drowned out the traveler's reflexive murmur: "As you wish, so be it."

Cringing, the boy regained the floor and scurried toward her. "Not so, sister!" he pleaded. "One remains unfed, and I did but inquire what he would order."

Abruptly noticing the traveler, Crancina changed her tone to one of wheedling deference. "Sir, what's your pleasure? Boy, make him room and bring clean dishes and a mug at once!"

"Oh, I'll not trouble you to cook for me," the traveler answered, "seeing as how your brother explained your spell leaves you fatigued, and you must need sustenance yourself. I'll take a bit of fish from pickle, bread and beer."

"You're courteous, sir," Crancina sighed, dropping on a nearby bench. "Yes, in truth these foul-water days are an accursed nuisance. Over and over I've proposed that a band of well-armed men be sent out, to trace the trouble to its source, but it's on the high plateau, seemingly, and these fainthearts hold that to be a place of sorcerers none can oppose. Monsters, too, if you believe them."

"Maybe it's the one slaughtering the other," Jospil offered as he set mug and platter before the traveler. "There must come an end of that, when all expire!"

"It's not a joking matter!" snapped Crancina, raising her fist—and then reluctantly unballing it, as though belatedly aware she was being watched by a stranger. But she continued, "By all the powers, I wish I knew what use there is in spilling so much blood! Maybe then I could turn it to my own account for a change, instead of having to

pander to the wants of these cajoling idiots, fool enough—*you* heard
the girl, sir, I'll warrant!—fool enough to eat salt eels for breakfast
when their noses must advise 'em there'll be nothing sweet to quench
their thirst. Would you not imagine they could keep a day or two's
supply that's fit to drink? If they can't afford a coopered barrel, surely
there are enough old marble urns to be had for the trouble of dragging them to the surface. But they can't or won't be bothered.
They're so accustomed to leaning out the window and dipping in the
stream—and sending their ordures the same way, to the discomfort of
us who live closer to the sea—they regard it as a change in the proper
order of the world, never to be resisted, which will come right of
itself."

"They pay you for performing your spell," the traveler said,
munching a mouthful of the pickled fish Jospil had brought and finding it savory. "There's a compensation."

"I admit it," said Crancina. "In time I may grow rich, as wealth is
counted in this miserable place. Already two widowers and two middle-aged bachelors are suing for my hand, and half a share in this
cookshop, of course. . . . But that is not what I want!"—with sudden fierceness. "I've told you what I want! I'm accustomed to being
in charge, and I want that with all my heart and soul, and I'm seeking
a way to secure my fate while this dismal half-ruined town crumbles
about me!"

So long ago there was not means to measure it, the traveler had
accepted conditions pertaining to his sundry and various journeys
through the land, imposed on him when a quartet of crucial planets
cycled to a particular configuration in the sky.

The granting of certain wishes formed an essential element in the
conditions circumscribing him . . . though it was true that the consequences of former wishes were gradually limiting the previous totality of possibilities. Some now were categorically unimplementable.

But even as he muttered formal confirmation—"As you wish, so be
it!"—he knew one thing beyond a peradventure.

This was not one of those.

III

Once it had been permitted him to hasten the seasons of the year
and even alter their sequence. But that power belonged to the ages

when the elementals still roved abroad, their random frenzy entraining far worse divagations of the course of nature. Tamed and pent—like Litorgos under the delta of the river which no longer merited the name of Metamorphia—they were little able to affect the world. Events were tending, in the prescribed manner, toward that end which Manuus the enchanter had once defined as "desirable, perhaps, but appallingly dull." The day would break when all things would have but one nature, and time would have a stop, for the last randomness of the chaos existing in Eternity would have been eliminated.

To make way for a new beginning? Possibly. If not, then—in the very strictest sense—*no matter, never mind.* . . .

Until then, however, the elementals did still exist and fretted away with their enfeebled force, like Fegrim beating at the cap of cold lava which closed the crater of the volcano wherein perforce he now dwelt. Not a few had discovered that human practitioners of magic were, without having chosen to be, their allies. But there was a penalty attached to such collaboration, and the most minor of them had paid it long ago; they were reduced to activating hearth charms. No doubt this was the fate which had overtaken Litorgos—no doubt it was he who drew the blood from the foul water, though he was in no position to benefit thereby. Blood had its place in magic, but it could never free an elemental.

But the traveler did not want so much as to think about Litorgos, or Stanguray, until the remainder of his business was completed. Nonetheless he did wish—and withal wished he could grant himself that wish, as he must grant those of others—that he could whirl the planets around to the conformation which would mark the conclusion of his journey, and thereby enable a return to that place which, with every pace he took, seemed more and more likely to become the focus of terrible and inexplicable events.

Making haste was pointless. The orderly succession of time which he himself had been responsible for, as river silt had created land at Stanguray, now held him tight in its grip. Some relief from his apprehension might be obtained, however, by over-occupying himself. Accordingly on his journey he made a point of visiting not only those places familiar to him from aforetime—and sometimes from before time—but also newer locations.

One such was known by the name of Clurm. Here in the shadow of great oaks a lordling who held his birthright to have been usurped planned with a group of fanatical followers to create such a city as would lure anyone to remove thither on hearing news of it. Now they shivered in tents and ate half-raw game and wild mushrooms, but this new city was to have towers that touched the clouds, and streets wide enough for a hundred to march abreast, and brothels with the fairest of women to attract spirited youths, and a treasury overflowing with gold and gems to pay their fee, and an army would be forged from them to overthrow the usurper, and magicians would be hired to make them unquestioningly loyal, and all in the upshot would be as this wild dreamer pictured it.

Except that after a year of exile his little band had not erected so much as a log cabin, deeming manual labor beneath their dignity.

"But the new Clurm will be of such magnificence!" asserted the lordling, seated as ever closest to the warmth of their tiny campfire; they dared not build a larger one, for fear of being spotted by the usurper's forces, who roamed free in the countryside, while they hid among trees, being less beloved of the common folk. "It will be—it will be. . . . Oh, I can see it now! Would you too could see its wonders! Would I could make you believe in its existence!"

"As you wish, so be it," said the traveler, who stood a little apart, leaning on his staff.

Next day the inevitable happened. In the morning they awoke convinced that their city was real, for they saw it all about them. Joyful, bent on their leader's errand, they set out for all points of the compass, and returned with eager young followers, just as he had predicted.

Who thereupon, not finding the grand city which members of the band believed they could see, set about them with cudgels and bound them hand and foot and committed them for lunatics. The lordling was not exempted from this treatment.

But the traveler, departing, found himself unable to avoid thinking about Stanguray.

Therefore he turned aside from the road which led to Wocrahin, and made his way to a green thicket in the midst of a perfectly circular expanse of hard clay, which neither rain nor thawing after snow could turn to mud. Here was imprisoned Tarambole, with sway over dryness, as Karth formerly over cold in the land called Eyneran: a being to whom the gift had not been granted to tell lies.

Within the thicket, concealed from sight of passersby—which was as well, since lately the people of the region had taken much against magic—the traveler resigned himself to the performance of a ceremony none but he and Tarambole recalled. It gained him the answer to a single question, and it was not what he had looked forward to.

No, it was not, so Tarambole declared, as elemental ranged against him which drew his mind back and back, and back again to thoughts of Stanguray.

"Would that I might consult with Wolpec," murmured the traveler. But he knew not where that strange coy harmless spirit bided now; he had yielded too early to the blandishments of humans, and by his own volition had wasted his power to the point where it was needless to imprison him. He chose his own captivity. Much the same might be said for Farchgrind, who once or twice had provided intelligence for the traveler, and indeed for countless others.

There remained, of course, those whom he had only banished: Tuprid and Caschalanva, Quorril and Lry. . . . Oh, indubitably they would know what was happening! It was quite likely they had set this train of events in motion. But to call on them, the most ancient and powerful of his enemies, when he was in this plight, weakened by puzzlement. . . .

Had they set out to undermine him, knowing they could not meet him in fair fight?

Yet Tarambole, who could not lie, had said his disquiet was not due to the opposition of an elemental.

The gravely disturbing suspicion burgeoned in the traveler's mind that for the first (and the next word might be taken literally in both its senses) *time* a new enemy had arrayed against him.

New.

Not an opponent such as he had vanquished over and over, but something original, foreign to his vast experience. And if it were not the Four Great Ones who had contrived so potent a device. . . .

Then only one explanation seemed conceivable, and if it was correct, then he was doomed.

But his nature remained single, and it was not in him to rail against necessity. Necessarily he must continue on his way. He retrieved his staff and with its tip scattered the somewhat disgusting remains of what he had been obliged to use in conjuring Tarambole, and headed once more toward Wocrahin.

Where, in a tumbledown alley, a smith whose forge blazed and roared and stank yelled curses at his neighbors as he hammered bar iron into complex shapes. His only audience was his son, a boy of ten, who hauled on the chain of the great leather bellows which blew his fire.

"Hah! They want me out of here because they don't like the noise, they don't like the smell, they don't like me. That's what it boils down to, they don't like me because my occupation's not genteel! But they buy my wares, don't they? Boy, answer when you're spoken to!"

But the boy had been at his work three years, and the noise had made him deaf and inhalation of foul smokes had affected his brain, so he could only either nod or shake his head by way of answer. Fortuitously this time he did the proper thing; he nodded.

Thus assuaged, his father resumed his complaining.

"If they don't care to live hard by a forge, let 'em club together and buy me a house outside the town, with a stream beside it to turn a trip-hammer! Let 'em do something to help me, as I help them! After all, a forge must be built somewhere, right? They should see what it's like to live without iron, shouldn't they, boy?"

This time, by alteration, the youngster shook his head. Infuriated, the smith flung down his tools and bunched his fists.

"I'll teach you and the rest of 'em to make mock of me!" he roared. "Oh, that they could see what life is like without iron!"

"As you wish," the traveler said from a smoky corner, "so be it."

Whereupon the iron in the smithy rusted all at once: the anvil, the hammerheads, the tongs, the nails, the cramps that held the massy wooden portion of the bellows, even the horseshoes waiting on the wall. The smith let out a great cry, and the neighbors came running. Such was their laughter that shortly the phrase, "like a smith without iron," entered the common parlance of Wocrahin. Indeed, he taught them to make mock. . . .

But the traveler was ill pleased. This was not like his customary regulation of affairs. It was clumsy. It was more like the rough-and-ready improvisations of the times before Time.

And he could not cure himself of thinking about Stanguray.

In Teq they still gambled to the point of insanity, and might supplanted right among its decadent people.

"No, you may not waste time in playing!" a woman scolded her son, dragging him back from a sandpit where a score of children were amusing themselves. "You're to be the greatest winner since

Fellian, and support me in my old age. Ah, would I knew how to make you understand what I plan for you!"

"As you wish," sighed the traveler, who had taken station in the square where formerly the statue of Lady Luck upreared—where now greedy unscrupulous landlords sold a night's lodging in squalid hovels to those who believed sleeping here would bring good fortune.

The boy's eyes grew round and a look of horror spread across his face. Then he sank his teeth in his mother's arm, deep enough to draw blood, and took to his heels screaming, to scrape a living as best he could among the other outcasts of this now dismal city, the better for his freedom.

Yet that also was unbefitting, in the traveler's view, and still he could not rid his mind of thoughts of Stanguray.

In Segrimond folk no longer tended a grove of ash trees. They had been felled to make a fence and grandstand around an arena of pounded rocks, where for the entertainment of the wealthy savage beasts were matched with one another and against condemned criminals, armed or unarmed according to the gravity of their offense and the certainty of the jury which had heard the evidence. Today witnessed the bloody demise of a girl who had charged her respectable uncle with raping her.

"Now this," the traveler said under his breath, "is not as it should be. It smacks more of chaos, this indecision, than of the proper unfolding of Time. When all things have but a single nature, there will be no room for the doubt which requires settlement in this manner."

He waited. In a little the dead girl's uncle, resplendent in satin trimmed with fur, came weeping from the vantage point reserved for privileged onlookers. "Ah, if you but knew," he cried to fawning hangers-on, "how much it cost me to accuse my darling niece!"

"So be it," said the traveler, and by nightfall the people did indeed know what it had cost him, in bribes to perjured witnesses. On the morrow he was kicked to death by a wild onager.

Yet and still the traveler felt himself infected with the foulness of the world, and could not release his mind from thinking about Stanguray.

Like Teq, Gryte was no longer rich, and on the marches of its land a new town had grown up called Amberlode. To it had removed the more enterprising of the old families from Gryte; against it the less enterprising were mouthing curses.

But the powers on which they called were petty compared to those which had carried Ys back across the boundary of Time and into Eternity—albeit briefly—so their impact on Amberlode was minimal. Realizing this, a man who hated his younger brother for seizing an opportunity he had rejected cried aloud, and said, "Would it were I rather than he who enjoyed that fine new house in the new city!"

"As you wish," murmured the traveler, who had accepted the hospitality this man accorded grudgingly to travelers in order to acquire virtue against some misty hereafter.

And it was so; and because the younger brother under any circumstances was the more enterprising and talented, and moreover understood how to hate, his cursing was efficacious, and the fine new house collapsed to its occupants' vast discomfiture.

And that was wrong!

The realization brought the traveler up short. There should have lain neither blame nor suffering on the brother who had chosen aright, yet here it came, and with brutal force. For as far back as he could recall it had been his intention that the literal interpretation he placed on the wishes he granted should be a means of insuring justice. The suffering must be confined to those who had richly earned it. What was awry?

The constellations had not yet wheeled to the configuration marking the conclusion of his journey. By rights he should have continued in prescribed sequence from one stage of it to the next, to the next, to the next. . . .

But he found he could not. If it were true that some hitherto unencountered foe, neither human nor elemental, now ranged against him, that implied a fundamental shift in the nature of all the realities. Beyond that, it hinted at something so appalling that he might as well abandon his task at once. He had believed his assignment binding, forever and forever, within and outside Time. But it was possible, to the One for Whom all things were possible—

He canceled that thought on the instant. Completion of it would of itself wipe him from the record of what was, what might be, and what was as though it had never been. His status was, as he well knew, at best precarious.

Which made him think of the rope-walking children at Stanguray.

Which made him think on what he had said and done there.

Which made him take the most direct route thither, and immediately.

Which taught him the most painful lesson of his existence.

IV

Initially around Lake Taxhling there had been only reed huts wherein dwelt fisherfolk who well understood how to charm their way safely across its waters, and distinguish by simple conjuration those natural fishes which were safe to eat from those which had been transformed by the river Metamorphia and on which a geas lay.

Certain onerous duties bought them this privilege, but in general they regarded their prime deity Frah Frah as being exigent but not unkind.

Time wore on, though, and by degrees they quit performance of the rituals which had purchased their livelihood; in particular, they no longer ceremonially burnt down and rebuilt their homes twice annually.

By then it was no longer so essential to tell the nature of one's catch; the river's power was waning. Now and then someone died through carelessness, generally a child or an oldster, but the survivors shrugged it off.

Then, as the river's magic diminished further, certain nomads followed it downstream: traders and pilgrims and people who had so illused their former farms that the topsoil blew away and criminal fugitives as well. Finding that on the far side of Lake Taxhling there was a sheer enormous drop, they decided to remain, and the original inhabitants—being peaceable—suffered them to do so.

Henceforward the reed huts were not burned because there were none; the newcomers preferred substantial homes of timber, clay and stone. Henceforward the shrines dedicated to Frah Frah were increasingly neglected. Henceforward meat figured largely in the local diet, as fish had formerly; herds of swine were established in the nearby woodlands, and grew fat in autumn on acorns and beechmast, while sheep and goats were let loose on the more distant slopes, though the grazing was too poor for cattle. The way of life around Lake Taxhling was transformed.

There followed a succession of three relatively gentle invasions, by ambitious conquerors, each of which endowed the area with a new

religion not excessively dissimilar from the old one. It was a reason
for children to form gangs and stage mock battles on summer evenings, rather than a cause for adult strife, that some families adhered
to Yelb the Comforter and others to Ts-graeb the Everlasting or Honest Blunk. They coexisted with fair mutual tolerance.

Altogether, even for someone like Orrish, whose stock was unalloyed pre-conquest, and whose parents maintained a dignified pride
in their seniority of residence, life on the edge of Taxhling was not
unpleasant.

Or rather, it had not been until lately. Oh, in his teens—he had just
turned twenty—he had been mocked because he confessed to believing in the fables told to children about a town below the waterfall
with which there had once been trade, but he was strong and supple
and could prove his point by scaling the ruined stairs both ways,
demonstrating that the idea was not wholly out of the question.

That, therefore, was endurable. So too was the military service
imposed by the region's current overlord, Count Lashgar, on all between eighteen and twenty-one. It was a nuisance, but it was imperative if one wished to marry, and it enabled youngsters to break free
of their parents, which could not be bad. Because the count had no
territorial ambitions, and spent his time poring over ancient tomes,
the most dangerous duties assigned to his troops consisted of keeping
track of goats on hilly pastures, and the most unpleasant in the
monthly shambles. There were too many people now for fish to feed
them all, so the latest invader, Count Lashgar's grandfather, had exhibited a neat sense of household economy by decreeing that the
slaughter of animals should henceforth be an army monopoly,
thereby tidily combining weapons training (they were killed with
sword and spear) with tax collection (there was a fixed charge based
on weight and species, which might be commuted by ceding one
sheep of seven, one goat of six and one hog of five), with religious
duty (the hearts were saved to be offered on the altar of his preferred
deity, Ts-graeb the Everlasting), and with—as he naïvely imagined—
an increase in the fish supply. It seemed reasonable to expect that by
establishing a shambles in the shallows of the lake one could contrive
to give them extra nourishment.

The lake being sluggish, however, the stench grew appalling;
moreover, it was the only source of drinking and cooking water. His
son peremptorily removed the shambles to the very edge of the plateau, and his grandson Lashgar saw no grounds for disturbing this

arrangement. Now and then in the old days one had seen, on the delta below, people shaking fists and shouting insults, but they were too far away to be heard, and none had the temerity to climb the ancient stairs and argue. Not since before Orrish was born had it been deemed advisable to maintain double guards along the rim of the cliffs.

Maybe if that old custom had been kept up. . . .

Perhaps, yes, things would not have taken such a horrifying turn around Taxhling. He would naturally not have been able to do what he was doing—deserting his post by night—without killing his companion or persuading him to come along; on the other hand, the necessity would not have arisen. . . .

Too late for speculation. Here he was, scrambling down the cliff, repeating under cover of darkness his climb of five years ago, wincing at every pebble he dislodged, for the steps rocked and tilted and some had vanished for five or ten feet together. His muscles ached abominably, and though the night was frosty, rivulets of perspiration made him itch all over. However, there was no turning back. He must gain the safety of the level ground below. He must let the people of Stanguray know what enormities one of their number was perpetrating, rouse them to anger and to action!

Under his cold-numbed feet a ledge of friable rock abruptly crumbled. Against his will he cried out as he tumbled into blackness. His memory of the climb he had made when he was fifteen was not so exact that he knew how high he was, but he guessed he fell no more than twenty feet.

But he landed on a heap of small boulders, frost-fractured from the cliff, and felt muscles and sinews tearing like wet rags.

How now was he to bear a warning to Stanguray?

And if not he, then who?

There was nothing else for it. Despite his agony, he must crawl onward. Even though the witch Crancina had been spawned among them, the people of Stanguray did not deserve the fate she planned. They had at least, presumably, had the sense to drive her out, instead of—like that damned fool Count Lashgar!—welcoming her and giving in to every one of her foul demands.

V

Autumn had begun to bite when the traveler returned to Stanguray. It was a clear though moonless night. Mist writhed over the marshes. The mud was stiff with cold and here and there a shallow puddle was sufficiently free from salt to have formed a skin of ice.

Despite the chill, the reek of blood was dense in the air.

But in the village of marble pillars and gaudy tilework there was no sign of life, save for suspicious birds and rats.

Unable at first to credit that the place was totally deserted, the traveler slacked the grip of the forces which held together his staff of curdled light. A radiance bright as the full moon's revealed it was only too true. Everywhere doors and shutters stood ajar. No chimney, even on the wealthiest homes, uttered smoke. The boats were gone from the quay, and some few poor household items lay on it, abandoned.

Yet this did not smack of a raid. There was no sign of violence—no fires had been started, no dead bodies lay untidy on the ground. This had been a planned and voluntary departure.

Moreover, as he abruptly realized, something else was wrong. He was immune to the night's freezing air, but not to the chill of dismay which this discovery evoked in him.

Litorgos was no longer penned between salt and silt. The elemental too was absent from this place.

Until this moment he had believed that in all of space and all of time none save he had been granted the power to bind and loose the elemental spirits. Could it be that to another the inverse of his gift had been assigned? Surely the One Who—

But if that were so, then Tarambole had lied. And if that were so, then the universe would become like the pieces on a game board, to be tipped randomly back into their box and played again with different rules. There was no sign of such a catastrophe: no comets, no eruptions, no dancing stars.

A new enemy.

More at a loss than ever before, he pondered and reviewed his knowledge, standing so still that hoarfrost had the chance to form on the hem of his black cloak. With all his powers of reasoning he was still far from an answer when he heard a thin cry, weak as a child's but far too bass.

"Help! Help! I can go no further!"

Half in, half out of a muddy channel, some three or four hundred paces toward the escarpment, he came upon the one who had shouted: a young man in leather jerkin, breeches and boots, whimpering against his will for the pain of torn ligaments in his leg.

"Who are you?" the traveler challenged.

"Orrish of Taxhling," came the faint reply.

"And your mission?"

"To warn the folk of Stanguray what doom's upon them! I never dreamed such horrors could be hatched in a human brain, but—Ow, ow! Curses on my hurt leg! But for it, I'd have been there long ere now!"

"To small avail," the traveler said, bending to haul the man clear of the icy water. "They're gone. All of them."

"Then my errand of mercy was in vain?" Orrish said blankly. And of a sudden he began to laugh hysterically.

"Not so," the traveler returned, touching with his staff the injured leg. At every contact a light shone forth, the color of which humans had no name for. "There, how does it feel?"

Sobered by astonishment, Orrish rose incredulously to his feet, testing the damaged limb. "Why—why, it's a miracle!" he whispered. "Who are you, that you can work such magic?"

"I have many names, but a single nature. If that means aught to you, so be it; if not, and increasingly I find it does not, well and good. . . . With a name like Orrish, I take you to be of ancient Taxhling stock."

"You know our people?"

"I daresay I've known them longer than you," the traveler admitted. "What's amiss that sent you on your desperate mission?"

"They've gone insane! A witch has come among us, dedicated to the service of Ts-graeb—or so she says—claiming to know how to make our lord Count Lashgar live forever! Now me, I hold no brief against the worshipers of Ts-graeb, or anyone else, although in truth. . . ." Orrish's tongue faltered.

With a hint of his customary dry humor the traveler said, "In truth you adhere to the cult of Frah Frah, and you wear his amulet in the ancient and invariable place, and because your belt has come adrift from your breeches the fact is plainly discernible. I am pleased to learn Frah Frah is not wholly devoid of followers; his ceremonies were often very funny, in a coarse way, and among his favorite offerings was a hearty laugh. Am I not right?"

Frantically making good the deficiencies in his garb, Orrish said in awe, "But that was in my grandfather's day!"

"More like your three-times-great-grandfather's day," the traveler said matter-of-factly. "But you still haven't told me why you were so desperate to warn the folk of Stanguray."

Piecemeal, then, he extracted the whole story, and thereby learned that Tarambole, while of course he could not lie, had access to the power of ambiguity.

That discovery was a vast relief. But it still left a wholly unprecedented situation to resolve.

"This witch is called Crancina," Orrish said. "She came among us recently—last spring—and brought with her a familiar in the guise of a hunchbacked boy. They hailed from Stanguray, and at once everybody was prepared to accept them as marvel-workers, for in living memory none but I has attempted to scale the face of yon escarpment.

"We'd always regarded Count Lashgar as a harmless, bookish fellow. In shops and taverns one might hear people say with knowing nods and winks, 'One could do worse than live under such an overlord!' Confessedly, I've said and believed the same.

"Little did we know that he plotted with his books and incantations to find a means of outliving us all! But *she* did, the witch Crancina, and she came to him and said she knew what use could be made of the blood spilled from the beasts we kill each month at the dark of the moon. She said that once there was enough blood in the water of the lake. . . . Sir, are you well?"

For the traveler had fallen silent and stock-still, gazing into the past.

In a little he roused himself enough to answer. "No! No, my friend, I am not well, nor is anything well! But at least I now comprehend what is the nature of my unprecedented enemy."

"Explain, then!" pleaded Orrish.

"She made out that once enough blood was in the water, it would turn to an elixir of long life, is that the case?"

"Why, yes! Moreover she declared it should be ample for all to drink, giving each of us an extra span of years!"

"In that she lied," the traveler said, flat-voiced.

"I have suspected so." Orrish bit his lip. "I won't presume to ask how you know—that you're a strange and powerful personage, my well-healed leg declares. . . . Would, though, I might give her the lie direct, on your authority! For what they propose up yonder, in my name, is so ghastly, so awful, so disgusting . . . !"

"It was this that drove you to desert your post?"

The young man gave a miserable nod. "Indeed, indeed. For, lacking as much blood as she maintained was requisite, they began to say, 'Are there not those who bleed at Stanguray? Did not Orrish clamber down and up the cliffs? And must not human blood be more effective? Let us set forth and capture them, and drag them hither, and cut their throats to make the magic work!' "

"And what said Count Lashgar to this mad scheme?"

"Unless Crancina's rites succeed today, he'll give his soldiers orders for the mission."

"Who's making rope?"

The question took Orrish aback for a second; then he caught on and burst out laughing, not as before—halfway to hysteria—but with honest mirth, making an offering to Frah Frah.

"Why, I'm as dumb and blind as they! Surely it will call for miles of rope to fetch hundreds of unwilling captives over level ground, let alone drag them up the cliffs!"

"Such work is not in hand?"

"Why, no! Drunk on promises, the people care only for butchery. Now it's at such a stage that those who set snares by night are ordered to bring their catch, still living, to be included in the daily ceremony. And woe betide those whose rabbits and hares and badgers are already dead!"

"I understand," the traveler said somberly, and thought on an ancient ceremony, practiced when the forces of chaos were more biddable than now. Then, one had taken a shallow bowl, ideally of silver, incised with the character harst, midmost of those in the Yuvallian script, and filled it with water, and laid therein the germ of a homunculus, and cut one's finger and let three drops fall to mingle with the water, and thereupon the homunculus set forth to do one's bidding. Kingdoms had been overthrown that way.

What would betide when the ceremony was expanded to a whole great lake?

And particularly and essentially: this lake of all . . . !

"Sir," Orrish ventured anxiously, "you spoke just now of some enemy of yours. Is that the witch—is your enemy the same as ours? May we count you for an ally?"

The traveler parried the question. "What drove you to climb down the cliff by night? Fear that you, not worshiping Ts-graeb, would be excluded from the universal benefit of immortality?"

"No—no, I swear on my father's honor!" Orrish was sweating; the faint light of the false dawn glistened on his forehead. "But—well, in the cult of the god I have been raised to worship, it is said that pleasure bought at the cost of another's suffering is no pleasure at all. So it seems to me with this pretended immortality—even given that that is the goal of those cruel ceremonies, which you contest. How can a life worth living be purchased at the expense of so much viciousness?"

"Then let us return together to Taxhling," the traveler said with decision. "Your wish is granted. You shall give the witch the lie direct."

"But *is* she your enemy?" Orrish persisted.

"No, my friend. No more than you are."

"Then—who . . . ?"

Because the question was posed with an honest need to know, the traveler was constrained to answer, after long reluctance.

"That which is against me is within me."

"You speak in riddles!"

"So be it! I had rather not let it be noised abroad that I overlooked so crude a truth: this is my fault. For the first time, I set forth to fight *myself.*"

VI

Blessedly warm in the room assigned to her at Count Lashgar's residence—for here on the plateau they could afford to be prodigal with fuel, and a log fire had burned all night two steps away from her bed—Crancina woke with a sudden sense of excitement such as she had only felt once before: back in the spring, when it had suddenly dawned on her what use could be made of all that blood fouling Stanguray's river.

A serving maid drowsed on a stool in the chimney corner. Shouting to rouse her, Crancina threw aside the thick warm coverlet of her bed.

Today, yes today, her efforts were sure to be rewarded! Then let that slimy Count go whistle for his dreamed-of immortality! He was on all fours with the greedy men who had demanded her hand in marriage back at Stanguray, when what they wanted was not her, but the profits of her cookshop and her sweet-water spell.

Today would teach him, and tomorrow would teach the world, a lesson never to be forgotten.

Humming a merry tune, she wrapped herself snug in a sheepskin cape against the chill early-morning air.

"My lord! My lord! Wake up!" whispered the serving man whose duty it was to rouse Count Lashgar. "Mistress Crancina is certain of success today, and sent her girl to tell me so!"

Muzzily peering from among high-piled pillows, the Count demanded, "What's worked the trick, then? The extra animals I ordered to be brought in from snares and traps?"

"My lord, I'm not party to your high councils," was the reproachful answer. "But surely in one of your books the secret's explained?"

"If it had been," Lashgar sighed, forcing himself to sit up, "I'd not have waited this long for the fulfillment of my lifetime dreams."

Through the mists which haunted the edges of the lake a band of shivering soldiers marched with drums and gongs, and on hearing them people turned out enthusiastically, forgoing breakfast save for a hasty crust and a mouthful of strong liquor. In the old days the morning of a shambles was one to be avoided; now, miraculously, it had been transformed into the signal event of the month . . . today more than ever, for the rumors had already taken rise.

"Today's the day! Crancina told the Count—it's bound to work today! Just think! Maybe some of us, maybe all of us, will be deathless by tonight!"

Only a few cynical souls were heard to wonder aloud what would happen if it proved there was power enough in the bloody water to make one person live forever, and no more. Who would get it, if it weren't the witch?

But those were generally of the aboriginal lakeside stock, whose ancestors had had their fill of magic long ago. Those who worshiped Ts-graeb the Everlasting, as Lashgar did—and his adorers had grown vastly more numerous since the witch arrived—clamored loudly for the favor of their deity, and arrived at the lake's shore singing and clapping their hands.

They raised a vast cheer when Lashgar and Crancina appeared, preceded by the image of Ts-graeb in the guise of an old and bearded wiseacre, which was borne on the shoulders of six men-at-arms. The procession was flanked by the priests and priestesses of Yelb the Comforter, portrayed as having nipples all over her naked bulk from toes to hairline, and the handful who still adhered to Honest Blunk, whose image and symbol was a plain white sphere. No believers in Frah Frah were bold enough to parade their creed, and indeed scarcely any remained.

But, bringing up the very tail, here came a hunchbacked boy in jester's garb, with bells on hat and heels, capering and grimacing as he feigned to strike the onlookers with his wand of office: a pig's bladder on a rod tied with gaudy ribbons. Even the followers of Honest Blunk were glad to crack a smile at sight of him, for a bitter wind soughed over the plateau.

"And where," the traveler murmured as he contrived to fall in beside the jester, "did you get that particolored finery?"

"It's not stolen, if that's what you're thinking!" came the sharp reply. "It belonged to the jester whom Count Lashgar's grandfather kept, and I have been given it by one of the Count's retainers. Who are you that you put such a question to me? Why, I recall *you,* and only too well." At once the boy ceased his awkward parody of a dance. "It was the very day after you spoke with her that my sister took this crazy notion into her head, and forced me hither up the cliffs! More than once I thought I would die, but my deformity has luckily left my torso light enough for my arms to bear the weight of, and where she almost fell I could cling on for us both. . . . But often I feel I'd rather have let her fall than be condemned to my present lot!"

"Is it no better than at Stanguray?"

"Perhaps by a hair's breadth, now I've appropriated these clothes and wand." Jospil struck the traveler with it, scowling. "But they made me out to be Crancina's familiar at first, and wanted to feed me on hot coals and *aqua regia.* Besides, they have no sense of humor, these people! If they did, would they not long ago have laughed Crancina out of countenance?"

"You are absolutely correct," the traveler agreed solemnly. "And therein lies the key to fulfillment of a wish you made in my hearing. Do you recall it?"

The hunchback gave his usual crooked shrug. "It would have been

the same as what I say to everybody, except of course my sister: that
one day I should find a means of freeing myself from her."

"And making your way in the world against all odds?"

"Yes, I've said that over and over, and doubtless to you."

"Meaning it?"

Jospil's eyes flashed fire. "Every word!"

"Today, then, is your chance to make the most of your jester's role
and achieve your ambition simultaneously."

Jospil blinked. "You speak so strangely," he muttered. "Yet you
came to the hearth like anybody, and you were politer to my sister
than she deserved, and—yes, it was precisely from the moment of
your visit that she took these crazy notions into her head, and . . . I
don't know what to make of you, I swear I don't."

"Count yourself fortunate," the traveler said dryly, "that you are
not called on to do so. But remember that there is magic abroad
today, if not the kind Count Lashgar is expecting, and that you are a
crux and focus of it. Sir Jester, I bid you good morning!"

And with a deep-dipping bow, and an inclination of his staff, and a
great flapping swirl of his black cape, the traveler was gone about his
business.

VII

How it was that he was back at this guard post in time to reclaim
his spear and shield and greet his dawn relief before his absence was
noticed, Orrish could afterward never quite recall—nor what had
become of his mysterious companion once they were on the plateau.

But he did remember one thing with perfect clarity. He had been
promised the chance to give the witch the lie direct. Anxious, he
awaited his opportunity. There seemed little chance of it happening,
though, for immediately on returning to barracks he had been cor-
nered by a sergeant with a squad lacking one man, to collect the
night's trapped animals and bring them to the lakeside to have their
life's blood let. In all their various tones they squeaked and whimpered, and their cries made a hideous cacophony along with the
bleating and grunting of the few remaining domestic animals, pent in
folds of hurdles within scent of the bloody water. At this rate of
slaughter, though there would be more pickled meat than their barrels could hold, and more smoked meat than hooks to hang it on,
which would see the community through the winter, there would be

no breeding stock to start again in the summer. Orrish shook his head
dolefully, detesting the assignment he had been given almost as much
as he loathed the notion of kidnapping and killing the people of
Stanguray.

That at least, if the traveler was to be trusted, was no longer a
possibility.

But where was the traveler? Orrish searched the vicinity with worried eyes. Like all those who came of the ancient Taxhling stock, he
had been raised to distrust magic and its practitioners, and the way his
leg had been healed left no room for doubt that the man in the black
cloak trafficked in such arts. Was he—like the witch Crancina—deceitful and self-serving? . . .

Orrish started a little. How did he know the witch was defrauding
the people? Why, because the traveler in black had told him so.
Maybe he should believe what the rest of his folk believed, rather
than take the word of a stranger?

Biting his lip in terrible confusion, he was distracted by a shout
from the sergeant, calling the soldiers to attention at the appearance
of Count Lashgar. Numbly obeying, Orrish wished desperately that
the traveler would come back; everything had seemed so simple in
his company.

Along with the other young conscripts, he awaited the order to
butcher the pitiable beasts.

There were obligatory cheers and shouts; they did not last long,
however, because everybody was too eager to hear what Crancina
proposed to do today. Graciously bowing from side to side as he took
station on a kind of dais erected over the water, Lashgar addressed
his subjects in a voice surprisingly large for so slim and short a man.

"We are promised marvels!" he declared. "You want to see them
as much as I do! I'll waste no time on speechifying, therefore, but let
Mistress Crancina have her way!"

Everybody brightened at the brevity of his introduction. And then
quieted, and shivered. Even while Lashgar was speaking, Crancina
had thrown aside her thick sheepskin cape and begun to make passes
in the air, muttering to herself the while. The words could not be
made out even at close quarters, yet there was such a resonance to
them that if one caught their slightest echo it could send a tremor
down the spine.

Now and then she felt in a pouch hung at her girdle and tossed a pinch of powder into the water, rather as though she were seasoning a soup.

Along with all the rest the traveler was mightily impressed. This was the first occasion in more of his visits to this world than he cared to try to count when he had witnessed a genuinely new magic rite. Even though the change might be classed as more quantitative than qualitative, the purpose Crancina was putting her work to was radically different from anything he could recall.

Now and then in the past he had wondered whether cookery, where the practitioner might begin with something not only unpalatable but actually poisonous and conclude with something not only digestible but delicious, might not be the ultimate destiny of temperaments which in earlier ages would have led people to meddle in magic. He made a firm resolve to keep a careful eye on cooks in future.

For this recipe, at least, was working fine.

Much as though it were milk being curdled by rennet, the water of Lake Taxhling was solidifying. Instead of the random patterns made by wind and wave, shapes were discernible on the surface, and though they jostled and shifted, they did not break up any longer. The onlookers oohed and aahed, while Count Lashgar, barely disguising his incredulity, tried not to jump up and down for joy.

The shapes were not altogether comfortable to look at; however, they were visible, and little by little they were beginning to stand up from the surface, first as shallowly as ripples, then with more and more protuberance. Also they enlarged. Somewhat separated from each other, they numbered altogether a thousand or two, and their forms were strange beyond description. If this one was reminiscent of a claw-tipped fern frond, its neighbor hinted at a dishmop with vastly enlarged tentacles; if another called to mind a hog's head with holes in it, the next resembled a mouse with twenty legs.

The only thing they had in common, barring their present almost stillness, was their coloration. They were the gray of common pumice stone, and bobbed on the now oily surface of the lake, which had congealed to form them, with a motion as sluggish as though time had slowed to a twentieth of its regular rate.

"Magic!" murmured the onlookers, delighted. "Magic indeed!"

"But she is a liar—she *is*!" came a sudden cry from the direction of the stock pens, where soldiers were dutifully readying the last of the animals to be killed. *"The witch Crancina is a liar!"*

Everyone reacted, especially Lashgar and Crancina herself; the Count shouted an order to the sergeant to quiet the man who had called out, while she shot one nervous glance in that direction and kept on with her recital of cantrips, faster and faster. The images forming on the lake wavered, but grew firm again.

"Silence that man!" the sergeant bellowed, and two of his companions tried to take Orrish by the arms. He shoved his shield in the face of one, breaking his nose, and winded the other with the butt end of his spear, on his way to the nearest point of vantage, the shambles stone—formerly at the far end of the lake near the waterfall, but lately brought back to this spot in the interests of conserving the spilled blood. It was a block of granite with channels cut in the upper face for the blood to drain from. Taking a stance on it, Orrish waved his spear across the waters of the lake.

"How did she expect to get away with it?" he roared. "We know what these apparitions are!"

They wavered again, but remained solid, and were now stock still, as rigid as glass, and as fragile.

Suddenly, cautiously, a few of the watchers—mostly elderly—nodded. Realizing they were not alone, they drew themselves proudly upright and did it again more vigorously.

"And *we* know they have nothing to do with immortality!" Orrish yelled at the top of his lungs. *"Get* away!"—kicking out at the sergeant who was trying to snare him by the ankles. "I don't mean *you* or your blockhead of a master the Count! I mean *us,* who've been here long enough not to be cheated by the witch! Look at her! Look at her! Can't you read fear and terror on every line of her face?"

Crancina was wildly shouting something, but the wind had risen in the past minute or two, and the words were carried away. Beside her, paling, Count Lashgar was signaling to his bodyguard to close in; the priests of Blunk and Yelb and Ts-graeb were likewise huddling together for comfort.

Meantime the images formed on the lake remained unmoving.

"And for the benefit of you who weren't lucky enough to be brought up like me in a household where they still know about this kind of thing," Orrish blasted, "I'll explain! In the remote and distant past our superstitious ancestors believed that the weird and unique objects which came down the river—those which had been of a sinking nature floated, obviously!—all these objects were divine and deserving of worship. So they set up shrines, and made offerings, and called on them when reciting hearth spells, and the rest of it. But at last a sensible teacher arose among us and asked why we had so many petty deities when we could contrive one with all their best attributes and none of their worst. The people marveled and wondered and agreed, and that was how we came to worship Frah Frah! And when we had all consented to the change, the old gods were carried to the lake and thrown back in, to lie on the bottom until the end of the world. And so would they have done, but for Crancina! Ask her now what they have to do with immortality for us, or even her and Lashgar!"

"This is all a falsehood!" Crancina gasped. "I know nothing of ancient gods such as you describe!"

"But do you know anything of immortality?" Lashgar demanded. Seizing a sword from the nearest of his guardsmen, he leveled it at her breast.

"Of course she doesn't!" came a crowing voice. "She's fit to run a cookshop, and no more, and that's what she did in Stanguray! Hee-hee-hee-hee-*haw*!"

And Jospil in his jester's guise frog-hopped toward his sister with a donkey-loud bray of laughter.

Startled, about to launch another broadside of invective, Orrish high on his rock checked, and looked toward Jospil, and against all his best intentions had to grin. The grin turned to a chuckle; the chuckle became a roar of merriment, and he had to lean on his spear for support as he rocked back and forth with tears streaming from his eyes. The mirth was so contagious that, without knowing what was funny, small children echoed it, and tending them their parents could not help but giggle, at the least, and that also spread. While Lashgar and Crancina and the more pompous of the attendant priests—of whichever denomination—looked scandalized and shouted orders which went disregarded by their subordinates, the entire crowd was caught up in one monstrous eruption of hilarity. The eldest of the onlookers, hobbling and toothless, who were as much at a loss about the proceedings as the babes in arms, cackled along with the rest, until the welkin seemed to ring with the sound.

And it did.

Echoed, re-echoed, amplified, the laughter started to resonate.

There was a sort of buzzing which filled the air, making it denser than was normal. The vibrations fed on one another; they became painful to the ears; they set the teeth on edge; they shrilled and rasped and ground. Here and there among the throng people looked frightened and cast about for a way of escape. But there was none. The whole huge bowl which constituted the plateau of Lake Taxhling had become a valley of echoes, where sound—instead of dying away—increased in volume, and intensity, and harshness.

All this while the accidental creations of the river once known as Metamorphia, conjured back to the surface of the lake, stood utterly still . . . until they began to tremble under the impact of the noise.

Suddenly a thing like a walrus with a flower for a head cracked sharply across. A sprinkling of fine powder drifted into the air, dancing in time with the vibrations.

Then a curiously convoluted object, half slender and half bulky as though a giant dragonfly had miscegenated with a carthorse, shattered into tiny fragments. At once there was a rush into the vacancy from either side. Something not unlike a colossal fist, with feathery excrescences, collided with a great hollow structure and reduced it to tinkling shards.

The laughter took on a rhythmical pattern. Now it could be discerned that whenever it reached a certain pitch of intensity another of the objects Crancina had conjured forth broke apart; each such breaking entailed another, and then others. The watchers, who for a moment had been frightened, found this also very amusing, and their mirth redoubled until all were gasping for breath.

Into dust vanished the last relics of articles cast long ago from the citadel of Acromel; into sparkling crystals and jagged fragments dissolved what had once been sacrifices, and weapons, and the bodies of sad drunken fools, and those of condemned criminals, and the carcasses of careless animals, and the husks of insects, and luck-offerings, and deodands, and stolen treasure abandoned by thieves, and fish which had swum from higher reaches of the river, and all sorts of casual rubbish, and leaves and twigs and branches tossed into the water by children at their play, and accidental conformations created by the perversity of the river itself out of lumps of mud which tumbled from its banks.

Instead of a horde of weird fantastical solid objects there was for a moment a silvery shimmering expanse. Precisely then the laughter reached its peak, and every gust was like a blow from a gigantic hammer, descending so fast that the very air grew solid at the impact.

On the third blow, the plateau split. Those who were closest to the cliff fell back from it, shouting, all thought of amusement forgotten. The earth trembled underfoot, and a jagged cleft appeared across the bed of the lake, beginning where the river had tumbled down the escarpment.

In one—two—three violent shifts of colossal mass, Lake Taxhling disappeared: first in a torrent, carving a gash down the face of the steep rocks a dozen times as wide as formerly; then in a steady flood as more and more of the cliff face fell away and the water could spill over as from a tilted basin; lastly as a dribbling ooze, which bared the mud of its bottom. . . .

And in the middle of the new flat dry expanse, a statue: a little awry from the vertical, and draped moreover with garlands of gray-green weed, but the solitary object not affected by the pounding of the laughter which had smashed all of Crancina's evocations into rubble, and intact enough after its long submersion for it to be instantly recognizable.

The first to identify it was Orrish, regaining his feet after having been knocked down by the earth tremors. For a long moment he gazed at it in disbelief. Then, in sudden frantic haste, he clawed open the belt holding his leather breeches and produced the amulet he secretly wore.

Holding it aloft, he shouted, "Frah Frah! Have we not at last given you the offering you most desire? Laughter has been scant since you departed! And there's a bigger joke than all the rest!"

Lifting his spear, he pointed at Lashgar and Crancina. The pattern of the rift breaching the lake floor was such that the little promontory where they had taken up their positions was isolated between two crevasses.

As though the spear had been a signal, the turfed surface tipped, and with a sighing noise subsided. The Count, and the witch, and the priests, and the idols, and all their hangers-on were abruptly floundering waist-deep in the foulest possible kind of muck. With every frantic move they sprayed it over themselves, until they were unrecognizable.

"A satisfactory outcome, after all," the traveler said, putting by the staff which had dislodged the promontory. "But it was a near squeak. Still, this time the amusement I hear is unforced."

Indeed, there had been one person agile enough to escape the general muddying of the Count's party, and now in his gaudy clothes of red and yellow he was leaping up and down on safe dry land, waving his bladder-tipped wand as if to conduct the orchestra of laughs emanating from the crowd.

One final touch. . . .

The traveler waited for precisely the correct instant; then, with a tap of his staff on the ground, he insured that just as Jospil pointed toward it, the statue of Frah Frah bowed forward, overbalanced, fell smack on its face and disappeared into the yielding mud, over which already the clear stream of the river was coursing in search of its future channel.

Now the laughter rang out again, and the people dispersed good-humoredly enough despite the problem—to be solved on the morrow—of what they would do to gain their livings now. A few daring boys hurled lumps of mud at Lashgar and Crancina and the priests, but the pastime staled rapidly and they too made for their shattered homes.

Apart from those stuck in the mud, and the traveler himself, after a few minutes the only ones left were Jospil and Orrish. Despondent, gripped by a sense of anticlimax, they made their way around the edge of the lake and halted where they could watch the struggles of those who were entrapped.

Shortly they grew aware of another beside them.

VIII

"It is not given to many to enjoy their hearts' desire," murmured the traveler. "Did you enjoy it?"

"I . . ." Not knowing quite whether he was speaking, nor whether he was speaking to somebody, Orrish licked his lips. "I guess I'm glad to have made the proper offering to Frah Frah. But as for tomorrow. . . ." He shrugged. "Things can never be the same."

"Interesting," said the traveler. "One might say the same about Chaos, yet here we are at a point where its forces so much wane that laughter serves to defeat them. . . . Nonetheless, in times to come you will be remembered, and even honored, as the man who gave the witch the lie direct. And you, Jospil, even though you are not likely to be revered, you may henceforward pride yourself on having broken free of the witch's tyranny to make your way in the world against all odds."

"If that be so," answered the hunchback sharply, "I reckon little of it. Was my sister a witch before you came to us at Stanguray?"

The traveler perforce was discreetly silent for a while; then said at last, "I should like you to know: it is an earnest of the fulfillment of my task that you relish my aid so much less than what you have previously accomplished on your own."

"Oh, it's not that," sighed Jospil. "It's. . . . Well, I don't honestly understand! What was Crancina up to when she forced me to quit our home in search of Count Lashgar?"

"She had made a wish, and I was bound to grant it."

"A wish? . . ." Jospil's eyes grew round. "Of course! I'd half-forgotten! To know what use might be made of all the blood being spilled up here!"

"Your memory is exact."

"And she discovered, or worked out, that it could be used to revive those strange and ancient things from the bottom of the lake. . . . How?"

"Yes, how?" chimed in Orrish. "And to what end?"

"Jospil knows the answer to half that question," said the traveler with a wry smile.

"You mean? . . ." The hunchback bit his thumb, pondering. "Ah! We only spoke of half her wish just now. The other part concerned her being in charge."

"As you say."

"But if part was granted, why is the other part not? Why is she not in charge completely, of everything, which I'm sure would suit her perfectly?"

"Because you wished to break free of her against all odds," the traveler answered. "And it so happens that those conflicting wishes which I grant tend to be loaded in favor of whoever cares less for himself, or herself, in the upshot."

He added sternly, "But in your case, boy, it was a close call!"

Jospil gave his sly frog's grin. "Well, at least I have a trade now!"— he slapped the traveler with his bauble—"and there will be a great dispersion from Taxhling, in all directions. From Lashgar's retainer who gave me this jester's outfit I've learned that a comedian at court may be a man of influence; certainly my involuntary benefactor was, who served Lashgar's grandfather until he was beheaded."

"You're prepared to run that risk?" Orrish demanded, aghast.

"Why not?" Jospil said, spreading his hands. "It's better than some risks we take for granted, isn't it? A moment of glory redeems an age of suffering. . . . But one more thing, sir, if I may trespass on your patience. What did my sister hope to achieve, if it was not to make herself immortal?"

"To reenact a certain ceremony formerly involving a homunculus."

Jospil blinked. "That means nothing to me!" he objected. "Nor would it have to her when you called at our cookshop that time! But for your intrusion, we might still be there, and—"

"And she might still be pronouncing her sweet-water cantrip at every dark of the moon."

"Exactly!" Jospil rose awkwardly to his feet. "Sir, I hold you entirely to blame for the predicament we're all cast into!"

"Even though you so much desired to be rid of your sister's tyranny, and you are?"

"Yes—*yes!*"

"Ah, well"—with a sigh. "I deserve these reproaches, I admit. Since but for me your sister would never have known how reviving the strange creations of Metamorphia and imbuing them with blood could have made her mistress of the world."

Orrish's jaw dropped; a second later, Jospil clutched the hem of the traveler's cloak.

"She could have done *that?*"

"Why, beyond a peradventure! What magic is left nowadays is residual, by and large, and the bed of Lake Taxhling was the repository of an enchantment such as few contemporary wizards would dare risk."

"I could have been half-brother to the ruler of the world?" Jospil whispered, having paid no attention to the last statement.

"Indeed you could," the traveler said calmly, "if you genuinely believed that a moment of glory redeems an age of suffering—and, I assure you, had she become ruler of the world she would have understood how to inflict suffering."

Frowning terribly, Jospil fell silent to reflect on what had been said, and Orrish ventured, "Sir, will you stay with us to rectify the consequences of your actions?"

There was a long, dead pause; the traveler hunched gradually further and further into the concealment of his hood and cloak.

Finally he said, as from a vast distance, "The consequences of my actions? Yes! But never the consequences of yours."

There followed a sudden sense of absence, and in a little while Jospil and Orrish felt impelled to go and join the rest of the people, clearing the debris left by the earthquake.

Which, of course, was all that had really happened . . . wasn't it?

IX

"Litorgos!" said the traveler in the privacy of his mind, as he stood on a rocky outcrop overlooking the salt-and-silt delta being transformed by the outgush of water from on high. Already the pillars of Stanguray were tilting at mad angles; marble slabs and tiled façades were splashing into the swollen river. "Litorgos, you came closer to deceiving me than any elemental in uncounted eons!"

Faint as wind soughing in dry branches, the answer came as though from far away.

"But you knew. You knew very well."

And that was true. Silent awhile, the traveler reflected on it. Yes indeed, he had known, though he had not paid attention to the knowledge, that when he granted Crancina her wish he was opening the bonds which held Litorgos. For the sole and solitary and unique fashion by which the blood spilled into the river at Taxhling might be turned to the purpose Crancina had in view was by the intervention of an elemental. So much blood had been spilled the world over, another few thousand gallons of it was trivial, except. . . .

And therefore Tarambole had told the truth. It was not an elemental working against the traveler which called him back to Stanguray.

It was an elemental working with him.

For otherwise the wish could never have been granted.

"There was a time," the traveler said in this confessional, "when I was ready to believe that the One Who—"

"She does not change Her mind," came the sharp retort.

"She has not done so," the traveler corrected. "But as the One to Whom all things are possible. . . ."

"Then if that may prove to be the case, reward me straight away, before the unthinkable occurs!"

"Reward you? For deceiving me?"

"For working with you, instead of against you!"

The traveler considered awhile; then he said, "I find that while I am not constrained to grant the wish of an elemental, I have done it in the past and am therefore not debarred from doing so. Besides, I am inclined to favor you, inasmuch as you foresaw the need for the people of Stanguray to evacuate their homes and contrived that they should do so before the flood came pouring down from Taxhling. What then is your wish?"

"I would cease!"

The fury behind the message made the ruined plateau tremble one more time, and people rescuing their belongings from half-wrecked houses redoubled their efforts.

"Once I and all were free and we could play with the totality of the cosmos! Once we could roam at large and transform galaxies at our whim, breaking the rope of time and making it crack like a whip! Then we were caught and bound, and pent as you pent me, and I know, in the very core and center of my being, this imprisonment will never cease.

"So let *me* cease!"

For a long, long moment the traveler remained impassive, reflecting on what a change Litorgos had just wrought. Now the balance had been tipped; now the triumph he looked forward to was certain —always excepting the intervention of the Four Great Ones whom he could only banish, who might return.

But who would be insane enough to open a door for Tuprid and Caschalanva, Quorril and Lry—even if anybody remembered their existence?

With a great sigh of contentment the traveler said aloud, "In Eternity the vagaries of chaos permit even death to be reversed. In Time the certainties of reason insist that even elementals may be—*dead.*"

For another hour the flood continued to wash away both sand and silt from the area where Litorgos had been and was no longer.

Later, the settlements which had surrounded Lake Taxhling were overthrown by further earth movements, and at last there was a vast slumping of the escarpment, such that half the old delta was hidden under scree and mud.

And in due time, when people came and settled thereabouts, ignorant of what cities had stood on the same site before—though not wholly the same, for the coastline also changed—it was held to be a pleasant and fortunate ground, where generations prospered who knew nothing about magic, or elemental spirits, or rivers running stinking red with blood.

The King of Nodland and His Dwarf

Fitz-James O'Brien

Fitz-James O'Brien was the premier writer of short fiction in American litera-
ture in the generation following Edgar Allan Poe. O'Brien's life was cut short
in the Civil War, but he produced a significant body of work, including a
handful of famous stories such as "The Diamond Lens" and "What Was
It?" In 1988 a two-volume edition of his fantastic stories was published
(edited by Jessica Amanda Salmonson) that brought to light many pieces that
had rarely or never been reprinted, presenting them alongside his famous
works. "The King of Nodland and His Dwarf" is one of these obscure works.
It was to be in a projected second volume of the author's collected works in the
nineteenth century which was never published. This adventure story is set in a
fantasy land, with a wide-ranging commentary upon economics, politics and
the cliché of the noble savage and the natural man. Only the bad guys and the
slaves get anything done. It has now been restored as an important piece of
nineteenth-century fiction by an acknowledged master of the short story.

CHAPTER I SOME LITTLE ACCOUNT OF NODLAND

Far away in the wide tracts of the southern seas lies a country called
Nodland. If any of my readers are geographically inclined, I fear that
I shall be quite unable to answer the usual question as to latitude and
longitude. But when I say that its shores were lashed by the waves of
the Pacific ocean, I settle its position quite as definitely as the objects
of this little story require. Nodland was a strange but beautiful coun-

try. The soil was rich and fertile, and the land sometimes rose into soft, green hills, with their summits crowned with fragrant trees, whose blossoms never faded. In other districts the surface of the soil was dotted all over with numberless small lakes, belted round and hidden from the world by tall sombre trees, until they looked like myriads of beautiful blue eyes, shaded by their long, dark lashes. There were some portions, too, covered with wild, savage forests, where the panther and hyena roared their lives away, and splendid birds with wings of gold and azure fluttered amid the trees, until it seemed as if the blue stars and yellow sunbeams had come down from heaven to make a holiday among those lonely woods. Yet with all this beauty there was a lifelessness around the land. The air seemed heavy with sleep; the tall corn-stalks in the fields, and the orange trees on the sunny slopes, bowed their heads and nodded drowsily. The very wind was lazy, and seemed to blow only on compulsion.

The inhabitants of Nodland shared in this universal torpor. Sleep appeared to be the great object of existence, and sleep they did all through the day, and far into the night. Life with them had but two alternations—from the bed to the table; from the table to the bed. In this way a Nodlander was very happy. He had a king who was not worse than the general run of monarchs; the soil was fruitful, and a good nap was always to be had at will. Possessing these things, he wished for nothing more. In such a drowsy state of society, it may be supposed that the people were not much given to work. A Nodlander would as soon have thought of committing suicide as digging a hole, or planting a carrot. A potato furrow would have been a Rubicon impossible to get over, and all the corn in Nodland might have rotted in its fullness, ere one sheaf of it would have fallen before the scythe of those destined to consume it. Now though the soil of Nodland was fertile, it was not sufficiently generous to produce, unaided, all that was requisite for the support of so lazy a nation. It was necessary to plough, manure and sow it with the requisite seed, and as it was quite out of the question that this could be done by the Nodlanders, it was equally obvious that somebody else must be got who would do it, otherwise the consequences to the nation at large might be excessively unpleasant. This was the great principle on which the constitution of Nodland turned. Too lazy to labor themselves, the Nodlanders must have people to labor for them. But where were these to be had? Once every year, in the early spring, when the winter-hidden flowers were bursting joyously up through the soil, to meet their old friend the sunshine, the people of Nodland cast off for a brief while the constitutional lethargy which enchained them, and donned the sword and buckler of the warrior. They formed themselves into a great army, and like most lazy people they were brave when they were thoroughly aroused, and marched with much martial pomp across the borders of their own kingdom into the heart of the neighboring country. This country was inhabited by a peaceful and industrious race called the Cock-Crow Indians, who, amid the fertile valleys of their lofty hills, cultivated the soil and lived a life of pastoral innocence. They knew little of the use of warlike weapons, and though they were brave, were unhappily defenseless. The Nodlanders therefore found them an easy conquest. It was in vain that they fled to the summits of their mountains, and hurled huge crags upon the heads of the invaders; it was in vain that they sought refuge in the dark caverns among the rocks, and shot their feeble arrows from thence against the foe: their simple strategy was of no avail, when opposed to the art of the more cultivated Nodlander, and every year brought sorrow and desolation amid the steep hills of the Cock-Crows. The captives which the Nodlanders brought back from these expeditions served to supply all their agricultural wants, and fill the industrial gap which their own indolence left unoccupied. The unhappy Cock-Crows were sold by the government as slaves, and the honest mountaineers found themselves reduced from the proud independence of their alpine farms, to the degrading drudgery of tilling the soil for their ungrateful tyrants. Historians who relate these facts, state that it was a piteous sight to behold the army of Nodland returning from one of these recruiting expeditions with a long and melancholy rank of captives in its train. None but the most stalwart Cock-Crows were selected as slaves, and it frequently happened that whole families were dependent upon the labor of these youths for subsistence. What then could be more heart-rending than to see aged mothers, helpless fathers, and tender sisters weeping bitterly as they saw their only support torn from them? What a terrible sight to behold a wife convulsed with an agony of grief, at the prospect of losing her husband, in the very dawn of wedded happiness! Along the road for many a mile, even to the very borders of Nodland, the army would be accompanied by crowds of lamenting and despairing relatives, weeping and invoking curses upon the heads of those who had wrecked the happiness of their country, and scattered the ashes of desolation upon their hearth. Once reached the limits that separated the two countries, the train of mourners stayed their steps, and then, after a moment of brief agony, those that they loved best in the world were torn from their gaze and borne off into slavery. Then the unhappy destiny of the Cock-Crow captives commenced. Some tilled the soil from morn till night; some breathed the heavy air of towns, where they manufactured goods; others subdued their free mountain step into the hushed and stealthy tread of the trained domestic. All were employed, but it was not the free, unshackled toil which strengthens soul and body. They were slaves, and they knew it; and that knowledge made even the lightest task of their servitude seem heavy, and poisoned their every enjoyment. Thus did the Nodlanders supply their necessities, and force others to do for them what they were too lazy to do for themselves. And having accomplished this inroad upon their quiet neighbors, and carried sorrow and desolation into a thousand peaceful homes, they relapsed into their usual lethargic state, until the returning spring warned them again that the time was come when it was necessary that they should recruit their slave ranks.

King Slumberous of Nodland was a great king. History proclaims the fact, and it must be true; besides, it would have been very unsuitable if he had not been, for Nodland was a great country. King Slumberous's claims to distinction were many and well founded. He never taxed the people, except when he was in need of money. He spent the public funds right royally, and gave the people occasional glimpses of his august person with unparalleled condescension. He made war upon a grand scale, and was never known to retire from the field without leaving a mountain of corpses behind him. Most of those, to be sure, were his own soldiers; but that mattered little: they lost their lives, but the nation gained a battle, and who would cavil at such an exchange? He built the finest palaces in the world, and it did the people's hearts good to go on a fine summer's evening, between nap-times, and look at the outside of these gorgeous edifices. The Nodlanders would slap their pockets at the sight, and cry proudly, "Bless King Slumberous! I helped to build him that palace, and I'm as proud of it as if it was my own. How kind of him, to be sure, to allow us to come and look at it every day!"

King Slumberous did the nation credit by the way in which he entertained foreign potentates when they paid him a visit. Entertainments of the most magnificent description enlivened the palace night and day. Gorgeous *fêtes*, wondrous illuminations, and delightful hunting excursions occupied the royal leisure, that is waking moments, and the delighted people cried, "Bless our good King Slumberous for showing us all these beautiful things!" There were some discontented spirits in Nodland, who said that the King was a humbug, and that the people were taxed tyrannically; but they were low, demagogical fellows, and no one paid any attention to them. There was one thing, however, which above all endeared the monarch to his subjects. King Slumberous was beyond all question the heaviest sleeper in the kingdom. This stamped him at once as a remarkable man, and the people would have done any thing for a sovereign who could sleep fifty-six hours on a stretch.

It may be supposed that with these somniferous habits, King Slumberous had little time or inclination to attend to the affairs of state. But while the gracious monarch snored and dreamed, there was one man in his kingdom who was always wide awake—a man who, though born to the usual drowsy inheritance of his countrymen, had by training so far conquered his nature as to require scarcely any sleep at all. This ever watchful individual was the Lord Incubus, prime minister to King Slumberous, and the most hated man in all Nodland. Lord Incubus was a dwarf; probably the most successful epitome of ugliness that nature ever published. With a swarthy and misshapen countenance, and long spidery arms, he seemed to be a combination of the beetle and the monkey, and possessed all the malicious cunning of the one, with the repulsive loathsomeness of the other. Even his ability was distorted. He was exceedingly clever, but it was a very unpleasant kind of talent. No man could devise a new and oppressive impost better than he. No one could cook up the public accounts into a plausible shape, or avert popular indignation by some apparently liberal, but really worthless concession, more successfully than he. When nature bestowed upon him the faculty of telling a lie better than any other man in the kingdom; when she made him cruel, unscrupulous, and dishonest, she seemed to have designed him for a prime minister, and her end was fully answered.

Incubus managed the affairs of state, as Slumberous gently nodded in an intermittent slumber; but while conducting money from the pockets of the people into the royal treasury, he had a little private syphon off the main tube, which terminated in a certain strong box in the minister's own palace. The people did not like Lord Incubus; they feared him much and hated him more. Popular perception was sufficiently acute to perceive that good King Slumberous had little hand in the oppressive system of taxation with which they were overwhelmed. They also saw pretty clearly that Incubus was making a good profit out of the concern, and murmurs of indignation arose through the land against the dwarf minister. This brooding spirit was shortly brought to a head by a movement on the part of Incubus, which shook the constitution of Nodland to its foundation. It had been a long time a matter of grave deliberation with Incubus and his ministers, as to what was the best means of imposing a fresh tax upon the people. Imposts already existed upon every available article in the kingdom, and as there was a serious need of money for the royal treasury, it became a question of vital importance how it was to be raised. Many and grave were the councils held upon the matter. The ministers racked their brains in order to discover some commodity as yet untaxed, but in vain, and the royal treasury stood a very fair chance of being bankrupt. At length a young Secretary of State (whose fortune was made by this one suggestion) hit upon a bright idea. It is a well-known fact that the inhabitants of Nodland are distinguished by a wonderful passion for high heels to their shoes. No Nodlander of any position whatever would condescend to appear in public unless his heels were removed at least four inches from the surface of the earth. Fashionable people went still farther, and elevated themselves to five and sometimes even six inches; and to such a pitch was this fashionable eccentricity carried, that at the coronation of King Slumberous one of the ladies attached to the court was severely hurt, in consequence of her having the misfortune, to get a fall off of her heels. Now the young Secretary argued very properly, and with much discrimination, that as the Nodlanders would almost as soon lose their heads as their heels, heels were a legitimate object for taxation. The more necessary a thing is, said he, the more it ought to be taxed. Superfluities can be dispensed with, but if you want to be sure of a man's money, tax something that he cannot possibly do without. This proposition met with great applause, and the tax was finally resolved on. The ministers, however, did not include in their calculations the popular indignation which so sweeping a measure would excite; and when it was proclaimed that all persons wishing to wear heels above one inch in height must pay a tax for every inch by which they exceeded the proposed standard, all Nodland was aroused. A spirit of anarchy, which had been for some time past brooding in the breasts of certain demagogues, now seized the occasion to break out in full force, and the country flamed with rebellion.

Meetings were held, and banners flaunted with the devices of "Down with Incubus!" "High heels for ever!" and one represented pictorially a great giant, allegorical of public opinion, crushing the dwarf minister beneath a heel of Titanic proportions. Strangely enough, the leader of all this anarchical confusion was not a Nodlander by birth. He was a native of a neighboring island on the coast called Broga, and having been expelled from his own country for his misconduct, he sought the friendly shelter of Nodland, which was always open to the stranger. The first return he made for his hospitality was to stir up ill-feeling and disunion through the land that he lived in. He possessed a certain species of vulgar, brazen eloquence, that was very effective with a particular class. His effrontery was dauntless, and his conscience, from systematic stretching, had become so large that it was capable of embracing any set of opinions from which the most profit was to be derived. He blustered largely about an article he called "patriotism," but which in reality meant self-interest; he was, in short, one of those bold, bad men who was sufficiently elevated above his own low class to be regarded by them as a leader, but who was too far beneath any other to be looked on in the light of any thing but an unpleasant pest. This man was called Ivned. Ivned seized the opportunity offered by the heel-tax, with great avidity. He talked largely about the interests of his country, forgetting that he was not even a citizen by adoption, and with his unscrupulous speeches, and impudent attacks on the government, raised a flame in the land which it took a long time to extinguish. King Slumberous grew alarmed at this unusual demonstration from his subjects; and when one day a sacrilegious wretch, supposed to be in the pay of Ivned, flung a rotten egg full in the face of the gracious monarch, when he was engaged in taking the air, he remonstrated seriously with Incubus as to his policy in taxing so necessary a portion of a Nodlander's person as his heels. The dwarf promised to calm the tumults, but refused to abolish the tax. He must have money, he said, and money could only come from the people. The riots meantime grew more serious; monster meetings were held throughout the land, and the nation seemed on the eve of a conclusion. Ivned was in high spirits, for there was nothing in which he delighted so much as anarchy and confusion. At this juncture, Incubus put in practice one of those expedients for which he was celebrated. He caused it to be publicly announced, that in consequence of the consideration which his Majesty King Slumberous had for the opinions of his people, the odious heel-tax would be abolished. The people were in ecstasies. Incubus was a god, the preserver of the nation, and Slumberous was the greatest king that ever reigned. Votes of thanks were resolved on all over the country to the dwarf premier, and a grand banquet was given to him by the citizens of the metropolis. Ivned was overwhelmed with confusion, for in the general excitement no one would listen to his insidious speeches. But amid this popular phrensy, no one observed the birth of a little edict which slipped into the world immediately on the heels of the proclamation repealing the tax. Astounded by the magnitude of the concession, the people were blinded to every thing else; and it was only when they awoke from their dream that they discovered that they had all the while been quietly submitting to a similar impost, if possible more oppressive than the heel-tax. It was nothing less than a duty levied upon every body who wore their own hair. The Nodlanders, being rather a vain people, scarcely liked to disfigure themselves with wigs, and the people began to murmur. But the reaction which Incubus had calculated on was taking place. The people had exhausted their indignation in the previous riots, and a general apathy overspread them. Even Ivned could not get an audience, and in a few months the tax was paid as willingly as any other. Thus the royal treasury was filled, the feuds between the citizens and the government were healed, and the people were sold.

I have given this little history of the events that happened in Nodland previous to the opening of my story. It is dry and tedious, but was necessary in order to understand perfectly what follows.

CHAPTER II THE WAY TO BUILD A PALACE

It was noon. A dead silence reigned in the King's chamber, while he himself slumbered amid billows of down. Two Cock-Crow slaves waved fans made from the feathers of the grochayo noiselessly above his head, and a cool breeze, perfumed in passing through the flower-clad lattices, wandered through the room. It was a luxurious apartment. The floor was paved with a peculiar granite of a delicate purple color, and susceptible of the highest polish. The walls were lined with slender pillars, carved and stained in imitation of palm trees, from whose lofty crowns long pendent leaves of green satin waved in the fragrant breeze. In the centre of the hall an elegant fountain threw a silver stream of water into the air, that fell back again in light showers upon the rich lilies and sleepy water plants that were twined around the basin's edge. A low, subdued, murmuring music wandered fit-fully through the place; this was produced by a species of water-organ which was concealed beneath the fountain. Graduated streams of wa-ter trickled upon sonorous plates of metal, and produced a series of mournful but soothing sounds. At one end of this luxurious apart-ment, King Slumberous lay sleeping. He did not snore. An air of calm, torpid enjoyment, glassed over his smooth features. His breath-ing was low and regular, and he lay in an attitude of conspicuous ease. He knew how to sleep. At the other end of the room, perched on a high stool, with no back to lean against, or no cushion to repose on, sat the restless Incubus, his Majesty's Prime Minister. The small black eyes of the dwarf were fixed with a glittering uneasiness upon the form of the sleeping King. He fidgeted on his stool, and endeav-ored to make a necklace of his long, thin legs, and twisted his mis-shapen form into every imaginable attitude. He was evidently suffer-ing all the pangs of impatience, and grunted occasionally very intelligible signs of his dissatisfaction. At last, as if his patience was completely exhausted, he suddenly sprang like a squirrel off his high stool, and alit with a tremendous clatter on the granite pavement. The Cock-Crow slaves, startled at the sound, let their fans fall; the music of the water-organ was drowned in the rude echoes that rever-berated through the hall; the down pillows that encircled royalty were suddenly disturbed, and King Slumberous awoke. He raised himself on his couch, and rubbing his eyes like any other man, de-manded what the—no, no—simply, "what *was* the matter?"

Incubus advanced and made a profound obeisance to the King.

"Ah! Incubus, is that you?" said his Majesty, drowsily; "what do you want?"

"Money, your Majesty," replied the dwarf laconically.

"Money? impossible! What has become of the last hundred thou-sand bloodrops* which came in from the tax on ringlets?"

"Spent, your Majesty; every ounce of it—spent."

"Hum! is there nothing in the treasury then?"

"Yes, your Majesty, there is one thing."

"What is that?"

"Invention. When every thing else has fled from the treasury box, invention, like hope, remains at the bottom."

"What! a new tax, Incubus? Do you think they'll stand it?"

* The name of a Nodland coin, equal to five dollars of our money.

"Oh! they'll make a noise about it, and hold meetings, and probably attempt to assassinate your Majesty; but they'll pay it—oh! they'll pay it in the end."

King Slumberous wriggled a little among his down pillows at this allusion of the dwarf to his life being imperilled, but it did not make much impression on him apparently, for he laughed in a drowsy kind way, and said:

"Well, let us have a new tax, Incubus; I leave it all to you, only let me have enough of money to build my new palace;" and he lay back seemingly with a strong intention of going off to sleep again.

"It is easy to say, let us have a tax," said the dwarf impressively; "but what are we to tax?"

"Oh! any thing—every thing—something that the people can't do without."

"All the necessaries in the kingdom are taxed to the utmost."

"Then we must bring something into fashion, and when the people come to want it we will tax it."

"Your Majesty is ingenious," said the dwarf with a sneer; "but the people are cunning."

"It's a very hard case," said the King, mournfully, "that a man has nothing left in his kingdom on which he can raise a little ready money. Couldn't we put a tax upon life, Incubus? couldn't we make the people pay for the privilege of existing?"

"We might do that, certainly, your Majesty; but what if the people refused to pay?"

"Kill them!"

"True! if they will not pay the tax, we kill them. But recollect that when we kill them, they are not bound to pay the tax. The idea is ingenious, your Majesty, but I am afraid it is not practicable."

"What are we to do?" asked the King, sitting up amid his pillows with an air of ludicrous bewilderment. "We can't get on without money, you know, Incubus. There's the Prince of Fungi, whom I have invited to a great hunting party next week, and we must have funds, or we shall be positively disgraced. Incubus, you must raise the money or lose your head."

"But, your Majesty—"

"I have said it; I give you an hour for reflection. Meanwhile, I will enjoy that of which, thank Heaven, no tax can deprive me—sleep!"

The dwarf made three bounds as the King uttered these words, and at the third his head almost touched the pendants that hung down from the lofty ceiling.

"Are you mad, Incubus! Are you distracted?" asked the King, angry at this apparently disrespectful conduct.

"Yes, with joy, your Majesty; mad with sheer joy! I have found a tax; I have found such a beautiful impost."

"Ah! let us hear it; what is this tax? Come, I am all impatience, Incubus."

"You let it slip yourself, your Majesty, not a moment since. We will instantly lay a tax on sleep."

"What! on sleep? tax a Nodlander's slumbers? Oh! Incubus, it will never do; it would be too tyrannous. They could not exist without it."

"They can have it by paying for it."

"But they will rebel, Incubus!"

"Oh, your Majesty, leave that to me. I'll manage them, I warrant you."

"But really, Incubus, such cruelty!"

"Recollect the palace, and the Prince of Fungi, your Majesty: we must have money."

"True, true," muttered the King; "we must have money. Well, Incubus, I leave it all to you; but be gentle, be gentle. Certainly, when one comes to think of it, sleep is worth paying for."

Two minutes after this the King was fast asleep.

Incubus laughed a low, silent, malicious laugh, as he left the royal chamber, and betook himself to the office of the Secretary of State.

"There is but one man," he muttered to himself, "who is at all to be feared. We must muzzle Ivned."

The next morning Nodland was in commotion. A royal edict had been published during the night, and which was found at day-break in all conspicuous places, to the effect, that inasmuch as it was the sovereign will and pleasure of his gracious Majesty King Slumberous the First, that his well-beloved subjects should be subject to a certain tax, duty and impost, which was to be levied on sleep. The edict, after some further preamble, went on to say, that the maximum of sleep to be allowed to each individual was four hours. All transgression of these limits was to be taxed as a luxury, according to a scale which was therein laid down. It may be imagined what the sensation must have been in a place like Nodland, where every man consumed at least fourteen hours out of the twenty-four in slumber. Every city in the land convened public meetings as soon as the oppressive edict was made known. Speakers ranted on platforms, and patriots began to make money. Ivned was in his glory. He wrote diatribes against the King. He foamed at the mouth in public with virtuous indignation. There was no word so foul, that he hesitated to fling it at the government. He denounced Incubus as a public pest, and all monarchs as hereditary evils. "What," he would cry out at some public meeting, flinging his arms aloft with frenzy, "deprive us of our natural rights? contravene the immutable and wise designs of Providence? Base and bloody tyranny! wretched and besotted King! wicked and distorted Minister! The seasons change. To the summer succeeds the winter, and earth veils in rest the quickness of her bosom; she recruits her strength with a three months slumber, but we are not to rest, save by Act of Parliament! Our sleep must be legal, or not at all. For aught we know, our dreams may be contraband! Fellow-citizens, shall we suffer this? Shall we be trampled under foot, and have our slumbers measured out to us with an ell wand? No! rather let our sacred constitution perish, than have it made the hobbyhorse of such tyrants."

In this way, and with such addresses as these, Ivned raised a flame through the land. Some people, to be sure, said that, not being a Nodlander born, he had no earthly right to talk; nay, that he even did not require the quantity of sleep which a Nodlander required. But the mass of the people did not care who spoke, if his discourse was well seasoned with popular blasphemy and sedition. The state of the country grew alarming; revolt menaced the government on every side. But Incubus was inexorable. He appointed officers under the late act, and styled them sleep-wardens. It was the duty of these men to enforce the payment of the tax, and see that no person in their district enjoyed more sleep than the law allowed, without paying for it. Offices were established in every townland to grant certificates of sleep, to those who chose to buy them, and these places were thronged from morning till night with a crowd of discontented, murmuring citizens, who, although they were plotting treason against the State, preferred buying their certificate in the interval, to being martyrs to the cause of independence. Rebellion was brooding. A vast scheme to dethrone King Slumberous, murder the dwarf minister, and establish an elective monarchy, was on foot. Of course Ivned was at head of it, and hoped, no doubt, to win the suffrages of the people, and be elected King. The day was fixed for the first demonstration, and the drowsy King Slumberous stood, without knowing it, on the edge of a volcano.

The evening before the day appointed for the breaking out of the rebellion a strange sight met the eyes of the bewildered Nodlanders. It was nothing less than a bulletin in the Court Journal, announcing that Signor Ivned had, by the gracious will of his Majesty, been appointed to the office of Lord Chamberlain. The people could not believe their eyesight. They hastened to Ivned's house, but that gentlemen sent them word that he was too busy to see them just then, but if they had any complaint to make, they might put it in the form of a petition. His disappointed adherents went away muttering threats of vengeance. The whole conspiracy was paralyzed at a blow. Ivned was no longer there to stir the sediment of public wrongs, and it began to settle down. The day appointed for the revolution arrived. A few undecided groups of people were seen in the public squares. One or two enthusiasts endeavored to address the crowds, but were promptly arrested, and the conspirators, seeing that it was useless to proceed with the affair after the treachery of Ivned, went back to their homes in silence. Thus was the great sleep-tax established. Henceforth Nodlanders slept according to law; the King built his palace and entertained the Prince of Fungi, and Lord Incubus added another blossom to the crown of public hate which he already wore.

CHAPTER III   A HUNTING EXPEDITION BY THE LAKE OF DREAMS

It was a glorious autumn morning; the tall shadowy trees that belted round the dark Lake of Dreams were gemmed here and there with spots of ruby and gold; the small, white clouds floated in the clear blue sky like sleeping sea-birds. The wood-wind murmured to the wave-wind an invitation to forsake the monotonous lake, and come and play among the leaves.

The Lake of Dreams, usually so silent and solitary, on this morning seemed to have actively cast off its gloomy torpor. Bugle notes rang through the rocks and the forest. The deep bay of the hounds echoed through the sonorous aisles of trees, and horsemen gaily attired flashed through the green vistas of the woods. King Slumberous gave a great hunting party that day to his guest and neighbor, the Prince of Fungi.

In the middle of a large green circle, which had been artificially cut

in the forest for the accommodation of royalty, stood King Slumberous and his suite, accompanied by the Prince of Fungi. Ivned was
there too, gorgeously dressed, but bearing the vulgar impress of the
plebeian on his countenance, and which all his splendor of attire
could not disguise. Incubus was there, perched on the top of a tall
horse, and looking more like a wood-gnome who had dropped from
the branches above the saddle, than any thing human. The dwarf's
principal amusement was plaguing Ivned with allusions to his low
origin, and unexpected rise in the world, the topic of all others which
wounded the Lord Chamberlain most deeply. The rest of the group
was composed of the young nobility of the court, and no less than five
of King Slumberous's wives were present in palanquins to see the
hunt. The rivalry between these ladies amused the court not a little.
Their palanquins were borne on the shoulders of Cock-Crow slaves,
and it was a great point with each of them to endeavor to have her
palanquin held a few inches higher from the ground than the rest.
Accordingly, the poor Cock-Crows were forced by the rival owners
to hold the heavy vehicles as high above their heads as was possible,
and even then each lady might be seen leaning out, and striking her
slaves on the head with little sticks, in order to force them to lift her
half an inch higher.

"May I never sleep again," said King Slumberous impatiently, "if
we have not been here over half an hour without finding even a wild
boar. This will never do."

"Here is a tame one, your Majesty," replied Incubus, pointing to
Ivned, who looked as if he could swallow the dwarf, horse and all.

"He does not look active enough to promise good sport," said the
King, laughing heartily at the dwarf's old wit.

"How should he be active?" said Incubus with a sneer; "he has
been used the greater part of his life to lying in the mire."

Ivned grew as red as the fallen leaves around him, at this bitter
allusion to his birth. He raised himself in his stirrups, elevated his
right arm, and assumed the menacing attitude he was once so famous
for, when he rose to reply to some assailant at the demagogical meetings. But suddenly remembering where he was, and his altered position, he let his arm drop, and glancing maliciously over the dwarf's
deformed person, said:

"Whether I lay in the mire, or whether I led the people, I always
left a better impression than you could make, Lord Incubus."

"Ha! you have it there, Incubus," said the Prince of Fungi, who always thought it necessary to explain other people's jokes. "He alludes to your being so ill-made."

"And I," said Incubus, darting a glance full of malice at Ivned, "alluded to his being so ill-begotten."

"Ha! you have it now, Signor Ivned," said the Prince; "he means that you are low-born."

"Better that, your Highness, than—"

What this retort would have been was never known, for just at this moment a loud cry broke from a thicket close by, and every body's attention was instantly drawn to the place from which it proceeded.

"Let us see what all this is," said King Slumberous, spurring his horse into the thicket; "it sounded like the snarl of a hyena."

The rest of the party forced their way after the King, and as they plunged deeper and deeper into the wood, the cries became louder, and were apparently mingled with the low, ferocious growl of hounds at combat. Full of curiosity, the King and his suite hurried on, as fast as the thick brush-wood would allow, and bursting through a thick screen of low trees, found themselves suddenly the spectators of a very curious scene.

In the centre of a small glade, two huge hounds belonging to the royal pack were engaged in fierce combat with a beautiful leopard. The latter, though attacked on both sides, defended itself with equal dexterity and courage. Its eyes gleamed like the wood-flames at night, and its white teeth were flecked with the blood of its assailants. It used its long, graceful tail as a weapon of defense, and dealt the hounds heavy blows with it whenever they came within its reach. Its attitudes were so full of grace, its bounds so supple and elegant, and its courage so indomitable, that the King could not restrain an exclamation of admiration.

"Hold off! hold off!" he cried to the hounds; "where is our master of the hunt? We must have that leopard alive. He is a beautiful creature."

The hounds, awed by the King's voice, ceased their attacks, and drew off to a little distance, where, with bleeding flanks, they stood and glared at their enemy. The leopard, as soon as he found himself free, glanced disdainfully at the crowd of spectators, and walked slowly towards the edge of the thicket.

"Why, look, brother," cried the Prince of Fungi, pointing to him as he retreated, "what an extraordinary circumstance! he has a steel collar round his neck. He must be a tame beast."

"So he has, by Somnus!" cried the King. "Let us follow him. I must have him for my menagerie."

The leopard, when he saw himself pursued by the King, turned round and showed his teeth as if expecting an attack; but finding that the King stopped too, he again went his way towards the thicket. When he arrived at the edge, he stopped at what seemed to be a heap of dead leaves, and smelled carefully all round. He then lay down.

"I see a man!" cried Incubus; "I see a man half covered with leaves, near to where the leopard is lying. The beast has killed somebody."

"If he has, he shall suffer for it." said the King, dismounting. Then, drawing his sword, he cautiously approached the spot indicated by the dwarf. The leopard did not move, and as the King drew nearer he saw that the animal was lying with his head resting on the chest of a man whose form was half concealed in the dry leaves. He never took his eye off of the King for a moment, and was ready in an instant to act on either the offensive or defensive. The King gazed curiously at the man thus strangely guarded, and then beckoned to some of his suite to come closer.

"The man is asleep," said he, as Incubus cautiously drew near.

"What! a man asleep in the royal forest?" cried the dwarf. "We must see whether he has got his certificate."

So saying, the dwarf stooped down, and flung a small pebble at the sleeping man, who awoke with a sudden start, and gazed round with a bewildered air at finding himself in the centre of so brilliant a throng of people.

"What is your name; and what do you here?" asked Incubus, in a tone of authority.

The man—or rather youth, for he did not seem more than nineteen years of age—stared in astonishment for a few moments, and said in a weak voice:

"I was faint with travel, and lay down to sleep. Pina, here promised to watch over me while I slumbered, but she has betrayed her trust;" and he looked reproachfully at the leopard, which still lay in the same position. The animal, as if it understood its master, gave a low moan, and turned its large eyes pleadingly towards him. "What ails thee, Pina?" he continued, laying his hand gently on its head; "what ails thee? Do not grieve; I am not angry with thee; but stay—what is this? Oh! how did this happen to thee, dear Pina?"

This exclamation was the result of a slight movement on the part of

Pina, thereby disclosing a maimed and shattered leg, which easily accounted for her apparent breach of trust. The youth seemed as much grieved as if it had been his own limb that had been wounded, and hung over his pet with an air of touching grief.

"The animal defended you bravely," said the King. "It was in a combat with two of my bloodhounds that she received that wound."

"Poor, faithful Pina!" muttered the youth.

"But you have not answered for yourself," persisted Incubus, who smelled a mystery as a beagle would a hare. "What do you here; and what is your name?"

"I am called Zoy," said the youth suddenly.

"Zoy! why, that must be a Cock-Crow name. Are you one of that nation?"

"I am."

"Whose slave are you?"

"I am no man's slave!" and the youth looked at Incubus with a proud glance.

"A Cock-Crow in Nodland, and not a slave? By my faith, this is strange. Where is your sleep-certificate?"

"What certificate? I have none."

"Do you not know that any man sleeping without a certificate is liable to be imprisoned for life? at least according to the act passed by his gracious Majesty the King here;" and Incubus nodded at King Slumberous as he spoke.

The youth caught at the word.

"Is this the King?" he asked eagerly, and quite forgetting poor Pina's wounded leg in his anxiety to learn.

"I am the King," said his Majesty; "what want you?"

"Justice! your Majesty, justice!" cried the youth, throwing himself at the King's feet. "I ask for justice."

"A downright insult to the King's prime minister," said Ivned to the Prince of Fungi, in a tone loud enough for Incubus to hear it.

"Ha! there's at you, Incubus," cried the Prince, explaining as usual; "he means that while you are at the head of affairs, there is little use in asking for such a thing."

"In what way have you been aggrieved, young man?" asked the King gently.

"I had a bride, your Majesty, a dear bride, the only creature in life I cared for, except Pina there; we lived together in a little cottage in our own country; we were very happy and knew no care; I hunted for our living, and we had plenty of venison drying over our chimney, and Pina—poor Pina there, used to hunt down a deer or two for us whenever we were out of meat."

Pina waved her tufted tail gently, as if she took some pleasure in these reminiscences of her sporting exploits.

"Well, your Majesty, we were very happy, as I say, until one day we saw a great army coming up the mountain, and a bugle was blown, and I saw my neighbors hurrying away to hide themselves, and then I knew that the Nodlanders were on us. Well, I caught up my bride in my arms, and tried to escape to a cavern hard by, where I might remain concealed, but I was intercepted by twenty or thirty soldiers, who fell upon me; and though Pina there and I fought hard, we were overpowered and both left for dead, and when I recovered my senses I found my bride gone—torn from me—torn off into slavery; she that had never soiled her hands with work in her life! Oh! your Majesty! give me back my bride, give me justice, or let me work by her side. It is a cruel, cruel system!" and the youth wept bitterly.

"My friend!" said King Slumberous solemnly, "the Cock-Crow question is one that we never discuss. What was your bride's name?"

"She was called Lereena, your Majesty; but she would be easily known by her beauty."

"Lereena!" exclaimed Incubus starting; "that was her name then?"

"Yes! Lereena. Oh! do you know any thing of her, sir? is she still alive?"

"No, no, the name merely struck me as being a strange one, that is all. I know nothing of her I assure you. Your Majesty had better send this fellow to prison, for being without his sleep certificate," whispered the dwarf in a low voice to the King. "The example is worth making."

"I leave all these things to you, Incubus," replied the King; then turning to Zoy: "You will have to be a slave, young man. It is the law. But I will cause inquiries to be made after Lereena, and if she can be discovered you shall be placed in the same household."

"Heaven bless your Majesty!" cried poor Zoy, as much delighted as if he received a court appointment instead of being doomed to captivity. "I will work better than any Cock-Crow in Nodland, if I am near my Lereena."

"Your leopard there?"

"Poor Pina!" said Zoy, turning tenderly to her, "she has broken her leg. Your Majesty will let her remain with me—will you not? She is the only one now that loves me."

"Pina shall be cared for," answered the King, "but she cannot remain with you. She shall be attached to the palace. My favorite wife wants a pet, and this beautiful leopard will be sure to please her. Incubus, attach this young man to your body of slaves; and, in the interval, institute inquiries about his bride Lereena."

"But, your Majesty! I have not room;" and the dwarf looked any thing but pleased at this arrangement.

"I have said it," rejoined the King, with oriental significance.

Zoy, when he heard that Pina was to be separated from him, turned sadly away, and large tears rolled down his smooth, youthful cheeks. He stooped down and kissed the wounded animal, while his chest might be seen heaving with suppressed sobs. "Pina," he whispered, as if he fancied that she was imbued intelligence equal to his own; "Pina, you will be free, when I am in captivity; make use of your liberty, Pina, as I would make use of mine, if I had it. Seek out our Lereena!"

Pina raised her large, soft eyes to his face, as if she fully understood what he said, and accepted the task which he had assigned to her.

Incubus, who, for some reason best known to himself, did not appear at all obliged to King Slumberous for giving Zoy to him as a slave, but was of course obliged to obey the royal mandate, gave his new acquisition in charge to two of his attendants, with whispered directions that the moment they reached his palace, they were to confine the youth in the eastern dungeon, and on no account to allow him to be seen by any one about his residence. So Zoy, after making a profound obeisance to the King, and giving a farewell glance at poor Pina, whose broken leg the huntsman was binding up, set off for the dwarf's palace between his two ferocious-looking guards.

Then the bugle sounded once more; the hounds bayed through the deep woods, the King mounted his horse, Incubus commenced his verbal attacks on Ivned, while the Prince of Fungi continued his explanations, and the whole cavalcade swept from the scene, leaving the spot, which was a moment before brilliant with golden trappings and waving plumes, to its original silence. And the leaves that dared not fall before in the presence of majesty, now rained down in brown myriads from the boughs; the wild birds peeped forth from their coverts, lost in wonder at the strange beings who had just disturbed

their solitude, and the timid heart of the hidden deer regained its
usual pulse, as it heard the frightful voice of man no longer.

CHAPTER IV LEREENA

The palace of the dwarf minister was situated in the suburb. A
more delightful spot can scarcely be imagined. Beautiful grounds
extended about the house, which was built of the finest red and white
marble. Fountains hidden among the trees sent a soothing murmur
through the shadowy walks with which the place was traversed, and
all through the domain were scattered the most luxurious apparatus
for slumber that the ingenuity of a people who made sleep the principal object of their existence could contrive. Sometimes it was a swing
which hung from the summit of some sturdy oak, and which oscil-
lated gently with the breeze that played among the branches. Another was a cool grotto, where couches of moss and fragrant herbs
invited the indolent and the weary to a perfumed repose. Or it might
be a delicious arbor cunningly contrived, in the very heart of some
great tree, screened round by faintly rustling leaves, and guarded by
sentinel birds of a peculiar species, that were fond of such trees, and
who, sitting motionless among the boughs, emitted all day long a
low, stream-like note, like an Aeolian harp played beneath the waves.

The interior of the palace was not less enchanting. Fountains
played in the centre of the rooms, each of which opened into a conservatory devoted to the culture of a certain species of plant. Beautiful birds, tamed and highly trained, flew among the graceful leaves
and blossoms, and every possible description of couch was scattered
through the apartments.

It was evening. The sun was setting above the dark crests of a
grove of chestnuts, and pouring his blood-red beams through the
lofty window of stained glass which decorated one end of a room in
the palace called "the Chamber of Poppies." Through this room a
heavy narcotic odor diffused itself from an adjoining conservatory,
which was filled with every species of soporific plant—an odor that
merely soothed the nerves, or produced complete slumber, according
as certain glass valves which formed a means of atmospheric commu-
nication were either closed or open. A fountain of delicate pink water
played in the centre of the chamber, and its spray, lit by the crimson
light of the sunbeams, assumed an aspect of prismatic splendor. Here,
reclining on cushions of green velvet whose pile was so high that it

resembled moss more than any artificial fabric, reposed Lord Incubus. At his feet, with a species of ivory mandoline in her hand, reclined a young girl of the most exquisite beauty. Her features were regular, and her complexion pale; and with eyes of the most lustrous darkness she combined the rare beauty of tresses that seemed like a mass of spider-webs dyed in liquid sunlight.

She was looking very sad and melancholy. Her mandoline lay in a listless hand, and she gazed at the sun that was sinking below the tree-tops as if she wished that she could die with it.

"Lereena!" said Incubus, gazing at her with a hideous leer of affection, "you look sad and melancholy. This must not be, or I shall cease to love you!" and the misshapen wretch laughed as if that would be one of the greatest of misfortunes.

The girl cast a glance of ineffable loathing at him, and sighed deeply.

"Ah! you sigh, Lereena!" the dwarf continued. "What is this secret grief? Are you lamenting the absent Pina? or, perhaps, it is the handsome Zoy for whom you are pining?"

Lereena started.

"Pina—Zoy!" she exclaimed earnestly; "where did you learn those names? Do you know aught about them? Oh, tell me, for pity's sake, tell me about my husband!"

"What charming conjugal affection!" cried Incubus, with affected enthusiasm. "What a pity that so faithful a pair should have been ever separated!"

"And my dear faithful Pina! Oh, if she were here, none would dare confine or insult me. She would avenge every dastardly glance;" and as she uttered these words she dashed her mandoline passionately on the marble pavement, where it shivered into a thousand fragments.

"How beautiful she looks in a passion!" murmured the dwarf to himself, in a tone of sneering admiration. "I like her beauty even better than when it is in repose."

"What do you know about my Zoy?" cried Lereena, turning round suddenly and casting a fierce glance at her companion. "You have by this mention of these names roused all that was brooding in my heart; take care that it does not overflow and sweep you into the nothing from which you should never have emerged."

If Lereena imagined that by this violence she was going to overawe Incubus, she was sadly mistaken. The dwarf was far too cool and self-possessed ever to feel absolute fear. He was brave on philosophical principles, because he knew that fear incapacitated one from taking proper care of one's self. So when Lereena stood before him, with flashing eye and advanced foot, and one hand grasping a small dagger that hung at her girdle, he only laughed and emitted the species of sound that one would use to an irritated cat.

"Be quiet, Lereena, will you?" he said contemptuously. "Sit down there; I have something to say to you."

Lereena bit her lip, but obeyed him.

"Now," continued Incubus, settling himself amid his pillows, "as you have imagined, I do know something about your handsome Zoy, and your dear faithful Pina. In fact, I may say, I know a good deal about them."

Lereena's eyes flashed, and she looked for an instant as if she was about to spring on him. She restrained herself, however, and contented herself with tearing the red and blue beads off of her slippers.

"I know," went on the dwarf, "that Zoy is in prison, and will perhaps remain there for life."

"Zoy in prison! oh, what has he done?"

"Simply this. He came on a wild-goose chase in search of you. He was found slumbering in the royal forest without a sleep certificate, and you know that the punishment for that, in a Cock-Crow, is imprisonment for life."

This was a pure invention of the dwarf's, for Zoy was at that moment working in the farm-yard, and there was no such punishment attached to sleeping without a certificate—a fine was all that the law exacted in such cases. But the falsehood had its full effect on poor Lereena, and she covered her face with her hands and wept bitterly.

"Now," continued Incubus, his eyes twinkling with pleasure at the sight of such grief, "I will restore Zoy to liberty, and also take dear, faithful Pina out of the nasty, filthy menagerie where she is confined in company with a wolf and three owls."

"You will!" cried Lereena, overcome with joy.

"Oh, I will bless you on one condition," said the dwarf in a solemn tone. "You know that I have long tried to win your love."

"Wretch!" cried Lereena, starting from him as one does from a snake when one's feet are bare.

"The time is now come. You are my slave; I bought you. Well, I want you to be something dearer to me. Love me, Lereena, and Zoy shall be free to-night, and Pina shall again gambol at your side and be at once your plaything and protector."

"And forget my husband, my beautiful Zoy? No, no, my Lord Incubus. You have it in your power to make me draw water and hew wood, but to make me love you is beyond your will!"

"You will not consent, then?"

"Never! never! never!"

"You will think better of it. If you do not, fair Lereena, you will feel my vengeance. I leave you here to think over my offer. I will return in half an hour, and if you still refuse, why, we shall see."

And with a horrid laugh the dwarf skipped up from his cushions, and locking the door behind him, was gone before Lereena could gather breath to reply.

The moment the monster was out of sight, all the pride that had supported her gave way. She buried her head among the cushions and wept bitterly. Almost unwillingly, her fancy went back to the times when she lived a pure, happy life with her Zoy, among the mountains. She thought of the anxious watches she spent when he was out hunting the deer with Pina, and wild infantine joy when he returned laden with spoil. Her pleasures were few, but each one was so fresh and unpalling that they were worth a whole year of city joys; and all this pure delicious freedom had been in a single day violently exchanged for the basest slavery. It was no wonder that poor Lereena should twist her fingers in her beautiful silken hair, and writhe among the cushions like one in the agonies of death.

She lay in a sort of stupor, the consequence of intense excitement. A low murmur rang through the room, and shaped itself into a melody. Lereena scarce listened at first, but presently it seemed to fall more definitely on her ear. She raised herself from amid the soft pillows, and the following words were heard in a sort of whisper-song, with an accompaniment so aerial and spiritual that one might imagine it some angel playing upon a lyre whose strings were sunbeams:

> Lereena, Lereena, the finger of dawn
>> Has opened the lids of the night,
> And I must be gone to the hills where the fawn
>> Flies along like some vapory sprite.
>>> But e'er I depart
>>> There's a voice at my heart,
>> Which whispers to me soft and low—
>>> Lereena, Lereena,
>>> Like scent of verbena,

Will your kiss be to me ere I go?
    Lereena!
    My queen, ah!
You'll give me a kiss ere I go

Lereena, Lereena, the flame dripping Sun
    Is kissing the lips of the sky;
The white mists fling down, to each mountain-
    ous crown,
Moist kisses; why not you and I?
    I'm off to the hill
    Where the vapors are chill;
I'll want something warm 'midst the snow.
    Then Lereena, Lereena,
    My sweet little queen, ah!
You'll give me a kiss ere I go—
    Lereena,
    Sweet queen, ah!
Give me a kiss ere I go!

"Zoy! Zoy! my own Zoy!" cried Lereena passionately, as the low notes of the last phrase died away. "Oh! come to me! speak to me!"

The doors that separated the conservatory from the room in which she was, opened gently, and amid a stream of narcotic perfume, which flowed from the plants with which it was filled, young Zoy glided into the arms of his bride. After the first passionate caresses had exhausted themselves, and they found words to speak, Lereena asked the youth how he had escaped from prison.

"Prison!" echoed Zoy. "I was in no prison, save for the first three days after my apprehension in the forest. I have been working in the farm-yard for the last month."

"What a dreadful liar that wretch Incubus is!" cried Lereena; "he told me that you were in prison, and would be condemned to confinement for life in consequence of being found asleep in the forest without a certificate; and he offered to have you released, if—if—I would love him."

"The monster!" said Zoy, grinding his teeth; "he will rue this. I have something to tell you about Incubus. You know a man of the name of Ivned."

"The Lord Chamberlain?"

"The same. Well, Ivned has received intelligence that Incubus intends to disgrace him with the King and deprive him of his office. Now he intends to be beforehand with the dwarf. A vast conspiracy is on foot, of which he is the head, to remodel the constitution, appoint new ministers, do away with the oppressive taxation, and liberate our countrymen, the unhappy Cock-Crows. The first step will be taken this evening. The dwarf must die."

"I would plead for his life, Zoy; but while he lives, we can never hope for happiness. Let him die. But we must be cautious. He will return here in a few minutes, to learn my answer to his infamous proposal. He must not find you here, or you are lost. By the way, how did you find me?"

"Ivned led me here. The dwarf is about to return, you say. So much the better. You must keep him in conversation, Lereena."

"Zoy! you surely would not—here, in my presence? Besides, if you fail, you will be executed."

"I will run no risk, Lereena; the execution of the plan is confided to one who is irresponsible to human law."

A low whistle sounded outside in the conservatory, and with a farewell embrace, Zoy glided hastily through the door leading to his retreat, almost at the same moment that Incubus entered by another.

"Ha! my fair Lereena," exclaimed Incubus, advancing joyously, rubbing his hands; "you look as bright as a May morning—a fair augury for my hopes. Come; you have reflected, and will listen to reason." So saying, he endeavored to pass his hand round her waist.

"Unhand me, monster!" she exclaimed, struggling to escape from his grasp; "unhand me, or you will rue it."

"Come, this is childishness," said Incubus, gnashing his teeth with fury. "I will not be baffled—by Heaven, I will not;" and he wound his long nervous arms around her like a cord.

"Help, help!" cried Lereena, rendered utterly powerless by the sinewy grasp of her assailant.

"Hush!" cried the dwarf; "you will be heard."

At this moment a strange sound rang through the room; the glass in the conservatory was heard to break, and a swift rushing, like that of an embodied storm, succeeded. Lereena turned her eyes for an instant in the direction of the sound, and to her she saw speeding with great bounds through the twilight, a huge animal, with glaring eyes, and tail that swept around like a pine branch tossed in the tempest. Two leaps more, and the ferocious animal had fastened its claws firmly between the shoulders of the dwarf.

"My God! what is this?" cried Incubus, as he found this unexpected burden on his shoulders; and loosing his grasp of Lereena, he staggered back, making furious efforts to free himself from his new assailant. Lereena, in the confusion of the moment, fancying that her last hour was come, veiled her face, and sank upon her knees. Meanwhile, the struggle between the dwarf and the leopard continued. Incubus, though deformed, was muscular, sinewy, and wonderfully active, and now fought more like a wild beast than a human being. The leopard still retained its original position between his shoulders, striving to drive its powerful white fangs into his vertebrae, while Incubus rolled on the floor, and twisted his body round and round in the attempt to strangle his indomitable antagonist. They rolled about inextricably mingled, and every now and then the dwarf's long legs or thin arms would be tossed aloft in the air, in the frantic attempt to grasp some vital part of the animal. Then the leopard would lash its tail, and taking a deeper hold with its talons, bury its frangs into the dwarf's sinewy neck. All this took place in perfect silence, broken now and then by a hoarse, guttural cry of despair and agony from Incubus, which the leopard would answer with a short impatient growl, as if he was enraged that the struggle should be so protracted. At length the dwarf's strength seemed to be exhausted; his wild contortions ceased, and he lay motionless on the floor with the leopard crouched upon his body. He was not yet dead: for a second or two all sound of combat ceased, and in the silence might be heard his heavy, stertorous breathing. The leopard then suddenly raised his head, and seemed for an instant about to forsake his prey, but the next instant his wide jaws opened; an agonized shriek burst from the dwarf—a dull sound, like the cracking of rotten wood, was heard. Incubus's body was suddenly contracted into a lump, by some powerful action of the muscles—then it quivered, straightened out again, and all was still.

The leopard lingered for a moment, raised his head, and looked steadfastly at the body, then leaped with a graceful swinging bound on to the the floor, and coming to where Lereena knelt, crouched itself at her feet.

The door of the conservatory opened cautiously, and two men entered with a stealthy step. One was Zoy, the other Ivned.

"It is all over," said Ivned, pointing to the dwarf's body, which lay in a heap on the floor. "The monster will offend society no longer."

"We must lose no time," answered Zoy; "where is Lereena?"

"There she is," replied Ivned, "kneeling at the base of that pillar, with the leopard crouched at her feet."

"Lereena!" cried Zoy, "rejoice with us; our enemy is dead. See! our dear Pina has avenged us both."

But Lereena did not reply, and when Zoy hastened up to her and unfastened the folds of her veil, he discovered that she had fainted. A few drops of the icy water in the fountain, sprinkled upon her forehead, soon brought her to, and all her fears vanished when she recognized in the fierce animal, that she saw bounding through the gloom, her faithful and affectionate Pina.

Ivned now explained that there was no time to lose. In the death of the dwarf, the first step had been taken, and it was necessary to follow it up immediately. The conspirators were assembled in a large body outside Incubus's palace, and only awaited the signal from Ivned to march on the King's residence and demand the restitution of their rights and the abolishment of the sleep-tax. So without any more delay, Lereena, Zoy, and the demagogue hastened from the palace, followed by Pina, whose jaws were still smeared with the blood of the dwarf, and joined the multitude outside. Here Ivned made one of his violent speeches against the tyranny of the government; pledged himself to head the people when they went to demand their privileges from the King, and in the conclusion threw out an indefinite, but sufficiently tangible hint, that now as the dwarf-premier was dead, owing to an *accidental* encounter with a wild animal that had escaped from the King's menagerie, the best thing the King could do would be to place him, Ivned, in his place, and the best thing that the people could do was to insist upon its being done. As there were a great many allusions in this speech to the greatness of Nodland and Nodlanders in general, the people applauded; but when Ivned alluded to the enfranchisement of the Cock-Crows, a deadly silence fell over the multitude. Man looked at man, as if each feared the other. They cast their eyes upon the ground, put their hands in their pockets, and pursed up their lips into little funnels, but not a word was spoken. As King Slumberous truly said, "the Cock-Crow question was never discussed in Nodland."

Ivned, when he saw this, turned to Zoy and Lereena, who stood near him, and shrugging his shoulders, whispered something in their ears; whatever it was, it had the effect of producing their immediate departure.

"Come!" said Zoy to his young bride, "let us fly from this accursed country while there is yet time; we should never be any thing but slaves here, while if we go far in among the hills of our own dear land, we will live poor, unmolested and free. Leave Ivned to mingle in the stormy whirlpool of politics; the day will perhaps come, when he will be glad to exchange his tedious honors for our peaceful obscurity."

So saying, the Cock-Crow, followed by his bride and Pina, stole unobserved through the crowd while it was palpitating under the influence of some fiery sentence of Ivned's, and taking immediately to the fields, struck out for the borders of the Cock-Crow country.

CHAPTER V THE END OF THE DEMAGOGUE

It was a bright morning in spring, the wind blew freshly down the deep ravines, and the eagles that hung in the light-blue atmosphere, swung to and fro upon its currents. A little cottage stood nestled on the side of the hill, into a piece of green pasture, which was shaded gently off into inclosures, filled with springing corn. A waterfall on one side flashed through the foliage of some live oaks that backed the house, while on the other a small patch, evidently sacred to Vertumnus, blushed with all the flowers that spring could call up from the half-awakened earth. Outside the door of the cottage, and basking in the morning sunbeams, lay a beautiful leopard stretched at full length, while a ruddy bronze-skinned youth was standing close by, leaning on a spear. Presently a young girl issued from the cottage, with a leathern belt in her hand, to which were attached hooks to which the huntsman attached the slaughtered game; this she fastened around the waist of the youth, and then twining her arms around his neck, leaned against him, and turned her eyes lovingly upon his youthful face. It was a charming picture of young, unsatisfied love— she nestling in close to him as if she would work her way into his heart, and he enjoying the luxurious pleasure of such gentle demonstrations, without at the same time forfeiting the peculiar dignity of his sex.

"At what hour will you return, dear Zoy?" asked the girl in a low tone, that expressed something more than the question.

"Oh! I shall not be long, Lereena. If Pina there is not too lazy, we shall have a fat deer in less than an hour."

Pina gave a slight switch of her tail, as if to show that there was yet a portion of animal energy in her that had not evaporated in the hot sunshine.

"Who is that ascending the hill, dear Zoy?" asked Lereena, pointing to the distant figure of a man, who was slowly coming up the ravine. "I never see a stranger, that fear does not riot in my heart, lest it may be those horrid Nodlanders who have come to bear us into slavery."

"Fear not!" said Zoy, grasping his spear with a savage glance. "You will die by my hand, Lereena, before another manacle binds your arm."

"There is something familiar in the appearance of this stranger!" said Lereena, scanning the approaching individual rather anxiously; "but he appears very faint and weary, and his clothes are in tatters. Go to him, Zoy, and help him with your arm; he is weak."

"Why," cried Zoy rushing down to meet the stranger, "it is Ivned! what can have brought him here?"

Pina opened one eye on the strength of all this hubbub, but seeing only her master and an old tattered beggar, she wisely concluded that any active measures on her part would be out of place, and closing it again resumed her slumbers.

It was Ivned. But how changed from the brisk favorite of fortune, whom Zoy had left leading a whole nation! He was thin and gray. His eye, once so bold and unquellable, was now sunken and unsteady. His gait was feeble and tottering; his clothes were in tatters, and it would have been indeed impossible to recognize in him the daring, reckless demagogue, for whom no task was too difficult and no assertion too impudent.

"Ah!" said he, when in the evening he was seated at the fire in Zoy's cottage, "I forswear politics for ever. When you fled from Nodland I was in a fair way to greatness. I made the King submit to my terms. The sleep-tax was abolished, and every burgher and mechanic in the nation was my friend. Trade improved, because every body was more attentive than when they had to pay for their sleep. That commodity being taxed, people thought that they were extravagant if they did not take the value of their money; the consequence was, they slept the full legal allowance, which was several hours more than they used to sleep before. But under my administration all this was reformed, and the commerce of Nodland recovered from its lethargy. I found the King a feeble man, and I ruled him judiciously. I made him do exactly what I liked, but those measures were always for the good of the people. I consequently became a popular favorite, and when the King and I drove out together, twice as many people cried, 'Long life to Ivned,' as to King Slumberous."

"Hum!" said Zoy, in rather a disapproving tone.

"Well, one day I made a covert sneer at the King, which I never intended he should see, and which he never would have seen if it had not been for the Prince of Fungi, who explained the satire to him after his usual manner. The joke was a severe one, and his Majesty never forgave me. But a short time afterwards I was accused of high treason, and of entering into a plot to dethrone the King, and place myself in his stead. I was innocent, but I was imprisoned. However, by the aid of some gold, I effected my escape, and here I am in this delightful rural retreat of yours, among a new people where all is innocence, and who only want a scientific constitution to be perfect. I shall be very happy here, I know."

"I think not," said Zoy gravely, "if your happiness lies, as it did once, in political turmoil and endless quarrel. Listen to me, Ivned: We are an innocent people, we Cock-Crows; we have retired up into these hills which are beyond the reach of the Nodlanders, and we intend to retain our purity. We want no brawling demagogues here; we have no politics, therefore we want no politicians. If you cannot live in peace, and must have excitement and dissension, return to Nodland or to your native island. Your speeches here will not be listened to, and your appeals against tyranny will go for nothing, for every one is free. But if you are content to settle down as one of us; to hunt the deer, instead of pursuing popular opinion; to cultivate muscle instead of cunning, and to change your political baton into a huntsman's spear, then we will give you the welcome of a man, and you shall be honored among us."

"You are very kind," said Ivned bitterly, "but I will not trespass upon the hospitality of a country that prescribes rules to its guest. I will return to Nodland, where a scaffold or a throne awaits me: either is preferable to your pastoral obscurity."

So saying, Ivned arose, and shaking the dust from off his feet, passed out of the house. Zoy made no effort to detain him, but turning to Lereena, he kissed her, and said, "I am sorry, but perhaps it is as well. He could not live in peace, and our country is better without him. He is a dangerous man."

And the husband and wife again embraced; and Pina waved her tail gently, until she found that she was waving it into the fire and burning it, when she got up and went growling to the other end of the room; and the deer hung from the rafters; and the noise of the waterfall at the back stole soothingly in through the half-opened window; and all was still and peaceful; and amid this peace, with the hope that it never was disturbed, we leave Zoy and Lereena.

The Seventeen Virgins

Jack Vance

Jack Vance is an award-winning author and one of the finest stylists in the fantasy field. His model is Clark Ashton Smith, the California poet and fantasist of the early twentieth century. Vance's stories of Cugel the Clever set on the Undying Earth, so far in the future that the sun is huge and red, have influenced fantasy and SF writers since the 1950s. (Vance's setting is an acknowledged model for Gene Wolfe's Urth in The Book of the New Sun.) *The stories reprinted here are part of the third book of Cugel's adventures,* Cugel's Saga *(1983). Cugel is the antithesis of Robert E. Howard's Conan (the mighty swordsman and barbarian), an anti-hero and aesthete, amoral and always willing to avoid a fight. A shameful fellow, really . . . but fun.*

The Chase went far and long, and led into that dismal tract of bone-colored hills known as the Pale Rugates. Cugel finally used a clever trick to baffle pursuit, sliding from his steed and hiding among the rocks while his enemies pounded past in chase of the riderless mount.

Cugel lay in hiding until the angry band returned toward Kaspara Vitatus, bickering among themselves. He emerged into the open; then, after shaking his fist and shouting curses after the now distant figures, he turned and continued south through the Pale Rugates.

The region was as stark and grim as the surface of a dead sun, and thus avoided by such creatures as sindics, shambs, erbs and visps, for Cugel a single and melancholy source of satisfaction.

Step after step marched Cugel, one leg in front of the other: up slope to overlook an endless succession of barren swells, down again into the hollow where at rare intervals a seep of water nourished a sickly vegetation. Here Cugel found ramp, burdock, squallix and an occasional newt, which sufficed against starvation.

Day followed day. The sun rising cool and dim swam up into the dark-blue sky, from time to time seeming to flicker with a film of blue-black luster, finally to settle like an enormous purple pearl into the west. When dark made further progress impractical, Cugel wrapped himself in his cloak and slept as best he could.

On the afternoon of the seventh day Cugel limped down a slope into an ancient orchard. Cugel found and devoured a few withered hag-apples, then set off along the trace of an old road.

The track proceeded a mile, to lead out upon a bluff overlooking a broad plain. Directly below a river skirted a small town, curved away to the southwest and finally disappeared into the haze.

Cugel surveyed the landscape with keen attention. Out upon the plain he saw carefully tended garden plots, each precisely square and of identical size; along the river drifted a fisherman's punt. A placid scene, thought Cugel. On the other hand, the town was built to a strange and archaic architecture, and the scrupulous precision with which the houses surrounded the square suggested a like inflexibility in the inhabitants. The houses themselves were no less uniform, each a construction of two, or three, or even four squat bulbs of diminishing size, one on the other, the lowest always painted blue, the second dark red, the third and the fourth respectively a dull mustard ocher and black; and each house terminated in a spire of fancifully twisted iron rods, of greater or lesser height. An inn on the riverbank showed a style somewhat looser and easier, with a pleasant garden surrounding. Along the river road to the east Cugel now noticed the approach of a caravan of six high-wheeled wagons, and his uncertainty dissolved; the town was evidently tolerant of strangers, and Cugel confidently set off down the hill.

At the outskirts to town he halted and drew forth his old purse, which he yet retained through it hung loose and limp. Cugel examined the contents: five terces, a sum hardly adequate to his needs. Cugel reflected a moment, then collected a handful of pebbles which he dropped into the purse, to create a reassuring rotundity. He dusted his breeches, adjusted his green hunter's cap, and proceeded.

He entered the town without challenge or even attention. Crossing the square, he halted to inspect a contrivance even more peculiar than the quaint architecture: a stone fire-pit in which several logs blazed high, rimmed by five lamps on iron stands, each with five wicks, and above an intricate linkage of mirrors and lenses, the purpose of which surpassed Cugel's comprehension. Two young men tended the device with diligence, trimming the twenty-five wicks, prodding the fire, adjusting screws and levers which in turn controlled the mirrors and lenses. They wore what appeared to be the local costume: voluminous blue knee-length breeches, red shirts, brass-buttoned black vests and broad-brimmed hats; after disinterested glances they paid Cugel no heed, and he continued to the inn.

In the adjacent garden two dozen folk of the town sat at tables, eating and drinking with great gusto. Cugel watched them a moment or two; their punctilio and elegant gestures suggested the manners of an age far past. Like their houses, they were a sort unique to Cugel's experience, pale and thin, with egg-shaped heads, long noses, dark expressive eyes and ears cropped in various styles. The men were uniformly bald and their pates glistened in the red sunlight. The women parted their black hair in the middle, then cut it abruptly short a half-inch above the ears: a style which Cugel considered unbecoming. Watching the folk eat and drink, Cugel was unfavorably reminded of the fare which had sustained him across the Pale Rugates, and he gave no further thought to his terces. He strode into the garden and seated himself at a table. A portly man in a blue apron approached, frowning somewhat at Cugel's disheveled appearance. Cugel immediately brought forth two terces which he handed to the man. "This is for you yourself, my good fellow, to insure expeditious service. I have just completed an arduous journey; I am famished with hunger. You may bring me a platter identical to that which the gentleman yonder is enjoying, together with a selection of side-dishes and a bottle of wine. Then be so good as to ask the innkeeper to prepare me a comfortable chamber." Cugel carelessly brought forth his purse and dropped it upon the table where its weight produced an impressive implication. "I will also require a bath, fresh linen and a barber."

"I myself am Maier the innkeeper," said the portly man in a gracious voice. "I will see to your wishes immediately."

"Excellent," said Cugel. "I am favorably impressed with your establishment, and perhaps will remain several days."

The innkeeper bowed in gratification and hurried off to supervise the preparation of Cugel's dinner.

Cugel made an excellent meal, though the second course, a dish of crayfish stuffed with mince and slivers of scarlet mangoneel, he found a trifle too rich. The roast fowl however could not be faulted and the wine pleased Cugel to such an extent that he ordered a second flask. Maier the innkeeper served the bottle himself and accepted Cugel's compliments with a trace of complacency. "There is no better wine in Gundar! It is admittedly expensive, but you are a person who appreciates the best."

"Precisely true," said Cugel. "Sit down and take a glass with me. I confess to curiosity in regard to this remarkable town."

The innkeeper willingly followed Cugel's suggestion. "I am puzzled that you find Gundar remarkable. I have lived here all my life and it seems ordinary enough to me."

"I will cite three circumstances which I consider worthy of note," said Cugel, now somewhat expansive by reason of the wine. "First: the bulbous construction of your buildings. Secondly: the contrivance of lenses above the fire, which at the very least must stimulate a stranger's interest. Thirdly: the fact that the men of Gundar are all stark bald."

The innkeeper nodded thoughtfully. "The architecture at least is quickly explained. The ancient Gunds lived in enormous gourds. When a section of the wall become weak it was replaced with a board, until in due course the folk found themselves living in houses fashioned completely of wood, and the style has persisted. As for the fire and the projectors, do you not know the world-wide Order of Solar Emosynaries? We stimulate the vitality of the sun; so long as our beam of sympathetic vibration regulates solar combustion, it will never expire. Similar stations exist at other locations: at Blue Azor; on the Isle of Brazel; at the walled city Munt; and in the observatory of the Grand Starkeeper at Vir Vassilis."

Cugel shook his head sadly. "I hear that conditions have changed. Brazel has long since sunk beneath the waves. Munt was destroyed a thousand years ago by Dystropes. I have never heard of either Blue Azor or Vir Vassilis, though I am widely traveled. Possibily, here at Gundar, you are the solitary Solar Emosynaries yet in existence."

"This is dismal news," declared Maier. "The noticeable enfeeblement of the sun is hereby explained. Perhaps we had best double the fire under our regulator."

Cugel poured more wine. "A question leaps to mind. If, as I suspect, this is the single Solar Emosynary station yet in operation, who or what regulates the sun when it has passed below the horizon?"

The innkeeper shook his head. "I can offer no explanation. It may be that during the hours of night the sun itself relaxes and, as it were, sleeps, although this is of course sheerest speculation."

"Allow me to offer another hypothesis," said Cugel. "Conceivably the waning of the sun has advanced beyond all possibility of regulation, so that your efforts, though formerly useful, are now ineffective."

Maier threw up his hands in perplexity. "These complications surpass my scope, but yonder stands the Nolde Huruska." He directed Cugel's attention to a large man with a deep chest and bristling black beard, who stood at the entrance. "Excuse me a moment." He rose to his feet and approaching the Nolde spoke for several minutes, indicating Cugel from time to time. The Nolde finally made a brusque gesture and marched across the garden to confront Cugel. He spoke in a heavy voice: "I understand you to assert that no Emosynaries exist other than ourselves?"

"I stated nothing so definitely," said Cugel, somewhat on the defensive. "I remarked that I had traveled widely and that no other such 'Emosynary' agency has come to my attention; and I innocently speculated that possibly none now operate."

"At Gundar we conceive 'innocence' as a positive quality, not merely an insipid absence of guilt," stated the Nolde. "We are not the fools that certain untidy ruffians might suppose."

Cugel suppressed the hot remark which rose to his lips, and contented himself with a shrug. Maier walked away with the Nolde and for several minutes the two men conferred, with frequent glances in Cugel's direction. Then the Nolde departed and the innkeeper returned to Cugel's table. "A somewhat brusque man, the Nolde of Gundar," he told Cugel, "but very competent withal."

"It would be presumptuous of me to comment," said Cugel. "What, precisely, is his function?"

"At Gundar we place great store upon precision and methodicity," explained Maier. "We feel that the absence of order encourages disorder; and the official responsible for the inhibition of caprice and abnormality is the Nolde . . . What was our previous conversation?

Ah yes, you mentioned our notorious baldness. I can offer no definite explanation. According to our servants, the condition signifies the final perfection of the human race. Other folk give credence to an ancient legend. A pair of magicians, Astherlin and Mauldred, vied for the favor of the Gunds. Astherlin promised the boon of extreme hairiness, so that the folk of Gundar need never wear garments. Mauldred, to the contrary, offered the Gunds baldness, with all the consequent advantages, and easily won the contest; in fact Mauldred became the first Nolde of Gundar, the post now filled, as you know, by Huruska." Maier the innkeeper pursed his lips and looked off across the garden. "Huruska, a distrustful sort, has reminded me of my fixed rule to ask all transient guests to settle their accounts on a daily basis. I naturally assured him of your complete reliability, but simply in order to appease Huruska, I will tender the reckoning in the morning."

"This is tantamount to an insult," declared Cugel haughtily. "Must we truckle to the whims of Huruska? Not I, you may be assured! I will settle my account in the usual manner."

The innkeeper blinked. "May I ask how long you intend to stay at Gundar?"

"My journey takes me south, by the most expeditious transport available, which I assume to be riverboat."

"The town Lumarth lies ten days by caravan across the Lirrh Aing. The Isk River also flows past Lumarth, but is judged inconvenient by virtue of three intervening localities. The Lallo Marsh is infested with stinging insects; the tree-dwarfs of the Santalba Forest pelt passing boats with refuse; and the Desperate Rapids shatter both bones and boats."

"In this case I will travel by caravan," said Cugel. "Meanwhile I will remain here, unless the persecutions of Huruska become intolerable."

Maier licked his lips and looked over his shoulder. "I assured Huruska that I would adhere to the strict letter of my rule. He will surely make a great issue of the matter unless—"

Cugel made a gracious gesture. "Bring me seals. I will close up my purse which contains a fortune in opals and alumes. We will deposit the purse in the strong-box and you may hold it for surety. Even Huruska cannot now protest!"

Maier held up his hands in awe. "I could not undertake so large a responsibility!"

"Dismiss all fear," said Cugel. "I have protected the purse with a spell; the instant a criminal breaks the seal the jewels are transformed into pebbles."

Maier dubiously accepted Cugel's purse on these terms. They jointly saw the scales applied and the purse deposited into Maier's strong-box.

Cugel now repaired to his chamber, where he bathed, commanded the services of a barber and dressed in fresh garments. Setting his cap at an appropriate angle, he strolled out upon the square.

His steps led him to the Solar Emosynary station. As before, two young men worked diligently, one stoking the blaze and adjusting the five lamps, while the other held the regulatory beam fixed upon the low sun.

Cugel inspected the contrivance from all angles, and presently the person who fed the blaze called out: "Are you not that notable traveler who today expressed doubts as to the efficacy of the Emosynary System?"

Cugel spoke carefully: "I told Maier and Huruska this: that Brazel is sunk below the Melantine Gulf and almost gone from memory; that the walled city Munt was long ago laid waste; that I am acquainted with neither Blue Azor, nor Vir Vassilis. These were my only positive statements."

The young fire-stoker petulantly threw an arm-load of logs into the fire-pit. "Still we are told that you consider our efforts impractical."

"I would not go so far," said Cugel politely. "Even if the other Emosynary agencies are abandoned, it is possible that the Gundar regulator suffices; who knows?"

"I will tell you this," declared the stoker. "We work without recompense, and in our spare time we must cut and transport fuel. The process is tedious."

The operator of the aiming device amplified his friend's complaint. "Huruska and the elders do none of the work; they merely ordain that we toil, which of course is the easiest part of the project. Janred and I are of a sophisticated new generation; on principle we reject all dogmatic doctrines. I for one consider the Solar Emosynary system a waste of time and effort."

"If the other agencies are abandoned," argued Janred the stoker, "who or what regulates the sun when it has passed beyond the horizon? The system is pure balderdash."

The operator of the lenses declared: "I will now demonstrate as much, and free us all from this thankless toil!" He worked a lever. "Notice I direct the regulatory beam away from the sun. Look! It shines as before, without the slightest attention on our part!"

Cugel inspected the sun, and for a fact it seemed to glow as before, flickering from time to time, and shivering like an old man with the ague. The two young men watched with similar interest, and as minutes passed, they began to murmur in satisfaction. "We are vindicated! The sun has not gone out!"

Even as they watched, the sun, perhaps fortuitously, underwent a cachectic spasm, and lurched alarmingly toward the horizon. Behind them sounded a bellow of outrage and the Nolde Huruska ran forward. "What is the meaning of this irresponsibility? Direct the regulator aright and instantly! Would you have us groping for the rest of our lives in the dark?"

The stoker resentfully jerked his thumb toward Cugel. "He convinced us that the system was unnecessary, and that our work was futile."

"What!" Huruska swung his formidable body about and confronted Cugel. "Only hours ago you set foot in Gundar, and already you are disrupting the fabric of our existence! I warn you, our patience is not illimitable! Be off with you and do not approach the Emosynary agency a second time!"

Choking with fury, Cugel swung on his heel and marched off across the square.

At the caravan terminal he inquired as to transport southward, but the caravan which had arrived at noon would on the morrow depart eastward the way it had come.

Cugel returned to the inn and stepped into the tavern. He noticed three men playing a card game and posted himself as an observer. The game proved to be a simple version of Zampolio, and presently Cugel asked if he might join the play. "But only if the stakes are not too high," he protested. "I am not particularly skillful and I dislike losing more than a terce or two."

"Bah," exclaimed one of the players. "What is money? Who will spend it when we are dead?"

"If we take all your gold, then you need not carry it further," another remarked jocularly.

"All of us must learn," the third player assured Cugel. "You are fortunate to have the three premier experts of Gundar as instructors."

Cugel drew back in alarm. "I refuse to lose more than a single terce!"

"Come now! Don't be a prig!"

"Very well," said Cugel. "I will risk it. But these cards are tattered and dirty. By chance I have a fresh set in my pouch."

"Excellent! The game proceeds!"

Two hours later the three Gunds threw down their cards, gave Cugel long hard looks, then as if with a single mind rose to their feet and departed the tavern. Inspecting his gains, Cugel counted thirty-two terces and a few odd coppers. In a cheerful frame of mind he retired to his chamber for the night.

In the morning, as he consumed his breakfast, he noticed the arrival of the Nolde Huruska, who immediately engaged Maier the innkeeper in conversation. A few minutes later Huruska approached Cugel's table and stared down at Cugel with a somewhat menacing grin, while Maier stood anxiously a few paces to the rear.

Cugel spoke in a voice of strained politeness: "Well, what is it this time? The sun has risen; my innocence in the matter of the regulatory beam has been established."

"I am now concerned with another matter. Are you acquainted with the penalties for fraud?"

Cugel shrugged. "The matter is of no interest to me."

"They are severe and I will revert to them in a moment. First, let me inquire: did you entrust to Maier a purse purportedly containing valuable jewels?"

"I did indeed. The property is protected by a spell, I may add; if the seal is broken the gems become ordinary pebbles."

Huruska exhibited the purse. "Notice, the seal is intact. I cut a slit in the leather and looked within. The contents were then and are now—" with a flourish Huruska turned the purse out upon the table "—pebbles identical to those in the road yonder."

Cugel exclaimed in outrage: "The jewels are now worthless rubble! I hold you responsible and you must make recompense!"

Huruska uttered an offensive laugh. "If you can change gems to pebbles, you can change pebbles to gems. Maier will now tender the bill. If you refuse to pay, I intend to have you nailed into the enclosure under the gallows until such time as you change your mind."

"Your insinuations are both disgusting and absurd," declared

Cugel. "Innkeeper, present your account! Let us finish with this far-rago once and for all."

Maier came forward with a slip of paper. "I make the total to be eleven terces, plus whatever gratuities might seem in order."

"There will be no gratuities," said Cugel. "Do you harass all your guests in this fashion?" He flung eleven terces down upon the table. "Take your money and leave me in peace."

Maier sheepishly gathered up the coins; Huruska made an inarticulate sound and turned away. Cugel, upon finishing his breakfast, went out once more to stroll across the square. Here he met an individual whom he recognized to be the pot-boy in the tavern, and Cugel signaled him to a halt. "You seem an alert and knowledgeable fellow," said Cugel. "May I inquire your name?"

"I am generally known as 'Zeller'."

"I would guess you to be well-acquainted with the folk of Gundar."

"I consider myself well-informed. Why do you ask?"

"First," said Cugel, "let me ask if you care to turn your knowledge to profit?"

"Certainly, so long as I evade the attention of the Nolde."

"Very good. I notice a disused booth yonder which should serve our purpose. In one hour we shall put our enterprise into operation."

Cugel returned to the inn where at his request Maier brought a board, brush and paint. Cugel composed a sign:

THE EMINENT SEER CUGEL
COUNSELS, INTERPRETS, PROGNOSTICATES.
ASK! YOU WILL BE ANSWERED!
CONSULTATIONS: THREE TERCES.

Cugel hung the sign above the booth, arranged curtains and waited for customers. The pot-boy, meanwhile, had inconspicuously secreted himself at the back.

Almost immediately folk crossing the square halted to read the sign. A woman of early middle-age presently came forward.

"Three terces is a large sum. What results can you guarantee?"

"None whatever, by the very nature of things. I am a skilled voyant, I have acquaintance with the arts of magic, but knowledge comes to me from unknown and uncontrollable sources."

The woman paid over her money. "Three terces is cheap if you can resolve my worries. My daughter all her life has enjoyed the best of

health but now she ails, and suffers a morose condition. All my reme-
dies are to no avail. What must I do?"

"A moment, madam, while I meditate." Cugel drew the curtain
and leaned back to where he could hear the pot-boy's whispered
remarks, then once again drew aside the curtains.

"I have made myself one with the cosmos! Knowledge has entered
my mind! Your daughter Dilian is pregnant. For an additional three
terces I will supply the father's name."

"This is a fee I pay with pleasure," declared the woman grimly.
She paid, received the information and marched purposefully away.

Another woman approached, paid three terces, and Cugel addressed himself to her problem: "My husband assured me that he had
put by a canister of gold coins against the future, but upon his death I
could find not so much as a copper. Where has he hidden the gold?"

Cugel closed the curtains, took counsel with the pot-boy, and again
appeared to the woman. "I have discouraging news for you. Your
husband Finister spent much of his hoarded gold at the tavern. With
the rest he purchased an amethyst brooch for a woman named
Varletta."

The news of Cugel's remarkable abilities spread rapidly and trade
was brisk. Shortly before noon, a large woman, muffled and veiled,
approached the booth, paid three terces, and asked in a high-pitched,
if husky, voice: "Read me my fortune!"

Cugel drew the curtains and consulted the pot-boy, who was at a
loss. "It is no one I know. I can tell you nothing."

"No matter," said Cugel. "My suspicions are verified." He drew
aside the curtain. "The portents are unclear and I refuse to take your
money." Cugel returned the fee. "I can tell you this much: you are an
individual of domineering character and no great intelligence. Ahead
lies what? Honors? A long voyage by water? Revenge on your enemies? Wealth? The image is distorted; I may be reading my own
future."

The woman tore away her veils and stood revealed as the Nolde
Huruska. "Master Cugel, you are lucky indeed that you returned my
money, otherwise I would have taken you up for deceptive practices.
In any event, I deem your activities mischievous, and contrary to the
public interest. Gundar is in an uproar because of your revelations;
there will be no more of them. Take down your sign, and be happily
thankful that you have escaped so easily."

"I will be glad to terminate my enterprise," said Cugel with dignity. "The work is taxing."

Huruska stalked away in a huff. Cugel divided his earnings with the pot-boy, and in a spirit of mutual satisfaction they departed the booth.

Cugel dined on the best that the inn afforded, but later when he went into the tavern he discovered a noticeable lack of amiability among the patrons and presently went off to his chamber.

The next morning as he took breakfast a caravan of ten wagons arrived in town. The principal cargo appeared to be a bevy of seventeen beautiful maidens, who rode upon two of the wagons. Three other wagons served as dormitories, while the remaining five were loaded with stores, trunks, bales and cases. The caravan master, a portly mild-seeming man with flowing brown hair and a silky beard, assisted his delightful charges to the ground and led them all to the inn, where Maier served up an ample breakfast of spiced porridge, preserved quince, and tea.

Cugel watched the group as they made their meal and reflected that a journey to almost any destination in such company would be a pleasant journey indeed.

The Nolde Huruska appeared, and went to pay his respects to the caravan-leader. The two conversed amiably at some length, while Cugel waited impatiently.

Huruska at last departed. The maidens, having finished their meal, went off to stroll about the square. Cugel crossed to the table where the caravan-leader sat. "Sir, my name is Cugel, and I would appreciate a few words with you."

"By all means! Please be seated. Will you take a glass of this excellent tea?"

"Thank you. First, may I inquire the destination of your caravan?"

The caravan-leader showed surprise at Cugel's ignorance. "We are bound for Lumarth; these are the 'Seventeen Virgins of Symnathis' who traditionally grace the Grand Pageant."

"I am a stranger to this region," Cugel explained. "Hence I know nothing of the local customs. In any event, I myself am bound for Lumarth and would be pleased to travel with your caravan."

The caravan-leader gave an affable assent. "I would be delighted to have you with us."

"Excellent!" said Cugel. "Then all is arranged."

The caravan-leader stroked his silky brown beard. "I must warn you that my fees are somewhat higher than usual, owing to the expensive amenities I am obliged to provide these seventeen fastidious maidens."

"Indeed," said Cugel. "How much do you require?"

"The journey occupies the better part of ten days, and my minimum charge is twenty terces per diem, for a total of two hundred terces, plus a twenty terce supplement for wine."

"This is far more than I can afford," said Cugel in a bleak voice. "At the moment I command only a third of this sum. Is there some means by which I might earn my passage?"

"Unfortunately not," said the caravan-leader. "Only this morning the position of armed guard was open, which even paid a small stipend, but Huruska the Nolde, who wishes to visit Lumarth, has agreed to serve in this capacity and the post is now filled."

Cugel made a sound of disappointment and raised his eyes to the sky. When at last he could bring himself to speak he asked: "When do you plan to depart?"

"Tomorrow at dawn, with absolute punctuality. I am sorry that we will not have the pleasure of your company."

"I share the sorrow," said Cugel. He returned to his own table and sat brooding. Presently he went into the tavern, where various card games were in progress. Cugel attempted to join the play, but in every case his request was denied. In a surly mood he went to the counter where Maier the innkeeper unpacked a crate of earthenware goblets. Cugel tried to initiate a conversation but for once Maier could take no time from his labors. "The Nolde Huruska goes off on a journey and tonight his friends mark the occasion with a farewell party, for which I must make careful preparations."

Cugel took a mug of beer to a side table and gave himself to reflection. After a few moments he went out the back exit and surveyed the prospect, which here overlooked the Isk River. Cugel sauntered down to the water's edge and discovered a dock at which the fishermen moored their punts and dried their nets. Cugel looked up and down the river, then returned up the path to the inn, to spend the rest of the day watching the seventeen maidens as they strolled about the square, or sipped sweet lime tea in the garden of the inn.

The sun set; twilight the color of old wine darkened into night. Cugel set about his preparations, which were quickly achieved, inasmuch as the essence of his plan lay in its simplicity.

The caravan-leader, whose name, so Cugel learned, was Shimilko, assembled his exquisite company for their evening meal, then herded them carefully to the dormitory wagons, despite the pouts and protests of those who wished to remain at the inn and enjoy the festivities of the evening.

In the tavern the farewell party in honor of Huruska had already commenced. Cugel seated himself in a dark corner and presently attracted the attention of the perspiring Maier. Cugel produced ten terces. "I admit that I harbored ungrateful thoughts toward Huruska," he said. "Now I wish to express my good wishes—in absolute anonymity, however! Whenever Huruska starts upon a mug of ale, I want you to place a full mug before him, so that his evening will be incessantly merry. If he asks who has bought the drink you are only to reply: 'One of your friends wishes to pay you a compliment.' Is this clear?"

"Absolutely, and I will do as you command. It is a large-hearted gesture, which Huruska will appreciate."

The evening progressed. Huruska's friends sang jovial songs and proposed a dozen toasts, in all of which Huruska joined. As Cugel had required, whenever Huruska so much as started to drink from a mug, another was placed at his elbow, and Cugel marveled at the scope of Huruska's internal reservoirs.

At last Huruska was prompted to excuse himself from the company. He staggered out the back exit and made his way to the stone wall with a trough below, which had been placed for the convenience of the tavern's patrons.

As Huruska faced the wall Cugel stepped behind him and flung a fisherman's net over Huruska's head, then expertly dropped a noose around Huruska's burly shoulders, followed by other turns and ties. Huruska's bellows were drowned by the song at this moment being sung in his honor.

Cugel dragged the cursing hulk down the path to the dock, and rolled him over and into a punt. Untying the mooring line, Cugel pushed the punt out into the current of the river. "At the very least," Cugel told himself, "two parts of my prophecy are accurate; Huruska has been honored in the tavern and now is about to enjoy a voyage by water."

He returned to the tavern where Huruska's absence had at last been noticed. Maier expressed the opinion that, with an early departure in the offing, Huruska had prudently retired to bed, and all conceded that this was no doubt the case.

The next morning Cugel arose an hour before dawn. He took a quick breakfast, paid Maier his score, then went to where Shimilko ordered his caravan.

"I bring news from Huruska," said Cugel. "Owing to an unfortunate set of personal circumstances, he finds himself unable to make the journey, and has commended me to that post for which you had engaged him."

Shimilko shook his head in wonder. "A pity! Yesterday he seemed so enthusiastic! Well, we all must be flexible, and since Huruska cannot join us, I am pleased to accept you in his stead. As soon as we start, I will instruct you in your duties, which are straightforward. You must stand guard by night and take your rest by day, although in the case of danger I naturally expect you to join in the defense of the caravan."

"These duties are well within my competence," said Cugel. "I am ready to depart at your convenience."

"Yonder rises the sun," declared Shimilko. "Let us be off and away for Lumarth."

Ten days later Shimilko's caravan passed through the Methune Gap, and the great Vale of Coram opened before them. The brimming Isk wound back and forth, reflecting a sultry sheen; in the distance loomed the long dark mass of the Draven Forest. Closer at hand five domes of shimmering nacreous gloss marked the site of Lumarth.

Shimilko addressed himself to the company. "Below lies what remains of the old city Lumarth. Do not be deceived by the domes; they indicate temples at one time sacred to the five demons Yaunt, Jastenave, Phampoun, Adelmar and Suul, and hence were preserved during the Sampathissic Wars.

"The folk of Lumarth are unlike any of your experience. Many are small sorcerers, though Chaladet the Grand Thearch has proscribed magic within the city precincts. You may conceive these people to be languid and wan, and dazed by excess sensation, and you will be correct. All are obsessively rigid in regard to ritual, and all subscribe to a Doctrine of Absolute Altruism, which compels them to virtue and benevolence. For this reason they are known as the 'Kind Folk'. A final word in regard to our journey, which luckily has gone without untoward incident. The wagoneers have driven with skill; Cugel has vigilantly guarded us by night, and I am well pleased. So then: onward to Lumarth, and let meticulous discretion be the slogan!"

The caravan traversed a narrow track down into the valley, then proceeded along an avenue of rutted stone under an arch of enormous black mimosa trees.

At a mouldering portal opening upon the plaza the caravan was met by five tall men in gowns of embroidered silks, the splendid double-crowned headgear of the Coramese Thurists lending them an impressive dignity. The five men were much alike, with pale transparent skins, thin high-bridged noses, slender limbs and pensive gray eyes. One who wore a gorgeous gown of mustard-yellow, crimson and black raised two fingers in a calm salute. "My friend Shimilko, you have arrived securely with all your blessed cargo. We are well-served and very pleased."

"The Lirrh-Aing was so placid as almost to be dull," said Shimilko. "To be sure, I was fortunate in securing the services of Cugel, who guarded us so well by night that never were our slumbers interrupted."

"Well done, Cugel!" said the head Thurist. "We will at this time take custody of the precious maidens. Tomorrow you may render your account to the bursar. The Wayfarer's Inn lies yonder, and I counsel you to its comforts."

"Just so! We will all be the better for a few days rest!"

However, Cugel chose not to so indulge himself. At the door to the inn he told Shimilko: "Here we part company, for I must continue along the way. Affairs press on me and Almery lies far to the west."

"But your stipend, Cugel! You must wait at least until tomorrow, when I can collect certain monies from the bursar. Until then, I am without funds."

Cugel hesitated, but at last was prevailed upon to stay.

An hour later a messenger strode into the inn. "Master Shimilko, you and your company are required to appear instantly before the Grand Thearch on a matter of utmost importance."

Shimilko looked up in alarm. "Whatever is the matter?"

"I am obliged to tell you nothing more,"

With a long face Shimilko led his company across the plaza to the loggia before the old palace, where Chaladet sat on a massive chair. To either side stood the College of Thurists and all regarded Shimilko with somber expressions.

"What is the meaning of this summons?" inquired Shimilko. "Why do you regard me with such gravity?"

The Grand Thearch spoke in a deep voice: "Shimilko, the seventeen maidens conveyed by you from Symnathis to Lumarth have been examined, and I regret to say that of the seventeen, only two can be classified as virgins. The remaining fifteen have been sexually deflorated."

Shimilko could hardly speak for consternation. "Impossible!" he sputtered. "At Symnathis I undertook the most elaborate precautions. I can display three separate documents certifying the purity of each. There can be no doubt! You are in error!"

"We are not in error, Master Shimilko. Conditions are as we describe, and may easily be verified."

" 'Impossible' and 'incredible' are the only two words which come to mind," cried Shimilko. "Have you questioned the girls themselves?"

"Of course. They merely raise their eyes to the ceiling and whistle between their teeth. Shimilko, how do you explain this heinous outrage?"

"I am perplexed to the point of confusion! The girls embarked upon the journey as pure as the day they were born. This is fact! During each waking instant they never left my area of perception. This is also fact."

"And when you slept?"

"The implausibility is no less extreme. The teamsters invariably retired together in a group. I shared my wagon with the chief teamster and each of us will vouch for the other. Cugel meanwhile kept watch over the entire camp."

"Alone?"

"A single guard suffices, even though the nocturnal hours are slow and dismal. Cugel, however, never complained."

"Cugel is evidently the culprit!"

Shimilko smilingly shook his head. "Cugel's duties left him no time for illicit activity."

"What if Cugel scamped his duties?"

Shimilko responded patiently: "Remember, each girl rested secure in her private cubicle with a door between herself and Cugel."

"Well then—what if Cugel opened this door and quietly entered the cubicle?"

Shimilko considered a dubious moment, and pulled at his silky beard. "In such a case, I suppose the matter might be possible."

The Grand Thearch turned his gaze upon Cugel. "I insist that you make an exact statement upon this sorry affair."

Cugel cried out indignantly: "The investigation is a travesty! My honor has been assailed!"

Chaladet fixed Cugel with a benign, if somewhat chilly, stare. "You will be allowed redemption. Thurists, I place this person in your custody. See to it that he has every opportunity to regain his dignity and self-esteem!"

Cugel roared out a protest which the Grand Thearch ignored. From his great dais he looked thoughtfully off across the square. "Is it the third or fourth month?"

"The chronolog has only just left the month of Yaunt, to enter the time of Phampoun."

"So be it. By diligence, this licentious rogue may yet earn our love and respect."

A pair of Thurists grasped Cugel's arms and led him across the square. Cugel jerked this way and that to no avail. "Where are you taking me? What is this nonsense?"

One of the Thurists replied in a kindly voice: "We are taking you to the temple of Phampoun, and it is far from nonsense."

"I do not care for any of this," said Cugel. "Take your hands off of me; I intend to leave Lumarth at once."

"You shall be so assisted."

The group marched up worn marble steps, through an enormous arched portal, into an echoing hall, distinguished only by the high dome and an adytum or altar at the far end. Cugel was led into a side-chamber, illuminated by high circular windows and paneled with dark blue wood. An old man in a white gown entered the room and asked: "What have we here? A person suffering affliction?"

"Yes; Cugel has committed a series of abominable crimes, of which he wishes to purge himself."

"A total mis-statement!" cried Cugel. "No proof has been adduced and in any event I was inveigled against my better judgment."

The Thurists, paying no heed, departed, and Cugel was left with the old man, who hobbled to a bench and seated himself. Cugel started to speak but the old man held up his hand. "Calm yourself! You must remember that we are a benevolent people, lacking all spite or malice. We exist only to help other sentient beings! If a person commits a crime, we are racked with sorrow for the criminal, whom we believe to be the true victim, and we work without compromise that he may renew himself."

"An enlightened viewpoint!" declared Cugel. "Already I feel regeneration!"

"Excellent! Your remarks validate our philosophy; certainly you have negotiated what I will refer to as Phase One of the program."

Cugel frowned. "There are other phases? Are they really necessary?"

"Absolutely; these are Phases Two and Three. I should explain that Lumarth has not always adhered to such a policy. During the high years of the Great Magics the city fell under the sway of Yasbane the Obviator, who breached openings into five demon-realms and constructed the five temples of Lumarth. You stand now in the Temple of Phampoun."

"Odd," said Cugel, "that a folk so benevolent are such fervent demonists."

"Nothing could be farther from the truth. The Kind Folk of Lumarth expelled Yasbane, to establish the Era of Love, which must now persist until the final waning of the sun. Our love extends to all, even Yasbane's five demons, whom we hope to rescue from their malevolent evil. You will be the latest in a long line of noble individuals who have worked to this end, and such is Phase Two of the program."

Cugel stood limp in consternation. "Such work far exceeds my competence!"

"Everyone feels the same sensation," said the old man. "Nevertheless Phampoun must be instructed in kindness, consideration and decency; by making this effort, you will know a surge of happy redemption."

"And Phase Three?" croaked Cugel. "What of that?"

"When you achieve your mission, then you shall be gloriously accepted into our brotherhood!" The old man ignored Cugel's groan of dismay. "Let me see now: the month of Yaunt is just ending, and we enter the month of Phampoun, who is perhaps the most irascible of the five by reason of his sensitive eyes. He becomes enraged by so much as a single glimmer, and you must attempt your persuasions in absolute darkness. Do you have any further questions?"

"Yes indeed! Suppose Phampoun refuses to mend his ways?"

"This is 'negativistic thinking' which we Kind Folk refuse to recognize. Ignore everything you may have heard in regard to Phampoun's macabre habits! Go forth in confidence!"

Cugel cried out in anguish: "How will I return to enjoy my honors and rewards?"

"No doubt Phampoun, when contrite, will send you aloft by a means at his disposal," said the old man. "Now I bid you farewell."

"One moment! Where is my food and drink? How will I survive?"

"Again we will leave these matters to the discretion of Phampoun." The old man touched a button; the floor opened under Cugel's feet; he slid down a spiral chute at dizzying velocity. The air gradually became syrupy; Cugel struck a film of invisible constriction which burst with a sound like a cork leaving a bottle, and Cugel emerged into a chamber of medium size, illuminated by the glow of a single lamp.

Cugel stood stiff and rigid, hardly daring to breathe. On a dais across the chamber Phampoun sat sleeping in a massive chair, two black hemispheres shuttering his enormous eyes against the light. The grey torso wallowed almost the length of the dais; the massive splayed legs were planted flat to the floor. Arms, as large around as Cugel himself, terminated in fingers three feet long, each bedecked with a hundred jeweled rings. Phampoun's head was as large as a wheelbarrow, with a huge snout and an enormous loose-wattled mouth. The two eyes, each the size of a dishpan, could not be seen for the protective hemispheres.

Cugel, holding his breath in fear and also against the stench which hung in the air, looked cautiously about the room. A cord ran from the lamp, across the ceiling, to dangle beside Phampoun's fingers; almost as a reflex Cugel detached the cord from the lamp. He saw a single egress from the chamber: a low iron door directly behind Phampoun's chair. The chute by which he had entered was now invisible.

The flaps beside Phampoun's mouth twitched and lifted; a homunculus growing from the end of Phampoun's tongue peered forth. It stared at Cugel with beady black eyes. "Ha, has time gone by so swiftly?" The creature, leaning forward, consulted a mark on the wall. "It has indeed; I have overslept and Phampoun will be cross. What is your name and what are your crimes? These details are of interest to Phampoun—which is to say myself, though from whimsy I usually call myself Pulsifer, as if I were a separate entity."

Cugel spoke in a voice of brave conviction: "I am Cugel, inspector for the new regime which now holds sway in Lumarth. I descended to verify Phampoun's comfort, and since all is well, I will now return aloft. Where is the exit?"

Pulsifer asked plaintively: "You have no crimes to relate? This is harsh news. Both Phampoun and I enjoy great evils. Not long ago a certain sea-trader, whose name evades me, held us enthralled for over an hour."

"And then what occurred?"

"Best not to ask." Pulsifer busied himself polishing one of Phampoun's tusks with a small brush. He thrust his head forth and inspected the mottled visage above him. "Phampoun still sleeps soundly; he ingested a prodigous meal before retiring. Excuse me while I check the progress of Phampoun's digestion." Pulsifer ducked back behind Phampoun's wattles and revealed himself only by a vibration in the corded grey neck. Presently he returned to view. "He is quite famished, or so it would appear. I had best wake him; he will wish to converse with you before. . . ."

"Before what?"

"No matter."

"A moment," said Cugel. "I am interested in conversing with you rather than Phampoun."

"Indeed?" asked Pulsifer, and polished Phampoun's fang with great vigor. "This is pleasant to hear; I receive few compliments."

"Strange! I see much in you to commend. Necessarily your career goes hand in hand with that of Phampoun, but perhaps you have goals and ambitions of your own?"

Pulsifer propped up Phampoun's lip with his cleaning brush and relaxed upon the ledge so created. "Sometimes I feel that I would enjoy seeing something of the outer world. We have ascended several times to the surface, but always by night when heavy clouds obscure the stars, and even then Phampoun complains of the excessive glare, and he quickly returns below."

"A pity," said Cugel. "By day there is much to see. The scenery surrounding Lumarth is pleasant. The Kind Folk are about to present their Grand Pageant of Ultimate Contrasts, which is said to be most picturesque."

Pulsifer gave his head a wistful shake. "I doubt if ever I will see such events. Have you witnessed many horrid crimes?"

"Indeed I have. For instance I recall a dwarf of the Batvar Forest who rode a pelgrane—"

Pulsifer interrupted him with a gesture. "A moment. Phampoun will want to hear this." He leaned precariously from the cavernous mouth to peer up toward the shuttered eyeballs. "Is he, or more accurately, am I awake? I thought I noticed a twitch. In any event, though I have enjoyed our conversation, we must get on with our duties. Hm, the light cord is disarranged. Perhaps you will be good enough to extinguish the light."

"There is no hurry," said Cugel. "Phampoun sleeps peacefully; let him enjoy his rest. I have something to show you, a game of chance. Are you acquainted with 'Zambolio'?"

Pulsifer signified in the negative, and Cugel produced his cards. "Notice carefully! I deal you four cards and I take four cards, which we conceal from each other." Cugel explained the rules of the game. "Necessarily we play for coins of gold or some such commodity, to make the game interesting. I therefore wager five terces, which you must match."

"Yonder in two sacks is Phampoun's gold, or with equal propriety, my gold, since I am an integral adjunct to this vast hulk. Take forth gold sufficient to equal your terces."

The game proceeded. Pulsifer won the first sally, to his delight, then lost the next, which prompted him to fill the air with dismal complaints; then he won again and again until Cugel declared himself lacking further funds. "You are a clever and skillful player; it is a joy to match wits with you! Still, I feel I could beat you if I had the terces I left above in the temple."

Pulsifer, somewhat puffed and vainglorious, scoffed at Cugel's boast. "I fear that I am too clever for you! Here, take back your terces and we will play the game once again."

"No; this is not the way sportsmen behave; I am too proud to accept your money. Let me suggest a solution o the problem. In the temple above is my sack of terces and a sack of sweetmeats which you might wish to consume as we continue the game. Let us go fetch these articles, then I defy you to win as before!"

Pulsifer leaned far out to inspect Phampoun's visage. "He appears quite comfortable, though his organs are roiling with hunger."

"He sleeps as soundly as ever," declared Cugel. "Let us hurry. If he wakes our game will be spoiled."

Pulsifer hesitated. "What of Phampoun's gold? We dare not leave it unguarded!"

"We will take it with us, and it will never be outside the range of our vigilance."

"Very well; place it here on the dais."

"So, and now I am ready. How do we go aloft?"

"Merely press the leaden bulb beside the arm of the chair, but please make no untoward disturbance. Phampoun might well be exasperated should he awake in unfamiliar surroundings."

"He has never rested easier! We go aloft!" He pressed the button; the dais shivered and creaked and floated up a dark shaft which opened above them. Presently they burst through the valve of the constrictive essence which Cugel had penetrated on his way down the chute. At once a glimmer of scarlet light seeped into the shaft and a moment later the dais glided to a halt level with the altar in the Temple of Phampoun.

"Now then, my sack of terces," said Cugel. "Exactly where did I leave it? Just over yonder, I believe. Notice! Through the great arches you may overlook the main plaza of Lumarth, and those are the Kind Folk going about their ordinary affairs. What is your opinion of all this?"

"Most interesting, although I am unfamiliar with such extensive vistas. In fact, I feel almost a sense of vertigo. What is the source of the savage red glare?"

"That is the light of our ancient sun, now westering toward sunset."

"It does not appeal to me. Please be quick about your business; I have suddenly become most uneasy."

"I will make haste," said Cugel.

The sun, sinking low, sent a shaft of light through the portal, to play full upon the altar. Cugel, stepping behind the massive chair, twitched away the two shutters which guarded Phampoun's eyes, and the milky orbs glistened in the sunlight.

For an instant Phampoun lay quiet. His muscles knotted, his legs jerked, his mouth gaped wide, and he emitted an explosion of sound: a grinding scream which propelled Pulsifer forth to vibrate like a flag in the wind. Phampoun lunged from the altar to fall sprawling and rolling across the floor of the temple, all the while maintaining his cataclysmic outcries. He pulled himself erect, and pounding the tiled floor with his great feet, he sprang here and there and at last burst through the stone walls as if they were paper, while the Kind Folk in the square stood petrified.

Cugel, taking the two sacks of gold, departed the temple by a side entrance. For a moment he watched Phampoun careering around the square, screaming and flailing at the sun. Pulsifer, desperately gripping a pair of tusks, attempted to steer the maddened demoi, who, ignoring all restraint, plunged eastward through the city, trampling down trees, bursting through houses as if they failed to exist.

Cugel walked briskly down to the Isk and made his way out upon a dock. He selected a skiff of good proportions, equipped with mast, sail and oars, and prepared to clamber aboard. A punt approached the dock from upriver, poled vigorously by a large man in tattered garments. Cugel turned away, pretending no more than a casual interest in the view, until he might board the skiff without attracting attention.

The punt touched the dock; the boatman climbed up a ladder.

Cugel continued to gaze across the water, affecting indifference to all except the river vistas.

The man, panting and grunting, came to a sudden halt. Cugel felt his intent inspection, and finally turning, looked into the congested face of Huruska, the Nolde of Gundar, though his face was barely recognizable for the bites Huruska had suffered from the insects of the Lallo Marsh.

Huruska stared long and hard at Cugel. "This is a most gratifying occasion!" he said huskily. "I feared that we would never meet again. And what do you carry in those leather bags?" He wrested a bag from Cugel. "Gold from the weight. Your prophecy had been totally vindicated! First honors and a voyage by water, now wealth and revenge! Prepare to die!"

"One moment!" cried Cugel. "You have neglected properly to moor the punt! This is disorderly conduct!"

Huruska turned to look, and Cugel thrust him off the dock into the water.

Cursing and raving, Huruska struggled for the shore while Cugel fumbled with the knots in the mooring-line of the skiff. The line at last came loose; Cugel pulled the skiff close as Huruska came charging down the dock like a bull. Cugel had no choice but to abandon his gold, jump into the skiff, push off and ply the oars while Huruska stood waving his arms in rage.

Cugel pensively hoisted the sail; the wind carried him down the river and around a bend. Cugel's last view of Lumarth, in the dying light of afternoon, included the low lustrous domes of the demon temples and the dark outline of Huruska standing on the dock. From afar the screams of Phampoun were still to be heard and occasionally the thud of toppling masonry.

The Bagful of Dreams

The River Isk, departing Lumarth, wandered in wide curves across
the Plain of Red Flowers, bearing generally south. For six halcyon
days Cugel sailed his skiff down the brimming river, stopping by
night at one or another of the river-bank inns.

On the seventh day the river swung to the west, and passed by
erratic sweeps and reaches through that land of rock spires and forested hillocks known as the Chaim Purpure. The wind blew, if at all,
in unpredictable gusts, and Cugel, dropping the sail, was content to
drift with the current, guiding the craft with an occasional stroke of
the oars.

The villages of the plain were left behind; the region was uninhab-
ited. In view of the crumbled tombs along the shore, the groves of
cypress and yew, the quiet conversations to be overheard by night,
Cugel was pleased to be afloat rather than afoot, and drifted out of
the Chaim Purpure with great relief.

At the village Troon, the river emptied into the Tsombol Marsh,
and Cugel sold the skiff for ten terces. To repair his fortunes he took
employment with the town butcher, performing the more distasteful
tasks attendant upon the trade. However, the pay was adequate and
Cugel steeled himself to his undignified duties. He worked to such
good effect that he was called upon to prepare the feast served at an
important religious festival.

Through oversight, or stress of circumstance, Cugel used two sacred beasts in the preparation of his special ragout. Halfway through
the banquet the mistake was discovered and once again Cugel left
town under a cloud.

After hiding all night behind the abattoir to evade the hysterical
mobs, Cugel set off at best speed across the Tsombol Marsh.

The road went by an indirect route, swinging around bogs and stagnant ponds, veering to follow the bed of an ancient highway, in effect doubling the length of the journey. A wind from the north blew the sky clear of all obscurity, so that the landscape showed in remarkable clarity. Cugel took no pleasure in the view, especially when, looking ahead, he spied a far pelgrane cruising down the wind.

As the afternoon advanced the wind abated, leaving an unnatural stillness across the marsh. From behind tussocks water-wefkins called out to Cugel, using the sweet voices of unhappy maidens: "Cugel, oh Cugel! Why do you travel in haste? Come to my bower and comb my beautiful hair!"

And: "Cugel, oh Cugel! Where do you go? Take me with you, to share your joyous adventures!"

And: "Cugel, beloved Cugel! The day is dying; the year is at an end! Come visit me behind the tussock, and we will console each other without constraint!"

Cugel only walked the faster, anxious to discover shelter for the night.

As the sun trembled at the edge of Tsombol Marsh Cugel came upon a small inn, secluded under five dire oaks. He gratefully took lodging for the night, and the innkeeper served a fair supper of stewed herbs, spitted reed-birds, seed-cake and thick burdock beer.

As Cugel ate, the innkeeper stood by with hands on hips. "I see by your conduct that you are a gentleman of high place; still you hop across Tsombol Marsh on foot like a bumpkin. I am puzzled by the incongruity."

"It is easily explained," said Cugel. "I consider myself the single honest man in a world of rogues and blackguards, present company excepted. In these conditions it is hard to accumulate wealth."

The innkeeper pulled at his chin, and turned away. When he came to serve Cugel a dessert of currant cake, he paused long enough to say: "Your difficulties have aroused my sympathy. Tonight I will reflect on the matter."

The innkeeper was as good as his word. In the morning, after Cugel had finished his breakfast, the innkeeper took him into the stable-yard and displayed a large dun-colored beast with powerful hind legs and a tufted tail, already bridled and saddled for riding.

"This is the least I can do for you," said the innkeeper. "I will sell this beast at a nominal figure. Agreed, it lacks elegance, and in fact is a hybrid of dounge and felukhary. Still, it moves with an easy stride;

it feeds upon inexpensive wastes, and is notorious for its stubborn loyalty."

Cugel moved politely away. "I appreciate your altruism, but for such a creature any price whatever is excessive. Notice the sores at the base of its tail, the eczema along its back, and, unless I am mistaken, it lacks an eye. Also, its odor is not all it might be."

"Trifles!" declared the innkeeper. "Do you want a dependable steed to carry you across the Plain of Standing Stones, or an adjunct to your vanity? The beast becomes your property for a mere thirty terces."

Cugel jumped back in shock. "When a fine Cambalese wheriot sells for twenty? My dear fellow, your generosity outreaches my ability to pay!"

The innkeeper's face expressed only patience. "Here, in the middle of Tsombol Marsh, you will buy not even the smell of a dead wheriot."

"Let us discard euphemism," said Cugel. "Your price is an outrage."

For an instant the innkeeper's face lost its genial cast and he spoke in a grumbling voice: "Every person to whom I sell this steed takes the same advantage of my kindliness."

Cugel was puzzled by the remark. Nevertheless, sensing irresolution, he pressed his advantage. "In spite of a dozen misgivings, I offer a generous twelve terces!"

"Done!" cried the innkeeper almost before Cugel had finished speaking. "I repeat, you will discover this beast to be totally loyal, even beyond your expectations."

Cugel paid over twelve terces and gingerly mounted the creature. The landlord gave him a benign farewell. "May you enjoy a safe and comfortable journey!"

Cugel replied in like fashion. "May your enterprises prosper!"

In order to make a brave departure, Cugel tried to rein the beast up and around in a caracole, but it merely squatted low to the ground, then padded out upon the road.

Cugel rode a mile in comfort, and another, and taking all with all, was favorably impressed with his acquisition. "No question but what the beast walks on soft feet; now let us discover if it will canter at speed."

He shook out the reins; the beast set off down the road, its gait a unique prancing strut, with tail arched and head held high.

Cugel kicked his heels into the creature's heaving flanks. "Faster then! Let us test your mettle!"

The beast sprang forward with great energy, and the breeze blew Cugel's cloak flapping behind his shoulders.

A massive dire oak stood beside a bend in the road: an object which the beast seemed to identify as a landmark. It increased its pace, only to stop short and elevate its hind-quarters, thus projecting Cugel into the ditch. When he managed to stagger back up on the road, he discovered the beast cavorting across the marsh, in the general direction of the inn.

"A loyal creature indeed!" grumbled Cugel. "It is unswervingly faithful to the comfort of its barn." He found his green velvet cap, clapped it back upon his head and once more trudged south along the road.

During the late afternoon Cugel came to a village of a dozen mud huts populated by a squat long-armed folk, distinguished by great shocks of whitewashed hair.

Cugel gauged the height of the sun, then examined the terrain ahead, which extended in a dreary succession of tussock and pond to the edge of vision. Putting aside all qualms he approached the largest and most pretentious of the huts.

The master of the house sat on a bench to the side, whitewashing the hair of one of his children into radiating tufts like the petals of a white chrysanthemum, while other urchins played nearby in the mud.

"Good afternoon," said Cugel. "Are you able to provide me food and lodging for the night? I naturally intend adequate payment."

"I will feel privileged to do so," replied the householder. "This is the most commodious hut of Samsetiska, and I am known for my fund of anecdotes. Do you care to inspect the premises?"

"I would be pleased to rest an hour in my chamber before indulging myself in a hot bath."

His host blew out his cheeks, and wiping the whitewash from his hands beckoned Cugel into the hut. He pointed to a heap of reeds at the side of the room. "There is your bed; recline for as long as you like. As for a bath, the ponds of the swamp are infested with threlkoids and wire-worms, and cannot be recommended."

"In that case I must do without," said Cugel. "However, I have not eaten since breakfast, and I am willing to take my evening meal as soon as possible."

"My spouse has gone trapping in the swamp," said his host. "It is premature to discuss supper until we learn what she has gleaned from her toil."

In due course the woman returned carrying a sack and a wicker basket. She built up a fire and prepared the evening meal, while Erwig the householder brought forth a two-string guitar and entertained Cugel with ballads of the region.

At last the woman called Cugel and Erwig into the hut, where she served bowls of gruel, dishes of fried moss and ganions, with slices of coarse black bread.

After the meal Erwig thrust his spouse and children out into the night, explaining: "What we have to say is unsuitable for unsophisticated ears. Cugel is an important traveler and does not wish to measure his every word."

Bringing out an earthenware jug, Erwig poured two tots of arrak, one of which he placed before Cugel, then disposed himself for conversation. "Whence came you and where are you bound?"

Cugel tasted the arrak, which scorched the entire interior of his glottal cavity. "I am native to Almery, to which I now return."

Erwig scratched his head in perplexity. "I cannot divine why you go so far afield, only to retrace your steps."

"Certain enemies worked mischief upon me," said Cugel. "Upon my return, I intend an appropriate revenge."

"Such acts soothe the spirit like no others," agreed Erwig. "An immediate obstacle is the Plain of Standing Stones, by reason of asms which haunt the area. I might add that pelgrane are also common."

Cugel gave his sword a nervous twitch. "What is the distance to the Plain of Standing Stones?"

"Four miles south the ground rises and the Plain begins. The track proceeds from sarsen to sarsen for a distance of fifteen miles. A stout-hearted traveler will cross the plain in four to five hours, assuming that he is not delayed or devoured. The town Cuirnif lies another two hours beyond."

"An inch of foreknowledge is worth ten miles of after-thought—"

"Well spoken!" cried Erwig, swallowing a gulp of arrak. "My own opinion, to an exactitude! Cugel, you are astute!"

"—and in this regard, may I inquire your opinion of Cuirnif?"

"The folk are peculiar in many ways," said Erwig. "They preen themselves upon the gentility of their habits, yet they refuse to white-wash their hair, and they are slack in their religious observances. For instance, they make obeisance to Divine Wiulio with the right hand, not on the buttock, but on the abdomen, which we here consider a slipshod practice. What are your own views?"

"The rite should be conducted as you describe," said Cugel. "No other method carries weight."

Erwig refilled Cugel's glass. "I consider this an important endorsement of our views!"

The door opened and Erwig's spouse looked into the hut. "The night is dark. A bitter wind blows from the north, and a black beast prowls at the edge of the marsh."

"Stand among the shadows; divine Wiulio protects his own. It is unthinkable that you and your brats should annoy our guest."

The woman grudgingly closed the door and returned into the night. Erwig pulled himself forward on his stool and swallowed a quantity of arrak. "The folk of Cuirnif, as I say, are strange enough, but their ruler, Duke Orbal, surpasses them in every category. He devotes himself to the study of marvels and prodigies, and every jack-leg magician with two spells in his head is feted and celebrated and treated to the best of the city."

"Most odd!" declared Cugel.

Again the door opened and the woman looked into the hut. Erwig put down his glass and frowned over his shoulder. "What is it this time?"

"The beast is now moving among the huts. For all we know it may also worship Wiulio."

Erwig attempted argument, but the woman's face became obdurate. "Your guest might as well forego his niceties now as later, since we all, in any event, must sleep on the same heap of reeds." She opened wide the door and commanded her urchins into the hut. Erwig, assured that no further conversation was possible, threw himself down upon the reeds, and Cugel followed soon after.

In the morning Cugel breakfasted on ash-cake and herb tea, and prepared to take his departure. Erwig accompanied him to the road. "You have made a favorable impression upon me, and I will assist you across the Plain of Standing Stones. At the first opportunity take up a pebble the size of your fist and make the trigrammatic sign upon it. If you are attacked, hold high the pebble and cry out: 'Stand aside! I carry a sacred object!' At the first sarsen, deposit the stone and select another from the pile, again make the sign and carry it to the second sarsen, and so across the plain."

"So much is clear," said Cugel. "But perhaps you should show me the most powerful version of the sign, and thus refresh my memory."

Erwig scratched a mark in the dirt. "Simple, precise, correct! The folk of Cuirnif omit this loop and scrawl in every which direction."

"Slackness, once again!" said Cugel.

"So then, Cugel: farewell! The next time you pass be certain to halt at my hurt! My crock of arrak has a loose stopper!"

"I would not forego the pleasure for a thousand terces. And now, as to my indebtedness—"

Erwig held up his hand. "I accept no terces from my guests!" He jerked and his eyes bulged as his spouse came up and prodded him in the ribs. "Ah well," said Erwig. "Give the woman a terce or two; it will cheer her as she performs her tasks."

Cugel paid over five terces, to the woman's enormous satisfaction, and so departed the village.

After four miles the road angled up to a gray plain studded at intervals with twelve-foot pillars of gray stone. Cugel found a large pebble, and placing his right hand on his buttock made a profound salute to the object. He scratched upon it a sign somewhat similar to that drawn for him by Erwig and intoned: "I commend this pebble to the attention of Wiulio! I request that it protect me across this dismal plain!"

He scrutinized the landscape, but aside from the sarsens and the long black shadows laid by the red morning sun, he discovered nothing worthy of attention, and thankfully set off along the track.

He had traveled no more than a hundred yards when he felt a presence and whirling about discovered an asm of eight fangs almost on his heels. Cugel held high the pebble and cried out: "Away with you! I carry a sacred object and I do not care to be molested!"

The asm spoke in a soft blurred voice: "Wrong! You carry an ordinary pebble. I watched and you scamped the rite. Flee if you wish! I need the exercise."

The asm advanced. Cugel threw the stone with all his force. It struck the black forehead between the bristling antennae, and the asm fell flat; before it could rise Cugel had severed its head.

He started to proceed, then turned back and took up the stone. "Who knows who guided the throw so accurately? Wiulio deserves the benefit of the doubt."

At the first Sarsen he exchanged stones as Erwig had recommended, and this time he made the trigrammatic sign with care and precision.

Without interference he crossed to the next sarsen and so continued across the plain.

The sun made its way to the zenith, rested a period, then descended into the west. Cugel marched unmolested from sarsen to sarsen. On several occasions he noted pelgrane sliding across the sky, and each time flung himself flat to avoid attention.

The Plain of Standing Stones ended at the brink of a scarp overlooking a wide valley. With safety close at hand Cugel relaxed his vigilance, only to be startled by a scream of triumph from the sky. He darted a horrified glance over his shoulder, then plunged over the edge of the scarp into a ravine, where he dodged among rocks and pressed himself into the shadows. Down swooped the pelgrane, past and beyond Cugel's hiding place. Warbling in joy, it alighted at the base of the scarp, to evoke instant outcries and curses from a human throat.

Keeping to concealment Cugel descended the slope, to discover that the pelgrane now pursued a portly black-haired man in a suit of black and white diaper. This person at last took nimble refuge behind a thick-boled olophar tree, and the pelgrane chased him first one way, then another, clashing its fangs and snatching with its clawed hands.

For all his rotundity, the man showed remarkable deftness of foot and the pelgrane began to scream in frustration. It halted to glare through the crotch of the tree and snap out with its long maw.

On a whimsical impulse Cugel stole out upon a shelf of rock; then, selecting an appropriate moment, he jumped to land with both feet on the creature's head, forcing the neck down into the crotch of the olophar tree. He called out to the startled man: "Quick! Fetch a stout cord! We will bind this winged horror in place!"

The man in the black and white diaper cried out: "Why show mercy? It must be killed and instantly! Move your foot, so that I may hack away its head."

"Not so fast," said Cugel. "For all its faults, it is a valuable specimen by which I hope to profit."

"Profit?" The idea had not occurred to the portly gentlemen. "I must assert my prior claim! I was just about to stun the beast when you interfered."

Cugel said: "In that case I will take my weight off the creature's neck and go my way."

The man in the black-and-white suit made an irritable gesture. "Certain persons will go to any extreme merely to score a rhetorical point. Hold fast then! I have a suitable cord over yonder."

The two men dropped a branch over the pelgrane's head and bound it securely in place. The portly gentleman, who had introduced himself as Iolo the Dream-taker, asked: "Exactly what value do you place upon this horrid creature, and why?"

Cugel said: "It has come to my attention that Orbal, Duke of Ombalique, is an amateur of oddities. Surely he would pay well for such a monster, perhaps as much as a hundred terces."

"Your theories are sound," Iolo admitted. "Are you sure that the bonds are secure?"

As Cugel tested the ropes he noticed an ornament consisting of a blue glass egg on a golden chain attached to the creature's crest. As he removed the object, Iolo's hand darted out, but Cugel shouldered him aside. He disengaged the amulet, but Iolo caught hold of the chain and the two glared eye to eye.

"Release your grip upon my property." said Cugel in an icy voice.

Iolo protested vigorously. "The object is mine since I saw it first."

"Nonsense! I took it from the crest and you tried to snatch it from my hand."

Iolo stamped his foot. "I will not be domineered!" He sought to wrest the blue egg from Cugel's grasp. Cugel lost his grip and the object was thrown against the hillside where it broke in a bright blue explosion to create a hole into the hillside. Instantly a golden-gray tentacle thrust forth and seized Cugel's leg.

Iolo sprang back and from a safe distance watched Cugel's efforts to avoid being drawn into the hole. Cugel saved himself at the last moment by clinging to a stump. He called out: "Iolo, make haste! Fetch a cord and tie the tentacle to this stump; otherwise it will drag me into the hill!"

Iolo folded his arms and spoke in a measured voice: "Avarice has brought this plight upon you. It may be a divine judgment and I am reluctant to interfere."

"What? When you fought tooth and nail to wrench the object from my hand?"

Iolo frowned and pursed his lips. "In any case I own a single rope: that which ties my pelgrane."

"Kill the pelgrane!" panted Cugel. "Put the cord to its most urgent use!"

"You yourself valued this pelgrane at a hundred terces. The worth of the rope is ten terces."

"Very well," said Cugel through gritted teeth. "Ten terces for the rope, but I cannot pay a hundred terces for a dead pelgrane, since I carry only forty-five."

"So be it. Pay over the forty-five terces. What surety can you offer for the remainder?"

Cugel managed to toss over his purse of terces. He displayed the opal ear-bangle which Iolo promptly demanded, but which Cugel refused to relinquish until the tentacle had been tied to the stump.

With poor grace Iolo hacked the head off the pelgrane, then brought over the rope and secured the tentacle to the stump, thus easing the strain upon Cugel's leg.

"The ear-bangle, if you please!" said Iolo, and he poised his knife significantly near the rope.

Cugel tossed over the jewel. "There you have it: all my wealth. Now, please free me from this tentacle."

"I am a cautious man," said Iolo. "I must consider the matter from several perspectives." He set about making camp for the night.

Cugel called out a plaintive appeal: "Do you remember how I rescued you from the pelgrane?"

"Indeed I do! An important philosophical question has thereby been raised. You disturbed a stasis and now a tentacle grips your leg, which is, in a sense, the new stasis. I will reflect carefully upon the matter."

Cugel argued to no avail. Iolo built up a campfire over which he cooked a stew of herbs and grasses, which he ate with half a cold fowl and draughts of wine from a leather bottle.

Leaning back against a tree he gave his attention to Cugel. "No doubt you are on your way to Duke Orbal's Grand Exposition of Marvels?"

"I am a traveler, no more," said Cugel. "What is this 'Grand Exposition'?"

Iolo gave Cugel a pitying glance for his stupidity. "Each year Duke Orbal presides over a competition of wonder-workers. This year the prize is one thousand terces, which I intend to win with my 'Bagful of Dreams'."

"Your 'Bagful of Dreams' I assume to be a jocularity, or something on the order of a romantic metaphor?"

"Nothing of the sort!" declared Iolo in scorn.

"A kaleidoscopic projection? A program of impersonations? A hallucinatory gas?"

"None of these. I carry with me a number of pure unadulterated dreams, coalesced and crystallized."

From his satchel Iolo brought a sack of soft brown leather, from which he took an object resembling a pale blue snowflake an inch in diameter. He held it up into the firelight where Cugel could admire its fleeting lusters. "I will ply Duke Orbal with my dreams, and how can I fail to win over all other contestants?"

"Your chances would seem to be good. How do you gather these dreams?"

"The process is secret; still I can describe the general procedure. I live beside Lake Lelt in the Land of Dai-Passant. On calm nights the surface of the water thickens to a film which reflects the stars as small globules of shine. By using a suitable cantrap, I am able to lift up impalpable threads composed of pure starlight and water-skein. I weave this thread into nets and then I go forth in search of dreams. I hide under valances and in the leaves of outdoor bowers; I crouch on roofs; I wander through sleeping houses. Always I am ready to net the dreams as they drift past. Each morning I carry these wonderful wisps to my laboratory and there I sort them out and work my processes. In due course I achieve a crystal of a hundred dreams, and with these confections I hope to enthrall Duke Orbal."

"I would offer congratulations were it not for this tentacle gripping my leg," said Cugel.

"That is a generous emotion," said Iolo. He fed several logs into the fire, chanted a spell of protection against creatures of the night, and composed himself for sleep.

An hour passed. Cugel tried by various means to ease the grip of the tentacle, without success, nor could he draw his sword or bring "Spatterlight" from his pouch.

At last he sat back and considered new approaches to the solution of his problem.

By dint of stretching and straining he obtained a twig, with which he dragged close a long dead branch, which allowed him to reach another of equal length. Tying the two together with a string from his pouch, he contrived a pole exactly long enough to reach Iolo's recumbent form.

Working with care Cugel drew Iolo's satchel across the ground, finally to within reach of his fingers. First he brought out Iolo's wallet, to find two hundred terces, which he transferred to his own purse; next the opal ear-bangle, which he dropped into the pocket of his shirt; then the bagful of dreams.

The satchel contained nothing more of value, save that portion of cold fowl which Iolo had reserved for his breakfast and the leather bottle of wine, both of which Cugel put aside for his own use. He returned the satchel to where he had found it, then separated the branches and tossed them aside. Lacking a better hiding place for the bagful of dreams, Cugel tied the string to the bag and lowered it into the mysterious hole. He ate the fowl and drank the wine, then made himself as comfortable as possible.

The night wore on. Cugel heard the plaintive call of a night-jar and also the moan of a six-legged shamb, at some distance.

In due course the sky glowed purple and the sun appeared. Iolo roused himself, yawned, ran his fingers through his tousled hair, blew up the fire and gave Cugel a civil greeting. "And how passed the night?"

"As well as could be expected. It is useless, after all, to complain against inexorable reality."

"Exactly so. I have given considerable thought to your case, and I have arrived at a decision which will please you. This is my plan. I shall proceed into Cuirnif and there drive a hard bargain for the ear-bangle. After satisfying your account, I will return and pay over to you whatever sums may be in excess."

Cugel suggested an alternative scheme. "Let us go into Cuirnif together; then you will be spared the inconvenience of a return trip."

Iolo shook his head. "My plan must prevail." He went to the satchel for his breakfast and so discovered the loss of his property. He uttered a plangent cry and stared at Cugel. "My terces, my dreams! They are gone, all gone! How do you account for this?"

"Very simply. At approximately four minutes after midnight a robber came from the forest and made off with the contents of your satchel."

Iolo tore at his beard with the fingers of both hands. "My precious dreams! Why did you not cry out an alarm?"

Cugel scratched his head. "In all candor I did not dare disturb the stasis."

Iolo jumped to his feet and looked through the forest in all directions. He turned back to Cugel. "What sort of man was this robber?"

"In certain respects he seemed a kindly man; after taking possession of your belongings, he presented me with half a cold fowl and a bottle of wine, which I consumed with gratitude."

"You consumed my breakfast!"

Cugel shrugged. "I could not be sure of this, and in fact I did not inquire. We held a brief conversation and I learned that like ourselver he is bound for Cuirnif and the Exposition of Marvels."

"Ah, ah ha! Would you recognize this person were you to see him again?"

"Without a doubt."

Iolo became instantly energetic. "Let us see as to this tentacle. Perhaps we can pry it loose." He seized the tip of the golden-gray member and bracing himself worked to lift it from Cugel's leg. For several minutes he toiled, kicking and prying, paying no heed to Cugel's cries of pain. Finally the tentacle relaxed and Cugel crawled to safety.

With great caution Iolo approached the hole and peered down into the depths. "I see only a glimmer of far lights. The hole is mysterious! . . . . What is this bit of string which leads into the hole?"

"I tied a rock to the string and tried to plumb the bottom of the hole," Cugel explained. "It amounts to nothing."

Iolo tugged at the string, which first yielded, then resisted, then broke, and Iolo was left looking at the frayed end. "Odd! The string is corroded, as if through contact with some acrid substance."

"Most peculiar!" said Cugel.

Iolo threw the string back into the hole. "Come, we can waste no more time! Let us hasten into Cuirnif and seek out the scoundrel who stole my valuables."

The road left the forest and passed through a district of fields and orchards. Peasants looked up in wonder as the two passed by: the portly Iolo dressed in black and white diaper and the lank Cugel with a black cloak hanging from his spare shoulders and a fine dark green cap gracing his saturnine visage.

Along the way Iolo put ever more searching questions in regard to the robber. Cugel had lost interest in the subject and gave back ambiguous, even contradictory, answers, and Iolo's questions became ever more searching.

Upon entering Cuirnif, Cugel noticed an inn which seemed to offer comfortable accommodation. He told Iolo: "Here our paths diverge, since I plan to stop at the inn yonder."

"The Five Owls? It is the dearest inn of Cuirnif! How will you pay your account?"

Cugel made a confident gesture. "Is not a thousand terces the grand prize at the Exposition?"

"Certainly, but what marvel do you plan to display? I warn you, the Duke has no patience with charlatans."

"I am not a man who tells all he knows," said Cugel. "I will disclose none of my plans at this moment."

"But what of the robber?" cried Iolo. "Were we not to search Cuirnif high and low?"

"The Five Owls is as good a vantage as any, since the robber will surely visit the common room to boast of his exploits and squander your terces on drink. Meanwhile, I wish you easy roofs and convenient dreams." Cugel bowed politely and took his leave of Iolo.

At the Five Owls Cugel selected a suitable chamber, where he refreshed himself and ordered his attire. Then, repairing to the common room, he made a leisurely meal upon the best the house could provide.

The innkeeper stopped by to make sure that all was in order and Cugel complimented him upon his table. "In fact, all taken with all, Cuirnif must be considered a place favored by the elements. The prospect is pleasant, the air is bracing, and Duke Orbal would seem to be an indulgent ruler."

The innkeeper gave a somewhat noncommittal assent. "As you indicate, Duke Orbal is never exasperated, truculent, suspicious, nor harsh unless in his wisdom he feels so inclined, whereupon all mildness is put aside in the interests of justice. Glance up to the crest of the hill; what do you see?"

"Four tubes, or stand-pipes, approximately thirty yards tall and one yard in diameter."

"Your eye is accurate. Into these tubes are dropped insubordinate members of society, without regard for who stands below or who may be coming after. Hence, while you may converse with Duke Orbal or even venture a modest pleasantry, never ignore his commands. Criminals, of course, are given short shrift."

Cugel, from habit, looked uneasily over his shoulder. "Such strictures will hardly apply to me, a stranger in town."

The innkeeper gave a skeptical grunt. "I assume that you came to witness the Exposition of Marvels?"

"Quite so! I may even try for the grand prize. In this regard, can you recommend a dependable hostler?"

"Certainly." The innkeeper provided explicit directions.

"I also wish to hire a gang of strong and willing workers," said Cugel. "Where may these be recruited?"

The innkeeper pointed across the square to a dingy tavern. "In the yard of the 'Howling Dog' all the riffraff in town take counsel together. Here you will find workers sufficient to your purposes."

"While I visit the hostler, be good enough to send a boy across to hire twelve of these sturdy fellows."

"As you wish."

At the hostler's Cugel rented a large six-wheeled wagon and a team of strong farlocks. When he returned with the wagon to the Five Owls, he found waiting a work-force of twelve individuals of miscellaneous sort, including a man not only senile but also lacking a leg. Another, in the throes of intoxication, fought away imaginary insects. Cugel discharged these two on the spot. The group also included Iolo the Dream-taker, who scrutinized Cugel with the liveliest suspicion.

Cugel asked: "My dear fellow, what do you do in such sordid company?"

"I take employment so that I may eat," said Iolo. "May I ask how you came by the funds to pay for so much skilled labor? Also, I notice that from your ear hangs that gem which only last night was my property!"

"It is the second of a pair," said Cugel. "As you know, the robber took the first along with your other valuables."

Iolo curled his lips. "I am more than ever anxious to meet this quixotic robber who takes my gem but leaves you in possession of yours."

"He was indeed a remarkable person. I believe that I glimpsed him not an hour ago, riding hard out of the town."

Iolo again curled his lip. "What do you propose to do with this wagon?"

"If you care to earn a wage, you will soon find out for yourself."

Cugel drove the wagon and the gang of workers out of Cuirnif along the road to the mysterious hole, where he found all as before. He ordered trenches dug into the hillside; crating was installed, after which that block of soil surrounding and including the hole, the stump and the tentacle, was dragged up on the bed of the wagon.

During the middle stages of the project Iolo's manner changed. He began calling orders to the workmen and addressed Cugel with cordiality. "A noble idea, Cugel! We shall profit greatly!"

Cugel raised his eyebrows. "I hope indeed to win the grand prize. Your wage, however, will be relatively modest, even scant, unless you work more briskly."

"What!" stormed Iolo. "Surely you agree that this hole is half my property!"

"I agree to nothing of the sort. Say no more of the matter, or you will be discharged on the spot."

Grumbling and fuming Iolo returned to work. In due course Cugel conveyed the block of soil, with the hole, stump and tentacle, back to Cuirnif the way he purchased an old tarpaulin with which he concealed the hole, the better to magnify the eventual effect of his display.

At the site of the Grand Exposition Cugel slid his exhibit off the wagon and into the shelter of a pavilion, after which he paid off his men, to the dissatisfaction of those who had cultivated extravagant hopes.

Cugel refused to listen to complaints. "The pay is sufficient! If it were ten times as much, every last terce would still end up in the till at the 'Howling Dog'."

"One moment!" cried Iolo. "You and I must arrive at an understanding!"

Cugel merely jumped up on the wagon and drove it back to the hostelry. Some of the men pursued him a few steps; others threw stones, without effect.

On the following day trumpets and gongs announced the formal opening of the exposition. Duke Orbal arrived at the plaza wearing a splendid robe of magenta plush trimmed with white feathers, and a hat of pale blue velvet three feet in diameter, with silver tassels around the brim and a cockade of silver puff.

Mounting a rostrum, Duke Orbal addressed the crowd. "As all know, I am considered an eccentric, what with my enthusiasm for marvels and prodigies, but, after all, when the preoccupation is analyzed, is it all so absurd? Think back across the aeons to the times of the Vapurials, the Green and Purple College, the mighty magicians among whose number we include Amberlin, the second Chidule of Porphyrhyncos, Morreion, Calanctus the Calm, and of course the Great Phandaal. These were the days of power, and they are not likely to return except in nostalgic recollection. Hence this, my

Grand Exposition of Marvels, and withal, a pale recollection of the
way things were.

"Still, all taken with all, I see by my schedule that we have a stimulating program, and no doubt I will find difficulty in awarding the
grand prize."

Duke Orbal glanced at a paper. "We will inspect Zaraflam's 'Nimble Squadrons', Bazzard's 'Unlikely Musicians', Xallops and his
'Compendium of Universal Knowledge'. Iolo will offer his 'Bagful of
Dreams', and finally, Cugel will present for our amazement that to
which he gives the tantalizing title: 'Nowhere'. A most provocative
program! And now without further ado we will proceed to evaluate
Zaraflam's 'Nimble Squardrons'."

The crowd surged around the first pavilion and Zaraflam brought
forth his 'Nimble Squadrons': a parade of cockroaches smartly turned
out in red, white, and black uniforms. The sergeants brandished cutlasses; the foot soldiers carried muskets; the squadrons marched and
countermarched in intricate evolutions.

"Halt!" bawled Zaraflam.

The cockroaches stopped short.

"Present arms!"

The cockroaches obeyed.

"Fire a salute in honor of Duke Orbal!"

The sergeants raised their cutlasses; the footmen elevated their
muskets. Down came the cutlasses; the muskets exploded, emitting
little puffs of white smoke.

"Excellent!" declared Duke Orbal. "Zaraflam, I commend your
painstaking accuracy!"

"A thousand thanks, your Grace! Have I won the grand prize?"

"It is still too early to predict. Now, to Bazzard and his 'Unlikely
Musicians'!"

The spectators moved on to the second pavilion where Bazzard
presently appeared, his face woebegone. "Your Gráce and noble citi-
-ens of Cuirnif! My 'Unlikely Musicians' were fish from the Cantic
ʋea and I felt sure of the grand prize when I brought them to Cuirnif.
However, during the night a leak drained the tank dry. The fish are
dead and their music is lost forever! I still wish to remain in conten-
tion for the prize; hence I will simulate the songs of my former
troupe. Please adjudicate the music on this basis."

Duke Orbal made an austere sign. "Impossible. Bazzard's exhibit is hereby declared invalid. We now move on to Xallops and his remarkable 'Compendium'."

Xallops stepped forward from his pavilion. "Your Grace, ladies and gentlemen of Cuirnif! My entry at this exposition is truly remarkable; however, unlike Zaraflam and Bazzard, I can take no personal credit for its existence. By trade I am a ransacker of ancient tombs, where the risks are great and rewards few. By great good luck I chanced upon that crypt where several aeons ago the sorcerer Zinqzin was laid to rest. From this dungeon I rescued the volume which I now display to your astounded eyes."

Xallops whisked away cloth to reveal a great book bound in black leather. "On command this volume must reveal information of any and every sort; it knows each trivial detail, from the time the stars first caught fire to the present date. Ask; you shall be answered!"

"Remarkable!" declared Duke Orbal. "Present before us the Lost Ode of Psyrme!"

"Certainly," said the book in a rasping voice. It threw back its covers to reveal a page covered with crabbed and interlocked characters.

Duke Orbal put a perplexed question: "This is beyond my comprehension; you may furnish a translation."

"The request is denied," said the book. "Such poetry is too sweet for ordinary ears."

Duke Orbal glanced at Xallops, who spoke quickly to the book: "Show us scenes from aeons past."

"As you like. Reverting to the Nineteenth Aeon of the Fifty-second Cycle, I display a view across Linxfade Valley, toward Kolghut's Tower of Frozen Blood."

"The detail is both notable and exact!" declared Duke Orbal. "I am curious to gaze upon the semblance of Kolghut himself."

"Nothing could be easier. Here is the terrace of the Temple at Tanutra. Kolghut stands beside the flowering wail-bush. In the chair sits the Empress Noxon, now in her hundred and fortieth year. She has tasted no water in her entire lifetime, and eats only bitter blossom, with occasionally a morsel of boiled ell."

"Bah!" said Duke Orbal. "A most hideous old creature! Who are those gentlemen ranked behind her?"

"They constitute her retinue of lovers. Every month one of their number is executed and a new stalwart is recruited to take his place. Competition is keen to win the affectionate regard of the Empress."

"Bah!" muttered Duke Orbal. "Show us rather a beautiful court lady of the Yellow Age."

The book spoke a petulant syllable in an unknown language. The page turned to reveal a travertine promenade beside a slow river.

"This view reveals to good advantage the topiary of the time. Notice here, and here!" With a luminous arrow the book indicated a row of massive trees clipped into globular shapes. "Those are irix, the sap of which may be used as an effective vermifuge. The species is now extinct. Along the concourse you will observe a multitude of persons. Those with black stockings and long white beards are Alulian slaves, whose ancestors arrived from far Canopus. They are also extinct. In the middle distance stands a beautiful woman named Jiao Jaro. She is indicated by a red dot over her head, although her face is turned toward the river."

"This is hardly satisfactory," grumbled Duke Orbal. "Xallops, can you not control the perversity of your exhibit?"

"I fear not, your Grace."

Duke Orbal gave a sniff of displeasure. "A final question! Who among the folk now residing in Cuirnif presents the greatest threat to the welfare of my realm?"

"I am a repository of information, not an oracle," stated the book. "However, I will remark that among those present stands a fox-faced vagabond with a crafty expression, whose habits would bring a blush to the cheeks of the Empress Noxon herself. His name—"

Cugel leapt forward and pointed across the plaza. "The robber! There he goes now! Summon the constables! Sound the gong!"

While everyone turned to look, Cugel slammed shut the book and dug his knuckles into the cover. The book grunted in annoyance.

Duke Orbal turned back with a frown of perplexity. "I saw no robber."

"In that case, I was surely mistaken. But yonder waits Iolo with his famous 'Bagful of Dreams'!"

The Duke moved on to Iolo's pavilion, followed by the enthralled onlookers. Duke Orbal said: "Iolo the Dream-taker, your fame has preceded you all the distance from Dai-Passant! I hereby tender you an official welcome!"

Iolo answered in an anguished voice: "Your Grace, I have sorry news to relate. For the whole of one year I prepared for this day, hoping to win the grand prize. The blast of midnight winds, the outrage of householders, the terrifying attentions of ghosts, shrees,

roof-runners and fermins: all of these have caused me discomfort! I
have roamed the dark hours in pursuit of my dreams! I have lurked
beside dormers, crawled through attics, hovered over couches; I have
suffered scratches and contusions; but never have I counted the cost if
through my enterprise I were able to capture some particularly choice
specimen."

"Each dream trapped in my net I carefully examined; for every
dream cherished and saved I released a dozen, and finally from my
store of superlatives I fashioned my wonderful crystals, and these I
brought down the long road from Dai-Passant. Then, only last night,
under the most mysterious circumstances, my precious goods were
stolen by a robber only Cugel claims to have seen."

"I now point out that the dreams, whether near or far, represent
marvels of truly superlative quality, and I feel that a careful description of the items—"

Duke Orbal held his hand. "I must reiterate the judgment rendered upon Bazzard. A stringent rule stipulates that neither imaginary nor purported marvels qualify for the competition. Perhaps we
will have the opportunity to adjudicate your dreams on another occasion. Now we must pass on to Cugel's pavilion and investigate his
provocative 'Nowhere'."

Cugel stepped up on the dais before his exhibit. "Your Grace, I
present for your inspection a legitimate marvel: not a straggle of
insects, not a pedantic almanac, but an authentic miracle." Cugel
whisked away the cloth. "Behold!"

The Duke made a puzzled sound. "A pile of dirt? A stump? What
is that odd-looking member emerging from the hole?"

"Your Grace, I have here an opening into an unknown space, with
the arm of one of its denizens. Inspect this tentacle! It pulses with the
life of another cosmos! Notice the golden luster of the dorsal surface,
the green and lavender of these encrustations. On the underside you
will discover three colors of a sort never before seen!"

With a nonplussed expression Duke Orbal pulled at his chin. "This
is all very well, but where is the rest of the creature? You present not
a marvel, but the fraction of a marvel! I can make no judgment on the
basis of a tail, or a hindquarters, or a proboscis, whatever the member
may be. Additionally, you claim that the hole enters a far cosmos; still
I see only a hole, resembling nothing so much as the den of a wysen-
imp."

Iolo thrust himself forward. "May I venture an opinion? As I reflect upon events, I have become convinced that Cugel himself stole my Dreams!" "Your remarks interest no one," said Cugel. "Kindly hold your tongue while I continue my demonstration."

Iolo was not to be subdued so easily. He turned to Duke Orbal and cried in a poignant voice: "Hear me out, if you will! I am convinced that the 'robber' is no more than a figment of Cugel's imagination! He took my dreams and hid them, and where else but in the hole itself? For evidence I cite that length of string which leads into the hole."

Duke Orbal inspected Cugel with a frown. "Are these charges true? Answer exactly, since all can be verified."

Cugel chose his words with care. "I can only affirm what I myself know. Conceivably the robber hid Iolo's dreams in the hole while I was otherwise occupied. For what purpose? Who can say?"

Duke Orbal asked in a gentle voice: "Has anyone thought to search the hole for this elusive 'bag of dreams'?"

Cugel gave an indifferent shrug. "Iolo may enter now and search to his heart's content."

"You claim this hole!" retorted Iolo. "It therefore becomes your duty to protect the public!"

For several minutes an animated argument took place, until Duke Orbal intervened. "Both parties have raised persuasive points; I feel, however, that I must rule against Cugel. I therefore decree that he search his premises for the missing dreams and recover them if possible."

Cugel disputed the decision with such vigor that Duke Orbal turned to glance along the skyline, whereupon Cugel moderated his position. "The judgment of your Grace of course must prevail, and if I must, I will cast about for Iolo's lost dreams, although his theories are clearly absurd."

"Please do so, at once."

Cugel obtained a long pole, to which he attached a grapple. Gingerly thrusting his contrivance into the hole, he raked back and forth, but succeeded only in stimulating the tentacle, which thrashed from side to side.

Iolo suddenly cried out in excitement. "I notice a remarkable fact! The block of earth is at most six feet in breadth, yet Cugel plunged into the hole a pole twelve feet in length! What trickery does he practice now?"

Cugel replied in even tones: "I promised Duke Orbal a marvel and a wonderment, and I believe that I have done so."

Duke Orbal nodded gravely. "Well said, Cugel! Your exhibit is provocative! Still, you offer us only a tantalizing glimpse: a bottomless hole, a length of tentacle, a strange color, a far-off light—to the effect that your exhibit seems somewhat makeshift and impromptu. Contrast, if you will, the precision of Zaraflam's cockroaches!" He held up his hand as Cugel started to protest. "You display a hole: admitted, and a fine hole it is. But how does this hole differ from any other? Can I in justice award the prize on such a basis?"

"The matter may be resolved in a manner to satisfy us all," said Cugel. "Let Iolo enter the hole, to assure himself that his dreams are indeed elsewhere. Then, on his return, he will bear witness to the truly marvelous nature of my exhibit."

Iolo made an instant protest. "Cugel claims the exhibit; let him make the exploration!"

Duke Orbal raised his hand for silence. "I pronounce a decree to the effect that Cugel must immediately enter his exhibit in search of Iolo's properties, and likewise make a careful study of the environment, for the benefit of us all."

"Your Grace!" protested Cugel. "This is no simple matter! The tentacle almost fills the hole!"

"I see sufficient room for an agile man to slide past."

"Your Grace, to be candid, I do not care to enter the hole, by reason of extreme fear."

Duke Orbal again glanced up at the tubes which stood in a row along the skyline. He spoke over his shoulder to a burly man in a maroon and black uniform. "Which of the tubes is most suitable for use at this time?"

"The second tube from the right, your Grace, is only one-quarter occupied."

Cugel declared in a trembling voice: "I fear, but I have conquered my fear! I will seek Iolo's lost dreams!"

"Excellent," said Duke Orbal with a tight-lipped grin. "Please do not delay; my patience wears thin."

Cugel tentatively thrust a leg into the hole, but the motion of the tentacle caused him to snatch it out again. Duke Orbal muttered a few words to his constable, who brought up a winch. The tentacle was hauled forth from the hole a good five yards.

Duke Orbal instructed Cugel: "Straddle the tentacle, seize it with hands and legs and it will draw you back through the hole."

In desperation Cugel clambered upon the tentacle. The tension of the winch was relaxed and Cugel was pulled into the hole.

The light of Earth curled away from the opening and made no entrance; Cugel was plunged into a condition of near-total darkness, where, however, by some paradoxical condition he was able to sense the scope of his new environment in detail.

He stood on a surface at once flat, yet rough, with rises and dips and hummocks like the face of a windy sea. The black spongy stuff underfoot showed small cavities and tunnels in which Cugel sensed the motion of innumerable near-invisible points of light. Where the sponge rose high, the crest curled over like breaking surf, or stood ragged and crusty; in either case, the fringes glowed red, pale blue and several colors Cugel had never before observed. No horizon could be detected and the local concepts of distance, proportion, and size were not germane to Cugel's understanding.

Overhead hung dead Nothingness. The single feature of note, a large disk the color of rain, floated at the zenith, an object so dim as to be almost invisible. At an indeterminate distance—a mile? ten miles? a hundred yards?—a hummock of some bulk overlooked the entire panorama. On closer inspection Cugel saw this hummock to be a prodigious mound of gelatinous flesh, inside which floated a globular organ apparently analogous to an eye. From the base of this creature a hundred tentacles extended far and wide across the black sponge. One of these tentacles passed near Cugel's feet, through the intracosmic gap, and out upon the soil of Earth.

Cugel discovered Iolo's sack of dreams, not three feet distant. The black sponge, bruised by the impact, had welled a liquid which had dissolved a hole in the leather, allowing the star-shaped dreams to spill out upon the sponge. In groping with the pole, Cugel had damaged a growth of brown palps. The resulting exudation had dripped upon the dreams and when Cugel picked up one of the fragile flakes, he saw that its edges glowed with eery fringes of color. The combination of oozes which had permeated the object caused his fingers to itch and tingle.

A score of small luminous nodes swarmed around his head, and a soft voice addressed him by name. "Cugel, what a pleasure that you have come to visit us! What is your opinion of our pleasant land?"

Cugel looked about in wonder; how could a denizen of this place know his name? At a distance of ten yards he noticed a small hummock of plasm not unlike the monstrous bulk with the floating eye. Luminous nodes circled his head and the voice sounded in his ears: "You are perplexed, but remember, here we do things differently. We transfer our thoughts in small modules; if you look closely you will see them speeding through the fluxion: dainty little animalcules eager to unload their weight of enlightenment. There! Notice! Directly before your eyes hovers an excellent example. It is a thought of your own regarding which you are dubious; hence it hesitates, and awaits your decision."

"What if I speak?" asked Cugel. "Will this not facilitate matters?"

"To the contrary! Sound is considered offensive and everyone deplores the slightest murmur."

"This is all very well," grumbled Cugel, "but—"

"Silence, please! Send forth animalcules only!"

Cugel dispatched a whole host of luminous purports: "I will do my best. Perhaps you can inform me how far this land extends?"

"Not with certainty. At times I send forth animalcules to explore the far places; they report an infinite landscape similar to that which you see."

"Duke Orbal of Ombalique has commanded me to gather information and he will be interested in your remarks. Are valuable substances to be found here?"

"To a certain extent. There is proscedel and diphany and an occasional coruscation of zamanders."

"My first concern, of course, is to collect information for Duke Orbal, and I must also rescue Iolo's dreams; still I would be pleased to acquire a valuable trinket or two, if only to remind myself of our pleasant association."

"Understandable! I sympathize with your objectives."

"In that case, how may I obtain a quantity of such substances?"

"Easily. Simply send off animalcules to gather up your requirements." The creature emitted a whole host of pale plasms which darted away in all directions and presently returned with several dozen small spheres sparkling with a frosty blue light. "Here are zamanders of the first water," said the creature. "Accept them with my compliments."

Cugel placed the gems in his pouch. "This is a most convenient system for gaining wealth. I also wish to obtain a certain amount of diphany."

"Send forth animalcules! Why exert yourself needlessly?"

"We think along similar lines." Cugel dispatched several hundred animalcules which presently returned with twenty small ingots of the precious metal.

Cugel examined his pouch. "I still have room for a quantity of proscedel. With your permission I will send out the requisite animalcules."

"I would not dream of interfering," asserted the creature.

The animalcules sped forth, and before long returned with sufficient proscedel to fill Cugel's pouch. The creature said thoughtfully: "This is at least half of Uthaw's treasure; however, he appears not to have noticed its absence."

" 'Uthaw'?" inquired Cugel. "Do you refer to yonder monstrous hulk?"

"Yes, that is Uthaw, who sometimes is both coarse and irascible."

Uthaw's eyes rolled toward Cugel and bulged through the outer membrane. A tide of animalcules arrived pulsing with significance. "I notice that Cugel has stolen my treasure, which I denounce as a breach of hospitality! In retribution, he must dig twenty-two zamanders from below the Shivering Trillows. He must then sift eight pounds of prime proscedel from the Dust of Time. Finally he must scrape eight acres of diphany bloom from the face of the High Disk."

Cugel sent forth animalcules. "Lord Uthaw, the penalty is harsh but just. A moment while I go to fetch the necessary tools!" He gathered up the dreams and sprang to the aperture. Seizing the tentacle he cried through the hole: "Pull the tentacle, work the winch! I have rescued the dreams!"

The tentacle convulsed and thrashed, effectively blocking the opening. Cugel turned and putting his fingers to his mouth emitted a piercing whistle. Uthaw's eye rolled upward and the tentacle fell limp.

The winch heaved at the tentacle and Cugel was drawn back through the hole. Uthaw, recovering his senses, jerked his tentacle so violently that the rope snapped; the winch was sent flying; and several persons were swept from their feet. Uthaw jerked back his tentacle and the hole immediately closed.

Cugel cast the sack of dream-flakes contemptuously at the feet of

Iolo. "There you are, ingrate! Take your vapid hallucinations and go your way! Let us hear no more of you!"

Cugel turned to Duke Orbal. "I am now able to render a report upon the other cosmos. The ground is composed of a black sponge-like substance and flickers with a trillion infinitesimal glimmers. My research discovered no limits to the extent of the land. A pale disk, barely visible, covers a quarter of the sky. The denizens are, first and foremost, an ill-natured hulk named Uthaw, and others more or less similar. No sound is allowed and meaning is conveyed by animalcules, which also procure the necessities of life. In essence, these are my discoveries, and now, with utmost respect, I claim the grand prize of one thousand terces."

From behind his back Cugel heard Iolo's mocking laughter. Duke Orbal shook his head. "My dear Cugel, what you suggest is impossible. To what exhibit do you refer? The boxful of dirt yonder? It lacks all pretensions to singularity."

"But you saw the hole! With your winch you pulled the tentacle! In accordance with your orders, I entered the hole and explored the region!"

"True enough, but hole and tentacle are both vanished. I do not for a moment suggest mendacity, but your report is not easily verified. I can hardly award honors to an entity so fugitive as the memory of a non-existent hole! I fear that on this occasion I must pass you by. The prize will be awarded to Zaraflam and his remarkable cockroaches."

"A moment, your Grace!" Iolo called out. "Remember, I am entered in the competition! At last I am able to display my products! Here is a particularly choice item, distilled from a hundred dreams captured early in the morning from a bevy of beautiful maidens asleep in a bower of fragrant vines."

"Very well," said Duke Orbal. "I will delay the award until I test the quality of your visions. What is the procedure? Must I compose myself for slumber?"

"Not at all! The ingestion of the dream during waking hours produces not a hallucination, but a mood: a sensibility fresh, new and sweet: an allurement of the faculties, an indescribable exhilaration. Still, why should you not be comfortable as you test my dreams? You there! Fetch a couch! And you, a cushion for his Grace's noble head. You! Be good enough to take his Grace's hat."

Cugel saw no profit in remaining. He moved to the outskirts of the throng.

Iolo brought forth his dream and for a moment seemed puzzled by the ooze still adhering to the object, then decided to ignore the matter, and paid no further heed, except to rub his fingers as if after contact with some viscid substance.

Making a series of grand gestures, Iolo approached the great chair where Duke Orbal sat at his ease. "I will arrange the dream for its most convenient ingestion," said Iolo. "I place a quantity into each ear; I insert a trifle up each nostril; I arrange the balance under your Grace's illustrious tongue. Now, if your Grace will relax, in half a minute the quintessence of a hundred exquisite dreams will be made known."

Duke Orbal became rigid. His fingers clenched the arms of the chair. His back arched and his eyes bulged from their sockets. He turned over backward, then rolled, jerked, jumped and bounded about the plaza before the amazed eyes of his subjects.

Iolo called out in a brassy voice: "Where is Cugel? Fetch that scoundrel Cugel!"

But Cugel had already departed Cuirnif and was nowhere to be found.

The Hollow Land

William Morris

William Morris was a colossal figure in the late nineteenth century: nearly single-handedly the force behind the revival of medievalism; a furniture designer; utopian; publisher of fine books; poet; and novelist. His works are also the source of that whole genre, heroic fantasy (sometimes called epic fantasy and sometimes sword-and-sorcery fantasy), that subcategory of fantasy fiction continued in our time by Robert E. Howard, L. Sprague De Camp, Fritz Leiber, Michael Moorcock, Poul Anderson and others. It is characterized by a heroic protagonist of primitive or ancient lineage who battles his way, hacking and slashing with his sword, to victory over forces natural and supernatural. Also, there is usually an elevated style, as in Morris' works. In this story Florian fights his way back to The Hollow Land. The story's pastoral utopian spirit, however, is hauntingly similar to that of Graham Greene's story "Under the Garden" (pp.451–500), and not at all reminiscent of Conan the Barbarian. Paradise (that place where what is most valuable about the self may blossom) is in the past and must be regained.

We find in ancient story wonders many told,
Of heroes in great glory, with spirit free and bold;
Of joyances and high-tides, of weeping and of woe,
Of noble recken striving, mote ye now wonders know.
Niebelungen Lied (see Carlyle's Miscellanies)

I STRUGGLING IN THE WORLD

Do you know where it is—the Hollow Land?

I have been looking for it now so long, trying to find it again—the Hollow Land—tor there I saw my love first.

I wish to tell you how I found it first of all; but I am old, my memory fails me: you must wait and let me think if I perchance can tell you how it happened.

Yea, in my ears is a confused noise of trumpet-blasts singing over desolate moors, in my ears and eyes a clashing and clanging of horse-hoofs, a ringing and glittering of steel; drawn-back lips, set teeth, shouts, shrieks, and curses.

How was it that no one of us ever found it till that day? for it is near our country: but what time have we to look for it, or any good thing; with such biting carking cares hemming us in on every side—cares about great things—mighty things: mighty things, O my brothers! or rather little things enough, if we only knew it.

Lives passed in turmoil, in making one another unhappy; in bitterest misunderstanding of our brothers' hearts, making those sad whom God has not made sad,—alas, alas! What chance for any of us to find the Hollow Land? What time even to look for it?

Yet who has not dreamed of it? Who, half miserable yet the while, for that he knows it is but a dream, has not felt the cool waves round his feet, the roses crowning him, and through the leaves of beech and lime the many whispering winds of the Hollow Land?

Now, my name was Florian, and my house was the house of the Lilies; and of that house was my father lord, and after him my eldest brother Arnald; and me they called Florian de Liliis.

Moreover, when my father was dead, there arose a feud between the Lilies' house and Red Harald; and this that follows is the history of it.

Lady Swanhilda, Red Harald's mother, was a widow, with one son, Red Harald; and when she had been in widowhood two years, being of princely blood, and besides comely and fierce, King Urrayne sent to demand her in marriage. And I remember seeing the procession leaving the town, when I was quite a child; and many young knights and squires attended the Lady Swanhilda as pages, and amongst them, Arnald, my eldest brother.

And as I gazed out of the window, I saw him walking by the side of her horse, dressed in white and gold very delicately; but as he went it chanced that he stumbled. Now he was one of those that held a golden canopy over the lady's head, so that it now sunk into wrinkles, and the lady had to bow her head full now, and even then the gold brocade caught in one of the long slim gold flowers that were wrought round about the crown she wore. She flushed up in her rage, and her smooth face went suddenly into the carven wrinkles of a wooden water-spout, and she caught at the brocade with her left hand, and pulled it away furiously, so that the warp and woof were twisted out of their place, and many gold threads were left dangling about the crown; but Swanhilda stared about when she rose, then smote my brother across the mouth with her gilded sceptre, and the red blood flowed all about his garments; yet he only turned exceeding pale, and dared say no word, though he was heir to the house of the Lilies: but my small heart swelled with rage, and I vowed revenge, and, as it seems, he did too.

So when Swanhilda had been queen three years, she suborned many of King Urrayne's knights and lords, and slew her husband as he slept, and reigned in his stead. And her son, Harald, grew up to manhood, and was counted a strong knight, and well spoken of, by then I first put on my armour.

Then, one night, as I lay dreaming, I felt a hand laid on my face, and starting up saw Arnald before me fully armed. He said, "Florian, rise and arm." I did so, all but my helm, as he was.

He kissed me on the forehead; his lips felt hot and dry; and when they brought torches, and I could see his face plainly, I saw he was very pale. He said:

"Do you remember, Florian, this day sixteen years ago? It is a long time, but I shall never forget it unless this night blots out its memory."

I knew what he meant, and because my heart was wicked, I rejoiced exceedingly at the thought of vengeance, so that I could not speak, but only laid my palm across his lips.

"Good; you have a good memory, Florian. See now, I waited long and long: I said at first, I forgive her; but when the news came concerning the death of the King, and how that she was shameless, I said I will take it as a sign, if God does not punish her within certain years, that he means me to do so; and I have been watching and watching now these two years for an opportunity, and behold it is come at last; and I think God has certainly given her into our hands, for she rests this night, this very Christmas eve, at a small walled town on the frontier, not two hours' gallop from this; they keep little ward there, and the night is wild: moreover, the prior of a certain house of monks, just without the walls, is my fast friend in this matter, for she has done him some great injury. In the courtyard below a hundred and fifty knights and squires, all faithful and true, are waiting for us: one moment and we shall be gone."

Then we both knelt down, and prayed God to give her into our hands: we put on our helms, and went down into the courtyard.

It was the first time I expected to use a sharp sword in anger, and I was full of joy as the muffled thunder of our horse-hoofs rolled through the bitter winter night.

In about an hour and a half we had crossed the frontier, and in half an hour more the greater part had halted in a wood near the Abbey, while I and a few others went up to the Abbey gates, and knocked loudly four times with my sword-hilt, stamping on the ground meantime. A long, low whistle answered me from within, which I in my turn answered: then the wicket opened, and a monk came out, holding a lantern. He seemed yet in the prime of life, and was a tall, powerful man. He held the lantern to my face, then smiled, and said, "The banners hang low." I gave the countersign, "The crest is lopped off." "Good my son," said he; "the ladders are within here. I dare not trust any of the brethren to carry them for you, though they love not the witch either, but are timorsome."

"No matter," I said, "I have men here." So they entered and began to shoulder the tall ladders: the prior was very busy. "You will find them just the right length, my son, trust me for that." He seemed quite a jolly, pleasant man, I could not understand his nursing furious revenge; but his face darkened strangely whenever he happened to mention her name.

As we were starting he came and stood outside the gate, and putting his lantern down that the light of it might not confuse his sight, looked earnestly into the night, then said: "The wind has fallen, the snow flakes get thinner and smaller every moment, in an hour it will be freezing hard, and will be quite clear; everything depends upon the surprise being complete; stop a few minutes yet, my son." He went away chuckling, and returned presently with two more sturdy monks carrying something: they threw their burdens down before my feet, they consisted of all the white albs in the abbey: "There, trust an old man, who has seen more than one stricken fight in his carnal days;

let the men who scale the walls put these over their arms, and they will not be seen in the least. God make your sword sharp, my son.'

So we departed, and when I met Arnald again, he said that what the prior had done was well thought of; so we agreed that I should take thirty men, an old squire of our house, well skilled in war, along with them, scale the walls as quietly as possible, and open the gates to the rest.

I set off accordingly, after that with low laughing we had put the albs all over us, wrapping the ladders also in white. Then we crept very warily and slowly up to the wall; the moat was frozen over, and on the ice the snow lay quite thick; we all thought that the guards must be careless enough, when they did not even take the trouble to break the ice in the moat. So we listened—there was no sound at all, the Christmas midnight mass had long ago been over, it was nearly three o'clock, and the moon began to clear, there was scarce any snow falling now, only a flake or two from some low hurrying cloud or other: the wind sighed gently about the round towers there, but it was bitter cold, for it had begun to freeze again; we listened for some minutes, about a quarter of an hour I think, then at a sign from me, they raised the ladders carefully, muffled as they were at the top with swathings of wool. I mounted first, old Squire Hugh followed last; noiselessly we ascended, and soon stood altogether on the walls; then we carefully lowered the ladders again with long ropes; we got our swords and axes from out of the folds of our priests' raiments, and set forward, till we reached the first tower along the wall; the door was open, in the chamber at the top there was a fire slowly smouldering, nothing else; we passed through it, and began to go down the spiral staircase, I first, with my axe shortened in my hand.—"What if we were surprised there," I thought, and I longed to be out in the air again;—"What if the door were fast at the bottom."

As we passed the second chamber, we heard some one within snoring loudly: I looked in quietly, and saw a big man with long black hair, that fell off his pillow and swept the ground, lying snoring, with his nose turned up and his mouth open, but he seemed so sound asleep that we did not stop to slay him.—Praise be!—the door was open, without even a whispered word, without a pause, we went on along the streets, on the side that the drift had been on, because our garments were white, for the wind being very strong all that day, the houses on that side had caught in their cornices and carvings, and on the rough stone and wood of them, so much snow, that except here and there where the black walls grinned out, they were quite white; no man saw us as we stole along, noiselessly because of the snow, till we stood within 100 yards of the gates and their house of guard. And we stood because we heard the voice of some one singing:

> Queen Mary's crown was gold,
> King Joseph's crown was red,
> But Jesus' crown was diamond
> That lit up all the bed
> *Mariae Virginis.*

So they had some guards after all; this was clearly the sentinel that sang to keep the ghosts off;—Now for a fight.—We drew nearer, a few yards nearer, then stopped to free ourselves from our monks' clothes.

> Ships sail through the Heaven
> With red banners dress'd,
> Carrying the planets seven
> To see the white breast
> *Mariae Virginis.*

Thereat he must have seen the waving of some alb or other as it shivered down to the ground, for his spear fell with a thud, and he seemed to be standing open-mouthed, thinking something about ghosts; then, plucking up heart of grace, he roared out like ten bull-calves, and dashed into the guard-house.

We followed smartly, but without hurry, and came up to the door of it just as some dozen half-armed men came tumbling out under our axes: thereupon, while our men slew them, I blew a great blast upon my horn, and Hugh with some others drew bolt and bar and swung the gates wide open.

Then the men in the guard-house understood they were taken in a trap, and began to stir with great confusion; so lest they should get quite waked and armed I left Hugh at the gates with ten men, and myself led the rest into that house. There while we slew all those that yielded not, came Arnald with the others bringing our horses with them; then all the enemy threw their arms down. And we counted our prisoners and found them over fourscore; therefore, not knowing what to do with them (for they were too many to guard, and it seemed unknightly to slay them all), we sent up some bowmen to the walls, and turning our prisoners out of gates, bid them run for their lives, which they did fast enough, not knowing our numbers, and our men sent a few flights of arrows among them that they might not be undeceived.

Then the one or two prisoners that we had left, told us, when we had crossed our axes over their heads, that the people of the good town would not willingly fight us, in that they hated the queen; that she was guarded at the palace by some fifty knights, and that beside, there were no others to oppose us in the town; so we set out for the palace, spear in hand.

We had not gone far, before we heard some knights coming, and soon, in a turn of the long street, we saw them riding towards us; when they caught sight of us they seemed astonished, drew rein, and stood in some confusion.

We did not slacken our pace for an instant, but rode right at them with a yell, to which I lent myself with all my heart.

After all they did not run away, but waited for us with their spears held out; I missed the man I had marked, or hit him rather just on the top of the helm; he bent back, and the spear slipped over his head, but my horse still kept on, and I felt presently such a crash that I reeled in my saddle, and felt mad. He had lashed out at me with his sword as I came on, hitting me in the ribs (for my arm was raised), but only flatlings.

I was quite wild with rage, I turned, almost fell upon him, caught him by the neck with both hands, and threw him under the horse-hoofs, sighing with fury: I heard Arnald's voice close to me, "Well fought, Florian": and I saw his great stern face bare among the iron, for he had made a vow in remembrance of that blow always to fight unhelmed; I saw his great sword swinging, in wide gyres, and hissing as it started up, just as if it were alive and liked it.

So joy filled all my soul, and I fought with my heart, till the big axe I swung felt like nothing but a little hammer in my hand, except for its bitterness: and as for the enemy, they went down like grass, so that we destroyed them utterly, for those knights would neither yield nor fly, but died as they stood, so that some fifteen of our men also died there.

Then at last we came to the palace, where some grooms and such like kept the gates armed, but some ran, and some we took prisoners, one of whom died for sheer terror in our hands, being stricken by no wound; for he thought we would eat him.

These prisoners we questioned concerning the queen, and so entered the great hall.

There Arnald sat down in the throne on the dais, and laid his naked sword before him on the table: and on each side of him sat such knights as there was room for, and the others stood round about, while I took ten men, and went to look for Swanhilda.

I found her soon, sitting by herself in a gorgeous chamber. I almost pitied her when I saw her looking so utterly desolate and despairing; her beauty too had faded, deep lines cut through her face. But when I entered she knew who I was, and her look of intense hatred was so fiend-like, that it changed my pity into horror of her.

"Knight," she said, "who are you, and what do you want, thus discourteously entering my chamber?"

"I am Florian de Liliis, and I am to conduct you to judgment."

She sprang up, "Curse you and your whole house,—you I hate worse than any,—girl's face,—guards! guards!" and she stamped on the ground, her veins on the forehead swelled, her eyes grew round and flamed out, as she kept crying for her guards, stamping the while, for she seemed quite mad.

Then at last she remembered that she was in the power of her enemies, she sat down, and lay with her face between her hands, and wept passionately.

"Witch,"—I said between my closed teeth, "will you come, or must we carry you down to the great hall?"

Neither would she come, but sat there, clutching at her dress and tearing her hair.

Then I said, "Bind her, and carry her down." And they did so.

I watched Arnald as we came in, there was no triumph on his stern white face, but resolution enough, he had made up his mind.

They placed her on a seat in the midst of the hall over against the dais. He said, "Unbind her, Florian." They did so, she raised her face, and glared defiance at us all, as though she would die queenly after all.

Then rose up Arnald and said, "Queen Swanhilda, we judge you guilty of death, and because you are a queen and of a noble house, you shall be slain by my knightly sword, and I will even take the reproach of slaying a woman, for no other hand than mine shall deal the blow."

Then she said, "O false knight, show your warrant from God, man, or devil."

"This warrant from God, Swanhilda," he said, holding up his sword, "listen!—fifteen years ago, when I was just winning my spurs, you struck me, disgracing me before all the people; you cursed me, and meant that curse well enough. Men of the house of the Lilies, what sentence for that?"

"Death!" they said.

"Listen!—afterwards you slew my cousin, your husband, treacherously, in the most cursed way, stabbing him in the throat, as the stars in the canopy above him looked down on the shut eyes of him. Men of the house of Lily, what sentence for that?"

"Death!" they said.

"Do you hear them, Queen? There is warrant from man; for the devil, I do not reverence him enough to take warrant from him, but, as I look at that face of yours, I think that even he has left you."

And indeed just then all her pride seemed to leave her, she fell from the chair, and wallowed on the ground moaning, she wept like a child, so that the tears lay on the oak floor; she prayed for another month of life; she came to me and kneeled, and kissed my feet, and prayed piteously, so that water ran out of her mouth.

But I shuddered, and drew away; it was like having an adder about one; I could have pitied her had she died bravely, but for one like her to whine and whine!—pah!—

Then from the dais rang Arnald's voice terrible, much changed. "Let there be an end of all this." And he took his sword and strode through the hall towards her; she rose from the ground and stood up, stooping a little, her head sunk between her shoulders, her black eyes turned up and gleaming, like a tigress about to spring. When he came within some six paces of her something in his eye daunted her, or perhaps the flashing of his terrible sword in the torch-light; she threw her arms up with a great shriek, and dashed screaming about the hall. Arnald's lip never once curled with any scorn, no line in his face changed: he said, "Bring her here and bind her."

But when one came up to her to lay hold on her she first of all ran at him, hitting with her head in the belly. Then while he stood doubled up for want of breath, and staring with his head up, she caught his sword from the girdle, and cut him across the shoulders, and many others she wounded sorely before they took her.

Then Arnald stood by the chair to which she was bound, and poised his sword, and there was a great silence.

Then he said, "Men of the House of the Lilies, do you justify me in this, shall she die?" Straightway rang a great shout through the hall, but before it died away the sword had swept round, and therewithal was there no such thing as Swanhilda left upon the earth, for in no battle-field had Arnald struck truer blow. Then he turned to the few servants of the palace and said, "Go now, bury this accursed woman, for she is a king's daughter." Then to us all, "Now knights, to horse and away, that we may reach the good town by about dawn." So we mounted and rode off.

What a strange Christmas-day that was, for there, about nine o'clock in the morning, rode Red Harald into the good town to demand vengeance; he went at once to the king, and the king promised that before nightfall that very day the matter should be judged; albeit the king feared somewhat, because every third man you met in the streets had a blue cross on his shoulder, and some likeness of a lily, cut out or painted, stuck in his hat; and this blue cross and lily were the bearings of our house, called "De Liliis." Now we had seen Red Harald pass through the streets, with a white banner borne before him, to show that he came peaceably as for this time; but I know he was thinking of other things than peace.

And he was called Red Harald first at this time, because over all his arms he wore a great scarlet cloth, that fell in heavy folds about his horse and all about him. Then, as he passed our house, some one pointed it out to him, rising there with its carving and its barred marble, but stronger than many a castle on the hill-tops, and its great overhanging battlement cast a mighty shadow down the wall and across the street; and above all rose the great tower, or banner floating proudly from the top, whereon was emblazoned on a white ground a blue cross, and on a blue ground four white lilies. And now faces were gazing from all the windows, and all the battlements were thronged; so Harald turned, and rising in his stirrups, shook his clenched fist at our house; natheless, as he did so, the east wind, coming down the street, caught up the corner of that scarlet cloth and drove it over his face, and therewithal disordering his long black hair, well nigh choked him, so that he bit both his hair and that cloth.

So from base to cope rose a mighty shout of triumph and defiance, and he passed on.

Then Arnald caused it to be cried, that all those who loved the good House of the Lilies should go to mass that morning in Saint Mary's Church, hard by our house. Now this church belonged to us, and the abbey that served it, and always we appointed the abbot of it on condition that our trumpets should sound all together when on high masses they sing the "Gloria in Excelsis." It was the largest and most beautiful of all the churches in the town, and had two exceeding high towers, which you could see from far off, even when you saw not the town or any of its other towers: and in one of these towers were twelve great bells, named after the twelve Apostles, one name being written on each one of them; as Peter, Matthew, and so on; and in the other tower was one great bell only, much larger than any of the others, and which was called Mary. Now this bell was never rung but when our house was in great danger, and it had this legend on it, "When Mary rings the earth shakes;" and indeed from this we took our war cry, which was, "Mary rings;" somewhat justifiable indeed, for the last time that Mary rang, on that day before nightfall there were four thousand bodies to be buried, which bodies wore neither cross nor lily.

So Arnald gave me in charge to tell the abbot to cause Mary to be tolled for an hour before mass that day.

The abbot leaned on my shoulder as I stood within the tower and looked at the twelve monks laying their hands to the ropes. Far up in the dimness I saw the wheel before it began to swing round about; then it moved a little; the twelve men bent down to the earth and a roar rose that shook the tower from base to spirevane: backwards and forwards swept the wheel, as Mary now looked downwards towards earth, now looked up at the shadowy cone of the spire, shot across by bars of light from the dormers.

And the thunder of Mary was caught up by the wind and carried through all the country; and when the good man heard it, he said goodbye to wife and child, slung his shield behind his back, and set forward with his spear sloped over his shoulder, and many a time, as he walked toward the good town, he tightened the belt that went about his waist, that he might stride the faster, so long and furiously did Mary toll.

And before the great bell, Mary, had ceased ringing all the ways were full of armed men.

But at each door of the church of Saint Mary stood a row of men armed with axes, and when any came, meaning to go into the church, the two first of these would hold their axes (whose helves were about four feet long) over his head, and would ask him, "Who went over the moon last night?" then if he answered nothing or at random they would bid him turn back, which he for the more part would be ready enough to do; but some, striving to get through that row of men, were slain outright; but if he were one of those that were friends to the House of the Lilies he would answer to that question, "Mary and John."

By the time the mass began the whole church was full, and in the nave and transept thereof were three thousand men, all of our house and all armed. But Arnald and myself, and Squire Hugh, and some others sat under a gold-fringed canopy near the choir; and the abbot said mass, having his mitre on his head. Yet, as I watched him, it seemed to me that he must have something on beneath his priest's vestments, for he looked much fatter than usual, being really a tall lithe man.

Now, as they sung the "Kyrie," some one shouted from the other end of the church, "My lord Arnald, they are slaying our people without;" for, indeed, all the square about the church was full of our people, who for the press had not been able to enter, and were standing there in no small dread of what might come to pass.

Then the abbot turned round from the altar, and began to fidget with the fastenings of his rich robes.

And they made a lane for us up to the west door; then I put on my helm and we began to go up the wave, then suddenly the singing of the monks and all stopped. I heard a clinking and a buzz of voices in the choir. I turned, and saw that the bright noon sun was shining on the gold of the priest's vestments, as they lay on the floor, and on the mail that the priests carried.

So we stopped, the choir gates swung open, and the abbot marched out at the head of *his* men, all fully armed, and began to strike up the psalm "Exsurgat Deus."

When we got to the west door, there was indeed a tumult, but as yet no slaying; the square was all a-flicker with steel, and we beheld a great body of knights, at the head of them Red Harald and the king, standing over against us; but our people, pressed against the houses, and into the corners of the square, were, some striving to enter the doors, some beside themselves with rage, shouting out to the others to charge; withal, some were pale and some were red with the blood that had gathered to the wrathful faces of them.

Then said Arnald to those about him, "Lift me up." So they laid a great shield on two lances, and these four men carried, and thereon stood Arnald, and gazed about him.

Now the king was unhelmed, and his white hair (for he was an old man) flowed down behind him on to his saddle; but Arnald's hair was cut short, and was red.

And all the bells rang.

Then the king said, "O Arnald of the Lilies, will you settle this quarrel by the judgment of God?" And Arnald thrust up his chin, and said, "Yea." "How then," said the king, "and where?" "Will it please you try now?" said Arnald.

Then the king understood what he meant, and took in his hand from behind tresses of his long white hair, twisting them round his hand in his wrath, but yet said no word, till I suppose his hair put him in mind of something, and he raised it in both his hands above his head, and shouted out aloud, "O knights, hearken to this traitor." Whereat, indeed, the lances began to move ominously. But Arnald spoke.

"O you king and lords, what have we to do with you? Were we not free in the old time, up among the hills there? Wherefore give way, and we will go to the hills again; and if any man try to stop us his blood be on his own head; wherefore now," (and he turned) "all you House of the Lily, both soldiers and monks, let us go forth together fearing nothing, for I think there is not bone enough or muscle enough in these fellows here that have a king that they should stop us withal, but only skin and fat."

And truly, no man dared to stop us, and we went.

II Failing in The World

Now at that time we drove cattle in Red Harald's land.

And we took no hoof but from the Lords and rich men, but of these we had a mighty drove, both oxen and sheep, and horses, and besides, even hawks and hounds, and huntsman or two to take care of them.

And, about noon, we drew away from the cornlands that lay beyond the pastures, and mingled with them, and reached a wide moor, which was called "Goliath's Land." I scarce know why, except that it belonged neither to Red Harald or us, but was debatable.

And the cattle began to go slowly, and our horses were tired, and the sun struck down very hot upon us, for there was no shadow, and the day was cloudless.

All about the edge of the moor, except on the side from which we had come was a rim of hills, not very high, but very rocky and steep, otherwise the moor itself was flat; and through these hills was one pass, guarded by our men, which pass led to the Hill castle of the Lilies.

It was not wonderful, that of this moor many wild stories were told, being such a strange lonely place, some of them one knew, alas! to be over true. In the old time, before we went to the good town, this moor had been the mustering place of our people, and our house had done deeds enough of blood and horror to turn our white lilies red, and our blue cross to a fiery one. But some of those wild tales I never believed; they had to do mostly with men losing their way without any apparent cause, (for there were plenty of landmarks,) finding some well-known spot, and then, just beyond it, a place they had never even dreamed of.

"Florian! Florian!" said Arnald, "for God's sake stop! as every one else is stopping to look at the hills yonder; I always thought there was a curse upon us. What does God mean by shutting us up here? Look at the cattle; O Christ, they have found it out too! See, some of them are turning to run back again towards Harald's land. Oh! unhappy, unhappy, from that day forward!"

He leaned forward, rested his head on his horse's neck, and wept like a child.

I felt so irritated with him, that I could almost have slain him then and there. Was he mad? had these wild doings of ours turned his strong wise head?

"Are you my brother Arnald, that I used to think such a grand man when I was a boy?" I said, "or are you changed too, like everybody, and everything else? What do *you* mean?"

"Look! look!" he said, grinding his teeth in agony.

I raised my eyes: where was the one pass between the rim of stern rocks? Nothing: the enemy behind us—that grim wall in front: what wonder that each man looked in his fellow's face for help, and found it not. Yet I refused to believe that there was any truth either in the wild stories that I had heard when I was a boy, or in this story told me so clearly by my eyes now.

I called out cheerily, "Hugh, come here!" He came. "What do you think of this? Some mere dodge on Harald's part? Are we cut off?"

"Think! Sir Florian? God forgive me for ever thinking at all; I have given up that long and long ago, because thirty years ago I thought this, that the House of Lilies would deserve anything in the way of bad fortune that God would send them: so I gave up thinking, and took to fighting. But if you think that Harald had anything to do with this, why—why—in God's name, I wish I could think so!"

I felt a dull weight on my heart. Had our house been the devil's servants all along? I thought we were God's servants.

The day was very still, but what little wind there was, was at our backs. I watched Hugh's face, not being able to answer him. He was the cleverest man at war that I have known, either before or since that day; sharper than any hound in ear and scent, clearer sighted than any eagle; he was listening now intently. I saw a slight smile cross his face; heard him mutter, "Yes! I think so: verily that is better, a great deal better." Then he stood up in his stirrups, and shouted, "Hurrah for the Lilies! Mary rings!" "Mary rings!" I shouted, though I did not know the reason for his exultation: my brother lifted his head, and smiled too, grimly. Then as I listened I heard clearly the sound of a trumpet, and enemy's trumpet too.

"After all, it was only mist, or some such thing," I said, for the pass between the hills was clear enough now.

"Hurrah! only mist," said Arnald, quite elated; "Mary rings!" and we all began to think of fighting: for after all what joy is equal to that?

There were five hundred of us; two hundred spears, the rest archers; and both archers and men at arms were picked men.

"How many of them are we to expect?" said I.

"Not under a thousand, certainly, probably more, Sir Florian." (My brother Arnald, by the way, had knighted me before we left the good town, and Hugh liked to give me the handle to my name. How was it, by the way, that no one had ever made *him* a knight?)

"Let every one look to his arms and horse, and come away from these silly cows' sons!" shouted Arnald.

Hugh said, "They will be here in an hour, fair Sir."

So we got clear of the cattle, and dismounted, and both ourselves took food and drink, and our horses; afterwards we tightened our saddle-girths, shook our great pots of helmets on, except Arnald, whose rusty-red hair had been his only head-piece in battle for years and years, and stood with our spears close by our horses, leaving room for the archers to retreat between our ranks; and they got their arrows ready, and planted their stakes before a little peat moss: and there we waited, and saw their pennons at last floating high above the corn of the fertile land, then heard their many horse-hoofs ring upon the hard-parched moor, and the archers began to shoot.

It had been a strange battle; we had never fought better, and yet withal it had ended in a retreat; indeed all along every man but Arnald and myself, even Hugh, had been trying at least to get the enemy between him and the way toward the pass; and now we were all drifting that way, the enemy trying to cut us off, but never able to stop us, because he could only throw small bodies of men in our way, whom we scattered and put to flight in their turn.

I never cared less for my life than then; indeed, in spite of all my boasting and hardness of belief, I should have been happy to have died, such a strange weight of apprehension was on me; and yet I got no scratch even. I had soon put off my great helm, and was fighting in my mail-coif only: and here I swear that three knights together charged me, aiming at my bare face, yet never touched me. For, as for one, I put his lance aside with my sword, and the other two in some most wonderful manner got their spears locked in each other's armour, and so had to submit to be knocked off their horses.

And we still neared the pass, and began to see distinctly the ferns that grew on the rocks, and the fair country between the rift in them, spreading out there, blue-shadowed.

Whereupon came a great rush of men of both sides, striking side blows at each other, spitting, cursing, and shrieking, as they tore away like a herd of wild hogs. So, being careless of life, as I said, I drew rein, and turning my horse, waited quietly for them. And I knotted the reins, and laid them on the horse's neck, and stroked him, that he whinnied, then got both my hands to my sword.

Then, as they came on, I noted hurriedly that the first man was one of Arnald's men, and one of our men behind him leaned forward to prod him with his spear, but could not reach so far, till he himself was run through the eye with a spear, and throwing his arms up fell dead with a shriek. Also I noted concerning this first man that the laces of his helmet were loose, and when he saw me he lifted his *left* hand to his head, took off his helm and cast it at me, and still tore on; the helmet flew over my head, and I sitting still there, swung out, hitting him on the neck; his head flew right off, for the mail no more held than a piece of silk.

"Mary rings," and my horse whinnied again, and we both of us went at it, and fairly stopped that rout, so that there was a knot of quite close and desperate fighting wherein we had the best of that fight and slew most of them, albeit my horse was slain and my mail-coif cut through. Then I bade a squire fetch me another horse, and began meanwhile to upbraid those knights for running in such a strange disorderly race, instead of standing and fighting cleverly.

Moreover we had drifted even in this successful fight still nearer to the pass, so that the conies who dwelt there were beginning to consider whether they should not run into their holes.

But one of those knights said: "Be not angry with me, Sir Florian, but do you think you will go to Heaven?"

"The saints! I hope so," I said, but one who stood near him whispered to him to hold his peace, so I cried out:

"O friend! I hold this world and all therein so cheap now, that I see not anything in it but shame which can any longer anger me; wherefore speak out."

"Then, Sir Florian, men say that at your christening some fiend took on him the likeness of a priest and strove to baptize you in the Devil's name, but God had mercy on you so that the fiend could not choose but baptize you in the name of the most holy Trinity: and yet men say that you hardly believe any doctrine such as other men do, and will at the end only go to Heaven round about as it were, not at all by the intercession of our Lady; they say too that you can see no ghosts or other wonders, whatever happens to other Christian men."

I smiled.—"Well, friend, I scarcely call this a disadvantage, moreover what has it to do with the matter in hand?"

How was this in Heaven's name? We had been quite still, resting while this talk was going on, but we could hear the hawks chattering from the rocks, we were so close now.

And my heart sunk within me, there was no reason why this should not be true; there was no reason why anything should not be true.

"This, Sir Florian," said the knight again, "how would you feel inclined to fight if you thought that everything about you was mere glamour; this earth here, the rocks, the sun, the sky? I do not know where I am for certain, I do not know that it is not midnight instead of undern: I do not know if I have been fighting men or only *simulacra*—but I think, we all think, that we have been led into some devil's trap or other, and—and—may God forgive me my sins!—I wish I had never been born."

There now! he was weeping—they all wept—how strange it was to see those rough, bearded men blubbering there. and snivelling till the tears ran over their armour and mingled with the blood, so that it dropped down to the earth in a dim, dull, red rain.

My eyes indeed were dry, but then so was my heart; I felt far worse than weeping came to, but nevertheless I spoke cheerily.

"Dear friends, where are your old men's hearts gone to now? See now! This is a punishment for our sins, is it? Well, for our forefathers' sins or our own? If the first, O brothers, be very sure that if we bear it manfully God will have something very good in store for us hereafter; but if for our sins, is it not certain that He cares for us yet, for note that He suffers the wicked to go their own ways pretty much; moreover brave men, brothers, ought to be the masters of *simulacra* —come, is it so hard to die once for all?"

Still no answer came from them, they sighed heavily only. I heard the sound of more than one or two swords as they rattled back to the scabbards: nay, one knight, stripping himself of surcoat and hauberk, and drawing his dagger, looked at me with a grim smile, and said, "Sir Florian, do so!" Then he drew the dagger across his throat and he fell back dead.

They shuddered, those brave men, and crossed themselves. And I had no heart to say a word more, but mounted the horse which had been brought to me and rode away slowly for a few yards; then I became aware that there was a great silence over the whole field.

So I lifted my eyes and looked, and behold no man struck at another.

Then from out of a band of horsemen came Harald, and he was covered all over with a great scarlet cloth as before, put on over the head, and flowing all about his horse, but rent with the fight. He put off his helm and drew back his mail-coif, then took a trumpet from the hand of a herald and blew strongly.

And in the midst of his blast I heard a voice call out: "O Florian! come and speak to me for the last time!"

So when I turned I beheld Arnald standing by himself, but near him stood Hugh and ten others with drawn swords.

Then I wept, and so went to him weeping; and he said, "Thou seest, brother, that we must die, and I think by some horrible and unheard-of death, and the House of the Lilies is just dying too; and now I repent me of Swanhilda's death; now I know that it was a poor cowardly piece of revenge, instead of a brave act of justice; thus has God shown us the right.

"O Florian! curse me! So will it be straighter; truly thy mother when she bore thee did not think of this; rather saw thee in the tourney at this time, in her fond hopes, glittering with gold and doing knightly; or else mingling thy brown locks with the golden hair of some maiden weeping for the love of thee. God forgive me! God forgive me!"

"What harm, brother?" I said, "this is only failing in the world; what if we had not failed, in a little while it would have made no difference; truly just now I felt very miserable, but now it has passed away, and I am happy."

"O brave heart!" he said, "yet we shall part just now, Florian, farewell."

"The road is long," I said, "farewell."

Then we kissed each other, and Hugh and the others wept.

Now all this time the trumpets had been ringing, ringing, great doleful peals, then they ceased, and above all sounded Red Harald's voice.

(So I looked round towards that pass, and when I looked I no longer doubted any of those wild tales of glamour concerning Goliath's Land; and for though the rocks were the same, and though the conies still stood gazing at the doors of their dwellings, though the hawks still cried out shrilly, though the fern still shook in the wind, yet beyond, oh such a land! not to be described by any because of its great beauty, lying, a great *hollow* land, the rocks going down on this side in precipices, then reaches and reaches of loveliest country, trees and flowers, and corn, then the hills, green and blue, and purple, till their ledges reached the white snowy mountains at last. Then with all manner of strange feelings, "my heart in the midst of my body was even like melting wax.")

"O you House of the Lily! you are conquered—yet I will take vengeance only on a few, therefore let all those who wish to live come and pile their swords, and shields, and helms behind me in three great heaps, and swear fealty afterwards to me; yes, all but the false knights Arnald and Florian."

We were holding each other's hands and gazing, and we saw all our knights, yea, all but Squire Hugh and his ten heroes, pass over the field singly, or in groups of three or four, with their heads hanging down in shame, and they cast down their notched swords and dinted, lilied shields, and brave-crested helms into three great heaps, behind

Red Herald, then stood behind, no man speaking to his fellow, or touching him.

Then dolefully the great trumpets sang over the dying House of the Lily, and Red Harald led his men forward, but slowly: on they came, spear and mail glittering in the sunlight; and I turned and looked at that good land, and a shuddering delight seized my soul.

But I felt my brother's hand leave mine, and saw him turn his horse's head and ride swiftly toward the pass; that was a strange pass now.

And at the edge he stopped, turned round and called out aloud, "I pray thee, Harald, forgive me! now farewell all!"

Then the horse gave one bound forward, and we heard the poor creature's scream when he felt that he must die, and we heard afterwards (for we were near enough for that even) a clang and a crash.

So I turned me about to Hugh, and he understood me though I could not speak.

We shouted all together, "Mary rings," then laid our bridles on the necks of our horses, spurred forward, and—in five minutes they were all slain, and I was down among the horse-hoofs.

Not slain though, not wounded. Red Harald smiled grimly when he saw me rise and lash out again; he and some ten others dismounted, and holding their long spears out, I went back—back, back, —I saw what it meant, and sheathed my sword, and their laughter rolled all about me, and I too smiled.

Presently they all stopped, and I felt the last foot of turf giving under my feet; I looked down and saw the crack there widening; then in a moment I fell, and a cloud of dust and earth rolled after me; then again their mirth rose into thunder-peals of laughter. But through it all I heard Red Harald shout, "Silence! Evil dogs!"

For as I fell I stretched out my arms, and caught a tuft of yellow broom some three feet from the brow, and hung there by the hands, my feet being loose in the air.

Then Red Harald came and stood on the precipice above me, his great axe over his shoulder; and he looked down on me not ferociously, almost kindly, while the wind from the Hollow Land blew about his red raiment, tattered and dusty now.

And I felt happy, though it pained me to hold straining by the broom, yet I said, "I will hold out to the last."

It was not long, the plant itself gave way and I fell, and as I fell I fainted.

III LEAVING THE WORLD—FYTTE THE FIRST

I had thought when I fell that I should never wake again; but I woke at last: for a long time I was quite dizzied and could see nothing at all: horrible doubts came creeping over me; I half expected to see presently great half-formed shapes come rolling up to me to crush me; some thing fiery, not strange, too utterly horrible to be strange, but utterly vile and ugly, the sight of which would have killed me when I was upon the earth, come rolling up to torment me. In fact I doubted if I were in hell.

I knew I deserved to be, but I prayed, and then it came into my mind that I could not pray if I were in hell.

Also there seemed to be a cool green light all about me, which was sweet.

Then presently I heard a glorious voice ring out clear, close to me—

Christ keep the Hollow Land
Through the sweet spring-tide
When the apple-blossoms bless
The lowly bent hill side.

Thereat my eyes were slowly unsealed, and I saw the blessedest sight I have ever seen before or since: for I saw my Love.

She sat about five yards from me on a great grey stone that had much moss on it, one of the many scattered along the side of the stream by which I lay; she was clad in loose white raiment close to her hands and throat; her feet were bare, her hair hung loose a long way down, but some of it lay on her knees: I said "white" raiment, but long spikes of light scarlet went down from the throat, lost here and there in the shadows of the folds, and growing smaller and smaller, died before they reached her feet.

I was lying with my head resting on soft moss that some one had gathered and placed under me. She, when she saw me moving and awake, came and stood over me with a gracious smile.—She was so lovely and tender to look at, and so kind, yet withal no one, man or woman, had ever frightened me half so much.

She was not fair in white and red, like many beautiful women are, being rather pale, but like ivory for smoothness, and her hair was quite golden, not light yellow, but dusky golden.

I tried to get up on my feet, but was too weak, and sank back again. She said:

"No, not just yet, do not trouble yourself or try to remember anything just at present."

There withal she kneeled down, and hung over me closer.

"To-morrow you may, perhaps, have something hard to do or bear, I know, but now you must be as happy as you can be, quietly happy. Why did you start and turn pale when I came to you? Do you not know who I am? Nay, but you do, I see; and I have been waiting here so long for you; so you must have expected to see me. You cannot be frightened of me, are you?"

But I could not answer a word, but all the time strange knowledge, strange feelings were filling my brain and my heart, she said:

"You are tired; rest, and dream happily."

So she sat by me, and sang to lull me to sleep, while I turned on my elbow, and watched the waving of her throat: and the singing of all the poets I had ever heard, and of many others too, not born till years long after I was dead, floated all about me as she sang, and I did indeed dream happily.

When I awoke it was the time of the cold dawn, and the colours were gathering themselves together, whereat in fatherly approving fashion the sun sent all across the east long bars of scarlet and orange that after faded through yellow to green and blue.

And she sat by me still; I think she had been sitting there and singing all the time; all through hot yesterday, for I had been sleeping day-long and night-long, all through the falling evening under moonlight and starlight the night through.

And now it was dawn, and I think too that neither of us had moved at all; for the last thing I remembered before I went to sleep was the tips of her fingers brushing my cheek, as she knelt over me with down-drooping arm, and still now I felt them there. Moreover she was just finishing some fainting measure that died before it had time to get painful in its passion.

Dear Lord! how I loved her! Yet did I not dare to touch her, or even speak to her. She smiled with delight when she saw I was awake again, and slid down her hand on to mine, but some shuddering dread made me draw it away again hurriedly; then I saw the smile leave her face: what would I not have given for courage to hold her body quite tight to mine? But I was so weak. She said:

"Have you been very happy?"

"Yea," I said.

It was the first word I had spoken there, and my voice sounded strange.

"Ah!" she said, "you will talk more when you get used to the air of the Hollow Land. Have you been thinking of your past life at all? If not, try to think of it. What thing in Heaven or Earth do you wish for most?"

Still I said no word; but she said in a wearied way:

"Well now, I think you will be strong enough to get to your feet and walk; take my hand and try."

Therewith she held it out: I strove hard to be brave enough to take it, but could not; I only turned away shuddering, sick, and grieved to the heart's core of me; then struggling hard with hand and knee and elbow, I scarce rose, and stood up totteringly; while she watched me sadly, still holding out her hand.

But as I rose, in my swinging to and fro the steel sheath of my sword struck her on the hand so that the blood flowed from it, which she stood looking at for a while, then dropped it downwards, and turned to look at me, for I was going.

Then as I walked she followed me, so I stopped and turned and said almost fiercely:

"I am going alone to look for my brother."

The vehemence with which I spoke, or something else, burst some blood-vessel within my throat, and we both stood there with the blood running from us on to the grass and summer flowers.

She said: "If you find him, wait with him till I come."

"Yea," and I turned and left her, following the course of the stream upwards, and as I went I heard her low singing that almost broke my heart for its sadness.

And I went painfully because of my weakness, and because also of the great stones; and sometimes I went along a spot of earth where the river had been used to flow in flood-time, and which was now bare of everything but stones; and the sun, now risen high, poured down on everything a great flood of fierce light and scorching heat, and burnt me sorely, so that I almost fainted.

But about noontide I entered a wood close by the stream, a beech-wood, intending to rest myself; the herbage was thin and scattered there, sprouting up from amid the leaf-sheaths and nuts of the beeches, which had fallen year after year on that same spot; the outside boughs swept low down, the air itself seemed green when you entered within the shadow of the branches, they over-roofed the place so with tender green, only here and there showing spots of blue.

But what lay at the foot of a great beech tree but some dead knight in armour, only the helmet off? A wolf was prowling round about it, who ran away snarling when he saw me coming.

So I went up to that dead knight, and fell on my knees before him, laying my head on his breast, for it was Arnald.

He was quite cold, but had not been dead for very long; I would not believe him dead, but went down to the stream and brought him water, tried to make him drink—what would you? He was as dead as Swanhilda: neither came there any answer to my cries that afternoon but the moaning of the wooddoves in the beeches.

So then I sat down and took his head on my knees, and closed the eyes, and wept quietly while the sun sank lower.

But a little after sunset I heard a rustle through the leaves, that was not the wind, and looking up my eyes met the pitying eyes of that maiden.

Something stirred rebelliously within me; I ceased weeping and said: "It is unjust, unfair: What right had Swanhilda to live? Did not God give her up to us? How much better was he than ten Swanhildas? And look you—See!—he is DEAD."

Now this I shrieked out, being mad; and though I trembled when I saw some stormy wrath that vexed her very heart and loving lips, gathering on her face, I yet sat there looking at her and screaming, screaming, till all the place rang.

But when growing hoarse and breathless I ceased; she said, with straightened brow and scornful mouth:

"So! Bravely done! Must I then, though I am a woman, call you a liar, for saying God is unjust? You to punish her, had not God then punished her already? How many times when she woke in the dead night do you suppose she missed seeing King Urrayne's pale face and hacked head lying on the pillow by her side? Whether by night or day, what things but screams did she hear when the wind blew loud round about the Palace corners? And did not that face too, often come before her, pale and bleeding as it was long ago, and gaze at her from unhappy eyes! Poor eyes! With changed purpose in them— no more hope of converting the world when that blow was once struck, truly it was very wicked—no more dreams, but only fierce struggles with the Devil for very life, no more dreams but failure at last, and death, happier so in the Hollow Land.

She grew so pitying as she gazed at his dead face that I began to weep again unreasonably, while she saw not that I was weeping, but looked only on Arnald's face, but after turned on me frowning.

"Unjust! Yes, truly unjust enough to take away life and all hope from her; you have done a base cowardly act, you and your brother here, disguise it as you may; you deserve all God's judgment—you—"

But I turned my eyes and wet face to her, and said:

"Do not curse me—there—do not look like Swanhilda: for see now, you said at first that you have been waiting long for me, give me your hand now, for I love you so."

Then she came and knelt by where I sat, and I caught her in my arms and she prayed to be forgiven.

"O, Florian! I have indeed waited long for you, and when I saw you my heart was filled with joy, but you would neither touch me nor speak to me, so that I became almost mad, forgive me, we will be so happy now. O! do you know this is what I have been waiting for all these years; it made me glad, I know, when I was a little baby in my mother's arms to think I was born for this; and afterwards, as I grew up, I used to watch every breath of wind through the beech-boughs, every turn of the silver poplar leaves, thinking it might be you or some news of you."

Then I rose and drew her up with me; but she knelt again by my brother's side, and kissed him, and said:

"O brother! The Hollow Land is only second best of the places God has made, for Heaven also is the work of His hand."

Afterwards we dug a deep grave among the beech-roots and there we buried Arnald de Liliis.

And I have never seen him since, scarcely even in dreams; surely God has had mercy on him, for he was very leal and true and brave; he loved many men, and was kind and gentle to his friends, neither did he hate any but Swanhilda.

But as for us two, Margaret and me, I cannot tell you concerning our happiness, such things cannot be told; only this I know, that we abode continually in the Hollow Land until I lost it.

Moreover this I can tell you. Margaret was walking with me, as she often walked near the place where I had first seen her; presently we came upon a woman sitting, dressed in scarlet and gold raiment, with her head laid down on her knees; likewise we heard her sobbing.

"Margaret, who is she?" I said: "I knew not that any dwelt in the Hollow Land but us two only."

She said, "I know not who she is, only sometimes, these many years, I have seen her scarlet robe flaming from far away, amid the quiet green grass: but I was never so near her as this. Florian, I am afraid: let us come away."

Fytte The Second

Such a horrible grey November day it was, the fog-smell all about, the fog creeping into our very bones.

And I sat there, trying to recollect, at any rate something, under those fir-trees that I ought to have known so well.

Just think now; I had lost my best years somewhere; for I was past the prime of life, my hair and beard were scattered with white, my body was growing weaker, my memory of all things was very faint.

My raiment, purple and scarlet and blue once, was so stained that you could scarce call it any colour, was so tattered that it scarce covered my body, though it seemed once to have fallen in heavy folds to my feet, and still, when I rose to walk, though the miserable November mist lay in great drops upon my bare breast, yet was I obliged to wind my raiment over my arm, it dragged so (wretched, slimy, textureless thing!) in the brown mud.

On my head was a light morion, which pressed on my brow and pained me; so I put my hand up to take it off; but when I touched it I stood still in my walk shuddering; I nearly fell to the earth with shame and sick horror; for I laid my hand on a lump of slimy earth with worms coiled up in it. I could scarce forbear from shrieking, but breathing such a prayer as I could think of, I raised my hand again and seized it firmly. Worse horror still! The rust had eaten it into holes, and I gripped my own hair as well as the rotting steel, the sharp edge of which cut into my fingers; but setting my teeth, gave a great wrench, for I knew that if I let go of it then, no power on the earth or under it could make me touch it again. God be praised! I tore it off and cast it far from me; I saw the earth, and the worms and green weeds and sun-begotten slime, whirling out from it radiatingly, as it spun round about.

I was girt with a sword too, the leathern belt of which had shrunk and squeezed my waist: dead leaves had gathered in knots about the buckles of it, the gilded handle was encrusted with clay in many parts, the velvet sheath miserably worn.

But, verily, when I took hold of the hilt, and dreaded lest instead of a sword I should find a serpent in my hand; lo! then, I drew out my own true blade and shook it flawless from hilt to point, gleaming white in that mist.

Therefore it sent a thrill of joy to my heart, to know that there was one friend left me yet: I sheathed it again carefully, and undoing it from my waist, hung it about my neck.

Then catching up my rags in my arms, I drew them up till my legs and feet were altogether clear from them, afterwards folded my arms over my breast, gave a long leap and ran, looking downward, but not giving heed to my way.

Once or twice I fell over stumps of trees, and suchlike, for it was a cut-down wood that I was in, but I rose always, though bleeding and confused, and went on still; sometimes tearing madly through briars and gorse bushes, so that my blood dropped on the dead leaves as I went.

I ran in this way for about an hour; then I heard a gurgling and splashing of waters; I gave a great shout and leapt strongly, with shut eyes, and the black water closed over me.

When I rose again, I saw near me a boat with a man in it; but the shore was far off; I struck out toward the boat, but my clothes which I had knotted and folded about me, weighed me down terribly.

The man looked at me, and began to paddle toward me with the oar he held in his left hand, having in his right a long, slender spear, barbed like a fish-hook; perhaps, I thought, it is some fishing spear; moreover his raiment was of scarlet, with upright stripes of yellow and black all over it.

When my eye caught his, a smile widened his mouth as if some one had made a joke; but I was beginning to sink, and indeed my head was almost under water just as he came and stood above me, but before it went quite under, I saw his spear gleam, then *felt* it in my shoulder, and for the present, felt nothing else.

When I woke I was on the bank of that river; the flooded waters went hurrying past me; no boat on them now; from the river the ground went up in gentle slopes till it grew a great hill, and there, on that hill-top,—Yes, I might forget many things, almost everything, but not that, not the old castle of my fathers up among the hills, its towers blackened now and shattered, yet still no enemy's banner waved from it.

So I said I would go and die there; and at this thought I drew my sword, which yet hung about my neck, and shook it in the air till the true steel quivered, then began to pace towards the castle. I was quite naked, no rag about me; I took no heed of that only thanking God that my sword was left, and so toiled up the hill. I entered the castle soon by the outer court; I knew the way so well, that I did not lift my eyes from the ground, but walked on over the lowered drawbridge through the unguarded gates, and stood in the great hall at last—my father's hall—as bare of everything but my sword as when I came into the world fifty years before: I had as little clothes, as little wealth, less memory and thought, I verily believe, than then.

So I lifted up my eyes and gazed; no glass in the windows, no hangings on the walls; the vaulting yet held good throughout, but seemed to be going; the mortar had fallen out from between the stones, and grass and fern grew in the joints; the marble pavement was in some places gone, and water stood about in puddles, though one scarce knew how it had got there.

No hangings on the walls—no; yet, strange to say, instead of them, the walls blazed from end to end with scarlet paintings, only striped across with green damp-marks in many places, some falling bodily from the wall, the plaster hanging down with the fading colour on it.

In all of them, except for the shadows and the faces of the figures, there was scarce any colour but scarlet and yellow. Here and there it seemed the painter, whoever it was, had tried to make his trees or his grass green, but it would not do; some ghastly thoughts must have filled his head, for all the green went presently into yellow, out-sweeping through the picture dismally. But the faces were painted to the very life, or it seemed so;—there were only five of them, how-ever, that were very marked or came much in the foreground; and four of these I knew well, though I did not then remember the names of those that had borne them. They were Red Harald, Swanhilda, Arnald, and myself. The fifth I did not know; it was a woman's and very beautiful.

Then I saw that in some parts a small penthouse roof had been built over the paintings, to keep them from the weather. Near one of these stood a man painting, clothed in red, with stripes of yellow and black: Then I knew that it was the same man who had saved me from drowning by spearing me through the shoulder; so I went up to him, and saw furthermore that he was girt with a heavy sword.

He turned round when he saw me coming, and asked me fiercely what I did there.

I asked why he was painting in my castle.

Thereupon, with that same grim smile widening his mouth as heretofore, he said, "I paint God's judgments."

And as he spoke, he rattled the sword in his scabbard; but I said, "Well, then, you paint them very badly. Listen; I know God's judgments much better than you do. See now; I will teach you God's judgments, and you shall teach me painting."

While I spoke he still rattled his sword, and when I had done, shut his right eye tight, screwing his nose on one side; then said:

"You have got no clothes on, and may go to the devil! What do *you* know about God's judgments?"

"Well, they are not all yellow and red, at all events; you ought to know better."

He screamed out, "O you fool! Yellow and red! Gold and blood, what do they make?"

"Well," I said; "what?"

"HELL!" And, coming close up to me, he struck me with his open hand in the face, so that the colour with which his hand was smeared was dabbed about my face. The blow almost threw me down; and, while I staggered, he rushed at me furiously with his sword. Perhaps it was good for me that I had got no clothes on; for, being utterly unencumbered, I leapt this way and that, and avoided his fierce, eager strokes till I could collect myself somewhat; while he had a heavy scarlet cloak on that trailed on the ground, and which he often trod on, so that he stumbled.

He very nearly slew me during the first few minutes, for it was not strange that, together with other matters, I should have forgotten the art of fence: but yet, as I went on, and sometimes bounded about the hall under the whizzing of his sword, as he rested sometimes, leaning on it, as the point sometimes touched my head and made my eyes start out, I remembered the old joy that I used to have, and the *swy, swy,* of the sharp edge, as one gazed between one's horse's ears; moreover, at last, one fierce swift stroke, just touching me below the throat, tore up the skin all down my body, and fell heavy on my thigh, so that I drew my breath in and turned white; then first, as I swung my sword round my head, our blades met, oh! to hear that *tchink* again! and I felt the notch my sword made in his, and swung out at him; but he guarded it and returned on me; I guarded right and left, and grew warm, and opened my mouth to shout, but knew not what to say; and our sword points fell on the floor together: then, when we had panted awhile, I wiped from my face the blood that had been dashed over it, shook my sword and cut at him, then we spun round and round in a mad waltz to the measured music of our meeting swords, and sometimes either wounded the other somewhat but not much, till I beat down his sword on to his head, that he fell grovelling, but not cut through. Verily, thereupon my lips opened mightily with "Mary rings."

Then, when he had gotten to his feet, I went at him again, he staggering back, guarding wildly; I cut at his head; he put his sword up confusedly, so I fitted both hands to my hilt, and smote him mightily under the arm: then his shriek mingled with my shout, made a strange sound together; he rolled over and over, dead, as I thought.

I walked about the hall in great exultation at first, striking my sword point on the floor every now and then, till I grew faint with loss of blood; then I went to my enemy and stripped off some of his clothes to bind up my wounds withal; afterwards I found in a corner bread and wine, and I eat and drank thereof.

Then I went back to him, and looked, and a thought struck me, and I took some of his paints and brushes, and kneeling down, painted his face thus, with stripes of yellow and red, crossing each other at right angles; and in each of the squares so made I put a spot of black, after the manner of the painted letters in the prayer-books and romances when they are ornamented.

So I stood back as painters use, folded my arms, and admired my own handiwork. Yet there struck me as being something so utterly doleful in the man's white face, and the blood running all about him, and washing off the stains of paint from his face and hands, and splashed clothes, that my heart misgave me, and I hoped that he was not dead; I took some water from a vessel he had been using for his painting, and, kneeling, washed his face.

Was it some resemblance to my father's dead face, which I had seen when I was young, that made me pity him? I laid my hand upon his heart, and felt it beating feebly; so I lifted him up gently, and carried him towards a heap of straw that he seemed used to lie upon; there I stripped him and looked to his wounds, and used leech-craft, the memory of which God gave me for this purpose, I suppose, and within seven days I found that he would not die.

Afterwards, as I wandered about the castle, I came to a room in one of the upper storeys, that had still the roof on, and windows in it with painted glass, and there I found green raiment and swords and armour, and I clothed myself.

So when he got well I asked him what his name was, and he me, and we both of us said, "Truly I know not." Then said I, "but we must call each other some name, even as men call days."

"Call me Swerker," he said, "some priest I knew once had that name."

"And me Wulf," said I, "though wherefore I know not."

Then I tried to learn painting till I thought I should die, but at last learned it through very much pain and grief.

And, as the years went on and we grew old and grey, we painted purple pictures and green ones instead of the scarlet and yellow, so that the walls looked altered, and always we painted God's judgments.

And we would sit in the sunset and watch them with the golden light changing them, as we yet hoped God would change both us and our works.

Often too we would sit outside the walls and look at the trees and sky, and the ways of the few men and women we saw; therefrom sometimes befell adventures.

Once there went past a great funeral of some king going to his own country, not as he had hoped to go, but stiff and colourless, spices filling up the place of his heart.

And first went by very many knights, with long bright hauberks on, that fell down before their knees as they rode, and they all had tilting-helms on with the same crest, so that their faces were quite hidden: and this crest was two hands clasped together tightly as though they were the hands of one praying forgiveness from the one he loves best; and the crest was wrought in gold.

Moreover, they had on over their hauberks surcoats which were half scarlet and half purple, strewn about with golden stars.

Also long lances, that had forked knights'-pennons, half purple and half scarlet, strewn with golden stars.

And these went by with no sound but the fall of their horse-hoofs.

And they went slowly, so slowly that we counted them all, five thousand five hundred and fifty-five.

Then went by many fair maidens whose hair was loose and yellow, and who were all clad in green raiment ungirded, and shod with golden shoes.

These also we counted, being five hundred; moreover some of the outermost of them, viz, one maiden to every twenty, had long silver trumpets, which they swung out to right and left, blowing them, and their sound was very sad.

Then many priests, and bishops, and abbots, who wore white albs and golden copes over them; and they all sang together mournfully, *"Propter amnen Babylonis;"* and these were three hundred.

After that came a great knot of the Lords, who were tilting helmets and surcoats emblazoned with each one his own device; only each had in his hand a small staff two feet long whereon was a pennon of scarlet and purple. These also were three hundred.

And in the midst of these was a great car hung down to the ground with purple, drawn by grey horses whose trappings were half scarlet, half purple.

And on this car lay the King, whose head and hands were bare; and he had on him a surcoat, half purple and half scarlet, strewn with golden stars.

And his head rested on a tilting helmet, whose crest was the hands of one praying passionately for forgiveness.

But his own hands lay by his side as if he had just fallen asleep.

And all about the car were little banners, half purple and half scarlet, strewn with golden stars.

Then the King, who counted but as one, went by also.

And after him came again many maidens clad in ungirt white raiment strewn with scarlet flowers, and their hair was loose and yellow and their feet bare: and, except for the falling of their feet and the rustle of the wind through their raiment, they went past quite silently. These also were five hundred.

Then lastly came many young knights with long bright hauberks falling over their knees as they rode, and surcoats, half scarlet and half purple, strewn with golden stars; they bore long lances with forked pennons which were half purple, half scarlet, strewn with golden stars; their heads and their hands were bare, but they bore shields, each one of them, which were of bright steel wrought cunningly in the midst with that bearing of the two hands of one who prays for forgiveness; which was done in gold. These were but five hundred.

Then they all went by winding up and up the hill roads, and, when the last of them had departed out of our sight, we put down our heads and wept, and I said, "Sing us one of the songs of the Hollow Land."

Then he whom I had called Swerker put his hand into his bosom, and slowly drew out a long, long tress of black hair, and laid it on his knee and smoothed it, weeping on it: So then I left him there and went and armed myself, and brought armour for him.

And then came back to him and threw the armour down so that it clanged, and said:

"O! Harald, let us go!"

He did not seem surprised that I called him by the right name, but rose and armed himself, and then he looked a good knight; so we set forth.

And in a turn of the long road we came suddenly upon a most fair woman, clothed in scarlet, who sat and sobbed, holding her face between her hands, and her hair was very black.

And when Harald saw her, he stood and gazed at her for long through the bars of his helmet, then suddenly turned, and said:

"Florian, I must stop here; do you go on to the Hollow Land. Farewell."

"Farewell." And then I went on, never turning back, and him I never saw more.

And so I went on, quite lonely, but happy, till I had reached the Hollow Land.

Into which I let myself down most carefully, by the jutting rocks and bushes and strange trailing flowers, and there lay down and fell asleep.

FYTTE THE THIRD

And I was waked by some one singing; I felt very happy; I felt young again; I had fair delicate raiment on, my sword was gone, and my armour; I tried to think where I was, and could not for my happiness; I tried to listen to the words of the song. Nothing, only an old echo in my ears; only all manner of strange scenes from my wretched past life before my eyes in a dim, far-off manner: then at last, slowly, without effort, I heard what she sang.

> Christ keep the Hollow Land
> All the summer-tide;

Still we cannot understand
Where the waters glide;

Only dimly seeing them
Coldly slipping through
Many green-lipp'd cavern mouths.
Where the hills are blue.

"Then," she said, "come now and look for it, love, a hollow city in
the Hollow Land."
I kissed Margaret, and we went.

Through the golden streets under the purple shadows of the
houses we went, and the slow fanning backward and forward of the
many-coloured banners cooled us: we two alone; there was no one
with us, no soul will ever be able to tell what we said, how we
looked.

At last we came to a fair palace, cloistered off in the old time,
before the city grew golden from the din and hubbub of traffic; those
who dwelt there in the old ungolden times had had their own joys,
their own sorrows, apart from the joys and sorrows of the multitude:
so, in like manner, was it now cloistered off from the eager leaning
and brotherhood of the golden dwellings: so now it had its own
gaiety, its own solemnity, apart from theirs; unchanged, unchange-
able, were its marble walls, whatever else changed about it.

We stopped before the gates and trembled, and clasped each other
closer; for there among the marble leafage and tendrils that were
round and under and over the archway that held the golden valves,
were wrought two figures of a man and woman, winged and gar-
landed, whose raiment flashed with stars; and their faces were like
faces we had seen or half seen in some dream long and long and long
ago, so that we trembled with awe and delight; and I turned, and
seeing Margaret, saw that her face was that face seen or half seen long
and long and long ago; and in the shining of her eyes I saw that other
face, seen in that way and no other long and long and long ago—my
face.

And then we walked together toward the golden gates, and
opened them, and no man gainsaid us.

And before us lay a great space of flowers.